An Ocean Between

An Ocean Between

A Novel
by

William D. Becher

Barton Publishers
Ann Arbor, Michigan

==

Publisher's Cataloging-in-Publication
(Provided by Quality Books, Inc.)

Becher, William D., 1929-
    An ocean between : a novel / by William D.
Becher. -- 1st ed.
    p. cm.
    Includes bibliographical references.
    LCCN: 99-69108
    ISBN: 0-9677283-4-7

    1. World War, 1939-1945--Evacuation of
civilians--Great Britain--Fiction. 2. World War,
1939-1945--Children--Great Britain--Fiction.
3. Children and war--Great Britain--Fiction.
4. World War, 1935-1945--Social aspects--England--
Fiction. 5. Bolivar (Ohio)--Fiction. 6. England
--Fiction. I. Title.

PS3503.E2385 2000   813'.54
            QBI99-901814

==

Barton Publishers
Ann Arbor, Michigan

First Edition

2 4 6 8 9 7 5 3 1

Dedication

To: Ruth, Vina, Ivy, Barry, Al, Laura and the seventy-eight other Hoover evacuees.

Foreword

In 1940 I was a ten year old boy whose main interests were build- ing rubber band powered model airplanes, carving rolling pins and can- dlestick holders on my wood lathe, riding a Silver King bicycle, reading Ellery Queen mysteries and Robert Payson Terhune stories about collie dogs, playing pickup basketball, sending Morse coded messages by flashlight to my friend a quarter mile away, and building rudimentary radio receivers. Besides *Captain Easy* and *Tim Tyler's Luck*, I found little to interest me in the newspapers. The war in Europe seemed ab- stract and far away. I liked school, felt obliged to like girls, played the saxophone, and had a springer spaniel named Waggy. I paraded around the house when I heard John Phillips Sousa marches on the radio, liked to pretend I was Captain Marvel or Batman, and stood at attention when they played the Star Spangled Banner. Except for living over a store that sold, among other things, candy and ice cream, I suppose you could call me a typical midwestern boy.

In mid September of that year I was sitting in my sixth-grade schoolroom in Bolivar, Ohio, regretting the end of summer vacation, when the teacher introduced Ruth Palmer, a new student, to us. I well remember his announcement and how it affected me. I had never known, or at least I thought I hadn't, anyone who lived farther away from Bolivar than Detroit, Michigan. Ruth was from London, England. Nearly all I knew about England was that it was ruled by a king and queen and was at war with Germany. I like to believe my heart skipped from all the educational opportunities her presence afforded. I suppose more realistically it had to do with early developing hormones.

Ruth was different from us. She talked with an accent, one I still find intriguing, wore clothes of slightly different style, and had many mannerisms that seemed strange. We were told she would be living with a family near Bolivar. The Hoover Company of nearby North Canton had invited her, and eighty-three others English evacuees,[*] to live in America until the war in Europe ended. I had little idea of what an evacuee was and, I suppose truthfully, did not care. I only recall my

---

[*] Laura Wales, another English evacuee, also attended our school. Un- fortunately, she was several grades behind us and I never knew her well.

decision that first day. I decided Ruth was special and should become a friend of mine. As any red-blooded young ten year old would do, I immediately set out to woo her with handwritten notes and offers of bonbons and ice cream. Much to my disappointment she rejected my proposals. We never walked in the moonlight, never watched sunsets together, never sipped sodas at the local malt shop, never danced to Jimmy Dorsey or Benny Goodman, and never kissed or held hands at the Wednesday night movies. We simply became classmates and good friends.

In this way we shared, at arm's length, most of World War II. During those years I watched the progress and failures of the Allied campaigns throughout Europe and the Pacific. I knew about Dunkirk, the fall of France, the London Blitz, Pearl Harbor, the North African campaign, the Russian front, Salerno, Anzio, Normandy, the Bulge, Guadalcanal, Iwo Jima, Okinawa, and all the other infamous battlegrounds. I had only a superficial understanding of the war, probably because I did not follow it closely. I bought war stamps, collected scrap paper, and waved the American flag; but almost never read Ernie Pyle, or followed the sordid details of the war published in our daily newspaper. My major exposure to current events was from the newsreels shown before the cartoons and double features at the nearby movie houses. I worried when one of our hometown boys left for the service, and wept with his friends and relatives when he was wounded, or killed in action. I never doubted that America would win the war. Sadly, I also learned little about the evacuation of Ruth and the other Hoover evacuees

Ruth remained in Bolivar until 1945 when, on a few days notice, she returned to England, upgraded her name to Ruthe, and disappeared from my world.

Later, while in college, I briefly resumed my friendship with Ruthe. We exchanged a few letters, I sent several CARE packages to help with the English shortages, and in the Spring of 1948 visited London for a brief stay. It was there I met her sister Lesley (Rosina Ivy) and her brother Albert who had also been Hoover evacuees, and Eric Davis, her friend. During the visit I heard more about the ordeals and joys of their evacuation, but the sights of war scarred England interested me more.

Several years later Ruthe wed Eric and raised two splendid children. I continued in school, became an electrical engineer and professor, and married Helen, a high school sweetheart whom I did date and kiss. We also had two wonderful children and have lived happily ever since.

In early 1993, nearing retirement, Helen and I decided to tour Europe. I had recently learned of Ruthe and Eric's address, wrote to them, and as part of our itinerary, visited with them. As we talked, and reviewed the past years, I became more and more enthralled with the history of the Hoover evacuation. For the first time, I realized what a poignant experience the evacuation must have been. It was difficult to imagine what wartime horrors and fears compelled parents to send their small children, children they loved, to a strange land. I wondered how they ever found the courage to say good-bye, not knowing when, or if, they would ever see them again. How did they suffer through those terrible, long years apart? I wondered how the children felt, sent to a strange country, with strange people, strange clothes, and strange customs. How did they deal with such a long stay? Did they resent their parents? Did they love their foster families? I wondered how the foster families felt. How did they react to a temporary commitment that turned into five years? Did they suffer when the children returned home? How could they part with children they had nursed and loved for five years? I wondered what adjustment problems the children, then young adults, had when they finally were back in England. Did they still know their parents? Did their parents know them? How did they relate to each other? Could the evacuees forget their foster parents? It seemed something worth exploring and a tale worth telling. I asked, then begged, Ruthe to write an autobiography. She declined.

Once back in America, I continued to think about the evacuation while lecturing on electrical principles to my students. By summer, I became convinced I needed more information. I searched the University of Michigan libraries and found many excellent books. They described the evacuation of English children, both within the United Kingdom and abroad. Some were about personal experiences, most were research findings. I visited with Stacy Krammes and Ann Haines of the Hoover Historical Center and Ms. Becky Hall of the North Canton Heritage Society in North Canton, Ohio and reviewed their collections of reference material and newspaper clippings of the Hoover evacuation scheme. I also visited with Dr. Kathryn Beck, a foster sister to one of the evacuees.

Continued correspondence with Ruthe and Eric concerning the evacuation prompted me to return to London for more research. Professor Hugh Griffiths of University College London kindly arranged a visiting professorship for me so that I could read at the British Library. I found many additional books during my three month stay in early 1994. During that time, Ruthe and Eric introduced me to Vina Williams, nee Vina Wales, another of the Hoover evacuees. Vina and Ruthe gave me more information about the evacuation and encouraged me to continue the research.

In 1995, I retired, and again visited London, continued to read at the British Library, and visited the British War Museum. With help from Mr. Roderick Suddaby, I reviewed the literature from the archives at the War Museum. During my stay I began writing the first draft of this book, with assistance from the ghost of Virginia Woolf, who, having once lived in the same building on Gordon Square where I lived, haunted its halls–or so I like to think.

Finally, in 1998, I returned to London one last time for a two month stay. During that time I attempted, with the help of some of those already mentioned, to insure the accuracy of many of the historic facts and English expressions used in the story. I shall not name the persons who helped so that all the blame for any inaccuracies rests where it rightfully belongs–with me. It was during this visit that I also had the opportunity to meet Mr. Barry Soundy, another of the Hoover evacuees. Barry filled in many additional details.

Writing the novel has been a long and arduous task for me. I feel much more comfortable writing treatises about electrical and computer engineering than I do about social events. It would have been better if Ruthe, Vina, or one of the other Hoover evacuees had agreed to write about their personal experiences. It undoubtedly would have conveyed the happenings and emotions in a more accurate light. I truly hope my book will cause them to reconsider.

The following is what I hope will convey some of the emotional experiences of those affected by the evacuation. It is fiction. It describes a tiny segment of the events of World War II, the evacuation of a group of English children from Pinnington, England to McKinley Heights, Ohio. The Bender Company is their sponsor. The story closely parallels the actual scheme sponsored by the Hoover Company of North Canton, Ohio. There were many other sponsorships, a few by private American organizations but most by the Australian, Canadian, English, and South African governments.

To add authenticity to the story, I left unaltered many of the actual places, times, public figures, and organizations. Others I altered deliberately. For instance, Pinnington; McKinley Heights, and the Bender Company are fictional. The references to historical dates and the progress of the war are mostly accurate, but none of the evacuees, their birth parents, their foster parents, their friends, or acquaintances are real. All personal experiences are imaginative, fictional extrapolations of the many tales I found during my search. None of the personal events as they are described actually happened to anyone I met, or know. No one should assume otherwise.

I hope the story will convey some of the courage, fear, heartache, melancholy, and happiness all those affected must surely have felt. And now, on to the story. Enjoy!

W. D. Becher
Ann Arbor, 2000

Acknowledgments

A very special thank you to the many who helped with this work, particularly to those mentioned in the Foreword: Ruthe and Eric Davis, Lesley Weatherley, Albert Palmer, Vina Williams, Barry Soundy, Stacy Krammes, Ann Haines, Becky Hall, Kathryn Beck, Hugh Griffiths, and Roderick Suddaby. Also a thank you is owed to Trista Waishkey, who helped me edit the manuscript, to Kathy King and Jan Stevens who helped me wind my way through the intricate process of printing, and, most importantly, to my wife Helen. Helen encouraged my visits to London; put up with my long hours writing, rewriting, and proofreading; consoled me when I was weary; inspired me when I became discouraged; and always loved me, in spite of my mood swings and nearly constant ill humor. Not only that, she also patiently read and commented on an early manuscript, then read and commented on a later version, and finally read the final copy. No more can be asked of a wife.

W.D.B.

Principal evacuees and their families

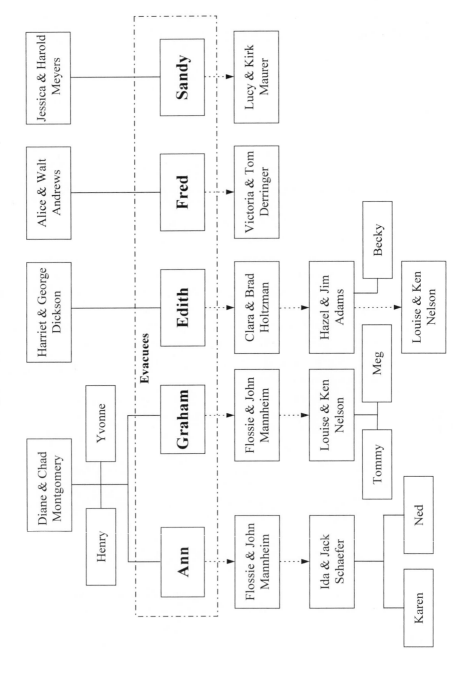

An Ocean Between

A Novel

by William D. Becher

PROLOGUE

In the late summer of 1939 all of England worried about the impending war with Germany. Although Prime Minister Chamberlain was still assuring the public that peace would prevail, no one truly believed him. Everyone recalled, in horror, the terrible war with Germany that had ended only twenty-one years before.

With all the advances in weaponry made during and after that war, many English people feared the dreadful forms of damage and ruin new technology would bring. They had seen how that deadly war had destroyed cities such as Ypres and how many had suffered, firsthand, the horror and devastation of the London bombing raids. As further reinforcement to these fears, they had heard of the awful, even more disastrous, results inflicted by aircraft during the civil war in Spain.

It was clear to most by 1939 that Adolph Hitler was an untrustworthy and unscrupulous dictator bent on overpowering the nations of Europe. In the six years since he had become German chancellor he had repeatedly espoused peaceful intent, only to follow each overture with another conquest. It began with the occupation of the Rhineland in 1936 and the seizure of Austria in March of 1938. During the following September, after Hitler assured the participants it would be his last demand, the Munich Agreement granting Germany the right to parts of the Sudetenland was signed. This, however, did not satisfy his expansionist ambitions and by March of 1939 Germany had quickly subjugated the Czechoslovakian Republic. It left little doubt that Hitler was pursuing an increasingly aggressive expansion in Europe.

An additional concern was the 1936 signing of the Rome-Berlin Axis agreement. With it came an ominous alliance between the two dictators–Hitler and the Italian, Mussolini–who the previous year had shown his own aggressive ambitions by assaulting Abyssinia. In August 1939 Russia and Germany signed a non-aggression pact, which added Russia to the increasingly fearful Axis alliance. The pact caused further worry, notably the fear that Poland was in imminent danger–in spite of the guarantee made the previous March by the English government to support Poland if it were ever attacked. England's hope for peace no longer looked as assuring as it had only days before.

Approximately one week later, on September 1, 1939, Germany attacked Poland. World War II became inevitable.

I - England

Chapter 1

Thursday, 31 August 1939

The Anderson shelter material was in the garden when Ann Montgomery came home from her Girl Guides meeting. It was the first air raid shelter she had ever seen. A rather drab gray steel covered the outside. Its arched shape reminded her of the Eskimo igloos she had studied last year, at least it would have, had its base been round instead of rectangular. This morning as they walked to their scout meetings Ann's older brother Graham told her the shelter would be 'corrugated.' She wondered what corrugated meant.

"I believe it describes the wavy shape of the metal," she thought. "Or, then again," she continued, "it jolly well might describe the overall inverted 'U' shape of the shelter itself." She could have asked Graham to define it, but hadn't, preferring instead to find out for herself. She had intended to stop by the library after the meeting and look for the word in the dictionary, but the Guides captain had kept them longer than usual and there hadn't been sufficient time. For certain she would do it tomorrow, before anyone discovered how stupid she really was.

After inspecting the shelter further, she continued to ponder its shape. "Come to think of it," she thought, "it more closely resembles the inside of a canal tunnel than an igloo."

No matter what corrugated meant, the shelter was much smaller than she had expected. Although she could stand upright in it, her father, who was nearly six feet tall, would need to stoop over whenever he was inside. Not only was the ceiling too low but the floor area was extremely small. She doubted if the entire family could fit inside without cramping them much too much.

"Now that Henry is working in Coventry," she rationalized, "Dad probably had not intended it for all six of us anyway."

She missed her big brother. He had a way of restoring her confidence whenever she worried, and certainly the threat of war demanded some sort of reassurance. She wished he had found work closer to home. Maybe then he would have been able to convince her England would never go to war, or at least he could reassure her it would not be as terribly frightful as everyone was predicting. She began to shiver. In an attempt to purge the threat from her mind, she tried to think of nicer things. But she failed, and her thoughts reverted to the shelter.

Dad had told her the workmen would plant it in the garden tomorrow. He said it would be quite different and much stronger once they added the ends, covered it with earth, and piled sandbags on top. "Silly Dad! Did he truly believe they could plant it? Maybe he thinks it will give us more room once it begins to grow," she chuckled.

Even with dirt and sandbags, she could not imagine the shelter providing much protection against those dreadful bombs everyone was expecting. She really had no idea what a bomb was, how it worked, or even precisely what it did. All she knew was that bombs could cause terrible damage. Some even said they could kill.

Mr. Hanfield, the headmaster, had told them there was little possibility of an actual raid in Pinnington. He said there were no important factories the Germans would want to bomb. But his assurances did not satisfy her and she remained scared, especially with the increase in war related activities just before school closed in July. Things such as learning how to put on gas masks, how to prepare the houses for blackouts, how to get to the school shelter, and how to protect oneself in an air raid weren't exactly peacetime subjects.

Ann gained what little positive hope she could muster from her mother who kept insisting they would never need to use the shelters. Diane was confident Mr. Chamberlain would find a way to avoid a war between England and Germany.

On the other hand, her father was considerably less optimistic. He did not think Chamberlain could maintain peace simply through talk and treaty, and was particularly fearful of the dire consequences if negotiations should fail. He remembered, firsthand, the terrible damage caused by the Zeppelin bombing raids on London during the Great War. "Furthermore," she had overheard him say quietly to Diane on several occasions, "given the progress of air technology since 1918, the raids are certain to be much more deadly than anything one can imagine."

Ann really did not completely comprehend everything, but what little she did understand greatly upset and depressed her. Ann was sorry she had overheard those conversations, but it was not her father's fault; she knew he would never mention those things if he thought she could hear him. He was not the sort of man who sought to frighten his children.

"Blimey, I'm tired. I thought the scoutmaster was never going to dismiss us today," Graham complained as he came up the garden path. "He's been trying to teach us Morse code–said it would come in handy if England goes to war. We learned half the alphabet today, and tomorrow he promises to give us the rest. It's been rather fun, but I soon became confused. I hope it comes easier with more practice."

He noticed Ann was looking at the shelter and frowning. He pointed to the shelter material and asked, in a feeble attempt at humor, "What do you think of your new home?"

"I think it's horrible," she replied, without pause. "It will never be home to me. It's so barren looking."

"Mum says the plans call for many modifications. She says Dad is going to considerable expense to make it a very special shelter. Once it's finished we'll have beds along each side and a table in between. You know Mum–by the time she has finished, it will be a very comfortable place to stay. She told me she plans to add a rug, some chairs, and the government recommended survival supplies. Dad's even ordered an electric light for the inside."

Graham thought about what he had just said and quickly added, "Although we need to be careful with lights, we must not violate the new regulations. The blackout must be total, no matter what." He was trying to sound authoritative like his dad and the other old gents in the borough.

"But we might need to remain there for ever so long. What will we do?" Ann asked–worrying about the length of the expected raids.

"Mum plans to put some magazines and books in there," he answered. "She said she'd add several games as well. That should help pass the time.

"But don't fret too much about it," he added with the confidence of a brash young lad and older brother. "The raids shouldn't last very long. The Germans will never be able to breach the British defenses; if they do, our antiaircraft units and RAF interceptors will quickly destroy them. You should see all the big guns they have installed around Northolt Aerodrome. Boy, will they surprise Jerry when he tries to bomb us. Those big guns will knock his aeroplanes right out of the sky. Before they know it, the Huns will be begging for mercy."

"Oh, Graham, you talk as if you believe going to war with Germany would be great sport."

"All I can say is, Hitler had better watch it. If he wants a war," Graham answered with schoolboy pride, "England will show him how it's done."

Before Ann could comment on Graham's optimism, Yvonne came around the house. She had just returned from visiting her girlfriend.

"Look at the two of you! Back from the scouts for just a few minutes and already into trouble. You both know Father doesn't want anyone mucking about with the shelter," she said as she tossed her haversack on the garden table.

"Oh, back off, Yvonne! Quit acting as if you're so much better than we are. Just because Dad gave you permission to continue in fifth form this year doesn't make you smarter than us; it merely indicates you're older," Graham retorted. "You're just jealous because you know Ann and I will do even better when we sit for our school certificate."

"Don't be silly, I'd never be envious of you two. You know perfectly well I received one of the highest matriculation marks ever at Pinnington County School. The headmaster says if I maintain my present performance level through the upper two forms, I should be able to earn a Higher School Certificate, with high marks, and eventually go to Oxford. Neither of you can ever hope do that. Let's face it, you have no hope of ever approaching the high standards I'm setting," she boasted. "The two of you are simply too stupid. You know very well, Graham, you'll never matriculate, you'll probably not even make it through standard fourth form this autumn. I'd wager they'll be asking you to leave county school in September, before you've been back in school one month; for certain they'll never permit you to sit for the certificate next April.

"As for you, Ann, even though you passed your scholarship in April, I'd be surprised if they let you stay in county school more than a year. They'll soon realize your passing was a fluke and off you'll go to senior school," she teased.

Ann knew that Yvonne was always trying to put her down and that most of what she said was not true, but the rebuke bothered her. She had always received high levels in all her studies, especially in English and maths, and had already been told she would be placed in the A stream this autumn, but still she worried that county school would be beyond her capability and, as Yvonne said, she'd be sent to senior school. "I'll probably never matriculate. I'm too dumb," she thought, her eyes beginning to tear. The idea of failing upset her; she wanted so badly to excel in school, for her parents' sake, as well as her own.

Yvonne sensed the teasing was having the desired effect. She continued her assault, "Actually, you'll probably not be able to stay in senior school. They'll make an exception and toss you out earlier than anyone else. You'll be the first in the United Kingdom to leave school at twelve, two years before the leaving age!"

Ann knew stupidity was not the only obstacle to advanced schooling.

It was difficult, if not impossible, for working-class people, especially the female working class, to qualify for higher education in England. Even if they did, there was little opportunity for them afterwards. She heard Cambridge University wouldn't grant degrees to women; women could attend the lectures and do all the work but weren't awarded a degree. That seemed terribly unfair. She wondered why Yvonne continued to entertain any notions of going on to university. Didn't she know how difficult it would be? She should be thankful Mum and Dad were letting her go on with fifth form this autumn; after all, that in itself was a first for anyone in the Montgomery family. Father had always said Montgomery's had no business staying in school more than ten years. Now he had agreed to let her stay for twelve. There was no way he would permit any further schooling, high marks or not, they simply could not afford the fee; but even if they could, according to him the working class had no right to so much education.

The idea that Yvonne would eventually be disappointed provided some solace to Ann, although it embarrassed her to think bad thoughts about Yvonne, after all she was her sister.

"Oh, don't be daft, Yvonne," Graham interrupted. "You jolly well know I'll receive a school certificate with high marks, and everyone knows how well Ann is doing.

"Besides," he continued, espousing what Ann had been thinking, "what makes you think any of us will ever benefit from school? You know we are a working-class family and there is little, or no place for us in higher education. Anyway, I have better things to do than go to school forever. We all do.

"For one thing, I plan to join the Army. Before you know it, they'll train me on one of those antiaircraft guns, and I'll shoot down any Jerry who even thinks of bombing us. I'll shoot down so many I'll be famous. Ace Montgomery, they'll call me. When the BBC interviews me, I'll say it was nothing, just part of my duty. When they ask me about my family I'll mention, with pride, my brother Henry, my sister Ann, and my mum and dad. When the interviewer asks if I have any other sisters, I'll have to admit I did but that we lost track of her. I'll say she never amounted to anything anyway; the last I heard she was a scullery maid. He'll fully understand about stupid sisters and tell me it's not unusual to have at least one poor performing black sheep in the family."

Ann could not hold back a snicker. She liked it when Graham teased Yvonne. She knew he was being silly, imagining himself a hero, but it made her feel good just to see Yvonne's angry countenance.

Yvonne was about to respond when Chad came out of the house.

She knew her father did not tolerate squabbles between his children, particularly when he was troubled. He was normally mild mannered and exceptionally loving but, on occasion, could also be quite stern. With the worry over the threat of war so prevalent these days, it was not the time to provoke him.

"Get away from that shelter!" Chad warned, his voice reflecting his irritation. "It's not a playhouse. I don't want anything disturbed before the work crew arrives tomorrow. If anything is missing or damaged they won't be able to finish. We can't tolerate a delay, there is no telling how soon we might need it. Now get out of here. All of you!."

"How could you, Father? How could you believe I would disturb that silly shelter of yours?" Yvonne thought indignantly. "You know I am always good, and much too intelligent to cause any damage to your precious shelter." Chad did not hear any of this–she chose to keep her objections to herself.

"Come now, Dad, that's ridiculous," thought Graham. "We shouldn't be able to destroy it that easily. After all, it was designed to withstand German bombs, wasn't it?" He, too, decided it prudent to keep quiet.

The last thing Ann wanted was to cause her father trouble. She wanted him to love her, not be angry with her. "I'm sorry, Daddy," Ann said, hoping he would forgive her, if not the others.

"I'm sorry too, dear," Chad answered, his voice softening considerably. "I didn't mean to shout at the three of you. I guess your daddy is getting too edgy, with all the bad news lately. Please forgive me?

"Why don't you go inside? Mother is busy hanging the blackout curtains she made. I'm sure she could use some help," Chad urged, smiling in an attempt to be more loving. "Her friend was just here and made some suggestions, changes which should make it easier to satisfy the regulations. Now mother worries she won't finish them in time. If she doesn't, we won't be able to turn on any lights tonight."

"Now scat!" he said, giving Ann a loving pat.

Diane Montgomery was indeed worried. Along with the effectiveness of her blackout curtains and all the ordinary everyday problems, she worried about the impending war, and, most of all, about the air raid shelter. She wasn't certain she could make the shelter comfortable enough, or sufficiently well-stocked, to support the many hours the family might spend there. Above all, she worried about its safety for, if war did come, the protection of her children was her prime concern.

She also worried about Henry. He was working now, had been for several months, as a machinist's helper in Coventry. It didn't pay much, but at least it was employment. She felt sorry for Henry, it had taken him such a long time to find even that. When he left school in '35, there was essentially no work anywhere. Full time employment had not been easy to find in England, hadn't been for ten years now.

Henry had not been particularly good in school. He probably could have studied harder, passed his scholarship exams and gone to county school, but, at the time, it seemed better to go to senior school where he could receive a less demanding education and leave school at the earliest possible moment. Everyone had agreed, less academic rigor would make him happier. But, even back then, Diane worried that going to senior school was unwise. However, once he had failed his scholarship there was nothing else he could do. Besides, times were tough and the family needed any additional money he might earn. He left school at the age of fourteen, the earliest age permitted. She realized now it was a mistake– she should have encouraged him to study harder. Maybe had she done so he would have passed his scholarship as her other children had done– but it was too late now.

If it had not been for the time spent as a restocking boy for Mr. Potts, the greengrocer, Henry would have been idle for nearly four years. But even then, Mr. Potts had to let him go during a business downturn in '37. It took Henry almost two years of searching before he finally found the work in Coventry.

Now, just as things were looking brighter for Henry, Parliament was talking about compulsory conscription. He was a strong, healthy, eighteen year old boy, just the type the National Service wanted. There was little doubt he would be one of the first to be called when conscription finally started.

"At least Yvonne will complete her education in two more years," Diane rationalized. She knew Yvonne wanted to continue into college or university but that would be impossible. She'll have to stop with her higher school certificate, even if she qualifies for a grant. "She'll be so upset–but, sadly, on Chad's meager income that is about all we can do. If she continues to live at home, her additional income will help meet our budget; if she leaves home, there'll be one less mouth to feed. In any case, the certificate should give her a slightly better chance of finding good employment.

"It is true, Chad has a good, secure position as a machinist at Bender Electric Limited but his wages have always been low. The family is scarcely surviving on his income," Diane worried. "Perhaps we should not have moved into this house in '37, but Chad insisted. He wanted to live in a 'real' house, he said at the time, and we certainly accomplished that. Pinnington is quite an improvement over that horrible East End flat. We have more living space, and the kitchen and bath facilities are much more modern. But, as nice as it is, the monthly rent is too high. Now, on top of that, we have all the additional expenses brought on by the threat of war. The cost of the Anderson shelter modification, by itself, is enough to send us to the poorhouse. I should have put my foot down when Chad ordered it, but he had insisted we should have nothing but the best.

"That bloody Hitler!" she said out loud.

Her voice surprised her. She did not ordinarily swear, or talk to herself, but most things were changing these days. "And not for the good," she decided.

Diane knew things could be worse. Tomorrow the government was planning a mass evacuation of school children and expectant mothers from the areas of London where air raids were most likely to occur. More than a million evacuees were part of the move. It included Chad's younger sister, Gladys, and her children, Fran and Ernie. Initially, Gladys' husband, Dave, had vehemently resisted, but the authorities convinced him it was the safest thing for his wife and children, and finally, however reluctantly, he signed the papers. Diane could not imagine Gladys, pregnant and in a strange place, adapting to a new life. In fact, she couldn't imagine it even if Gladys had not been pregnant. If ever there were two people who could not adjust to new situations, it had to be Dave and Gladys. They were East Enders through and through. She was thankful Chad did not have his sister's temperament; Gladys was such a crude, ignorant, and opinionated person.

The government was sending the evacuees to places where air raid attacks were not expected. These so called reception areas included the less populated parts of South and Western England, Wales, and even locations near London, some as close as Hatfield. Diane was glad they had not chosen Pinnington as a reception area; she would have hated to host one of the evacuated families, especially if it meant having someone like Gladys and her children living with her. She was happy they had not considered the air raid threat bad enough to designate Pinnington as an evacuation area either; at least her children were not involved in the evacuation. On the other hand, since Pinnington was neither a reception nor evacuation area the authorities must not have completely ruled out the possibility of air raids. She simply couldn't make up her mind whether this was good or bad. "Maybe, if we're lucky, we'll never need to decide; maybe we won't go to war," she told herself hopefully.

She wondered how the reception area hosts would manage the extra expenses. She and Chad certainly would not have been able to assume the additional costs of an evacuee living in their house. From what Gladys had told her, to ease the burden, evacuees who could were asked to contribute a small percentage of the bill, with the government making up the rest. But knowing how such things went, the total stipend would more than likely not cover everything; there almost certainly would be many unforeseen expenses. And even if that wasn't a hardship, she still felt sorry for any host who had to put up with children from the poorer parts of London; these children could be horrible, ill mannered monsters at times.

There was one thing Diane had no doubts about, however. No one would ever evacuate any of her children–even if she were ordered to do so. She wanted her children with her–right where she could watch them–and know they were safe. Not knowing what was happening to them and not seeing them every day would be much too difficult. She loved her kids. Neither Hitler, nor anyone else, was going to come between her and the children.

"Oh, Mother! Those curtains look simply awful!" Yvonne said, as she came in through the backdoor just ahead of Ann and Graham.

"Now don't be impolite, dear," Diane scolded, as she pinned the remaining hem on one of the front bow window curtains. "You just wait until I'm finished, you'll see, we can keep the light from escaping and still maintain a very pleasant decor inside. It's all in the way we treat the lining."

Ann agreed with her sister. She, too, thought the blackout curtains were destroying the charm of their house. She said nothing. She did not wish to have her mother annoyed with her; it was trouble enough to have already upset her dad. It would never do to upset her mum too.

She hoped the enforcement of the regulations would be brief. The curtains looked so horrible from the outside, particularly when closed. At least there was no reason to close them during daylight hours, but even when they were open they still partially showed from outside. Their drab color added a spookiness to the house, almost as if no one lived there. What a shame it was to do that to any house.

It had been a lovely house, with the bow windows in the parlor downstairs and in her bedroom above. The bows were a special part of the house's charm. Now the curtains were destroying that beauty. It made her sad, but at least it didn't prevent her from sitting on the built-in window bench during the daytime. Over the past two years, she had spent many hours sitting there, looking at the lovely flowers in both her mum's garden and Mrs. Wilson's next door. It was the one place where she could find the peace and solitude she seemed to need more than ever since turning eleven; it was a special retreat, a place where she could think and dream, where she formulated her plans for growing up, for her life in England, and most importantly, for finding her prince charming.

Unfortunately, because she shared the room with Yvonne, she could only sit on the window seat when Yvonne wasn't home. Yvonne had always claimed to be 'in charge' of the room and, out of shear orneriness, would never let Ann sit there. Sometimes, when her sister did spiteful things such as that, Ann would find herself wishing Yvonne had already finished school and was living by herself.

It delighted Ann when the family had moved to Pinnington. It was a wonderful detached house, not a flat in a row house like they had in the East End. She knew of no one who had as lovely a house–except, of course, for the other families in the development who had identical houses. Even those lacked the charm of her own, perhaps because her parents were so clever at caring for the garden and making the inside and outside of the house so homey.

The bow windows were not the only things that made her proud; she thought the front exterior was quite lovely too. Ann specifically liked its colors. The house was mostly a pale red brick with brown window trim and brown eaves. Deep red colored tiles covered the area between the parlor and bedroom windows. Above the bedroom windows was a triangle of off-white stucco. The remainder of the wall was pebbledash colored to match the stucco. Brown rustic wooden irregular boards crisscrossed the stucco. The stucco and boards reminded Ann of pictures she had seen of Ann Hathaway's cottage and gave her a feeling of being important.

The house was wired for electricity, and the kitchen contained many modern appliances. There was a gas cooker with pilot lights enabling one to turn on any burner simply by rotating a knob. The cooker had a grill for preparing grilled dishes, and the oven even had a temperature control. Mum, an excellent cook and baker, used it to make many delightful roasts and scrumptious tarts. The ice chest kept their food fresh and made it possible, when the ice was fresh, to keep ice cream and to chip off ice cubes for their cold drinks. They even had a pop-up electric toaster, a rarity in Pinnington; no one she knew had one of those. It had been a special Christmas present from Dad last year and must have cost a fortune. Mum often used it to toast bread to go with the morning cup of tea. It was jam and either toast, crumpets, or tarts that ranked as Ann's favorite foods. She had difficulty deciding which.

Hot or cold water was available at the sink simply by turning on one of two taps. There were hot and cold water taps in the bathroom upstairs too, a set at the washbasin and one in the large, deep washtub. Ann made frequent use of this tub, soaking for long periods–unless Yvonne was home demanding her turn. The toilet was in a separate room next to the bathroom. It flushed automatically by simply pulling on an overhead chain. Individual coal burning fireplaces in each room effectively combined to keep out the English wintertime cold and dampness.

Their flat in the East End had almost none of these conveniences.

Perennials, planted by her mum when they first moved in, edged the grassy front garden and nearly filled the rear garden. Although everyone considered her mum responsible for the garden's beauty, some of the credit had to go to her dad who enjoyed working alongside Diane. Together, they had spent many of their free hours digging, planting, and hoeing. It was truly a labor of love for both of them. Aunt Gladys had once praised the rear garden as the loveliest country garden found in England, but Ann was almost certain Gladys had been exaggerating. Nevertheless, it was indeed the focus of the property's beauty. Now an Anderson shelter would destroy most of their hard work.

Diane and Chad had debated the shelter's location the night before. Diane wanted to save as much of the garden as possible but Chad insisted they place it as far from the house as they could, just in case a bomb hit the house and started a fire. He wanted room for the family to escape. Unfortunately, the one spot in the back that would have damaged the flower bed the least was too low for good drainage. The only alternative was to place it in the middle of the rose garden, which meant the loss of every rose bush. Diane had argued with Chad, but he was persistent, and when he brought in the welfare of the children, she finally agreed. It was the welfare of the children that usually influenced Diane's decisions. It was the major consideration for Chad as well.

Ann felt bad about their decision, but so did everyone else.

The greatest disadvantage with living in Pinnington compared to the East End was the inconvenience getting to the Underground. Whereas the tube station was only a few blocks from their East End flat, there was no direct access in Pinnington. They could take the Underground to central London, but it meant first catching the No. 17 bus to Northolt, taking the pull and push steam train to Ealing, and finally the Central Line to the high-street. Transfers obtained when boarding the bus permitted travel all the way on the same ticket. Ann liked traveling into London, but it was Graham who truly loved the rides. He was always finding excuses to take them.

Up until now Chad and Diane had rarely permitted Ann to travel without them–one time last year with Graham to see Gladys, and again two weeks ago with her friend Sheila to the cinema house. Sheila and

Ann saw Robert Donat in *Good-bye Mr. Chips* that day. Ann felt so very grown-up riding the tube without her mum and dad; although, secretly, she was glad to have Sheila with her.

Now there was a new impediment to travel which made Ann even more reluctant to go without her parents. The government was removing all street names and direction signs. According to Ann's Guides captain, its purpose was to impede spies who might be lurking about. She told the troop no one was to provide assistance to anyone who asked for directions. This confused Ann. If the signs were gone and no one was willing to provide directions, how could any legitimate stranger find his way to any new place? Sometimes grownups didn't make much sense.

After dinner, as they usually did, the family gathered in the parlor. As darkness came they pulled the blackout curtains. As Chad was going outside to check for light leakage, there was a rap on the door. Diane answered. It was old Mr. Whitwell wearing his steel ARP helmet. He carried an electric torch in one hand and a notepad in the other. A canvas pouch containing a gas mask was draped over his shoulder, and his warden whistle hung on a lanyard around his neck.

"You folks are in violation of the new blackout ordinance. I must report it to the Air Raid Protection Board," he said, trying hard to sound authoritative as he strutted back and forth. It had the opposite effect on Chad. He thought old man Whitwell was taking his new authority much too seriously and began smiling. "This is no laughing matter, it's important," Mr. Whitwell whined. "The new laws are here to protect you. If you people won't obey them, England is going to have a damn hard time keeping those Jerries away."

"That's comical," Graham thought, "if there is a total blackout what use is his torch?"

"Come now, Ezra, give us some slack," Chad said, slightly irritated by the accusation he was too cavalier about the blackout regulations. "We hung the curtains only today and it was just a few moments ago that it became dark enough to check for leakage. I was on my way out to see how effective they are when you knocked on the door."

"Well, you must fix it immediately, Chad. I won't tolerate violations in my area. I am demanding one hundred percent compliance with the regulations."

"Where's the light getting through, Ezra?" Chad asked, his anger growing.

"It's on the lower bow window. Near the top."

While the men were talking Diane continued to inspect the curtains.

"Yes, here it is," she said, "I had the top of this curtain pinned improperly."

She climbed onto a stool and within a minute had it fixed. "There, I think that will do it. Now you may check it, Mr. Whitwell," she said courteously.

Before Ezra could organize his gear Chad had gone outside to inspect it. He saw no light escaping. "Yes, Ezra, I think she found the trouble."

"All right, then," Ezra said, making an entry in his notepad. "I won't report you this time–since you fixed it so promptly. However, be forewarned; I will be keeping an eye on the Montgomery house. If it happens again I'll issue a citation, and that means paying a hefty fine."

"Yes, yes, Ezra. Be assured, we'll be careful in the future," retorted Chad, growing increasingly more irritated each time Ezra warned him of the consequences of a further violation. "Now good-day, Ezra! I have other things to do this evening."

"Good-bye, Chad. Say good night to Mrs. Montgomery. And most importantly, remember, England could be at war any minute now, it's the duty of every citizen to help all they can in the war effort."

"Good night, Ezra!" Chad sighed.

After Ezra left, Chad tapped on the door and told Diane to turn out the lights so he could enter. He wanted no light to escape through the opened door. Once inside he suggested a design for the door curtains whereby they could enter without turning out the lights. "I will work on it this weekend, after I finish my work at Bender Limited," he promised.

With Ann and Graham in bed and Yvonne visiting her girlfriend Elaine, a noticeable quiet settled over the house. It was the time Diane enjoyed the most, a time when she and Chad could talk without interruption. Ann also enjoyed this time too. Her bedroom was directly over the parlor and the muffled voices of Diane and Chad below gave her a feeling of contentment and security. Usually she heard little of their conversation before dropping off to sleep. Tonight, however, she was on edge and heard much more of what they said.

"I placed stakes in the garden marking the four corners of the shelter. Will you make certain the workmen place the shelter exactly where I want it?" Chad asked. "Insist they follow the modification plans just as they are drawn. I don't want any mistakes–our lives may depend upon it someday."

"Of course, dear," Diane agreed.

"Make certain they install it with the shelter entrance facing our house. We want the shortest path between the house and the shelter. There may be times when we must get in there in a hurry."

"Oh, Chad, do you really think we'll use it?"

"It's almost certain, love. I can't imagine Chamberlain making headway with those Nazi idiots. Believe me," he continued, "if war does come, it's going to be very hard on us. The Germans surely will launch air attacks on London. When they do, all hell is going to break loose. Look what happened in Spain. The dive bombers nearly flattened some Spanish areas. Jerry clearly could do the same to our cities–and much more. We could lose entire English cities, the London area included. The raids could kill thousands of people. That's the advantage of evacuating women and children to the countryside."

"Well, even so, I wouldn't evacuate our children. I want them right here with me, where I can watch over them, and know they're safe," Diane declared.

"Don't be silly. How can we guarantee their safety? The shelters only protect against flying splinters and falling parts; they offer no protection when hit directly. A bomb landing too close is certain to kill everyone inside. I am no longer as convinced as I once was that it would be better to keep them here rather than send them away.

"Fortunately we may never need to make that decision," he continued. "Thank goodness Pinnington is not a primary target area. One of its few manufacturing facilities is Bender Limited. If they stick to producing electric appliances the Germans should leave them alone. On the other hand, they're beginning to manufacture a few weapon parts. If the trend continues it could change things considerably. Pinnington also has several aerodromes nearby–they surely would be targets.

Believe me, if I were an aristocrat with plenty of money I certainly would look into sending my kids to a safer place. As for us working-class blokes, what chance do we have to do something like that? We must depend solely upon the government evacuation programs."

Ann heard these comments and began to worry. Would she be brave enough to sit through an air raid? What would she do? What if they sent Yvonne, Graham, and her away from home? She would miss her mum and dad terribly. Perhaps too much. "Oh, Mum, it frightens me!" she said softly and began to sob. "I don't want to die. I don't want to lose you, Mum. ... Or you, Daddy. ... Or Graham. ... Or Henry. ... Or even you, Yvonne. Please, Lord, don't let England go to war. Please protect us. Please don't let them send us away. Please!"

It took a long time, but finally Ann fell asleep.

Chapter 2

Friday, 1 September 1939

The workmen arrived early and were extremely efficient; by 11 o'clock they had packed their tools and left. Afterwards, Diane had little doubt their training taught them to erect shelters, not to save gardens; not a single rose or rosebush remained. The rose garden was in ruin. "How cloddish," Diane thought, "don't they have any appreciation for beauty?

"If this indicates the damage expected from war, I want no part of it," she said to herself facetiously–she was well aware now, or thought she was, of the destruction war would bring.

The shelter was different from what she had expected, it looked much more secure than it had before. The ends had been sealed off with concrete blocks and the shelter was partially buried. Sand bags covered the portion of the shelter not in the ground. Five steps led down through a sandbag lined passageway to a thick wooden door on one end.

Inside there were four bunk beds, two on each side. A small table took up most of the aisle space between the two rear bunks. "It's poor planning," she thought, feeling somewhat frustrated, "there are five in the family, six when Henry is home. Where, in the name of heaven, will the extra two people sleep?" She supposed they would need to add several sleeping cots, but exactly how baffled her, there really was no place to put them. "On the other hand," she tried to excuse the inadequacy, "who'd be able to sleep if bombs were falling all around?" She made a mental note to discuss the sleeping arrangement with Chad when he arrived from work.

When pulled shut, the entrance door was nearly airtight. To provide ventilation the top of the shelter contained a small air vent. Chad hoped to eventually attach a fan and filter to the vent, if he could ever find one. Diane shuddered when she recalled the filter's purpose, the prevention of poison gas from seeping into the shelter. She didn't like to think about gas warfare. It was too horrible to contemplate; instead she worried how they would manage with all the heat trapped in the shelter in the summertime.

The workmen had not only been mindless of the garden but had been messy as well. Debris lay everywhere; and it was immediately obvious a thorough cleanup of the area and a scrubbing down of the shelter interior was necessary. With all the additional work, she didn't see how she could finish everything herself. She would ask Ann and Graham for help when they came home from scouts and Yvonne when she came back from Elaine's. At least she had already assembled the bulk of the supplies. Thank goodness Chad had insisted on that last evening; it was one less thing to do today.

Diane had just filled her pail with water and was on her way to the shelter when Mrs. Wilson shouted over the back fence, "Turn on your wireless. The Germans have attacked Poland!"

Diane rushed back into the house, thinking as she went, "We need a wireless set in the shelter, it would keep us informed of what was happening."

The BBC commentator was summarizing the situation, "It has now been confirmed; the German training ship *Schleswig-Holstein* fired on the Polish coastal fort near Danzig this morning. The British government is interpreting the incident as a serious hostile act. Because of its treaty with Poland, England has no other choice; it is committed to assist them in every way possible. Accordingly, our prime minister issued an ultimatum to the German government at 9 o'clock this morning. The ultimatum said if Germany did not cease and desist at once England would consider the attack a clear act of war and would respond by declaring war on Germany. Parliament is in the process of making the necessary plans for going to war, including the national mobilization plan. Stay tuned for further details as they are announced."

The commentator then added that, coincidentally, the previously scheduled 'Clean Out Scheme' had begun this morning according to plan. The operation, which was progressing smoothly, would move a million children and expectant mothers from London to outlying reception areas. Travelers were warned that altered train schedules would continue until the transfer was complete, hopefully by Monday when everyone was scheduled to be in their new homes. All children who remained in the evacuation areas were reminded school would not be starting next week.

Diane wished everyone were home. She felt so alone with so many thoughts going through her mind. War was inevitable now; the peace she had hoped for would not happen. What a difference it would make in their lives. Most certainly Henry would be going into the Army now; who could tell about Chad, he was 47 years old last month. They probably wouldn't want men his age, but there was no guarantee. The announcement certainly placed additional urgency on completing the shelter. Should she wait for Ann and Graham to start carrying out provisions and supplies? What about the anti-shatter tape for the house and car windows? They should have done that last evening.

She wished she could ring-up Chad and talk to him, but she knew Bender Limited frowned on calls from home. She resigned herself to wait until after work.

The Guides captain suppressed the news of the German attack as long as possible, but there were too many visitors during the morning. The news soon leaked to one of the girls. After that, it spread quickly. Ann was weaving a lanyard in crafts when she first heard the news. Afterwards, she had tried to pay attention while the lieutenant listed the various characteristics of the deciduous trees of England but found it too difficult to concentrate. Concentrating was not much easier during animal studies, or the group sing either.

Ann's initial reaction had been discouragement; last night's prayer had apparently gone unanswered. "How quickly He displayed His scorn for my wish," she thought disappointedly. "He could have bided His time at least two or three days." She could hardly wait to go home; there was so much she wanted to ask her parents.

The boys learned about it while playing football. It excited Graham. Although he knew war was terrible, the idea of it fascinated him, and he looked forward to it with boyish enthusiasm. Most of the remaining hours were spent discussing the implications of the attack and the effect it would have on England. Graham did not quite understand all the things the scoutmaster said–he had never really understood politics. He only understood that Hitler was a bad man and deserved all the punishment England could inflict. In an unusual move, the scoutmaster assembled both the boys and the Guide girls near the cricket pitch at the end of the day and led them in a small prayer for England and for the king and queen. He dismissed the children after the singing of *God Save the King*.

There was a frenzy of activity at the Montgomery household that evening. Diane, Ann and Graham were kept busy stocking the shelter with supplies. Chad applied tape to the house windows and tried to tidy-up what remained of the back garden. Even Yvonne, who usually complained about being asked to help, pitched in. On a day as serious as this she knew crossing her father was not the thing to do; it would only lead to unpleasantries for everyone.

"They must really believe we're about to be invaded," Chad said. "One of the chaps at the factory said he could barely recognize the sea-coast areas. The Army has strung barbed wire barricades along all the beaches and have sunk wooden pilings into the sand. They probably hope to delay landing craft coming on shore.

"They must also fear an airborne assault," he continued, "most of the open fields now have old cars, tractors, and other pieces of farm machinery setting all over them. I guess they placed them there to interfere with the landing of enemy aeroplanes and gliders. It's unbelievable how quickly the signs on the roadway have disappeared," Chad said. "They certainly are giving sign removal a top priority."

"Would the Germans really try to land, Father?" Ann asked, her mouth quivering and almost bursting into tears.

"I'm afraid so, Ann," he answered.

"But don't you worry, dear. We'll never let Germany take our island," he added, trying to calm her fears.

Chad, although he knew the shelter still required many adjustments and changes before it would be entirely ready, decided it was late, approved everyone's work, and suggested they quit for the night. No one objected. Afterwards, the family assembled in the parlor and turned on the wireless. The BBC had canceled all regularly scheduled programs. Every channel contained discussions of the war in Poland and what it meant to Britain.

One commentator observed that Parliament was working long hours and would announce many new emergency acts, edicts, and laws within the next few days. "Most urgent on their agenda–beyond, of course, the advice and assistance Parliament is providing the Prime Minister concerning the ultimatum sent to Germany–is compulsory conscription of all the young lads of Great Britain. It can be expected," he continued, "young women will also be asked to assist. War will bring an urgent need for replacement of many young chaps working in the factories, in the offices, and on the farms. It will be necessary to enlist the support of women for many civil defense duties as well. The government sees no reason why, in this time of dire emergency, women cannot handle many of these very important tasks. All people must give their fair share–and even more than what is fair–toward the defense of the British Isles."

He added, "God save the king!"

"Oh, Chad," Diane worried, "that means Henry will be called to duty. Oh, the poor boy, he is so young, so innocent, and only now finally settled into a good job."

"I am afraid so," replied Chad.

Chad thought about his own military service in the Great War. He recalled those times too vividly, the trench warfare, the gas attacks, the artillery fire, the killing. Now Henry, his son, would be immersed in another war. He desperately did not wish those terrible, terrible days at the front on Henry. He wondered what tragedies and difficulties this war would impose on the family. He knew there would be many. He tried desperately, for the sake of the children, to maintain a confident, unworried appearance but, in spite of all his good intentions, he still looked downcast and heartsick. It was difficult, feeling as insecure as he was, to look otherwise.

"I suppose this means the government will ask me to do something for the war effort," complained Yvonne. "How can I do my studies and help too? There won't be time to relax or play."

"You need to start acting a little more mature, Yvonne," Diane scolded. "There are more important things to consider than your personal convenience. Start thinking about your family and your country for a change. The way you've been acting lately you remind me of a spoiled child–thinking only of yourself. Perhaps we should start calling you Lady Yvonne, or maybe Princess Yvonne."

The effect the news was having on everyone disappointed Diane. Chad was obviously much more worried than he showed, and the children seemed terribly upset. She attributed Yvonne's recent bad manners to the stress of the troublesome times. Nevertheless, she wished Yvonne would act a little more grown-up. She was fifteen years old now; she owed it to the others to set a better example.

Diane particularly worried about Ann. She apparently was taking the news badly, had been noticeably quiet ever since the broadcast. She knew Ann worshipped Henry. This talk about his conscription could not possibly have lifted Ann's spirits; she needed to find some way to help her. Graham was troubled too, but he was a boy; the excitement and adventure would shore his spirits. She was almost certain she could count on him when the need arose.

"Good heavens!" she thought, "If the wretched war should persist, Graham might be conscripted too. Oh, Graham! You're only fourteen; you shouldn't need to fight for your country."

"Graham! Ann! Yvonne! Come here. Let me hold you for a minute," she said, opening her arms to them.

"Mother, what's wrong?" Yvonne asked.

"I love you, Mother," Ann said, as she tightened her grip around Diane's waist.

It was early morning. Ann felt herself lift off the ground. She was soaring–flying freely above the treetops as a graceful swan. What freedom! She flew higher and higher until her wings would go no further.

She darted into a white fluffy cloud. When she reappeared, the sun was shining brightly from a deep blue sky. She looked to her left. Graham was there. She looked again–it couldn't be Graham. Whatever it was, it had huge feathered wings where arms should be. No! It was an eagle! It was flying so fast. Faster than any bird–any thing–she had ever seen. Suddenly, without warning, it darted earthward. Its beak pointed directly ahead, its talons in front, opened, as if ready to seize whatever it saw.

As Ann dipped her wings to see more clearly, she saw Yvonne lying in the garden. There was no bomb shelter. The rose bushes were blooming where the shelter had been. Yvonne wore pink shorts and a small white halter. She was basking in the sunlight, pretending to read her school book. Suddenly she saw the eagle and screamed, "Dad! Mum! It's coming directly toward me!"

Ann and Graham were at the other end of the garden. They ignored her scream; their thoughts were on the bird. Ann felt helpless. "Stop!" she cried. "Stop it, Graham!"

The eagle dove on, then–unexpectedly–disappeared.

Ann's focus shifted to the house. She saw a purple clematis climbing the latticework near the front door. The wind was gently blowing the curtain out of her unscreened bedroom window. A window shade flapped in the adjacent window. Then a huge dark cloud appeared and began to blot the sky. A shadow engulfed the house. Black shutters covered the windows. They blocked the outside air from reaching the room. Although once again flying high overhead, Ann felt the suffocating effects of the sealed bedroom. She began to gasp.

While she watched with horror, the house turned black and began to melt, then vanished. All that remained was the garden, but the roses had withered. Ann noticed the shelter. Henry was there, he had just finished painting it. He had used a bright orange paint. Paint covered his hands and face, but he was wearing a well pressed, immaculate army uniform. He looked at the eagle, which still raced directly toward the garden. As if to shield it from the eagle's fury, Henry threw his body across the shelter. He vanished. The eagle continued downward.

The eagle by now had become a vulture. Graham, his feet planted firmly on the ground and rifle in hand, tried to shoot, but the gun refused to fire. In desperation, he threw the rifle at the approaching bird. It merely bounced off its breast.

"Stop!" Diane screamed, "Please go away!" To no avail.

Everyone started to disappear. First Yvonne, then Graham, then Diane, and finally Chad. Ann was soon the only one left. Try as she would, she could find no place to land.

She spied Mr. Whitwell still wearing his ARP helmet. "Help me! Please help me?" she pleaded. "My wings are tired, so very tired!" But Mr. Whitwell did not see her.

"Ann, Ann, wake up!. You were having a nightmare."

It was her mother. She cradled Ann in her arms. Ann felt so safe in her mother's arms. She knew she must never, ever, leave her mum.

No, never!

Chapter 3

Sunday, 3 September 1939

It was a quarter past eleven; the wireless had been on all morning. The family listened as they continued to prepare the shelter. Suddenly the announcer interrupted the program to bring a message from the Prime Minister, direct from No. 10 Downing Street.

Prime Minister Chamberlain sounded grave as he said, *"This morning the British Ambassador in Berlin handed the German government a final note stating that unless we heard from them by eleven o'clock that they were prepared at once to withdraw their troops from Poland a state of war would exist between us. I have to tell you now that no such undertaking has been received, and that consequently this country is at war with Germany. ..."*

No one in the Montgomery family heard any more of the message. There was a stunned silence. What everyone had feared, finally had happened. England was at war. Now the blackout curtains, the gas masks, the shelter, and Mr. Whitwell and his ARP helmet took on new meaning. They were no longer merely precautionary measures in the event of a war; they were going to be used in an actual war.

Diane held the girls tightly. No one seemed to mind. Ann said nothing but found comfort in her mother's arms. Yvonne, surprisingly, held Diane the tightest. Even Graham briefly joined the group putting his arms around them, giving them a hefty squeeze and taking comfort from their mutual solace.

Chad reminded them it was no time to feel sorry for themselves. England was at war. It was the responsibility of the Montgomery family, just as it was the responsibility of all English families, to do whatever was necessary to end the terrible thing as quickly as possible. "We can begin," he said, "by reviewing the tasks still needed to finish the shelter.

"I realize," he added, "we have been working on it since Friday, but there is still much to do. And it must be done quickly. It's hard telling how soon we might need it."

As he finished talking, the air raid sirens began to blare. Everyone went into a state of panic. They started towards the shelter until someone noted they had forgotten their gas masks. Everyone ran back into the house and searched eagerly for the masks. Graham, who needed help from Diane, was the last to find his. Again, they started for the shelter. Diane remembered the wireless and returned for it. Chad went back for the first aid kit. Yvonne looked for a magazine she hadn't read. Graham ran upstairs to get his binoculars. Ann looked in the toy box for her favorite rag doll–not certain why she wanted it. She had not played with dolls for a long time but it seemed to make her more comfortable holding it tightly.

Finally, the confusion subsided, and they were all in the shelter. Chad snapped on the light and closed the door. Almost immediately they realized Chad had been correct; they still had many things to do. Using the beds for seats would be acceptable if it was for a short spell but would be intolerable for any lengthy stay. If the electricity failed the shelter would go dark. The air became stuffy after only a few minutes, and they nearly panicked. Soon everyone was thirsty. If they drank too much they would deplete their inadequate water supply. They decided to put off drinking a little longer.

Soon they were speculating on the duration of the raid. Ann hoped it would be short, Graham was certain it would take hours, and Chad guessed it would be over soon. It was then that Diane remembered the games and magazines. With all the other things requiring her attention, she had forgotten them. If they had to wait long, they would have nothing to occupy their time. Only Yvonne had a magazine, one of little interest to the others. They would soon discover many other items needed to help survive the closeness, inconvenience, boredom, and, most prevailingly, fear.

Fortunately, after only ten minutes the sirens wailed again. When Yvonne anxiously exclaimed that the 'all clear' had sounded, Graham, authoritatively, corrected her. "It's a 'raid-passed' signal," he said. "An 'all clear' signal means the air is safe after a gas attack." The family, as did most of their fellow countrymen, never used the more precise definition; they, like Yvonne, continued to say 'all clear' after each raid.

A commentator came on the wireless soon afterwards and assured the listeners the alarm had been false. The wardens had mistakenly identified a lone aeroplane flying overhead as hostile. The Montgomery family was thankful it had been a false alarm, and, even more so, thankful to have had an opportunity to test their preparation without real danger. They were never as unprepared again. The false alarm had provided a valuable lesson.

It was not long after the air raid alert that Diane, who had been monitoring the wireless, called the family together to listen to the commentator's most recent announcement. He said both houses of Parliament on Saturday had empowered the government to conscript all men between the ages of eighteen and forty-one. Quickly responding this morning, the prime minister had already ordered the mobilization of all military reserve units and authorized the increase of all existing units to full strength by conscription. Since they had anticipated the Act for several days, the government was prepared to respond immediately. It meant many English lads could, before the day was over, expect to receive telegrams ordering them to report for duty.

"What's it all about, Dad?" Ann asked.

"I'm afraid it means Henry will be serving in either our Army or Navy within a few days," Chad answered, his face reflecting his agony. "You'll soon be able to boast that your brother is in the service."

"At least now he'll have steady employment," Diane quipped, trying to ease the tension she felt.

"Oh, Daddy, will he be required to fight?" Ann asked. "Will he need to fight those nasty old Nazis?"

"I hope not, Ann," Diane answered, her voice almost a moan. "Let's hope the war ends long before Henry completes training and is ordered into battle."

"I'd be surprised if the war ends soon enough for that," said Chad, regretfully. "It could be a long time before England brings Hitler to his knees. From what the *Independent* says, Germany has many weapons now, in spite of all the limitations the Allies placed on her after the last war. Why the governments of the world ever permitted such a belligerent nation to rearm is beyond me."

"I'd like to fight those filthy Huns," boasted Graham, excitedly. "I'll join the Army and show them a thing or two!"

"This war isn't for you, Graham," Chad admonished. "It can't possibly last until you're old enough to fight. Once the air raid madness gets in full swing, the war should quickly end–neither nation can last many months if they start dropping bombs on each other's cities." He continued, "They'll probably never call me either. I'm too old. Most likely, Henry will be the only Montgomery family member called on to defend England. It will be up to the rest of us to do all we can–any way we can–to support him and the other boys while they fight this war for us."

Throughout all this, Yvonne sat silently. The last few hours had had a much greater impact on her than she, or any of the others in the family, realized. It frightened her. She did not want to be in a real air raid. She liked her life as it was and did not want things to change. All she wanted was to complete her upper levels and get the Higher School Certificate so that she could go on to college or university. She was not certain exactly what she wanted to study–she would decide that later. She was doing extremely well in biology, perhaps she would become a botanist, or biologist, or maybe even a doctor.

She knew everything depended on two things. She had to convince her mum and dad she should go on with her education, and she needed to pass her examinations successfully. She wasn't too concerned about the examinations. She thought that, with sufficient study, she could write them; she had never had any problems with examinations. As for going on with her education, that was a different story. The family was not too well off financially, and it would be difficult without some sort of assistance. The certificate, with the possibility of a paid fee grant, would help. It represented the first real opportunity for any Montgomery to raise herself above the working class. It was the family's big opportunity to escape that wretched existence and attain the status she thought they deserved. The problem was, her mum and dad did not appreciate the opportunity–or even the need. Now the war added further impediments to all her plans. Maybe it would even cause all her dreams to be shattered.

But the threat to her school career was not the only reason she was silent; it also had to do with the safety of the family. She loved her family, even though she had failed to show it recently. She was sorry she had acted the way she had, especially now that such dire times lay ahead. "Poor Mum, she worries so much about us. And poor Dad, he's trying so hard to prop up the family's spirits. It must be difficult for him to display confidence when he fears the worst. There must be times when he must wish he could sit down and have a good cry."

Her brothers and sister were also of more concern to her than she pretended. "Graham–cocky Graham–tries to be so brave and tough," she thought, "but he fools no one. He's just as scared of this war as the rest of us.

"And poor, mild mannered Henry; he never was one to get into scrapes. How could he be a soldier? How could they ask such a timid, kindhearted boy to go into battle? What if he couldn't do it? What if it's too much for him?" It seemed to her as if it were too much to ask. She thought for a minute and said to herself, "No, there's nothing he couldn't do. One thing to say for Henry, he has always had the fortitude to finish anything he started. Never mind his poor school performance, his interests leaned toward practical, not abstract or intellectual types of activities. Perhaps they'll ask him to be a mechanic in the Army."

Yvonne felt the sorriest for Ann. Although she found it difficult to admit, even to herself, she loved Ann more than any of the others. Ann was such a fragile, timid, sweet little girl; the beauty of the family, with her tall slender body and her dark brown hair. Yvonne had always thought Ann's deep dark brown eyes were particularly attractive. They gave Ann the look of someone who was in deep thought, which, of course, most of the time she was. She was such an intelligent, serious girl–and yet so witty. Ann would surely grow into a charming woman–if only the world would let her survive.

Yvonne knew how much the possibility of war, and now the war itself, had deeply upset Ann. Late at night she often heard Ann crying. Those were the times she wanted to hug her, but for some unexplained reason, she hadn't. Neither sister seemed to be able to show the other her true feelings anymore. Yvonne wished they could change.

A progress report on the evacuation of the women and children from London followed the mobilization announcement. Diane looked at Chad, "When I last talked to your sister, Gladys, she said they were prepared to leave whenever the authorities issued the evacuation orders. She and the children should be in their new homes by now."

"You're undoubtedly right. They've left by now," replied Chad, "although it is difficult to believe they actually went through with it. Dave was completely against the program and swore no one in his family would ever be evacuated."

"Where are they headed, Mum?" Ann asked.

"No one knows. They weren't told anything before they left," she replied. "They only knew their assembly point. Further instructions were to be given as needed. It had something to do with security."

"In the country, more than likely," Chad volunteered.. "Maybe they'll be relocated to a farm in south or southwest England–or even Wales or western England."

"Oh, how terrible," Ann exclaimed. "I wouldn't want to live on a farm, with all those dirty pigs, cows, and other animals. I don't see how farmers put up with such smelly creatures."

"Me neither," empathized Yvonne, imagining herself milking cows or tedding hay.

"How long must they stay?" Ann asked.

"That's difficult to say," Chad answered.

"You don't suppose they'll be there until after Christmas, do you?" Ann asked. "I think it would be too lonely being away from home over Christmas."

"Of course not, dear," Diane laughed. "The war will never continue that long."

"They're being sent away from the air raids, aren't they? Why aren't we being evacuated?" Ann asked, a look of concern on her face.

"Any raids will probably be concentrated on strategic areas, places where there are a large number of factories. The authorities decided to move the women and children from those zones to safer parts of the country. You're not going because they don't expect the Germans to drop bombs in neutral areas, residential areas like ours," Chad assured her.

"Then why did we build the shelter?" Graham asked.

"It's only for precautionary purposes," Chad answered confidently, trying to minimize the need to worry.

The mention of air raids reminded every one of the shelter experience they had just been through and the dreaded, but still not fully comprehended, damage bombs could inflict. They all became silent, each trying to find some way to face the unknown crises that surely lay ahead.

A knock at the front door interrupted their thoughts. It was Mr. Wilson. "Your son is on the phone. He wants to speak with you, says it's quite urgent."

"Well, it's as we expected. Henry's been called into the service," Chad announced when he returned from the Wilson's. "He received the telegram just a few minutes ago. He reports for examination on Tuesday. Plans to come home tomorrow after telling his supervisor at the machine shop. He hopes to catch the eleven o'clock bus."

"Notified on Sunday?" Diane observed. "Since when do they conduct business on Sunday?"

"Get used to change, Diane. We'll be seeing many new practices before this war is over," Chad explained.

"Oh, poor Henry. I'm frightened for him," Ann lamented, then added, "And so proud!"

* * *

At four-thirty the BBC carried a special news program. It began with a reconfirmation that the morning air raid alert had been a false alarm. There followed a list of special precautions the government had instituted: it was closing, until further notice, all places of entertainment, including indoor and outdoor sports gatherings; school starting dates in the evacuation and neutral areas would be delayed at least one week; and the banks and stock exchange would not open until Tuesday. The commentator then itemized the special safety measures each person should follow: everyone should keep off the streets as much as possible; keep their gas masks with them at all times; carry their names and addresses clearly written on an envelope or luggage tag; and eliminate all lighting on the roadways. He emphasized the importance of the last item, since inadvertent light after sunset constituted a grave danger to public safety because it provided an excellent beacon for German bombers.

At six-thirty the king addressed the nation over the wireless. He began, *"In this grave hour, perhaps the most fateful in our history, I send to every household of my peoples, both at home and overseas, this message."* He continued, *"For the sake of all that we ourselves hold dear and of the world's order and peace, it is unthinkable that we should refuse to meet the challenge."* He ended by saying, *"To this high purpose, I now call on my people at home and my people across the sea. I ask them to stand firm and united in this time of trial."*

The Montgomery's sat in silence after the speech. They all wondered what other horrors were in front of them.

Although they were not aware of it until a few days later, around nine o'clock that evening a German submarine, lying in wait off the coast of North Ireland, torpedoed the outward bound passenger liner, *S.S. Athena* from Glasgow. The casualties included one-hundred twelve dead, twenty-eight of whom were American citizens. The attack on a ship carrying civilian passengers outraged the world. In defense, Hitler accused Churchill of deliberately placing a bomb on board to influence German-American relations.

There were some who believed him.

Chapter 4

Wednesday, 29 May 1940

Surprisingly, during the period between September 1939 and the end of May 1940 Germany did not bomb Britain as had been expected, and, as a result, the fear of air raids slowly decreased. The civilians began to seriously doubt raids would ever occur and eventually the war became known, somewhat facetiously, as the "phony war." All of this increasingly relaxed attitude occurred in spite of the repeated warnings by government officials that the threat was not over. Prime Minister Chamberlain unintentionally fanned it still further on April 4 when he publicly declared Britain was now strong and Hitler had missed the bus.

At the start of the war the air raid threat had closed all cinema houses. As the apparent danger lessened the government rescinded the restriction, providing the patrons a much needed means to relax and relieve some of their war related tensions. Graham, noting the local public cinema had reopened, repeatedly asked permission to go. Finally, convinced by Chamberlain's speech that the bomb threat was minimal, Chad and Diane gave their permission. Playing at the time was *The Lion Has Wings*. It did much to bolster Graham's confidence. After seeing the German Luftwaffe turn back, terrified at the sight of Britain's massed balloon barrage, Graham was convinced England would someday end the war victoriously. He related his optimism to the Montgomery family at dinner that evening and was surprised they did not share his confidence and enthusiasm

Chad and Diane were well aware a state of war still existed. England was slowly finding itself more isolated in Europe with each collapse of another government. On September 17, Russia invaded Poland and England found itself opposed, not only to Germany but to Russia as well. In November Russia continued its aggression with an attack on Finland. Although Finland made a valiant effort to ward off the attacks, by March of 1940, it capitulated and signed an armistice with Russia. In April, German forces invaded and quickly overran Denmark. A German invasion of Norway followed, and, although Britain tried to assist Norway with ground attacks at Navrik, Trondheim, and other Norwegian places, it only served to delay the eventual German victory. By May a successful withdrawal of the British forces from Norway was all England could salvage.

Things were not going well for Britain at sea either. The German Navy, particularly with the deployment of their U-boats, was causing havoc in the waters around the United Kingdom and in the Atlantic Ocean. Each month they were sinking large numbers of British transport ships carrying vital war materiel, even after the formation of large convoys escorted by fighting ships. Losses were heavy for the British Navy, as well. In September, the Germans sank the British aircraft carrier *Courageous* in the English Channel; in October, the British battleship *Royal Oak was sunk* at Scapa Flow.

Not only did these losses at sea and the invasions of the northern European countries continually remind everyone that a real war existed, but things were becoming worse on the home front as well. Rationing of petrol began immediately after the start of the war. Because it limited the monthly purchase to only ten gallons, the transportation mode of many English families changed.

The Montgomery car spent most of its time in the garage. They used it only when necessary. For a short period Chad had considered the increasingly popular idea of substituting town gas for petrol. It involved rigging a gas storage bag in a wooden frame on the car roof. However, he was glad he had delayed building it, not only because of its unwieldy construction and dangerous design, but because rationing soon also included town gas. Instead Chad and Graham often hitch-hiked to work and school. It was a form of local transportation increasingly encouraged by the government. Chad, however, forbade, Ann, Yvonne, and Diane to do this. It meant buses, steam trains, and tube trains were their only means of transportation.

Some people used horses. This was one aspect of the war that pleased Ann. She enjoyed seeing the horses tied outside the shops while the riders made their purchases.

Except for the horses, Ann did not like shopping anymore. The shop windows, with all the added shatter-preventive tape pasted across them, made it difficult to tell them apart. The sandbags piled in front compounded the difficulty even more and from the bus and tram windows it was nearly impossible to find a shop. A translucent material, interwoven with a net to prevent bomb blast damage, had been applied to each window leaving only tiny diamond shape cutouts near their centers. It restricted her view so much that she could never be certain where to get off.

Keeping autos in the garage was not a total disadvantage however. Permanent storage reduced the threat of a serious accident at night. At first, when a total blackout was in effect, it was nearly impossible to see. The number of collisions between cars, between cars and pedestrians, and between pedestrians increased significantly. To ease the danger people began painting the curbs white and a small slit in the headlamp blackout masks helped to show the auto's location. To prevent pedestrian accidents, people carried luminous walking sticks or wore luminous arm bands and artificial flowers. Even pets wore blackout coats with white and red spots and a bell.

Food rationing began in January 1940 with butter, sugar, bacon, and ham the first items rationed The list soon grew to include mutton. To ease expected shortages and in response to the government's request for homeowners to grow as many vegetables as possible, Diane and Chad planted vegetables in every available garden space. The only space not used was the pathway to the shelter. Not a flower remained. It nearly broke Diane's heart to give up her few remaining flower beds for so few veggies.

Because of the mobilization of many of the young men and the increase in manufacturing plant production there was a growing shortage of workers. To overcome this, the government encouraged women to go to work. Diane accepted the challenge and began working at a munitions factory newly established near Pinnington. The labor shortages also had an impact on Chad whose weekly working hours increased significantly. Even so, after the mobilization of Henry, Chad added more hours by joining the Local Defence Volunteers. He thought it was the least he could do to show support for his son in the Army. These extra duties kept Diane and Chad away from home for long periods and, as a consequence, Ann, Graham and Yvonne often found themselves on their own.

In October 1939, England sent the British Expeditionary Force into Europe in support of the Belgium and French armies. By April 1940, Henry, his training completed, joined this force on the Belgium-France border.

It did not take long before Henry found himself actively engaged in the war. On May 9, concurrent with their heavy incendiary air raid on Canterbury in southeast England, Germany launched a major offensive through Holland, Belgium and Luxenbourg. On May 12, in support of this Blitzkrieg, German parachute troops landed in both Holland and Belgium. By May 15 Holland capitulated. Three days later, the Germans entered Brussels and by May 28 Belgium surrendered. It left England, members of the English Commonwealth, and France the only nations resisting the German Army. Henry was part of that resistance.

On May 10, Neville Chamberlain resigned and a vote of confidence installed Winston Churchill as the new prime minister and minister of defence.

By May 29, a large part of the British Expeditionary Force had withdrawn to the French port of Dunkirk. Once again, England found itself withdrawing from battle. Between then and June 4 a mass evacuation successfully transported most of the British and French troops across the English Channel back to England.

The people of England were discouraged. The Montgomerys had additional concerns. They were fearful Henry would not be among the survivors. They waited anxiously for word of his successful return.

Chapter 5

Sunday, 2 June 1940

Because the news had been so worrisome and depressing Chad and Diane decided it would benefit everyone to do something special. Ann's upcoming birthday on Tuesday was just the excuse they needed. Because everyone worked on Tuesday they chose Sunday for a birthday party. It would not be much–food rationing limits saw to that. However, with a few shortcuts Diane was able to bake a small birthday cake. She added twelve candles and planned to served it with peaches from a tin she had been saving for just such an occasion. She wanted to do more, but with her expanded work hours, it was difficult to do even that.

To make the celebration a little more special they invited Gladys and her family, which now included their four month old infant, Nancy. Diane was looking forward to seeing everyone again. The two families had not been together since the London evacuation. It would be interesting to learn why the Haskells were no longer in the program. As she understood it, the authorities were still encouraging everyone to remain in the reception areas. Many had heeded this advice, while the Haskells, and many others, had left their foster families and returned home. Diane had not heard why.

It would be good for Ann to play with other children again; maybe they could bring her out of her doldrums. Ernie and Fran were quite a bit younger than Ann, but she had always enjoyed their company. Now that school was on a half time basis she saw little of her schoolmates. Mostly she played alone in the afternoons and always seemed to be sad. It worried Diane. The war was turning her daughter into a somber little girl. Going to see *The Hunchback of Notre Dame* with Charles Laughton and Maureen O'Hara had helped, but tube and bus travel proved too difficult, and they had not gone to the cinema since. Now Ann was as sad as ever.

Graham would enjoy seeing the two children too. He liked to tease them. She knew it annoyed Gladys, but she did not intend to stop him, not as long as Gladys did not correct Ernie's vulgar tongue and rough play. "I do believe every tenth word out of his mouth is a swear word," she mumbled to herself in disgust, "but what can I expect when his dad is less well behaved. And to make matters worse, he encourages his children to follow his example." She hoped the past year had improved their terrible manners but seriously doubted it. She had gone ahead with the invitation anyway–surely they could not cause too much damage in one afternoon.

"Oh fie! It was nasty on the tubes today," Gladys said as she removed her hat. "I've never seen so bloody many people. It was all we could do to jam the kiddies into the Underground car. Thought for a moment there we'd lost Ernie after leaving the station," she teased.

"Wouldn't a been much of a loss, luv," Dave said as he playfully cuffed Ernie across the head. "Hello, Diane. Chad. Graham.

"Oh! There's my sweetie. Hi, Yvonne. My, what a looker you've become. I bet the boys don't leave you alone nowadays," he said planting a big wet kiss on the side of her face, much to Yvonne's disgust. "I supposed you'd be in the Women's Land Army by now; a wholesome girl like you. Bet you'd make a real good farmer: feeding the pigs, milking cows, pulling all those teats. Har! Har!" he laughed.

Yvonne was embarrassed. Diane did not appreciate his banter either.

"Now, where's the birthday girl? Ah, there you are! Come here and give your uncle a great big hug," he said, as he slapped Ann on her bottom. Ann always hated that. Uncle Dave had always touched her, especially on her bottom. He most definitely was not one of her favorite people.

"Hello, Uncle Dave," Ann replied somewhat coolly, trying to avoid his kiss. "How are you, Aunt Gladys?"

"My oh my, Ann, how big you've become. Why, before you know it, you'll be a woman with children of your own," Gladys said. "What a honey you're becoming. I'll bet the lads are pounding at your door all the time now. Come here. Give your aunt a great big hug."

Ann was always glad when the Haskell introductions were over. They never were pleasant. Ernie always greeted her with a punch, or pulled her hair, or some other obnoxious boyhood tease. She wished he wouldn't have come or, at least, would go play football with Graham and leave her alone.

"What a silly hat," she thought to herself. "You would think the last thing Ernie would want to do would be to play soldier in a tin hat. Isn't there enough war going on these days without playing army?"

On the other hand, Ann liked Fran. She was a sweet, shy little girl, in many ways, much like Ann. Even though Fran was much younger, Ann always felt a special kinship toward her. Playing with Fran gave her the feeling she was playing with a doll. It made Ann feel grown-up.

"Come on, Fran," Ann said, "I'll show you the new coloring book Mum and Dad gave me for my birthday. You'll like it. It contains outlines of Mickey Mouse and Donald Duck."

"Oh, Ann, I'm so sorry. Dave and I did not have time to shop for a birthday gift," Gladys said. She looked expectantly at Ann. "I hope you will forgive me?"

Diane knew it was a lie. She suspected the real truth was they didn't have the money needed to buy the gift; they were usually without funds. Dave was a stevedore with a small wage. Unfortunately, he liked his ale, and much of what wage there was went to satisfying his thirst.

"What a pity," she thought, trying to contain her anger. "One bob– or even five shillings–could have bought something. They could have spent at least that much so as not to disappoint Ann."

"Oh well, we can't pick our relatives," she tried to rationalize but couldn't quite stop thinking about the Haskells' irresponsible behavior. "Thank God Chad is not like his sister. Or maybe Gladys was once like Chad? Dave more than likely changed her. I don't see how she puts up with him. He's such a roughneck. I could never live with a man like him; he'd make me daft in no time."

"What's the latest on the hero?" Dave asked Chad, "Do you have any idea where Henry is now? I hear, as we speak, a major effort is underway to withdraw our boys from Dunkirk."

Chad's face lit up. "We had some good news last evening," he said enthusiastically. "Henry called to say he was back in England. He came across the Channel in a small civilian craft. It seems our Navy has enlisted every craft it could find–naval, commercial, civilian–to help our boys get out of Dunkirk. Henry says he saw plenty of action but, thank God, came through it all with nary a scratch. He expects to be home tomorrow, or Tuesday at the latest. They're giving him a seven day leave."

"Ah! Now that's good news. Gladys, did you hear? Henry is safe and on his way home!" Dave said, turning to his wife.

"That's wonderful! I'm so happy for you, Diane. It must be miserable, having a son in the service. I expect you miss him terribly. I know how I missed Fran and Ernie when I was in Denham. I could barely sleep at night, always worried how they were, and if they were being treated properly," Gladys consoled, giving Diane a little hug.

"It won't be long now before we beat those damn Huns," Dave assured her. "Convoys fill every road now and everywhere you look you see lads dressed in service uniforms. We met several convoys on our way here from the Underground station. Had a devil of a time finding our way without street signs. Good thing I remembered exactly where you lived.

"When the Germans landed their parachute troops in Holland and Belgium in May, I thought for certain England was a goner. I would have thought Hitler would have landed his troops here by now. Let's hope Henry, and his buddies, taught old Jerry a lesson. I guess we aren't going to be the pushovers he thought. Never mind we had to pull out at Dunkirk. It was only a tactical redeployment. We'll be back, Mr. Hitler," Dave boasted, "and set you on your arse.

"I hear you are a Local Defence Volunteer now? Diane tells us you spent a few days at Wimbledon learning how the LDV operates? It must be tough, working long hours too?"

"I am only too glad to offer my services to the Crown. It's the least I can do considering all Henry has been through," Chad replied. "As Mr. Churchill recently said, 'If Germany keeps taking countries, we soon will have no allies to pamper.' We best be doing everything we can to stop that madman.

"I hear they now have another group. The Home Defence Battalion. It's mission: to defend our coastline. They've been recruiting old chaps living along the coast, chaps like us–between forty-one and fifty-five years old. Soon everyone will find himself in one form of service or another," Chad added. "They've even started recruiting women for work and service."

"You should see the barrage balloons they have hanging over the docks now," Dave observed. "I don't see how Jerry could possibly get a bomber through that maze. From what I hear, he's now regularly hitting southeast England. Those poor devils down in Kent and East Sussex counties are taking quite a beating. The funny thing is, it's the same areas where they sent the evacuees. Now they are evacuating kids from there. It doesn't make any sense, but then, the entire evacuation scheme never made any sense to me. That's why I brought the wife and kiddies home. I want them with me. Not off somewhere, minding some aristocratic farmer, or working as a slave for some foster family who's getting wealthy from the exorbitant compensation they're given."

"Besides," Dave added, after pausing for a moment, "all those government warnings were just idle bureaucrat threats. There will be no bombing raids here in London. I'm certain of that. We're too well defended now."

"I don't know, Dave," Chad argued. "If France should fall, then Hitler could concentrate all his energy and resources on us. I should think we'd see air raids in London then."

"You don't think Mr. Churchill would have permitted the theaters and restaurants to reopen if he thought there'd be more air raids, do you?" Dave asked, somewhat incredulously.

"I don't believe that's why he reopened them," Chad protested. "People need rest. The cinema, theaters and restaurants are good forms of relaxation."

"Who can afford any of them? With prices what they are, we can't make use of them," Dave complained.

"By the way, Dave, we have our air raid shelter in good shape now. Would you like to see it?"

"Sure would. We considered one, but where would we put it? There just isn't any place for a shelter around our flat. Our plan is to go into the tube stations–if there ever is a serious threat."

On the way to the shelter Chad and Dave met Diane and Gladys. The women were returning from the shelter where Gladys had been nursing Nancy. "That's a splendid shelter, Chad," Gladys complimented him. "You and Diane should be proud of the way you fixed it. It's as pleasant as any home. A wee bit cramped, perhaps, but otherwise, the interior is comparable to almost any flat I know of," Gladys continued, realizing she was exaggerating. "Now let's have a look at that garden," she said turning toward Diane.

"The Suttons seeds have us extremely pleased. We used them everywhere. Just look how healthy everything is. Would you believe it? The seeds came perfectly packed and labeled, and only cost half a crown," Diane said as she started towards the garden.

"That's a bargain–if I've heard one," said Gladys. "From the looks of everything, you'll be having plenty of veggies this year; it would cost a small fortune to buy them at the greengrocer's. I always said you had a green thumb, Diane."

As they entered the shelter, the men could hear Diane complaining about the latest pricing of Christy linen towels. "What started off at only three shillings each, is now six shillings eleven pence at Marks and Spencers. Too much for our budget."

Gladys agreed, although she really had no idea of the price of Christy towels. She never bought anything as expensive as that. Dave's income, after the bitters, would not permit it.

"Want an ale, Dave?" Chad offered. "I keep a supply of it here in the shelter. You never know how long you're going to be here. I like to be prepared," he added, and laughed.

"Blimey, Chad, you really do have the comforts of home in here," Dave noted, a hint of jealousy showing on his face.

"I don't know, Dave," Chad mused, bringing up a subject he had been waiting to discuss with him, privately. "If we had the opportunity to send our children to a safe haven I don't know how seriously Diane and I would consider it. Some days we wouldn't give the slightest thought to sending them, and then on other days we probably would want them to go, especially now that it looks as if things will get much worse before they get better. Hitler has been bombing England more and more lately. Contrary to what you said, I expect eventually he will bomb London, or worse, send his troops here. If France falls, I'd wager an invasion will follow shortly."

"You want no part of an evacuation, or the bloody confusion con-nected with it, Chad. Those damn government officials don't know a tinker's darn about how to run a program—or how to treat women and children. I should know, the way they treated my family was a bloody disgrace."

"I've been meaning to ask you about that, Dave. What happened?"

Dave told Chad how they had received a description of the plan sev-eral weeks before the evacuation began and how the authorities had held a rehearsal the week before. Both Fran and Ernie were eligible since they were not under five or over fifteen years old. Gladys was eligible because she was pregnant. At the time, Gladys thought the evacuation was a good idea, but Dave did not. He had tried to persuade her to stay home, but she would not listen. She wanted to move her children, and herself, as far away as possible from the expected German air raids. She also thought it would be an excellent opportunity for the children to broaden their experiences and would provide her with much better medi-cal care than she could get if she were to remain in the East End.

It sounded simple. There was to be no cost to the evacuees. They were to pack their bags, one per person, and be prepared to leave on a moment's notice. They weren't told the departure date and time until the morning of the actual evacuation. When it came, they quickly as-sembled at the school and marched from there to the train station where they immediately boarded the train and departed for their assigned reception area. Dave had no chance to give them a proper good-bye; he was at work when the order came.

It all began on September 1. In less than four days, nearly one and one-half million evacuees were transported to reception areas. Within another week, the count had gone much higher, so high that some London schools were forced to either close indefinitely or offer only half day schedules. In places where schools had closed and no alternatives were available, the children were often required to give up school entirely.

Chaos and confusion started almost immediately for the Haskell family. Gladys found herself separated from Fran and Ernie before they left the station. It would be several weeks before she could determine where her children were. Fran, separated from her mother, became sick and no one on the train knew what to do for her. Ernie, worried and disgusted from the lack of help, threw a temper tantrum which led to the threat of removal from the train. When their train finally arrived at its destination, the escorts discovered it was a neutral area not a reception area. Only after many hours of frantic search was an alternative destination finally found. Because of the delay Fran and Ernie, along with all the other tired and discouraged evacuees, had to be held over the first night in a southern Wales school building.

The next day, all the families who had volunteered to accept evacuees came to the school and, as everyone looked on, selected the child they wanted. It was embarrassing for the children who were not selected early, they soon considered themselves undesirables. Forced to stand in front of the group until chosen, they heard comments such as, "That one looks good," and "I don't want that one, he's probably a troublemaker," and even, "Don't pick him, he looks like a filthy beast." To compound matters, Fran and Ernie were not selected by the same family. Fran went early in the process, Ernie nearly last. The families lived on opposite sides of town. Although Ernie had never been a sensitive boy, the realization that he was one of the least wanted bothered him. It led to disciplinary problems with his first parents, which continued with each of his subsequent foster families.

Fran had considerable difficulty adjusting to her new home and missed Gladys and Dave deeply. She cried herself to sleep nearly every night, and, although her foster mother was aware of her melancholy, she did nothing to ease Fran's sadness. She simply laughed and said little seven year old Fran was nearly grown and had no business acting like a child.

Ernie, much to his embarrassment, began to wet the bed at night. Each time he did he would be scolded severely and made to wash the sheets himself. The confrontations always ended with Ernie swearing and doing mean things. Before long he was transferred to another family with much the same result. Finally, out of desperation, Ernie devised a plan to run away and, although he did not know how, to make his way back to his dad in London. Before doing so he visited Fran, who pleaded with him not to leave her. Succumbing to her wishes he changed his mind, but now, more frustrated than ever, he became almost completely incorrigible. After several confrontations with the police, he soon had the reputation as one of the worst evacuees in southern Wales.

While all this was happening Gladys, after a considerable delay in the reception hall in Denham, moved in with an old man and woman who had never had children of their own and always had lived alone. It was impossible for them to develop any semblance of mutual respect or tolerance. Disagreements and misunderstandings were common. Almost from the beginning everyone knew the relationship could not last long.

Ernie's reputation eventually reached Denham where Gladys heard about it. Knowing where Fran and Ernie were, she immediately asked to be transferred closer to their area but the authorities denied her request. Instead they granted her permission to visit the children once each month. In mid November, during one of these visits, the police threatened to put Ernie in a reformatory. It was the final humiliation. Gladys immediately decided to call Dave and talk about bringing the family home.

In October, the government had asked Dave, because his wage had improved, to begin contributing a small amount towards the support of his family. The fee, coupled with the absence of bombs falling on London, made it easy for Dave to decide. By Christmastime everyone was back in London. Nancy was born in late January, and now in June the family was still convinced they had made the right decision. They refused the second evacuation in March even though, by then, almost everyone was convinced an invasion was imminent. They hadn't even changed their minds when bombs started dropping nearer and nearer to London. They had considerable company—many other families felt the same way.

"You may have a point," Chad commented, after hearing Dave's story. "It appears the government did not do a creditable job. Of course, it's what you might expect from all those bureaucratic nincompoops."

"Don't misunderstand me, Chad. The evacuation did not make everyone unhappy. They treated the children well in many of the reception areas, and many families are quite pleased with the program. It's just not something that Gladys and I would ever choose to do again."

"I suppose Diane and I would need to do some serious thinking before we sent our children away. We would have to weigh very carefully their safety here against all the risks of evacuation. One thing we both agree upon already: we don't relish sending them away. We love them too much. Thank God there is no need to make such a decision."

"Chad. Dave. Come in now," called Diane. "We want to sing happy birthday to Ann and give her the birthday cake."

For a few minutes everyone forgot the war. They laughed at Ann when she couldn't blow out every candle on her first try. Then Chad offered a toast. "Ann, here's hoping by this time next year, there will be only peace and serenity surrounding you. Let this be your last birthday under threat from Germany, or any other evil nation."

"Hear! Hear!" They all said in unison, as they joined in wishing her happiness. They sang the birthday song, with Dave horribly out of tune. Everyone smiled but were careful not to let Dave know he was the cause of their amusement.

With the cake eaten, Dave and Gladys decided to leave. "It's dangerous out there after dark," Dave said. "We had better go now so we're home before dusk. The sliver of light from car headlamps is causing real difficulty. To avoid head-on collisions all the autos are staying close to the curb. In so doing the drivers forget to watch for pedestrians and, before you know it, one of the buggers runs you down. I've had a number of close calls."

There were many hugs and kisses, and then they were gone.

"It's peaceful already," Diane observed, as she closed the door.

As was their usual practice, before they retired, the Montgomery family huddled around the wireless. Afterwards, Ann was pretty certain she would sleep well, playing with Fran and Ernie had tired her, but more importantly, there had been no particularly bad news reported to upset her.

Chapter 6

Tuesday, 4 June 1940

In the past, Ann had only known Henry was somewhere in either Belgium or France, his letters had been censored and he could reveal nothing more. Now she knew exactly where he was; he was home with her, on a seven day leave. It could not have been a nicer birthday present. She was so happy to see her brother again, so proud of what he had done and how handsome he looked in his army uniform.

Once home, the news that Henry had been at Dunkirk spread rapidly. Everyone was eager to hear what he had done and what he had seen; but when they talked with him or tried to praise him, they found an extremely reticent soldier. He would look modestly at the floor and say simply, "I just did my duty." They learned very little but still called him a hero.

The details did not concern Ann–she knew whatever he did, it had to be a valiant effort. Henry was special. He was an ideal big brother. He had always been so kind and gentle, helped her when she needed help, encouraged her when she needed encouragement, and supported her when she needed support. She attributed much of her academic success to him. It was Henry who told her how important school was; how she should always strive for the highest goals. He told her a proper education would yield great rewards, a good husband and a pleasant life.

But she also felt sorry for Henry. She knew Henry told her these things, not only because he wanted what was best for her, but because he had also once wanted them for himself. It was too bad the Montgomery family had been so poor when he was a boy, he never had a chance for a good education, never had a chance to matriculate. Even county school was beyond his reach. It had always been expected he would go to work when he reached the leaving age, no one had ever questioned it. It was what all working-class boys did. That was probably why Henry had not done well in school. Early on, he must have seen there was no point in studying hard. He knew he would be going to work at fourteen, no matter how well he performed.

Now here he was home, once again encouraging her to study, telling her their family circumstances had changed, now she could go on with her education, get her Higher School Certificate, possibly even go to college or university. Ann smiled. It was so nice hearing this advice from Henry again.

For months Graham had been telling everyone how proud he was to have a brother in the Army and how he hoped someday to follow him into the service. He personally preferred the RAF, where he could fly Spitfires or Hurricanes, but, if they wouldn't permit that, it would be enough if he could wear the air force blues. If he ended up in the Army, that would be all right too.

"Come here," Henry said when he first saw Graham. "Let's see if you're man enough yet to take me on?"

Graham gladly accepted the challenge and grabbed Henry around the waist. Henry responded with an arm lock around Graham's neck. They wrestled briefly, fell to the floor, rolled around trying to pin each other, and giggled incessantly.

Diane could not believe the strong looking soldier scuffling with Graham was her son. It amazed her how much he had filled out since she last saw him; the Army most definitely had turned him into a different person. There was no doubt about that. It made her sad to realize she had lost her little boy. No longer could she cradle him in her arms, cuddle him, or look after him. In place of the boy there now was a man. A man with a sad look in his eye, a look of someone who had experienced the horror and irrationality of war, had been mentally scared and known terror, had faced pain and death, had killed, maimed and disfigured. She wondered why this had had to happen and what had made the years pass by so quickly. She wished she had paid more attention to him–hugged him a few more times–while he was with her. Now, here he was, a soldier home from battle. "In a few days, off to ..." She wondered where. "Oh, Henry! What terrible things await you? You're my son, you mean too much to me, I can't let you go!"

"Enough of that!" She did not intend to let her fear of the future interfere with the happiness she felt at the moment. He was home–with her–and that was the most important thing.

Diane quickly put a stop to the playful, and sometimes over zealous, tussle. The boys had always done that, had always enjoyed a good-natured romp together, had always been pals. However, today she insisted on maintaining peaceful tranquillity in her home. The terrible and brutal fighting that was overtaking the world thoroughly disgusted her. She wanted these few days with Henry to be calm, sweet, and, most importantly, gentle.

Even Yvonne, who lately had been increasingly reticent and showed almost no emotion, could not restrain herself when Henry first arrived. She threw her arms around him, gave him an enthusiastic hug, and placed kisses on both sides of his face. It surprised everyone, including her. She had always treated Henry with reserve. This time, however, somewhere deep in her mind, so deep that even she could not hear it clearly, was a nagging realization that this might be one of the last times she would ever hug him.

"We missed you, Henry. I'm so happy to have you home again. We all love you so much," was all she could say before she left the room sobbing.

Chad had waited most of the day for a good opportunity to take Henry aside and ask how things had really been at Dunkirk. The opportunity arose after teatime when the children were busy playing and Diane was busy with the wash-up.

"Let's have a brew and sit a spell," Chad said. "I'm sorry, son, all I have is Benskin's. Gnat's water seems to be all that's been available these past few weeks."

"That's all right, Dad. Anything tastes good after all those army rations." He chuckled, sat there for a few minutes, then sighed, "It's good to be home, Dad."

"It is good to have you, son. Tell me, how was it over there? Was it bad?"

"Not at first. I joined the outfit in November, not long after the unit got there. We were on the Belgium-France border. We dug in immediately and everyone thought our defenses were secure.

"It was peaceful until the morning of May 10 when we learned the Jerries had invaded Holland and were rapidly advancing toward our line. I don't know what the newspapers reported, but the Germans have well-trained troops, use highly mechanized equipment, and possess impressive heavy armor. They moved so rapidly we didn't have a chance. They call their tactic a Blitzkrieg, that's German for lightning warfare, which makes sense. They moved almost as fast as lightning. We could barely defend ourselves, Dad. Our equipment was too inferior. None of us: England, France, Holland, or Belgium had anything that could stand up against theirs."

"Why weren't the Allies better prepared for this war, Dad?"

"We've been hearing tales about the German armor. I suppose we must blame Chamberlain and all the other MP's. No one seemed to pay much attention when Germany began disregarding the terms of the armistice. Every time Hitler violated something, we would protest and he would promise never to do it again, and, remarkably, we would believe him. I'm afraid everyone wanted peace so badly that they were willing to believe almost anything. Hitler somehow convinced the world leaders he was a peaceful person.

"Now it's too late, and they know differently," Chad added, almost apologetically.

"When Holland capitulated on the fifteenth our unit was sent into Belgium to reinforce the defenses there," Henry continued. "Before we were in position, the Germans entered Brussels, and by May 20 they were at Abberville. Our unit engaged them first near Arras. Blimey, they fought tough! Thought for a while, Dad, I would never see you and Mum again. Somewhere around the twenty-third–I don't know exactly what the date was with all the confusion and action that was going on– we learned the generals had pulled our rear guard at Boulogne. Shortly after that we headed for Dunkirk.

"The Germans nearly cut us off along the way, but we finally fought through their lines with only minor casualties. Some of the poor blokes in the other units weren't so lucky. Later we learned quite a few were taken prisoner.

"On the twenty-eighth, we were told that Belgium had surrendered and that the British and French armies were the only remaining units fighting the Huns. The next day our company took up a position as part of the perimeter defense. The fighting was bloody awful there, Dad. The German armor pounded us almost constantly. Whenever they quit, the Jerry Luftwaffe would either dive bomb or strafe us. I lost quite a few of my mates in that battle."

Henry stopped for a few moments, swallowed back his tears, then continued, "Good men, all of them! I wish there were some way to tell each of their families personally how courageous and heroic they were."

"Some of it is beginning to make the newspapers, Henry," Chad tried to reassure him. "Everyone agrees, the British Army put up a brave and outstanding fight at Dunkirk. I am certain the families already know what their sons did, if not in actual fact, at least in their hearts. Don't feel you must do something, Henry. You can't accept responsibility for everything. You've done your share, fighting your way off that beach. You did your best, and that's all anyone can ask of you."

"I never saw so many boats, Dad. We heard there were nearly nine hundred gathered in the harbor. There were big ones, little ones, military, commercial, and even pleasure craft. We boarded the first boat available. My group made it onto a fishing trawler. It smelled, but what a relief it was to be off that beach.

"We felt like sitting ducks until we got off. There was no place to hide–three days on that hellish place, with gun barrels that never cooled down. We made it back to Britain on the first. If it had not been for the fog cover we probably would never have gotten back." He added, "I guess the last of the British made it out last night."

"Today the news reported the French in Lille surrendered on the thirty-first," Chad said.

"Yes, I understand the last of the French to get out are all over here now," Henry speculated.

"Anyway, you made it, lad, and with honor. That's what's important," Chad said with both relief and pride.

"Oh, Dad, it scared me. I'm so ashamed," Henry apologized. "I could have fought so much better, done so much more. If only I hadn't been so frightened, I know I could have saved some of the chaps who died."

"You mustn't think that way, Henry," Chad scolded. "You did your best, which, I might add, was quite a bit. Believe me, son, it was no picnic in the trenches in the Great War, and it scared all of us. You would need to be mad to react otherwise. There's no disgrace in being scared."

"I know one thing for certain," Henry added after regaining his composure. "After re-issue of my kit and a wash-up, my entire unit–to a man–is eager to get back to the front and have another go at them."

"I know you are. I wish I could join you, son. I'd feel better if I were out there fighting along side you. We would smack the hell out of them! Wouldn't we, boy?" Chad said, patting Henry on the shoulder.

Although neither Chad nor Henry had noticed, Ann had walked past the window just as Henry began telling Chad about the campaign. She hadn't wanted to eavesdrop, but when she heard Henry talking it had piqued her curiosity. Instead of passing by she sat down and listened to their conversation. Afterwards she wished she hadn't. For the first time she fully realized how horrible the war had been for Henry and the grave danger he still faced. Her worry for his safety became almost unbearable. She could only hope the government would label Henry a hero and excuse him from all future fights. Anything else did not seem fair.

"Please, God? My Henry is a hero. Don't make him fight any more," she prayed.

"Come on, men. That's enough man talk for now. It's time to eat. Dinner is ready," Diane called from the house.

After the dinner wash-up, the family gathered around the wireless to hear the latest news. There were glowing reports about the magnificent effort of the BEF and French forces at Dunkirk. Ann almost burst with pride knowing Henry was part of it. She gave him a kiss and a special hug. Everyone smiled. They too were proud.

None of the other news stories were as upbeat. There were reports of more bombing raids in Britain and from the description it was clear the raids were in southeast England but, as was the rule now, no specific city was named so they could not be certain. The most disturbing part of the program was the summary of the report Churchill had given to Parliament that afternoon. He'd warned that France was in danger of being overrun by Germany unless the French Army could establish a line of defense somewhere between the Belgium border and Paris. Should they be unsuccessful, England would be the only free European nation left and, undoubtedly, would be Hitler's next target. He noted that Germany had gained control of the countries of Europe mostly by invasion and saw no reason why the same tactic would not be used against England. Churchill fully expected a fight on English soil. He was confident England would ultimately be victorious but stressed that destroying the wicked tyrant would require the help of everyone: man, woman, and child.

Yvonne gasped. "They're going to ask me to help. Aren't they?" No one replied. No one could believe how self-centered Yvonne had become.

The news commentator followed the report with a brief reminder of the special preparations everyone should take. He stressed the importance of effective blackout precautions, the ramifications of careless talk and rumors, the need for adequate protection during air raids, the review of plans to fight fires, and the continued necessity to keep gas masks always available. He ended with a review of useful action plans, when the invasion came.

"Oh, Chad," Diane sobbed, "Will they invade?"

"There doesn't appear to be much doubt. The government is certainly taking it seriously. Look at all the precautions: they still haven't replaced a single sign post or name of a town anywhere; they are asking almost every capable person to join the LDV, and there are military convoys regularly passing through town, probably moving into defensive positions. I heard recently they are encouraging children to evacuate Kent, South Downs, and East Anglica. As Churchill said, 'if Hitler defeats France, Britain will be alone.' Since it doesn't look as if the United States will help, it's reasonable to conclude we're next on Hitler's list.

"What worries me the most," Chad continued, "is the use of gas. I can't see any reason why he won't use it here in Britain. We're an island. It's much easier to deploy it here, especially if he does it before he invades. As insane as it seems, I really believe a gas attack is inevitable."

"We spent a major portion of our army training program preparing for gas," Henry noted. "There's little doubt the government expects it. Why else would they have issued all the gas-masks to the civilians during the past several years."

The conversation upset Diane. "Would he gas children?" she asked.

"Don't worry about us, Mum," Graham responded. "We can take care of ourselves. They've shown us in school how to use the masks properly."

"I suppose he would, Diane. He's not demonstrated any concern for his enemies so far, no matter who they are," Chad answered. "The trouble is, there's no area in Britain safe from a gas attack, or from an invasion or air raid for that matter. It would be difficult to find a safe place anywhere on the island. That's one of the reasons I have doubts about the government evacuation schemes. Should they ever decide to evacuate Pinnington, it's not clear to me there would be benefit in sending the children away. From what Dave was telling me on Sunday it doesn't sound too well organized either. I think my preference would be to keep Ann, Graham and Yvonne right here with us."

"Aren't they sending some children overseas?" Diane asked. "That would get them safely out of harms way."

"Yes, they're sending children to Australia, Canada, and South Africa. There are even some plans to use America."

"Yes! Send me to America," Graham exclaimed. "I would love to see some cowboys and Indians."

"But they're mainly privileged children," Chad continued, ignoring Graham's remark. "I understand E.J. Newton from Bender Limited is planning to send his kiddies to the U.S. Of course, he can afford it; it would be much too expensive for us. Besides, he has friends and acquaintances over there who will take good care of them. Who do we know in any of those countries? No, I don't believe the evacuation of children will ever be a viable option for the Montgomery family."

Ann was pleased to hear her dad say that. Although she worried about the gas, the bombs and the parachutists, she didn't wish to leave home. Actually, what she really wanted was for everybody to remain in the parlor—forever. But of course that was impossible, Henry was returning to his unit next Monday. She was not looking forward to his going.

For a few moments it occurred to her maybe–just maybe–Yvonne could leave without causing too much grief, but, as she thought about it further, she realized she really wanted everyone to stay, including Yvonne.

When Diane returned to work the next morning, everyone congratulated her on the heroic deeds of her son Henry. They all wished only the best for him. Her supervisor asked if Henry could make a quick visit to the factory, to provide a few words of encouragement to the crew. He said Henry's participation at Dunkirk impressed everybody and said it would boost morale to hear from a national hero. Diane knew Henry would be reluctant to talk about where he had been, or what he had done. She also knew it would be difficult to avoid questions about things that were to remain secret, especially with all the interest the Dunkirk invasion had generated. "Besides," she told herself, "he would be scared to death giving a speech to a large audience." She decided to make an excuse for him.

"I'm sorry, Bert, Henry is out with a few of his friends today. He doesn't plan to get home until later this evening. Poor lad, he's trying to see everyone before he completes his seven day leave. You recall how you wanted to see your mates during the Great War, don't you?"

"Aye, that I do. Probably having a leg over with his girl friend about now. That would be my guess. How well we all remember them days, eh, Diane?" Bert asked, trying to be funny.

The glare from Diane's eyes clearly showed she was not amused.

The shiny open-air phaeton sped swiftly along the avenue. Ann, her hair swirling over the seat back, could see the gray manor house in the distance. Ezra Whitwell sat on the seat beside her, intent on the road ahead, his hands firmly gripping the steering wheel. Graham and Yvonne were in the rear seat. Graham laughed and begged to accelerate; the auto raced faster. Fright engulfed both girls; they pleaded to stop; the auto raced faster.

Ann saw Henry. He stood in the rapidly approaching intersection, in a bobby uniform. He blew his whistle and frantically waved his arms, ordered them to stop; the auto raced faster. They passed Diane, standing on the curb. She was crying. Ann waved to her, but Diane did not see; the smoke was too thick.

Suddenly Chad appeared beside the speeding vehicle. He ordered them to stop. Ezra pulled to the side of the roadway and shut off the engine. "Daddy did it," cried Ann. "Daddy saved us from going so fast!"

"Where are you going?" Chad asked, looking sternly at Ezra. "To America," Ezra shouted. "I am taking your kiddies to America!"

A dark shadow enveloped the auto. Ann looked up to see a giant floating in the bucket hanging under a gray balloon. The man was dressed in a German uniform. Bandoleers and guns hung on each shoulder. He sneered and clutched at Ann. Just as he was about to grab her there was a large puff of smoke. Ann looked at everybody. They had all put on their gas masks. Ann reached for her mask carton. It hung from her shoulder. It was empty! She had lost it! She coughed and began to suffocate. Loud explosions erupted around her. An orange glow, the reflections from her house, enveloped the auto. The house was burning, then quickly disintegrated.

"Move on, children," her dad shouted. "Get out! Whilst you can!"

Ezra restarted the auto and soon was speeding again. Ann looked back; she could see Pinnington, it was burning! Little remained. "You should have studied geography harder," Miss Anders, her school teacher, cried. "Now you will forget Pinnington."

When they came to the sea Ezra stopped the car. "I have reached the end," he said. "You must go on from here alone."

"But how, Mr. Whitwell? How can we? There is no boat," Ann sobbed.

"We will build a raft!" shouted Graham excitedly.

"Look! Over there! It's Henry," Yvonne cried.

Ann saw Henry. He was sitting in a small boat. His uniform was ragged and dirty, his head bandaged and bleeding. He looked tired, as if he wanted to lie down and rest. "Quickly, children!" he pleaded. "Sail away, before it's too late."

"Where to?" asked Ann. "Where should we go?"

"Over there," Henry answered, pointing westward.

Ann looked. She could see nothing, except water and the setting sun. It etched the edge of the overhead clouds, caused golden spires to radiate outward. The horizon looked peaceful and serene. "I don't want to go!" she cried. "We haven't said good-bye to Mum or Dad!"

"Go, children, before it's too late! All except you, Yvonne." screamed Henry, then disappeared.

Ann felt a chill on her shoulder, she opened her eyes and saw her bedroom window. Everything was as it had been before. She pulled the covers securely around her shoulders and closed her eyes.

Her sleep was sporadic the remainder of the night.

Chapter 7

Tuesday, 18 June 1940

Ken Nelson was becoming increasingly concerned about the war in Europe. No country seemed capable of stopping Germany's evil war machine; the countries had fallen like tenpins. He couldn't understand how Hitler had rebuilt his military capability so rapidly. Apparently Ken's stint in France in 1917 had been for naught. It certainly had not ended all wars as the Allies had hoped. It had managed little more than to cost many of his buddies their lives. Now there was a possibility the U.S. could be dragged into another war.

President Roosevelt was sounding more belligerent each day. Ken thought F.D.R. should be mindful of his earlier promises, especially those made during the election campaign. He most definitely should not be inflaming an already tense international situation. Only a week ago Monday, referring to Italy's declaration of war on England and France, Roosevelt uttered the now often repeated phrase, "The hand that held the dagger has struck it into the back of its neighbor." Statements like that could only stir the international pot and lead to war. The president had no right to antagonize Italy and jeopardize the neutrality of the U.S. "It was almost as if the he wanted us involved," Ken mused.

Ken questioned whether U.S. involvement would do any good anyway, especially with so little time apparently left. Germany, Russia and Italy already occupied most of the European countries, and it looked as if France was on the brink of collapse. If France fell, England would be the only remaining country with any hope of stopping Hitler. And if what the newspapers were reporting about English military strength was true, it did not look promising for England either. Once Britain fell, there would be no major European nation left.

"How crazy it is," Ken thought, "madmen like Hitler, Stalin, and Mussolini are taking over Europe, and apparently there's nothing anyone can do. It's a good thing Congress had the foresight to pass the Neutrality Acts back in the mid thirties. Those acts should keep us out of the present European quagmire. Thank God we have an ocean between us."

However, at the moment the war in Europe was not Ken's major worry. He was more concerned about his wife and how he would nurse her back to good health. When Tommy contracted infantile paralysis and died last fall, Louise lost her enthusiasm for life. There seem little anyone could do for her. Doc Riley assured Ken that, eventually, she would fully recover but that the mending would take time. He urged Ken to be patient, but Ken was beginning to have his doubts; there had been little, if any, improvement since the funeral. Each day she moped around the house, depressed, and said almost nothing. He longed for the old Louise, the happy and contented one, not the one who could think only of their dead son, Tommy.

Ken missed him too. There were times when it seemed unfair. Why did polio have to strike him? It was such a terrible disease. What had Tommy done to merit so much suffering? Those last several months nearly broke Ken's heart, watching him, completely at the mercy of the iron lung machine, slowly fading away. Now at least Tommy was no longer in pain; it really was better for him this way, free at last from that terrible disease. He wished Louise could understand that.

If for no other reason, Louise needed to get better for Meg's sake. They owed so much to Meg. She had been such a good trooper through-out Tommy's illness. She never gave either of them any trouble–not once during those two long years. Since the funeral, she had practically taken over the housework. It was an awful lot to ask from their fourteen year old daughter. Ken wondered if there was something special Louise and he could do for her, perhaps on her birthday next October. Maybe they could think of something to give her more involvement with school activities and friends. Meg was an excellent student, but all those months helping at home had left Meg little time to socialize. She had participated in none of the special programs at school this past year; in-stead, she spent her time working and studying. Ken knew it had to change quickly, or it ran the risk of ruining Meg's life.

Thank goodness business was beginning to pick up at Bender Electric. One thing to be said for the European war, it was beginning to generate more work for the plant. Ken wondered how much more it needed to improve before there no longer would be idle young men spending their time in the barbershops and beer taverns. He knew the WPA, PWA, CCC, and all those other work programs of Roosevelt's had reduced unemployment, but those were all efforts intended primarily to create jobs. What was really needed was work targeted towards making useful things, products that improved the standard of living or made things better around the house–the sort of products Bender Electric had always made. He was not foolish enough to believe military items, like the products the plant was now beginning to produce, would improve the standard of living, but at least it decreased unemployment. He was willing to compromise good intentions for decreased idleness. The Depression had been going on long enough.

"Oh, well," Ken thought, "Roosevelt is at the end of his second term, he will be out of office next year. Maybe the Republicans will replace him with someone who will keep us out of war and solve this unemployment mess too." He not only thought of Roosevelt as a war monger but believed he was wasting too much of the nation's wealth on his New Deal programs. Ken truly believed if F.D.R. continued to spend the way he had, the country would be bankrupt within a few years. A major change in federal policy was the only hope for the nation's salvation.

If he hadn't had such a good position at the plant, Ken would have given serious consideration to becoming personally involved locally in the upcoming presidential campaign this fall. However, he had decided against it; he feared if his political affiliation became known it might alienate one of his bosses and jeopardize his job. With Louise so sick, losing his job was the last thing he needed.

It was at about this time that Ken had the new thought. He had heard rumors one of the executives in the Bender English Division was sending his three children to McKinley Heights. Rumor said he wanted them safely out of Britain before the Germans invaded the island. The children would be staying at the home of a Bender vice president. It was unfortunate the children were from such an important and wealthy family. If they had been from an ordinary family, perhaps Louise and he could have volunteered to keep one of them. It would be, at least temporarily, like adding an additional member to the family. If it were a boy, it might help take her mind off Tommy or be just the spark Louise needed to escape her doldrums.

Then, as quickly as the idea had occurred, he forgot it. Although Oakton was an upper-middle-class suburb it was not of the same quality as the west side of McKinley Heights. Oakton could not offer the exclusivity he was certain those wealthy children required.

The town of Dexter Hills, not too far south of McKinley Heights and Oakton, was a pleasant little town nestled in the Shiawasse River valley amid the hills of eastern Ohio. For the first seventy-five years the town and its surrounds were populated mainly by shopkeepers and German immigrant farmers. Once the automobile became practical, the town slowly grew as workers from nearby industrial plants chose it as a place to live. By the late 1920's, a sizable portion of its residents worked in the steel mills and other nearby manufacturing industries. The change was unfortunate. Most of its able-bodied men lost their jobs after the crash of '29 and during the years of the Great Depression that followed. Until the industrial surge caused by the war in Europe, most of the young men remained out of work, and the town suffered severe economic hardship. By 1940, even with the increased manufacturing activity, unemployment remained high. To pass their time, many of the idle men hung out daily at Klink's tavern, making it the most rowdy spot in Dexter Hills. It was also the target of much contempt, particularly by the ladies of the local churches.

Oliver Schumacher was a resident of Dexter Hills, a schoolboy, the son of one of the frequenters to Klink's tavern, and a newsboy for the local newspaper. As he did almost every day, before he began his delivery route, he scanned the paper for items that might be useful to him in his special summer school project. One article in particular caught his eye. It described the evacuation of children from English industrial centers to the safer rural areas. Towards the end of the article was a brief paragraph which described the growing interest several U.S. charitable organizations had in evacuating children from England to America.

It was an interesting idea. He wondered what would happen if some organization in Dexter Hills were to sponsor a group of these children. Having boys from a foreign country as classmates would be a new and different experience. It certainly would decrease the boredom in school. Foreigners from any country would be interesting, but if they were from England they would at least speak English. It would be much easier to understand boys who spoke his language. "What fun," he thought, "to learn about their strange customs and especially to hear all about the war from children who had actually been there."

The thought did not remain with Oliver for long; it was merely a whim, nothing that could ever conceivably happen, Dexter Hills was too poor to sponsor anything as expensive as bringing children all the way from England to the United States. He had no intention of ever thinking about it again; there were more important things to do. He still needed material for his school assignment, something of international importance or human interest. The evacuation article met the interest criteria but, unfortunately, was too short. He needed an article with more substance.

Oliver had not done as well in school last year as he had hoped and not nearly as well as Mr. Ramsay, his teacher, had expected. Because Nathan Ramsay believed Oliver, with a little encouragement and a lot less interference from his obnoxious, tavern carousing father, had the potential to excel academically, he had offered to work with him during the summer. It was nothing formal, nothing official that concerned the Dexter Hills Board of Education, simply a "friendly bit of free tutoring to help the kid," as Nate told his wife. Oliver had done well in the science and math areas; it was only in the social sciences where he needed improvement. Nate suspected no one at home had ever properly motivated Oliver to read. He hoped a daily reading assignment, with a report at the end of the summer, might help. If nothing else, it would develop a habit of reading the news regularly, a habit Oliver's good-for-nothing father more than likely never encouraged.

Oliver did not mind the assignment. He actually looked forward to it each day. He had always welcomed academic challenges, but his performance had dropped off recently, due probably to the many distractions at home. In the earlier grades when topics were not as complex, it didn't matter as much, but now he needed to concentrate when he studied. And that was difficult with all the abuse at home. He was particularly worried about seventh grade this fall. It was the first year of junior high, and the older kids talked about how different it was from grade school, how much more difficult the topics were. School did not start until September, until then he would work with Mr. Ramsay. Perhaps in nearly three months he would be ready to take on the rigors of junior high. If he wasn't ready, it wouldn't be because he hadn't tried.

That is, he would be ready if his father left him alone. It was becoming increasingly more difficult to suffer through the beatings his father gave him after a night at Klink's. It had been going on for as long as he could remember. When he was younger, the abuse had been less severe, but lately it had become nearly intolerable. There were times when Oliver didn't think he could suffer through one more thrashing. Increasingly, Oliver thought of fighting back, particularly now that it was happening so often. He knew it would increase the old man's rage, but he thought he was big enough now, strong enough to take him on, and win–maybe then his dad would stop. It might be possible, particularly since he was beginning to suspect his dad was a coward. He had noticed recently how often Ludwig backed down whenever confronted by someone at Klink's; it was only at home where he acted so tough. If it were true, if his dad really had a yellow streak, his chances of whipping him were pretty good. In some ways, he hoped he was wrong, if he wasn't it would hurt almost as much as the abuse itself.

It wasn't only the beatings Oliver minded, the difficulties they caused with his studies and athletics bothered him almost as much. Pretending everything was normal when your body ached, as his so often did, was the most troublesome part. It was terribly difficult to hide the bruises. The bruises were the main reason Oliver was reluctant to tryout for basketball this fall, if he undressed in front of the guys they would almost certainly see them and know what had happened. He was tired of making up excuses; in fact, he had nearly convinced himself not to go out for any junior varsity sport–it simply wasn't worth it. It saddened him, though, because he enjoyed participating, especially in basketball.

As for his schoolwork, it was nearly impossible to do well on the homework assignments after one of the beatings; he simply couldn't concentrate. Many times it was simpler to ignore the assignment and receive a failing grade than it was to work through all the pain.

Oliver planned to leave Dexter Hills someday, not because he didn't like the town, the town was pleasant enough, but because he wanted a career involving airplanes. He wasn't certain exactly what the involvement would be, at times he thought of being a pilot and at other times he wanted to be an engineer, one who designed things. He really didn't know much about either profession, especially not aeronautical engineering. No one he knew in Dexter Hills could help him, not even Mr. Ramsay. Ramsay was a good teacher, but he had a liberal arts degree and knew almost nothing about the engineering sciences.

But college was six years away, plenty of time to choose a career, what he needed to do now was finish reading the newspaper. If he didn't start delivering soon, people would start complaining about his service. They expected him to be prompt; after all, he was making a penny a paper each day.

He also had another reason to start peddling his papers. When he passed Vicky's house she might be there. One of the best things about his route was that it went by her house. Sometimes she would be in the yard and he would stop and talk to her. He liked Vicky. Why shouldn't he? She was popular, certain to be a junior varsity cheerleader this fall and was very pretty.

It was getting late. He returned to the news.

Oliver did not completely understand the headlines, *"The Pétain-led French Government Asks Germans for Armistice."* Oliver supposed it meant France was giving up; Germany had won another victory. That had to be bad. The news seemed to be so dismal lately: last Wednesday the French IX Corps and the Scottish 51st Highland Division had surrendered at St. Valery; on Saturday the British and Canadian troops were withdrawn from Brest; and on Sunday Paris fell to the Germans.

Oliver tried to imagine how it must feel to be French and realize you lost and hereafter would be living under German rule. He wondered how the English people felt now that they were the only major European power still at war with Hitler. He wondered how long England would survive by themselves, and how long it would be before they were invaded.

But all that must wait; it was time to start delivering papers.

Oliver could not sleep. For reasons he did not understand, he kept thinking about the evacuation of English children. Finally, after successive periods of dozing off and reawakening, he fell into a deep sleep. While in that sleep, he dreamed.

He wore a suit of armor. The horse he was riding was white. They were inside a large arena. The crowd cheered. He waved to them as he rode around and around the arena. The cheers grew louder. He stopped in front of the king and queen and coaxed his horse into a bow. The king nodded. The queen waved her kerchief.

Suddenly trumpets began to blare. The parade was beginning. There were horsemen and chariots. Clowns did their tricks while pretty young maidens threw flowers from their trugs. Knights in full armor rode by in ordered pairs and soldiers on foot, each carrying swords and shields, marched in rigid formation. There were horse drawn cages filled with wild roaring lions and ferocious tigers.

Suddenly his suit of armor changed into tattered rags. He stood in the narthex of a magnificent old cathedral; through the door came the euphonious strains of an organ. On the throne sat the king, his queen by his side. The coronation was about to begin. The lord mayor began to read a proclamation, then suddenly stopped and looked at the boy in rags. Everyone looked. The king glared, the queen frowned. They were unhappy. He saw no place to hide.

He ran from the hall, found refuge at the edge of a large lake. He faced the east across the water. On the far shore stood a young girl. She was dressed in white. He saw her dark brown hair and her long slender body. Her deep dark brown eyes entranced him. On her left foot was a slipper. Her right foot was bare. Behind her, the sky was dark. Lightning jumped from cloud to cloud, from cloud to earth, from earth to cloud. The thunder roared. It frightened her. She pleaded for help. "Help me get across the lake," she begged, "I can not find my way." He wanted to help. There was no bridge, no canoe.

"How can I?" he asked, "There is no way."

Oliver awoke to find himself covered with perspiration. He knew he had been dreaming but, at first, could not recall the theme. Then he remembered, not the king and queen or the knights or the soldiers, but the girl standing on the eastern shore. She was the loveliest girl he had ever seen. He must see her again! He wondered how? She had only been a dream.

Chapter 8

Monday, 8 July 1940

E.J. Newton sat in his office on the second floor of the Bender factory in Pinnington. He was deep in thought and looked worried. The company had been undergoing a major shift in production these past few months, and the changeover was not going as well as he had hoped. There were too many problems his engineers had never encountered before. Now, with production parts becoming scarcer each day and the ever increasing shortage of manpower, the promised delivery date was in serious danger of slipping. He had been on the telephone most of the morning trying to find a solution. Although the Ministry of Defence had been sympathetic they offered no significant assistance. They simply warned him it would be unacceptable to delay shipment of the Bender selsyns beyond the scheduled August 30 delivery date.

He had talked to Mr. Bender this morning, but the transatlantic telephone call had not solved his problems. W.T. had been unable to offer any suggestions, other than to remind him Bender Electric always stood behind its promises. He emphasized the importance of prompt delivery; the parts were vital to the war, and future business depended on successful completion of the contract. Although W.T. had given permission to go over budget if necessary, it really would not help much. Lack of funds was not the problem; it was the scarcity of a trained labor force.

To make matters worse, W.T. had nothing new to report on Jenny, John, and Charles. They still had not arrived in New York. He had tried to find out, but even with his influence, he could not obtain any shipping schedule or passenger list detail. The information was considered secret; the U-boat threat was simply too great–as it had been for nearly a year now. The best W.T. could do was promise to cable E.J. the minute the children arrived.

This lack of news would not make their mother happy either. She was becoming increasingly alarmed about the time it was taking to cross the Atlantic. The journey had never been as long on any of her trips. She worried something terrible had happened to the children's ship. E.J. could offer little to console her. He knew schedules had been significantly lengthened now that ships were sailing in convoy and constantly changing course, all to evade those damn U-boats, but still, he was surprised it was taking as long as it was. The recent disclosure of the torpedoing of the 20,000 ton liner *Lancastria* did nothing to reassure anyone. The sinking had been a real tragedy, of the 5,000 passengers on board, nearly 3,000 had died. However, E.J. did not want to think anymore about the implications of that horrible incident; it was too gruesome.

Even with all the danger, E.J. was convinced staying with American friends until the war ended in Britain was the proper thing for his children. At least they would be safe from the threat of war on British soil–once they arrived. Things certainly looked bleak for the United Kingdom. Only last Thursday Churchill had warned Parliament of the imminent danger of an invasion by the Germans. Everyone expected the attack would come either by airborne assault or a seacoast landing. The defense of the island was solely up to Britain now. They stood alone against the German tyranny. Romania had capitulated to the Axis demands last week, a result of the Russian occupation in late June. Even France had fallen. It had been nearly three weeks since the evacuation of all remaining British troops from Cherbourg. E.J. wondered if the war would ever turn in England's favor.

Even so, there were a few good things. Twenty thousand Polish troops had come out with the British at Cherbourg; they'd be a great help with home defenses. On July 3, British warships destroyed the remainder of the French Navy at Oran, and, only yesterday, the Navy took control of all the French vessels moored at Portsmouth and Plymouth. E.J. was thankful the French Navy had been neutralized before Hitler could use it against Britain, "It was time England had at least one victory."

E.J. was glad Mr. Bender had agreed to his proposed evacuation scheme. It would help alleviate some of the ill will he knew was circulating among the Pinnington employees. He really could not understand all the fuss. Why shouldn't he send his children to America? After all, he was paying for it. Since when in England was it wrong, for those who had money, to use it however they saw fit? The upper classes had been doing it for centuries. "If we can afford to send our children to public school, why can't we send them overseas?" he reasoned. "At least now, with the scheme approved, the company will be giving all its children an opportunity to go to America. It will be a wonderful adventure with little cost to the employees and will cost Britain and the United States almost nothing since it will be financed entirely by Bender Electric." He did not see how anyone could object to his children going now. "That, at least, is one good thing Mr. Bender told me this morning," E.J. muttered to himself.

Things had moved quite rapidly since he first proposed the scheme two weeks ago. The Children's Overseas Reception Board program, introduced by the government last month, formed the model for his program. Although CORB, as it had become known, had only started June

17, there already had been more than two hundred thousand applicants. If CORB was any indication, E.J. believed the Bender scheme should be quite popular among the Bender employees. From the preliminary survey, he estimated that approximately one hundred Bender children would participate.

To expedite things even more, committees had been working on the plan simultaneously in both Pinnington and McKinley Heights. Fortunately, E.J. knew the director of CORB, Mr. Geoffrey Shakespeare, who, most graciously, had shared many details concerning CORB's rules and procedures. This made the work of the Pinnington committee much easier. They had completed many details by the time the McKinley Heights department heads gave their final approval on Friday. Along with news of this approval came word the McKinley Heights employees were enthusiastically looking forward to hosting the children in their homes. That had given the committees a much needed boost in morale.

The help from CORB had been a blessing as the committee still needed to work all weekend polishing details and preparing the first letter announcing the eligibility requirements, program rules, and a preliminary draft of the procedures. Some of the committee members had wanted to delay the announcement until everything was finalized. They objected to the release of a letter with sketchy information. Fortunately, the committee overruled their objections. E.J. was pleased; in spite of a number of important items still requiring a decision, all employees would receive the letter by the end of the day. He was eager to get it distributed, a delay could easily scuttle the entire scheme.

It was a good plan. They would ask the evacuees' parents to commit to a token weekly fee for their children's support. Most importantly, the commitment was voluntary, if necessary the company would pay the entire fee. Lack of personal financial resources would not prevent participation of any child. The company would pay all travel expenses and would assume liability for all medical expenses incurred during the children's stay. The sons and daughters of all current Bender Limited employees would be eligible to participate. The only qualification was that they must be no less than five or more than fifteen years of age and in good health. Mothers could not accompany their children.

What the Bender group did not realize as they formulated the program was Prime Minister Churchill's objections to evacuation of any child from the British Isles. The large numbers wishing to participate in the CORB program had upset him. He thought it reflected poorly on the British people and "their will to carry out the war to the fullest extent possible," as he had said in one of his public speeches. The prime minister's attitude created one of the major difficulties in implementing the

Bender scheme. The governments of both Great Britain and the U.S. required special permits before the children would be allowed to go, and there were few officials in either government with sufficient nerve to challenge the displeasure of Mr. Churchill.

E.J. could only hope everything would come together in time. He had heard there were a number of other private evacuation schemes being organized, and he was attempting to obtain more procedural information from them. Only last Thursday, he had heard that both the Kodak Company of Syracuse, New York and the Hoover Company of North Canton, Ohio were organizing evacuation programs similar to the Bender scheme, and he had been attempting ever since, without success, to talk to their committee chairmen. He also had heard that, besides the CORB program, there were private schemes being readied for shipping children to Australia, Canada, New Zealand, and South Africa, but he still had not contacted any of the organizers of those groups and still had to find out more detail.

In McKinley Heights, the committee concentrated its efforts on seeking cooperation from American political and social groups. This was an important responsibility since there were many US immigration rules that had to be circumvented before the scheme could be implemented. One of the groups contacted was the U.S. Committee for the Care of European Children. It had only been created on June 20 but, with Eleanor Roosevelt as the honorary administrative chairman, everyone had high hopes it would be immensely influential in helping to arrange the required immigration waivers. Once the children arrived in McKinley Heights, local committees had been asked to direct the program. The committees asked included the Family Service Society, the Children's Bureau of Bear County, and the Catholic Community Service. They all had expressed an interest in the scheme and were willing to cooperate in whatever manner they could.

E.J. felt fairly comfortable sending the letter today even though there was still a possibility he might need to cancel the scheme later. If he had to, he did not think it would cause too much grief. He was taking a chance, he knew, but in times like this, decisions had to be made more by gut feelings than by fact.

But he could not spend all his time on the Bender evacuation scheme. He had an organization to run!

As he was leaving for the production control meeting the telephone rang. It was a cable from Irma Williams, the children's nanny who had accompanied them on their trip to America. She reported they had arrived safely in New York several hours earlier. Everyone was well, and the trip had been uneventful. There had been no U-boat incidents, as far as she knew. The children were still somewhat homesick, especially John, but it was only natural for a six year old to miss his mum and dad. Jenny, the nine year old, charmer that she was, had made many friends while on board, and Charles had been a sweet, well mannered baby throughout the journey. A reporter from the *McKinley Heights Sentinel* met them at the pier. Irma was almost certain they would be receiving a celebrity's welcome when they reached McKinley Heights–at least that was what the reporter had told her.

E.J. was relieved. He called his wife at once. He was eager to tell her the children had arrived safely.

Perhaps the children of the employees would be safe after all. He hoped so.

Chapter 9

Monday, 8 July 1940

Graham and Ann spent most of their free hours collecting scrap metal and newspapers or running other errands for the war effort. This particular Monday, however, they had completed their work early and had joined other children at the nearby playground. They were playing Identification Parade, a game that had become popular recently. The boys were in one group, the girls in another. All the boys were hiding out-of-view behind a shed. They had selected Graham to represent the group. He placed his gas mask over his head, wrapped a sheet around his body, and stepped into view. It was the girls' responsibility to determine who was under the disguise.

This game disgusted Ann, especially when Graham was under the sheet. She never had difficulty recognizing him, all she had to do was look at his shoes. She could have called out his name immediately but chose to keep quiet. She believed it unfair for a sister to identify her brother. Besides, Ann thought it was a silly game. She would have much preferred to play something else. Singing was her favorite, particularly group singing. She enjoyed the feeling of camaraderie that resulted from singing in a group. It made her feel so close to everyone; she usually forgot most of her troubles when she was singing. She didn't mind which songs they sang; she liked them all, even *Umbrella Man, Run Rabbit Run,* and other childish songs of that sort.

*   *   *

While Graham and Ann were playing, Yvonne, much to her regret, was at the local church cutting and rolling bandages for the Red Cross. It did not seem fair that her mum and dad were always volunteering her services for the war effort these days–at least it was not fair to do it so often. Everyone was calling it a phony war now; some were even saying the war would be over soon. If it was phony, why did they keep volunteering her services for all these extra things? Why was she–never Graham–always the one to receive the nastiest of assignments? They said it was because she was older, but she was only a little over a year older. She suspected her parents really didn't like her as much as they liked Ann and Graham. She even thought at times it was their dislike for her that caused all the trouble between them. Why else were they pulling her out of county school at the end of this term and ruining her chance of receiving the Higher School Certificate and going to university? It was too bad the county school no longer charged a penalty when upper form students dropped out early, maybe if they still did her dad wouldn't have been so quick to do it. The bloody war had been responsible for that too; it released her parents from their original financial obligation. They said they wanted her to withdraw because they could use her extra income if she worked, but she wondered if that was the only reason; perhaps they were afraid she was becoming too well educated for the likes of them. She wished she were young again, young enough to do all the things they were letting Ann do these days.

Working each day still exhausted Diane, and it was good to be home. She thought she would never grow accustomed to working in the munitions factory. She felt terribly tired. It was Monday, the first day back after a Sunday off always made her particularly weary. She should have called Ann and Graham in from the playground to help when she arrived, but she needed time for a little peace and rest before she started dinner. Besides, Chad said he would probably be late tonight. They had some new project at the factory, and he needed extra time to set up the machines. She decided to let the children stay out a little longer. She flopped down on the sofa and soon fell asleep.

"Hey there, sleepyhead, wake up!" Chad said, as he gently shook Diane. "Are you going to sleep your life away?"

"Oh, Chad, you're home!" she answered sleepily "I must have dozed off."

"Dozed off? It is half past six. What time did you get here?"

"The usual time, half past five. I don't know why I'm feeling so tired. We had better call the children; they were in the playground earlier," Diane said, quickly getting off the sofa.

"No. Let them stay there a bit longer. Something happened at the factory today, and I think we should talk about it.

"Without the children around to hear," he quickly added with a note of caution in his voice.

"Now what dreadful thing has happened?"

"Not dreadful," Chad corrected, "but awfully serious. I'm afraid we have a difficult decision to make, one that concerns the children, Diane–and, truthfully, I have no idea what we should do."

"What is it, Chad? What now? I'm sick to death of this war and all the things it's doing to all the families." She sighed, then added, "Particularly to ours."

Chad pulled a letter from his pocket. "The company sent this letter to all employees who have children. You can read it later, but in essence, it says our children can go to the United States and remain there until the war is over and it's safe to return. Similar to the evacuation of Fran and Ernie–only to the U.S. instead of a remote British countryside. The company will make all the arrangements, find accommodations for the children during their stay, and cover most of the expenses. All the parents must supply is a very nominal weekly fee for the children's billets. I have been thinking about it and believe our budget could cover the stipend." Seeing the look of horror on Diane's face he quickly added, "That is, if we agree."

"All we must supply is a nominal weekly fee? It seems to me we need to supply much more than that, Chad! Don't we need to supply our children? Our children, Chad!

"Our children!" she repeated a third time, then grew silent for a few minutes. Finally, she continued, "Don't even consider it. I'm not going to give up my children! Do you recall what you said when Dave and Gladys were here? You were against evacuating them then. Weren't you?"

"But this is different, Diane. It's a private evacuation, sponsored by Bender Electric. The government will be excluded from this one. They won't have the opportunity to botch it as they did with the Haskells. Besides, things have changed for the worse since then. France is gone. Russia is still after more territory. Even Mussolini is getting greedier. You heard what the members of Parliament are saying. Everyone believes, without France, it is only a matter of days until Hitler invades Britain. Do you want your children living under Nazi rule, Diane?"

"But, Chad, they are our children. Our children!" Diane was almost shouting. She started to cry.

"E.J. believes in this program. As you know, he already has sent his children. He used his own money. What better assurances can there be? He certainly would not have sent his children if he hadn't thought it a good idea. It's obvious he wanted them out of England. The factory is modeling its scheme after the CORB program we have been reading about in the news. You know how popular that program is."

"Those bloody upper classes are always sending their children away. They don't particularly care to keep their children around them; they send them to school, they send them on trips with an escort while they stay home, and they leave them at home with a nanny while they travel. You know as well as I do they don't relate to their children the way we do. We love our children, damn it! We want them with us all the time."

Diane was angry. She was swearing more these days, especially when she was angry, and, as usual, once she did she regretted it. She decided to keep her remaining objections to herself, at least temporarily, until she had time to regain her composure. "Must we decide tonight?" she asked.

"No, we have a few days."

"Then let's think about it some more. We'll discuss it later. Perhaps ask the kiddies how they feel about it. I don't believe Graham would mind going, but I am almost certain Ann and Yvonne would be against it." She hesitated a minute, and then added, "On second thought, maybe we should wait until we know better how we feel. We can broach the subject with them later."

"You're right. It's too early to ask for their opinion. We should have our minds made up first. There is one thing you should know, however; it only involves Ann and Graham. Unless I misunderstood the rules, Yvonne will be too old to qualify."

"Oh, Chad, will she be left out again? It will bother her terribly, you know? Growing up has been such a difficult adjustment for her. Although she always derides Graham and Ann about their youth and brags about her maturity, the transition to womanhood is harder for her than she'll admit. She's having such a difficult time accepting her responsibilities as a young adult. As you know, she's always complaining about replacing play with work. Although I'm certain she has no desire to go to America, she'll grab onto this as one more indication we are persecuting her. The poor thing believes the world has picked her out especially to torment, particularly since we decided to pull her out of county school."

"Yes, it really is a shame," Chad agreed. "If we decide to send our children, they should all go. Let's think about it overnight, see how we feel in the morning. You had best prepare dinner before I'm late for the LDV. I'll call the children."

"It's really not fair, Chad. You have already spent a long day at the factory and now must spend more hours taking care of your Local Defence Volunteer duty. You're hardly ever home anymore."

"Now, Diane, we've discussed that. It's my duty. How else will we stop Jerry when he invades? Besides, it's an honor to be serving my country again. I know it is not the real army, but it's the best I can do at my age."

"If only Yvonne had your dedication to duty," Diane sighed. "Maybe then she wouldn't always complain so."

Diane and Chad discussed the scheme again on Tuesday evening but still could not reach a decision. The thought of losing the kiddies, for who knew how long, made it difficult. At times they persuaded themselves not to send them, but then they would think of the threatened German invasion. At other times they would decide it best to send the children, but then they would think of the U-boat dangers in the Atlantic. They would think of the children's safety should the Germans bomb Pinnington and would decide to send them. They would think of little Ann and Graham living with strangers in America and would decide against sending them.

Chad and Diane had good reason to worry about the bombing threat. So far, most of the German fly-overs had been either reconnaissance flights or sporadic and tentative forays with not much damage. Then, suddenly on Wednesday, the onslaught intensified. The Germans began harrying British convoys in the English Channel and struck the English seaports from Dover to Plymouth. Although no one knew at the time, the so called Battle of Britain had begun.

Diane and Chad heard the heavy air strike announcement on the BBC six o'clock news. Although the commentator did not identify precisely where the strikes occurred, it was apparent they involved major English cities and that damage had been severe. The announcement weighed heavily on their thoughts about the scheme. They both began to think more positively about sending the children; the benefits of safety suddenly seemed more important.

"What did they say about the billets?" Diane asked. "Would Ann and Graham be kept together once they arrived in America?"

"They said there could be no guarantees since it depended on the availability of homes and the particular wishes of the foster parents involved. Still they assured us they would make every effort to keep siblings together whenever possible. They sound sincere in wanting to treat the children with compassion and concern."

"It would devastate Ann if she were left by herself. I can't imagine her staying with a family without Graham; she is such a sensitive child," Diane worried. She then changed her mind once again and said, "Oh, Chad, I don't think we should send them!"

"I agree, Diane, maybe we shouldn't. You know, there's also the danger in crossing the Atlantic. The U-boat menace is growing each day. Simply getting across safely may soon be impossible. The officials have assured us the trip will be by convoy which should reduce the odds of being torpedoed, but still it is a worry."

"Torpedoed! Oh, I hadn't thought about it exactly that way! How can we send them, Chad?"

"I don't know, Diane. I don't know!"

On Thursday the *Daily Express* ran an editorial urging nonessential people to evacuate London. The editorial painted an extremely bleak picture of the expected bombing raids. That same day the *Evening Standard* said people should stay home. It argued that the inconveniences and dangers of evacuation far exceeded the air threat. Since the Montgomery's read the *Daily Express*, they leaned toward sending Ann and Graham. A talk that evening with Mr. Wilson, who read the *Evening Standard*, changed Chad's mind back toward keeping them in Pinnington. Both Chad and Diane continued to vacillate on the pros and cons all evening.

On Friday, July 19, Hitler sent a peace offer to England. He said that if he could retain all the territories he presently occupied, he was willing to live in peace with Britain. There was little debate over the British government's response. Even before the government sent a formal rejection to Hitler, the BBC and the British press had already rejected the idea. Peace was unacceptable under the stated conditions.

This rapid and firm public response left no doubt Germany would retaliate against Britain in an all out effort. The expected invasion seemed certain. It was late Friday night when Diane and Chad finally concluded they should put their selfish feelings aside and enroll Ann and Graham in the scheme. It still took several more days before they were sufficiently confident to tell the children.

On Monday, July 22, after dinner, they called Ann and Graham into the parlor and told them of the planned trip to America. They made it plain the children had no choice; they would be going, barring any last minute changes in the Bender plan.

"It will be just like a holiday," Diane promised.

Both children were excited. "Oh, Mum! Oh, Dad! That will be top notch!" Graham exclaimed. "We'll be able to see America firsthand. I know we'll simply love it there. I've seen it in the pictures at the cinema. I think it will be a grand experience."

"Will we see cowboys and Indians?" Ann asked.

"I'm afraid not," Chad laughed. "You'll be staying with friendly people who work at Daddy's company in McKinley Heights, Ohio. There aren't any cowboys and Indians in McKinley Heights."

"There will be big cars, Ann. Really nice homes with huge gardens. It will be just like in the pictures." Graham advised her.

"Do we know who we'll be staying with, Mum?" asked Ann, a worried look taking over her countenance.

"No, Ann, you don't know them now, but, once you arrive, you quickly will. They'll be nice people–they must be good or they wouldn't be so unselfishly inviting you into their home."

"How long will we be there?" Ann asked.

Chad answered. "We can't be certain, but I would guess no more than one-half year, or maybe–at the longest–one year."

"Oh, Mum, I don't want to stay an entire year. I want to remain here with you."

"Don't you understand, dear, you must go. It's better that you leave Pinnington. With the threat of the air raids and invasion increasing each day, it's the only safe thing to do."

Ann asked the first of a long list of questions that immediately came to mind, "Will you be bombed, Mum? Will you and Daddy be killed? What will happen to Graham and me if you are?"

"Of course we'll be all right, Ann," Diane tried to assure her. "We simply think it will be less inconvenient for you if you're in the U.S. while conditions are bad here."

"I don't want to go," Ann said resolutely.

"Now don't argue. You and Graham are going, and that's final," Diane said firmly.

Ann did not understand. If her mother loved them, how could she think of sending them away? It was a thought that would linger in Ann's mind for a long, long time. "Don't you love us anymore, Mum?"

"Look, Ann, we're doing what we believe is best for you. Don't accuse your mother of not loving you. I won't tolerate it," Chad scolded, somewhat defensively.

"He doesn't love me either," Ann thought. This idea, also, remained with Ann for a long, long time.

Ann began to cry. "Don't cry, Ann. I'll be there with you. I'll take care of you," Graham said, trying to console her.

"What's happening? Why will you take care of her, Graham?" Yvonne inquired as she walked into the parlor. "Why is everyone looking so serious? Why is Ann crying?"

"We're being evacuated to America," Graham boasted, excitedly.

Yvonne looked at her parents, "Am I going too?"

"No, Yvonne, this is a scheme sponsored by Bender Electric, and, unfortunately, you're too old. You don't qualify under their rules. You'll stay here with Mum and me. You will help England win this war. She needs your support; we need your company," Chad said, trying to defuse her disappointment.

"You might know," complained Yvonne, "once again old Yvonne gets nicked by the cruel finger of fate. Did you really try to include me, Dad? Or did you do as you always do? You probably bloody well didn't try to send me. Did you?" She began screaming, "You don't give a damn about me! You and Mum never have. You hate me, don't you?"

"That will be enough, Yvonne. Go to your room." Chad shouted.

"Oh, Yvonne, how could you talk so cruelly?" Diane asked.

"Who's cruel? Who's the Scrooge? It's not me! It's the two of you!. You have always hated me. Haven't you? First you took away my one chance to receive a university education and now you won't send me to America where I'd be safe. You want me dead. I hate you–both of you!" she screamed

"Yvonne, go to your room!"

"Don't order me around, Dad. If I'm old enough to stay here and work in this bloody awful war, then I jolly well am old enough to do as I please. You shan't boss me around anymore."

She looked at Ann and Graham, "I hope the two of you never come back!" Before anyone could respond, she turned and stomped out of the house. She would remember this day for a long, long time, too.

"Mummy, Mummy, will Yvonne ever forgive us? Please, please? I don't want to go to America. Can I stay here with Yvonne, and Daddy, and you? I love you!" Ann pleaded.

"No, Ann, Dad and I made the decision. It's final. The two of you are definitely going."

It broke Diane's heart. She realized how terrible Ann must feel. She knew telling someone you were sending them away sounded terribly harsh. She knew it must seem as if she didn't love Ann. But what could she do? She had to save her children. "What if the Nazi's invade England? And win! What would happen if the Germans gave England the same treatment they are giving the Dutch, the Belgians, the French, and the citizens of all the other countries? She also understood Yvonne's feelings. Would Yvonne ever forgive her? She was so mistaken–the real truth: Chad and she would have gladly sent Yvonne, if the rules had not excluded sixteen year olds. Thank God Graham is only fifteen, at least he can go."

Diane thought about the war. It was destroying her family; even though she had never heard a bomb explode, or the report of a German rifle, her family was being wounded. It seemed somewhat ironic.

She wondered if she had made the right decision. Only time would tell.

Chapter 10

Tuesday, 23 July 1940

Worrying about their final choice kept Diane and Chad awake even after Ann and Graham had been told they were going. They talked for hours, carefully reviewing, for one last time, their decision. They knew, whatever they did, it would impact heavily on the life of each child, as well as on their own. They did not want to be wrong. If they kept them home, they might die in an air raid or suffer under Nazi rule. If they sent them to America the children would be lonesome and homesick. If it was a lengthy stay, the children might quit loving them, perhaps lose sympathy for their English heritage as well. Because it was selfish to think of anything but their safety, the troubled parents finally decided they had made the right choice but still fell asleep with what was, perhaps always would be, a lingering doubt in their minds.

The first thing Chad did upon arrival at the factory on Tuesday was to register Ann and Graham for the evacuation. Once he did, he felt a huge sense of relief; the period of indecision was over; he was happy for the first time in weeks. There'd be no turning back now. His children's fate had been sealed.

He shuddered as he repeated that last thought over and over again. "My children's fate has been sealed? My God! What have I done?" he asked himself. There was no doubt that the choice still worried him. It wasn't over. It would never be over. There would always be a question; only time would prove it right or wrong.

And what about Yvonne? What would happen to her? She certainly had been angry Monday evening. In one way he didn't blame her, life was not easy with the war and all its ramifications. On the other hand, she was no longer a child; it was time she accepted things as they were, not as she wished them to be. She still did not seem to realize everyone had his or her place in the world. She shouldn't expect more than was due, especially when it came to school. He had tried to explain it to her when he told her he was withdrawing her from county school. True, she had matriculated with extremely high marks. There was no doubt she was intelligent enough to continue, even to be successful at university, but she was a Montgomery. The Montgomery's had their place in society, and it definitely wasn't as members of the educated upper crust. He could not understand why she couldn't see that. How many times had he tried to explain it? Each time he tried had only made her angrier.

He had hoped once she knew her schooling was definitely over, she would settle down and accept her fate. Unfortunately, it hadn't happened that way. She still was discontented, maybe even more so now. "Perhaps, once she finds steady employment her attitude will change." he tried to assure himself. "One thing's for certain, we had better find something to convince her soon, before she does something she shouldn't. If we don't do it quickly, one of us is going to say something, and our relationship will be destroyed forever, that is if we haven't already said too much."

Once again his mind reverted to the scheme. "At least the registration is complete and no longer an option. It's over. Finished. Good or bad, I can't change it anymore. Perhaps now everyone can get on with their life, resigned to their role in the scheme of things–whatever fate has in mind. The 'scheme' of things. The Bender 'scheme.' Now there's a strange coincidence of words," he thought. Was it humorous? He thought so. He needed something–anything–to relieve the strain of these past two soul wrenching weeks. He sighed briefly and relaxed ever so slightly.

The remainder of the morning raced by relatively quickly. It had been a long time since he felt as relieved and relaxed. It was as if a huge burden no longer hung over him. He could not recall when work had been so pleasant. He appreciated the reprieve.

*   *   *

As he usually did, he ate lunch with George Dickson, a machinist's helper who worked in his department. He had known George for several years. He could not say they were good friends; a better description would be good acquaintances. Even though George was highly opinionated and as stubborn as an ox–and as big as one–he liked George. George often questioned, usually with a negative bent, many of the things Chad took for granted. He had a way of forcing Chad to look at things from a different point of view, often to make him think more objectively. Even so, Chad was thankful he only spent one-half hour listening to all of his negative criticisms each day. He could never survive an entire day listening to all his complaints. "George's poor wife," he thought, "How does she tolerate all his negativity? It's a wonder she puts up with him." He discarded the last thought, decided it was none of his business.

Their talk centered on the Welsh boxer, Tommy Farr. Farr had just fought Joe Louis for the world heavy weight championship. They were both impressed with Farr. They hadn't expected Tommy to last more than a few rounds, certainly not fifteen.

Just before they returned to work, Chad mentioned that Diane and he had finally decided to send Ann and Graham to America and how relieved he was to have the decision behind him. George looked surprised. "What took you so long? I registered my daughter, Edith, over a week ago."

"My wife and I couldn't make up our minds what to do. Its effect on the kiddies, especially my daughter, Ann, concerns us. We were afraid sending her away might make her too homesick. She's become quite the homebody lately, has been very depressed. We don't know what a trip like this might do to her. And that's just one of many questions. If we keep our children here with us we can look after them and know they are well, but they might get hurt. If we send them away they will be safer, but they won't be under our cognizance and supervision. The decision is a tough one."

"Chad," George sighed, "let your children grow up! It won't harm them to be homesick. They need knocking around a bit as they get older, a little time away from home will be good for them. I certainly am not going to worry about Edith. She's twelve now, almost old enough to find her own way in this world. It's almost time for her to leave the nest anyway. Sending her to America is an excellent way to force her to fly a little earlier."

"But won't you and your wife miss her?"

"Not I, mate," he snorted. "I'll be glad to see that girl gone. She's getting brattier and brattier the older she gets. She has given me nothing but cheek and sass this past year. I can barely stand the bloody girl. She's just like her mother, sits around whining about how much better things could be. They both need a good whipping. They've needed one for some time now."

"What does your wife think about your daughter going?" Chad asked. "My wife is having difficulty adjusting to the idea. She still is not certain she'll be able to say good-bye when that day finally arrives."

"What does my wife think? Ha!" George laughed. "What difference does that make? It doesn't matter what she thinks. It's my decision. I'm the head of my household. I make all the decisions. My family does what I say, and when I tell them to do it." He looked at Chad quizzically, "Now don't tell me you permit your wife to tell you what to do?"

"Of course I do, George. She has as much right to say what she thinks as I do."

"I imagine the next thing you'll be telling me is the two of you are a team," he chuckled. "Blimey! You have it all screwed up, Chad. This is the twentieth century. Don't you know that man is supposed to be the head of the house? Why else do you think men hold all the important positions in the world. If men must earn the living; that certainly should give them the right be the final authority in all matters of any importance."

"You're wrong, George, women have feelings too, just the same as we do. They want a say in their future too. They deserve a good, happy, responsible life, every bit as much as men do. And to do so, they have a right to participate in all the decision making processes."

"Next you'll be telling me you believe Bender Limited should start taking advice from these women. I'll bet you'd even let them take on supervisory positions someday. I suppose you also believe they should keep their jobs after the war. I say they're here only to help during this crisis, to do the menial tasks we men don't like doing. Bender Limited had better not keep them one day longer than needed. If it does, the factory will bloody well have a strike on its hands. When the men return from military service there won't be enough jobs for everybody, even with all the shortages brought on by the war. Imagine if the women are still working once the war ends. Why, it would be a blooming disaster. Men would be sitting at home twiddling their thumbs while the women-folk are out working–at jobs that rightfully belong to us men. Besides, who would look after the house and babies if the women don't stay home? Certainly not the men, that's women's work. It's been that way for as long as I can remember, and I for one want to keep it that way."

"Come off it, George. I imagine next you'll tell me you believe women should be belted occasionally."

"Why not? When the girls do something wrong, it's only fitting we set them straight."

Chad could not believe what he had just heard. In all the time he had known George, he had never heard him speak about women in this manner. "What a terrible attitude," Chad thought. He wondered if George really treated his family the way he said, or whether it was just the idle boast of a brash man. If George truly believed in what he was saying, Chad should start looking for a new lunchtime companion. He certainly did not want a friend that harbored those kinds of ideas.

In the meantime he thought it prudent to change the subject. He returned the talk to the Brown Bomber. "Is there anyone in the world that can fight Louis and win?" he asked.

Edith Dickson, born in April of 1928, had developed into a witty, precocious young girl. An excellent student, she sat for her scholarship in April of 1939 and had passed with high marks. It entitled her to enroll at East Valley County School last September. Now, after the first end-of-year examination, she had been placed in the A stream. Her ultimate ambition: to study at university, specialize in pharmacology, and work as a chemist someday. But that was mostly a dream. Her dad was firmly against her taking over, what he described as, "a man's line of work." This bias, however, did not prevent him from wanting her to get a job; he already had outlined his plans for her contribution to the family coffers when she left school in '42. Her only hope: somehow, to convince him to let her continue beyond the leaving age, sit for her matriculation in three years, her Higher School Certificate in five, and go on to university.

But at the moment her main concern was his decision about going to America. Although she had been told it was an excellent evacuation plan, she had no desire to go. She had heard of the terrible experiences some of the children had when they were evacuated in '39, especially when it came to schooling. Limited facilities, teaching staff, and organization in most communities restricted the quality of the schooling they were offered. The last thing she wanted was to end up in some mediocre school.

There were, of course, exceptions. In some communities, where the number of evacuees was small, they had been placed in classes with the local children; in others, they were kept in separate groups but were taught by London teachers who had accompanied them. In both cases, the teachers were able to maintain a semblance of a normal program, but neither appeared to be viable options if she went with the Bender group. First of all, not all Bender children would come from the same school or school level so there wouldn't be a sufficient number of teachers to maintain separate classes for everyone. In fact, rumors were circulating that no adult would accompany the children, which Edith thought ludicrous. They certainly needed escorts; they couldn't be expected to travel all the way to America all by themselves. After all, they were only children. Even if the rumors proved false and escorts did go along, the escorts undoubtedly could not all be teachers, especially with a teacher shortage in England already. Undoubtedly the best Bender evacuees could hope for would be integration into the existing American classes. But how could their education be good? The classes would be taught by American teachers. What would they know about the educational needs of English children? How could American teachers prepare her for matriculation, or to become a chemist? She decided she would learn almost nothing during the stay. The trip would be a total waste.

"Mum, can't you do something? Can't you make Daddy change his mind?" She pleaded with her mother, Harriet.

Harriet Dickson was a tiny, fragile woman who loved her daughter dearly. Edith was the one person in her life who really mattered. Now George was sending Edith away. She knew she should do something to stop him but was afraid to challenge his authority. Once made up, there was no way of changing his mind. He was set in his ways and neither argument, reason, nor threat could change him. She also knew the consequences if she tried.

"You know how Dad is, Edith. There is nothing we can do. Heaven knows I want you to stay, I love you, and would do anything to keep you here with me," she answered. She tried to smile, "Look on the cheery side, love. You'll be in America, safe from air raids and invasion."

"But I want to go to school, Mum. I want to be a chemist someday. If I don't keep up with my studies, I'll never make it."

"They have good schools in America. Some say they're even better than ours. They give everyone an equal chance for education over there, no matter who they are. A person can be upper-class, middle-class, or even lower-class like we are, and still qualify for university work. I wager you'll find some nice people to live with," she continued, trying to sound hopeful, "people who will encourage you to study. More than likely, when you return home you'll be able to go on as if nothing ever happened–maybe even qualify for more advanced studies; perhaps even be qualified to do more than you would if you had stayed here. Why–if you're there long enough–you might even matriculate in America."

"But what can I study over there, Mum? Their culture is so different. Most of their studies will probably focus on how they gained their independence from Britain. What forms of government will they study? Will they study our Parliament? What interest will they have in Shakespeare? Keats? Faraday? Maxwell? When they study social subjects, what societies will they study? Perhaps they'll ignore our country altogether. Oh, Mum, please! Please, can't you do something?"

Although Harriet was not a scholar and had not progressed nearly as far as Edith in school, she understood Edith's concern. She thought about her schooling. Had she been able to continue on, maybe, just maybe, her life would have turned out better. She had been doing well in her studies when her dad made her leave school and go to work. She could recall, all too well, how devastated she had been at the time.

Once out of school, her life became pure drudgery. About the only kinds of jobs available for uneducated girls at the time was service work. Positions had been scarce even in service. The work she finally found was extremely degrading; she emptied chamber pots, scrubbed floors, and scraped burnt pots and pans for Lady MacPhearson. She did not wish to see Edith doing the same type of miserable work.

She had to thank George though. He had rescued her from all that. It was true, he knocked her about quite a bit since then, but it was such a small price to pay for all the good he had done. He had given her a home, a lovely child, saw to it that they had ample food on the table, and even scheduled her time so she could sit down late at night and rest. "George had been a handsome lad," she remembered. She wondered why he had picked her from all the girls she was sure he could have had.

When George came home from work that evening he looked tired. It had been an exceptionally busy day at the factory, and all he wanted was to sit down and relax. "Where's my tea, Harriet?" he shouted, rather meanly from the parlor. "You've always had it ready when I got home. What's wrong today? What are you doing? Instigating a bloody strike or rebellion?"

"I'm sorry, George, the grocer was out of tea today. He assured me once rationing begins he should have more on hand; he shouldn't run out as often then. With rationing everyone will be able to purchase their fair share. He said he expects a fresh supply in a day or so. However, you must remember, it won't be much. They're only going to authorize two ounces per week per person."

"That's only six ounces each week for us! What do those blokes on the Ration Board think a family like us is going to do? That's less than I drink in a week by myself. What will you and Edith do? You had better start thinking of something the two of you can substitute."

"The news is now saying margarine and cooking fats will be next. I don't know how we'll ever manage. Soon they'll be rationing everything."

"Well, you better get off your ass and do something, Harriet. Snoop around. See if there are any black market chaps who can help us," George ordered.

Harriet knew this was not the time to discuss Edith's evacuation, but decided to do so anyway. She hoped his preoccupation with rationing–and its threat to his stomach–might keep him from paying close attention to what she was suggesting. Maybe she might just slip it through. "You know, George, we really should reconsider sending Edith to ..."

"To the United States," he answered before she had completed her sentence. "Don't send Edith to the United States? What are you trying to do, Harriet? You stupid bitch! I told you a week ago! The decision is final. She's going!"

"But, George, I was just thinking ..."

"Damn it, Harriet, don't think. Keep your mouth shut. I want no lip from you."

George grabbed Harriet by the neck with one hand and slapped her violently with the other.

"Stop it, Dad!" Edith screamed. "Leave Mum alone. You beast! She was only asking for my sake. It's me you should be hitting."

George released Harriet and lunged at Edith. "You smart ass!" he screamed. "It's time to teach you some manners, girl. You young people don't have any respect for your elders these days. I'll beat some sense into that flea-sized brain of yours."

Edith was too quick for George. He lunged at her but missed. She quickly ran from the room. She did not know which way to turn but knew she had to hide somewhere. His awful temper had been growing worse each day, but never this outrageous. She would lock her door, or sleep on a park bench if she had to. Or someplace? She certainly wouldn't, couldn't, let him get to her. Whenever he was this angry it took several days until he cooled down.

"How I hate that man! How I'd like to get away from the blighter, permanently!" she thought. "Some day, some how, I'll make him pay for abusing Mum and me."

It was at that moment Edith made a decision. She would willingly go to the United States. While there, in spite of losing the English education she sought, she would take advantage of every opportunity she could. She would study conscientiously and would somehow obtain the pharmaceutical training she needed. Afterwards, she would not return to England, she would make America her permanent home. She resolved never to suffer under her father's tyranny again. Once she became a successful chemist, she would send for her mum, take her away from her dad's stupid rage. "We'll live in a cute little cottage somewhere in America. And Mum will have a pretty garden. There'll be no shouting or hitting. Dad won't be there to interfere."

She hoped what her mum had said about good schools in America was correct.

Chapter 11

Friday, 2 August 1940

The decision to send the children to America continued to plague Diane even after Chad submitted the registration papers. There still remained much doubt about the wisdom of what they had done. Diane mulled each point over and over, reconsidering the same arguments they had struggled through during the past month. Nothing new, she had gone over everything many times before. She would envision her lonely, empty house and decide to cancel the registration. She would imagine Pinnington after a devastating air raid and conclude her only choice was to let them go. There would be moments when she visualized the children alone in the U.S. and would resolve to keep them at home. Other times she would remember the threat of a German invasion and would conclude it best if they left. She would suffer through long periods pining for Henry and want the children with her. She would think of the shortages in England and want them to leave. There would be times when she would imagine not knowing their situation, wondering if they were sick or well, happy or sad, successful with their studies or having difficulties, and she would decide to keep them in Pinnington.

She was still vacillating when the letter arrived from Bender Limited. It contained the first formal instructions for the scheme. The actual departure date depended on the availability of suitable transportation. The children might leave at any time and on short notice. It emphasized the need for absolute confidentiality regarding departure details and cautioned them not to share travel information with anyone. Failure to maintain secrecy, it warned, might provide the enemy with information that could place the children's ship in danger from U-boat attack. Diane and Chad fully complied with these instructions. They discussed the details with no one, including the children. They were determined not to jeopardize Ann and Graham's safety.

All good-byes were to be said in the assembly area. Parents would not be permitted to accompany their children beyond that point. "I don't know if I can say good-bye that soon," Diane said, her eyes filling with tears.

"You must, the children's safety, perhaps their lives, depends on leaving quickly. The longer it takes or the more publicity the scheme gets, the greater the opportunity for the Germans to learn about the trip and to react accordingly. I know it will be difficult but we must be strong–for the kiddies' sake. It's going to be difficult for the children, too. We must make the departure as easy as possible," counseled Chad. "Now let's have a look at the list of recommended take-along items. Do you have it, Diane?"

"It's such a meager list," she complained, as she handed it to Chad. "How can they expect the children to be gone for such an extended period with so few clothes?"

"They don't. It includes only essentials–enough to get them to America. They'll need many more things once there; especially with the weather extremes in Ohio." Chad paused, then added, "That's the re-markable thing about this scheme, Diane. Those wonderful people are not only sharing their homes with our children but will also be feeding them and providing their wardrobes. Can you believe it? Those folks, who know absolutely nothing about our children, have committed them-selves to months, maybe even a year, to serve as their parents, to treat them as if they were their real mother and father."

He immediately realized his mistake, he should not have mentioned the role of mother and father. Diane burst into tears. "Are they trading us in for new parents? Will we no longer be their mum and dad?" she moaned. "If they stay for a year will they forget us? Oh, Chad, are we giving our children away?"

Chad tried to assure her. "Of course not." He pulled her close to him and put his arms around her in a tender, but fruitless, attempt to comfort her. "They're our children, Diane. They'll always be. Hope-fully, they'll love those kindhearted people and will respect America, but they will always be our children and will always think of England as home. Don't worry. As busy as we are now, with our long working days and ever increasing volunteer work, the year will pass quickly. That is, if it is a year; it's difficult to believe the war can last that long."

His words did not satisfy her. She was still sobbing when Ann entered the room. "What's wrong, Mum? Why are you crying?" she asked.

"Nothing important, sweetheart. Mother merely bumped her elbow, and it hurt a bit. It's much better now," she fibbed, drying her tears. "Bender Limited sent home the list of things needed during your holiday in America," she added. "Let's look at it together, see if we need to purchase anything before you leave."

Ann really was not interested in the list. She had not changed her mind—she still did not want to go. However, since there was little doubt she and Graham were going, she reluctantly accepted her fate. She would try to be the little soldier all English children were expected to be these days, but it was difficult feigning interest and trying to be a good soldier when one was asked to leave her beloved country.

The thought of being a soldier made her think of Henry. "Poor Henry. He must have felt awful when he had to leave in June. At least I know where I am going; he had no idea. He just had to go wherever they send him—probably back into battle." She wondered how he put up with it. "Henry is such a hero. If they asked me to fight, I'd run and hide somewhere, not obey their stupid orders. I must give him a great big hug when I see him again—just to let him know how much I love him and how I miss him." She decided it would be the grandest hug she had ever given.

"What's on the list?" Ann asked bravely.

Chad read the list. The suggested items for Ann read:

	gas mask	1	warm coat & Mackintosh, if possible
1	cardigan or woolen jumper	1	pair warm gloves
1	hat or beret	2	pair stockings
1	warm dress or skirt and jumper	1	pair strong boots or shoes
1	change of under clothes, including vests, knickers, etc.	1	pair plimsoles
2	cotton dresses or overalls with knickers	2	pair pajamas
		1	towel
6	handkerchiefs	1	hairbrush and comb
1	toothbrush and paste	1	face flannel or sponge
	sanitary towels	1	linen bag
	sewing outfit		stationery and pencil
	Ration card		Identity card
	Birth Certificate (if possible)		Bible or New Testament

The list was similar for Graham. It included:

	gas mask	1	overcoat and Mackintosh,
1	suit		if possible
1	pullover	1	hat or school cap
2	shirts (coloured)	2	pair stockings
2	undervests	2	pair underpants
2	pair pants	2	pair pajamas
1	pair boots or shoes	1	pair plimsoles
6	handkerchiefs	1	comb
1	toothbrush and paste	1	face flannel or sponge
1	towel		stationery and pencil
	Ration card		Identity card
	Birth Certificate (if possible)		Bible or New Testament

"Why do we need those silly gas masks? Aren't we going to America where there is no war?" Ann asked.

"Of course you are, honey," Chad replied, "but you need to get there and must keep it available until you are well out at sea."

"Goodness," exclaimed Diane, "there are things on this list that I'm ashamed to send. They're so tattered and worn. We had better buy a few items. Graham wore his suit most of last school year and it's quite shabby looking. Besides, he has nearly outgrown it." She sighed, "He's growing so fast now. He'll need new boots too. Ann needs a new skirt and jumper and at least one new dress. I am ashamed to send her in the Yvonne hand-me-downs she has been wearing lately."

"That'll be a problem, Diane," Chad cautioned, "I'm afraid we don't have sufficient ration coupons to purchase everything you mentioned. Perhaps we can talk to the local haberdasher and dressmaker? We could ask if they would let us borrow against our future ration allotment. I'll inquire at both places after work on Monday."

"If need be, we could also use Yvonne's too."

Ann wondered what Yvonne would do when she discovered they were giving away her clothing coupons. She did not mention it however; she did not want to bring up all of Yvonne's complaints again.

Diane worried the items would not fit in the luggage space permitted. Each child could only take one suitcase, about twenty-six by eighteen inches, and a haversack or attaché case. The haversack was to contain enough items for two or three nights. The children were urged to keep their passport, ration cards, sleeping clothes, soap, towel, toothbrush and tooth paste in it. All frocks were to be clean and laundered. Also, the instructions said each child should bring food and thirst quenching fruit sufficient to last twelve hours. To avoid waste and litter, no bottles were permitted, only a half pint carton filled with either milk or water. No chocolate either, it would make them too thirsty.

"We'll need to buy two suitcases and one more haversack," Diane reminded Chad.

"I understand they're now making cardboard suitcases that meet the specifications. They made them for the London evacuees last year and are currently being used in the CORB program. I'll also check on this at work on Monday. See if they are still available and, if so, where they are sold."

The following week brought news of the Soviet Union annexation of the Baltic states of Estonia, Latvia, and Lithuania. Russia justified her aggressive deed by accusing them of military conspiracy. It was becoming clearer each day that England would be adding Russia to her list of warring enemies soon.

A second letter arrived from Bender Limited on Wednesday. It contained additional instructions concerning the evacuation process and further stressed the need for rapid embarkation and rigid security once the actual process began. Also included was a letter from E.J. Newton. In it he said the children are going to a new country and should expect to find many customs different from those they now knew. It claimed there will be differences in the meaning and use of words and expressions; many things they are used to in Britain would not be available in America; and many things in America would not have been heard of in England. "All in all, though," the letter continued, "you can expect to have a jolly good time on your adventure." He closed by reminding the children that America would be looking at them as representatives of England. He urged everyone to always present themselves in a manner that brought honor and pride to their English heritage.

"What a super trip!" Graham exclaimed as he entered the room and heard the last of the letter. "It surely will be a splendid holiday: a voyage on the sea, a new land to explore, new people to meet, and new customs to learn."

But Graham was the only one who felt good about the trip. Ann still thought of it as a horrible idea and wished desperately she could remain in England. Diane continued to doubt her decision. Chad knew he would miss Ann and Graham and had difficulty at times holding back his tears. More and more, he wished he had decided against sending them. Yvonne continued to resent the trip, not so much because she could not go with them but more because remaining behind meant she soon would be working in a defense factory. She was not looking forward to work. She still believed she should continue with school and still hoped she could find some excuse to do so. During her job interviews she had even tried to project a poor image of herself, hoping it might discourage her hire. But she knew she was only delaying the inevitable–it was only a matter of days until she would be at work. They needed workers too badly to be choosy.

Ann was hot, thirsty, and tired. She gasped for breath. Never before had she been in such close quarters. She and all the others were wondering what was happening. Only minutes before some men had packed them tightly in the corral. She did not recognize who they were. She only recognized them as cowboys, funny looking cowboys wearing steel helmets with pointed silver gewgaws on top. Several of the more impatient in the herd kicked the gate violently with their hooves. Their reward: a swift prod with the huge stick each jailer carried. She wished she weren't a horse; she longed to be a little girl again, back with her mum and dad.

Graham was there too. He stood stiffly on the opposite side of the corral, a saddle, haversack, and two suitcases strapped firmly to his back. A gas mask dangled from the saddle horn. She tried to move toward him, but it was too crowded. He looked so lonely and sad.

Suddenly the corral was gone. They were standing on the deck of a large ship. She could see no land, only water everywhere. Wherever she looked large fish with bulging eyes stared at her. The fish wore the same ridiculous helmets as the cowhands in the corral. Suddenly a huge whale, mouth open, lunged at her. Certain it would swallow the ship, she whinnied with fright.

Still later, she was a little girl again, this time standing in a train station, the station of a large city. It was not London. She did not recognize it. A crowd of children, most about her age, huddled impatiently near a taxi stand. A very good friend, she could not recall her name, stood beside her. They laughed, entered a cafe, and sat at a long narrow table. Suddenly a waiter appeared. He, too, was wearing a gray steel helmet with pointed silver gewgaws on top. He pointed to a giant trough. "Eat!" he shouted.

"We can't. There are no knives, no spoons," Ann complained.

"Stupid swine," he roared, "use your hands. *Mach schnell!*"

Ann had no desire to use her hands. They were wrinkled and dusty.

Suddenly the door swung open. A tall man entered. His face bore a heavy tan from days in the sun. A Stetson sat cockily on the back of his head; a red bandanna hung around his neck. "How strong and handsome you look," Ann thought as he swaggered to her table.

"A cowboy! You are a cowboy?" she asked.

"Don't eat it, Annie," he drawled, grabbed the waiter by his helmet, and hurled him as hard as he could. He sailed through the swinging doors, the cowboy in close pursuit. As they tussled in the dusty street, the cowboy lost his hat. For the first time, Ann could see his face. It was Henry!

Just before she woke, Ann stood at the water's edge. The morning sun peeked over the horizon. She watched as the sky changed from an early morning gray to a brilliant gold. "Somewhere. Somewhere over there," she said, pointing toward the east, "is England–and England is my home. My mum and dad live there. Someday I'm going home."

A few minutes after she woke she forgot the dream. Her only recollection was that it had been something troubling. But she could not let one bad dream upset her. Tomorrow was going to be a very important day in her life; she should be thinking about it instead.

Chapter 12

Friday, 9 August 1940

Diane woke Ann and Graham early. It was the day the children were leaving for America–the day Diane had been wishing would never come. But there was little time to think about it; there were too many things still to do.

The committee had sent word early yesterday morning. It triggered frantic activity at the Montgomery household. Fortunately, Diane had already planned to finish shopping for the items the children needed and had asked her supervisor for the day off. Even so, it was all she could do to complete everything. Besides shopping, there remained the final wash-up of clothes, the ironing, a careful check that everything was ready, the packing of the suitcases, and the many other small details she had somehow neglected to finish before.

She had anticipated difficulty persuading the merchants to manipulate the ration coupons but was pleasantly surprised. As soon as she mentioned her children were being evacuated to America, most were sympathetic and eager to help. Only a few grumbled and thought everyone should remain in England and "take a common stand against the Jerries," but even they had difficulty finding reasons for the children to stay. Naturally, because of the confidentiality of the departure, Diane could not reveal how urgent things were, but everyone seemed to understand and made themselves, and the items she needed, immediately available.

Even with all the cooperation, the shopping had taken much longer than Diane had planned. She, with much help from the children, spent the remainder of the day, and most of the night, finishing everything. In a way, it was fortunate she was busy because it provided little time to think of how she would feel when the final good-bye came, or how she would feel during all those future lonely days to come. But all those worries were still there, in the back of her mind, and a sadness permeated all her thoughts throughout the day.

Now here it was, the fateful hour when her children were leaving home–perhaps forever, although she never admitted that possibility, not even to herself.

"I made a very special breakfast for you this morning," she told the children. "Come down as soon as you're ready." She had been hoarding ham and eggs ever since the first Bender letter came and had used every available ration stamp for this special meal. She fried potatoes and red tomatoes, piled a dish high with various types of cheese, filled a bowl of mixed fruit, prepared many slices of toast spread with real butter and orange marmalade she had miraculously found at the shop only a few days before, and made hot cocoa and tea. At the last minute, she even added hot porridge to the menu.

For the first time in weeks, the entire family sat down together, but no one ate with enthusiasm, and afterwards food remained on all their plates. Everyone was more interested in trying to store the remaining precious moments in his mind. They all knew it would be the last meal together for a long time to come. It even occurred to some that they might never be together again, but that horrible thought was quickly suppressed.

"Did you wash carefully this morning, Graham?" Diane asked.

"Yes, Mum, I was careful to wash everywhere–even behind my ears," he replied, trying valiantly to be lighthearted.

"Is everything packed and ready to go?" Chad asked. "If we're to be on time we must leave in a few minutes."

"All that remains is to brush their teeth and pack their toothbrushes," Diane answered.

Ann and Yvonne said nothing. They sat in silence. Both were deep in thought. They were thinking of what was about to happen: in effect, both girls were about to lose a sister, at least temporarily.

"Why are you so quiet, Ann?" Chad asked, trying to find some way to ease the situation. "You should be excited. Imagine, before long you will be on a big ship sailing for America. Not many children your age will ever be able to boast of an experience like that."

"I know, Daddy," Ann answered, trying to be brave and not cry.

Chad looked at his watch, "Oh! Look at the time. We must leave immediately. Come on, kiddies, finish up. Let's get cracking."

With toothbrushes packed, a final check of the contents of the suitcases, inspection of each child's appearance, a hug, a kiss, and the children, with Chad in the lead, left the house.

Diane did not go with them. She couldn't. Saying good-bye in the assembly area would have been too difficult. She watched the car back down the driveway and disappear around the bend. She could hold out no longer. She collapsed on the floor and sobbed violently. Her kiddies were gone. "Would she ever see them again? Would they be all right? Would their new mum and dad take good care of them?" Her sobs grew louder as her heart nearly broke.

Yvonne did not cry. Although she knew she would miss Graham and Ann, she could not cry, and did not understand why. She tried to comfort Diane. She put her hand on Diane's shoulder; it was all she could think to do, but it helped much more than she realized. Diane still had one of her girls at home with her. "Thank God for that," she sobbed.

Ann looked out the rear window as they drove down the street. She watched her favorite house grow smaller and smaller and finally disappear behind the trees. She could still feel Diane's good-bye hug and the kiss on her cheek. They had been so warm and gentle. "Oh, Mummy, when will I see you again? Couldn't you have kissed me once more before I left?" she pined. Tears welled in her eyes, but she did not cry. Evacuees do not cry. The instructions said they should be brave little soldiers; it was their patriotic duty.

Graham talked excitedly about the trip, "Do you think we'll sail in a convoy, Dad? How long will it take to cross the Atlantic? From what port will we embark? What are the chances we'll see a U-boat?"

Chad did not try to stop Graham. He was thinking about the upcoming departure. He marveled at how well Diane had held up during the good-bye and worried whether he could do as well. He thought about his decision. "Oh, God, what have I done? I can't go through with it! Help me. Please?" he prayed.

They pulled into the special car park area reserved for the evacuees. There was mass confusion: parents were unloading the suitcases; coordinators were rushing around trying to organize the rapidly expanding crowd; people were standing in small groups anxiously talking. Many of those assembled, especially those with several children leaving from the same family, did not talk to the other groups; it was not a time when families wished to share the company of their children, or practice the niceties and formalities required with outsiders. They hoped simply to find a way–somehow–of saying good-bye to their children.

Chad unloaded the suitcases and haversacks then gave Ann and Graham some last minute advice, instructed them not to lose their passports and other papers, then checked them to assure himself they could manage their luggage. Chad turned to Graham, "Son, I want you to promise me you'll look after Ann. I'm depending on you to care for her on this trip. Do everything you can to stay together in America; she needs your support and help." He put his hand on Graham's shoulder and patted him, as one man would another.

Graham realized the responsibility his dad was assigning and accepted it with enthusiasm and self assurance. "You can count on me, Dad. I will take good care of her," he promised. He knew the gravity of his promise and felt quite manly making it.

"Hello, Chad! I see your wife decided to send the children. Har, har!"

"Oh, hello, George," Chad said, annoyed with the intrusion.

"Meet my missis, Chad. Chad, this is Harriet. Harriet, Chad. I work with Chad at the factory, Harriet."

"I'm pleased to meet you, sir," she responded obediently. "Is your wife here?"

"Diane couldn't come. She had to work." Chad lied. He looked at the girl standing beside Harriet, "Is this Edith?" he asked, trying to quickly divert the topic away from Diane and his lie.

Ann and Edith looked shyly at each other and smiled.

"Yes this is Edith," George replied. "Edith, say hello to Mr. Montgomery."

"Hello," she said with stifled enthusiasm.

"Hello, Edith. I would like you to meet my children, Graham and Ann."

Graham and Ann exchanged greetings with Edith.

Ann immediately knew she liked Edith. They were nearly the same age and there was a look in Edith's eyes, a sad look that told Ann they shared many common feelings. Edith, too, saw something in Ann she liked. They tacitly decided to become friends on the trip.

"That's a fine looking lad you have there, Chad," George said. He then added what he considered real humor, "Graham would make a good boyfriend on the trip, Edith. Give him a good look."

Edith responded with a look of disgust aimed directly at George. Graham blushed.

The trip coordinator soon interrupted their conversation, instructing the children to pick up their identity tags at the special tables in front of the buses. Once they were given their group numbers, they were to continue directly to the bus designated for their group, give the bus driver their suitcases, and board immediately.

The parents and the children said hurried last minute good-byes during the walk to the buses. The children then obediently boarded, and the buses quickly pulled out of the car park. Almost before anyone had time to react, the children were gone.

Chad waved good-bye, turned, and hurried back to his car. He did not want anyone to see his tears. "Oh, Graham! Oh, Ann! What have I done?"

Chad would spend the remainder of his life trying to formulate an acceptable answer.

Chapter 13

Friday, 9 August 1940

The children, their boxed gas masks hanging at their side, were silent as the double-decker buses pulled out of the car park. Each child was thinking about the families they were leaving behind and the difficult farewells they had just said. Everyone realized they were beginning an extended journey and knew they would sorely miss their families. Some were in tears, others, less sensitive to the significance of their departure, looked forward to the adventure that lay ahead.

The good-byes would have been even more difficult had they not happened as quickly as they had. The original plan had been to perform all the processing functions and present an official farewell in the car park but, at the last minute, E.J. Newton decided to move these functions to the Grosvenor House in central London. He hoped it would minimize the time in the assembly area, prevent meddling by emotional parents, and start an earlier adjustment of the children to the separation. It worked better than he had expected, the children had simply boarded and, almost before anyone had time to be sad, or have second thoughts, the buses were on their away.

The group consisted of eighty-four children plus several escorts. Originally one hundred children had enrolled in the program, but sixteen withdrew in the last few days before departure. The parents of these sixteen, after much soul wrenching, concluded they could not bear to part with their children, and in each case, felt as guilty about not sending their children as those who sent theirs did.

The children represented many departments from Bender Limited. Among the parents were metal workers, cabinet makers, machine operators, clerks, managers, salesmen, accountants and solicitors. In most cases the children were traveling by themselves, the sole child from a family. In a few cases, there were two, or even three, siblings from one family. Many had brothers or sisters still at home who were either too young or too old to qualify. A few had brothers or sisters serving in one of the armed forces or the Medical Corps.

To Ann's delight, they placed Edith on the same bus with Graham and her. When they boarded Ann made certain she sat beside her. Graham sat across the aisle, and next to him was a thirteen year old boy named Fred. Fred, the son of Alice and Walt Andrews, was a handsome lad with a good sense of humor and a keen interest in athletics. Walt was a foreman at Bender Limited.

"Hi, my name is Graham," Graham said, smiling at Fred. "That's my sister, Ann, across the aisle. The girl sitting next to her is our friend Edith."

"Hi, Graham," Fred responded, relieved to be talking with someone. "I'm pleased to meet you. My name is Fred."

"Where's your home, Fred? We're from Pinnington. Dad is a machinist at the factory."

"I'm from Northolt. My father is in Shipping and Receiving. He's a supervisor on the loading dock; he makes certain the crews load the lorries correctly."

"Do you have any relatives in America?" Fred asked. "I understand the boy two seats in front of us will be staying in California with relatives. The two girls, up a row and to his left, will be living in Canada."

"No, we have no one in America. Ann and I will be staying with complete strangers." Then Graham added, more to assure himself than to provide Fred with additional information, "It shouldn't be too bad, though. They'll most likely place Ann and me with the same family. We specifically asked them to billet us together."

"I will be with strangers too. It is kind of scary, isn't it? Imagine living with foreigners, people we don't already know."

"It sure is. Those bloody Jerries are causing us lots of trouble. It's going to be exciting, though, living in America. In fact, it should be super. There'll be no gas masks, no blackouts, and plenty of oranges and ice cream. If we're lucky, we might see a cowboy or an Indian."

"Oh, I don't think so. They don't have cowboys and Indians running around the streets shooting at each other. Those are just wild west stories made up for the picture shows, they aren't what it's really like–at least that's what my Dad says," Fred argued, trying to sound knowledgeable by disagreeing.

"I suppose you're right, but wouldn't it be exciting if we really did see an Indian?" Graham asked, a little embarrassed that he sounded so ill informed.

Before they could continue the conversation the escort, sensing some of the children were already beginning to miss their families, suggested a group sing-along. "Let's sing, children. Do you know the *Barrel Song*? Here we go! One, and a two, and a roll out the barrel, we'll have a barrel of fun ..."

At first only a few voices joined in, soon others began to sing, and, finally, after a few more measures, most of the children were laughing and, although not with great enthusiasm, were politely singing. The songs, while temporarily easing some of their pain, did little to dispel their growing homesickness.

As the bus drove east on Bayswater Road one of the children, who had been peering through the small diamond shaped opening in the shatterproofed window, spotted an antiaircraft gun emplacement in Hyde Park. The children excitedly began to vie for a turn to look through the openings in their windows. Many had seen antiaircraft gun installations before but never so many, or ones with such impressive guns. Soon everyone was talking excitedly about the guns and the singing stopped. Some of the older children noticed the trenches and knew they were public air raid shelters. Not wishing to frighten the youngsters they said nothing.

The Grosvenor House impressed Graham and Ann. They had never been in such a grand building, particularly one with such soft, plush carpets, shiny door knobs, and elegant fixtures. The huge crystal chandelier hanging in the grand ballroom caught everyone's eye as they entered. At one end of the ballroom, the officials had set up tables to process the children; at the other end they had piled the children's suitcases and haversacks. The children searched for their luggage and began forming a check-in queue. At first Ann could not find her suitcase and was certain she had lost it–one of the last things Diane had specifically cautioned her not to do. Finally, with the help of Graham, and much to Ann's relief, they spotted it hidden behind another.

The queue moved slowly. Eventually, Ann and Graham reached the check-in table where the officials verified they had brought their birth certificate, passport, ration card, and health papers and gave them red badges and luggage ID tags. Each had the name *Bender* printed on it in big black letters along with their name and address. After the children had tagged their suitcases, the porters loaded the suitcases onto a wagon and carted them to the buses for transportation to the ship. The children kept their haversacks and gas-masks and waited in two small rooms adjacent to the ballroom, the girls in one room and the boys in the other. The separation from Ann caused Graham a few moments of concern; he had promised his parents he would keep Ann in his eyesight, and already he had failed. He felt better only after one of the escorts assured him he would see Ann again as soon as they finished their health examinations.

Ann stayed close to Edith during the examination, particularly when the girls were asked to remove their outer garments. It embarrassed her to disrobe in front of the other girls, but Edith eased the situation when she pointed to the fancy knickers some of the other girls were wearing. Ann agreed, she had never seen undergarments quite as frilly. She told Edith she was glad hers were more comparable to what most of the girls were wearing. Later Edith quipped, "It's too bad the boys aren't here to see those knickers," then added, "imagine how foolish the boys must look in their underpants." Ann blushed. She thought it rather vulgar, but the banter had accomplished its intended purpose; before long Ann had forgotten her embarrassment and was, more or less, comfortable parading around partially undressed in front of the others.

Afterwards, everyone returned to the ballroom where E.J. Newton gave a small sendoff speech. Ann would remember little of what he said that morning, except for one major part: he urged them to keep in mind they would be guests in America, and as such they should always be on their best behavior. He hoped, once the Americans came to know them, they would say, "Aren't these British children nice! They always say 'please' and 'thank you' and always try to make everyone very, very happy." It was something she would think of often, and apply throughout her stay.

By the time the ceremonies ended, Ann and Edith had begun talking with Sandy, a slightly built, eleven year old girl from Uxbridge. Soon another friendship among the evacuees was formed.

Sandy was hungry and thought it time to eat the food their mothers had packed. After much discussion Edith and Ann persuaded her to wait a little longer. It was fortunate they had, a few minutes afterwards the waiters wheeled in several large tables. None of the children had seen tables like these, even before the war. On them were all types of sandwiches, a tray of assorted fresh vegetables, a tray of apples with a few grape clusters added for color, a variety of sweet biscuits, pitchers of milk, an urn of tea, and even a bowl of fruit punch. Several excited exclamations arose from the children. Bender officials wanted to send the children off with a fond memory of England and had done so with this impressive farewell lunch. In later years, the children would often think of this gesture fondly.

It would have surprised no one had the children been greedy as the queues filed past the table, but an unexpected thing happened, each child, recalling what Mr. Newton had just said in his speech, took only moderate portions. They were trying to be polite–although a few succumbed to youthful appetites and returned for a second helping. Even Graham, who had questionable table manners at home, behaved like the gentleman he could be.

After lunch the children re-boarded the buses and proceeded on what seemed to those who knew their way around London a rather circuitous route to Euston Station. They rode through Piccadilly Circus and saw all the pedestrians scurrying along Regent Street. They passed Trafalgar Square with its boxed statue of Lord Nelson and surrounding antiaircraft gun emplacements, this time the reaction to the guns was more subdued, the children had already become somewhat accustomed to defense installations. They made their way up Shaftesbury Avenue, passing the partially sandbagged theaters, turned north on Charing Cross Road to Tottenham Court Road, and, finally, east on Euston Road to the station.

At the station, the children boarded the train through doors on the side of the cars directly into their assigned coach compartments. Because the train was crowded there were fewer seats available than normal, and they had to crowd close together. A corridor running along one side of the car with access to the other compartments and the loo located at one end provided some relief but visiting between the groups was discouraged and long lines soon formed at the toilet. With uncomfortable seats, little opportunity to move about, and memories of saying good-bye to their families still fresh in their minds, everyone soon became tired, irritable, and more homesick than before.

Perhaps, had they known where they were headed–the port where they would embark, the expectation would have made some of them feel better, but no one knew. Even the escorts had not been told. Only the driver and guard knew their destination. In wartime, the fewer who knew the less chance the enemy had to interfere with transport plans.

The escorts once again tried to start a song session, but it soon failed. The effects of compartmentalization, the large noon luncheon, and the early morning wake up began to take a toll. Although some of the older children stayed awake and watched the changing countryside, most dozed off. Graham and Fred counted antiaircraft installations the train passed and tried to count barrage balloons floating over the cities. They abandoned balloon counting when the number became too large to finish the count before the balloons passed beyond their view.

Throughout the trip there was a steady flow of traffic to the loo. On one occasion several older children carelessly left one little five year old in the corridor. Alone, she quickly became disoriented and lost. It was tragic to see her standing in the corridor, holding her little doll, crying, and calling, "Mummy!" It caused considerable disruption among the older passengers on board but finally, with their help, she was reunited with her group and the crisis ended. The Bender representative in charge of the scheme severely reprimanded the escort assigned to the little girl's group and promised her she would never serve as an escort again.

Two hours after leaving the station, the escorts finally permitted the children to eat the snack their mums had prepared. The children ate in near silence. The food brought back memories of their mum. They realized it was the last of her food they would taste for a long, long time to come.

It was nearing dusk when the train finally pulled into the station. There were no signs and the children remained ignorant of where they were. They also did not know of the plans to board the liner *S.S. Caerleon* after a quick evening meal.

The meal, served at the city cathedral by a group of women volunteers from the congregation, was not as grand as their luncheon at the Grovsenor House had been; wartime reality was back in effect. After dinner Mr. Geoffrey Shakespeare, the Director of CORB, who had happened to be in the city on CORB business, gave a brief speech. Again Ann remembered only the main points from the speech. He told them they were going to new, wonderful homes where they would be warmly received and have great experiences. He cautioned them that no matter what happened they must never let down their guard; they should always act with dignity, politeness, and responsibility. He said people would judge those they had left behind, and the cause for which they fought, by the behavior of every one of them. He then distributed a book titled *The Token of Freedom*, which, he said, men from all nationalities wrote some two thousand years before. He said it characterized all the reasons Britain was fighting for and urged everyone to study it carefully. He emphasized they were all representatives of Britain, and, as such, they had a responsibility to act like ambassadors. They had to be much more grown-up than they really were. He ended by admonishing them to be polite, but on the other hand, never let the Yanks take advantage of them.

As they boarded the buses for the ride to the pier, the air raid sirens sounded. Soon they heard bombs exploding and felt the pressure from the concussions. The escorts immediately ushered the children out of the buses into a nearby public shelter. They stayed there nearly four hours while the bombing continued, interrupted occasionally by short periods of quiet when the only sounds came from the wail of the ambulances and fire lorries, and the cries of others in the shelter with them. Most of the children were frightened. It was their first experience with exploding bombs and the first time for many in a shelter without their mums and dads. With their growing fear came increased loneliness and a tremendous desire to go home. A few of the younger children cried while the older ones, who did not want the others to know how homesick and frightened they also were, held their tears in check.

By the time the all clear sounded it was too late to load the remaining supplies on the *Caerleon* and join the convoy before daylight. This meant a delay in the sailing time until the following evening and a delay in putting the children on board. As a result, the escorts arranged temporary sleeping quarters in a local grammar school basement. Because it was late, the hurried accommodations were primitive. The children slept on mattresses hurriedly placed on the concrete floor. Loo facilities were inadequate for such a large group and everyone waited in long queues to use the loo, to wash up, and to brush their teeth. It was nearly three o'clock before the children were finally in bed.

Excited, homesick, tired, hungry, and uncomfortable in their inadequate sleeping quarters the children did not sleep well. They made many trips to the water fountain for drinks and to the toilet. The muffled sound of sobs filled the room throughout the night. With few exceptions, the children wished their parents had not sent them on this journey.

Edith was one of those who still thought it was a good idea.

Chapter 14

Saturday, 10 August 1940

Diane was the first to hear it. She put her ear closer to the wireless. "Come here quickly, Chad!" she shouted

"What's wrong?" Chad said, still tucking in his shirt tail as he raced down the stairs.

"I just turned on the BBC morning news. They're talking about a heavy raid on one of the coastal cities last evening. Listen to what they're saying." She increased the volume.

"There have been numerous casualties and major damage to the port facilities. Several ships received extensive damage. Many on board have serious injuries, some are dead." The commentator continued, "The RAF responded to this vicious attack in their usual heroic manner. Ground observers report the German attackers suffered heavy losses. RAF losses were light. Also reported were many civilian casualties, and damage to buildings in the city has been severe. The name of the city is being temporarily withheld in the interest of security. We shall bring you further reports on this terrible tragedy as soon as additional information is available. I repeat: the Germans bombed one of Britain's major seaport cities last night. The city suffered heavy damage. Please stay tuned."

"Oh, Chad, you don't suppose Ann and Graham were there?"

"I doubt it, Diane. What do you think the chances are that, out of all the seaports in England, they ended up in that particular one?" He tried to sound confident but felt uneasy and concerned.

"I know it's where they went–I just know it," Diane fretted. "Something tells me they were in that raid. Oh, I do hope no one was hurt! How can we find out if they're all right? Call someone, Chad."

"No one is going to know; security is too tight. I'm certain they'll notify us as soon as they can if something happened to the children; we need to be patient a little while. Until then, we're going to have to depend on our faith. Thank God our children will be safely settled in America soon; I don't believe I can take much more of this worry."

"But what if they don't get there? We shouldn't have sent them, Chad. It's just what we always feared–we don't know if they're safe or injured. If they were here with us right now there'd be no worry. Oh, Chad! We've made a mistake! A horrible mistake!"

"You can't think that way. Who knows for certain where the Germans will bomb next? Perhaps tonight they'll bomb Pinnington. Ann and Graham are as safe where they are as they would be here–or will be before long. In a few days they'll be in the U.S. From then on they'll be out of this terrible war altogether. Forever! Had they remained with us they'd be in danger every day, for weeks, perhaps months, to come."

Chad did not believe what he was telling Diane. He only knew they would go mad if they didn't hang on to at least some semblance of hope. "I must leave now. I'll be late for work," he said.

He turned quickly, grabbed his coat, and walked out the door. He did not want Diane to notice his tears.

Chapter 15

Saturday, 10 August 1940

Graham did not mind the early morning call. The crying, coupled with an uncomfortable bed, made it nearly impossible to sleep. It had been a difficult night. Ann, and many of the other children, kept waking up, crying, and wanting to go home. He had tried to comfort Ann, but nothing he could do seemed to ease her deep feelings of despair.

Edith also had had difficulty sleeping. To pass the time, she and Graham had talked. By morning he better understood why she was so eager to leave home. He thought it sad someone as intelligent as she could have such an unsympathetic father. In a way, it reminded him of Yvonne. Poor Yvonne, she had wanted more schooling too. Both their fathers seemed set on limiting their children's education–the big difference, her dad was not as mean as Edith's. He was kind, loving, and generous. His only fault, he believed working-class people should be happy with what they had; they had no right to climb above their own social group.

As they talked, Graham realized America represented something entirely different for Edith than it did for him. He wanted adventure and safety where she wanted education and career. He hoped the trip to America would help her realize her ambition of becoming a chemist but was less sympathetic when she said, "Once out of England, I'm never coming back."

Her statement bothered him. He couldn't understand why anyone would want to live anywhere but in England. After all, it was his home. He loved England. It was his country. If he could, he would gladly fight for the right to live in England–just like Henry was doing. "But, you have no choice," he reminded her, "you're under strict obligation to return as soon as it's safe to do so. American immigration officials insisted on it as part of the agreement to admit the Bender evacuees." This surprised Edith. She had not heard that before, or, thanks to her dad, many of the other scheme details.

His dad had told him everything–Graham wondered why Edith's father hadn't shared more things with her.

After the children were up and about, local volunteers served breakfast. It consisted of hot porridge, a slice of toast without butter, and hot Ovaltine. The children did not particularly relish the menu but, because they were hungry, ate it with gusto and soon finished.

Throughout the meal there was much talk about the air raid. "Wasn't it simply awful?" Sandy remarked. "I hope there isn't another one today."

"Graham says the Germans usually bomb at night so I guess we're safe until then," Ann assured her.

"We'll probably board this morning," Edith speculated. "I overheard one of the escorts say the ship should have sailed last night, so I imagine the ship's captain is eager to leave."

"The only thing," said Graham, who had just walked over to make certain Ann was all right, "they probably don't want to do much loading during the daylight."

"Why not?" Fred, who was with Graham, asked.

"They like to load in secret. If a reconnaissance pilot were to fly over during the day he could see the cargo. If he thought it important enough, he would issue a report over his wireless, and have a U-boat waiting for us," replied Graham, displaying much more confidence in the accuracy of his information than he actually had. Most of what he said was sheer speculation on his part.

"You mean one of those horrible U-boats might chase us once we're at sea?" Sandy asked, a look of fear on her face.

"It could happen," Graham sighed. "They might even sink us." He wondered why so many children knew so little–hadn't their parents told them anything?

Seeing Sandy's look of horror, Edith tried to console her, "Don't worry, Sandy, it's a big ocean and extremely difficult to find small ships. There is too much water to look everywhere."

"Who would want to torpedo a ship carrying people?" Ann asked, trying to put Sandy's mind at ease. "Aren't they after ships carrying guns and ammunition, and things like that?"

"Besides," interjected Fred, "after the sinking of the *Andora Star* last month, our government no longer permits British passenger ships to sail unless they're in a convoy. We'll not be sailing until we're part of one."

"Navy destroyers, escorts, and battleships sail with the convoys," Edith assured Sandy. "That makes them pretty safe. We should have no difficulty getting across the Atlantic."

All these words of assurance did little to ease Sandy's fears. "I hope we can stay together on the ship," she said.

"I agree," said Ann. "Let's ask our escort if we three girls can share a cabin. I would also feel better if you and Fred were in the cabin next to mine, Graham. Would you ask if that would be possible?"

"I sure will, Ann," Graham promised, feeling better now that there was something specific he could finally do for his sister.

The captain had a problem. He did not know whether to load the passengers during the day or wait for nightfall. If they boarded early, they ran the risk of a daylight bombing, but the sailing time would be more flexible. On the other hand, if he waited until night, the passengers would be safer, but another raid might once again delay the departure. He couldn't keep the convoy waiting; he had to put to sea tonight; there was no question about that. He finally compromised. He decided to board the passengers at dusk. He relayed his plan to the escorts but, as a precaution, instructed them to let him know of their whereabouts at all times. If his plans changed, he would notify them immediately.

The escorts, after discussing the delay, decided the children needed entertainment while they waited, something to distract them from thinking so much of home. They planned a picnic in a nearby park and afterwards a visit to the maritime museum only a few blocks from the wharf. Although the head escort agreed they had to keep the children occupied, the threat of another air raid continued to worry her. She wasn't certain the museum would be a safe place to be if a raid should develop. After being assured the children would never be far from a public air raid shelter, she reluctantly gave her approval.

Ann liked the park. There was a small pond where the children could watch the ducks swimming and a small playground with swings, slides, and a seesaw. Ann and Edith chose the playground and because the group was large spent most of their time waiting a turn. They didn't seem to mind, they enjoyed talking with the other girls while standing in line. The more they talked the more they found to say, and the more they liked the others. It made Ann happy to think that only after one day she had found so many new friends. She was especially pleased she had found Edith. Edith was definitely going to be one of her best friends.

While the girls were taking their turns, Graham and Fred played cricket with equipment the escorts had borrowed from the school. The game was played with considerable difficulty. To prevent enemy airborne landings a trench had been dug through the cricket pitch. Even with so many special rules they had to devise because of it, it didn't seem to interfere with their fun. Graham and Fred, who managed to be on the same team, won. It was Fred who made the most runs and caught the ball to make the final out.

Later, after they had tired of cricket, the two boys joined Ann, Edith and Sandy at the pond. Lying on the grass, they looked at the blue sky, each lost in thought. "It's difficult to imagine that beautiful blue sky filled with aircraft, dropping bombs and shooting at each other," Fred remarked dreamily. "It's so peaceful now. I could lie here forever, listening to the ducks quacking and the nightingale singing, feeling the breeze on my face, and watching the birds fly overhead."

It was not so much what Fred said but the tone of his voice that immediately caused the group to think of home. Even Edith could not resist the melancholy feeling. All five of the children in their own way felt the pangs of homesickness. Each tried to hide his feelings.

Ann thought how fortunate it would be to have a boyfriend as romantic as Fred. Graham interrupted her thought, saying, "It would be peaceful looking, if not for the bloody bomb damaged buildings down the street." He had hoped what he said would bring everyone back from feeling so homesick, but it didn't.

They continued to think of home. They placed their arms over their eyes, as if to shade the sun, and tears began to flow. Even lunch did not alleviate their depression. The children's mood dipped lower yet when the escorts demanded ration stamps for the food they had just eaten.

Graham and Fred enjoyed the afternoon tour of the museum. They had a lengthy discussion about the various types of navy ships and the purpose of each. Both boys tried to make the other believe he was an expert on naval matters. Each learned many things about the British Navy, its history, and its weapons. When the boys left, Graham thought Fred's knowledge of ships was terribly limited–certainly not up to his level of understanding. Not surprisingly, Fred thought the same about Graham.

The group had not been in the museum long before the order came to proceed to the docks for immediate embarkation. They quickly boarded the buses and rushed to the pier.

As they climbed off the bus the children strained for a glimpse of the ship that would carry them to America. Unfortunately, crates waiting to be loaded cut off their view. No one seemed to mind; they assumed they would be boarding soon and would see it then. It was not to be, however. They remained in the small waiting room for nearly five hours with no place to sit except on the dirty floor, no food to eat, nothing to drink, and with limited toilet facilities. The children soon became tired, restive, and irritable which made them increasingly more homesick. Some of the younger children began to think they would be there forever and would never see home again.

Then, just before dusk, they were escorted to the processing area in preparation for boarding. The excitement of finally doing something improved their attitude considerably. However, when they arrived at one of the checkpoints the children received their first glimpse of the liner they were to call home for the next unknown number of days. The *S.S. Caerleon* disappointed everyone. They had expected to see a clean, freshly painted ship similar to those seen in travel pictures posted on the Underground walls before the war. Instead they saw a weather beaten, black and buff ship. Paint covered most of its portholes, particularly the lower ones, and black smoke belched from the large funnel rising near the center of the ship's top deck. At times, when the wind shifted, the smoke made them cough. They could see many passengers already on board. They stood at the railings of the numerous decks. The number of decks surprised the children; there were many more than expected; most had imagined no more than one or two.

"Oh, Mum," Ann thought, "why did you send us? We can't sail on a dirty old scow like that. It will surely stink. Come and get me. Come take me back home. Please!" She knew how foolish her thoughts were, but, try as she would, she could not suppress them.

Finally, after an additional lengthy wait, the escorts told the children to fetch their luggage in the pile previously off loaded by the bus driver and form queues in front of any of the tables set up for final processing. The children scrambled for their luggage. At first, they could not find their own and a frantic search developed, but eventually they had it sorted and were lined up, luggage in hand. The processors carefully checked their passports and began collecting their identity cards and ration books. Many children rebelled; one of the last instructions received from their parents had been to always keep these items in their possession. Now total strangers were asking them to surrender those sacred possessions. Considerable time passed before the escorts could convince the children the men asking were not German spies or a secret advanced airborne contingent bent on stealing their papers.

Finally, with the processing completed, the children, tired, hungry, disillusioned and homesick, walked up the gangplank, ready, if not eager, to set sail for a new world on the other side of the ocean.

They still had little idea of the profound effect this journey would have on their lives.

Chapter 16

Saturday, 10 August 1940

There would be eight hundred passengers on board the *S.S. Caerleon* when it left England. The manifest included two hundred and ten British youngsters, all part of one evacuation plan or another. The eighty-four children from Bender Limited were among the evacuees. Accompanying the youngsters were forty escorts and one doctor, all of whom were scheduled to return to England immediately after safe delivery of the children. Most of the other passengers were English and Polish military personnel on special assignment to America or Canada. A few were American diplomats or civil service workers returning from duty in Britain. Most of the grown-ups were men.

The Bender children struggled going up the gangplank, particularly the smaller ones. They were hungry and tired and hoped food would be waiting and cabins quickly assigned once they were on board. Each child carried his suitcase, haversack or cloth bundle, and gas mask. A few had camera cases hanging over their shoulders. The cases contained additional personal items; security regulations prohibited cameras.

Ann nearly dropped her suitcase part way up the gangplank. Had it not been for the older boy behind her, it would have fallen into the water below. The accident embarrassed her. She blushed and thanked him. "If you hadn't grabbed it when you did I surely would have lost it." She paused, then added, smiling. "It's wonderful how everyone from our group is so kind and helpful. Mr. Newton would be proud of how well mannered you are." The compliment caused the boy to blush too.

When he reached the top Graham was impressed. The captain was standing in the gangway greeting every child with a smile and a pleasant welcome. When he said, "Nice to have you on board, laddie," and shook his hand, Graham knew it would be a grand trip. He couldn't imagine anything going wrong with such a pleasant chap in charge.

After everyone was on board the escorts assembled the children on the promenade deck where members of the ship's crew issued a small food parcel to each child, which was not to be eaten until they were in their cabins. The smallness of the package worried them. They were certain it was too skimpy to sate their hunger and began to wonder if it was indicative of what else they could expect during the voyage. Several of the children tried to sneak a peek at the contents and received a harsh upbraiding from a crew member who, they would soon learn, was the first mate. He turned to them and, in a stern authoritative voice, said, "There are certain rules on the *Caerleon* that you must always follow. The captain is a strict disciplinarian. He expects you to obey all the rules rigorously and follow all orders faithfully and precisely. Anyone disobeying will be punished. By international law and treaty, the captain is king on this ship. You are expected to obey all his instructions."

Ann had never before heard orders given in such gruff, harsh tones, not even from her county school headmaster who had a reputation for being quite stern. It upset her. She thought about how kind and gentle her mum and dad had always been and how silly it had been when she thought their scoldings were unfair. "I wish I could go home. If I were in Pinnington now, I would never complain again, not about anything they did," she lamented. Then it occurred to her, since leaving yesterday almost all her thoughts seemed to be about her mum, dad, and home. "Good heavens, that must have been the thousandth time I've wished I were home. I need to snap out of it," she told herself. "I must try to get over being so sullen. I must think happier thoughts."

When the mate finished his lecture, he huddled with the escorts. A few minutes later they began announcing cabin assignments. As Ann had asked, they placed Edith, Sandy, and her in the same cabin along with a girl named Elizabeth. Graham and Fred shared a cabin farther down the passageway with two boys named Steve and Stewart.

Once the escorts completed the assignments, a seaman led the children down several companionways to their cabins on one of the lower decks. The size of the cabin disappointed Ann; she had thought it would be more spacious. It was meant for two people but recently had been modified to hold four. Two hammocks, one above the other, hung in each of the two alcoves where the original bunks had been. The room contained one small wash basin and an extremely small built-in chest of drawers. The chest contained four drawers; one drawer for each girl. There was a porthole in the wall opposite the door, a tightly secured bolt held it shut and thick ugly opaque paint blanked out the view.

Midway down the passageway were two rooms each containing several loos, or heads as the sailors called them. All the cabins along the passageway, from bulkhead to bulkhead, shared these facilities. The port side heads were for the girls and those on the starboard for the boys. A wash-up area where the children could take baths was adjacent to each of the heads, separated only by a dividing partition. "To conserve hot water you must schedule your baths," the seaman told them. "But it may not be a serious problem. You may soon discover you don't wish to take many baths. The bathtubs have salt water taps."

The journey was not starting as Ann had expected. She was depressed, homesick, and eager to go to bed. The musty smell of the cabin especially disturbed her. Until she got used to it, she found it difficult to breathe. Apparently there had been no attempt recently to freshen the cabins. "Probably they hadn't been aired in many months," she thought. If she could sleep, perhaps she could forget this terrible ship–at least until morning. Perhaps things would be better after a long night of sound sleep.

The girls were beginning to transfer the things needed from their haversacks to the chest when a whistle blew and a voice boomed over a loudspeaker in the passageway. It explained it was a lifeboat drill, they were to proceed, at once, to the main deck. Members of the crew had been stationed in each passageway to assist in guiding everyone to their lifeboat stations. Immediately, cabin doors flew open, and excited children began to pour out of the cabins.

The simultaneous emergence of so many children caused major congestion. After considerable chaos, including much giggling among the children, angry scolding by the escorts and harsh commands by the seamen, order prevailed and the jam of children began to progress slowly toward the companionways. When the children reached their lifeboat stations, the captain was waiting. The smile Graham had observed before was no longer evident. "Ladies and gentlemen," he said, his eyes directed at the children, "this is the first of many lifeboat drills we will have. These drills are important for the safety of everyone on board this ship. Your first task is to memorize the precise route between your cabin and your lifeboat station. I expect, from now on, you will proceed to your station in a more organized and speedy manner. Whenever the alarm sounds, everyone must respond immediately, no matter where you are or what you are doing. Furthermore, at all times you must–I repeat, you must–be aware of the shortest route to your station. This means you must quickly memorize the relationship between your lifeboat station and each area of the ship where you are authorized to be.

"Once you have arrived at your station, you will queue in pairs, one pair in front of the next so as to form two columns facing the lifeboat. The seaman stationed at your boat will demonstrate how to get into the boat. Should it be a real emergency, not a drill, the seaman in charge of each boat will tell you when you should load. Upon his command, you will march smartly to your boat and climb in rapidly. You must, I emphasize must, obey all commands quickly and without argument.

"Are there any questions so far?" He paused and glared at the passengers.

He continued, "Good! Now we will issue each passenger a life jacket. You are to keep it with you at all times, regardless of where you might be. If I see, or hear of, any of you without your jacket you will be disciplined. That is a promise." Graham was certain the captain looked directly at him. Several of the children grinned. "Children," the captain warned, "this is no laughing matter, this is serious business. Your life, all our lives, depends on the faithful and precise adherence to every instruction."

The captain began issuing more instructions, "When you arrive at your station you must be wearing your life jackets with the straps drawn tight. The seamen will now demonstrate how to put them on and will help those who need further assistance. Each time you arrive at your station, you older children should check the jackets of the younger ones. Make certain they are tied properly. Your escort will designate which child you are to help, but do not hesitate to help others should it become necessary.

"The North Atlantic can be extremely cold, even in August. It can be so cold that no one could survive for any length of time without adequate clothing. It is important, whenever possible, to bring with you a warm overcoat, a hat to shield the sun, strong shoes, a mug for drinking, your gas mask, and any other special things you might need, for instance any special medications you require. I suggest you keep the items by your hammock at night and in a place where they can be easily found during the day. Each of you will be receiving a torch. Bring it along with you to all drills. I caution you, however, not to turn it on unless someone specifically instructs you to do so. Blackout rules are as important–perhaps more important–at sea as they are on land. On the sea U-boats and aeroplanes can see small lights from great distances at night.

"If a torpedo strikes us and we must abandon ship, use your torch wisely. The batteries will not last forever. The light from your torch may be the only thing that makes your rescue possible."

"Torpedoes! Abandon ship!" Ann thought, "How dreadful!" Now that she was on board it seemed much more threatening than when her dad had first mentioned it. But Ann and Graham were fortunate, their parents had already told them about the threat of torpedoes. Many of the other children had not been so well informed, they had never heard of the threat until the captain mentioned it. These children were suddenly worried and afraid. They listened intently as the captain continued, "Furthermore, you saw how disorderly you were when the alarm first sounded. You and your escorts must work on this immediately. This type of disorganization must not happen again. I shall conduct another drill shortly–perhaps yet tonight. Be prepared!

"Now permit me to end on a more pleasant note. On behalf of myself and the crew, I would like to welcome each of you to the *S.S. Caerleon*. It is our sincere desire to transport you safely across the Atlantic. Let's hope it is a pleasant and trouble free journey.

"I suggest you now return immediately to your cabins and retire. Tomorrow will be a busy day. We have many things planned for your health and pleasure while on board. Good night, ladies and gentlemen. Good night, children. May God bless you all, and God save the king."

Everyone returned to their cabins, and after a brief meeting called by the escort to discuss the route to their lifeboat, the children opened their food packages, quickly ate the nearly stale food, and climbed into their hammocks. Sleeping in a hammock was a new experience for most of the children. It took several spills before they mastered the technique and finally quit giggling long enough to settle down and fall asleep. For a second night, there were many tears shed in the privacy of their beds. U-boats and home were the central themes in most of their prayers and subsequent nightmares.

While the children slept, the *S.S. Caerleon* weighed anchor and sailed out of the harbor. England soon disappeared in the darkness. Shortly other ships, some of them Navy warships, joined the *Caerleon*. No one could see them. It was a pitch black night. Slowly Batch Z_1 of convoy OC_{108} began to form. When assembly was complete the convoy immediately set sail through the Irish Sea toward the North Atlantic.

The Bender children were no longer at home.

Ann woke to a new sound, water rushing past the outside cabin wall. She was too drowsy and tired to investigate and soon was asleep again.

Suddenly she found herself standing on the main deck. She could see a name printed in bright red colors on the gray life preserver hanging on the gunwale. It read, "*S.S. Plum Pudding.*" There were no clouds in the deep blue sky. The sun was shining brightly. A warm, pleasant breeze caressed her face and ruffled her hair. It felt delightful. She was happy and contented. She had no recollection of leaving her mum and dad two days before.

The ship moved swiftly. She turned and saw its giant white wake spreading as it fell behind. "It must reach all the way to England," she yelled, not certain why she was shouting.

Suddenly a water spout appeared in the east and moved toward the ship, threatening to overtake it. The captain grabbed the wheel and spun it violently. The ship lurched to the left. The spout followed. He spun the wheel again. The ship rapidly altered its course, yawing to the right. The water spout continued onward, and onward, closer, and closer. When the spout and bow met, lifeboats began falling into the sea.

A sudden flash of lightning found Ann alone in the only lifeboat afloat. There were upturned and broken boats scattered everywhere. She turned to look for the ship; it was gone. Sunk. Only bubbles remained, marking where it had slipped into the sea. Apparently no one but she had escaped the fury of the whirling wind.

A giant eagle appeared, swooped down and grabbed the rope hanging from the bow of her lifeboat. It began towing Ann westward, accelerating each time it flapped its wings. Soon the boat was racing faster than the *S.S. Plum Pudding* had ever gone. The wind rushing past her head blew Ann's hair wildly. Suddenly, a large shark broke from the surface of the sea, its momentum propelling it high into the air. It snapped at the eagle, missed, then snapped again. On the second try it caught the eagle in its jaws. Together, they plunged into the sea.

The boat lay still in the water. Ann was frightened, thirsty, alone. She looked to the east, saw nothing; she looked to the west, saw nothing; she looked into the sea, a face looked back at her; a face she didn't recognize. He begged her to follow. She grabbed the oars and began rowing with all her energy. She could not keep up. "Wait!" she cried. He sped on, growing smaller and smaller, then disappeared beyond the horizon. When she could go no farther, she ceased to row, gave up all hope of ever reaching the shore. She began to cry.

"Wake up, Ann. Wake up!" the voice said.

She opened her eyes. It was Edith. "You were crying, Ann. Was it a bad dream?"

Ann knew it had been a dream, but there was something about the face that looked pleasant. For some reason–it was an eerie thought–she was almost certain she would see that face again, but next time not in a dream.

She went back to sleep and dreamed of Pinnington, of her mum and dad, and of the doll she had left behind. The dream made her somber once more, but even so she did not wake until nearly half-past five the following morning.

Chapter 17

Sunday, 11 August 1940

There was no clock in the cabin, she didn't know the time. She only knew that it seemed frightfully early. She could not even tell whether it was daytime or nighttime, the paint on the porthole made that impossible. She would just lay there for now, in her hammock. Maybe she could recall her dream. She vaguely remembered Edith talking to her during the night. She couldn't be certain if Edith had been part of the dream or if she had actually asked why she was crying. Her dreams were usually like that. They would be vivid at the time but would rapidly fade from memory once awake. She would have to ask Edith when she woke.

Just then she became aware of the sound of rushing water. It came from the ship's hull; the ship was moving. She recalled hearing that same sound during the night; that must have been when they left the harbor. That part had not been a dream, she was now certain of that. They must be at sea, on their way to America!

It was strange to know she was no longer in England–no longer at home. Her mum and dad were still there, but she wasn't. She momentarily had a feeling of desperation. If she should need them, they wouldn't be there to help. She was on her own now. True, Graham was still with her, but he was only a young boy, not much older than she was, and he could not offer much support. "It's strange," she thought, "this added responsibility should make me feel more homesick. Instead, it seems to have given me strength and determination, more than I ever knew I had."

A bell sounded somewhere outside along the passageway. It was the ship's bell, time to get up. She rose from the hammock, placed her feet on the deck, and suddenly realized the deck was not stationary. It was difficult to stand, not only was it rocking backward and forward but also pitching from side to side; it wouldn't take much of this to make one ill. "I say, Edith. Sandy. Elizabeth. That was the wake-up call. It's time to learn how it feels to walk on a swaying deck."

There was no response.

"Come on, you sleepyheads." she teased. "Don't you remember?

Miss Lewis told us to hop out of bed as soon as we heard the ship's bell. It's time to wash for breakfast; time to rise, you lazy things."

The three girls moaned. "It's too early and much too cold to get up," Edith complained, pulling the cover over her head. "Tell Miss Lewis I decided to stay in bed until autumn."

"I'm famished," Ann said, ignoring the comment. "Aren't you? Remember how hungry we were last evening?"

"I changed my mind. I'm not hungry anymore," Sandy lied in order to sleep a few minutes longer. She had no sooner uttered the words when she began to feel queasy and for a brief time thought she would be sick. But the feeling quickly passed, and then she realized how hungry she actually was. She leaped out of bed, eager for breakfast. Unfortunately, she had not remembered she was in a hammock and her legs became tangled in the ropes. She tumbled awkwardly to the floor.

"Careful, Sandy," Elizabeth giggled. "You're a sailor now. You'll need to get off the hammock more gracefully than that." Everyone laughed.

"Gracious," Sandy complained, "those hammocks are much more stable than I realized, they make quite a difference compared to the floor. The floor's moving much more than the hammock did. I can barely stand up." Hearing this, the other girls climbed out of their hammocks; stumbled, staggered, and finally stabilized themselves. They laughed at their clumsiness.

After brushing their teeth and splashing water on their face, they dressed and tidied the cabin. "What time is breakfast?" Elizabeth asked.

"Miss Lewis wasn't certain what the schedule would be. She said to wait in our cabins; she'll come for us as soon as they're ready to serve," Edith answered.

"Miss Lewis seems like a charming person," Ann observed. "I believe she'll be a good escort."

"Too bad Mrs. Hosely couldn't have stayed with us all the way to America," Sandy sighed. "I wonder why the escorts from London had to leave when we boarded last evening."

"It had something to do with their availability," Edith volunteered. "Mrs. Hosely has other duties and could only be away from home a few days. She simply didn't have the time to travel all the way to America and back."

"Then why didn't Miss Lewis escort us from London?" Sandy asked.

"Because it took time to arrange to be away from home for such a long time. She told me she barely had her work done before she was due on board Friday evening," Edith answered.

A knock on the cabin door interrupted their conversation. "Come on, children," Miss Lewis said. "It is time for breakfast. Follow me to the dining saloon."

In order to feed so many, the passengers had been divided into smaller groups and served at several sittings. Even so, the saloon was nearly full when the girls arrived. The Bender group had a special reserved area. Graham, Fred, Steve and Stewart were already sitting at their table laughing boisterously. They were catapulting forks into their water glasses. Ann thought the boys' manners were disgusting. "Graham, mind your manners," she whispered. "What will the other passengers think of us? Remember what Mr. Shakespeare told us. We represent England and must always endeavor to be polite."

"Oh don't be an old sod, Ann," Graham replied, as he banged his fist on the handle of the crude catapult he had constructed from the table silverware. A fork flew along a miscalculated path and ended not in the glass but on the deck.

"You might not believe it but, so far, Graham is the champ," Fred laughed. "He put four consecutive forks into the glass."

Ann blushed with embarrassment but did not scold Graham any further.

Soon the stewards served breakfast. It was a much better breakfast than the one served the previous morning at the grammar school. The children ate as if they were famished. Many of the boys asked for second helpings and the stewards, much to the boys' surprise, served it without argument. There was much laughter and talk during the meal. Afterwards, the captain stepped onto the raised platform at the front of the saloon and warned the diners there would be another practice lifeboat drill after the last breakfast sitting. He stressed the need for "preparation, execution, and cooperation," then announced a contest between lifeboat sections. The section first to their station with everything properly in hand would be declared the winner.

Afterwards, Miss Lewis met with her group in the passageway outside one of their cabins. She reviewed lifeboat procedures, reminded them of what articles they were to bring with them, diagrammed the route, and described the behavior she expected from everyone. As she left, she asked, "Shall we make our lifeboat section the winning one?" The response was a hearty "Yes!"

Soon afterwards, the anticipated lifeboat drill began. This time the children grabbed the correct items, moved quickly into the passageway, climbed the companionways, and marched smartly to their lifeboat. The seaman had previously selected Graham to check several of the younger children's life jackets. He was very proud of his assignment and conscientiously, and in near military style, performed his duty.

The drill not only ensured a safer journey but provided an opportunity for the children to breathe fresh sea air and, for the first time, observe the surrounding sea in the daylight. Seeing the other ships in their convoy excited the boys. They could see ships in every direction. "Look over there! That's a corvette!" exclaimed Steve.

"That's a destroyer next to it!" Fred shouted. "I don't think we'll hear from Jerry on this trip. We have too much naval power for him to risk it."

"Our Navy will blast the German U-boats clear out of the water, that is if any dare get close," boasted Graham. "Old Adolph's navy is no match for the British Navy."

"Settle down, boys," the mate scolded, "We're here for a lifeboat drill, not to hold a social get-together. Save your comments until after we're finished."

"This is just like the bloody Navy," Fred muttered, under his breath.

With everyone assembled, the seamen demonstrated briefly how to board the lifeboats. Graham immediately sensed a danger in this procedure. There were many places where something could go wrong and, if it did, one could easily end up in the sea. He did not relish a dunking of that sort; he would have to be careful.

Afterwards, the captain assembled the children around him and told them he was still unhappy with their performance. There would be no contest winner, none of the sections had done well enough to merit an award. Graham and Fred thought he was being unfair; they thought their group had performed well enough and deserved the award. Miss Lewis disagreed. She told them their only recourse was to do even better the next time. They agreed to follow her suggestion; they wanted desperately to win the contest.

The group had just returned to their cabins when the alarm sounded again. They grabbed their coats and life jackets and quickly made their way back to the lifeboat. It was obvious by now that the captain was serious and wanted them properly prepared. They admired his concern but groused about three drills in less than twelve hours. After the drill, the captain announced lifeboat number four had won. Fred and Graham's boat was number six. It disappointed them to have failed. Someone suggested they try even harder, but no one had much enthusiasm for the idea. They were tired of all the silly practice. They wanted no more trips to their lifeboat. They thought they had done well enough. One of the children even facetiously proposed they not participate if the captain sounded the alarm again. Everyone laughed. Fortunately, no one took the suggestion seriously. It never occurred to any of them the next time might be a real emergency; they still were not fully aware of the danger they were in.

After the last lifeboat drill, the escorts began to organize the children's day. They chose an ambitious schedule designed to keep the children overly busy. Their plan: to distract the children from thinking of home in the hope it would slow the increasingly serious cases of homesickness. Unfortunately, it would prove to be only moderately successful.

The schedule called for the children to rise early each morning with the breakfast sittings following soon after. Each child was to complete his wash up and be properly groomed and dressed before breakfast. After breakfast they were to return below decks to tidy up their cabins and then proceed to a special recreational area on the upper deck. Each child was expected to join in some strenuous activity. To keep the children on schedule, each escort had a whistle she blew when she needed to assemble the children quickly. Those sick and unable to play, and everyone during inclement weather, were sent to an activity room on the main deck where they selected a less strenuous activity such as checkers, chess, Parcheesi, or table tennis. In mid morning they were to assemble in the entertainment hall where different programs would be offered each day. The programs would include lectures and music presented by various knowledgeable and skilled adult passengers and crew members. No one was to return to their cabin until just before lunch; the captain would conduct an inspection while they were participating in the morning activities. Any cabin found lacking in tidiness would receive demerits handed out at lunch.

The Bender children were assigned to eat with the first lunchtime sitting at precisely noon. There was no need to coax anyone that first day, after the morning activities they had huge appetites and were eagerly waiting outside the saloon doors when twelve o'clock arrived.

A rest period was scheduled immediately after lunch. They were to lie in their hammocks and write letters, read, or sleep. An adequate supply of stationery was issued so no one had an excuse not to write.

On that first day, Ann had intended to write to her parents. She had promised them she would, but every time she wrote the line *"Dear Mum and Dad"* she would start to cry–it triggered too many memories. She finally gave up and slept instead.

Graham was too busy swapping stories with Fred, Steve, and Stewart to write. Besides, he reasoned, the letters would not be posted until they arrived in America anyway; he could wait until almost in port without causing a delay in the first letter reaching home.

To accommodate the large group, they divided the children into two smaller subgroups for the afternoon session starting at two o'clock. Everyone was to attend either a crafts workshop or watch a motion picture in the cinema. The groups alternated daily between the two activities. During crafts, children with other previous interests, such as Guides and Scouts, were assembled for their own special activities.

The first sitting for dinner was at five p.m. While one group ate, the other group was to use the time to bathe and wash their smalls. After dinner the children gathered and sang songs. The younger children were to be in bed at half-past seven, the older ones by half-past eight, but usually no one got to sleep until half-past nine, or sometimes ten o'clock. In spite of the escorts' admonitions, it usually took that long for the older children to quit frolicking and talking.

Ann looked forward to bedtime the first evening. She had enjoyed the songfest but the day had been stressful and tiring. There had been too many new experiences and activities.

Chapter 18

Monday, 12 August 1940

While everyone slept, the convoy sailed from the Irish Sea into the North Atlantic, and along the way it encountered the leading edge of a low pressure system with its concomitant winds. Although no storm ensued, the sea turned decidedly more turbulent, and as it did, the hammocks swung farther from side to side.

Sandy was the first to wake. The first thing she noticed was a lingering nausea. She supposed she had eaten too much at dinner and thought little of it. The second thing she noticed was the pitch and roll of the ship; they were much more violent than they had been the night before. The third thing was how well the hammock compensated for the ship's motion, although she wished it would do more. She tried to get up, felt vertiginous, immediately lost her balance, and decided to climb back into her hammock. She gulped several times, trying to ease the queasy feeling, and wondered how much longer before the others woke.

Elizabeth and Edith were next to wake. Both were also feeling nauseated. "Golly! My stomach feels terrible this morning," whispered Edith, not wanting to wake Ann who was still sleeping peacefully. "I must have eaten too much last evening."

"That's odd," replied Sandy, "I was just thinking the same thing."

"Me too," said Elizabeth.

By this time Sandy was feeling worse. Not certain how much longer she would be able to control the nausea, she decided it time to go to the loo–just in case. "I think I had better get down to the head," she said as she opened the cabin door. Before she could step into the passageway she hurriedly added, "Extremely fast!"

It surprised Sandy to see several other girls hovering around the toilets when she arrived. A few were hunching over them, some were retching, and several were bent over in apparent pain. The sight of the sick girls nauseated Sandy even more. In a few minutes she was vomiting. "Oh, heavens," she thought, "this is horrible. I must find some way to ease this dreadful feeling." Unfortunately there was nothing she could do.

Just then Edith burst into the room, her hands clutching her mouth. She did not reach a toilet before she too became sick. The girls began to panic; they wondered what was happening to them. All they could think of was last night's dinner. The food must have been bad. It was odd though, nothing looked or tasted spoiled; everything had seemed so inviting and delicious.

Ann entered with Elizabeth. Ann was laughing, "Oh don't be silly, you'll be all right, Elizabeth. It's just a mild case of upset stomach, it'll pass in a few minutes." Her words did not convince Elizabeth who was looking even more peaked and pale.

When Ann looked around and saw the other girls, she changed her mind and began to worry. With so many sick girls something had to be wrong. They must have been poisoned. She should tell one of the escorts. She quickly hurried down the passageway to Miss Lewis' cabin. "Miss Lewis," she said pounding on the door. "Miss Lewis, it's Ann Montgomery. Come quick! Quite a few of the girls are sick!"

Ann heard a muffled reply from inside the cabin. "We can't, Ann. We're too sick." Ann thought the voice belonged to Miss Lewis, but she could not be certain. It was much weaker and shakier than she remembered. "Please call Dr. Peters, Ann. Neither of us can help the girls," continued the voice.

Ann was not certain she knew the way to Dr. Peters' cabin, but she had little choice, everyone was sick and needed immediate help. It was up to her. She raced down the passageway and up the companionway to the deck above. She looked frantically for a clue to where doctor Peter's cabin was. As she raced down one of the passageways, she met one of the ship's officers. "Whoa there, child," he said, grabbing her gently by the arm. "What's the hurry? What's wrong?"

"Oh, sir!" Ann pleaded breathlessly. "Come quick! To the deck below! All the girls are sick! Even Miss Lewis, our escort. I don't know what's wrong; I think something poisoned them!"

The officer laughed, "No, child, I would bet they weren't poisoned. My guess is they're seasick."

"Seasick!" Ann exclaimed. She had never given that a thought before. "What can we do for them?"

"We had best have a look to be sure, but I'm almost certain that's what it is. It usually happens when the sea is as rough as it is today. Let's see now, what was the name of your group's doctor?"

"Dr. Peters," Ann answered.

"All right, I'll find Dr. Peters and the ship's doctor too. You go back down to your deck and tell everyone to stay calm. A doctor will be with them shortly."

"Thank you, sir," Ann replied.

She stopped first at the girls' head and tried to assure everyone it was nothing serious. "Nothing serious!" Edith screamed at Ann. "Nothing serious? You should know how I feel. It's worse than ..." She could not complete her sentence. She had to get back to the toilet before she had another accident.

A few minutes later Graham knocked on Ann's cabin door. "Ann, are you all right? Stewart and I woke up sick this morning. I don't know what's wrong."

"Many of the girls are sick too," Ann told him. "One of the officers told me he thinks they're seasick. He's fetching the doctor right now. I'll tell them about the two of you when he gets here."

Graham was both surprised and ashamed. He had not figured he would get seasick. "Seasick? Not Graham Montgomery–a future admiral in the British Navy."

The dining saloon was much less crowded the next few days. At one point Ann was the only one sitting at her table. Surprisingly, Ann adapted well to the moving deck and was never bothered by it. She enjoyed having the table to herself, especially with the overabundance of food. On one of those occasions, the steward suggested she order all the desserts on the menu. Against her better judgment she took his advice, felt like an aristocrat eating all those delectable sweets, but later that night came close to joining the others in the loo. Fortunately, she quickly recovered and, afterwards, vowed never to act so piggish again.

There were almost no children on the upper deck while the seasickness persisted so Ann had few playmates. To compensate, she made friends with a handsome deck steward. They talked of many things. She told him about her parents and he told her of some of his adventures while serving in the Navy, gave her a tour through sections of the ship normally off-limits to the children, and said she reminded him of his daughter who was about the same age. He confessed how much he had hated leaving port this time. After the air raids, he had not had a chance to check with his family and worried they might have been hurt. Ann told him she was concerned about her family too, and cried when she told him how much she feared for Henry's safety. Together they consoled each other, as best they could–it helped to share their concerns.

Ann especially enjoyed the morning her steward friend–she never learned his name–pointed out the flying fish. She had never imagined such fish existed and stood for a long time at the rail watching them. She liked looking at the fish almost as much as attending the cinema showings.

She had to admit, though, the *Laurel and Hardy* picture, which had been shown on Sunday, was quite hilarious.

Chapter 19

Thursday, 15 August 1940

The escort told Graham his area in the cabin was not neat enough to pass the captain's inspection and suggested he clean it. He did not take her advice; he thought he was too sick to do such an unpleasant task at the moment–perhaps he would take care of it later. Instead, he joined the other boys in the recreational area on the upper deck. On the way he hoped there would not be another lifeboat drill; he didn't think he could stand one more, at least not the way he was feeling.

Most of the other boys had recovered and were playing shuffleboard and volleyball. Graham sat on a deck chair and watched. The girls played similar games on the port side of the ship and he could clearly hear their giggles and shouts. "Come on, Graham, you have to start playing sometime. It might as well be now," Fred coaxed. "Join our team."

Graham declined, "No thanks, Fred. I think I'll sit here and simply watch you chaps play."

"Well, at least move your chair over here where you can see the girls. Haven't you noticed? Some of them are pretty spiffy," sighed Fred.

"What are you talking about, Fred? They're only girls."

"I know, Graham, that's the point. They are girls!" Fred corrected. "Can't you understand? That's what makes it so grand."

This exchange confirmed what Graham had been thinking: Fred had gone a little daft. It seemed girls were the only thing he wanted to talk about since they met. "What is it about girls that makes Fred think they're so special? They're kiddies just like we are–nothing more, only creatures we boys must tolerate," he thought to himself. What he said instead was, "Yes, I know what you mean. Several of them look quite lovely. I'd normally be excited, but not today; I still don't feel up it." He thought that would do it, thought it would make Fred believe he was a red-blooded British boy, a boy with ripe hormones. In truth, he didn't particularly care for girls.

"You can't fool me," teased Fred. "You're an old sod, aren't you? I'll bet you haven't even kissed a girl yet."

"Maybe we could slip away and explore some of the other parts of the ship this afternoon?" Graham suggested, trying to change the subject.

"That's a good idea," Fred said excitedly, "I'd like to sneak up to the sky deck and see some of those first-class beauties."

By lunchtime, Graham felt much better. For the first time in three days he was in good spirits and, more importantly, hungry again. More to impress Fred than because he believed what he was saying, he teased Edith. He told her being seasick had been good for her, had slimmed her down to what was almost a good weight. "A few more weeks without food and you'll be quite attractive," he said. It was a mean thing to say– she was far from being overweight, she weighed five stone twelve, only a few pounds more than Ann. She knew he was teasing but, just to be sure, refused to eat any more desserts during the trip.

But the teasing did not continue. The captain destroyed Graham's euphoria when he announced the results from his morning cabin inspection. He made a special point to single out cabin 24-D and asked the lad responsible for the lower, rear hammock to come forward.

"That's your hammock!" giggled Steve, looking at Graham.

The captain's announcement caught Graham by surprise. He had forgotten about Miss Lewis' warning. It had completely slipped his mind; never once had he given any more thought to it. Now everyone at his table was laughing at him, especially Edith. He did not know what to do. "I'm sorry, sir," he said, shuffling his feet and looking down at the floor as he stood before the captain.

"I have never seen such a disgrace in my life. That cabin of yours deserves a prize; it's the most untidy mess I've ever seen on the *Caerleon*. Everyone in the saloon laughed. "What's worse, I found your life jacket in the cabin. You didn't have it with you. Did you?"

Graham cringed and whispered, "No, sir."

"That's a major mistake, young man," the captain scolded. "Clearly you chose to ignore my specific instructions. I'll not tolerate such disobedience from you, or anyone else, not from a crew member and not from a passenger. I am so outraged that I find it difficult to think of an appropriate punishment."

The scolding began to worry Ann. She wondered what the captain would do. She hoped he wouldn't throw Graham in the brig, like they had in the picture show they had seen the other day. She hoped the captain hadn't seen it.

The captain continued, "Have you read *The Scarlet Letter*, by Hawthorne, son?"

"Yes, sir," Graham replied meekly.

"Not only do I expect you to return immediately to your cabin and put on your life jacket, but, as with the red letter in that story, I'm ordering you to wear that jacket continuously until this time tomorrow. It will be your badge of dishonor. When others see you, it will remind them of what a despicable boy you've become. Permit me to clarify further: You must wear it all the times. That includes while you are cleaning your cabin, while you are eating, while you are playing, and even while you sleep. I will ask the other boys in your cabin, on their honor, to report to me if you do not follow these instructions. Do you understand, lad?"

"Yes, sir! I do, sir," Graham responded, standing rigidly at attention. Surprisingly, Graham did not mind the reprimand, or the punishment. In reality, he found it amusing–actually quite clever–and certainly not unreasonable. It was how he had always thought military service would be. He could imagine enlisting when he was old enough. It would be fun to be in the Army, trying to outwit the sergeants and officers, like Errol Flynn had done in *Gunga Din*, and helping to win the war by shooting at the Germans. Of course, he would need to wait until he was old enough.

There was one regret, however. It interfered with Fred and his plans to explore the ship. He couldn't sneak around the ship unnoticed while wearing a life jacket. He guessed they would have to postpone the exploration until later.

"One thing more," the captain added, "as further punishment, I'm ordering you to assist the deck steward this afternoon. You can help him swab down the sky deck and wash the deck chairs."

This seemed a bit more harsh than the previous punishment, and Graham no longer found it quite as humorous. None of other children sitting at the his table found it amusing either; he was from their group, and he was beginning to embarrass them, but no one disputed the punishment; they thought it just and that Graham deserved all he had gotten.

The evacuees, minus Graham, saw a documentary on midwest America that afternoon. Graham was sorry he couldn't attend because he had specifically wanted to see it. He wanted a better understanding of life in McKinley Heights, Ohio. But there was nothing he could do about it. To make the most of his situation, he would be as cheerful around the deck steward as he could possibly be.

As it turned out, the steward was a pleasant chap, by coincidence the one who had befriended Ann several days before. He didn't ask Graham to do much, mostly they talked. Graham suspected the easy assignment was due to Ann's friendship and worried that if the captain saw he hadn't been working he might add an even harsher punishment. Finally Graham garnered sufficient nerve to tell the steward of his concern. The steward laughed and whispered confidentially that the captain was not as much of a tyrant as he seemed. He further confided that the captain had instructed him to go easy on Graham. Hearing this, Graham resolved to follow all the captain's orders to the fullest for the remainder of the trip. "Any bloke as good as that deserved to be obeyed," he told himself.

It was late afternoon when the first explosion occurred. Graham had been watching the ships nearest the *Caerleon*. Suddenly, Graham saw two large plumes of water rise near the ship off the port side. Within several seconds there were two additional explosions off the starboard side. The pressure from the accompanying concussion waves nearly knocked Graham to the deck. "Blimey!" cried the Steward, "those two ships have been hit! Run, lad! Get to your lifeboat as fast as you can. We could be next!"

The explosions terrified Graham. He was uncertain what to do. He was already wearing his life jacket and had on a heavy coat. He decided it prudent to obey the steward and made his way to his lifeboat. By the time he arrived, things were happening all around him. The lifeboat alarm had sounded and passengers were pouring out of the companionways and assembling in front of their boats. Seamen were rapidly working on the lifeboats, apparently readying them for use. Graham could not help noting how much more orderly everyone was, compared to how they had been a few days before, in spite of all the excitement. He admired the captain even more than he had just a few moments earlier. The captain's insistence on so many drills had paid off.

Soon the others in his group arrived, and they assembled in two columns as instructed and waited for the dreaded order to abandon ship. While they waited, they heard another explosion aft of the ship, followed closely by several larger explosions. Although they could not see what had happened, rumors quickly spread that a torpedo had hit another ship. There had to be a German U-boat somewhere close at hand. Everyone expected the *Caerleon* would be next. Some of the children began to cry. The escorts tried, as best they could, to maintain calm within the group. There followed a series of explosions from depth charges discharged by the destroyers in a futile attempt to sink the submarine.

Then there was silence. Although no one knew it at the time, the threat had ended. The large explosion they heard a few minutes before was the U-boat's last torpedo. The U-boat would need to return to its base before it could carry on any more sorties.

After what seemed to everyone an eternity, the captain finally told the passengers to return to their cabins and to standby for further instructions. An eerie quiet settled over the ship. No one said anything as they trooped back to their cabins, this time with a noticeable change in their demeanor. Everyone realized–for the first time–this was not a pleasure cruise to America, it was a dangerous–possibly deadly–voyage.

As they slept that night their dreams were morose and frightening. They continued to see the three convoy ships sinking. In the morning there would be less laughter than before. Although no one knew it, each child had grown much older. It had only taken a few minutes.

Chapter 20

Saturday, 17 August 1940

Saturday, 17/8/40
Somewhere at sea

Dear Mum, Dad, and Yvonne,

I am writing this during our rest hour. After lunch each day, we have time to either sleep or write letters. Today I decided it was time I tell you a little about what your "little girl" has been doing. (Actually, I started to write last Wednesday but decided to start over today. I was not happy with what I wrote. Too childish!)

I am well. I did not get seasick like many of the children. Most are better now. What a terrible thing it was for them. It was good for me though, since so few wanted to eat there was plenty of food for the rest of us. The food is delicious here on the ship. We have a very good cook. I probably have gained half a stone by now. I bet when you see me you'll say, "My goodness, how fat Ann has become! She is not our little girl any longer." (Tee, hee.)

I hope everything is going well in Pinnington. Graham and I were talking about you yesterday. We imagine the house seems bigger now that the two of us are not there to take up all that space. (More for you, Yvonne?) We are certain it is neater–now that we're not there to clutter. It would surprise you if you saw how neat we keep our cabins. The captain is very strict and inspects our cabins each morning. Woe to anyone who does not tidy up properly.

We cannot tell you what ship we are on, or where we are. (As if we knew!) The captain says the restriction is for security purposes. We may not even describe several events that have happened to us along the way. You would not believe some of the things we have experienced! What adventures we've had! I'll tell you about all of them when I get home. In the meantime, I will write them down so I won't forget anything.

I have made some lovely new friends on this trip. Edith, the daughter of Dad's friend, George, and I have become very close friends. (Do you remember her, Dad? We met her in the car park in Pinnington.) We share a cabin with two other girls. Their names are Sandy and Elizabeth. Sandy is 11 years old and Elizabeth is 10. They are both splendid girls. We have already had some jolly good times together. I hope we'll be able to continue seeing each other once we arrive in America. It will not be so lonely if we can talk to some friends occa-sionally. Here she had crossed off "occasionally" and substituted "often."

Our schedule says we must get up early in the morning–5:30 a.m. (Ugh!) We go to bed quite early–8:30 p.m. (Double Ugh!) Because it is so early, we usually do not fall asleep right away. Instead we talk in the dark. (There are no windows in our cabin, they have all been painted over.) We tell ghost stories and act silly. Elizabeth is particularly witty and keeps us laughing. (I should not be writing this–Miss Lewis will know about our folly! She must read our letters before we post them to ensure we do not give away any military secrets.) I would tell you what a super person Miss Lewis is—and what lovely things we say about her at night—but it might embarrass her. You will simply have to imagine how pleasant and helpful she is.

Graham is staying in a cabin just down the passageway from us. He shares his cabin with boys named Fred, Steve, and Stewart. They all seem to be good chaps. I imagine Graham will tell you about them in his letters, so I will say no more.

Gee, by the time you get this we will be in America! Since we can not post our letters until we arrive, I suppose I could have waited until then. I thought it better to write now. This way you will receive an extra letter and will know more about what we have been doing. I hope you are doing the same!!!

Well, it is almost time for our rest period to end so I must say good-bye. Tell everyone I said hello. I will write again when we arrive so don't worry about how we are. I hope you do not mind receiving two letters?

Please write to me. I would love hearing from you. Hint: Letters from each of you would give me more mail.

> *Love,*

> *Ann*

P.S. No need to censor this, Miss Lewis. I have no idea where we are; just that we're somewhere on a very big ocean.

*   *   *

> *Sunday*
> *18 August 1940*

Dear Mr. and Mrs. Montgomery,

As you can see by Ann's letter, we escorts must review the children's letters to make certain they divulge no military information. I apologize for the intrusion into the privacy of your daughter's letter. This, I fear, is one of the many unfortunate difficulties created by this nasty war. Let us hope the military will soon put an end to this monstrous conflict and we can return to normal times.

I am enclosing this note simply to assure you Ann is all right and getting along splendidly. She is a fine young girl and is a joy to be around. She has made many friends and everyone comments on what a polite young lady she is. You can be proud.

In closing, permit me, again, to assure you Ann has adjusted well to this adventure. I am certain she will have a pleasant and fruitful stay in America. It is a pleasure to be her friend and escort.

> *Sincerely,*
>
> *Virginia Lewis*

P.S. Your son Graham is doing well too. We all agree he is full of spirit and always good for a laugh. Now if we can just get him to write a letter to you!

Chapter 21

Sunday, 18 August 1940

On Thursday, 15 August, approximately one hundred German Henkel-111 bombers and forty ME-110 fighter escorts raided Tynesdale on the northeast coast of England. At the same time, eight hundred German planes raided southern England in a diversionary ploy to tie up the RAF interceptors. Seven British Hurricane and Spitfire squadrons responded to these simultaneous attacks. When the battle ended, the Germans had lost seventy-six aircraft, the British thirty-four.

Diane and Chad, sleepy from the lack of a good night's sleep, heard about the air battle at seven o'clock on the Saturday morning news program. Although many of the details were censored and not available, it was apparent the air war in England was escalating drastically. The news did not surprise them; they had just spent the week in and out of the shelter and listening to the nearly incessant drone of fighter aircraft taking off and landing at the nearby Northolt Aerodrome. No bombs had fallen in Pinnington yet, but, even so, there had been many air alerts and all clears and little opportunity for sleep.

"Is it going to get worse?" Diane asked Chad.

"I expect it will," Chad answered gloomily. "Thank God we sent the children away."

"Perhaps, Chad. Perhaps! I would feel much better if Ann and Graham were here so I knew they were all right," she said.

"You still believe we made a mistake?" he asked, incredulously.

"I don't know. I, truthfully, am not certain," she sighed.

The air battle escalated throughout the day. The Germans began attacking the nearby airfields and the air war spilled into the skies over Pinnington. Chad and Diane watched some of the battle from the door of their shelter. By Sunday evening, causalities on both sides had increased significantly. By then, Diane was nearly in tears.

*   *   *

To: *Ann & Graham Montgomery*
%   *Bender Electric Company*
      100 Bender Place
      McKinley Heights, Ohio, USA
           Sunday, 18 August 1940

Dear Ann and Graham,

We still have not received any news about you. Dad and I imagine by now you are well on your way to America and are having a wonderful time. You are more than likely meeting wonderful people and seeing all sorts of new things. Dad said he saw many nice children in the Bender group the day you left, so I am certain you have new friends by now. You certainly are lucky children to be participating in the scheme. Remember to thank Mr. Bender when you meet him.

I'll enclose the brief note I wrote last Sunday with this one. We couldn't send it before because we didn't know your address. The Bender Company has <u>finally</u> decided they will collect our letters and forward them in bundles to the McKinley Heights factory for distribution. Dad will take the envelope to work tomorrow and these two notes should be waiting when you arrive. At least I hope so. I will attempt to maintain this weekly writing schedule, but cannot promise it with certainty. Dad and I have been unbelievably busy since you left and, unfortunately, the outlook does not offer any immediate improvement.

Dad is still working too many hours. He has his regular Bender Limited work and now all the extra duties because of his Home Guard activities. (They changed the name to Home Guard from LDV.) But not to worry, he says he does not mind the extra duties, so long as he knows it helps win the war.

I too continue to be very busy. There is my work at the factory and, of course, the housework that always needs doing, war or not. Of course, nothing gets dirty now that you two are not here to mess up things. – I am only joking! – I would gladly clean up after the two of you if you were back home. The house seems very lonely without you. I miss you!

Penciled in the margin at this point was the note: *Dad says my promise would last only one or two days–then I would start nagging the two of you to do it yourselves. Ha, ha!*

The letter continued: *We hope you are well and are having many laughs with the other kiddies. Nothing new has happened here.*

Yvonne is still spending much of her free time cutting and rolling bandages at St. John's while she waits for her defence assignment.

When not at St. John's, she's with her friends. We see very little of her. She is not here today, but if she were I am sure she would send her love. I will have her write to you before long.

We have not heard from Henry since you left. We still do not know where he is or what he is doing. We trust that God is looking after him.

Please take care of each other. Graham, remember to insist the two of you stay together in America. Ann, follow your big brother's advice.

Well, there is much work to do before bedtime. I will sign off for now and promise to write regularly, if at all possible.

Dad sends his love and I do too.

> *Love,*
>
> *Mum*

Chapter 22

Monday, 19 August 1940

After the torpedo attack the demeanor of the *Caerleon* passengers changed. Solemnity replaced their previous jocund attitude. There were no more complaints about the lifeboat drills. Everyone responded to each alarm seriously, carefully followed instructions, and listened intently afterwards to suggestions for improvement. Rumors, however, grew in number and spread quickly. After nearly every drill, many insisted it had not been a practice exercise but a real alert caused by a U-boat nearby. But, fortunately, there were no additional official U-boat sightings during the trip.

Realizing the need to lift passenger morale and recognizing their greater camaraderie, the captain reduced many of the shipboard formalities, relaxed the rigid schedules, and removed some, but not all, of the compartmentalization restrictions–he still had to maintain some class distinctions so as not to upset some of the more haughty, class-conscious passengers traveling in first class. He gave the children more free time and opened the topside deck areas to everyone. Ann and Edith, quick to take advantage of this change in policy, were among the first to avail themselves of these new deck liberties. They spent many hours lounging on the open decks, discussing with each other their hopes, ambitions, dreams, and concerns.

"What's wrong with our fathers?" Ann asked. "Why don't they want their children to receive as much education as possible? My dad acts the same as yours when it comes to schooling. He wouldn't let

Yvonne remain in county school, even though she wasn't required to pay any fees. And your father is eager for you to leave school so you can go to work. Don't they know more schooling will help all of us obtain a better life?"

"My dad knows. He simply believes no one in our family has a right to be a chemist, especially a girl. He says we have our place in society, thinks it improper to assume privileges meant only for the gentry. When I asked him to remove my name from the evacuation list so I could earn a Higher School Certificate and go to college it really upset him. He became angry and pushed Mum and me around."

"Pushed the two of you around, Edith? Are you saying he hit you?"

"I'm afraid so, Ann. It takes very little for him to fly into a rage. He has been that way for as long as I can remember. I've had many bruises to show for it, and poor Mum has fared even worse. He broke her arm several years ago. On another occasion, she had a concussion and was in bed for over a week. I never understood why she puts up with him. I would've sent him packing a long time ago."

"Gosh, Edith, my dad would never strike any of us. Doesn't your dad love you and your mum?"

"I suppose, in his own perverse way, he does, but I'm through putting up with the bugger. I've decided I'll make the most of this trip to America. I plan to do everything I can to better my chances of becoming a chemist. I'm going to study hard and insist on placement with a family who thinks positively about education. What I would really like is to find a school that trains chemists in the U.S. and then find some means to attend–even if I must remain in America after everyone else goes home. I'll do whatever is needed; just as long as I can become a chemist and can keep away from my old man. I truthfully don't care if I never see him again, at least not until I finish school and have my pharmacology degree."

"There are other subjects besides pharmacology. There's music, poetry, literature, ..."

"Those are okay, but they don't interest me that much."

"Finding a good career is all right, Edith, but what about falling in love? Don't you dream of meeting some handsome lad–and marrying him?"

"Not until I finish school. It would only interfere with my goal. As I just said, I'm not going to let anything get in the way. Besides, I can't imagine a boy good enough to change my mind. I certainly don't think I could fall in love, especially after watching what my mum has been through. How does one ensure they don't marry some blighter like Dad?"

"What about sunsets, rainbows, rain on a spring day, a baby laughing, cuddly animals? There are so many wonderful things, Edith. You shouldn't go through life ignoring them, simply for the sake of your ambition."

"Ann, you're nothing but a romantic. You have to face reality. We'll never have enough leisure time to enjoy those things fully. We'll never be poets, or scholars. The destiny of our class is to work. The best we can hope for is to get all the education we can; then, perhaps with luck, we may be able to do something we enjoy, something that will give us respectability, like being a chemist, for instance. You know, Ann, there are no prince charmings. Those are just fairy tales. There are only men who want a wife to clean their house, cook their meals, and make their babies. That's not my cup of tea."

"But cleaning houses, cooking meals, and taking care of children would be okay, if they were for the right man. There must be someone who would be worth keeping house for; one who would work hard, bring in a good wage, and provide a comfortable home."

"Your trouble, Ann, is you're an idealist. You think, once you marry, you'll have all the peace and contentment you want. I know better. I've seen what ugly creatures men can be–no correct that, what ugly creatures men *are*."

"But they can also be sweet and gentle. My dad has always been that way. He loves my mother, looks after her with tenderness and kindness, and has never had anything but concern for his children. He's always treated us with love and compassion while maintaining enough discipline to let us know the difference between right and wrong. No, Edith, I do not believe it's the way you say. One must simply be careful to avoid those horrible men who don't love their wives and family."

"You're still describing my dad?" Edith laughed. "He certainly is no prince charming, more like Ivan the Terrible. Just how are you going to know what he'll be like after you're married? Men can be all peaches and cream before marriage. But afterwards? Watch out! Do you think my mother would have married him had she known beforehand?"

Ann had never thought much about any of this before. She had often dreamed of a prince charming, but she never thought seriously about marriage. She wondered how girls ever selected who they should marry. But she needn't worry, that was a long way off for her. This conversation had become much too serious–too grown-up. She was enjoying her early years and intended to stay a child for a long time, or at least until she returned to England. She would think more about it then.

But thinking about the return started her worrying about the months she would be away. She began to wonder how many there would be, how long until she saw her mum and dad again. She wished she were back in England with them. Her eyes clouded with tears.

Just then Sandy came around the corner and interrupted Ann's thoughts. "Hi, girls! The two of you look so comfortable lying there on those deck chairs. Mind if I join you?"

"Not at all," Edith said, "pull up a lounge chair and rest awhile."

"Where've you been this morning, Sandy?" Ann asked, trying to secretly wipe her eyes so no one would notice she had been crying.

"I just finished dancing class. We've been rehearsing for tonight's show. I believe we have a jolly good program planned for you," Sandy replied, boasting just a little. She thought she had reason to be proud. She had never danced before, but after only a few days practice she was already good enough to perform in a show. Maybe she was not quite ready for the Covent Garden Opera House, but still, she thought she was already much better than all the other dancers.

"I understand Graham and Fred are singing in a group. Did I hear correctly?" Edith asked.

"Yes, I stayed for a few minutes after dance class and listened to their rehearsal. They're not bad–for amateurs," Sandy observed, a little perturbed the topic had been diverted from her dancing prowess.

"I wish we had joined the chorus," Ann lamented. "At the time, I thought it would serve me better to attend the lecture series on America. Unfortunately, most of the sessions have not been worthwhile. They've been presented by officers, crew members, and passengers, none of whom seem to have much to tell us. I don't know why the escorts bothered to hold the series. What do you think, Edith? You went with me."

"I think they knew their topics, they just didn't know how to present them," suggested Edith. "I forgive them though–after all, they're not professional speakers, just amateurs."

"The only good talk was the one by that nice gentleman with the funny mustache. I thought his description of midwest America both humorous and informative," Ann added, trying to soften what earlier must have sounded as unfair criticism.

"Yes, but you may have a bias. I thought the two of you would never stop talking afterwards. What did you possibly have to say to him?" Edith asked. She added, with a chuckle, "Just because he likes you is no reason to recommend his lecture."

Ann blushed and pretended she hadn't heard Edith's tease. "The comparisons he made between Britain and America were helpful. Don't you think? I never imagined there would be so many differences. The only thing: he didn't delve into the things in sufficient detail; that's what I was talking to him about. We still have no clear idea of what to expect when we arrive."

"What do you think you'll find?" Fred asked, as he joined the group. "I don't expect the natives will have good manners, after all, the Americans are quite primitive compared to us."

"That's not too unexpected, is it?" interjected Graham who was with Fred. "The U.S. wasn't even a nation two hundred years ago. England must surely be much more highly advanced; it's been around so much longer."

"I wish they had offered school lessons on the way over," Edith lamented. "It would have been much better than wasting time dancing, singing, and lying on deck chairs all day."

"How could they?" observed Graham. "We have no school teachers on board."

"Thank goodness!" exclaimed Fred. "I have no desire to go to school until I absolutely must."

"What's wrong?" Edith asked, looking with concern at Sandy. "Why are you rubbing your neck like that?"

"Was I? Gee, I don't know," Sandy replied. "For some reason my neck has been itching all morning."

"You should ask Dr. Peters to take a look at it," Ann advised.

"Oh, it is nothing. It's just a little rash. It will be all right," Sandy assured everyone. There was a noticeable hint of worry in her eyes. "If Mum were here, she would take care of it for me in a jiff," she said. It was an inadvertent slip. She didn't want them to think she needed her mother.

As always happened whenever someone mentioned their mum, dad, or home, a pall immediately fell across the group. Everyone began to think of England and their families–they once again were homesick.

"Come on, people," Edith coaxed. "Let's leave this deck before the sun burns us to a crisp. Let's go down to Neptune Hall and see if they're playing any games we can join; or perhaps we can play a game of whist. There are enough of us here to play."

"I would rather play netball," Fred said.

"That's a good idea," Graham added. "We will choose sides, half the boys and half the girls on each team. I'm certain we can find others to join us when we get there."

"Or we could explore the ship," Fred said, changing his mind.

"That's a good suggestion," Ann said. "It's better than playing games."

Everyone agreed exploring was what they should do.

They spent the next hour sneaking through doors marked with *OFF LIMITS* and *FIRST AND SECOND CLASS PASSENGERS ONLY* signs. The size of the *Caerleon* impressed them, they had not realized how little space had been allocated to the third class passengers. The elegance of the first class passenger facilities impressed them even more. They began to appreciate the advantages of being an aristocrat.

Sandy, more timid than the rest, was unhappy and complained most of the time they were in the upper-class sections. She worried they would be caught and disciplined. She did not wish to be reprimanded in front of everyone at dinner that evening; Graham's ordeal had convinced her of that.

Had she only known. She was in no danger: the captain had instructed the crew to scold trespassers only if they annoyed the other passengers.

The evening program was a success. The audience enthusiastically applauded the children for their industry, skill, and good spirits. Several remarked that the children were good ambassadors for England; the performers had apparently taken the admonishments of the scheme officials to heart.

After the show, a snack table was provided in the dining saloon as a special treat for everyone. The children still found it difficult to believe it possible to have so much food, particularly so many sweets. But even with this cornucopia of goodies before them, many of the children remained sad. The snacks could not compensate for the lingering melancholy of the children. It had now been ten days since they had left home.

The next morning Graham awoke from a sound sleep. He sensed something was wrong. He looked at the clock on the chest of drawers. It was a quarter to five. As he sank back into the folds of his hammock he heard the fog horn. The horn was what had wakened him. Although he knew he shouldn't, he climbed out of his hammock, put on his trousers, heavy coat, and life jacket; quietly slipped out of the cabin and made his way to the main deck.

Everything was shrouded in almost total darkness. He carefully inched his way across the deck to the railing and as his eyes became accustomed to the night he realized fog enveloped the ship. Looking down, where normally he would have seen the ship's wake he could see only fog. In the distance, he could hear the foghorns of other ships. First came one, then another, and then the answer from the *Caerleon's* horn. As he stood there, captivated by the eerie envelope of fog, the ship shuddered to a halt. The sound pattern of the horns from the other ships slowly began to fade. He wondered why.

Although Graham knew he should return to his cabin, the fog and the foghorns fascinated him. He remained on deck until just before the wake up calls began, then inched his way back to the companionway and quickly returned to his cabin. He was back in the hammock just as the ship's bells sounded half-past five.

Everyone talked about the fog at the breakfast table. By then they had heard of Graham's adventure and asked may questions; his daring had added to his celebrity. Fortunately, no one told the escorts, and more importantly to Graham, no one told the captain.

It was late afternoon before the fog lifted and the ship could resume its journey. As it did, the children noticed there were no other ships around. The *Caerleon* was alone. The convoy had disbanded and the British Navy had deserted them. Being alone at sea worried the children; they were now easy prey for the German U-boats. As their fears grew, Steve suddenly exclaimed, "Look! Over there. Isn't that land?"

It was only after the captain briefed them that they knew they were off the shore of North America, looking at the coast of Newfoundland. The ship had safely crossed the Atlantic. The trip was nearly over. Arrival time in New York harbor was expected on Wednesday. Everyone began to prepare for disembarkation.

That night the children's tears were not for home and family but for a new fear. Living in America was beginning to frighten them. They started to worry that it might not be as nice as they had thought. It was not because they had learned any new, disturbing things about America, it was simply because their new life was now so close at hand.

Between aspen, birch, and pine covered hills lay a large clear lake. No wind blew. The lake was mirror flat; none of the aspens quaked. Just off the eastern bank, high in an aspen tree, was an aerie. In the nest sat a mother eagle, her wary eye on her brood of eaglets. On the western shore, opposite, an old male eagle tormented his eaglet son. The only sounds were those of the mother coddling her young and the scolding male.

"No!" screamed the old male, as he tried to seize the little bird with his talons, "I am better, you are the worthless one. You will never be as fine. You will never fly as high. You will never be as mighty."

The eaglet began to move away. "Do not fly from me!" the eagle screamed, lashing out at his progeny. The eaglet darted to one side of the nest. Being older and not as quick, the old eagle missed. Frustrated, he tried again ... and again ... and again ... always missing. Finally, the young eaglet could stomach no more. He screamed, "That's enough, old eagle. Leave me be. I have tired of your abuse. I shall make my own destiny. I shall be bigger than you, faster than you, smarter than you. Your rule is over. I have won! He spread his wings and flew away."

The old eagle pursued but could not catch him, then watched, helplessly, as the eaglet flew eastward, across the lake.

While the old and young eagles fought, the mother eagle on the opposite shore had coaxed her brood to leave their nest, to sample the world. They resisted. They were afraid to spread their wings and fly. "I will fall!" sobbed the smaller, the last to hatch. "I will never learn to fly."

"Oh yes you will, my sweet little bird," said the mother, knowing all eaglets eventually spread their wings and fly. "Have courage, my pet. You are an eagle. You are meant to fly. Leave the nest. Go out into the world, be free of my influence. Fly! Wherever your heart takes you."

"I'm afraid, Mother. I'm afraid!"

"Worry no more, child; the day has come." The mother then gently nudged her youngest over the edge.

The young eaglet plunged earthward. "I cannot fly," she cried. But as she neared the ground she spread her wings. The air filled her feathered underside, and she began to soar. Her fall had turned to flight. "I am flying! Oh, I am flying!" she shouted joyously. "I did it! I have won."

She moved her wings and began to rise. Enthralled with this new skill, she flew in a large circle, increased the radius, and circled once again. She explored the land below, saw the lake under the blue sky, saw the setting sun reflecting a golden stripe across the lake. Entranced by the beauty, she forgot her fright. She experimented more, the circle grew larger, and larger. Suddenly, she remembered her mother and turned toward the nest. It was empty. Her mother had gone. Her family had gone. She was alone. She was sad, homesick; tears beaded in her eyes. She turned towards the sun and flew westward across the lake.

The two young eaglets met. Each attracted to the other. Each saw things in the other that caused new feelings, feelings they did not quite understand.

They soared playfully. First one followed, then the second. They flew high. They soared close to the water. They flew quickly. They flew slowly. They surveyed the heavens, the water and ground below, scanned it all with sharp eyes. A mouse skittered across an open field. Down swooped the eagle. Soon mouse and eagle were on a tree branch, the young female next to them. Together the eagles shared the meal.

Afterwards, their appetites sated, she moved close to him. They gently touched. Their feelings stronger still. Suddenly, lightning flashed in the west. The wind blew harder, colder. It became difficult to perch. She lost her grip, disappeared, blown toward the east. The male eaglet tried to follow but eddies overcame. He plunged downward toward the sea.

The storm ended. She looked back; he was gone. He looked for her. She was gone.

Ann woke in her hammock. "What a strange dream," she thought. Several hours later Oliver woke in his Dexter Hills bed. He too marveled at his dream.

Neither could decipher what the dreams meant.

Chapter 23

Wednesday, 21 August 1940

While Chad was at work he received the following memorandum:

Date: *21 August 1940*
To: *Families of Evacuee Children*
From: *E. J. Newton*

Mr. W. T. Bender has just informed me that the liner S.S. Caerleon arrived safely in New York Harbor this morning with the Bender kiddies on board.

All children are well and send their love.

Chad was never happier in his life. He immediately telephoned Mrs. Wilson and asked if she would run next door and ask Diane to call him. When Diane telephoned back he read the memo to her. Diane asked him to read it twice. She wanted to be certain she had not misunderstood. "Oh, Chad, they are there. We needn't worry anymore. They have safely crossed the Atlantic!"

Tears of happiness streamed down Chad's face. He imagined Diane was doing the same. He was correct, she was also crying, not only because she was happy, but because she was sad. "Now there's an ocean between us," she told Mrs. Wilson.

II - America

Chapter 24

Wednesday, 14 August 1940

Stan Roberts could not believe it was the middle of August already. It had been nearly two months since W.T. had asked him to direct the McKinley Heights phase of the evacuation. Where had the time gone? The Pinnington children were arriving next week, and there was still much to do. From the very onset of the project, there had been one unexpected difficulty after another.

The arrival date was a good example; information about English shipping had been extremely difficult to obtain. The English government had classified all departure and arrival dates and refused to provide any estimates. Finally, after several frantic telephone calls by Mr. Bender to his friends in Washington and New York, the cablegram had come this morning. The ship was expected in New York harbor sometime towards the end of next week, much earlier than Stan had originally thought.

It left him with only eight or nine days before the children arrived. Fortunately, since he planned to entertain them at Camp Bender for at least a week before sending them to their assigned homes, preparation for their arrival was the only major hurdle that absolutely had to be cleared before then. Everything else had a few additional days–but not many, he would still need to hurry. Matching the children with foster families was his major problem; he needed every minute he could find for that effort. The children's earlier arrival would make the task that much more difficult–or would it? Maybe it wasn't as bad as it sounded. Since they would be here earlier than planned, the children could be interviewed sooner. That way their precise needs could be identified, perhaps even before he had the final list of foster families. Then there would be less wasted time readjusting the assignments; they would only need to compile the housing list once. One thing was for certain, though, somehow all the children had to be placed with foster families in the next three weeks if they were to start school with everyone else.

When he was first given the assignment, he hadn't thought it would be a particularly difficult one but how wrong he had been. He knew now it would take a miracle to complete everything on time. It would not have been so bad if he could have approached it as he had other projects; he simply would have studied the alternatives, made a few reasonable decisions, and issued instructions on how he wanted things done. It was the petty politics that had impeded progress with this assignment; there were just too many politicians, government agencies, and benevolent groups involved.

First off, each child needed a visa before they could enter the U.S. Stan hadn't thought visas would be a major problem; after all the children would only be here until the war ended. Surely the American government would never be so insensitive as to deny these poor little kiddies safe refuge until then. Unfortunately, the U.S. Neutrality Acts passed in the mid 1930's mandated a stringent isolationist policy and, among other things, set rigid rules and limitations on immigration. When he approached the government officials, they cited these Acts as an excuse for why they couldn't help. It was not until he talked the local newspaper editor into publishing an article describing the children's plight that positive things began to happen. Fortunately, a national newspaper had picked it up, and once it was printed, there was a huge sympathetic public outcry. This reaction, and support from the U.S. Committee for the Care of European Children and the local congressman, finally pressured the Department of State into agreeing, however reluctantly, to issue the visas. But even then they insisted Bender Electric create a special trust fund to guarantee each child would go home as soon as the emergency was over. The fear was that without it the children might someday become public wards. Stan felt good about the resolution but had little time to enjoy his success; there were so many other problems still demanding his attention.

In early July, the Bender Electric employees had been surveyed to determine who would be willing to provide a foster home for the children. The number of enthusiastic replies had been impressive. It was this overwhelming response that had led the department heads to unanimously approve the program. At the time, Stan had been elated, there seemed little doubt billets could be easily arranged for the hundred, or so, children E.J. had told him to expect.

By the middle of the month, the U.S. Committee for the Care of European Children, or USCCEC as they then called themselves, had heard about the Bender program and started imposing its own rules, regulations, and demands. Before long, not only was it necessary to satisfy USCCEC but, in Britain, CORB also wanted to approve all major plans. The required multitude of additional reports, justifications, and approvals nearly caused the program to collapse. Fortunately, E.J.

Newton had friends in CORB and easily handled that interface so their demands did not directly involve Stan, except for the annoyance of sending wire copies of all his committee's major actions and waiting for their approval. It wasted so much valuable time that on several occasions Stan had serious thoughts about giving up.

As planning progressed however, Stan realized one way to minimize interference from USCCEC and CORB was to enlist the services of local volunteer community groups. By using them to either make, or at least approve, many of the decisions his committee would normally have made on its own, it served to mollify the meddling bureaucrats. The local organizations accepted these responsibilities with enthusiasm and good intention. Unfortunately, their involvement also brought with it other major complications. Jealousies and rifts between the groups began to develop. Each wanted full authority over the program and insisted on acting independently of the other groups, especially when it involved newsworthy activities which were certain to be mentioned in the local newspaper. It was not difficult for Stan to conclude at these times that the groups were more interested in publicity for themselves than in the welfare of the children. Believing it best to let them sort out their differences themselves, he tried to stay out of their politics; there simply was not enough time left to risk his embroilment in petty controversies. Whenever things started getting too far out of hand, he would call the groups together and, using all his skills to influence and coerce, would guide the rather naive chairwomen to some sort of joint innocuous compromise. But all this took time too!

In spite of all the difficulties, the program had continued to progress. Each candidate foster family had been carefully screened and interviewed and in Stan's opinion the choices, for the most part, were satisfactory. There were only a few selections that troubled him; some families, much like the local organizations, seemed to be more interested in impressing the McKinley Heights community than in caring for the children. Since any unilateral action on his part would undoubtedly have lead to a lengthy hearing and ultimately created additional animosity between the increasingly belligerent groups, he decided to ignore the problem. He hoped the bad choices would be eliminated during final matchups of children and families.

As time grew shorter, one of his main worries became the growing number of families who were withdrawing their offer to care for a child. It seemed that as the decision date approached, more and more families were having second thoughts. If the trend continued it was possible there would be an insufficient number of families left to accommodate all the children. Unfortunately, because of the uncertainty over the specific needs of these children, the only thing he could do was wait to see how everything worked out after they arrived. If there were too many special cases he wasn't quite certain what he would do.

The plan now was to meet the children in New York, remain there overnight, and transport them by train to McKinley Heights the following day. The one night stay would permit him to take care of any last minute logistical problems that were certain to arise and give the children a little time to adjust to being back on firm soil–find their land legs, so to speak.

When he was absolutely certain about the date of arrival, he would make the hotel reservations. Stan wanted everything to be right; he wanted to be certain the accommodations were as luxurious as the company could afford. He knew the children would be tired and homesick. Good accommodations would distract them from thinking too much about home; and perhaps more importantly, would give them a good first impression of America and the hospitality they could expect. He chose Hotel McAlpin. It was not too far from the pier and close to the railway station. The hotel had assured him rooms would be available as long as they had a one-day notice. The Pennsylvania Railroad Company agreed to add several deluxe Pullman parlor cars for the group's exclusive use on its journey to Ohio. Stan hoped the luxury of these cars would make the train ride a trip to remember and would give the children a better opportunity to rest after their long journey.

Buses would transport the children to Camp Bender when they arrived in McKinley Heights. Although their stay at the campgrounds was intended to orient and process them and determine their foster homes, it would not be all business. There would be plenty of recreational and entertainment activities to enliven their stay. The committee still needed to complete some of the details, but Stan was pleased with the events that had been scheduled so far. If he had anything to do with it, no one was going to be homesick while they were in camp. Unless he had overlooked something, he could not see how, as busy as they would be, anyone would have time to pine for home.

The local newspapers and radio stations had first written about the Bender scheme nearly a month ago. The amount of community interest the children generated since then had startled him. Numerous newspaper articles had appeared already, and a number of the local reporters wanted to know when the children would arrive in New York. Many New York newspaper reporters had also called, wanting more detail and kept asking for the arrival time. The company could certainly have used all this interest for free publicity but Mr. Bender, bless his soul, had made it clear, nothing was to detract from the children's welfare and happiness. He instructed Stan to proceed discreetly; he wanted to keep the initial reception private if at all possible. Stan could notify the local press, but beyond that, there was to be no press releases.

By noon on Monday, almost everything Stan could think of was either in place or being worked on. He hoped he had considered every detail. "With luck," he thought, "we might just be able to successfully complete this project after all."

Chapter 25

Monday, 19 August 1940

Excitement was beginning to grow for the families in the McKinley Heights area who had volunteered their homes to the evacuees. The day was approaching when the children would arrive and matchups finalized. The Nelson family of Oakton was one of the families eagerly awaiting the outcome.

When Ken first learned about the scheme, he had wasted no time. It was just what he had wished for, an answer to his prayers. These children, unlike the well-to-do Newton children, were from ordinary working-class English families; any of the youngsters should fit in quite nicely in the Nelson household. He quickly offered to billet one of them. The result had been almost miraculous. The thought of having another child in the house had returned a sparkle to Louise's eyes, something Ken had not seen since Tommy first contracted polio. Ever since he had told her they might be getting a young visitor, she had been making plans.

Ken didn't think there was any chance the committee would turn them down, especially since they had agreed to accept either a girl or a boy. Louise had preferred a girl, but it really didn't matter; she would welcome either. Meg agreed with her mom, either would be fine; but she did think a girl, about her age, would be the best choice. But even setting this aside, how could the committee deny them? They had more than enough room in the house for the child and his salary, although not outstanding, was adequate to feed and clothe another person. They were devout people, involved in many community activities and organizations, and had already raised a fine young daughter, which should count for something. The interview had certainly gone well enough. Although it might have been his imagination, he could have sworn the interviewer winked at the close of their meeting; that must have indicated they were high on her list. He had also dropped many hints at the plant about his desire to billet a child–as well respected as he thought he was at Bender Electric, that should improve his chances.

It was his understanding that they would make final assignments soon after the children arrived which, rumors now suggested, would be sometime towards the end of this week. If so, he estimated the Nelson's would have a visitor in their home well before Labor Day.

It surprised Ken when Louise said at breakfast, "Kenneth, let's give the new child Tommy's room. We could spruce it up a bit, perhaps wallpaper it and buy some new drapes. I think we could find a pattern suitable for either a boy or a girl; that way we could do it now and have it ready before she arrived." She laughed and added, "Or he."

Ken couldn't believe what he was hearing. Louise had scarcely entered Tommy's room since he passed away, and now, all of a sudden, she was talking about remodeling it. "That's an excellent idea, Louise. I thought we would use the spare bedroom, but it really is too small to be comfortable. Tommy's room would suit so much better."

"It's also much brighter, the sun shines in during the afternoon. I think the spare bedroom is too dark and gloomy for a long term guest. We could move in the double bed from the spare bedroom, that way the child could invite visitors for a stay over now and then. I know how much Meg likes to do that."

"Let's do it, Louise! You'll need to hurry though. My guess is our guest will be here–in our home–by the end of the month. You'd best start shopping today for the things we need."

"What do you need?" Meg asked as she spooned oatmeal into her bowl and sat down for breakfast.

"Mom wants to redo Tommy's room for our English guest," Ken answered excitedly.

"Gee, that sounds great. May I go with you, Mom?" Meg asked, noting the look on her mother's face. She couldn't recall the last time she had last seen such a pleased and excited look.

"We'll try to be there when the stores open. I'll get ready as soon as we wash the dishes, but first, I want to look in the phone book for Mr. Stohl's telephone number. I hope he's available on such short notice. He did such an excellent job wallpapering Tom and Victoria's room last spring. I'd like to have him do ours."

"Go ahead. Call him, Mom. I'll do the dishes," volunteered Meg. "I've already bathed and only need to change my clothes."

"I'll help with the dishes," Ken said, to the surprise of both Louise and Meg; he normally never offered to do dishes.

*   *   *

Next door Dr. Thomas Derringer and his wife Victoria were also discussing the Bender scheme. "I'm afraid I can't change it, Victoria. The Medical Society meeting is next week and I must be there. I'm presenting my paper on poliomyelitis. The meeting's in Chicago. There must be some sort of arrangement we can make to take care of this Bender business. I definitely want you there with me. You can spend the day shopping at Marshall Fields, and in the evening we can take in a stage show. You deserve a vacation."

"But they haven't assigned a child to us yet. Louise told me yesterday, Ken is almost certain, from what he heard at work, the children should arrive in McKinley Heights very soon–more than likely, later this week. They will probably make final assignments sometime next week. I don't think it's wise to go before they're made. They might not give us one of the children if we're not here."

"Oh, I think I can pull a few strings to ensure we won't be overlooked."

"You must be positive, Tom. My appointment as president of the Garden Club depends on it. You know how important it is to make a good impression on the girls. Being a foster mother to an evacuee is just the kind of publicity I need to win the election."

"Is it worth it, Victoria? Do you realize the commitment you're making? The child could be with us for six months–maybe even a year–however long the war in Europe continues. Are you certain you can handle a child? What if he's a naughty boy? What if he gives us a difficult time? You know how little patience you have with children. Whenever your sister brings her kids here you are always in bed with a headache the next day. I truthfully think you'd be better off if we forgot the whole idea."

"No, Tom, I have my mind made up; I want a foster child. It's important for my image. Besides, we can put her in the servants' quarters. There's a spare bedroom down there. Sarah won't mind if we crowd her a little. We've been spoiling Sarah, anyway. I don't know what she does with all that room as it is. The child will be out of the way down there. We can ask Sarah to tend to her day-to-day needs. Then all we'll need do is to put up with her on those special occasions when we ask her to dine with us. Certainly, we can expect her to behave and mind her manners for at least one meal now and then."

"You talk as if it's certain they will give us a girl. What if it's a boy?"

"Oh, I think we can count on a girl. I talked to Mrs. Welch, the head of the Family Service Society. I believe I made my desires perfectly clear to her, and she had better do as I ask, or I'll see to it she no longer runs the society. She knows I mean it."

"Victoria, sometimes I think you should slow down a bit. You soon won't have any friends left. You demand too much attention in every organization you join."

"Let's face it, Tom, it gets me where I want to be, and where I should be for your sake. It's what you need, a well-known wife, one who has the proper connections and knows the right people. If you're going to run a successful–and financially fruitful–practice you need to focus more on wealthy people. They're the ones who are willing to pay top fees."

"I entered medicine to make people well, Victoria, not to earn money."

"That's all well and good, but unfortunately you chose a wife who needs expensive clothes, a big house and elegant jewelry. I want to live in the exclusive part of McKinley Heights someday, Tom. The only way we'll ever get to Clairmont is for you to make more money, and the way to do that is to make friends with rich people."

"Well, I hope you know what you're doing, Victoria. I think you're wrong, but if that's what you want, all right, that's what we'll do. I'll talk to Stan Roberts this morning and make certain they won't forget us should they make the final assignments while we're gone."

Victoria seemed satisfied with his promise and changed the subject. She thought the curtains in the bedroom they had wallpapered last spring were beginning to look shabby. "Can we buy new ones?" she asked. She knew the question was unnecessary, Tom always agreed to buy anything she wanted.

John and Flossie Mannheim had no children. They had tried for a number of years, but after further testing, the doctor told them conception was impossible, John was sterile. Flossie had accepted the diagnosis and was resigned to a childless marriage, however, when Bender Electric announced the evacuee program, she changed her mind. The many advantages of fostering a child described in the announcement convinced her they should apply. In fact, her enthusiasm was so great that she persuaded John to ask for two children. She thought asking for more than one child would impress the committee and better their chances.

She was correct. Among all the applicants there were only a few willing to assume responsibility for more than one child. Because there were so few, the Mannheim's were marked as potential parents with the highest priority, even though the investigating social worker had recommended against giving them a child. She had detected what she thought to be personality problems.

Although the committee had not shared with Brad and Clara Holtzman, or any of the other applicants, what they were planning, the Holtzmans were on the high priority list. They had impressed the caseworker during their interview. She was certain they would provide one of the best home environments of all those she had interviewed. Their house was neat and comfortable; they were young, loved each other, were religious, and, most importantly, they obviously loved children. Without a doubt, they would provide a nurturing environment for any child. After the interview she made a simple notation in her casebook, "High priority! By all means, give this couple a child," and had underscored it.

The final count, obtained from E.J. late last week, indicated eighty-four children were on the ship. Of these, five would be staying either in Canada or California with relatives. There were children from forty-one separate families, including one family who had sent five children. As Stan had feared, the total count of available homes was low. On Friday it had decreased to only sixty-two. Not many were willing to accommodate more than one child and some even insisted on selecting the sex of their child. It was clear, final assignments would be extremely difficult, caution had to be exercised to ensure all children had homes; there would be no room for error.

But they had to consider the children's wishes too. They couldn't do that until the youngsters were interviewed. They could do nothing more until the children arrived at Camp Bender. Stan hoped the matchups would become more apparent after that.

Chapter 26

Wednesday, 21 August 1940

It was Wednesday after lunch. Stan and W.T. were at Pier 14 on the west side of Manhattan. Word had apparently spread among the news agencies. A large contingent of news reporters and photographers from McKinley Heights, Akron, and Cleveland, as well as the local New York newspapers were there. As the *S.S. Caerleon* slowly moved into its berth, they could see a large group of children on the sun deck waving excitedly. The Bender children were almost certainly in the group, but Stan and W.T. had no idea where.

Stan looked at the children and thought about all the long hours he had spent on this project. The smiles on the their faces and their jubilant excitement made all his hard work worthwhile. He knew he would remember the moment for a long time; it nearly brought tears to his eyes. When he looked at W.T. he had to smile. W.T. had always been such a reserved person, someone who seldom displayed any emotion, but here he was, jumping up and down and waving to the children. It was almost as if he were a boy again. No doubt about it, W.T. was enjoying himself.

Yesterday had been different. On Monday afternoon, Stan had finally received the cable he had been waiting for; it indicated the *S.S. Caerleon* was expected to arrive in New York on Tuesday morning. He had immediately booked reservations on a Pullman sleeper for W.T. and himself and barely had time to finish everything before leaving McKinley Heights early Monday evening. Miss Perkins, his secretary, remained in McKinley Heights to take care of any last minute details. She planned to catch a later train and arrive around noon on Tuesday.

It was fortunate she had delayed her schedule. In all the confusion, Stan had forgotten his promise to notify the local press. The train was about to leave when he remembered. Too late to call the newsmen, he quickly telephoned Miss Perkins and asked her to take care of it. Efficient secretary that she was, it was promptly done, along with many of the other last minute details Stan had failed to do.

The trained pulled into Pennsylvania Station on Tuesday morning shortly after breakfast. Stan and W.T. grabbed a taxi and went directly to the pier. They tipped the cabdriver generously and asked him to deliver their bags to the Hotel McAlpin. He gave the cabby detailed instructions on what to tell the hotel desk clerk. Fortunately, the driver was dependable and delivered the instructions accurately. Stan was thankful for that; he had been afraid the driver might keep their bags or, at a minimum, mishandle the instructions.

It surprised Stan to find McKinley Heights reporters already waiting at the pier; somehow they had arrived in New York before him. He supposed it was because they had more experience arranging quick trips. They waited at the pier all day looking for the ship. As the hours dragged on, Stan became increasingly anxious. "It is surprising," he thought, "how many terrible images one can conjure in one's mind when he's ignorant of what is actually happening." He imagined many things: a torpedo had hit the ship; the ship had struck a mine; or someone had botched the arrival date. It was late evening before they learned the ship had been caught in a fog bank and would arrive a day late.

After hearing the news they went to the hotel. Miss Perkins had arrived and, in her usual manner, had already rearranged all the schedules caused by the delay. W.T. was so pleased with all she had done, and so relieved nothing serious had happened to the ship, that he invited her to join Stan and him for dinner. As was his habit, W.T. selected a very posh restaurant, one that impressed both of his guests. Neither had ever dined in such an elegant setting or received such impressive service before, but both agreed the food was nothing special. They did not complain to W.T. about that however.

It was an exciting morning for the children. The schedule called for them to rise early, eat quickly, pack, and be ready to disembark before noon. Ann and the others found it difficult to fill their suitcases carefully; they were too excited and giddy to take things seriously. Some packed so poorly they had to sit on their suitcases before they could close them, all of which added to the frivolity of the occasion. "I hope this doesn't pop open as we walk down the gangway," Edith snickered. "I would hate to have that handsome sailor we met last night see my smalls."

Everyone laughed, except Elizabeth who blushed; she was unfamiliar with talk of that kind.

After they finished packing, the girls followed Miss Lewis to the main deck where the group was assigned an interior passageway to wait for further disembarkation orders. Soon afterwards, Graham and his cabin mates joined Ann and the other girls. Everyone was in a jovial mood. Filled with curiosity, they began sneaking into the lounge to glimpse the rapidly approaching harbor through the starboard portholes. Once the New York skyline, appeared they could no longer be restrained. Although instructed otherwise, Miss Lewis acceded to their pleas and moved the group to the sun deck.

As the ship sailed through the upper bay of the Hudson River Ann exclaimed, "Oh, look everyone. There's the Statue of Liberty!"

"Blimey! Look at it. They've painted it green! I always thought the Statue of Liberty was silver," Fred noted.

"That's not paint," Edith corrected him. "It's copper oxide. The French made the statue out of copper. Copper turns green when it weathers."

"Whatever it is, she's beautiful," Sandy observed.

The ship soon sailed past the statue and entered the Hudson River. The children could now clearly discern the individual buildings of the skyline. "Look at that tall spire. It really towers over the other ones. Does anyone know what it is?" Steve asked.

"That's the Wall Tower building," Ann answered.

"How do you know that?" Sandy asked.

"They showed pictures of the New York buildings in one of the lectures I attended while you were at dance class."

"Look at that tall building farther up the island. It looks taller than the others. Is it the Empire State Building? It must be ninety stories high," Graham guessed.

"It is the Empire State Building all right," Ann answered. "I believe it is ninety-five stories high."

"No, it is one hundred and two stories," Edith corrected. "We just finished reading about it in school this past year. Look at the gray one further along, the one with the fancy, pointed top. That must be the Chrysler Building."

"I believe that's one of the Rockefeller Center buildings," Ann said, pointing further up the island but being careful to be a little less definite of what it was she had identified.

As the children marveled at the skyline, several tugs met the ship and began guiding it slowly toward the dock. The children could see people waiting on the pier as the ship neared its berth.

"Look how everyone is waving. Let's wave back," cried Steve over the noise of the tooting tugs and the excited shouts from other passengers. At that moment, no one felt homesick; no one was thinking of home, their new adventure was filled with too much excitement. For many, however, it would not be long before they once again suffered the pain of homesickness.

Disembarkation took much longer than expected. Immigration officers insisted on carefully processing everyone before they could leave the ship. As time passed, the children became more and more impatient to go ashore. At one of the final check stations, a seaman asked the children to turn in their gas masks. "I'm sorry, sir, but I'll keep my gas mask, if you do not mind," one of the young boys said, resolutely.

"It's all right now, sonny, you're in America, there's no danger of a gas attack here," the seaman counseled. "Give me your mask so I can take it back to England for someone else to use. Please?"

"My Dad said I should always keep it with me. I don't wish to disobey him just because we're in America," the boy argued. It took the assurances of Miss Lewis, the chief escort, Graham, and some of the other older boys before he was finally convinced to part with it.

Afterwards, the captain stood at the head of the gangplank and shook hands with everyone and wished them good luck as they left the ship. When Graham approached, the captain greeted him with a big smile and an enthusiastic handshake. "You remind me of my son," he told Graham. "You both have lots of spunk. Keep up your spirit, lad. You'll be a great man someday."

Graham smiled as he walked down the gangplank; the captain liked him after all. The compliment had capped a good voyage, and now he was ready to take a look at New York, and then America; he was eager to get started. Unfortunately the immigration officials had other plans. They directed the children into a portside building where a group of medical officers waited to examine them. No one could believe they had to go through another medical examination; they had already gone through one at the Grosvenor House just twelve days before.

For the most part, the results of the examinations were satisfactory and the children passed through quickly. Unfortunately, Sandy's case was different. The examiner noticed the rash on Sandy's neck and asked about it. She told him she first noticed it on Monday and immediately consulted Dr. Peters who had diagnosed it as nothing more than a reaction to the strong shipboard soap. The medical examiner frowned. "I'm sorry, miss," he apologized, "I'm afraid we must retain you until we complete a detailed dermatological examination. I'm confining you to our detention center on Ellis Island until someone can look at you more completely. You probably won't be delayed more than a day or two."

"But I don't know anything about America, sir. I can't travel alone, I need to stay with my friends. Please, sir, don't make me stay," she pleaded.

"We'll talk to your escort and make arrangements for you to rejoin your group after your examination and release. It's the best I can do. Now please go with this gentleman. He'll show you where to wait for transportation to the island."

When Miss Lewis finally persuaded the officials into letting her talk with Sandy, she found Sandy in tears. "I'm sorry, Sandy, I tried, but I'm afraid there is nothing more I can do, today. I can't change their minds. I don't expect you'll be going to McKinley Heights with the others tomorrow.

"At least you're not the only one retained. Several children from the other groups that sailed with us–you may have met some of them–are also being held for more detailed examinations. No one appears to have anything serious, but they want all of you to see specialists before they'll sign your release. The best I could do was to obtain the officer's promise that he'll keep all of you together in one group tonight. It'll give you some company. Tomorrow I'll make certain either I, or one of the other escorts, will remain in New York until your release. Afterwards, we'll get you to McKinley Heights as quickly as we can. You shouldn't be separated from the others very long."

"Oh, Miss Lewis. I'm frightened! I wish I'd never come to America," she sobbed. "Can't you do something more? I know you will do all you can, but I'm still afraid I'll be forgotten. I'm really scared, Miss Lewis."

"I know you are, honey. We simply can't do anything more today. Dr. Peters has tried to convince them it's nothing serious, but they won't accept his word; they say he isn't licensed to practice medicine in America. You're just going to have to get through one night on your own. I promise you, we'll not leave you here any longer than we must. I'll talk to the Bender people as soon as I leave here, perhaps they can do something. In any case, someone will be back for you, hopefully by tomorrow."

Before Virginia Lewis left, she made certain all the children were together as promised and everyone properly introduced. She wished she could do more but could think of nothing else. When she left, several of the children, including Sandy, were crying. It nearly broke Virginia's heart.

Later that evening, as soon as she could, she told Mr. Bender what had happened. He became extremely upset and cursed the officers. He said he could do little until people were in their offices in the morning but would personally look into it just as soon as possible. He also promised that Sandy would have a personal escort to McKinley Heights if she wasn't released in time to accompany the others. He then generously offered the best travel accommodations he could arrange for all the children detained. It did not matter to him that no one but Sandy was in the Bender group. "They're still kids," he observed. Even with all his kindness, Virginia spent a troubled night. She worried, somehow, she had let Sandy down. Sleeping in the Ellis Island retention center seemed a terrible way to spend one's first night in America.

After the other children successfully passed the medical examinations, the officials permitted them to leave. The first person they saw as they passed through the exit gate was Mr. Bender. What a welcome he gave them. His enthusiasm, friendliness, and deep concern for every one immediately captured their hearts. They fell in love with him at once. Although no one could recall later who said it first, someone called him Captain Ben. Before long they all began affectionately calling him by that nickname. They would use it fondly throughout their stay in America and long afterwards. It was one of the most pleasant memories that always came to mind when they thought of America.

Before boarding the special buses for the trip to their hotel, and much to the surprise of W.T. and Stan, the entire Bender group, led by the chief escort, formed a semicircle around the two men and began singing *There'll Always be an England*. They followed it with a rather weak rendition of *The Star Spangled Banner* and a hardy *God Save the King*. They ended the program with one of the lads shouting, "Are we downhearted?"

"No!" was their unanimous response.

"I can't hear you," he shouted.

"No!" shouted the group, louder than before.

"I still can't hear you."

There followed an overpowering, "No!"

The reporters took many photographs of the children while dockside and more as they boarded the buses but only managed a few brief interviews. When they complained to Stan, he promised to make the English visitors available again–after they had checked into the hotel and had a brief rest.

"Would you look at that," exclaimed Graham. "We have bobbies on motorbikes in front of us and bobbies behind us. They're all wearing Colt revolvers! It's almost as if we were in the Wild West–except they're on motorbikes, not horses."

"They're known as policemen here," Ann corrected.

"Or cops!" someone shouted from the rear of the bus. They all broke into laughter.

As the escorted caravan made its way through the streets of New York, the children excitedly looked at the many new sights. Impressed with the missing protective webbing, they rolled down the bus windows and shouted greetings to the pedestrian onlookers. Many stopped to look or wave at the noisy, arm waving procession as it sped past, most smiled, and some shouted back.

The notice the evacuees were receiving from everyone and the apparent friendliness of the New Yorkers impressed them. With all this attention, it was difficult for them to think of themselves simply as commoners on a visit; it felt to most that they had become celebrities. This feeling of importance would continue for weeks to come. Eventually it would become a problem for some.

Chapter 27

Wednesday, 21 August 1940

The motorcade stopped in front of Hotel McAlpin, and eighty-three tired, excited, and noisy children climbed out of the buses and swarmed into the lobby. Guests of the hotel stopped to look at them, wondering who they were and why they were dressed as they were. Many of the boys wore navy blue trench coats, short pants with long stockings and cricket caps. Some had open-collared shirts but most wore buttoned collars with colored neckties. The girls wore either skirts and tailored blouses with neckties or cotton dresses. Some had ribbons in their hair, others wore straw or cotton hats. Many of the girls had on white stockings and plimsoles. A few were carrying dolls. Almost all the children had knapsacks slung over their shoulders and carried cotton or woolen outer coats; all struggled with their suitcases. It only took a few minutes listening to their chatter to guess they were not from America.

"Hello there, dear," one of the ladies said to Ann. "Where are you children from, sweetie?"

"Hello, madam," replied Ann, trying to act as dignified as she could. "We have just come from England. There's a war on over there; our parents sent us over here to escape the German air raids."

"Are your parents with you?"

"I'm sorry to say, they're not," Ann answered. "Mum and Dad had to remain in England–to help defeat that awful Mr. Hitler."

The lady's husband interrupted, "I wish you'd turn around and go home. Don't get us involved in your damn war. You limeys asked for it. You deserve whatever you get. Had you spent the thirties reinforcing your defenses instead of trying to pacify the Germans, you wouldn't be in the trouble you're in today. There'd be no need for anyone to fight Hitler. He wouldn't be the only nation prepared to fight. Now your government wants to get us involved, wants to borrow our arms and ships. Why don't you leave us alone? Don't embroil us in another of your stupid wars. Go back home where you belong! Being here will only cause us more problems."

"John! She's only a child! You shouldn't talk to her that way," the lady protested.

Ann did not completely understand what he had said, but she sensed he intended it as an insult. He had referred to her as a "limey." It upset her; she had never been called that before. Not certain how she should respond, she answered, "You have a very lovely country, sir. I can easily see why you want to keep it that way. I hope Mr. Hitler leaves you alone. It would be a shame to have him bomb a nice city like New York. If he did, then you might need to send your children away to some strange land too. Just like my mum and dad had to do. You wouldn't like that very much, would you?"

"You poor dear. Never mind him. He's just an old grump today." The lady apologized, then added, "I hope your stay in America is very pleasant."

"Come on, Ann. They're ready to take us to our room," Edith interrupted.

Ann felt relieved. She finally had an excuse to leave this terribly rude man. "Excuse me, madam. Excuse me, sir. It's been lovely meeting the two of you. I hope you have a nice evening." She turned quickly and walked away. The man mumbled something as she left, but she did not hear what it was.

Fred and Graham could hardly believe what they saw. They had never seen such plush quarters. It was almost like being in a fairy tale. The first thing that caught their eye was the large basket of fruit on the entryway table. There were enough bananas, oranges, apples and grapes to satisfy them for days. The selection outdid anything they had seen on the trip so far. Fred could not resist. He took a banana, peeled it, and ate it greedily. "This is really something," he exclaimed.

Graham in the meantime had gone into the washroom. "Look at this," he exclaimed. "Isn't this what they call a shower? I've heard of them. There's no need to sit in the tub. You simply stand in the tub and let water fall on you–just like standing in the rain. And look at this fancy toilet! Have you ever seen one with gold handles, Fred?"

"This is unbelievable! Just feel this bed, Graham. Have you ever felt anything so soft? And look, there's a telephone on the table beside the bed," Fred exclaimed.

"Look at the view, Fred. You can see the Empire State building from here. Would you believe how high we are? From our room number I'd guess, we're on the forty-fifth floor. And look, the label on this box says its an air conditioner!" Graham began pushing the buttons on the control panel and soon cool air was coming from the vents. "Blimey! We can cool the room if it gets too warm."

"Turn it off, Graham. It'll get too cold in here."

"Not to worry. See. This control switches it from an air conditioner to an electric heater. We can heat the room, as well."

"Look at this, Graham. This card says we can order food from the café just by ringing number 3-4-4. Let's try it!"

"I don't think we should, Fred. How would we pay?"

"Oh, nonsense! It doesn't say anything about paying. It probably comes with the price of the room."

Fred picked up the telephone and dialed the number. When the café maitre d'hôtel answered, Fred asked what sweets were available, hesitated while he mulled over the choices, then said, "Please send two pieces of apple pie to room 4508. Thank you. ... Yes, a scoop of ice cream on each would be jolly nice. ... Oh yes, we could use something to drink. Two cups of tea. Please. ... A large pot? Yes that would be even better. ... Certainly we want cream. ... Ten minutes? Yes, thank you, sir. ... Bellhop, you say? We shall be waiting for him."

"I hope we're not in trouble, Fred," Graham worried.

The boys inspected the remainder of the room and looked in all the cupboards and closets. They tested the radio, or wireless as they called it, and marveled at the number of different stations they heard. They laughed at the advertisements and were amused when they discovered the radio was also an alarm clock. "That clock bloody well won't be of much use to me. I'm going to sleep for days and days," Fred declared. "I like this room so much I think I'll tell Captain Ben I have decided to stay here in New York, not continue on to McKinley Heights."

A knock at the door interrupted him.

Graham opened the door and found a bellhop with a linen covered portable cart. On it were beautiful china teacups, a large silver tea pot, a lovely sugar and creamery set, and two huge pieces of apple pie, each covered with a large scoop of vanilla ice cream. The bellhop pushed the cart into the room and carefully arranged the napkins. "Will there be anything else, gentlemen?" he asked, lingering at the door with his right hand slightly extended, palm up, toward the boys.

"No, we have everything we need. That will do nicely, thank you," Fred answered. Then he added, "For now."

The bellhop hesitated a few seconds more. Finally the boys understood—he wanted a tip. Neither had any money; Miss Lewis was still holding it for them. "We're terribly sorry," Graham apologized. "I'm afraid we can't give you a tip. We just got off the boat from England and we have no cash. Please forgive us? Perhaps later."

"You lads just arrived from England, eh?" the bellhop asked. "I've only been in New York a few months myself. I'm from Canada. My mother comes from England. Near London, I believe; I don't recall the name of the town. Where do you lads live?"

"I'm from Pinnington, and he's from Northolt," Graham answered. "We left England to escape the German air raids. They call us evacuees. We're on our way to McKinley Heights, Ohio."

"Pinnington! My goodness, that's the town! That's where my mother lived. She's from Pinnington, too."

"Your mother is from Pinnington? Imagine that!"

After talking excitedly for several minutes about things they had in common, the bellhop said, "Well, lads, I best be getting back to work. You have a good stay in New York, and a pleasant journey to McKinley Heights. The best of luck to you both."

When the door closed the boys gobbled down the pie al a mode, as the maitre d'hôtel called it, took a long shower, and engaged in a boisterous water fight which left pools of water covering the bathroom floor. By the time they finished dressing, clothes were scattered everywhere; the suite was in disarray, the sun had set, and lights were beginning to show in many of the skyscraper windows.

"Would you look at the buildings, Fred," Graham exclaimed, as he stood looking out the window in amazement. "Have you ever seen so many lights?"

"It's really something. Isn't it?" was all Fred could say. The number of lights, their color, and the sheer beauty of the view nearly overwhelmed him. "There's certainly no blackout in New York," he quipped.

The evacuees were to meet in the lobby on the ground floor. 'G' stood for the ground floor in English lifts. Graham could find no 'G' button on the lift controls. He pushed the 'B', the only other unnumbered button. When the lift stopped and the door opened he knew it was not the floor he wanted. 'B' apparently stood for basement. Graham pushed the '1' button. They stopped on the ground floor. "That's a strange method of assigning floor numbers," Graham observed. "Didn't Americans know the first story *added* to a building should be labeled '1' not '2'?"

"Boy! Are they mixed-up over here," Fred observed. "They can't even label the floors of the building correctly."

All these strange customs would take time to understand. The boys hoped their stay in America would be long enough to learn a few of them. But they were making progress; for instance, they already knew the Americans called it an elevator not a lift.

At dinner, the boys were not as hungry as the other children and had difficulty eating all the delicious food. When Ann asked why, Graham told her about the apple pie and ice cream. She couldn't believe the boys would do such a bold and devilish thing. All three of them laughed when the waiters brought the dessert. It was a huge piece of apple pie– or what Ann would call an apple tart–with a large scoop of vanilla ice cream on top.

After dinner, the children were ushered into a huge conference room filled with reporters waiting to conduct interviews. The rush of reporters and photographers, with their flashing cameras, frightened several of the younger girls who had never seen flashbulbs before. They clasped their dolls as though they were their only friends. Several of the boys, curious about the devices, politely asked for the spent bulbs after each flash.

For over an hour, the reporters interviewed the children, fascinated with the cute things the children said. Snippets of the interviews appeared in the newspapers the next day both in New York and Ohio. Included were many quotable and poignant statements[*], among them: "I'm glad I'm here, but I miss my daddy." "England is the center of a great empire. I'm grateful to have been born into this empire." "We're servants to England." and "I am eager to get back." They demonstrated pride in their country with statements such as: "We're all British and we feel certain that we will win the war." "England will never give up so long as there are British men with equipment to defend themselves." "I don't believe the Jerries can ever whip Johnny Bull." and "Our country has lost battles in many wars but has a reputation for winning the last one in every case." They talked about the differences between England and America: "We have no ice in England, you know." "Ice cream is not common in England." and "They have gum in England, but we are not allowed to use it. Chewing gum in school or in the presence of elders is a punishable offense." They complimented America: "America is the most beautiful country in the world. It has lights." They talked about the war: "Turn out them lights! You see, we're so used to the blackout." "The night before we left England we were in an air raid scare and were taken to a shelter ... near the docks." "At my home we usually have a cup of tea after air raids." and "We had an air raid back home. Forty-five dive bombers, but Spitfires and Hurricanes drove them off. They didn't do 'nutten! I wasn't scared. I stood outside. I wanted to count them." None of the children said anything about the torpedoes or the sunken convoy ships. The captain had asked them not to tell and, as loyal little seamen, they obeyed his orders. "Not one single German showed up during our ocean trip," was volunteered by one faithful child.

---

[*] These are samples of actual statements made by the Hoover children during their North Canton, Ohio interviews in 1940.

As one reporter put it, "The main themes that permeated all of the children's comments were that they were brave little Englishmen thankful for the hospitality offered by the Americans, and that the Germans were evil monsters who had caused them to be sent away from England and their parents."

When the interviews were over, the children were sent back to their rooms. No one complained. They were ready for a good night's sleep, although many of them were still too excited to sleep. Instead they had pillow fights and talk sessions until, finally, too exhausted to stay awake, they fell asleep. Some dreamed of parades and special banquets. The attention from the reporters had reinforced the idea that they were famous and should be treated accordingly.

Chapter 28

Thursday, 22 August 1940

When Stan saw the morning newspaper, he immediately issued a warning to the escorts: the evacuees were not to hear the news before they boarded the train. He did not want the children to worry about the escalating dangers at home.

A front-page article summarized the ongoing air battle between the English RAF and the German Luftwaffe and predicted dire consequences. The air war over England had been raging almost continuously now since July 10 and was particularly intense on August 15 when ferocious air battles occurred all along the southeast coast. The number of planes shot down on both sides had been heavy. Although the British had added to the German losses with recent expanded bombing raids on strategic targets in Germany and airfields in France, Belgium, and the Netherlands, there was no sign of any immediate reduction in the air war over England. In fact, there were some who thought Germany, in retaliation, might expand the scope of its raids, making the skies over Britain even more dangerous. The article speculated that London and its suburbs would be among the expanded targets.

If this proved true, the children's parents would soon be under attack.

Graham woke to the ring of a bell. At first he was not certain what was ringing, then finally recognized it as the telephone beside his bed. He answered it.

"Good morning, this is the front desk," the voice on the telephone said. "This is your wake-up call. The time is six-thirty. The temperature outside is sixty-two. The forecast is for sunshine with a high of seventy-eight. It promises to be a fine day."

"I bloody well don't care," Graham thought, but instead answered, "Thank you."

He then recalled Miss Lewis' instructions last night. She had requested wake-up calls for everyone and had promised to make them as late as possible. It meant Fred and he would need to hurry this morning. "Come on, Fred, wake-up. We must hurry if we want to eat before we board the bus."

"Humph," Fred replied, pulling the covers over his head.

Although sleepy, the children were in a festive mood when they assembled for breakfast. The selection of food continued to impress them. Most could not recall ever seeing some of the varieties of fruit offered. It had been a long time since they had eaten jelly-filled doughnuts or drank freshly squeezed orange juice. The cocoa was a treat also; many refilled their cups several times.

After breakfast they returned to their rooms, quickly fetched their belongings, and reassembled in the hotel parking lot. "A strange name for a car park," they told the escorts. The escorts agreed.

The children immediately boarded the buses and proceeded by motorcade to the Pennsylvania Railroad Station. Signs taped to the side of each bus read, "Bender Electric Ltd. Evacuees, Pinnington, England." Again people stopped, stared, waved, and shouted as the buses passed, and, as they had done the day before, the children amiably returned the greetings. At one intersection, while the buses stopped briefly for a traffic light, a woman rushed up to the bus and handed a box containing bubble gum through the window. The children yelled with joy, quickly unwrapped the gum, and began chewing. At the train station, W.T. and Stan laughed to see the busload of children blowing huge bubbles as they stepped down from the bus.

The children boarded the train, and, as they settled in, the train pulled out of the station. Almost before they realized it, they were under the Hudson River heading toward New Jersey and on the final leg of their journey to Ohio.

Although Ann felt tired, she found it difficult to rest. She could not stop watching the scenery whizzing by as they passed through the Allegheny Mountains of Pennsylvania. She had never seen mountains quite like the Alleghenies; they were blanketed with trees, far different from the pictures she had seen of Ben Nevis, the famous mountain of the Scottish Highlands. The mountainous countryside continued almost to the end of the trip, where the mountains had been replaced by large rolling hills. She was not certain how far they had traveled but guessed it must have been hundreds of miles. The topography around McKinley Heights certainly differed from Pinnington's; not only were the hills much higher, but distances seemed much greater; everything seemed so much farther apart. She wondered if she would ever adapt to this strange country. She didn't think so.

The train arrived at the Pennsylvania Station in McKinley Heights at six-twenty-two p.m. It was nearly two hours late, delayed by roadbed reconstruction in Pennsylvania. The long journey had tired the children. They were also terribly hungry. It had been over six hours since they had their noonday snack and now it was even past their teatime. The snack had been a box lunch. It consisted only of a sandwich, a small bag of potato crisps, which to their amusement were labeled chips on the package, a Coca-Cola, an apple, and several biscuits, or cookies as the steward had called them. The Coke, as they would soon call it, was a special treat; it was the first one they had tasted. Six hours later, however, the memory was no substitute for, what seemed to be, the last throes of hunger.

Some of the more thoughtful children began to worry that the special treatment received in New York had not been for their benefit. They suspected Bender Electric had done it solely to impress the reporters. Now that the trip was nearing an end and there were no reporters around maybe they intended to starve them. Maybe the Americans were going to treat them like beggars. They did not discuss these fears with each other, too afraid that saying it out loud might make all their worries come true.

But they were not as worried as Stan and W.T. The plan had been to provide a light noonday lunch on the train, then give them a special banquet at Camp Bender soon after they arrived. They knew now, because of the delay, the children were hungry. To compensate they hoped to shorten the ceremony at the train station, quickly proceed to the campgrounds, and after the banquet, take them to their sleeping quarters.

Stan did not know what to do. He could not telephone anybody in McKinley Heights, there were no train stops long enough for a long distance call before they arrived. Any program changes would need to wait until then. He wondered what parts of the ceremony he could cut. He had invited several political dignitaries and was certain they would not be willing to forego their speeches. He had originally hoped to give the evacuees an opportunity to hear music played by their peers. He had invited the McKinley Heights High School Band to the ceremony. Unfortunately, the band director had declined his offer–the band did not organize until school started in September. As a second choice, Stan had asked the McKinley Heights Community Band. In a way, it was a better solution; they were better instrumentalists, the music would be much better. But he supposed they had accepted the invitation only to gain more public exposure; if that were the case they wouldn't be willing to cut their part in the program either.

He had scheduled an informal get-together at the end of the program, intended for the McKinley Heights folks to introduce themselves. That was probably a segment he could eliminate, there would be other opportunities for everyone to meet later in the week. The only other part of the program he could cut was his speech, but that would only save about three minutes. It looked as if it would be quite late before they could feed the children. He hoped the chef could keep everything warm until then. "Maybe, there will be a last minute impromptu solution," he hoped.

There was a large crowd on the station platform as the children stepped off the train. The band was playing *Rule Britannia*. All the activities impressed the children, particularly the presentation by the McKinley Heights mayor of a little "key to the city" to each of them. A speech by Captain Ben followed. He welcomed them as guests of Bender Electric, "... for as long as it takes to rid the world of the tyrant, Adolph Hitler." The president of the Children's Bureau of Bear County told them she was impressed with the kindness and generosity of the families who had volunteered to keep the children, "... while the war rages on in Europe." After the speeches, the band director announced the playing of the British National Anthem. He cautioned everyone not to confuse *God Save the King* with *America*. The crowd laughed. The children wondered what he meant, stood proudly at attention during the Anthem, and continued to listen respectfully as the band closed the program with *The Star Spangled Banner*.

The reporters and town folks quickly gathered around the children at the end of the ceremony to ask questions. Much to Stan's disgust, it took nearly fifteen minutes before he finally could get the last child onto the McKinley Heights school buses. Under police escort, they motored directly to Camp Bender. Ann could not believe how popular they continued to be. She felt like a princess when the people waved along the way and particularly when the people who had gathered at the entrance cheered as the buses drove into the camp.

Camp Bender was a recreational facility reserved for the enjoyment and private use of Bender employees and their families. It consisted of a twenty acre wooded area not far from McKinley Heights. In the middle of the grounds stood the Center building with its dining hall, theater, recreation facility, and administrative and meeting rooms. A large outdoor swimming pool was directly behind the Center. A recreational field separated the sleeping cabins from the Center on three sides. On the fourth side were tennis courts, a ball diamond, a volleyball court, and a playground with several swings, a teeter-totter, and a slide. The area beyond the cabins was wooded. Footpaths and horse trails wound through the woods. A horse stable bordered the east end of the camp.

The children were greatly impressed by the camp facilities as the buses wound their way into the campgrounds. "Do you imagine we'll be permitted to use any of those?" Ann asked Graham as they were exiting the bus.

"Probably not," Graham surmised. "They're most likely reserved for use by the factory executives."

"I doubt it, Graham," Fred interrupted. "The Americans are not as conscience of social structure as we English are. They have fewer class distinctions here. I'll bet all Bender employees use the facilities, regardless of their rank in the company. They won't discriminate against us. Look at all they let us do at the hotel in New York. Captain Ben socialized with us as if we all were his equal. Why wouldn't he and the others do the same here?"

"I hope they do," Ann added.

"I don't believe they will," Graham said, still convinced Fred's assessment was wrong. "I bet they keep us in our place; let us know we're inferior to them; after all, they're still the gentry and we're still only working-class blokes."

The children went directly from the buses to the dinning hall. The escorts instructed them to neatly pile their haversacks and suitcases in the cloakroom, wash their hands, and choose a place at the dining table. It was the announcement they had been waiting to hear. Immediately, there was loud shouting and a wild scramble. Happy that they were about to eat, they carelessly tossed their haversacks and suitcases into the cloak room, and after a superficial wash up, hastened to find seats next to their friends, if one was available, otherwise in any empty seat they could find. Although the escorts asked them to wait until after the blessing before starting to eat, somehow all the bread on every table mysteriously disappeared before Mr. Bender rose and asked them to bow their heads.

"Dear, Heavenly Father," he began. "Thank you for choosing such lovely children to visit our humble community and for safely escorting them across the troubled sea. We pray we will be gracious hosts during their stay, sharing with them all the love that is in our hearts and providing all the care they so richly deserve. Please show us the way so they might benefit from this–their great adventure. Help us to support them in body, mind and soul. Please, gracious Father, watch over these children, their families in England, their new families here in America, and all of us who love them so dearly. And please, dear Lord, put a quick end to the horrible war that continues in Europe, so these children can quickly return to their English homes. For this, and for the bountiful feast set before us, we give most gracious thanks. Amen."

For a brief moment there was silence. The prayer had reminded the children of their parents and families. Tears came to many eyes. But nostalgia soon dimmed as the servers, with a flourish, brought the Waldorf salads from the kitchen. Their melancholy disappeared completely as the servers set platters of Swiss steak, smothered in onions and gravy, in front of them. Next came large bowls of mashed potatoes, cooked carrots, green peas, and candied beets. The children ate greedily, controlled almost entirely by their empty stomachs. When they finished, nearly every bowl was empty–except for the peas. Peas were apparently not as popular as the other vegetables.

The glasses of iced tea caused special interest. They, at first, complained that tea should be hot when served, but after cautiously sipping the iced drink, they changed their minds and were soon asking for refills, some requesting extra ice.

The availability and use of ice in America continued to fascinate them. Most had never seen ice cubes before their meal in New York. Some were still uncertain how to manage the cubes. Some thought it bad manners to leave them in their glasses and attempted to eat them. Others spooned them from the glass. Not knowing quite what to do with them and feeling somewhat mischievous after their long train ride, they began tossing the cubes at each other. Fortunately, strawberry ice cream and chocolate brownie desserts arrived just in time to stop the impending food fight.

After dinner, Stan announced that the boys would sleep in the camp cabins and the girls at the Bender Inn in downtown McKinley Heights. The children wondered what "downtown" meant. One of them finally mustered the courage to ask. Stan apologized and explained it was the same as their "high street." They all agreed American's had humorous names for certain things. Stan assured them they would soon discover many more differences. He said it would take time before they were familiar with all the American expressions and encouraged them to ask for clarification whenever they heard something they did not understand.

His second announcement came as a sad surprise. The escorts would be returning to New York early in the morning, the children should say good-bye before leaving the dining hall. The children would meet the new counselors, all from the McKinley Heights area, when they got to their sleeping quarters.

The announcement devastated the children. The escorts were their last remaining solid tie to England. Now they would no longer have even that. "Oh, Miss Lewis. Don't go," Ann said, and began to cry. "We want you to stay here with us."

"I'm sorry, Ann. I wish I could. I enjoyed being with you children— every minute of it. Unfortunately, before we left, I agreed to return to England on the first ship available. I love all of you, but I must go back. Don't you understand? There are other children in England who are waiting to come to America. I need to escort them, too."

"But we'll never see each other again," Ann continued to plead.

"But we will, dear. I'll write to you. And you can write to me. Once this war is over, let's promise to arrange a get-together back in England."

"Come on, Ann," Graham urged, "remember what Dad said. We must be brave soldiers while we're here. We must keep a stiff upper lip and do what is best for England. Someday everything will turn out all right. Someday we'll see her again."

Graham turned to the other children who had been in Miss Lewis' group. "Let's give a cheer for Miss Lewis," he said. "She has done an excellent job getting us safely, and happily, here to McKinley Heights. Hip! Hip! Hurrah!"

"Hip, hip, hurrah!" they shouted.

The same cheer followed at the other tables. Every group felt the loss of their escort in much the same way. A cheer was the only means the children had to thank them.

"Thank you, children. I shall never forget you." Miss Lewis said, looking fondly at each child through eyes filled with tears. She wondered if she could leave in the morning. She truly understood what brave little troopers these wonderful children were—leaving their mums and dads and coming all this way to a strange new country. She wondered how their parents had ever said good-bye. "This bloody war!" she repeated to herself again and again.

* * *

Perhaps it had been the big dinner, maybe it was Miss Lewis leaving, maybe the strange bed, or maybe she was still homesick; whatever it was, Ann had difficulty sleeping. She tossed for several hours. Many thoughts and fears raced through her mind. The last before finally falling asleep was the family in whose house she would be staying. She hoped they would be a good family, with a kind and generous mum. She supposed it was more likely she and Graham would get a mum who would treat them like Cinderella's stepmother; she would probably be mean!

Her dreams included scrubbing dirty floors, the washing-up of dinner dishes, the scraping of burnt pots and pans, and the emptying of chamber pots. It was not a restful sleep.

Chapter 29

Friday, 23 August 1940

The limousine pulled into Camp Bender just before five o'clock. At first, Ann could only see Captain Ben and Miss Perkins. They were sitting on the rear seat and were apparently talking to someone. As they came closer, she could see a little girl sitting on the seat facing them. The auto stopped in front of the Center building, and the chauffeur opened the door; it was only then that Ann recognized the girl. It was Sandy, she looked very sad.

Ann bolted from the playground. "Sandy, Sandy, you're here!" she shouted.

Sandy's countenance changed immediately, a broad smile lit her face. With open arms, she rushed towards Ann. "Oh, Ann," she cried, "I'm so glad to see you. I thought I'd never get here." The two girls embraced.

"How was Ellis Island? Was it awful?" Ann asked.

"It was horrible! I felt so alone," Sandy answered, her voice quivering slightly. "It was so dirty. The officials were impersonal and mean. Most of the people being held there couldn't speak English. If it hadn't been for the other children from the *Caerleon*, I think I would have died. The officials treated us as if we were criminals. They seemed more interested in keeping us locked up than checking how healthy we were.

"For a while I didn't think they would ever look at my rash. I was certain I would never get to McKinley Heights, never see any of you again," Sandy continued, babbling as if she had not spoken to anyone for weeks. "After waiting for what seemed like years, Miss Perkins finally arrived. Even then, she had to make a huge fuss before they agreed to examined me. They released me late yesterday afternoon. The doctor couldn't understand why I had been detained. He said Dr. Peters' diagnosis was correct, it was merely a rash, probably brought on by the soap. They found nothing wrong with the others either. It seems terribly unfair, having kept us there when there was no need."

"Last night we stayed at a hotel called the Waldorf-Astoria. You should have seen the hotel: thick plush carpets, gilded chandeliers, a huge bedroom, and lifts that went so fast it nearly took one's breath away. Last evening Miss Perkins took us to a very fancy restaurant. I don't believe I have ever eaten so much, or had such delicious food. But none of that compares to arriving at the McKinley Heights station this afternoon and seeing Mr. Bender. Just knowing I had caught up with the Bender group meant more than anything. It's so good to be here with you, I was so afraid I would never see any of you again."

"You'll like Camp Bender, Sandy. They're treating us almost as if we were members of the Royal family. You wouldn't believe the meals we've had." Ann boasted.

"You wouldn't believe the meals I had on the Island, either," Sandy complained.

"Why don't you stay in the room with Edith and me? That is, if you wish to share?" Ann suggested.

"That would be great," Sandy said, somewhat excitedly, already sensing an improvement in her life.

"Let's arrange it now," Ann said, turning toward the door to the Center.

"That's an excellent idea. It would be one less thing I must do," Miss Perkins said as she climbed out of the limousine. "You children go in and tell them that you want to share. Either Mr. Bender or I will join you in a few minutes."

The girls were in a gay mood when they entered the administrative offices. Sandy had just said something that made both of them laugh and they were still giggling as they approached the woman sitting at the desk. "This is Miss Sandy Meyers. She is one of the evacuees. She has just arrived. She was detained at Ellis Island. We would like to share our room with her. My name is Ann Montgomery; my roommate's name is Dickson; Edith Dickson. Our room number is 315."

"Oh yes, we have been expecting you, Miss Meyers," the woman said. She turned to Ann, "I'm sorry, miss, but we don't permit three girls in one room. We have reserved another for Miss Meyers. Let me see ... Oh yes, it's room 236."

"That room's not even on the same floor as ours," Ann objected. "Our bed is big. We can easily sleep three. Sandy, Edith, and I are great friends, and we really want to be together."

"There is no need to plead, miss. We have assigned her to 236. The decision is final," the woman said, somewhat irritated. She returned to her work, ignoring the girls still standing before her.

"Who will share the room with me?" Sandy asked.

"You will have the room all to yourself, honey," the woman answered, annoyed at being interrupted again.

"But I don't want to be alone, not after spending that horrible night at Ellis Island! Please, let me stay in their room?"

"We have rules. We are not going to change them just for you," the woman retorted, her face beginning to turn red.

"That's unfair," snapped Ann.

"Now look, young lady, we have neither the time nor the resources to deal with all the silly whims of you children. We have seventy-eight–seventy-nine now–children to take care of; we cannot make exceptions just to satisfy a few spoiled little girls' wishes."

Ann glared at the woman. "Come on, Sandy, we're not going to accomplish anything with this snippy woman." The girls turned and left the office before the woman could say anything more.

As they were leaving the building they met Mr. Bender. "Oh, hello, Captain Ben," Ann greeted him. "Can you help us, sir?"

Sandy was surprised. Ann seemed much more friendly with Mr. Bender than she expected, especially with the way she had addressed him. She had never heard him called 'Captain Ben' before. She would ask Ann about it later, when they were alone.

"What's wrong, girls?" Mr. Bender asked, a concerned look on his face.

Ann told him about the room assignment. "It's really sad!" she continued. "Sandy doesn't want to be alone. If we don't mind sharing our bed, why shouldn't she be able to stay with us if she wishes?"

"I don't understand why they did that," he said, thinking out loud. "They had instructions to do everything possible to make you children comfortable." He paused for a moment, realizing he should not be making these comments to the girls, then continued, "Let me see what I can do. You girls wait outside while I talk to them."

He closed the office door behind him but they could still hear the muffled sounds of raised voices. "You shouldn't have said anything to Mr. Bender, Ann. That woman will be angry if you caused her trouble– and it sounds as if you have," Sandy warned.

"Nonsense. One must stand up for her rights," Ann replied indignantly. "Besides, what can she do to me?"

"People have their methods, Ann."

They were interrupted by Mr. Bender who had just come back. He looked at the girls with a friendly smile. "Go on in, girls. I believe Miss Klienschmitt will take care of your room request now."

When the girls re-entered the office Miss Klienschmitt's face was red. She was quite angry; her voice quivered as she talked. "I've had another look at the room layout. I believe we can accommodate your wish, we'll add a rollaway bed," she said without looking at either girl. "Just give Mr. Bender's chauffeur your room number, Miss Montgomery. He'll take Miss Meyers' things to the Inn. You'll find them in the room when you get there this evening, Miss Meyers."

"Thank you, Miss Klienschmitt," Ann said.

She did not respond. "Somehow I'll get even with that little trollop," Miss Klienschmitt said to herself as they closed the door behind them.

At dinner that evening, the children sat at long tables. Each table had twenty place settings. Mr. Bender, his wife, and the other company officials and their spouses sat at an elevated table at one end of the dinning hall. Sandy and her three cabin mates sat together at one of the other tables. Graham and his shipmates sat opposite the girls. Everyone was eager to hear what had happened at Ellis Island. They listened intently while Sandy described her ordeal.

Afterwards, Sandy asked about the camp and what activities she had missed. They assured her she hadn't missed anything significant. The schedule had been simply to rest and relax. It consisted mostly of free time and had actually been rather boring. Apparently the company thought they needed time to adjust to their new life and locale. The formal activities were scheduled to start with a private showing of the film *Pinnochio* at the local cinema tomorrow morning.

"Movie house, or picture show," Fred corrected, "They don't call it a cinema over here."

"Or motion picture theater," Elizabeth snickered.

"Or flick," Stewart added. They all laughed. They wondered if they would ever learn all the strange new names for everything.

"Afterwards, they are planning a swimming party," Edith continued. "On Sunday morning they expect us to go to church. We have our choice of which denomination we wish to attend."

"This morning they explained the differences between the American churches and compared each to our churches in England," Ann explained. "Graham and I have decided the best church for us is the Episcopal Church."

"A picnic is planned for Sunday afternoon," Edith continued. "They have not completed the schedule for the remainder of our stay, but they said they will show us William McKinley's monument someday next week."

"Who is William McKinley?" Steve asked.

"The twenty-fifth president of the United States," Edith answered. "The person after whom this city was named. Other things on the agenda include a visit to the local art museum, to a natural history museum at a nearby university, to a baseball game in Cleveland, a tour of a rubber plant in Akron and a steel mill in Canton, and, of course, to the Bender plant here in McKinley Heights."

So many plans surprised Sandy. She began to understand what Ann meant when she said they had been treated like royalty.

Graham described some of the camp facilities. The horse stables particularly caught Sandy's interest. Horses were her favorite animals; she hoped to ride someday.

For dinner the chef wanted to give the children a very special treat in celebration of their first full day in McKinley Heights. He started with a green salad topped with a specially seasoned ranch dressing. It was highly successful. The children, after cautiously sampling it, ate enthusiastically. By the time they finished, everyone was in a cheerful mood.

The menu planned consisted of hamburger sandwiches, freshly sliced tomatoes, fresh green beans, applesauce, and fresh roasted corn-on-the-cob. He knew American children relished this menu, especially the corn. He had spent a good bit of time carefully selecting the ripest and biggest ears of corn he could find. He stacked the corn on platters as high as possible and, for special effect, instructed the waitresses, women volunteers from the Women's Aid Society, to hold the plates high above their shoulders as they entered the dining room and, with a flourish, place two platters on each table. He fully expected the children to shout with delight, as American children would, when they saw the steaming ears of corn.

Instead, to his surprise, when the corn was placed in front of them, the children's mood deteriorated rapidly. They looked with horror at the platters and a strange hush settled over the hall. Next came the hamburger sandwiches, also served with great flourish. By the time the sandwiches were placed on the tables a murmur arose at every table.

The children whispered among themselves. "What the bloody hell is this?" Fred whispered to Graham.

"Pig food!" Graham answered in disgust.

"They don't expect us to eat this trash, do they?"

"Wouldn't you know," Graham complain. "Corn! We've been here only one day and already they're feeding us a pig's meal! I can't believe it."

This was typical of the conversations at each table, followed often by a defiant grumble, "Don't anyone eat the corn! We're children, not pigs. They have no right to humiliate us this way."

Mr. Bender and his wife looked at each other, so did Stan and his wife. Finally, Graham garnered his nerve and rose to his feet. Looking directly at Captain Ben, he said, "I'm sorry, sir. You can't expect us to eat this," he paused, then added, "this corn! It's something we only feed to pigs in England. We simply cannot permit you to demean us in this manner."

Graham's comments were sufficient to inspire others. Almost in unison the other children joined in the protest, chattering among themselves and shaking their heads in agreement; refusing to eat the corn–or anything else. They were thoroughly insulted.

Mr. Bender's face reddened. Stan sensed his anger. He knew he had to do something quickly. "Children, children," he pleaded, "please don't be upset. We consider corn-on-the-cob a delicacy here in America. This corn differs from what we feed our pigs. What you're talking about is field corn. This is sweet corn. Try it. Please? Sweet corn is good for you and really delicious."

Stan did not convince any of them. They were, however, embarrassed. They realized they had been rude and perhaps had acted too hastily. They had grossly misunderstood the good intentions of their hosts. But even so, they still were reluctant to taste this, so called, American delicacy.

Ann stood up. "Please accept our apologizes, sir? We were not aware of the different types of corn. I fear we've behaved badly. I, for one, will try it, since you say it is good." She sat down, selected an ear, studied it carefully, trying to decide how to eat it, and finally began scraping the kernels off the cob with her knife.

"No, dear," Stan's wife said, smiling. "It's more fun to eat it directly from the cob. You hold it with your hands. Do what I do." She picked up an ear and began demonstrating. The children watched and slowly began to nibble on theirs. They were unimpressed. It was not as terrible as they had anticipated, but it tasted awfully dull.

Mrs. Bender, who had been watching all this, rose to her feet. "There's one more thing, children. Before you eat, you should spread it with butter. Then apply salt. Here, I'll show you." The children watched closely, then followed her example.

"Good! Now let's eat!" she said. The children took cautious bites, and then began eating enthusiastically.

"Before you go further," W.T. interrupted. The children stopped. They held their breath. Had they angered Captain Ben? They wondered what sort of scolding he was about to give them. "Most of us eat across the ear–along the rows–not around the ear," he said, laughing. "We don't worry about getting our hands greasy from the butter either. We simply use our napkins when we're finished."

They laughed and began to eat vigorously, especially when they discovered that ketchup added extra flavor to their hamburgers. After finishing the watermelon, everyone was full, but still managed to eat a few chocolate chip cookies. They vowed that the next time they would mind their manners better. They would, as a minimum, try new dishes before complaining.

Stan wondered what other cultural misunderstandings were still to come. "No wonder there are conflicts between nations," he thought. "It starts with little misunderstandings between people, grows, and eventually involves nations." He wondered if the children would return to England with a clearer understanding of the differences between their two countries and, afterwards, if they'd have a better tolerance for the differences. "Perhaps their visit will yield bigger benefits than simply providing them with a safe haven. Maybe, ultimately, it will contribute to a better understanding between Britain, the United States, and the rest of the world."

The evening ended with a songfest around a roaring campfire. The songs ranged from old folk songs to modern American songs. Favorites included *Clementine*, *Tipperary* and *Oh Susanna* and the more humorous *Bamboo King* and *Bill Grogan's Goat*. *The Barrel Song* was high on the children's list of favorites but some of the more modern songs, particularly *South of the Border*, and *Oh Johnny*, also were quite popular.

The selections had been carefully chosen by the counselors so as not to mention the war, England, or anything else that might trigger sad memories of home. They had wisely decided to leave those for another day. The last song, *God Save the King*, was proof that the decision they had made was a good one. Afterwards everyone was noticeably quiet as they left the fire; apparently it had triggered melancholy thoughts of home.

Chapter 30

Friday, 30 August 1940

It was nearly eleven at night. The Dutch vessel *Volendam* was off the north coast of Ireland, two hundred and fifteen miles from the River Clyde. The sea was calm. Among the passengers were three hundred and forty-one English evacuees, asleep in their cabins. Suddenly, an explosion and the sound of alarms interrupted their sleep. There was little panic. They had been through many lifeboat drills before. They obediently donned their life jackets, wrapped themselves in blankets, and proceeded to their lifeboat stations.

There was unusual confusion topside. The passengers, who had not heard the explosion complained; they thought it an inappropriate hour to conduct a drill. Those who had heard the explosion screamed and hugged each other in fear. The crew members shouted, pointed, and frantically ran from lifeboat to lifeboat. Because they did not speak English, their instructions were difficult to interpret.

When smoke began pouring from several vent pipes everyone finally understood; it was no drill. A torpedo had struck the ship, and it was sinking. They climbed into the lifeboats, and were lowered towards the sea. In the crew's haste, one of the boats tipped, spilling its occupants. The others made it successfully. Some rowed quickly away from the sinking ship. Others helped those still in the water. Eventually, all passengers found safety in lifeboats, and the wait for rescue began. To keep the children calm, the escorts led them in song. The song they chose: *There'll always be an England*.

The survivors were eventually rescued by the English vessel, *The Bassett Hound*, the British tanker, *Val de Losa*, and the Norwegian ship, *The Olaf Forstenes*.

With all on board, the vessels turned toward Scotland and two days later arrived in the port of Gourock where a large welcoming contingent awaited them. The greeting party included volunteer women with hot food and warm clothing, medical personnel, curious onlookers and visiting dignitaries. Among them, a concerned Geoffrey Shakespeare, the director of CORB. He knew, even though no one had suffered any major physical trauma other than severe seasickness due to rough seas, the future of his program was in serious trouble. He wondered how much longer the government would permit the transport of United Kingdom children overseas.

There was a glass window at the front of the room; the other three walls were solid. There was no ceiling. The straw made her scratch behind her ear. Ann had never scratched her ear with her foot before; at least not as she could recall. It felt good.

"Out of my way," growled the collie pup next to her. He tumbled over her and his tail tickled her snout. She sneezed.

"Stop that!" snarled the spaniel, as he nipped at her front paw.

"What unfriendly pups," she thought, scratching behind her other ear. "When will someone adopt me? When will I sleep in my own doghouse?"

"That one, Mama," the little boy urged. "Let's take that one. Please?"

"Not that one. She's too ugly," the man groaned. "Look at her paws. They are much too big."

"Look at her face," the woman chuckled. "Have you ever seen such sad looking eyes? It will be a wonder if anyone chooses that mutt."

They all laughed.

"But I like her," the little girl insisted.

"We'll take the other one," the man said, pointing at the collie.

Ann watched as the clerk picked the collie up by his scruff and handed him to the boy. "I love him, Daddy," the boy cooed.

"He is so cuddly," the little girl said. "You are so right. He is much nicer than that mongrel. Thank you."

The next couple came later that same day. They chose the spaniel.

The terrier went next. Then the boxer, the St. Bernard, and finally the spitz.

After that, only the mongrel remained. "Shoot it," someone suggested.

"No, drown it," another laughed.

Ann buried her head in the straw and whimpered. "Mother! I want my mother. I don't like being a mongrel."

The parrot mimicked, "Mongrel."

Chapter 31

Friday, 30 August 1940

During the first days in America, everyone the evacuees met treated them with interest and concern, told them how grand they were, and said how pleased they were to have them as visitors. By the end of their first full week in camp, all the children, even those who had not thought so before, were convinced they were very special and important.

Their stay at Camp Bender had been one continuous series of exciting and pleasurable events, many that showcased American culture. The counselors fed them American beef steaks and roasts, showed them American movies, taught them to sing American songs, and presented lectures on American customs. The children read American newspapers and American comic books, used American plumbing, and saw girls and boys wearing American style clothing. They chewed gum, drank cherry Cokes, ate *Clark* and *Three Musketeers* candy bars, sipped chocolate and strawberry sodas, gorged themselves on banana splits, played the jukeboxes, and ate popcorn while watching *Over the Rainbow* and *Mickey McGuire* at the movie theater.

They laughed at the American method of eating. They could not understand why anyone would cut several pieces of meat with the knife in their right hand and the fork in the other, lay the knife down, transfer the fork to the right hand, and, only then, eat the pieces. They decided it was terribly inefficient compared to their method. Always holding the knife and fork in the same hands made much more sense to them.

They rode in big oversized automobiles and heard many words of American slang including "guys," "uh-huh," "yea," and "nah." They learned the difference between the penny, nickel, dime, quarter and half dollar and marveled at the simplicity of computing prices and making change using the American dollar system. They asked why the quarter was "two-bits," why the dollar was a "buck," and why the ten dollar bill was a "sawbuck." It disappointed them when no one provided a plausible explanation.

In spite of all the exciting activities and experiences, the children still missed home. It had now been over three weeks since leaving. Why hadn't they received any letters? Their mums and dads had promised they would write often. Was it possible their parents would not keep those promises? They began to question why their parents had sent them to America. While not confiding with one another, most began to believe the evacuation was simply an excuse to get rid of them. They felt orphaned and insecure. They compensated with increased letter writing and often cried in the privacy of their beds at night. Because they did not share their feelings with others, each thought he was unique. It made the burden much harder to endure.

Ann's letter was typical of those written during the stay at Camp Bender.

No 4

Camp Bender

McKinley Heights, Ohio, USA

Friday, 30 August 1940

Dear Mum, Dad, and Yvonne,

I hope this letter finds you happy and well. I have not received any letters from you yet. I expect you are quite busy, with the war and every-thing—but—I do hope you can find the time to write soon. (Real soon!) I will not mind if it is only a short note. Graham and I miss you very much and would like to receive something.

As you can see from the letterhead we are still at the camp I de-scribed in my previous letter. We have been having a good time here. A "swell" time as the Americans would say. (Their talk is certainly differ-ent from ours. I suppose, eventually, I will become accustomed to their slang.) We have been eating all types of goodies and have been to the cinema several times now. The entertainment has been superb. They had a magician here at the camp several nights ago. You would not be-lieve how clever he was. We couldn't figure how he did his magic tricks. Afterwards, Graham thought he could mimic several of the tricks, but when he tried to demonstrate every one of them failed. We all had a good laugh over his awkwardness. I guess Graham will never be a ma-gician. Ha, ha!

A week ago Thursday, when we said good-bye to Miss Lewis, our ship escort, we thought we would never find another "friend" quite as nice. To our great surprise we have indeed found another. Our coun-selor now is Mrs. Albright. She is a fine lady and takes good care of us. She even gives us hugs when we need them. I hope the people I am to live with are as nice as she is.

Speaking of living with someone—tomorrow we are to learn who our foster family will be. I do hope Graham and I like them—whoever they are. But don't worry, they will NEVER replace you. You are our real family. Everyone was hoping we could remain at the camp a few more days, but I guess we cannot stay here forever. We must begin our new life tomorrow.

Well, it is time to go to the campfire sing-along, and I don't want to be late. I especially enjoy that part of the camp program. It is so lovely sitting there, watching the sparks fly into the night sky, and listening to the voices of the children in song. At times, some of the songs make me think of home, perhaps a little more than I should.

With love and kisses, X X X O O O X X X

Your daughter–always,

Ann

X X X O O O X X X

P.S. Notice I have started to number my letters. It will help you detect missing ones. (We worry letters may not make it across the Atlantic; they might be torpedoed.) Do you think you should number yours? If you did, we also would know when one was missing.

P.P.S. Just so you can verify all my previous letters: I wrote No. 1 on the ship, sent No. 2 from New York, and posted No 3 last weekend.

The purpose of the children's extended stay in Camp Bender was, of course, not solely to acclimate the children to American culture but, more importantly, to determine each child's personality and background through interviews and, with that information at hand, to match them with suitable foster families. However, the matching process proved more difficult than anticipated, particularly since there were no "experts" only local volunteers available for the work. It was late Friday afternoon before they finally completed the entire billeting plan. All that remained was approval from the committee on Saturday morning. Mrs. Dorothy Studer, the head of the Children's Bureau and Stan's appointee responsible for billeting, thought the match was about as good as possible, although far from ideal. She was proud of work she and Vi, her secretary, had accomplished during the past several weeks and believed Saturday would prove to be a very satisfying day for her.

Saturday, unfortunately, did not go exactly as she had hoped. Soon after she woke, she received an urgent telephone message from Vi. Vi had just received a request from Dr. and Mrs. Weber. They had been on a cruise off the coast of Baja California and had returned home on Friday afternoon. They heard about the foster program and hoped it was not too late to enroll in the plan. They wanted a boy.

"That's nonsense, Vi, we have the assignments set. It's entirely too late to consider their application. The program was announced weeks ago. Have they been away all that time?"

"No they haven't," Vi answered. "Mrs. Weber apologized for not calling sooner. They heard about the program the week before they left but the doctor had several emergencies during the week and, not realizing the program would move as rapidly as it did, had not turned in their application. He would have, had he known."

Vi added, "As you know, Dr. and Mrs. Weber are very prominent in the community. They can do our organization plenty of good–or plenty of bad, depending on how we treat them. If you recall, they gave a large sum to the McKinley Heights Art Institute last year."

"What should we do, Vi?"

Vi Klienschmitt sensed an opportunity. "Why don't you send Graham Montgomery to the Webers?" she said.

"That would separate the Montgomery children," Dorothy objected. "You know we're trying to keep families together whenever possible. The Montgomery children are scheduled to live with the Mannheims. We shouldn't split Ann and Graham."

"From what I've heard, the girl is not too keen about being billeted with her brother anyway. I don't think they'd complain too much if we separated them and sent only Ann to live with the Mannheims."

"No! I'm not going to do that. It's important to keep siblings together whenever we can. We simply must find another way."

Vi hid her disappointment. "Another possibility is to send Stewart Jamison to the Webers. The only difficulty then–there would be no one left for Ken and Louise Nelson."

"Do you recall how badly the Nelsons wanted a child? Frankly, I'd like to keep Stewart with them if possible. On the other hand," Dorothy thought aloud, "the Nelsons are accommodating people. They probably wouldn't fuss too much if we didn't give them a child."

"I agree, they probably wouldn't say anything. They're too nice to complain," Vi concurred. "Do you want me to make the change? We're running late. I need to type the final list before your eleven o'clock meeting."

"Yes, I know. It needs a quick resolution. If there are any loose ends we'll never get a committee consensus today. A delay would be terrible. Monday is Labor Day, it would be Tuesday before we could get the committee together again. School starts next Wednesday. Any delay would mean the children could not start the first day of the term. They really should not miss the first day of school; it would only make starting that much more difficult for them. The committee must assign the billets today, as planned."

She paused for a minute to think. Finally she said, "All right, go ahead with the change. The Jamison boy will live with the Webers. I had better call the Nelsons. What's their telephone number?"

Ken was upset. "You can't do that to us, Dorothy. Please?" he pleaded.

"I'm sorry, Ken. There just aren't enough children to satisfy everyone. Since your home is not in McKinley Heights, you didn't make the final cut. I did everything I possibly could. I simply could not persuade the committee to send another child to Oakton. They want to keep as many of the children here in McKinley Heights as they can," she lied. "We already are sending a boy to the Derringer's; but that was a special case."

"Dammit, Dorothy, Oakton is only seven miles from McKinley Heights. It can't make that much difference. You've known me for a long time, how can you do this to us? You know how badly Louise needs a youngster around the house. This disappointment will set her back weeks."

"Now, Ken, don't start swearing. I'll not put up with it. I'd hang up on you here and now if you weren't such a good friend."

"I'm sorry, Dorothy. I lost my temper. But don't you understand? I'm desperate. I must do something to help Louise. You can't believe how much she's been looking forward to this foster child. She's been making so many plans; she even redecorated the bedroom and has bought all sorts of things. Please see if you can't do something to change this decision." Ken thought for a second, then asked, "Come to think of it–what makes the Derringers so special?"

"Believe me, Ken, there is nothing I can do right now. Do you know how influential Victoria is in the community? Whatever she wants, she gets. No one could override her wishes, even if they tried. Perhaps something will come up after we announce the assignments this afternoon. I promise you, your name will be at the top of our list. You'll get first priority for any reassignment."

"I consider that a promise, Dorothy. I'll hold you to it."

It was a dejected Ken who hung up the telephone. He wondered how he would tell Louise. He worried she might not get through the disappointment.

*   *   *

Assignments began after lunch. The procedure, approved by the committee, invited all the foster families to the Center building where they would be introduced to their new wards. Because of the limited number of staff available to administer the introductions, they staggered the meetings throughout the afternoon and evening. The schedule was the work of Vi Klienschmitt.

Edith and Sandy were among the first to meet their foster families. Neither girl had time to say good-bye to Ann, or tell her where they were going. Later on, Ann heard both girls would be living somewhere on the east side of McKinley Heights.

Not much later Fred left with his foster family. From the way it looked to Ann and Graham, he had drawn a good billet. His foster parents were Dr. and Mrs. Thomas Derringer of Oakton. Dr. Derringer was a medical doctor, and both parents were impeccably dressed. "What a lucky boy Fred is. Dressed as they are, it's a good bet they're an upper-class family, or wealthy family, as the Americans prefer to say," Graham remarked.

About half way through the afternoon, Steve and Stewart left. Elizabeth followed soon after. All three would be living in McKinley Heights. It was about then that Ann and Graham began to worry. They noticed none of the families had taken more than one child. Graham was not certain, but he thought he had seen several children from the same family go to different homes earlier. Then later, there was a spurt of multiple child billets and Graham and Ann's hopes of being billeted together increased.

By six o'clock, they were beginning to wonder if they would be assigned to any family; especially after several people, who looked like foster families, came into the Center, looked at the remaining children, shook their heads in apparent disgust, and left without a child. Was it possible Ann and Graham had failed to impress their foster family? Was it possible they would have no billet?

Later still, they were the only two children remaining with no prospective parents left in the building. It nearly broke their hearts. They wondered what was wrong with them. Were they that unattractive? "Why haven't we been selected?" Ann asked Graham.

"I don't know, Ann. I don't know," he said, wondering what his parents would say if they knew he had failed to find a home for Ann.

The counselors were beginning to straighten the room in preparation to leave when John and Flossie Mannheim came rushing in, nearly out of breath. "We're so sorry, Mrs. Studer. We know we're late. We didn't receive your message until a few minutes ago," John apologized. "We hadn't heard you were making assignments today until the Schmidts, from down the street, told us they had picked up Jenny. We immediately called your office and were told we should have been here earlier. We're truly sorry; we got here as fast as we could. We can't understand what happened. Did someone try to reach us earlier?"

"I tried to call you this afternoon. In fact I tried several times. No one answered," Vi volunteered.

"That's odd. We were home all day. What number did you call?"

"Klondike 5-6733."

"Oh, that explains it. Our number is Klondike 5-6738," Flossie said. Vi looked at Ann, then quickly looked away. Ann wondered why Vi was smiling. It looked almost as if she were amused by something.

"Well, you're here now," Dorothy sighed. "Children, please meet Mr. and Mrs. Mannheim. Flossie, John, this is Ann and Graham Montgomery."

"How do you do, Mr. and Mrs. Mannheim," Ann answered, with a slight curtsey. "Curious," she thought. She had not heard one name today that had not seemed to be of Germanic origin. She wondered if everyone in McKinley Heights had German ancestors. She guessed it had to do with the history of the town. After all, last week the speaker told them that before 1905 it had been called West Dresden. German immigrants originally had settled the region. That was undoubtedly why, but wasn't it ironic? English children had been sent to a German community to escape German tyranny.

"Hello," said Graham.

"It's so nice to meet you, Ann and Graham," replied Flossie, smiling pleasantly. "Please call us Aunt Flossie and Uncle John, dears."

"Hi there, kids," John said, holding his hand out to shake hands with Graham.

"They seem like fine people," Graham thought, very relieved. "It looks as if Ann and I will be all right."

"Our house is just down the road, about a quarter mile," said John.

"Oh, good," thought Ann, "Edith, Sandy, and I will all live in McKinley Heights. We may even be in the same school. What good fortune."

The new "family" left the Center in John and Flossie's late model Packard automobile. The motor car impressed Graham. It indicated that Ann and he were going to an upper-class billet.

"Wait till Fred discovers he's not the only lucky person," Graham grinned.

Chapter 32

Saturday, 31 August 1940

Fred could not believe his eyes when the Cadillac turned into the driveway. The Derringer home stood on a small swell overlooking a large carefully manicured garden–or "lawn" as he would soon learn to say. The main section of the house was immense. The cream-colored trim was a perfect complement to the red of the exterior brick siding. A large porch ran along its entire front. Eight giant pillars rose from the porch floor to the underside of the roof overhanging the second story. The pillars reminded Fred of *Tara*, the southern plantation home he had recently seen in the cinema picture *Gone With the Wind*. A large rustic chandelier hung halfway down from the porch ceiling on a sturdy iron chain. Projecting from the two ends of the house were two wings, each slightly smaller than the main section.

He had never seen such a well maintained house. The windows sparkled, apparently cleaned in the last several days; the shades were perfectly aligned, and the curtains hung uniformly in all the windows; the shutters and trim looked freshly painted, not a speck of paint was spilled on any brick; nothing looked out of place or missing.

He could see four stately chimneys rising between the wings and the main section; another at the end of each wing. A number of flues protruded from each chimney. "It should be a warm house in the wintertime with all those fireplaces," Fred mused. He had often wished his bedroom had a fireplace in it. The fireplace in the parlor at home just didn't provide enough heat to the rest of the house on those cold winter days. Now maybe he would be warm.

The driveway wound along a tree lined lane until it reached the pond. From there it gently turned to the left and continued up the swell to a three-car garage attached to the rear of the house. Two automobiles were in the garage: a very sporty convertible, carefully maintained and apparently driven only on special occasions, and another less ostentatious auto, slightly smaller than the Cadillac. To the west of the house stood a large orchard separated into areas of apple, peach, cherry, and pear trees. A stand of maple, pine, dogwood and birch trees bordered the rear and east side of the house. Fred could see that someone had worked hard maintaining the estate; he felt sorry for whomever it was who had to do all the work.

Once they reached the house, he could no longer see any of the neighboring houses. The dense foliage around the perimeter of the estate hid the other homes from view. The isolation impressed him. It certainly did not compare to his home in England. His home, and those of his friends, had only tiny gardens and shared sidewalls with each of its neighbors. Only upper-class families had detached homes with surrounding acreage.

He was going to be living in a rich man's home; he had serendipitously become one of the gentry. He marveled at how lucky he was.

"Well, Fred, this is your new home," Tom said. "What do you think of it?"

"It's super! You certainly have a lovely home here, Mister–er Doctor–er ... ?" he said, stumbling over the proper title for Tom.

Tom laughed, looked at Victoria as if he wanted her approval and said, "I understand, son. It's difficult to know how to address us. I suggest you call me Dr. Derringer. And of course Mrs. Derringer should be called Mrs. Derringer." He was proud of what he thought was a friendly gesture on his part.

Fred thought differently, but answered politely, "Yes, sir–I mean, Dr. Derringer."

"You poor boy. You must be terribly hungry," Victoria said, sounding very sympathetic. "Would you like something to eat?"

"Yes, please, ma'am–er, Mrs. Derringer. We had an early lunch today, before they started making the assignments. I could truthfully use something to eat," he replied politely.

"Then come with me. You may have a snack. Afterwards Sarah will show you to your room. Just put your belongings inside the garage there. You can fetch them later." Victoria led Fred down several steps to a basement door. The door opened into a kitchen where a woman was busy scrubbing several greasy pans.

"Sarah, I would like you to meet Fred Andrews. He is our English guest. He will be staying with us. Fred, this is our maid, Sarah."

"Hello, Sarah," Fred said, smiling.

"Hello, Master Fred," Sarah responded with a slight nod.

"Sarah would you please fix a snack for Fred. Not too much though, we don't wish to spoil his dinner."

"Yes, madam."

"It's already four-thirty," Fred thought. "If a snack this late won't spoil my appetite, dinner must be very, very late. I guess I really am in the home of aristocrats."

"Afterwards, show Fred his room and help him settle in," Victoria ordered. "We will talk again later, Fred." She turned and quickly left the kitchen.

Sarah fixed Fred a very delicious snack. As Fred sat eating at the small kitchen table he commented on his good fortune. "Would you believe it, Sarah, only a little over three weeks ago I was in England living in a small attached flat and worrying about German air raids. Now here I am, in a huge mansion, about to dine with Dr. and Mrs. Derringer."

"Oh, Master Fred," she sighed, "I believe ..."

"Now see here, Sarah," Fred interrupted, "please don't call me Master Fred. I much prefer Fred–if you don't mind."

"It's strange," he thought, "I like Sarah more than I do Mrs. Derringer, even if she is only their cook and maid." Then, smiling, he added another thought, "I guess I don't fit into this upper-class snobbery very well."

"But, Master Fred–I mean Fred, I believe you misunderstood Mrs. Derringer," Sarah said, rather apologetically. "You'll not be eating with them. You'll be eating here in the kitchen with me."

The news surprised Fred. He was certain it was some sort of mistake. The children had been told the people would treat them as members of the family, not as servants; at least it was what he thought he had heard. He wondered who'd made the mistake, the Derringers or the counselors. He was confused, and now more curious than ever to know what the Derringers expected of him

"Your bedroom will be down here in the basement; next to mine."

"Well, that's good news, Sarah. If this is where you sleep, it most definitely will be good enough for me. Even without a room upstairs, my quarters certainly will be better than my bedroom in our Northolt flat," he said, trying to sound chipper.

"It shouldn't surprise you if they assign you some pretty hefty chores, either," Sarah continued. "The Derringers are notorious for taking advantage of everyone. If I know those two, you will be doing all sorts of tasks here at the house. I can only hope they'll leave you ample time to attend school."

"Well at least I'm a boy," Fred joked. "If they wanted someone to serve as a houseboy or gardener, they must be thankful I didn't turn out to be a girl."

Unbeknownst to Fred and Sarah, Victoria was at that same moment raving to Tom about the mistake. "I cannot believe it, Tom! How dare they give us a boy instead of a girl? I know I made my request perfectly clear. I will fix Helen Welch's wagon at the next meeting. She will regret this."

"Calm down, Victoria. Helen probably had no choice. Dorothy Studer was in charge of the billet selections; she's probably the one who made the final decision. But you shouldn't complain, determining the assignments of all those children must have been a difficult task. It's a miracle they did as well as they did. You know, when you think about it, a boy around the house won't be so terrible. In fact, we might even benefit by it. Fred looks like a healthy young boy; he can help around here immensely." He thought for a minute, then smiled and said, "Maybe he will participate in the Oakton school sports program. I would like it if we had an athlete here in the house. It's been a long time since I played ball. It would be interesting to get back into Oakton athletics, even as a foster dad, just to see how things have changed. Lately, I've been too busy working to pay much attention."

"Quit thinking only of yourself, Tom. What about me? Don't my needs count for anything?" she said in disgust. Her mind jumped back to the injustice she was being asked to bear, "You wait and see, my day will come—I'll reckon with both Helen and Dorothy before many more days have passed."

On Sunday morning, Fred chuckled as he read the article in the Oakton Herald. It listed his name among the English evacuees and said he was the guest of Dr. and Mrs. Thomas Derringer of Oakton. It complemented the Derringers, and the other generous families, for taking the poor waifs into their homes—and especially into their hearts. A direct quotation attributed to Mrs. Victoria Derringer stated, "Fred is such a dear boy. We enjoy his living with us and love him so very much. We already think of him as our son."

Fred wondered what room they would have given him if they had decided to think of him as their servant.

The initial experiences in the foster homes were varied. None were quite the same as Fred's. Some quickly adjusted to their new family and environment; some at first had difficulties with the differences, then adapted as time passed. Some never became comfortable.

Little Jenny Parsons went to live with Lucinda and Raymond Schmidt in McKinley Heights. She immediately settled in as one of the family. Before the first evening was over, she had shown her new "mum" the clothes she had brought from England and, together, they planned a shopping spree to purchase the missing items she needed for school. When Jenny went to bed that first night, and for many nights afterwards, her new mom and dad tucked her in and insisted her prayers include a special thought for her English mum and dad.

Several days later, Mrs. Schmidt wrote a letter to Jenny's parents. She called Jenny an angel and told them how happy and pleased she and Raymond were to have Jenny staying at their house.

The foster parents fought back tears when Bobby Preston worried because there was no bomb shelter in their back yard. He would not go to bed until they convinced him the German bombers could not reach McKinley Heights. They had no sooner tucked him in when he thought he saw a spy lurking in the shadows of his bedroom. They promised to keep the hallway light burning all night, but before he would agree to the light, they had to assure him they were not violating any blackout regulations.

Janice Mudge found it difficult to accept her new family. She said her new mummy and daddy were far too different from her folks in England–she thought they were such odd looking people. For nearly a week, her only friend was the doll she had carried with her all the way from England. Everything began to change after her foster mother gave her a Mickey Mouse doll. At first Mickey was her only friend but gradually, through extended conversations between Janice and Mickey, he persuaded her to accept her new parents.

Roy Barkley had a difficult start with his new family. His foster parents, Earl and Mary Summers, could not meet him at the Center. Earl, a member of the clergy, had funeral services to perform that afternoon. Immediately following the service was a reception dinner for a newly appointed deacon of Earl's church. Because Mary had to accompany Earl to both functions, they asked a member of the congregation to collect Roy from the Center. She agreed to entertain him during the afternoon and deliver him to the parsonage after the reception. While waiting, the woman asked Roy to accompany her while she ran several errands. The errands took longer than anticipated and she and Roy did not arrive at the parsonage until almost eight o'clock that evening.

The first meeting between Roy and his new parents proved awkward. By then Roy was tired, hungry, sleepy, and cross. He refused to answer questions, picked at the snack Mary had prepared, and complained about everything. Mary, trying to ease the tension and to make him feel more at home, suggested they should buy some new trousers for school, and a belt to hold them.

"I like my short pants," he retorted, indignantly. " and have no use for a bloody belt. I am a braces bloke–I am."

"But you will need something much warmer than those short pants in another month or so, Roy. It gets quite cold here in McKinley Heights in the wintertime," Mary argued. "You would freeze to death if you went out in your short pants."

"No thank you, ma'am," Roy said stubbornly. "These will do just fine. I'll be returning to England long before wintertime."

Some of the tension was explained when Earl and Mary discovered it was Roy's birthday. They apologized for not knowing and offered to celebrate it with a party, within a day or two, just as soon as one could be arranged. Roy told him he did not want a party, not unless his sisters could be there to celebrate with him.

"Where are your sisters?" Mary asked.

"I don't know. They took them away this afternoon. They didn't tell me where. They said I was too little to understand where it was." His eyes began to tear as he pleaded, "Could you find them, and ask them to stay here?"

"No, Roy, I'm sorry, we only have room for one child, but we'll find them. They must be staying with a family nearby. They shouldn't be too far away. It's too late to do anything tonight, but we'll start searching tomorrow, immediately after church. Don't you worry. We'll find them."

"I hope so," said Roy, his voice quivering.

The next morning Mary noticed Roy had wet his bed. She changed the sheets without saying anything to Roy. She hoped it was only a temporary problem.

On Sunday, Earl found Roy's sisters. They were billeted with a couple on the street immediately behind the parsonage. It was only a two minute walk between the two houses. The news greatly relieved Roy. For the first time he began to smile. His sisters, along with some of the other neighborhood children, came to a quickly arranged birthday party on Monday afternoon. Within a week Roy was wearing trousers, he no longer wet the bed, and considered Mary and Earl two of his very best friends.

Ann and Graham both believed the Mannheims would be a super couple to stay with. Both Flossie and John seemed friendly and helpful.

The only difficulty, as far as the children could see, was Flossie's excessive talking. She talked from the time they left the Center until they reached home. She was still talking as they entered the house. "I can't tell you how much it excites John and me to have the two of you with us," she continued. "I am certain we will get along splendidly–as long as you obey our simple rules."

"Rules?" thought Graham, "Why does she mention rules?"

"You see," she babbled on, "we believe you children must be taught obedience and good manners. How else can you grow into outstanding citizens? Of course, we know you want to be good citizens. We want to surprise your parents when you return home. We want them to marvel at your improved manners. We want them to say, 'Why thank you, Mr. and Mrs. Mannheim. You have trained our children exceptionally well. Their manners are now quite exemplary. Thank you so very much; you have done much better than we could ever have hoped to have done ourselves.'"

She paused only long enough to take a breath, "Don't you agree children? Wouldn't it be nice, hearing your parents congratulating you on your improvement? Don't you think it would be a nice surprise, going home without all those uncouth manners you surely must now have?"

Before either could respond she continued. "Starting in the morning we will begin going over the rules we have established for your good behavior. Tonight we will simply relax and enjoy ourselves, we know all those strenuous activities at Camp Bender must have tired you. It must have been terribly traumatic, coming all the way across the Atlantic only to discover how little you know about proper manners. As I said, tonight we won't worry too much about it. Tomorrow, however, we expect both of you to buckle down, start towing the line, start obeying the captain, so to speak. Isn't that right, Uncle John?"

"Right," said John meekly.

"What in bloody hell is she saying?" wondered Graham.

"What is this all about?" Ann worried.

After a delicious supper of sausage and beans and a huge dish of apple strudel they excused themselves early and gave–upon the insistence of Flossie–goodnight kisses to both of their foster parents. The children found their rooms pleasant and the beds softer than any they had known since leaving Pinnington. After climbing into bed they were asleep within a few minutes. They were much more tired than they had realized.

*   *   *

"Wake up, you sleepy head. Wake up!" said a voice Ann did not recognize. "Come on now, *Mädchen*, it is no time to be sleeping. It's time to rise." Although still in a daze, Ann pulled her legs from under the covers and placed her feet on the floor. "That's more like it, girl. Come, there are things to do; there's a life to live. Breakfast will be in fifteen minutes. That should give you ample time to wash and dress. Put on your better clothes; we are attending the early service at church this morning."

Now Ann remembered. She was at the Mannheims' house. It was Flossie Mannheim calling her.

"And still talking," Ann noted. The incessant talking was already becoming tiresome.

Ann had not known she had to dress up this morning. Had Mrs. Mannheim said something last evening, Ann would have told her that her only good dress needed laundering; the only thing she had left to wear was a blouse and jumper. She knew it was not the most appropriate thing to wear to church, but at least it was clean and pressed. She would explain at breakfast. Surely Flossie would forgive her this one time.

At breakfast Ann smiled when she saw Graham. He looked terribly sleepy, as he usually did in the morning. He had crudely parted his hair and it was apparent he had made only a lame effort to comb it. There were wrinkles in his shirt and his necktie had been carelessly knotted. He looked as sad and sleepy as she felt. "What time is it?" he asked.

"It's six-fifteen," Flossie said sternly. "Now, young man, you march back to your room and make yourself more presentable. You look a sight! Uncle John and I will not go to church with anyone who looks as unkempt as you." She turned to Ann, "And look at you. We're not playing in the park. We're going to church, to worship God. We must dress nicely when we worship Him. You go back to your room and put on something more appropriate. Didn't I ask you to do so earlier? And hurry, you two, the hands of the clock do not wait for sloppy children filled with sloth."

"This is the best I can do," Graham complained. "Everything else is too dirty to wear."

"What! You neglected to keep your clothes neat and clean? I cannot believe it. Now what can we do? Why aren't your things ready this morning? Have you been shirking your laundry?" she ranted.

"Why didn't you tell us last evening we were to dress up this morning?" Graham asked. "We could have taken care of our clothes had we known."

"Don't sass me, you little heathen," Flossie screamed. "Just because you come from an uncivilized nation doesn't mean you may act like a barbarian in our house. You are not in England anymore; you're in the United States of America. You are in a civilized country now. You will act civil!"

"I was not sassing anyone, ma'am. I was simply observing a fact," Graham replied indignantly.

"What is she talking about?" Ann asked herself. "We're as civilized as they are–in fact, we're even more civilized. We have Shakespeare, Byron, Dickens, and ... Also, our country has been around much longer than America has. That must account for something."

"Well, what are we going to do? You can't go to church looking like that." Flossie continued.

"You could help them a little, show them what you want, help with their grooming, dear," John said meekly.

"How can they ever become independent citizens if we start coddling them, John?"

"Just this once, Flossie. Please?"

"Oh, all right. Immediately after dinner it's back to the bathroom, Graham. I expect you to wash your face, neatly comb your hair, and, if you can't properly knot a necktie, Uncle John will help you. If you don't believe you can handle these simple assignments, mister, tell me now."

"I can do them," Graham replied sarcastically.

"As for you, young lady, what is your excuse?"

Ann explained her good dress was soiled.

Finally, after another tirade from Flossie, Flossie agreed Ann could wear her blouse and jumper. "But only this once," Flossie harped, "We will do much better next time. Now let's eat our breakfast. I have fixed both of you lovely bowls of mush."

"Mush!" both children cried simultaneously.

"We don't like mush, Aunt Flossie," Ann pleaded.

"Now look here, you little insubordinate snip," Flossie screamed. "I will not have any more of your nonsense. Today we are being served mush–and today we will eat mush!"

"No ma'am, I won't eat that slop," Ann cried.

"You will sit there until you do, you little snot!"

By seven-fifteen Flossie had a decision to make. Was she going to give up on Ann eating the mush or would she have to forgo taking them to church? She couldn't decide which was best. Rearing children was not going to be as easy as she had thought. She believed her stern approach was the right way to go; she just didn't know how to make it work. One thing she knew for certain though, she was the boss. These stubborn children were not going to undermine her authority.

"All right, if you won't eat your warm mush before we go, you'll eat it cold afterwards, every last spoonful, and nothing else before then."

At church, Flossie was all smiles. She told everyone she and John "were so fortunate to have this wonderful opportunity to entertain these little darlings from England." She said she already loved them so much she could barely control herself. "They're such little angels." she boasted.

Graham looked at Ann. Ann looked at Graham. Neither one could understand how she could say these things. Church was no place to tell fibs. Didn't she know that? How could she behave so differently here from what she had at home this morning? They were living with a hypocrite–to put it politely. They began to wonder what they would do if things continued as they had started.

Chapter 33

Tuesday, 3 September 1940

Fred marveled at his good fortune. Even though the Derringers had given him a bedroom in the basement it was much better than his room at home. It contained everything he needed: plenty of closet space for his clothes, a lamp for reading in bed, a desk for doing his homework, and a wireless to listen to the short-wave bands. He had already picked up a station in Canada and one in Mexico and hoped someday to pick up the BBC in England. He supposed it would be difficult to do because of all the wartime restrictions on radio transmissions, but it was worth trying every chance he had.

What impressed him the most about the house was its centralized heating and air conditioning system. Even though it would be some time before winter came to Ohio, when the temperature suddenly dipped on Sunday evening Tom had fired the furnace. It worked wonderfully. Within minutes, all the rooms in the house, including Fred's basement room, were warm and comfortable. As Tom explained it to Fred, all but one of the chimneys on the roof were connected to fireplaces. But the fireplaces were not used to heat the rooms but were there primarily to enhance the ambiance of each room. The remaining chimney came from the major heat source for the house, an oil-fired furnace. A system of air distribution ducts led from the furnace to each room.

It seemed awfully complicated to Fred and a terrible waste of fireplaces.

The Tuesday before had been an extremely hot August day, the day the evacuees' schedule included the McKinley Heights cinema. While Tom was explaining the furnace, Fred had commented on how nice and cool the cinema had been. It surprised Fred when Tom told him that on warm days the Derringer house would be just as comfortable as the theater had been. The same air ducts used to supply warm air from the furnace were also used to supply cold air from the air conditioner. Fred was fascinated, home air conditioning was something he had never heard of before; he wondered if rich English families had similar systems.

Later, Sarah told him the Derringer system was quite new and unique, only a few families in Oakton presently owned air conditioners.

Fred hoped there would be one more hot spell before winter. He wanted to determine, first hand, how well the Derringer air conditioner worked. If there weren't any more hot days this year, there probably wouldn't be another opportunity to see the system in operation. His Dad had assured him his stay would not be long, he fully expected to be back in England long before the first warm days next spring.

"It's not that way at home," he told Sarah. "We don't have air conditioning or central heating. We only have coal burning fireplaces, one in almost every room. The problem with them is the constant stoking needed and length of time required before the room is comfortable, but even then the heat isn't even. On cold winter days, we must bundle up and sit close to the fireplace to feel reasonably warm.

"But we don't spend much time in many of the rooms when it's cold," Fred recalled. "Several years ago, Dad installed a special coal stove in our kitchen. Mum almost always keeps a small steady fire burning in it. She likes having the oven and grill always hot and ready for cooking and it's great in the wintertime. The kitchen is so warm and cozy. The family spends most winter evenings sitting by the oven, taking in its warmth, and listening to the wireless."

"Mum loves that stove," Fred continued to reminisce. "She says with its steady heat she knows exactly how things will cook, and how long it will take. You wouldn't believe how good her puddings taste.

"But I'm afraid the war is changing all that; it's causing almost everything to run short these days. When I left home, Dad worried he might not be able to buy coal much longer; it was becoming quite scarce, probably even more so now. I wish my folks would write, so I knew what has been happening over there. I don't understand it. I should think I would have received at least one letter by now."

"It takes time for mail to cross the Atlantic," Sarah advised him. "Try to be patient."

In spite of Sarah's earlier warning, Fred still had not been assigned any household chores. He thought the delay might be due to yesterday being a holiday in the United States. Dr. Derringer was probably waiting until Labor Day, as the Americans called it, was over. Last evening, when Dr. Derringer called him to his study, he was certain he would be given a work assignment. Instead, Dr. Derringer said he was taking Fred to the Bear County fair. He said it would give Fred a good, comprehensive look at the northeastern Ohio farm products. He then bored Fred with a lengthy description of American county fairs. He told him the local farmers displayed their livestock, garden products, and crafts and competed for prizes in each category. The winners won ribbons, blue for first prize, red for second, and yellow for third. He followed this with a long description of the judging criteria used and explained in great detail all the things Fred would see. By the time he had finished, Fred was almost certain fairs in the U.S. were quite similar to English country fairs, although he couldn't be positive. He had never been to a country fair in England. He didn't know why–perhaps his parents, having always lived in the city, had no interest in farm products.

Fred worried that, much like his parents, he would find little to interest him. That was until he heard Sarah's description of the fair. She told him about the horse racing, sideshows, food, games, Ferris wheel, and the many other rides on the midway. It might be a grand day after all.

Sandy was surprised when she entered the fairgrounds with her foster parents, Kirk and Lucy Maurer. There, standing in front of the ticket booth, was Fred. He was with two adults who, she assumed, were his foster parents. A large group of reporters surrounded them. She could hear only snippets of what Fred was saying.

"I am very grateful to Dr. and Mrs. Derringer for their generosity and support here in the United States.

"They are treating me as if I were their son.

"It's such a lovely house.

"Yes, I miss England, and my parents, very much.

"Everyone in America has been so kind to us. I wonder how we will ever repay them."

Suddenly Fred noticed Sandy. "Oh! There's Sandy! Miss Sandy Meyers. She's another of the Bender evacuees."

Immediately the reporters turned to Sandy and began asking questions and snapping her picture. The loss of interest in "her evacuee" annoyed Victoria Derringer. She attempted to coax the reporters' attention back to Fred. "We're looking forward to the start of school tomorrow, eager for Fred to attend our American school system," she said. "It will enable him to compare it to his English system." When they continued to ignore her, she added, "We considered enrolling Fred in an academy, but Fred prefers the less demanding public school. Dr. Derringer and I believe he made a wise decision. He needs time to adapt before enrolling in one of our more demanding institutions."

Fred was confused. He had not discussed the selection of school with either of them. She had pointed to the school on their way home from Camp Bender and asked if he would enjoy attending. He had answered simply, "Yes, ma'am." There had been nothing to suggest he was making a selection. If there had been a choice, he certainly would not have chosen a public school. He really did not think he was smart enough to attend a public school. He wondered why she apologized for enrolling him in such a prestigious place. She had even claimed it was less difficult. He didn't understand. Even if it was not up to the standards of the public schools in England, schools like Harrow or Eton, it still would be too demanding for him. He could not wait to tell his mum and dad he was going to public school. The news was certain to surprise them.

Fred did not discover until Wednesday when he talked with the school principal that private schools in the U.S. were the equivalent of public schools in England. Public schools in the U.S. were the equivalent of English county or senior schools.

Once the reporters had snapped their pictures and asked their questions, they moved on to other interests at the fair. After Fred and Sandy had introduced the Derringers to the Maurers, Kirk asked the Derringers to join Lucy and him at a concert in the pavilion and suggested the children might enjoy looking around the midway by themselves. "Here's a quarter, Sandy," he said. "Why don't you buy Fred and yourself an ice cream cone and some soda pop? Or whatever you wish."

"Here's two dollars, Fred," Tom said, in an attempt to outdo Kirk and Lucy. "Take a run down the midway and have a good time. Win a kewpie doll for Sandy; or maybe she would like to ride the Ferris wheel? Go ahead, enjoy yourselves. We'll meet you at the poultry barn in an hour."

A look of concern appeared on Lucy's face. "I wouldn't recommend riding the wheel, Sandy. It's too dangerous," she cautioned.

Sandy and Fred, ignored Lucy's advice, they rode on several of the "dangerous" rides (including the Ferris wheel and the roller coaster), shared cotton candy, and talked about their new homes. They assured each other they were happy and said their billets were better than expected. They worried about school, wondered what differences they would find there, and talked about their shipmates. Sandy had heard that Ann and Graham were still together and that their billet was somewhere in McKinley Heights. She thought Edith was also in McKinley Heights. She looked forward to seeing them in school tomorrow. As far as Fred knew, he was the only evacuee billeted in Oakton. He hoped he was wrong. Otherwise, it was going to be a lonely stay in the U.S.

They found it difficult to say good-bye. He promised to call her within a few days. She agreed to tell him as soon as she knew Edith's or Ann and Graham's addresses. They both had tears in their eyes when they approached their foster families at the barn.

Things had not gone well in the Mannheim house. Flossie and John had planned to take the children to the fair after the noon meal but the children were not cooperating. "Now look, Ann, you cannot continue to do this. You must start eating what we set in front of you. Your refusal to eat is just plain bullheadedness," Flossie said, her voice quivering with disgust. "I guess we made a mistake on Sunday. We shouldn't have pitied you; we should have forced you to eat the mush. You surely must agree, I cannot permit you to get away with such gross disobedience a second time. If you refuse to eat your beef liver, you cannot go to the fair."

"I don't care," Ann replied defiantly. "I told you before you served it to me that I don't like liver, that I never liked liver, and that I never will like liver. To tell you the truth, your mashed potatoes are lumpy and your gravy tastes like lard. I refuse to eat any of this garbage."

Ann knew her actions were outrageous, but she could not help it. Flossie Mannheim had been treating both Graham and her like convicts ever since they had arrived on Saturday. It was time to take a stand.

"Eat it! You little slut!" Flossie screamed, insulted by Ann's unkind critique of her potatoes and gravy.

"Don't call my little sister a slut! You bloody ... ," Graham paused, trying to think of a good insult. "old German hag!" he yelled.

It was the first time he or Ann had referred to the Mannheim Germanic ancestry. In fact, it was the first time any of the evacuees had vocalized what they had tacitly noticed about the bloodline of the majority of the McKinley Heights residents.

"Now wait a minute, son," John interrupted angrily. "We're Americans. We're not Germans. We were born here; our mothers and fathers were born here, and even some of our grandparents were born here. We are patriotic, perhaps more so than most Americans. Don't accuse us otherwise."

"Well! You act like Nazis," Graham accused him.

"Take that back!" Flossie cried.

She glared at Graham for a minute, then slapped him.

"Don't you dare strike my brother," cried Ann, tears rolling down her cheeks. She hurled her dinner plate at Flossie. It struck Flossie on her forehead, food side first. Mashed potatoes and gravy began sliding down Flossie's face. Flossie looked comical. Graham and Ann could barely keep from laughing.

"My God, you children are heathens!" Flossie cried as she lunged at Ann.

"Leave her alone," screamed Graham. To protect Ann, he jumped in front of Flossie. By this time Ann had risen from the table. "Come on, Graham! Let's get out of this madhouse!" she urged. They bolted from the kitchen, slammed the screen door behind them, and ran to the nearby playground.

"Now what are we going to do, Flossie?" John asked in frustration.

"Call the police!" she shouted.

"We can't do that!"

"Why not? They need to be arrested. Those brats should not be running loose. They're a danger to society."

"Now settle down, Flossie. Let's think this through carefully."

When tempers had calmed, John said, "Let's face it, Flossie, we can't handle them. Maybe it's us. Maybe it's them. Whoever is at fault, we can't continue as we are. Should we call Mrs. Studer? Tell her to come and get the children?"

"What will my girlfriends say?" Flossie protested.

"The problem is beyond worrying about what your girlfriends might think, Flossie."

John called Mrs. Studer. Although reluctant at first to do so, Dorothy agreed to come to the house immediately.

When she arrived, she reviewed the altercation with Flossie and John, then found Ann and Graham in the playground and listened to their version. She finally decided it was in everyone's interest to find another home for the children.

She asked the children to collect their things, but they refused to return to the house. It was only after the Mannheims volunteered to remain out of sight until they had gone that the children cautiously entered, quickly gathered their belongings and left.

In her haste, Ann forgot the doll her mum had packed for her in England. She never asked Flossie for it, and Flossie never sent it.

Chapter 34

Wednesday, 4 September 1940

Whoever it was who said if something could go wrong, it would go wrong, was certainly correct, at least as far as Dorothy Snyder was concerned. In spite of all of their careful preparations, no one had really planned for an irreconcilable conflict between the children and their foster parents. Now it had happened and here she was, uncertain what to do. The only thing she knew for sure was that her guests could not sleep in her bed for many nights; sleeping on the couch, with her husband at the lodge, was not a pleasant way to live.

The children were still sleeping. She imagined they were both emotionally drained after the events of yesterday. She had spent a long time last evening consoling them and discussing the problem. By the time they had finally gone to bed she was convinced the fault rested primarily with Flossie Mannheim. What could Flossie have been thinking? Had she no empathy for the children? Her goal of well mannered children was laudable, but why hadn't she taken the time to evaluate their manners beforehand? It seemed to Dorothy the children's manners were really quite good. Flossie simply did not seem to know how to treat children. Had she shown love instead of uncompromising discipline, she would have accomplished much, much more. Certainly the children would still be living with Flossie, not with her.

After the children had gone to bed, she had tried to talk with Flossie again, but John refused to call her to the phone. He said she had a severe headache and could not be disturbed. Dorothy doubted he was telling the truth; she was almost certain she could hear Flossie whispering in the background. Not being willing to discuss the problem reinforced Dorothy's belief that she should never have selected John and Flossie in the first place. She should have heeded the social worker's advice, rejected the Mannheims' application right away. She should have known better than to deviate from the normal procedure. She shouldn't have overridden the advice.

The truth was, at the time, she had few choices. There were simply not enough families to handle all the special requests of the children. Had all the families, who originally expressed an interest in the program, kept their promises this would never have happened. More than enough homes would have been available. The scarcity of multiple child homes had been the major problem, right from the beginning. It was the reason they had placed Roy and his two sisters in different homes. Regretfully, the situation was still no better; no new offers had come in recently, in spite of another plea to the community. Placement was a major problem before last Saturday and would be even more so now that all the children had been assigned to families.

She planned to visit the office this morning, just as soon as she saw to the needs of Ann and Graham. One thing was certain, they would not be starting school with the other McKinley Heights youngsters today. They needed to establish an address before their school assignment could be made. She could have sent them to the school in her district, but it made no sense to enroll them in one school today, then change it tomorrow. She didn't think a few days delay would hurt the children too much, but still she would have to find a home in a hurry.

"Good morning, Mrs. Studer," Graham said, yawning as he walked into the kitchen.

"Hello, Graham. I was just going to call you. Your breakfast is nearly ready. I'll call Ann, then we can sit down together."

"No need to call her, ma'am," Graham indicated. "I already did. She is on her way down now."

"Why thank you, Graham. That was nice of you, and it helps a lot. I'm in a bit of a hurry this morning. I must go to the Center shortly and try to find a home for the two of you."

"We truly are sorry for all the bother, Mrs. Studer. We hope it's not causing too many problems."

"Don't fret about that. It's perfectly fine. We're here to help, whatever your needs."

"Good morning, Mrs. Studer," Ann said, sleepily.

"Ann, you're not dressed," Graham scolded. "Didn't I tell you to dress before you came down? We start school today."

"I was too sleepy," she murmured.

"It's okay, Graham, she needn't hurry. You aren't going to school today. We'll put that on hold until we know where you will be staying."

"Have you decided what to do with us?" Ann asked.

"No, honey, I haven't," Dorothy replied, looking somewhat dejected. "I'm going to the Center when I finish here. I'll try to find a new home as quickly as I can, but you should plan on staying here at least one more night. I seriously doubt whether I can complete all the arrangements in one day. I promise, though, I'll do everything possible to have you settled in by tomorrow evening."

When Dorothy returned late in the afternoon, Graham met her at the door and asked anxiously, "Have you decided anything, Mrs. Studer?"

"Nothing yet, Graham. Miss Klienschmitt and I have been calling families all day. We still haven't found anyone willing to accept two children. It's very discouraging."

"Ann and I have been talking about that," Graham volunteered. "If it helps, we would consider living with separate families. America is not as threatening to us as we originally thought it would be. Naturally we prefer to be together but, if it's not possible, we think it would be all right to separate us–as long as we're with families who are helpful, caring, and kind."

"That's good of you, Graham. It would help considerably. What's your feeling about this, Ann? Would it be acceptable to you?"

"Yes, ma'am," Ann answered. She paused, then added, "So long as it is not with another lady like Mrs. Mannheim."

Dorothy laughed. "Don't worry, dear, I promise to find a friendlier family."

The evening newspaper contained a picture of Fred and Sandy eating cotton candy at the Bear County Fairgrounds. The caption read, *"English Children Enjoying Bear County Fair: Miss Sandy Meyers (left) of Uxbridge and Mr. Fred Andrews of Northolt."*

The article accompanying the picture carried the headline, *"Area Couples Enjoy English Evacuees."* The article said:

Dr. & Mrs. Thomas Derringer, of Oakton, enjoyed a day at the Bear County Fair Tuesday with Fred Andrews of Northolt, Middlesex, England. Mr. Andrews is living with the Derringers. He recently arrived from England under an evacuation program sponsored by the Bender Electric Co. of McKinley Heights. The program provides sanctuary

*from the bombing of Britain. The children will remain in the U.S. until
the war in Europe ends.*

*Mrs. Victoria Derringer, chairman of the McKinley Heights Art
Group and an active member of the Oakton League of Christian Women
said, "I am thrilled for the opportunity to serve as a foster parent for
one of these little darlings. Freddie already seems like one of the family.
We love him dearly." She hopes the war in Europe ends soon but dreads
the thought of losing Fred.*

*Dr. Derringer practices medicine at Highman Hospital where he is
the senior orthopedic surgeon. Fred will be attending Oakton Jr. High
School this Fall. He said he is looking forward to an American education because he knows it will be a "top notch program."*

*His friend, Miss Sandy Meyers is staying with Mr. and Mrs. Kirk
Maurer of McKinley Heights. She is the daughter of Mr. and Mrs.
Harold Meyers of Uxbridge, Middlesex, England. She will be attending
the Warren G. Harding Elementary School in McKinley Heights this
year. She is "very glad to be in McKinley Heights" and thinks
"everyone in the United States is super."*

*A total of seventy-nine boys and girls are staying in the McKinley
Heights area as part of the Bender program. Their fathers are employ-
ees of Bender Electric Ltd., Pinnington, England, a subsidiary of Bender
Electric.*

"Now we know where Fred and Sandy are living," Ann said excitedly.

A brief description of the sinking of the Dutch liner *Volendam* was
next to the article about Fred and Sandy. Graham scanned it, then, when
he realized what it was about, carefully read it. "Would you look at
this," he said. "The Germans sank a ship coming from Britain. The article says there were three hundred forty-one English evacuees on board.
Fortunately, there were several ships nearby that could rescue them.
They saved everyone–but many were in their life boats for a long time.
Those poor devils! It took several days before everyone was back in
Britain. I'm glad our ship wasn't sunk when we came across the Atlantic!"

"Let me see!" Ann said, trying to read the article over Graham's
shoulder. She read it with much greater interest than she had given any
of the previous articles concerning the war. This one seemed much more
personal.

*　　*　　*

No 5
Mrs. Dorothy Studer's Home
McKinley Heights, Ohio, USA
Wednesday, 4 September 1940

Dear Mum, Dad, and Yvonne,

Well here it is only five days since I wrote my last letter (See the number above). I know it is rather soon to be writing again, but I thought it would interest you to know what Graham and I have been doing.

We went to the home of a Mr. and Mrs. Mannheim on Saturday night but are now waiting for a new home. Our stay with the Mannheims did not work out so well. They were opinionated people of <u>German</u> ancestry. (I suppose nationality is not relevant since almost everyone here has a German background, but it seemed so at the time. Did you know they once called McKinley Heights, West Dresden?) The Mannheims ordered us to do many things against our will. A little of that was okay, but they carried it to the extreme. Finally, we had a huge fight and Mrs. Studer (the Bender representative in charge of billeting) came by and rescued us.

Now don't worry about this. We are temporarily staying with Mrs. Studer–at her home. She is a very fine lady and is taking good care of us. She hopes to find a permanent home for us by tomorrow.

They are having difficulty finding families willing to take more than one child, so Graham and I have volunteered to accept separate homes– if we must. We are already becoming familiar with American ways and no longer feel so intimidated. I will miss Graham, but it will be all right. They have promised to let us visit each other often.

Wasn't it terrible what happened to the children on the Volendam? Thank goodness we arrived safely. I would not have enjoyed spending that much time in a lifeboat!! I understand most of the children were very seasick. Ugh! Those poor souls!

We still have not received any letters from you. I hope my letters are reaching you in better time than yours are reaching us. They tell us mail is slow because of the war. We hear the Jerries have been bombing Britain quite a bit lately. I pray no bombs have dropped on Pinnington. Be sure to use the air raid shelter if they do!!!

Have you heard anything from Henry? Do you know where he is now? I often think of him and hope he is all right. My love to him– wherever he is.

Well, it's getting late and I must get some sleep. I want to be alert tomorrow when I meet my new family.

Love to you all,

Ann

P.S. You would not recognize me. We have such grand food here. I bet I have gained a stone. Ha. Ha. It is just a joke, I am not fat–yet!

Ann slept better that night than she had for many nights. Surely Mrs. Studer could find suitable places for Graham and her–homes with love and compassion.

Ann dreamed she was a kitten snuggled next to the warm furry belly of the mother cat. Beside her lay Graham, Yvonne, and Henry. They were kittens too. The father cat sat close by, watching over his brood. She could hear the soft purr of her mother. She felt so warm, so content.

She trusted Mrs. Studer.

Chapter 35

Thursday, 5 September 1940

"Of course he can stay with us, Dorothy," Ken Nelson said excitedly. "Didn't I say we wanted a boy? Louise will be thrilled. We don't care if he is fifteen. Actually, that is ideal. Our daughter will be fifteen in October. Having someone in the house who is her age will be good for her. She has been working so hard and hasn't been socializing as she should. A foster brother in her class at school might be the catalyst she needs to become more involved in social activities."

"We really appreciate your agreeing to this on such short notice. After the shoddy treatment I gave you on Saturday it wouldn't have surprised me had you turned us down," Dorothy Studer apologized.

"Nonsense, you were only doing what you had to do. No one blames you. I admire you for volunteering to take on this assignment. It must be terribly difficult to satisfy everyone–and frustrating at times–especially when you are doing it for free. Anyway, I think a boy will be just what Louise needs to get back on her feet. We owe you a great deal, Dorothy."

"We will bring Graham some time around twelve. I'm sorry we must bring him at lunchtime. I hope you don't mind."

"No, that will be fine. Eating with a youngster is a good way to get to know him. I'll try to make it home around then, so I'm there to greet him too. But if your schedule changes, bring him whenever you can. Someone will be home all day."

"Exactly where is your house?"

"Go down Elm Street, until you come to Park. Turn right on Park. We're the fourth driveway on the left. Ninety-four Park is our address."

"Ninety-four Park? Isn't that next to Dr. & Mrs. Derringer?"

"Yes, Tom and Victoria are our next door neighbors."

"Next door neighbors. That is wonderful. Did you know they have one of our children? A boy. As I recall Fred Andrews is about the same age as Graham–perhaps a little younger."

"I didn't know they had one of the children. I haven't seen the Derringers for some time. I thought they were in Chicago. Does Graham know he will be living so close to another Bender evacuee?"

"He probably doesn't. We haven't distributed any list of addresses yet."

"Good! We'll surprise him then. I'll call Tom. Maybe the boys can visit later today. It should please both of them to see a familiar face."

"There's one other thing: Graham has a sister Ann. We're placing her on a farm near Dexter Hills. We promised Ann and Graham they would be able to visit each other regularly. I hope this is okay with you."

"The poor kids. The separation must be terribly difficult for them. Rest assured Ann will always be welcomed here. We'll see to it they visit each other often. I really wish we could take Ann too, but our house is just not big enough for two children."

"No need to apologize. Taking Graham is help enough."

Graham liked the Nelson house when it came in view. It was not as big, or as elegant, as the house he saw through the trees as they drove into the driveway, but it was much bigger and more stately than his home in Pinnington. The English Tudor style reminded him of England. He had never dreamed of living in such an elegant home. The big lawn and huge maple trees reminded him of an English country estate he had once seen.

"Hello, Graham. Welcome to our home," Ken said, cordially shaking his hand and smiling warmly.

"How do you do, sir."

"Permit me to introduce you to everyone. Graham, this is Mrs. Nelson. Louise, this is Graham."

"It pleases me to meet you, Graham. I'm so glad you have agreed to stay with us," Louise said, hugging him tightly and kissing him on the cheek. "But let's decide here and now what you should call us. I know how awkward it is for young people to know what to call us old folks. Now, as I see it, you have two choices. You may call us 'Aunt Louise' and 'Uncle Ken', or you may call us 'Mom' and 'Dad'. Truthfully I prefer 'Mom' and 'Dad', but I don't wish to take anything from your real parents. If calling us that makes you uncomfortable, use 'aunt' and 'uncle'. Whichever you decide will be perfectly fine with us."

Graham thought for a moment. He could see nothing wrong with 'Mom' and 'Dad'. He did not think it would diminish his feelings for his mum and dad. Whatever the Nelsons preferred seemed okay to him. "I would like that, ... Mom. I would consider it an honor."

"Oh, how nice, Graham. Selecting Mom makes me very happy. I hope I can live up to it."

"Now I would like to introduce you to Meg. Graham, this is our daughter Meg. Meg, Graham. I guess if you called us Mom and Dad you should call her 'Sis'."

"Hello, Meg. I mean, 'Sis,'" he laughed. He knew he was staring, but he could not quit looking at her. He had never seen such a beautiful girl. "How lucky to have a sister who looks as pretty as she does," he thought to himself as his face turned pink with embarrassment.

Louise smiled when she saw Graham's reaction. "Meg, please show Graham to his room. Graham, you will probably want to wash before we eat. Meg will point out the bathroom to you. Whenever you are ready, please come back downstairs. I don't want to rush you, but we should eat shortly or Meg will be late for school and Dad will be late for work. Lunch will be ready when you are."

"Thank you, ma'am."

"No, Graham. Remember? We agreed to call me Mom."

"Sorry, Mom," he said, emphasizing her title.

Graham enjoyed lunch. He could not remember when he had last eaten with such thoughtful and jovial people. Certainly it had not been in America. He particularly liked the way Mom and Dad Nelson were always teaching while they ate. They discussed important news events, talked about the books they were reading and played word games. He could see he would learn many things from these people. He quickly decided this was going to be a good place to stay; he would be happy with the Nelsons. He hoped Ann would do as well.

After lunch, Ken told Graham about Tommy. He said he hoped Graham's being there would help Louise get over the death of their son. Graham hoped so too. He promised himself he would be particularly attentive to his new mom.

"I want you to think about this very carefully, Ann," Dorothy said, looking at Ann with concern.

"Yes, Mrs. Studer, I have thought about it. I would enjoy staying with the Schaefers." Ann answered.

"You understand? It's a farm, much less modern than the Mannheim home, much more primitive than your home in England."

"I know. I don't believe I'll mind. I have always liked animals and this is a wonderful opportunity to be around them."

Dorothy did not feel comfortable with the idea. She almost wished Ann had said no. It would have ended consideration of the Schaefer farm for any future billets. They seemed to be sincere enough. That was not the problem. She just did not think a child, reared in the city, would easily adjust to farm life.

"Living on a farm is much more difficult than living in the city, Ann. There are always chores to do and farmers get up much earlier in the morning. I must emphasize again, you will not have all the modern conveniences you had at home."

"It's all right, Mrs. Studer. Honestly. Please don't worry about it. I'll be okay. I have already caused you too much trouble. I know it is difficult to find new billets now. If the farm is available, and you believe the people will treat me fairly, I'll be happy to stay there."

"All right, Ann, we'll go ahead with the assignment—just remember; you must make a special effort to get along with the Schaefers. We can't move you again. Do you understand that?"

"Yes, ma'am. You're telling me I must not ask for another change. Once I'm there, I must stay there. I promise to try very hard so I don't inconvenience you again."

The Schaefer farm was nearly one mile from the village of Dexter Hills. Ann and Mrs. Studer arrived at the farm around three o'clock. Ida Schaefer was in the kitchen when they came to the door. She was about to put two apple pies in the oven and apparently had wiped her hands on her apron just before answering the door. Flour spotted her apron and arms.

"Hello. Please come in. You must be Ann," she said in a friendly tone.

"Yes, this is Ann. Ann, I would like you to meet Mrs. Schaefer," Dorothy said, pleased with Ida's pleasant disposition.

"Hello, Mrs. Schaefer," Ann said extending her hand. "It's very good of you to invite me here. Thank you."

"No need to thank me, child. It pleases us to have you here. Why, we were at our wits end, we didn't know how we were going to milk all our cows. You're the answer to our prayers. Now we have a pair of strong hands to help us." Ida winked at Dorothy and laughed.

Ann was almost certain Mrs. Schaefer was jesting but not entirely. The thought of milking a cow horrified her. She tried to control the look on her face and hoped it didn't show; it was difficult to disguise her feelings. She wondered if she should admit she had no idea how to milk a cow. Then she remembered the promise she had made to Mrs. Studer. "I'll be very glad to help out–wherever I can, ma'am," she said bravely.

Ida saw the frightened look on Ann's face and laughed. It was a very hearty laugh. Ann instantly liked Ida. "Oh, child, I was only teasing. Don't you worry your pretty little head. We won't work you to death. We'll give you time off for school. You can do your chores before and after school. We'll even give you a day off–once a month." Again, she roared with laughter.

Ann laughed too, now certain Ida was only teasing.

Ida grabbed Ann and gave her a big hug. It was the first strong, loving hug Ann had had since she left Pinnington. It felt good. She was pretty sure she would like this farm.

Ida turned to Dorothy. "I'm sorry the mister isn't here to greet you. He, and our son Ned, are working in the field. They won't be back until suppertime. I know he would have liked to meet you."

"Don't worry, Mrs. Schaefer. We'll have many opportunities to meet later. The company plans to invite everyone–the children, the foster parents, their families, and the Bender program administrators–to a banquet every so often. We'll use it as an opportunity to compare notes and–well–just an opportunity to have some fun together."

"That sounds lovely. We'll look forward to those banquets. Won't we, Ann?"

"Oh yes, that would be splendid. Then I'll be able to visit with some of my friends," Ann said hopefully.

"Don't worry, honey. I'm sure your friends would enjoy a day on the farm. We'll invite them for a day now and then. We don't want you to be lonely," Ida said, sensing Ann was beginning to miss her pals.

They unloaded Ann's things from Mrs. Studer's auto, said good-bye, and then Ann and Ida were alone. "Well, dear, I think the apple pie is ready. Shall we have a look?

"What do you think? Does the crust look brown enough to you?" Ida asked.

"Oh yes, Mrs. Schaefer. It looks luscious."

"The menfolk will be in from the fields in another hour or so. I had best start making supper soon. We'll wait until suppertime to eat the pie; that is, if you can wait that long."

Ida pulled a tin from the cupboard and with a wink, pulled off the cover and offered Ann a ginger cookie.

"Oh yes, ma'am, I can wait." she answered, smiling as she bit into the cookie.

"Now that will never do. You can't keep calling me 'Mrs. Schaefer' and 'ma'am'. I wouldn't know who you meant. What say you call me 'Aunt Ida'? Would that be all right?"

"Aunt Ida? Oh, yes, I think that would be lovely." Ann did not think she could ever confuse Aunt Ida with Aunt Flossie.

"Great! Aunt Ida it will be. Now, let me show you to your room. I'm afraid it is nothing fancy, but at least the mattress is soft, and we have plenty of covers to keep you snugly and cozy when winter comes."

Chapter 36

Thursday, 5 September 1940

"I'm busy at the moment. Would you please see who is at the door, Graham?" Ken asked.

It seemed odd. Graham wondered why Ken would ask him to answer the door. He had only been there a few hours and could not be expected to know whoever it was, or what to do once he met the person. "But if that's what Dad Nelson wants, who am I to question him," he told himself.

When he opened the door he understood. "Fred!" Graham exclaimed, "What are you doing here?"

Fred was grinning. "Hi, Graham. How are you doing, old chap?"

"How did you know I was here?"

"I live next door. I'm your neighbor! Can you believe it? Mr. Nelson called our house a little while ago, told us you were here. He suggested I come over and surprise you."

"It certainly is a nice surprise. I can't believe it."

"Isn't it great? We'll be in the same school. But what are you doing here? I thought you and Ann were staying with a family in McKinley Heights?"

"Ha! We were," Graham laughed, "but it didn't work out. It was a terrible couple of days. I'll tell you about it–when we have lots of time. Mrs. Studer brought me here at noon today. Afterwards, she was going to take Ann to a farm near a town called Dexter Hills. Gee, it's great to learn we're going to be neighbors."

"It certainly is. They separated you and Ann, did they? Bad show. To a farm, you say?"

"After we left the McKinley Heights home, they couldn't find any family willing to keep two children. We finally offered to let them find separate homes for us. I hope it wasn't a mistake and Ann will be all right. She assured me she didn't mind." As if he was trying to convince himself, he added, "The Nelsons have already said Ann can visit here as often as she wishes. That should help a little.

"Congratulations! I saw your picture in last night's newspaper," Graham said, changing the subject. "I guess I'm talking to a celebrity." He slapped Fred on the back and added, "May I have your autograph, Mr. Andrews?"

"Oh, 'tweren't nuttin'," Fred answered, feigning embarrassment and attempting, unsuccessfully, to mimic an ignorant character he had recently seen in a picture show. He then lowered his voice and asked quietly, "How do you find the Nelsons? Is everything all right?"

"I think they're super, Fred. I really believe I have drawn a lucky billet."

Graham also began to whisper. "You should see my new sister. She's quite a nice looking girl. You'll like her."

"Hey, don't keep me waiting. I'm always interested in meeting comely girls," Fred teased.

Graham introduced Fred to the Nelsons. Afterwards, he took Fred to his room where they talked about many things. The thought of starting school worried Graham, even after Fred told him how nice he had been treated by everyone and how much he liked Betsy Ross Junior High, especially the sports program. They exchanged what each knew about the billets of their friends and talked at length about their new homes. Fred tried to clarify the newspaper account. He told Graham that the Derringers were not treating him as their "son" as the article claimed. Instead, he said, they had given him a room in the servants' quarters which, although extremely pleasant, was not exactly the same as living with them. He assured Graham he did not mind eating his meals in the basement with Sarah but did mind not having many opportunities to talk with the Derringers.

When Fred left, both boys were feeling much better about their stay in America and each hoped his good fortune would continue.

94 Park Ave.

Oakton, Ohio, USA

Thursday, 5 September 1940

Dear Mum, Dad, & Yvonne,

Please excuse the long delay between letters. There simply has not been time to write. Bender Electric kept us unbelievably busy while in camp. We went swimming almost every day, saw a number of picture shows, attended many lectures about America, had very scrumptious meals, sang by the campfire, and played numerous games including softball–a game somewhat akin to our rounders. You would have been proud of me, I hit a two bagger. (I'll explain all about it when I return home.)

Now that I have a permanent home I (hopefully) will write more letters.

After several days of living with a horrible family, I finally found a good one here in Oakton. Their names are Mr. Kenneth and Mrs. Louise Nelson. Oakton is a suburb about six miles south of McKinley Heights. The Nelsons have a daughter, Meg, who will be fifteen next month. They lost a son last year to Infantile Paralysis (Polio). Mr. Nelson is assistant comptroller at Bender Electric.

The Nelsons have a lovely house. You wouldn't believe how big it is–it's almost as if I were living with the gentry. Of course, here in America they are not as conscience of class structure as we are. They classify people as either rich, middle-class, or poor, but even then, I'm told, there is much more intermingling. For instance, the family next to us is much richer than the Nelsons and has a huge house and garden– much bigger than this one. I would imagine the Nelson family is considered upper middle-class or, maybe only middle-class–I still haven't completely grasped their social structure.

Fred, one of my evac friends, is staying with these wealthy neighbors. He is not as lucky as I am though. My family treats me like a son;

his treats him as they would a servant. He must eat and sleep in the servants' quarters in the basement!

I am rather ashamed of one thing, though. I hope it doesn't upset you too much. Ann is not with me here at the Nelsons'. Instead, she is staying on a farm some miles south of McKinley Heights. Our counselors had difficulty finding a family willing to accept two children. Finally, Ann and I agreed it would be all right if we stayed in different homes. I did, however, make everyone promise that we could visit often. Ann has been a good soldier about the arrangement. I believe everything will work out well. She seemed excited about living on a farm and appears to have already adjusted to life in the U.S. She doesn't seem to be homesick anymore.

I have not talked to her since we moved (her family does not own a telephone) but hope to do so before Sunday night. Please, Dad? Do not be too angry with me? I know I promised to keep her with me, but it was the only thing to do. There really was no other choice.

You would not believe how the first family treated Ann. I think maybe they were Nazi sympathizers and hated the English. Their name was Mannheim. German! That is suspect, is it not? They were extremely strict. Whatever they asked us to do, we had to follow to the letter, even when it made poor sense. On Tuesday, Mrs. Mannheim reprimanded Ann very severely. I felt I had to do something. I argued with her and then all h__l (Excuse me, Mum?) broke loose. Finally, the Mannheims called Mrs. Studer to referee. Mrs. Studer is the person in charge of placing Bender evacuees. After we explained to her what had happened, she agreed with us and took us home with her. We stayed at her house two nights. Now both of us have new homes. In some ways the disagreement reminded me of Fran and Ernie's evacuation experience in Wales last year.

Anyway, it's over now and everything looks rosy.

I will start school tomorrow–two days late because of the change in billet. But that's okay. I'm looking forward to school but worry they might not fit me into the proper program level. Fred told me he had all sorts of difficulty his first day. The headmaster knew nothing about our system and could not determine in which form (they call them grades here) he belonged.

Mrs. Nelson explained to me this evening that they separate American schools into grades. The student's performance determines when they promote him–they say "pass him"–to the next higher grade. She believes I will be placed in the tenth grade. (Fred is two years younger than me and is in eighth grade.) They call the seventh and eighth grades junior high school. Starting with the ninth grade, they call it simply high school. First year high school students are known as "freshmen", second year students are "sophomores", third year students are "juniors", and fourth year students are "seniors". The principal (equivalent to our headmaster) will decide tomorrow if I qualify as a sophomore. I hope I do because Meg is a sophomore, and we could study together.

I hope you understand all this! It's very complicated and confusing, isn't it? Not like our English system.

No matter where they put me, I still will be able to walk to school with Fred and Meg. Betsy Ross Junior High School is next door to Oakton High School. It will be great to have their company.

Well, dears, it is getting late and I should turn out the lamp here on my writing desk and go to bed. Would you believe it? My bedroom is so large that I have a writing desk of my very own. It will be a super place to study. The room makes me almost believe I have become a prince.

Take care and say "hello" to all my old chums.

Love and kisses,

Graham

P.S. Ann and I are still waiting for a letter from you. We both miss you terribly.

Chapter 37

Thursday, 5 September 1940

Ida Schaefer was proud of her kitchen. Although not modern, it was large and neat. An old wood burning stove stood on the west wall opposite the outside door. Its built-in boiler provided the hot water needed to cook, wash, and bathe. The wash area, to the right of the door, consisted of a sink with a small hand pump at one end and a drain board at the other. A window above the sink looked eastward over the well-kept yard. Beyond the yard was the barn. Inside the kitchen, to the left of the door, was the icebox. A worktable, with storage space below, ran along the south wall. A window above the worktable faced the wooded area behind the house. A three-cornered cupboard stood in the northwest corner. Between the icebox and cupboard were two doors; one provided access to the pantry, the other to the cellar stairs. An archway between the stove and cupboard led to the dining room.

Even with the abundant cookbooks, spice jars, canisters, and other kitchen tools stored on the shelf above the worktable and the pots, pans, utensils, and dishes stored in the cupboard and in the storage space below the worktable, the kitchen looked neat and orderly. There was no doubt it was a clean and often scrubbed room.

Jars of canned fruit and vegetables, evidence of many hours of work, filled the pantry. A smell of newly baked bread mingled with the smell of ginger from the cookie tin on the pantry shelf, the spices stored in the cupboard, and the musty smell emanating from the damp cellar below.

The dining room, sparsely furnished, contained a large old oak table in the center surrounded by eight heavy chairs. A china closet with a large mirror stood on the north wall. There were two windows, one faced south overlooking the same woods seen from the kitchen; the other faced west looking towards a small pond. A porch outside the west wall of the dining room connected to the living room through a door at the north end of the porch. A door on the west wall of the dining room connected to a small vestibule. Two doors from the vestibule led to a downstairs bedroom and the second floor stairway. There was an archway between the dining and living rooms.

The living room contained a mohair sofa, two overstuffed chairs, a straight chair, and, dominant to the room, a large upright piano. Small tables with ornate kerosene lamps sat next to the sofa and each chair. Sitting on the piano top was a small lamp and a large collection of garishly framed photographs of family members. A battery operated console radio with one of the new electric tuning eyes sat along the wall not far from the sofa.

The downstairs bedroom, used by Ida and Jack, was barely large enough to hold a double bed, a chest, and a small dressing table. The pieces formed a matched colonial style maple set and clearly showed the wear from long and hard use.

There were three small bedrooms and a small bath area upstairs. The bath contained a copper bathtub and a small wash basin. There was a medicine chest, with a mirrored door, mounted over the basin. A pitcher filled with water sat on the stand beside the wash basin. There was no running water. To make room for the tub it had been necessary to remove the door. A curtain hung over the doorway where the door had been. A small window provided light.

"That's Ned's room, and that's Karen's," Ida said, pointing to two of the bedrooms. "This one is yours, Ann."

Neat lace curtains hung at each window of the freshly painted room. From one window, Ann could see the pond and, beyond it, several tree covered hills. From the other, she could see the woods. A four poster bed was the central piece of furniture. An old badly scarred table, meant to serve dual purposes of both a dressing and a writing table, stood in one corner. There was a coal oil lamp on the table. A small portable cupboard provided space to hang clothes. The drawers underneath the dressing table provided space for folded clothes.

Neatness was what impressed Ann the most. Everywhere she looked, everything was clean and tidy. Although the house was old and sparsely furnished, Ann felt a special, warm feeling towards it. She wasn't certain why; it wasn't something easily identified, but there was some sort of underlying charm, something most homes did not have.

"Oh, I like it, Aunt Ida," Ann said, starting to hug Ida. Thinking a hug might be too bold, she backed away.

"Come here, child," Ida said, holding out her hands. "We can hug if you wish. You will find we are a family who often hug."

She took Ann in her arms and held her tightly for a long time. It was the second time Ida had hugged her in only a few minutes. It felt so good. Tears formed in Ann's eyes. "How different from the Mannheims," she thought.

"Now then, I will leave you for the time being. You might wish to unpack your clothes and freshen yourself," Ida said, as she released Ann. "Do you have running water and electricity in your home in England?"

"Yes, ma'am, we do."

"Then I fear you'll find living here a little rustic in comparison. I hope it doesn't bother you too much. We hope to have electricity by next summer. Once we do, we can install an electric pump and have running water. Until then, we must put up with some inconveniences. The toilet is outside and the hot water for washing is in the boiler on the kitchen stove."

Ann thought all this was ironic. Everyone had been saying how much more modern America was compared to England, but here she was, about to live in a home that was more primitive than anything she had known, perhaps even more primitive than Aunt Gladys'. "Oh I don't mind, Aunt Ida," she replied politely, while silently wondering if she would ever adjust to outside toilet facilities.

"I suggest you rest for a while after you unpack. Ned promised me he would show you around the farm after supper. Although you are free to explore yourself, I think it best if you wait for him. There are a number of areas where you should know what to look for to keep out of trouble. Ned will point them out to you. To reach the toilet, we call it the 'outhouse', go through the kitchen door and follow the path. The toilet is behind the tool shed. It's the little building with the quarter-moon cutout above the door. You can't miss it. If nothing else, you'll be able to smell it." Ida laughed at this last statement.

Ann unpacked her things, hung them up, and, failing to think of any other excuse to delay, went downstairs and followed the path to the out-house. "I'll never be able to sit in there," she thought as she approached it hesitatingly. "The smell is horrible–and look at all the spider webs! How can people live this way?" Using as much resolve as she could muster, she finally managed to enter. Much to her surprise, she quickly overcame most of her initial fears. It wasn't quite as bad as she had anticipated.

Afterwards, she headed back to the house. About half way to the kitchen door, she met a large white gander. "What a handsome swan," she said mistakenly, and reached to pet it. Suddenly, the gander lunged at her and began nipping at her ankles and knees. Ann turned and ran down the path, screaming, the gander in pursuit.

Ida was at the sink when she heard Ann scream. She looked out the window, saw what was happening, and rushed out the door. By then Ann had circled around the yard and was nearly to the kitchen door. "Shoo!" Ida yelled, waving her arms and swatting at the gander. "Leave her be! Get out of here, Gus! Scat!"

The gander, sensing Ida meant what she said, stopped, turned, and waddled away. "Don't let old Gus intimidate you, Ann. Just show him you're the boss. He'll leave you alone."

Ann was not certain she believed Ida's advice, and even if she did, she wondered if she could convince 'old Gus' who the boss really was. She did not look forward to the next trip outside alone.

Back in her room she began to feel extremely melancholy and homesick. It was the worst she had felt since arriving in Ohio. Everything seemed hopeless. She had promised Mrs. Studer she would stay on the farm, but here she was, in a place where there was little chance she could ever endure all the inconveniences and hardships. "If only I were home," she thought as she collapsed on the bed and began to sob. Soon she was asleep. She slept until Ida called her for supper.

"Have you spent much time on a farm?" Jack asked.

"No, sir. I haven't. The closest I've been to a farm is the London Zoo."

"My, my! Then you're in for a lot of new experiences. What do you know about the care and feeding of farm animals?" Jack continued.

"I'm sorry, Mr. Schaefer. I fear you'll find I'm quite naive about everything when it comes to farming."

"Here now, that will never do. Let's put a stop to it. Right now!" Jack said, looking rather sternly at Ann.

Ann's heart sank. Why was he angry? Couldn't he understand? She simply did not have any farm experience. She was willing to learn– but he had to give her a little time!

"This is important, Ann. I want you to remember it well," Jack ordered. "Ida told me you agreed to call me 'Uncle Jack'. None of this, 'Mr. Schaefer' nonsense. Call me 'Uncle Jack'. Please." His laugh was almost as hearty as Ida's.

Ann was relieved. She smiled and answered, "Yes, sir. I mean: yes, Uncle Jack."

"When we're finished eating, I'll take you on a tour of the barn and a little walk around the farm," Ned said, smiling.

"I would like that. I haven't seen anything outside; except the toilet and old Gus. Oh! excuse me? I guess you call it the outhouse," she said, trying desperately to use the proper words. She wanted badly to fit into this family.

"I hear Gus chased you today," Karen teased.

"Aunt Ida told me I must show him who's the boss. I hope I can do that. Right now I'm not so certain," Ann answered, slightly embarrassed.

"Don't fret about it, child," Ida interrupted. "It'll take several days to learn the ins and outs around here. Before long you will be a farmer, just like the rest of us."

"Be careful, Ann. Can't you see what they're doing? They aim to take advantage of your innocence. They'll load you with all the nasty chores. All the things they don't want to do themselves," Karen said with a smile.

"Look who's talking," chimed in Ned. "It's mostly your chores that Ann will be doing. You're the one who shirked her duty, Karen. It's you who chose a career as a barmaid, rather than as a farm girl."

"You're simply jealous, Ned. You know perfectly well you would leave the farm right now if you could figure an honorable way to do it," Karen snapped back. She turned back to Ann. "Don't let them burden you with too many chores, Ann. They will, you know? Why they had me so loaded down with work that I had almost no time for anything else. They had me working from dawn to dusk. The only way I could find relief was to find work at Klink's Tavern."

"Yes, you poor dear. We certainly overworked you. It took the rest of us about fifteen minutes to take over all your duties," laughed Jack.

"Actually, Dad and I saved half an hour each day. Now we don't need to fix the things Karen was always breaking," Ned teased.

"Well, just be careful, Ann. They're all slave-masters," Karen warned.

"That's enough teasing for tonight," Ida scolded. "Poor Ann will be ready to leave us before her first day ends. Don't believe anything they said, Ann. They just love to tease. Now let's have some dessert and coffee."

After a second piece of apple pie, Ned took Ann to the barn. He explained how the cows were fed and milked, introduced her to the new piglets, let her pet the workhorses, showed her the roosting hens in the hen house, chased away the angry rooster, explained the operation of the new separator in the milk house, demonstrated the potato sorter and bagger, looked at the new brood of baby chicks, and let her play with several of the cats outside the milk house. Afterwards, he took her to the top of the knoll just behind the house where she could see most of the one hundred-fifty acre Schaefer farm.

"It's too bad you weren't here earlier, Ann," Ned said. "We just finished the potato harvest yesterday. In order to pick the potatoes we hire additional help. Most are local school children. Had you been here you would have met some of your schoolmates. Now you must wait until next Monday."

"On Monday? School starts next Monday?" Ann asked. "I thought it started Wednesday?"

"It did in McKinley Heights and Oakton, but in Dexter Hills and the other farming towns it starts later. The farmers need all the extra help they can get this time of year. It gives us a few more days to work the farm. A extra few days help considerably."

"It would have been nice to have met them before school started," she agreed. "To be honest, going to school has me worried. I imagine it's frightfully different from what I'm used to in England. Mostly though, I worry the children won't accept me. They'll probably treat me as a foreigner–which, of course, I am."

"Oh, I wouldn't worry about it, Ann. You'll find American children are quite friendly. You seem very bright. You shouldn't have any difficulties with your studies. I bet before long you'll be at the top of the class."

"I hope you're right. I hope they like me and treat me fairly. If not, it will be a lonely stay for me." Ann continued to fret.

"Now don't you worry about that. If you have any problems, just come to me, Karen, or Mom and Dad. We're here, whenever you need us. We want you to have a good time while you're here. We don't want anything to go wrong. I'll always be available at school too. That's one of the advantages of going to school in Dexter Hills. The school is small and all the classes meet in the same building. I'll be a sophomore this fall."

"Thank you, Ned. Your kindness and concerns are very helpful. If I'm treated as well on Monday as I have been by the Schaefer family today, there certainly should be nothing to fear.

"Even so, I find it difficult being so far from home, and so new to all your customs. For instance, I assumed you mean 'autumn' when you say 'fall', and I've never heard of a 'sophomore' before. You have such different names for everything.

But mostly, I don't even know which school level I'll be assigned to on Monday." Her eyes filled with tears.

Ned, feeling sorry for her, put his arm on her shoulder. "It's all right to feel sad and lonely. I would, too–anyone would in your situation. Honestly, before you know it, you'll feel much better. You'll soon be wondering why you ever felt so sad. Once you make new friends, things will look much rosier. I well remember my first time at summer camp. The camp and the counselors were very pleasant and helpful, but all I could think of was my family back home. It took several days meeting with new friends before I finally overcame the homesick feeling. But once I did, I had a wonderful time. Before you know it, you'll have so many friends and things to do, you'll be as happy as a lark."

Ann continued to cry. She supposed Ned was correct but found it difficult to imagine ever thinking about her mum and dad and not crying.

"Let's see. How old are you Ann?" Ned asked, trying to divert her thoughts.

"I was twelve - on June 4."

"I'm fifteen. You should be three grades behind me. That would put you in seventh grade. You'll be in junior high school. Starting with the ninth grade we call it simply high school."

"I suppose junior high school compares to our county school. That was where I was when I left England. I was in what we call the first form, just about to go into second form. What if I don't have the proper background for seventh grade?"

"Don't fret. You're smart enough. Anyway, all subjects start over again in the seventh grade. They just go into everything in greater detail, and move at a little faster clip. Karen and I will help you if you run into difficulty. Besides, our principal, Mr. Hartline, is a good person. He won't place you where you don't belong; he'll put you in the proper grade.

"Did I hear correctly? Your brother is staying in Oakton and your girlfriends are in McKinley Heights?" Ned asked, once again trying to change the subject to keep Ann from feeling sad.

"Yes, Graham is living with Mr. and Mrs. Nelson in Oakton. Sandy is in McKinley Heights; her picture was in the newspaper last night. I'm not certain where Edith is."

"Well, just so you know, Mom and Dad plan to invite them to the farm as soon as possible. They can come whenever and as often as you wish. I expect you'll be having sleepovers. Karen always did. And of course, Graham can visit whenever he wants. He's welcome to stay over, too. He can sleep with me when he comes."

"Thank you for telling me that. It would be nice to see them again," Ann responded, drying her tears. "I really am lucky to live here. You're all so good to me."

"We're the lucky ones, Ann. We're going to enjoy having you here. Now let's go over to the pond and see if we can find the wild ducks that nest there."

Ann looked at Ned. He certainly was a handsome young man, so tall, so wiry, and with such curly brown hair. Particularly outstanding was his wonderful smile. Ned was certainly special. She could not wait to tell Edith about him. She knew Edith would agree with her. "Perhaps Edith and he would someday be lovers," she thought momentarily.

What Ann would remember most about her walk through the farm that day were the smells. The mixed smell of straw, cow urine, and slightly soured milk in the cow barn, the smell of hay in the hayloft, the acrid smells of the pigpen and chicken coop, the musty smell of the silo, the smell of the straw in the strawstack, the smell of grease near the farm machinery, and the smell of the fresh clean country air blowing across the fields. At first, she thought she would never like those smells. In later years, she would look back on all of them with fond memories.

"Ann. Yoo-hoo, Ann!"

She could hear it plainly. Who was calling? Was it her mother? It sounded like her! "Mama! Mama!" Her voice reverberated as if in a well.

There was no answer.

"Mama!" She tried to cup her hands around her mouth, hoping to make her voice louder. She couldn't. She had no hands. She had no arms either. Where they should have been were two giant, triangular-shaped wings, brilliant orange in color and trimmed along each edge in brown. Streaks of brown segmented each wing. Beneath these was a set of large, cone shaped wings colored much the same as the ones above.

Her body was long, tubular, and dark brown. Two large antennae protruded from just above her eyes. She could not see her eyes, but somehow she knew they glowed iridescently.

An then she realized what she was. She was a butterfly!

"Mama," she cried again. "Mama!"

There was no answer.

She saw the garden. It was her garden. The one in Pinnington. There was no Anderson shelter. The garden was in gorgeous bloom, much prettier than she had ever seen it. Not the way it looked the day she left.

She flitted from flower to flower, from tree to tree, from flower to tree, from tree to flower. There were rhododendrons, azaleas, magnolias, flowering pink and white cherries, and weeping birch. In one damp corner, nestled among the flowering trees and shrubs bloomed pink primulas. Scilla-bluebells mixed with white wood anemones and pale blue pulmonarias formed a patchwork carpet along one edge. A path meandered between borders of pulmonarias, polyanthus, daffodils, cowslips, forget-me-nots and small pink and yellow tulips. Narcissus, mixed with bluebells and aconites, covered a slowly rising bank near the rear of the garden. Flowering wisteria sinensis behind domes of clipped box decorated the house.

She darted to the left; she flitted to the right. She flew to the top of the trees. She tasted the dew on the white snowdrops, sipped on the juices of the wild strawberries, and felt the cool spray of the bubbling fountain.

"Mama," she cried again.

There was still no answer.

Chapter 38

Friday, 6 September 1940

Oliver could hardly believe school would start next Monday. It seemed the summer had gone by much too rapidly to do everything he had planned. Although he had made progress on Mr. Ramsay's summer assignment, there was much more he had hoped to do. Perhaps it was his fault, he still looked at the *Captain Easy*, *Terry and the Pirates*, and *Gasoline Alley* comic strips before reading the news, but at least now he found more of the articles of interest than he had in the beginning

He had not expected to find Mr. Ramsay's assignment as interesting as it was. He especially enjoyed reading about the war in Europe and the American reactions to it. He had never realized how horrible war could be or how intense and varied the disagreement between Americans had become. He supposed he sympathized more with those who said the U.S. should assume a more active role in the war, but he harbored no strong convictions one way or the other. Perhaps if he had to pay the higher taxes, or really thought the young men of Dexter Hills would have to go to war someday, as some people feared, he would have leaned more towards isolationism. The only thing he knew for certain was that he did not want Dexter Hills subjected to the terrible bombing presently going on in England and Germany.

There was one thing he had no doubts about however. In fact he was so sure of it, he was making it the theme of his final report to Mr. Ramsay. If the United States should ever decide to join in the fight against Germany, the war would be over in a hurry. Hadn't it taken the U.S. only a little more than a year to finish the last war? America, if it so chose, could quickly put an end to all those senseless hostilities. The idea that America's effort might not be as successful this time around, or even more incredulously, that America might lose had never occurred to him. After all, the U.S. always won their wars; it was inconceivable it would start losing now.

But Oliver had more important things on his mind today. He and his dog Stripes were heading for the old fishing hole just beyond the railroad overpass south of town. He was hurrying since he needed to be back in time to peddle papers; he didn't want to upset any of his customers. His dad had said this morning they would be working all weekend, cleaning the basement and garage. Oliver figured this would be his last chance to fish before school started, and maybe even for the remainder of the year. He had decided, in spite of the bruises, to tryout for the junior varsity baseball and basketball teams this fall. Eligibility for JV was one of the more exciting things about the seventh grade. Oliver could at last begin participating in real athletic contests instead of those silly intramural games. He knew the town folks didn't consider JV very important, but it was a necessary step if one had any hope of joining the high school varsity teams. Since he intended to keep his paper route, there would be little time for fishing once the season started with all the added practices and games he'd be attending.

Oliver was thinking about his chances of making the baseball team as he walked along the railroad tracks and was not paying particular attention to either side of the roadbed. Thus it startled him when Stripes began to growl. "What is it fella?" he asked, as he tried to see what had caught Stripes' attention.

Surprised to see something in the small clearing several yards to the side of the roadbed, partially hidden by a large clump of brambles, Oliver felt a little shiver run down his spine. Then he realized it was only a ragged tramp sitting there. Hoboes usually did not cause Oliver much concern; it was not unusual to meet them walking along the railroad tracks. They didn't scare him, at least not unless he came upon them unexpectedly, as he had this time.

Grandpa Schumacher often complained to Oliver about the number of tramps passing through Dexter Hills. He was always saying it would be a grand day when the U.S. economy recovered sufficiently "and all those bums got back to work." A tirade usually followed about F.D.R. and his "useless WPA and PWA programs and his foolish waste of taxpayers' money." "Those programs have not made one damn bit of difference," he would say, "there are still too many tramps and too many idle men." This would then lead to another of his favorite speeches which always ended with the statement: "Most hoboes are just plain lazy and wouldn't do a lick of work–even if you paid them a fortune."

Grandpa also told Oliver there was no need to be particularly afraid of hoboes, as long as one did not threaten or tease them. "Generally, if you let them alone," he said, "they're harmless. They are just men down on their luck and usually don't cause any trouble–other than pestering everyone for handouts." On this advice, Oliver was not reluctant to talk to them and had done so on several occasions, often finding their stories interesting.

"It's okay, Stripe. Don't be alarmed," he said, patting Stripe on the head. "Hi, mister. Don't worry. Stripe won't bite. He just likes to pretend he's mean."

"Hello, son. Where're you off to? Thinking of riding the rails?"

Oliver laughed, "No, sir, Stripe and I are just heading down to our favorite fishing hole to see if we can catch a few bluegill. Where are you headed?"

After asking the question he realized it was rather foolish; he knew hoboes often had no specific destination in mind, or if they did, they wouldn't say. "Oh, I don't know, sonny. I may go here; or maybe there. It makes no difference. Only thing for certain, I'll be going somewhere, hopefully somewhere new."

"Gee, that sounds like fun. I bet you have been to many interesting places in your journeys here and there," Oliver replied, trying to interject a little humor into their conversation by paraphrasing part of the tramps rather evasive answer.

"You bet I have. Would you believe it? Just two years ago I was traveling around the English countryside. I would still be there, except for all that German ruckus. Once Germany started occupying one country after another, I thought I'd better find someplace safer than Europe. Besides, at the time, it had been extremely difficult to find work in England. When I heard Roosevelt was making things better here in the U.S., I decided to come home. Soon afterwards, I had an opportunity to grab work on a tramp freighter. It was out of Liverpool and bound for America, so I took it. Unfortunately, things aren't really much better over here. All F.D.R.'s promises were mostly political blather, there still isn't much work for an able-bodied man anywhere these days. That's especially true in Dexter Hills; there just doesn't seem to be any work around here."

"Sorry. I know what you mean, most of the young men in Dexter Hills are out of work these days. Grandpa says the WPA and PWA programs should have helped more than they did. He predicts it'll take a significant increase in the production of arms for Europe before there'll be any noticeable increase in employment in America," Oliver replied, trying to sound as if he understood the national unemployment problem. "What kind of work did you do on the freighter?"

"I stoked coal. For five long weeks that's all I did. I hardly ever got a chance to breathe fresh sea air during that entire miserable trip," he complained. "The captain made us stay down below nearly all the time. It was really a rotten job. The Statue of Liberty looked awfully good to me as we sailed into New York harbor. Fortunately, I only signed on for a one-way trip to New York."

"Gee, you were in England! Did you find it interesting?"

"I suppose you could say so."

"Did you ever meet the king and queen?" Oliver asked, smiling at his joke

"As a matter of fact I did. I was in London during the king's coronation. They didn't invite me to any of the balls," he said, with a grin on his face, "but I was standing on a street corner when his chariot passed. It was really something to see. The chariot had gold trim and was pulled by eight beautiful horses. You should have seen the fancy uniforms worn by the coachmen and the king's guards." He leaned forward, close to Oliver, and whispered, as if he were revealing a huge secret, "Of course I can never be certain, but I think the queen winked at me as she went past. It looked to me as if the king was arguing with her afterwards. He probably was pleading with her to stay in the carriage. I think she wanted to stop the parade so she could talk with me. Unfortunately, I seem to always have that sort of effect on women. They just can't resist my good looks. I have tried to prevent it, but it always seems to happen."

Oliver laughed and went along with the story. "I don't suppose you ever heard from the queen after that?" he said.

"Well now, that's not entirely true. Afterwards, the word on the London streets was that the queen was offering a reward to anyone who could help her meet the handsome chap she saw standing on the Mall. Not too surprisingly, she indicated the gent had been standing at the precise spot where I had been. I thought about visiting Buckingham Palace and identifying myself–just to relieve her misery–but then I decided it was in the best interest of England not to. England had just gone through the abdication of King Edward, and I didn't think the country could stand another scandal so soon. I decided the queen would just have to suffer through her great disappointment."

"That was extremely benevolent on your part," Oliver snickered.

"Well, I saw m'duty, and I did m'duty. It's the way I am–always willing to sacrifice for the good of the country," he chuckled.

"I would like to go to England someday," Oliver mused. "I think it would be super to visit a great city like London. I suppose the people there are quite different from us?"

"Oh, I don't know. There really is very little difference. You meet some that are better and some that are worse. It depends on who you meet, just as it does here. Now take you and me, for instance, we are both good blokes, but I venture we wouldn't have to hunt very far to find a rotten potato, somebody we could easily hate."

"I suppose you're right, but I'd need to meet a few Englishmen before I'd be convinced of what you say."

"I assure you, lad, there are many wonderful Britons. I hope one day you'll get the opportunity to meet one of them."

"Perhaps I will. The newspaper reported some English children have recently come to McKinley Heights and plan to stay until after the war. They're called evacuees. Maybe, if I'm lucky, I'll meet one or two of them before they go home. McKinley Heights isn't far from here."

"I hope you do," the hobo replied. "They're terribly lucky kiddies. From what I read, it's almost certain Hitler plans to invade England this fall. If he's successful, England will no longer exist as an independent country. If those children were still there they might be shot or at least placed under Nazi tyranny. It's what has happened to the poor French people, and the Dutch, and all those other countries he's invaded."

"You're probably right," Oliver responded. Then, not wishing to reveal how little he understood about England, he apologized, "I've been on vacation from school all summer and have not kept up with the situation in England as much as I should, but I agree, things are bad." Having said that, it was time to fish. He called Stripe, bid the hobo well, and continued on to the fishing hole.

As Oliver sat on the bank watching his bobber, he continued to think about England and the evacuees. "Gee, wouldn't it be something if one of them came to our school," he thought. "Maybe he would be in the seventh grade with me. The two of us might become good buddies. I bet my understanding of current events and world geography would make him pleased to meet me. Come to think of it, knowing him might even improve my understanding of the world." The thought left him when his cork disappeared under the surface.

That evening, after delivering his papers and eating supper, Oliver joined some of the other boys in a pickup softball game at the high school ball diamond. As usual, the game attracted spectators. Among them, much to Oliver's delight, was Vicky Johnson. Vicky was, without a doubt, the most popular girl in Oliver's class. She had caught the eye of not only Oliver but almost every other boy in school, from the fifth grade through the tenth; perhaps even beyond. Oliver and Vicky had been classmates ever since the first grade and he had never had difficulty talking to her before but, for reasons he did not understand, it had become noticeably more difficult this past few weeks. Nowadays, he always seemed to be bashful and nearly speechless every time he was around her. As he looked at Vicky from his left field position, he promised himself tonight would be different, tonight he would find the courage to talk with her and, perhaps, even to walk her home after the game.

Unfortunately, Oliver made several fielding errors and was too ashamed to carry through on his after-game plan. Much to his dismay, he had once again missed an excellent opportunity to establish the new sort of friendship he was seeking.

Vicky was becoming frustrated too. Perhaps Oliver would never be smart enough to notice the little discrete signs she had been giving him. She was beginning to think maybe it wasn't his stupidity, maybe he just didn't think she was nice enough. But that seemed highly unlikely, considering the effect she was having on all the other boys. Surely Oliver should be affected the same way. She decided to try a new tactic. "Have you heard? One of the Bender Electric English evacuees will be staying with the Schaefer's this fall," she said to her friend Audrey, loud enough for Oliver to hear. "As I understand it, most of the children in the group are around our age. There's an excellent chance one of the boys will be in our class this year."

"Wouldn't that be great," Audrey responded, sensing Vicky was trying to make Oliver jealous. "I saw a picture of the group. The boys are all so handsome. Any one of them would be nice to meet. Can you imagine? How wonderful it would be to have a sophisticated Englishman as a boyfriend."

"It certainly would be lovely. How worldly those boys must be. Think how it would be to sit on the porch swing at night and listen to an Englishman whisper poetry in your ear," Vicky sighed, thought a minute, then added, "with one of those heavenly English accents. It would be like having your own movie star. Someone like Cary Grant!"

"Or Ronald Coleman!" Audrey cooed.

"Ooh!" they both squealed.

"Think how lonely he would be! Far away from home, in need of a real companion," Audrey said dreamily.

"Maybe he'd let me be his special companion," Vicky volunteered.

Oliver knew they were teasing. The only response he could think of was to act as if he had not heard them. "Hey, John, wait for me!" he yelled to his buddy, "I bought a new *Katzenjammer Kids* comic book today. Want to come over to the house and read it tonight?"

"How immature!" Vicky observed to Audrey. "Imagine reading comic books when he could walk me home. I'm afraid I have a great deal to teach that boy."

But Oliver was no longer thinking only about Vicky. He couldn't believe what he had just heard, one of the evacuees was living on the Schaefer farm and actually would be attending Dexter Hills school this fall. "Gosh, it was only this afternoon when I first wished for that," he thought, "Now it's really going to happen. Even if Vicky might find the boy attractive, I still hope he's in our class. There are so many things I want to ask him. By golly, should it happen, school might be even more fun than I had hoped. I can hardly wait to meet him on Monday."

When he mentioned the English evacuee at dinnertime that evening, it came as no great surprise when Oliver's father grew angry. It was his usual response to anything Oliver said, or did. "Don't tell me we're going to have a limey in our school. Damn it, we pay enough taxes now without having to support one of those foreign kids," he complained. "I suppose it's another of Roosevelt's cockamamie schemes. If the people don't vote that idiot out of office in November they must have rocks in their heads. I swear if F.D.R. is permitted to stay in office for a third term, the U.S. deserves everything bad that happens to it."

Chapter 39

Friday, 6 September 1940

"Ann. Ho, Ann."

Opening one eye Ann could see the flickering light of the kerosene lamp. She looked at the window, it was still dark outside. Could someone be calling her? Why so early, she wondered. "What's the matter?" she asked, sleepily.

"It's time to get up, sweetie," Ida said, pulling the covers off Ann and gently kissing her cheek. "If you're going to school on Monday, we need to get you outfitted today. That means a trip to McKinley Heights. What fun we'll have looking for school clothes, but first there are chores to do."

At the moment, school clothes were of no interest to Ann. The only thing she wanted was to go back to sleep. "A few minutes sleep is what I really I need," she thought. She turned over and tried to ignore Ida.

"Come on, Ann, the rooster will be crowing any minute now. "Up and at 'em, Miss Montgomery! There's no time to sleep; there's an entire barnyard full of animals waiting for you. We have cows to milk and chickens to feed. Don't neglect them on your first day at work, it'll make them too sad," Ida teased. "I'm going back down to the kitchen now; if you're not down there in five minutes–well, let's just say, you'd better be there."

Ann knew she should get up, but Ida had gone. She rolled over, pulled the covers tightly around her neck, and stared at the shadows flickering in the light of the kerosene lamp. It had been a difficult night. She knew she had had a dream but could not recall the details. Her only memory was that after it was over she woke up, missed her home, felt bad, and cried for a long time. "It's strange," she thought. "Why would I be homesick now? It's silly. For the first time since leaving home, I finally feel happy and secure."

Ida and Jack seemed awfully nice; and she liked Ned and Karen. Although she realized she had many adjustments to make, she was looking forward to life on this Ohio farm. She shouldn't be homesick now. She wondered why she had felt so melancholy and what had caused her to cry. Perhaps, after the excitement of traveling and the special attention she had grown used to this past month, the letdown had left her depressed; or maybe it was simply because she was finally going to have a normal, settled life again. "Now that's dumb," she thought, "as if everything were settled. One of the scariest days of all still remains. School begins on Monday. I'll be entering a strange school–in a foreign country. That's anything but normal. How will I make new friends? What if everyone hates me? Will I be able to adjust to an entirely different curriculum?" She began to cry again.

A few minutes later Ann heard Ida putting the skillet and teakettle on the stove and soon afterwards the sizzle of frying bacon. She seemed so much hungrier this morning, she wondered why. Perhaps it was the fresh country air. The window had been open wide all night and the cool breeze and clean air seemed to relax her. Except for her dream, she had slept soundly, snuggled under the thick, warm quilt. It was the soundest sleep she had enjoyed since leaving home, even so, more would feel even better. But soon the aroma of the bacon became much too luring; she jumped out of bed, quickly dressed, and rushed downstairs.

"There you are," Jack said, looking very stern, as he sat near the cook stove pulling on a pair of socks. "It's a good thing you got here when you did, young lady. I was about to come up there and pull you out of bed. Didn't I say yesterday there would be much work to do? To get it all done we must start early–we can't sleep until almost noon."

"Almost noon? It must be five o'clock in the morning!" Ann thought. She didn't know how to respond. He looked so gruff. Perhaps she was wrong? Perhaps the Schaefers were just like the Mannheims? Maybe all American families are mean and unfriendly?" She looked down sadly and said nothing.

"Har, har, har!" laughed Jack.

"You'll have to get used to Jack's warped sense of humor, Ann," Ida said, smiling. "He'll tease you, and tease you. He never lets up, never gives anyone a moment of peace."

"That's for certain!" added Ned as he came into the dining room. "Don't take anyone seriously in this house. It's a custom here to tease everyone about everything."

Just then Karen entered the kitchen. "It must be difficult for strangers, adjusting to all your pranks, Daddy. Simply ignore whatever Dad and Ned say, Ann. Even if they tried, they couldn't be serious."

"Odd," Ann thought, "Ned seemed awfully sweet and serious last evening when he showed me around the farm."

"Karen's right, Ann. Have we told you what a mixed-up girl she is?" Ned asked.

"No, you haven't," Ann answered, a questioning look on her face.

"There you have it! If everything we say is untrue and must be ignored, then what we don't say must be true. So what Dad didn't say must be true. Karen must be a mixed-up girl," Ned reasoned. "Isn't that right, Dad?"

Ann wasn't at all certain she understood his logic. She didn't know how to respond, so she said nothing.

Ned looked at Jack and they both began to laugh. Karen laughed too and gave Ned a playful poke in his ribs.

Ann was relieved. She began to smile. Everything was going to be all right here. She must simply learn to be less sensitive to the teasing. She could do that–if she tried real hard.

"I thought we would get our chores done this morning, then see what we can find in the clothes chest. Heaven knows, we'll need quite a few things if we're going to dress you properly for school," Ida said, as much to herself as to Ann. "There are some skirts and dresses Karen wore when she was younger; we can alter them for you."

"Ann doesn't want all hand-me-down clothes," Jack complained. "Surely we can buy some new things for her?"

"Of course, Jack, I intend to buy those things this afternoon. But first I wanted to see what was available for makeover. We don't have unlimited resources, Jack."

"Oh, Missis–er, I mean, Aunt Ida–please don't buy anything for me. I'm happy with what I have now," Ann pleaded. She was embarrassed to think the Schaefers were spending money on her. She knew how much of a problem money had always been for her parents; it undoubtedly was for the Schaefers too.

"Nonsense, girl. The Schaefer family never sent any of their children to school dressed improperly. We're not going to change our ways now, not as long as I have anything to say about it," said Jack, a serious look on his face.

"That's right, Ann," Karen joined in, "I can truthfully say Ned and I always wore nice clothes to school. As much as we kid around, we are a close family and always look out for each other. Now that you're one of us, we'll be looking out for you, too."

"Don't fret, child. We have enough cash to do what little is necessary," Ida tried to assure her.

"But you have already done enough, just by inviting me to stay here. You don't need to buy clothes too. I don't want to be any more of a burden than necessary."

"Your mom and dad are the ones with the burden, Ann. We really appreciate their stand against that paperhanger, Hitler. Fortunately for us, England is willing to fight him. Without your country's stand, it would not be long before we were at war with Germany, and no one relishes that alternative. Don't you ever worry about being a burden; the least we can do is take care of you," Jack scolded. "Consider it our small contribution to your country's heroic stand. We're so happy you decided to come live with us, Ann. Just having such a nice little girl like you staying here with us is ample payment for everything."

After Ann had helped Ida wash and dry the breakfast dishes, she accompanied Karen to the hen house where Karen demonstrated two of Ann's newly assigned chores, gathering eggs and feeding the chickens. Ann, at first, worried she would not like barn work but, after watching Karen, she decided the tasks were more play than work. The way the chickens, or brooders as Karen called them, defended their eggs impressed Ann. But she felt sorry for the wishful mothers-to-be, they needed some baby chicks to look after. She asked Karen if they could leave a few eggs for the hens. But Karen told her the brood had to be managed carefully. If they didn't, the balance would go awry and soon the daily supply of eggs would be in jeopardy. Until Jack decided otherwise, Ann would have to be content collecting every egg. Ann was disappointed, it would have been fun to have had more of those cute little furry yellow balls to cuddle.

Although Ann knew it was mean, she found an amusing method of feeding the chickens. Instead of simply standing in one place and feeding them, she would toss a handful of corn on the ground, wait until the chickens had nearly finished eating, then go to another spot and throw another handful. It kept the chickens running towards her. The way the chickens looked as they ran amused her. It made her think of old dowagers running about. She would have to describe it to her parents in her next letter.

Which reminded her–it was time to send another letter home. But maybe she should put it off until the postman came with the mail, maybe today would be the day she received a letter from her mum and dad. She wanted to receive that letter so badly.

*   *   *

They spent most of the morning searching through Karen's out-grown clothes. Fortunately, Ida was one of those mothers who never threw any of her children's things away. There were many outfits that fit Ann with little, or very little, alteration, as well as larger sizes Ida thought could be altered without losing their style. Ann could not believe how enthusiastic Ida became assembling the new wardrobe. It was almost as if Ida were the person receiving the clothes. Her knowledge of fashions and her eagerness to start the alterations convinced Ann she was in good hands. It was obvious that Ida enjoyed sewing and was an excellent seamstress as well.

Dinner, the big meal at the Schaefer farm, came at noon during the summertime while the children were not in school. When the family sat down to eat, the discussion once again centered on Ann's wardrobe. How little they had to buy surprised everyone. They agreed that Ida and Ann had made excellent choices and that Ann would look nice this year in school. Ann felt particularly excited. She had never had anything that even began to compare to what was already hanging in her closet. No one she knew had ever had so many clothes. Not wearing a school uniform was going to have some definite benefits. Of course all the advantage was hers, not Ida and Jack's. She felt sorry for Jack, he had to pay for all the things Ida planned to buy. "But, this is America," she mused, her naive idea of American life still showing. "They're so cavalier about spending. I'll just have to adjust to this new way of thinking."

After they washed the dinner dishes, Ann and Ida drove to McKinley Heights in the Schaefers' old Hudson automobile. Ann thought it wonderful that Ida knew how to drive. Diane had never learned, nor had the mothers of any of Ann's friends. Ann had always assumed only men drove automobiles. She wondered if someday she might drive.

The size of the McKinley Heights shopping area did not impress Ann. It contained the necessary shops and stores but did not compare with the high street area of London. She knew it was unfair to compare McKinley Heights with London. A more appropriate comparison would have been between the shopping areas of McKinley Heights and Pin-nington, or maybe the larger Uxbridge. Ann, however, preferred the London comparison–it made her country's facilities far superior to those in the U.S. and that made her proud, as Mr. Shakespeare and Mr. Newton had instructed her to be. She had to admit though, the merchandise selection in American stores seemed so much better than what they had in the English stores. The war, of course caused most of the shortages but, to someone as young as Ann, the shortages had always been there.

Ann was certain most of the clothes they bought would be entirely too warm, especially the parka, galoshes, and mittens. In spite of Ann's protests, Ida insisted they all be fur lined. Even the hood was fur lined. Ann thought the need for so much lining strange, she could not imagine ever wearing them; it could never get that cold. Nevertheless, she was very happy. All the new things reminded her of Christmas—but even for Christmas it seemed excessive. She had never had so many before.

She could not wait to tell Graham and her parents about her good fortune.

Chapter 40

Saturday, 7 September 1940

News of the war in Europe filled the Saturday newspaper. The headline, *"London Bombed Last Night,"* particularly caught Oliver's attention. With more interest than usual, he carefully read the article.

A large sortie of German aircraft, estimated at more than sixty-eight, caused considerable damage in London, England last night. Especially hard hit was the dock area in the East End. Damage was severe, numerous buildings were destroyed and many more were left with serious damage. Also hard hit was the Oxford Circus area near the center of the shopping district where a large number of incendiary bombs were dropped. The resultant fires were difficult to control. Debris on the streets prevented fire equipment from getting near many of the conflagrations and numerous shops and buildings were lost. However, by early morning most fires were under control. The fire warden reported those still burning would be in hand shortly.

It is impressive to see the positive spirit of the British citizens during these trying times. Ignoring the damage, most activities were functioning near normal this morning. The dock workers were back at their jobs and stores in the high street area opened on time. Almost one hundred percent of the sales staff reported to work. When asked about the bombing one determined sales lady said, "Hitler does not have enough aeroplanes to keep us from our duties. Before this is over he bloody well will wish he had never done this to us." That was the general sentiment voiced by everyone who this reporter interviewed.

Winston Churchill, the Prime Minister, voiced much the same opinion this morning when he said, "If Hitler wants a fight, that is what he will get." He particularly praised his air force pilots, pointing out the heavy losses they inflicted on the German raiders, especially the large number shot down as they entered English territory. He would not give estimates of destroyed aircraft on either side but assured everyone that the results strongly favored the British.

Others in the government are less optimistic, however. One official, who did not wish to be named, said the Germans were severely testing England's military resources. He believes the heavy raids are a precursor to a German invasion and told this reporter he expects it almost any day now. He then hastily added, "If an invasion does come, Hitler will soon discover England is much better prepared than he realizes. The will and determination of the British people will ultimately prevail and repel that wretched heathen."

Until the raid last night, attacks on London have been small and sporadic and almost entirely confined to the southern suburbs. Most major air attacks on Britain, which have been going on for nearly two months now, have concentrated on the airfields and industrial areas and have become increasingly more intensified in recent weeks.

Surprisingly, there were no major raids outside London reported last night. Some officials speculate this may represent a change in tactics by the German High Command. This would be consistent with the public statement issued by Hitler on Wednesday. Apparently reacting to the recent retaliatory RAF air attacks on Berlin, he was quoted as saying "If they attack our cities we will simply erase theirs." Reports from Germany say Hitler had promised the German people the effects of war would never reach German soil. "Now they know otherwise," one British official boasted.

Oliver knew he was late and should start delivering his papers but an editorial caught his attention. It read, *"Arms Lease Approved, Debate Continues."*

On Thursday the English House of Commons voted final acceptance of the loan of fifty American destroyers to Great Britain. The draft of this agreement was first publicly revealed on August 14 and is in exchange for a ninety-nine year lease of U.S. air and naval bases in the West Indies and Newfoundland. Included was assurance these vessels would not fall into another power's hands, either by scuttle or by surrender.

President Roosevelt has praised the agreement as another step towards an early restoration of peace in Europe. He stressed that these destroyers came from the last war and, although now obsolete, once refurbished, would be useful for combating the German submarine wolf-packs presently harassing shipping in the Atlantic.

The heavy attack on London last night has already caused renewed concerns over the wisdom of further U.S. aid to Britain. Several U.S. officials, who do not wish to be named, agree that if Britain loses its fight with Germany they fully expect America will be a future target of Hitler's maniacal attempt to conquer much of the world. If this should happen, they say, America will experience destruction and hardships unlike anything it has ever experienced before. They feverishly believe the only way to prevent such a catastrophe is to provide Britain with this additional aid. One official told this reporter he fears it is already too late.

Others, just as strongly believe, America has no business meddling in European affairs. They cite the cost to the U.S. in lives and dollars during its involvement in the Great War. With the country still racked with the greatest depression it has ever known, these "America-stay-out-of-it" advocates believe there are no resources available for an endeavor of this sort. "Let's take care of our own first" is the motto often heard. One official, who wished to remain anonymous said, "In 1917 our leaders assured us U.S. involvement in the war would produce world peace. Where is that peace? It is now twenty-three years later and Europe is again at war. What is there to ensure things would be any different this time?"

Many officials fear Germany will interpret this additional assistance to Britain as an act of war and hereafter would treat the U.S. as an active participant. Others say Hitler would not dare declare war on the U.S. They say he already has his hands full with Britain. Others argue Britain can only continue if it receives this loan from the U.S.

There are no signs these differences of opinion can be resolved soon. The only thing everyone agrees to is, now that England has signed the agreement, we will soon know the ramifications.

The editorial rather overwhelmed Oliver. On one hand, Oliver could see that it was better to stay out of the European dispute, on the other, there were compelling reasons to assist England. He could understand why it would upset Hitler if the U.S. began assisting England, but it seemed to him the country was already providing assistance by offering refuge for the evacuees. Perhaps all this would form the basis for an interesting debate in school this fall, especially with the evacuee attending Dexter Hills. Maybe he could participate in the debate. The point of view of an Englishman would make an interesting contribution. Oliver decided to suggest this idea to the teacher once school started. It could be just what he needed to shore up his new scholarly image and might even earn him some brownie points.

As he often did, Oliver slowed down as he neared Vicky's house.

He was glad he had. As he came around the corner he could see her in the front yard. She was practicing tumbling, probably the routines she would use on the JV cheerleader squad this fall. This time he would be brave; he would ignore his timidity and say something. "Hi, Vicky," he said, with only a slight quiver in his voice.

"Oh, hello, Oliver," Vicky responded, in a sultry voice. Her voice should have told him she was not as startled as she pretended, but he was too much under her spell to notice such subtleties. "I didn't see you coming. It's nice to see you. What have you been doing this after-noon?" she asked.

Even though he would be late getting back to cleaning the garage and his dad would be angry, he stopped. "I just finished peddling my papers," he answered quickly, then realized how stupid and immature the phrase must sound. "I see you're practicing for cheerleader tryouts," he noted, trying desperately to find something that sounded more sophisti-cated than "peddling my papers."

"I'm not really practicing–just having a little fun while I'm waiting for dinner. I don't need to practice; I won't have any difficulty making the squad," Vicky boasted. "I was sorry you didn't stop to talk with me last evening at the ball diamond."

Oliver's heart skipped a beat. "What a fool I've been," he thought. "She wanted me to talk to her yesterday. Why didn't I do as I had planned?

"I really didn't have time. I needed to finish some work at home– had promised my dad I would do it before dark," he lied. "Otherwise, I assure you, I would have gladly stayed and talked," he continued, com-pounding the lie.

"Could you stop by this evening? I would love to go to the library. I can't go unless you take me. The last time I became so absorbed in the books I forget the time. By then it was dark and I had a horrible time getting home. I don't believe I have ever been so frightened. If you were with me I wouldn't need to worry; I'd have someone strong to protect me."

It was a poorly contrived ruse, something he should have easily rec-ognized, the library closed early on Saturdays, long before dark. He shouldn't have been so gullible, should have laughed and turned her down. Instead, he wanted to believe her and ignored the faulty logic. "I'd like that, Vicky. You won't believe this, but I had also planned to go to the library this evening. I still have a few things I must research for Mr. Ramsay before school starts on Monday," he said, continuing to fib. "I've been doing a special project for him this summer and have some last minute facts to check."

"Then it'll be convenient for both of us. That's a lucky break. What is it you need to know?"

Oliver panicked. He hadn't expected Vicky would ask him for a topic. He said the first thing that came to his mind, "I need to find more information about London. It's population, climate, history. Stuff like that."

"Why England?"

Now what would he say? He remembered the news item. "I'm studying the effects of the war on the city of London. They were heavily bombed last night, you know?"

"I don't pay any attention to that silly war in Europe. Lucky for you though, I hear someone from England is enrolling at Dexter Hills this fall. I understand he's an evacuee and that most of the evacuees are from London. If so, you can interview him. That should give you some good firsthand information," she said. "Stop by to pick me up at six-thirty tonight."

He hoped he could finish the garage by then. But it probably wouldn't be a problem; his Dad usually was at Klink's long before that. "Six-thirty it is. I'll see you then!" he promised.

"See you, Ollie," she said, then turned and walked towards the house.

Oliver sat on his bicycle for several moments before he left. No one, other than his mother, called him Ollie. Not even his best boyfriends used that name. "Wow! Imagine calling me Ollie," he thought, "Vicky must really like me." A smile crossed his face. He began to whistle as he rode away.

That evening Vicky and Oliver went to the library and afterwards spent time sitting on Vicky's front porch talking, munching on cookies, and drinking lemonade. Before the evening was over they had agreed to sit next to each other in as many classes as they could in school. Although they had not specifically said so, when they parted they both assumed they were going steady.

Before Oliver went to sleep, he turned on the radio. The commentator was reporting another raid on London. It had been a daylight raid. The raid involved approximately three hundred seventy-five German bombers. One thousand fires resulted. Any one of fifty-nine of these in peacetime would have been considered a major disaster in itself. Nine were uncontrollable and reduced entire districts to rubble before they burned out.

That night two hundred fifty more German bombers attacked the city. Little did anyone know but the London Blitz was now well under way.

Chapter 41

Sunday, 8 September 1940

% Mr. & Mrs. Jack Schaefer
RFD #1 Dexter Hills, Ohio, USA
8 September 1940 (No 6)

Dear Mum, Dad, & Yvonne,

This letter comes soon after my last one. I hope you don't mind. (Ha. Ha.) I thought it important to tell you that <u>finally</u> I have a home here in America–at least it looks as if it is final. Unless I tell you something different you may use the above address for all your future letters. (I still have not received any letters from you. You <u>are</u> writing, aren't you?)

My prediction–see my last letter–has come true. Graham and I are no longer living together, which seems to be okay. Although I have not talked to him yet, Mrs. Studer said he is staying with a good family living in Oakton, Ohio. I believe the family is well off, i.e., rich. Their name is Nelson. That is about all I can tell you now. I imagine Graham has (or soon will) write all about it. My foster parents say Graham and I will be able to visit <u>shortly, and often,</u> so I should see him before long and will know more after we talk.

As for my new family, you would not believe how wonderful they are. It's quite an improvement over the Mannheim's. (Ugh! Let's forget the Mannheim's!!!) Their names are Ida and Jack Schaefer. We have agreed I will call them Aunt Ida and Uncle Jack. They seem to be very lovely people. They have two children, Ned who is 15 years old, and Karen, who is 18. Ned is still in school and Karen has just graduated (equivalent to completing her six forms and receiving a higher school certificate). Now that Karen has finished school she is working as a barmaid at a local pub. (They call them 'bars' or 'taverns' in America.)

I know you won't believe this but I am sitting here writing by an oil lamp (also called a kerosene lamp). You see, I am living on a <u>farm</u>! Can you imagine? A farm! Picture your sweet little city girl–a farmer now! The farm is very nice but quite rustic. There is no electricity, no *running water, and a coal furnace heats the house with warm air circulated to each room through registers. Imagine, no nice cozy fireplaces like yours to sit by on those cold winter English evenings. They have not fired the furnace yet. The days are usually warm and the nights not too chilly. I'll tell you how well it works once the weather turns cold.*

Aunt Ida keeps a very neat house. She must do all her cooking on a wood burning stove. All the water for laundry (and bathing) comes from a hand pump. We use the stove to heat all our wash water as well. There is no inside plumbing. We must go outside to the toilet. Except for the spiders and odor, it has not been too inconvenient, yet, I worry, though, how it will be once winter comes. They tell me winter is considerably colder here than what we have in Pinnington–sometimes well below zero with plenty of snow. Brrr!!

I have just read the above paragraphs again and fear you may get the idea the farm is a bad place to live. On the contrary, it is very pleasant and I am convinced I will enjoy my stay here. There are many animals to play with, and according to Uncle Jack, some will require my care. He has already assigned me the chore of collecting the eggs and feeding the chickens. Karen tells me I can expect many more assignments. She says Uncle Jack is a taskmaster, but I think she is exaggerating a bit–he seems like a very sweet, warmhearted person.

You should see my bedroom. It's a lovely room with pretty wallpaper. I even have a desk for letter writing and school studies. That's where I am writing this letter. I enjoy having a separate room, but I must admit, Yvonne, I miss talking with you at night. I wish you were here with me, or better still, I wish I were back in Pinnington with all of you.

Now for some good news! Aunt Ida insisted I needed a large assortment of clothes for school. (They do not wear uniforms in school here.) Yesterday she sorted through all the clothes Karen had outgrown. She gave me the good ones. Most fit perfectly, those that don't she plans to alter. You would not believe how lovely they are. I have never looked so good in my entire life. But that's not the whole story! In the afternoon, the two of us went shopping in McKinley Heights. Aunt Ida wanted to buy the things we couldn't find in Karen's wardrobe. I now have a fur lined anorak and fur lined boots. Both things are lovely. It's difficult to imagine needing such warm things, but she assures me I will, once the weather turns cold. She also bought me some smalls (she called them panties) and vests (petticoats).

Poor Aunt Ida and Uncle Jack! I'm certain they couldn't afford to buy all those expensive things. I protested, then begged them not to do it, but they insisted. They certainly are treating me superbly. I cannot tell you how wonderful they are to me.

I realize this letter is already too long but I must tell you one more thing. Tomorrow I start school. I will be attending school in Dexter Hills. Ned tells me they will probably interview me first to determine where I belong. He thinks they will put me in either the sixth or seventh grade–I think seventh grade correspond to either our first or second forms. He says it's better if they place me in the seventh grade since it is part of junior high school. It has a more flexible curriculum and schedule than sixth grade. Sixth grade is the last year of, what they call, elementary school. Ned will be in tenth grade, also called the sophomore year. (High school includes the ninth through twelfth grades; junior high, the seventh and eighth grades.) Sounds complicated doesn't it? Ned assures me it will soon all make sense to me and I will enjoy going to school in America. I worry though! I am rather anxious about starting tomorrow.

I miss all of you and wish I were back in jolly old England even though, according to the papers here, you are having a rough time of it. I hope the air raids around London haven't damaged Pinnington. I worry about you every time I read the news, or see a newsreel. PLEASE! PLEASE! _WRITE SOON!!_

Love to you all,
X O X O X O X O
Ann

Also written that evening, unbeknownst to Ann, was the following note from Ida.

RFD #1, Dexter Hills, Ohio USA
8 September 1940

Dear Mr. and Mrs. Montgomery,

Please excuse my intrusion on what I am certain is a very busy and worrisome time for you. I simply wanted to ease any concerns you have about your daughter Ann. She is a lovely young lady who displays exemplary manners. It is a pleasure to have her staying here with us, and I believe she is enjoying her visit. You have certainly done an admirable job with her upbringing. We have not met your son Graham yet, but, from all the reports, he is an outstanding young boy as well. Ann is eager to see her brother again, and we are looking forward to meeting him. Although our first priority is to enroll Ann in school and settle her into a routine here at home, we expect to invite Graham soon–hopefully next weekend.

As you well might imagine, we have been extremely busy. Ann arrived on Thursday and school starts tomorrow. It provided little time to prepare her. Although the clothes you sent are quite suitable for school, knowing how our daughter Karen was always in need of new things, we decided to supplement Ann's wardrobe. Unfortunately, Jack (Mr. Schaefer) and I are not wealthy so we are unable to buy all new things. Because of the Depression that has plagued the U.S. this past decade, there has been little work in Dexter Hills (or for that matter, throughout America), hence little cash to buy anything but the necessities. To cut costs where we could, we examined Karen's closet and selected items she had outgrown which either fit Ann or could be easily altered. We bought essentials (mostly winter togs) where Karen's old wardrobe had nothing suitable to offer.

I hope this doesn't offend you. I know some parents do not want their children wearing second-hand clothing, but I want to assure you that everything is clean and no one will view anything as a hand-me-down. The truth is we spoiled Karen with too many clothes while she was growing. She wore some only a few times, many still look brand-new. Everything remains stylish as well. We can thank the Depression for that; there have been few style changes in recent years.

We have a very modest farm here in northeast Ohio and, although we lack many of the modern conveniences, we believe it will provide a pleasant and healthy environment for your daughter until she returns to you. If you could see our farm I think you would agree. I might add that our two children have grown up healthy and happy, which is further testimony to its suitability.

We did not attend church services this morning. We felt Ann had undergone ample adjustments for one week and chose to delay church until next Sunday. We are a Christian family and believe strongly in Christian principles and values and intend to make them available to Ann as well. However, we do not wish to impose our beliefs on your child if you think it inappropriate. If you find our proposal objectionable, we will be happy to comply with any changes concerning Ann's spiritual education you wish to make. We look forward to your instructions. Incidentally, we are Lutherans.

I have shared the above details with you to convince you Ann is being properly cared for and hope it will ease your minds. I hope to continue with additional letters as time progresses. If at any time you find we are doing something that does not meet with your approval, please, please, tell us. We will do everything within our power to rectify our error. We look forward to a letter from you whenever you find the time.

Again, let me say how much we appreciate and enjoy the opportunity to care for your daughter. Jack and I have often talked about how difficult it must have been for you to send your children so far away from home. We truly hope, in some humble way, we can ease that burden.

May the Lord bless you and keep you, and watch over both our families during these trying times. With the hope your horrible war ends soon and you once again have your children with you, I remain

Very truly yours,

Ida Schaefer

P.S. Please have no concern about us intruding into private matters between Ann and yourselves. You may write anything you like to her without fear we will read it. We have a firm policy in our household, we never read each other's mail–unless invited to do so. We will treat anything you write to Ann as confidential. Likewise, we will not censor, or read, anything Ann writes to you.

The headmaster was wearing a dark gown and mortarboard. "Ann Montgomery?" he said, glaring directly at Ann.

"Here, sir," she replied. A chill ran up her spine. None of her previous teachers had ever looked as stern.

"Ah! There you are. We have been expecting you!" He paused and examined her carefully. "You have quite a reputation. You are one of those evacuees, aren't you? One of those troublemakers?"

Frightened, she could not look at him. Instead, she looked at her desk. Its surface was scarred and uneven. There were initials everywhere. Most were her own, A.M. A few were different. Some were O.S., others were C.J. One, freshly carved, was A.S., another A.J. "How can I write on this horrid surface?" she asked herself.

"Where are your books?"

"Here they are, sir," she replied, reaching for her satchel. It was empty. Her books had disappeared! She heard someone snicker in the back of the room. She turned to look. It was one of her classmates. Everyone was pointing–at her– everyone began to laugh.

"I am sorry, sir. The books seem to be missing."

"Missing? How could that be? he asked. "Didn't you have them when you entered the room?"

"Yes, sir."

"Then you couldn't have lost them. Look under your desk," he ordered, impatience reflected in his voice. "Are you so incompetent that you misplaced your books? On the first day of class!"

"I looked everywhere."

"They're not there," she heard someone say The children laughed harder.

"Someone must have taken them," she cried.

"Nonsense," the headmaster shouted. He looked at the class, "Has anyone stolen Ann's books?"

"No, sir," they cried in unison.

"I thought not," he said. "Why would any of these sweet little American kiddies steal your books? These are the children of a God fearing nation. We only rear honest children in this country." He sighed, then angrily added, "But alas, all this will change. We now have criminals amongst us. Little heathens. Bad mannered little brats. English evacuees."

"Evacuee brats! Evacuee brats! Evacuee brats!" the children chanted.

"No!" Ann cried. "I'm not a brat. I'm not bad. I'm good. I always tell the truth. I lost my books–they surely were stolen."

"Get out! Get out!" the headmaster screamed. "No one is permitted to insult my children!"

Ann rushed towards the door, tears streaming down her cheeks. As she ran she stumbled over a satchel in the aisle. It contained her books. "Here they are!" she shouted. "I found my books! Please don't hate me. Please?"

"It's too late! Leave this minute, and never come back!"

"Wake up, child," Ida said. "You had a terrible dream."

"Oh, Aunt Ida," Ann sobbed. "They were horrid! I can't go to school tomorrow. They won't like me."

"Oh, Ann, you poor dear. Don't worry, they will love you, honey. Honest, they will. I promise."

Ida took Ann into her arms. Ann could hear Ida's heartbeat. It reminded her of her mum's. When she had nightmares her mum would hold her the same way. Soon Ann was back asleep. Ida gently laid her back in bed, tucked the covers around her, and kissed her lovingly on the cheek.

Ann dreamed of a small burbling brook, of autumn leaves, and humming birds.

241

Chapter 42

Monday, 9 September 1940

Graham woke thinking about Ann. He had only learned yesterday that she was not starting school until this morning and he was confused. It had started in Oakton and most other areas last Wednesday. It had to do with Dexter Hills being a rural district. Supposedly it gave the children a few more days to help on the farm but he wondered if it was worth the wait. Three additional days didn't seem significant. But no matter what the reason, this would be her first day and he worried how things would go for her.

What concerned him the most was that he had not talked to her since they parted on Thursday. He had planned to talk with her over the weekend but no one knew her telephone number. Mr. Nelson–that is Dad Nelson–promised he would see Mrs. Studer today and either obtain a telephone number or, if there wasn't any, get directions to the farm. Graham hoped Dad Nelson didn't forget, one way or the other, he had to talk with Ann before the day was over and hopefully see her yet this week.

Graham was worried. He knew so little about her new living arrangements, only that she had gone to a farm near Dexter Hills, with a family whose last name was Schaefer. What if they were mean? What if she were sad? Or sick?

He had failed miserably; he had not stayed in touch as he was supposed to do. He hoped she didn't think he had abandoned her. He wished now he had kept his promise to his dad, had never agreed to separate billets. He should not have compromised, should have insisted they remain together. It was, of course, too late to rectify his error now, but, at a minimum, he needed to make certain everything was all right.

"If only Ann's first school day goes as well as mine did on Friday," he thought. "Maybe then she could forgive me."

Things were certainly looking bright for him; he had no complaints as far as his own life was concerned. He was pretty certain he was going to enjoy his stay in America. So far the Nelsons were great hosts; Meg was turning out to be a wonderful foster sister; Fred was his next door neighbor; and school looked as if it would be enjoyable.

Originally, Louise had planned to accompany him to his meeting with the principal on Friday, but he had been afraid his new classmates would tease him if they saw him there with his "mother" and asked her not to embarrass him. After a lengthy discussion and considerable support from Meg, he convinced her she was not needed; he could talk to the principal alone. It was good he had; everything turned out much better than he had ever dared to hope. It might have turned out quite differently if she had gone along. His program might not have been as good.

Mr. James, the high school principal, had been quite helpful. After a lengthy review of Graham's English program, he recommended ninth grade rather than tenth. He said the material Graham had covered in England, in some cases would give him a slight initial advantage over his classmates while in others he would need to do a little extra work. But in a few weeks, he assured Graham, everything would even out and from then on he and his classmates would be on equal footing. He also thought the ninth grade would provide a better foundation for subsequent school work should Graham's stay last a number of years. It made sense to Graham, although he couldn't imagine staying more than one year. He quickly agreed, his only regret: Meg would be a grade level ahead of him, he would not be in any of her classes.

When Graham expressed an interest in airplanes, Mr. James recommended the college preparatory option. He explained it provided the most comprehensive educational foundation and the greatest career flexibility. With it, assuming he did well in high school, he would be qualified to study engineering, or whatever else he decided to pursue, at a college or university. Initially the idea excited Graham; it was the first time he had really ever dared think seriously of going to college. Then, recalling his father's opposition to advanced schooling, Graham asked what would happen if he chose not to go to college. He was relieved when Mr. James told him the program would still permit him to chose a vocationally oriented occupation, perhaps he could be a machinist or airplane mechanic. The college preparatory option would involve a little more studying but its flexibility made it a safer choice. He finally made up his mind after Mr. James added that it would undoubtedly increase his chances of matriculating once he returned to England.

Other than the requirement to elect the ominous sounding Latin I, Graham was pleased with his final class selections. He thought he could master them rather easily. They included American History, English I, General Mathematics I, Physical Science I, and Physical Education. He looked forward to American history. He knew England was responsible for much of the United States' early development and at one time had ruled over the American colonies; it would be interesting to see what the Americans had to say about that period. He thought English would be easy, after all wasn't he an Englishman. Mathematics and science couldn't be much different from what they taught in England, neither depended upon the country where they were being studied. "The laws of mathematics and science are certainly international," he told himself, chuckling at his clever substitution of "international" for "universal." And finally, he thought physical education had to be fun. "What a wonderful idea. Imagine receiving school credit for playing games!"

By the time he had finished with Mr. James, he had missed Latin, but all the other classes had gone well. The classmates had been helpful and seemed friendly enough; he liked the teachers; the textbooks looked interesting; and the homework assignments had been shorter than expected.

He was both surprised and pleased to find Fred in his physical education class. Normally eighth graders did not mix with ninth graders but "Physical Ed," as the students called it, was one of the few exceptions. Limited facilities in Oakton forced students from junior high to use the high school sports facilities and to share classes with the freshmen. While Fred, as an eighth grader, was limited to junior varsity sports, Graham was eligible for either junior or senior varsity. But the option made little difference to Graham. With no sports background he entertained no thought of qualifying at any level other than the most elementary and signed up with Fred for junior varsity softball. Fred had no doubt he would make the final cut; after all, he had been quite successful at cricket back home. On the other hand, Graham thought a miracle was needed for him to make the team. He hoped he would; he'd be embarrassed if he didn't, especially since he wanted to impress Meg. It was going to be difficult to wait until tryouts and preliminary practice sessions were over to know for certain.

The three children had much to talk about when they walked home together after school on Friday. They talked briefly about softball, but, to the amusement of both Graham and Meg, Fred had been mostly interested in the girls he had met. He said he had fallen deeply in love with Betty Lou in second period, but then met Anna Marie in fourth period. Anna Marie quickly became another "girl of his dreams." Still later, in seventh period, he discovered Jo Ann who was so attractive it nearly caused him to swoon.

While Fred had tried to decide on a strategy for remaining friendly to all three, Graham described his classes to Meg. They were delighted to discover that they would be in the same Latin class. Meg, who also was in the college preparatory program, needed Latin too and, since it was only offered in alternate years, she was taking it this year. "That's wonderful," she exclaimed. "We'll be able to study together. I'm going to need all the help I can get."

"Why's that?" Graham asked. "I thought you were one of the top students."

"Because the Latin teacher has the reputation of being a taskmaster. They say she gives long and difficult homework assignments and tough examinations. Wait until you see the homework she assigned this morning."

It was the only blemish on the otherwise perfect day for Graham.

When Louise learned Graham and Meg had only one class together, she was greatly disappointed; she had hoped they would share many classes as tenth graders. She suspected Mr. James had made a mistake. In her opinion, Graham could easily compete at the higher level; he was an extremely sharp boy. She regretted having let Graham talk her into not going with him to see Mr. James. She debated going in and complaining on Monday but, after discussing it with Ken, had decided to drop it; Graham seemed happy, and she supposed, in the long run that was best for everyone.

The weekend had also gone well for Graham. Already there was no doubt his stay with the Nelson family was going to be a wonderful experience. Louise spent Saturday morning with him arranging his room to make it easier for him to study and introducing him to the neighbors. In the afternoon, after he had finished his homework and Latin studies, he and Meg played several games of checkers and several sets of tennis. The checker match was even, neither player could win consistently, but the results at tennis had been less pleasing. He had never played before and lost every set. Undaunted, he assured Meg he would practice and practice until he could trounce her every time. "Ha," responded Meg, "that will be the day!"

In the evening, they listened to the radio. When Graham called it the wireless it sparked a long discussion concerning their language differences. Each laughed at the other's vocabulary. Milk and cookies–or as Graham would say, "milk and biscuits"–ended the night. Both Meg and Graham slept soundly after a most pleasant, but tiring, day.

On Sunday, after going to church, Louise invited family and friends to an afternoon picnic. By late afternoon, Graham was certain he had never before met so many people or eaten so much food in a single afternoon. Ken agreed. He teased him, saying he had never seen an eater like he was, a boy who could stuff himself with hamburgers and then attack the watermelons as if he had had nothing to eat. Everyone laughed. That is, except Meg who, in an attempt to defend Graham, had been unmercifully teased herself. They laughed at her and told her she sounded like a mother defending her child. Seeing Meg blush, Graham thought he should say something in her defense. He tried to think of something clever. When he couldn't, he kept quiet and later wished he hadn't. He felt he owed her something. After all, wasn't he her "brother" now?

Sunday evening Graham had difficulty falling asleep. The party had triggered memories of similar get-togethers in Pinnington. He thought of his dad, his mum, Yvonne, and Henry. The pangs of homesickness overcame him and he spent most of the night awake, thinking of home, and wishing he were back in England. He vowed he would write a letter to his folks on Monday evening–after school.

"Perhaps that's why I'm so worried about Ann this morning," he thought, as he dressed. "I'm homesick for her, too."

Fortunately, the challenge of his second day in school occupied most of his thoughts. He found the course work more interesting and demanding than he anticipated and quickly realized winning a place on the softball team was just as difficult as he had imagined. By evening, he had forgotten his resolve to write his letter.

He did not write the letter the next night, or any night that week. Although he didn't realize it, school and his new family was quickly replacing his previous life. His new interests were making it much easier to adjust to life in America. Unfortunately, the adjustment for Ann, and many of the other evacuees, was not going to be nearly as rapid.

Chapter 43

Monday, 9 September 1940

The day had finally arrived, Ann's first day in an American school. Now, by evening, she would have answers to all the uncertainties, or at least most of them. She would have a list of her subjects, have met her classmates, and have an idea of how they would treat her. She was not very hopeful. She questioned, as she had since the first day when her parents told her she was coming here, whether she had the intelligence to compete successfully in this strange new, totally different environment.

Adjustment to the American school system seemed insurmountable. She considered not going to school, running away instead. It would not be difficult. She would simply disappear after finishing her chores. But that was silly, she knew a twelve year old girl could not survive on her own for very long, especially in a strange country. Where would she go?

What would she do? Then she remembered her promise to make Britain proud. Running away would never do. She decided she would go to school, but it would be with great apprehension.

Trying to appear nonchalant as she entered the house, she set the egg basket in the pantry, carefully washed her hands, and without speaking, sat down at the breakfast table. Everyone could see she was troubled and on the verge of crying.

"Well, Ann, this is your big day," Jack said, looking at her sympathetically and smiling. "I imagine you are eager to meet your new school chums?"

"Oh yes," she lied.

"I'm driving Ann to school today. Tell the school bus driver he should expect to see her this evening," Ida told Ned.

Turning to Ann she explained, "I'm going with you and talk with Mr. Hartline. I want to be certain he assigns you to the grade level you rightfully belong. Did you prepare the list of school subjects you studied last year?"

"Yes, ma'am, I did," Ann answered, somewhat relieved to learn Ida would be with her, "but it was difficult. It may not be of much help, it's not complete. Listing the courses was easy, but including the details wasn't. It's hard to remember everything we covered."

"Don't fret about it. Any facts you have will be helpful. The more he has the easier it'll be for him. Even without it, I'm certain he'll quickly determine where you belong. He's a conscientious and thorough principal. He'll question you about anything he doesn't understand."

"Look at the time!" Ned exclaimed, "The bus will be here any minute. I'd better finish."

"It is late," Ida agreed. "We'll leave as soon as you're ready, Ann."

It was a common practice for Dexter Hills Junior and Senior High School students to arrive early the first morning of each school year. It gave them first choice of homeroom seats. Because it seemed to improve the children's disposition most teachers allowed them to remain in those seats throughout the year. Of course, the teachers always had the right to overrule, especially when they felt it necessary to separate troublemakers and over-talkative friends.

Oliver and Vicky were among the first into their homeroom. As many others did, they considered sitting together vital to their new budding romance. Their promptness paid off, they secured seats next to each other. When her friend, Audrey, sat directly in front of her, Vicky was completely satisfied, that was until Oliver's buddy, John, sat down. She was certain he would garner too much of Oliver's attention. How could she monopolize Oliver if John was directly behind him? She tried, unsuccessfully, to coax John into moving.

The school building surprised Ann. It was smaller than she had anticipated. Her school buildings in Pinnington were much larger, so were the school buildings she saw during the Bender tour of the McKinley Heights schools. But as she thought more about it, she wasn't surprised, there were less than three-hundred houses in Dexter Hills, even with the children bussed in from the surrounding farms, total enrollment had to be small.

The three-story red brick construction was typical of school buildings built in eastern Ohio in the late 1920's. Three tiers of large windows overlooked a carefully manicured front lawn. A flag pole, with a large American flag flapping in the breeze, stood in the center of the lawn. The main entrance to the building was by either of two large swinging doors located at the front of the building near the north and south ends. Inside, stairs led down to the first floor and up to the second and third floors. The classrooms on each floor opened to corridors ending at each of the stairs. The rear of the building contained a combination auditorium and gymnasium. The classrooms for the elementary grades occupied most of the first floor and a portion of the second floor. Junior high classrooms used the remaining rooms on the second floor. All high school classrooms were on the upper floor.

Ann and Ida arrived in Mr. Hartline's second floor office shortly before the first bell sounded. He met with them briefly, but soon excused himself, "To take care," as he said, "of those activities that always occupy a principal on the opening day of each school year." The delay concerned Ann. She was certain it was deliberate, a clever ruse to make her agonize a little longer. Ida tried to convince her otherwise but it did little good, Ann continued to fret. It was nearly lunchtime before he returned. After what seemed to Ann an excessive number of questions and a lengthy period of indecision, he finally concluded Ann belonged in seventh grade.

Because there were only a few minutes left before lunchtime, Mr. Hartline suggested Ann wait until noon. He would introduce her to each of her morning class teachers during lunch. She could get her books and assignments from them before afternoon classes started. Until the bell rang, Ann was to wait in his outer office. This delay, compounded by Ida's decision not to wait any longer, caused mixed feelings. On one hand, Ann was happy to postpone facing her new classmates, but on the other hand, she was disappointed the initial meeting with the teachers was still to come.

Another girl was waiting in the outer office. She was somewhat younger than Ann. After several minutes Ann overcame her initial shyness, "Hello, my name is Ann. Are you waiting to meet your teachers too?"

"Hi! I'm Margie. Yes, I was late this morning, I arrived only a short time ago. The secretary asked me to wait until she had time to escort me to my classroom. My family just moved here. It's my first day. I'll be in fifth grade."

"You're lucky they knew where to place you so quickly," Ann said, trying to be friendly. "They weren't certain where to put me. I just finished a lengthy session with Mr. Hartline. He finally decided I belonged in seventh grade."

"Why didn't he know which class you should be in? Don't you know where you were last year? Did you fail or something?"

"No, I didn't fail," Ann laughed. "I'm from England. Our school system differs from yours. Mr. Hartline had difficulty comparing the two programs."

"I thought you sounded funny. Does everyone in England talk the way you do?" asked Margie, her curiosity piqued.

"There are some variations. It depends upon where in England one lives. But regardless, our manner of talking is most proper. After all, English is our language; we invented it. We should be the authorities on how things should be pronounced. Wouldn't you think? You Americans simply borrowed the language from us, you aren't the experts," Ann answered, somewhat annoyed at Margie's comment. "It's your accents that are funny. Wouldn't you agree?"

Margie found it difficult to believe anyone with Ann's accent could serve as a model but, sensing Ann was becoming defensive, she changed the subject. "Where are you from in England?" she asked.

"Pinnington. It's a suburb of London."

"Gee, you're from London. I've read about London. It's big, isn't it? We moved here from Cleveland. I always thought Cleveland was big, but I guess it doesn't compare to London."

"Where's Cleveland?" Ann asked, naively.

Margie could not believe Ann had to ask where Cleveland was. Everyone knew that much. "North of here, on Lake Erie," she answered. Then, convinced the English hadn't taught their children anything useful, she decided to go on to something else, "Why don't we eat while we wait?"

The girls barely had time to finish before Mr. Hartline returned and hurriedly asked Ann to come with him. Because he seemed so impatient Ann did not take the time to say good-bye or arrange to meet Margie later. "I must find out where Margie lives so we can visit some time soon," Ann promised herself as she accompanied Mr. Hartline along the hallway. "Margie is a little young, but she seems pleasant enough. Maybe we can be friends anyway. She might very well be the only friend I ever make while I'm here."

Most of Ann's teachers were friendly and helpful, the only exception was Mr. Teasley, her homeroom teacher. He appeared more curt than the others. She hoped it was only her imagination. With each teacher, she had to answer many questions, mostly about England. They expressed sorrow over the terrible German air raids on London and were concerned for her parents' safety. The lunch period was almost over by the time Ann finished with the last teacher. Ann only had a brief peek at her school books and assignments before afternoon classes started. The books all seemed understandable. It did not look as if English or geography would be too difficult, but general math–she called it maths–differed considerably from all the maths books she had seen before and was a little more worrisome, but even it seemed doable.

She barely made it to general science, her first afternoon class, before the bell rang. As she entered the room she quickly sensed an underlying camaraderie between everyone and, much more ominously, a hostile attitude towards her. She supposed it was because they had been classmates for many years; she was an outsider. They examined her carefully as she entered. Few smiled. No one volunteered to show her to a seat. She finally asked one of the girls where she should sit.

"Any empty seat you see," came the girl's snooty answer.

She chose a seat at a vacant desk, but, before she could sit, a boy quickly slid into it. She nearly sat on his lap. She began to blush.

"Sorry. This seat's taken," he said, a grin on his face. Everyone laughed.

She tried another but again a boy beat her to it. "Doesn't she even know how to find a seat?" one of the girls whispered, loud enough for everyone, including Ann, to hear. They all laughed and Ann blushed even more.

Just then the teacher entered and the class grew quiet. He looked at Ann, as if he wondered why she was still standing. He said nothing, he simply stared. Ann quickly sat in the nearest seat she could find.

During roll call, when he called her name, she answered, "That would be me, sir." Several of the girls giggled.

The teacher called the next name on his list. There was commotion in the back of the room as some of the larger, more athletic looking boys began to laugh. "Oh, I say, old chap! That jolly well ought to be me, sir!" one of them volunteered, in a poor imitation of Ann's accent.

Everyone laughed. Ann's face turned a deep shade of red. The teacher, Mr. Casey, who was also the athletic coach, looked at Ann and laughed too. "Is there a foreigner in our midst?" he asked. "Do I detect a limey accent?"

Ann was not certain how, or indeed if, she should answer. She did not appreciate being called a limey, particularly in the disparaging tone Mr. Casey had used. "I'm English, if that is what you mean, sir," she replied, her voice quivering with embarrassment.

"Well isn't that just grand," Casey retorted. "Now, perhaps, we can find out why the Europeans didn't arm themselves when they had the opportunity in the 30's; why they permitted Hitler to overrun their countries so easily; and why England is so weak now." He thought for a moment, then continued, "Yes! That will be our class project this year. We'll compare American and European military science and technology. We'll attempt to determine why America's technology is so superior to Europe's; and why England's scientific understanding and productivity are so inferior to ours. We'll use Miss Britain here as our resource. Certainly, she must be an expert on these matters. After all, she has a much better education than the rest of us—at least that is what I've been told."

Most of the children laughed. It shocked a few, the ones who felt sorry for her. "How could Casey say such rude things?" they asked themselves. They knew they should challenge him but no one dared.

Ann did not participate in any of the subsequent discussions that hour. She sat silently, nearly in tears. Although embarrassed, no one could bring themselves to apologize to her after class.

Home economics followed general science. Ever since Karen had described it, Ann had looked forward to it. It would be useful to know how to be a good housewife and a good opportunity to learn about American methods of cooking and housekeeping. Although no one from general science helped her or would talk to her, the building was not that large and Ann managed to find the classroom with relative ease. She found a seat near the front and smiled when Miss Frank, one of the teachers she had met earlier, came in.

Miss Frank began by introducing Ann to the others and briefly describing the Bender evacuee program. Several of the girls, who had been in general science, snickered at first but, as they learned more, soon were as interested as the others. Miss Frank asked if someday, after Ann knew everyone better, she would tell them about England. Ann agreed–reluctantly.

After class, Bonnie Hoffmeyer introduced herself. The girls soon discovered they both were in the next class. They agreed to sit next to each other and, although there was to be no talking, whispered while Mr. Spencer, the music teacher, auditioned each student. Ann's voice quivered during her trial but Mr. Spencer, pretending not to notice, said nothing. Afterwards, Bonnie admitted that she too had been frightened. Knowing she had not been the only nervous person helped Ann. It made her feel much better and, more importantly, let her know there was at least one friendly person in her Dexter Hills junior high class.

The entire seventh grade class reassembled in their homeroom the following period. Once again, wherever Ann tried to sit, someone would tell her the seat was reserved. She was still standing when Mr. Teasley entered the room. "Class, I want you to meet Miss Ann Montgomery," he said. "She is visiting us from England and I want all of you to give her a warm welcome." He then turned to Ann, welcomed her, told her how pleased he was she had come, and wished her a pleasant stay.

"This row isn't full. Why don't you sit here, Ann?" he said, pointing to where Vicky was sitting. "Would everyone please move over one seat? That includes you, Vicky."

Vicky's face reddened with anger. If she obeyed she would no longer be behind Audrey and, even worse, Ann would be between Oliver and her. "That's unfair, Mr. Teasley," she protested. "We came to school early this morning, just to choose the seat we wanted. Now you're making us change. Move someone else!"

Mr. Teasley grew extremely irritated. It looked as if he was about to strike Vicky. Ann began to shiver. "See here, Miss Johnson, don't tell me what to do. It's my room. I'm in charge of this room–not you," he snapped. "What I say is law. The sooner you realize it the better off we'll all be. Do you understand?" Vicky shook her head. "All right then, move! Do it! ... Now!"

Vicky had heard of Mr. Teasley's temper. She complied without further comment. Silently she promised to get even with the new girl. She was not certain how, only that, somehow she would teach that limey not to come between Oliver and her.

The seating arrangement pleased Ann, it was directly in front of her new friend, Bonnie. But Mr. Teasley worried her. Obviously he had a temper. She had never seen a teacher display such uncontrolled rage. She wondered when she would see it again. She hoped it wouldn't be soon.

At first, Oliver was sorry to see Vicky move, but as he thought about it, it really didn't make that much difference. Sitting together had been Vicky's idea, anyway. They could talk before and after school. As far as he was concerned that was enough. After all, he had planned to be more serious in school this year, sitting next to a girlfriend would only be a distraction. Besides, he was now next to the English girl. Who would have ever guessed last week, when he talked to that hobo, that he would be sitting next to one of the evacuees today? What a marvelous opportunity to learn more about England. He looked at Ann expectantly. Then for the first time he noticed how pretty she was. That certainly was another plus.

At suppertime, Ann could barely eat after Karen told her about the telephone call she had gotten from Ken Nelson. Because the Schaefers had no telephone, he had called her at Klink's and asked Ann to telephone as soon as she could. He said Graham wanted to talk with her and make plans to meet.

It was difficult for the Schaefers to make telephone calls. They had to use the Ekenwilders' telephone, something Jack was not keen on doing. He did not like asking favors from his neighbor, but knowing how upset Ann was after her first school day, he agreed to make this one exception. Somewhat reluctantly, he accompanied her, and on the way he asked her to keep her conversation with Graham short. He did not want to burden the Ekenwilders any longer than necessary. "How dreadfully inconvenient," Ann thought. "It's just the same as in Pinnington. I never could talk very long on the Wilson's telephone either."

The moment they met her, the Ekenwilders liked Ann. Her good manners and sweet disposition impressed them. When Jack apologized for Ann's and his intrusion, Mrs. Ekenwilder scolded him and said, "You know you may use our telephone anytime." She turned to Ann and, shaking her finger at Jack, she added, "Don't listen to that old grouch, Ann. Whenever you want to telephone your brother, you are more than welcomed to come over and use ours. Anytime. Tell your brother he may leave messages with us as well. Whenever he wishes. We'll relay them to you as quickly as we can.

"We don't want that to be the only reason to visit us either," she continued. "Our children are grown now and have all left home. They have families of their own. We seldom see them; Jeb and I are quite alone these days. It would make us extremely happy if you would come over and keep two lonely old people company. Often! It would be wonderful to hear the voice of a sweet young lady around the house again."

Ann could not believe how kind they were. She knew Mrs. Ekenwilder's invitation was sincere and promised to visit again real soon. She wished her schoolmates had been as friendly. With the exception of Bonnie and Margie, no one had treated her very nice.

In spite of Jack's explicit wish, Graham and Ann talked a long time that evening, sharing all their experiences since their separation. School was the major topic. They did not talk about Pinnington–thoughts of home still caused too much pain, especially for Ann. Before hanging up, it was agreed, Graham would visit the farm on Saturday.

Chapter 44

Tuesday, 10 September 1940

Fred was in good spirits when he met Graham on his way to school. He was comfortable with his classes, having easily completed his homework the night before; he was confident the coach wanted him on the team because he had done well at softball practice yesterday, and most importantly, he had managed to maintain good relationships with Betty Lou, Anna Marie and Jo Ann. None of them had yet discovered he was flirting with the other two.

"Did you see the catch I made on second base yesterday?" he asked.

"I envy you, Fred. You seem to be a natural at softball. I don't know how you do it. I wish it were as easy for me," Graham lamented.

"I wasn't always as athletic as I am now. It takes time. With more practice, you'll get better," Fred assured him.

"I hope so. If I don't, I won't be on the team this year," Graham muttered. "Poor Ann, I feel sorry for her," he continued, changing the subject. "She was terribly upset last evening."

"Blimey, it sounds as though Dexter Hills is not a friendly town," Fred said sympathetically after Graham had described Ann's first day in school. "Her classmates must be a bunch of snobs. Thank goodness they're not like that in Oakton. We certainly are lucky."

"I need to see her. She needs lots of encouragement," Graham said. "Unfortunately, we can't get together until this weekend."

"Just knowing you're coming should be of some cheer."

"I've never known her to be so dejected. I hope she'll be all right until then. She even talked about faking an illness so she could stay home from school this morning. I advised against it, but I'm not certain she listened. Golly, Fred, I really goofed. I should never have agreed to the separation."

"You had no choice," Fred consoled. "Don't be so hard on your-self."

"It's difficult not to be. Ann needs help, and I am not there for her. I promised my parents I would look after her. Now here I am, in America not even a month and already I failed to keep my promise."

"After she's been in school a few days, she'll make friends and feel differently."

"I suppose so," Graham replied, although he still was not convinced. "At least she likes her foster family. They're treating her well. She seems to like living on the farm, too. A letter from Mum and Dad would help more than anything. She's been so homesick. I know she'll feel much better once we receive a letter. The absence of any word is beginning to get to her. Have you received anything from your parents, Fred?"

"As far as I know, no one has. I suppose it takes a long time to get letters across the Atlantic. They come by boat, just as we did and I don't imagine our letters have high priority. They don't contribute to winning the war. The ships are probably loaded with much more important things."

This turned their conversation to the war in England. They talked about the news reports describing conditions over the weekend in London. The Germans were dropping bombs on London both during the day and at night now, and there appeared to be no letup in sight. It was forcing the civilians into the shelters on a routine basis. Casualties were heavy. One news story estimated two hundred eighty-six killed and at least one thousand seriously injured in one raid on Sunday night alone. Amazingly, the raids had little effect on British morale. They only seemed to make everyone angrier and more determined than ever to withstand the bombing and repel the German invasion when it came. Reading about the stoic resignation of the people made Fred and Graham proud of their English heritage.

The reports that German bombers had been releasing their lethal loads over large, apparently random, areas in and around London, hitting as many civilian homes as strategic targets were their major concern. They feared for their parents' safety. After discussing it for several minutes, both boys fell silent. They said little more after that, they simply walked on in silence.

Just before entering the school building, Fred briefly mentioned the eighth grade assembly scheduled that afternoon. It had a two-fold purpose: to let student organizations advertise their planned activities; and to begin the process of officer selection. He was looking forward to the election. "I'll be able to see American democracy in action," he said, as they parted.

The assembly began with the moderator calling the group to order. As a first agenda item he asked everyone to stand for the singing of the National Anthem. Afterwards they would recite the Pledge of Allegiance.

The American flag was standing to the left of the podium. The students rose, faced the flag, stood at attention, and began to sing. Fred rose with the others and faced the flag. As they sang, he began to ponder what he was doing. He was an English citizen. The *Star Spangled Banner* was not his anthem. He did not believe it disrespectful toward England to stand at attention while they sang another nation's anthem, it was done all the time at international events. However, to show his loyalty to England he decided not to sing. It would make little difference anyway, many of the other students were not singing. But the Pledge was another matter. It would be an act of treason for him to pledge his allegiance to the flag of the United States. He still owed his full commitment to England, even if America was generously providing him with refuge from the war. But if he did not recite it some of his classmates would notice and perhaps be upset. It probably wasn't the wisest thing to do but, darn it, he had to be loyal. Before the music stopped he made his decision, out of duty to England he would refuse to say the Pledge. He would be firm if anyone objected, it was a just decision.

When the anthem ended, he sat down. The boy standing next to him, who had become his friend only that morning, nudged him, "No, Fred, we stand while we recite the pledge to our flag."

"Sorry, old man," Fred replied, "I'm an Englishman. I can't give allegiance to your flag. It just wouldn't be fitting."

His friend recalled reading a newspaper article describing a recent Supreme Court decision. School authorities had expelled two children from Pennsylvania for refusing to salute the flag. The children claimed saluting violated their religious scruples. The court sustained the state's ruling and upheld the suspension. "You really should stand, Fred. It's against the law not to," he pleaded.

The other children began reciting, "I pledge allegiance to the flag of the United States of America, and to the ..."

Several boys noticed Fred and began pointing him out to their neighbors. By the end of the Pledge most of the children around him had stopped reciting and were staring at him. "Mr. Chairman," called one of the students, recalling his teacher's instructions about addressing the chair, "there is one amongst us who refused to pledge his loyalty to our flag."

Others agreed and added their voice to the objection. Disorder quickly engulfed the assembly. The moderator, following the official procedure, pounded his gavel and called for order. The children ignored his command, became increasingly more hostile, and began shouting obscenities at Fred. Fred continued to sit, apparently unperturbed. Finally, one of the boys could restrain himself no longer. He swung his fist and struck the side of Fred's face. The blow glanced off harmlessly, but made Fred angry. He rose quickly and began flailing his arms wildly, hitting several boys nearby. The offended boys joined the melee. Several girls began screaming.

The fracas drew the attention of the teachers who rushed toward the trouble spot. One grabbed Fred by the collar. Another grabbed one of the other boys and demanded an explanation.

"That boy won't participate in our Pledge of Allegiance," one of the girls whined.

"He wouldn't stand and recite it. He must be a Nazi," cried someone else.

"Is what they say true, young man?" asked the teacher holding Fred.

"I don't mean disrespect, sir," Fred answered. "It's just that I'm British. I can't, in good conscience, pledge my allegiance to another country's flag."

"Traitor!" "Foreigner!" "Spy!" the students chanted.

The teacher, an isolationist who privately resented having any British evacuees enrolled at Oakton Junior High, had heard enough. "Come with me, you scoundrel!" he ordered. "You're going to the principal's office. He'll set you straight. We won't tolerate troublemakers–obstinate foreigners–causing disruptions during our assembly." He roughly pulled Fred into the aisle and marched him out of the auditorium. "How could you refuse to salute the American flag?" the teacher asked, shaking his head in disgust.

As they left the assembly hall, Fred noticed the other boy had been released. All the students were returning to their seats. No one else was being taken to the principal's office.

At the receptionist's desk the teacher paused long enough to state why he was there and proceeded immediately into the principal's office. "We have a problem here," he announced indignantly. "This boy has been fighting in eighth grade assembly. We have witnesses who say he caused the fight. Even worse, he refused to pledge his allegiance to our flag. He refused to stand while the others were reciting it. We cannot tolerate troublemakers. I demand you discipline him severely."

The principal found it difficult to believe Fred was a troublemaker. He had spent considerable time with him the first morning assessing his grade level. He didn't appear to be a bad boy. "Is it true, Fred? Did you start the fight?" he asked.

"No, sir. I did not start it. One of the other boys did. He hit me first."

"Why did he strike you? Did you refuse to say the Pledge, as Mr. Haines claims?"

"Yes, sir, I don't deny that."

"Why? Why won't you recite the Pledge?"

"Because I'm English, sir. I cannot, in good conscience, make a pledge to another country's flag. I'm sorry. I don't mean to be disrespectful, but I simply don't believe it proper to make a pledge I can't keep. My loyalty must remain with England," Fred replied, his eyes focused on the floor instead of on the principal.

The telephone interrupted their conversation. The principal talked briefly, looked at his watch, gathered some papers from his desk, and headed for the door. "I have a meeting now. We'll attend to this later. Be here immediately after school, young man. We'll decide what to do then."

"In the meantime," he said, looking at Mr. Haines, "ask my secretary to contact this boy's parents. Set up a telephone meeting between the parents and me. I want to discuss this with them."

Fred was upset as he entered the classroom. A discipline problem at school was the last thing he wanted to be involved in. He surely didn't want to upset Dr. and Mrs. Derringer. They'll be terribly disappointed. Still, he thought what he did was proper. It was appropriate because he had done it out of loyalty to Britain. It's what he had been told to do. He could still hear Mr. Shakespeare's words, "Never let down your guard, never let the Yanks take advantage of you."

Somehow he managed to survive the day despite torments from many of his classmates. Afterwards, when he learned the principal had again postponed their meeting—until he could meet with Fred's parents—he was relieved at first, then concerned. He would have to face the

Derringers at home and, more than likely, be the first to tell them what had happened. He did not look forward to seeing their reaction. This would probably destroy their faith in him. He supposed he wouldn't blame them if they sent him packing.

Softball practice was particularly difficult that afternoon. The team members were uncertain how they should treat Fred. They did not want to associate with a traitor. On the other hand, because he was a very good ball player, they did not wish to keep him off the team and jeopardize a potential winning season. But the coach made it easy, he said he understood how Fred felt. Although he did not sympathize with Fred's method, he respected Fred for sticking to his principles and thought it unfair he was the only one reprimanded. He, for one, was not going to judge Fred, he was going to ignore the controversy and, for the good of the team, would forget the incident had happened. The team members, their consciences greatly relieved, agreed and welcomed Fred back into their fold.

Graham and Fred walked home together after practice. Although Graham tried various methods to lift Fred's spirits, all his good intentions failed. Nothing he did or said seemed to help. Fred was quiet and refused to discuss the incident, or any of the other happenings. When they arrived home he quickly said good-bye and hurried into the house.

Fred knew he was in trouble when Sarah told him Dr. Derringer wanted to see him in the study.

Chapter 45

Saturday, 14 September 1940

Ann was excited. It was difficult doing chores while thinking of all the things she wanted to tell Graham. He had said he would arrive around ten-thirty. By ten o'clock she was nearly in a panic, almost certain something had happened to cancel his visit.

"Calm down," Ida told her, "your brother will be here. He's not late, there's still plenty of time. Why don't you help me with this bread while you're waiting?" She had just finished adding the yeast and was about to begin kneading the dough. "Start with this," she said, pushing the dough towards her.

It took Ann several minutes to master the technique, but soon she was working the dough like an experienced baker. Because Ida always baked large batches of everything, and today was no exception, Ann was still busy when Ken Nelson's car turned into the driveway. When Ann heard it, she gave a little squeal, ran out the door, spied Graham getting out of the car, put her arms around him, and gave him a hug and kiss. "Whoa, Ann! Take it easy. You don't want to hurt him," Ida cautioned good-naturedly. Then she began to laugh, "Gracious! Look at your brother, he's covered with flour! The least you could have done was wipe your hands before you hugged him."

Neither Ann nor Graham seemed to mind. They were already excitedly sharing their recent experiences. Ida looked at Ken and smiled, "I suppose it makes no sense trying to talk to them now. We'll let them be. Would you care for a cup of coffee?" Ken declined. He had too many things to do at work and asked if it would be all right if he didn't return for Graham until late evening. Ida assured him it was; it would give the children plenty of time to visit.

"Come with me. There's some things I want to show you," Ann said, grabbing Graham's hand and pulling him towards the barn. "Later I'll take you to a special hideout I found. It's such a peaceful place. You'll like it. I go there whenever I want to simply sit and think. It will be a good place for you to tell me all about what you've been doing!"

"Be back in time for lunch!" Ida called as the children disappeared around the shed.

Ann took Graham into the hen house and explained how she gathered the eggs each morning. She showed him the pigsty and horse paddock, demonstrated how to milk cows, explained the use of the cream separator, and described how they used the churn to make butter. They chased several cats around the tool shed and spent time playing with a litter of kittens they found in a corner of the tractor shed. Graham particularly liked a calico kitten and held it tenderly as they discussed school.

There were many tears as the children reminisced about home and how much they missed their mum and dad. They wondered if Yvonne had started working, and worried about Henry who had so many important military things to do, whatever they were. The absence of any letters from home troubled them. They assured each other it was due to slow transatlantic mail service but still thought it possible, however unlikely, that the family had abandoned them and no longer cared.

"Although some of the children have been pleasant to me, you wouldn't believe how badly others have acted, especially the boys," Ann complained. "Having boys and girls together at school certainly is different. I still haven't adjusted. The boys are such a tease and cause so many problems. For instance, our class meets in homeroom first period. Yesterday I arrived a little earlier than usual. Some of the boys in the last row started throwing spitballs at me. They aimed for the back of my head and some stuck in my hair. It was awful! They made them by putting wads of paper in their mouth until they turned soggy. I didn't want to touch them and didn't know what to do. I finally shook my head to get rid of them. By the time Mr. Teasley came everyone was laughing. He wanted to know why, but no one would say. When he saw the spitballs on the floor he became angry and insisted someone tattle."

"Did you tell him?" Graham asked.

"No, I couldn't. He's very strict and metes out very severe punishments. I couldn't snitch on the boys. That would have only worsened our already fragile relationship. They treat me badly enough as it is.

"But things seem to be improving. Everyday I'm getting to know a few more children. Some are quite nice, a few boys, mostly girls. I have one particularly good friend already. Her name is Bonnie. We chum around together most of the time now."

"Speaking of bad boys," Graham said, "I should tell you about Fred." He told her about the problem with the Pledge and its aftermath. "On Wednesday they placed Fred on detention and his foster parents, who were extremely upset with him, took away his privileges. But through it all, he stuck to his principles. He would not apologize and refused to recite the Pledge publicly. Wednesday night Dr. Derringer confronted Fred and demanded an explanation. Fortunately, he was able to convince Dr. Derringer that he was not being obstinate. He said he was merely trying to be a loyal English subject."

"What finally happened?" Ann asked.

"Dr. Derringer and Fred talked with the principal the next morning. After a lengthy discussion they agreed Fred would stand while the class recited the Pledge but he did not have to recite it."

Graham continued, "On Friday morning, the principal met with the Oakton Junior High School classes. He asked for volunteers willing to pledge their allegiance to the Canadian flag. No one volunteered. He then asked if anyone was willing to pledge allegiance to the British flag. No one volunteered. Finally he asked for a show of hands of those willing to pledge allegiance to any flag other than that of the United States. No one raised his hand. He then asked them if they thought it fair to require Fred to do what they would not do themselves. The students looked at each other and shook their heads. Having obtained their concurrence, he apologized to Fred and announced hereafter both *The Star Spangled Banner* and *God Save the King* would be played at all

Oakton school assemblies, in honor of America and the visiting English children."

"Then the decision affects you, too?"

"Yes, although a few resent it, the ruling applies to Oakton High School as well. I finally can follow my conscience. I must admit, I was not as brave as Fred. I was afraid to make it an issue. Instead, I stood for the Pledge and mumbled along with the others. Now I don't need to pretend I'm reciting it."

"I don't know why I didn't object too. I guess I didn't think enough about it. It makes me feel somewhat ashamed. Perhaps I should suggest we do the same thing at Dexter Hills? Mr. Hartline seems reasonable. Maybe he would agree," Ann mused.

"By the way, Fred told me when the children heard *God Save the King* it confused them," Barry laughed. "They insisted it was not our anthem but their song, *America*."

The hayloft was the next stop on the farm tour. They spent considerable time chasing each other and rolling in the hay. Soon Ned heard their laughter and climbed into the hayloft with them. "What are you two doing?" he asked.

Before long Graham and Ned were climbing among the rafters and jumping into the hay below. They repeated it many times, Ann did not participate, it seemed much too dangerous. Several more months would pass before she would muster the necessary courage to take her first leap. Once she did, however, it became one of her favorite farm sports.

After lunch they went to the hideout. It was on a bluff overlooking the Shiawasse River valley. From it, they could see Dexter Hills approximately one mile away. Not much was visible, only a few houses built on high ground and the steeples of the four Dexter Hills churches. Most of the village hid behind the hills or under the canopy of giant maple and oak trees. The trees were still green with only a slight hint of the soon to be seen colors of autumn. A narrow column of white smoke rising from the brickyard kilns contrasted with the bright blue afternoon sky. White, fluffy clouds dotted the sky and a breeze, warmed by the September sun, blew gently across their faces. The serenity and beauty of the spot touched Graham. "Oh, Ann, this is wonderful," he said as his eyes glazed over and he sank into the tall grass. "I see why you call it your special place. I could sit here forever, just thinking; just as you said you do."

They spent most of the afternoon lying in the grass, talking, and occasionally dozing. They discussed their American life, their new friends, England, and, at great length, their family.

That evening, to the delight of Ida, Graham was exceptionally hungry and ate heartily. The fresh air had enhanced his appetite and Ida's cooking was the best he had tasted since leaving home–perhaps even before then. He could have eaten more, but after the third helping of mashed potatoes, a fourth chicken drumstick and two helpings of green beans he was too polite to ask for more. Fortunately, Ida served apple pie for dessert, and his two pieces helped satisfy his hunger. On several occasions, Ida and Jack watched Ann and Graham and smiled, not because of Graham's appetite but because Ann had such a contented look. They had never seen her quite so happy.

After supper Ann, Graham, Ned, and Karen played Chinese checkers until Ken, Louise, and Meg came for Graham. Ida was quick to apologize for Graham's appearance. "Would you look at him–he has soiled his nice clothes. I'm afraid he's been into some things he shouldn't have. You know how children play."

Louise laughed, "I should have known he couldn't spend a day on a farm without getting dirty. The next time he visits we'll choose more appropriate clothes. But don't worry, there was no harm done. I'm certain everything will come clean in the wash."

Before they left, Graham insisted Ann take Meg to the barn to see the kittens. Afterwards, on the way home, he sat in the back seat with Meg and described all that had happened during the day. He told her how much he loved the kittens and raved about Ann's retreat. "You've never seen any place like it, Meg. I won't be happy until you see it."

Meg looked at Graham and reaffirmed her earlier thought: he was such a pleasant fellow. The sparkle in his eyes, the childlike enthusiasm for Ann's hideout, and, especially, his tenderness with the kittens were all so precious. She was glad Graham was the one chosen to come live with them.

Two fishermen sat silently in their boat, patiently watching the bobbers floating quietly above their carefully baited hooks. The only sound, an occasional gurgle as each wave playfully rippled beneath the bow. As if awakened by the early morning light, a mist rose mysteriously from the shining clear waters of the lagoon. A bugle call by a loon broke the silence and echoed off the aspen lined shores. Tiny white clouds, tinted along their edge by the rising sun, drifted slowly toward the east. There was peace in the world. The small girl smiled. She felt safe, secure, sure of herself.

"Hoo-woo-hoo," cried the loon, in its melancholy manner.

The man's eyes were heavy. He was nearly asleep when the bobber bobbed. He woke then drifted back to near unconsciousness as the cork once again became motionless. It bobbed once more, steadied, then dipped again. The man's eyes shot open, alert. "I think I have a nibble," he whispered.

Suddenly, the cork disappeared. The line went scurrying away from the boat, then turned and raced back. "A strike," shouted the girl. The pole bent as the line again sped away.

As if on cue, the wind began to blow and the little clouds began to amalgamate into one thick, black, threatening shroud. The force of the wind troubled the little girl. She asked if it would blow her away; then uttered one tiny girlish sob.

"Don't cry," someone said, although no one was there, "I am here to help."

The water surface broke apart where once the line had entered. A giant pike stood on its tail, splashed, shook its head, and plunged backwards. Advantaged now, within its realm, it looked viciously at the boat, swam forward with increasing speed and hostility.

"Shall I gaff it?" one man cried.

"It's too late," came the hopeless answer from the other.

As the fish struck the hull, the boat divided almost in two, one man in one part, the second in the other. Water cascaded over what remained of the deck. "You poor people! You are sinking!" the girl cried.

"We know," they said in unison, then leaped into the lake.

She watched as they tried to stay afloat. They struggled some more, then once again, but all was in vain. She saw the look, their fear as water engulfed their faces. Then they were gone. "Did it swallow you? Where have you gone?" she asked. "You poor, unfortunate souls. Have you drowned? It would be so unfair if your families could not say goodbye."

The pike laughed. "*Sehr gut,*" it cried, then swam away.

One of the fishermen reappeared. She smiled. He did not return her smile. He looked helplessly toward shore, splashed hopelessly, looked frantically at her as if to plea for help, then sank again, the water emanating a loud squish as it closed over his head.

She began to cry.

The wind subsided. The black cloud dissipated, replaced by tiny white puffs, tinted with gold. She watched as they drifted slowly eastward. Once again, the bugle call of the loon broke the silence and echoed off distant shores. Peace had been restored. The lake was calm once more, content to have eaten well; only pieces of wood, perhaps from a boat, gave evidence of its meal.

She did not smile, did not feel safe, secure, or self assured. "Mama! Daddy!" she screamed.

"Graham. Yvonne.

"Henry!"

Chapter 46

Friday, 20 September 1940

Oliver thought about Ann as he peddled home from his paper route. He had been thinking about her more and more lately. He supposed being from another country was what made talking with her so intriguing. Sitting next to her in school was really fortunate; it gave him a chance to ask many questions and, as a result, each day he was learning many new things about England. He was also getting to know her better, and everything he discovered convinced him she was a very nice person.

He had to be careful though, for some reason Vicky seemed to have developed a dislike for her. She was becoming increasingly more irritated each time he talked to Ann. He could not fully understand why. He wasn't doing it to antagonize Vicky. All he wanted was to expand his knowledge of the world. And he certainly wasn't trying to woo Ann–if that's what Vicky thought. But it didn't matter anyway, a petty jealousy was not going to interfere with such a grand opportunity, especially since there was no telling how soon she would be leaving. The war in England could wind down at any time, and once it did, she would leave, and the opportunity would be gone forever.

It was in geography class where he had the most time to talk to her. Vicky was not in that class so he could talk more openly. He had been asking many questions. In particular, he wanted to learn more about her experiences in the war: what life was like under the threat of air attacks and an invasion, what she did during the air raids, how scared she was when she first learned England was at war–things such as that. But she didn't have much to say about those things, mostly she talked about Pinnington, London, and her life before the war had started.

One day they found Pinnington on a map in the library and together they had traced the bus and Underground route from Pinnington to Buckingham Palace. Oliver was curious about the Underground. He knew it was doubling as an air raid shelter now, but he really couldn't understand why it had been built under the ground in the first place. It was difficult to believe traffic congestion could ever warrant putting the trains below the streets, especially since he had never witnessed a serious traffic jam in Dexter Hills or McKinley Heights. Ann had laughed at how naive he was and explained some of the differences of living in a city of seven million people compared to a town of only five hundred. Afterwards, he wondered which would be the better place to live. The fact that most people in London would be strangers while almost everyone was an acquaintance in Dexter Hills seemed to be a plus for Dexter Hills. But then he thought that maybe London would be nicer; at least then one wouldn't need to put up with the small town busybodies who were always prying into everyone's personal business.

Later, as he rode up his driveway, something told Oliver his dad was angry. He wasn't surprised. He had expected it, ever since old lady Herbold interfered last night. She was always doing that sort of thing. He wished she would stay out of the family's business. Her meddling had caused Oliver much grief and worry over the past year. She had no right gossiping about his dad and especially about his dad's drinking. Everyone already knew Ludwig Schumacher was a lush; there was no need for her to shout it over the back fence. It only made things worse for Oliver.

Every time his dad heard her raving, or even when it was only rumored that she had, it was Oliver who was the butt of his rage. Fearing his dad might be angry, he decided it was a poor time to be coming home. He quickly turned around and was nearly down the driveway when his dad staggered out of the house. "There you are, you bastard. Where the hell have you been? Get in here! Immediately!" he ordered, as he stumbled on the door threshold and fell, striking his head on the porch floor. "Ow!" he cried. Then he was silent.

Oliver could see blood running down his dad's forehead. Apparently his head had struck the banister as he fell. Thinking the fall had seriously hurt him, Oliver jumped off his bicycle and ran to the porch. "Dad, Dad! Are you all right?" he asked, as he knelt down beside him.

"Who put that goddam threshold there? Probably that bitch, Selma Herbold," he said, opening his eyes and staring drunkenly at Oliver. He lay there for a moment, staring. "It's damn well nobody's business," he screamed. "I'll do anything I want. No old busybody is going to tell me I'm a drunk. Go to hell, Selma!"

Oliver took a pillow from the swing and placed it under his dad's head. "It's all right, Dad. Don't worry about Selma."

Suddenly Ludwig grabbed Oliver's arm, cursed some more, and pulled Oliver to the floor beside him. "You little troublemaker," he screamed. "You complained to her. Didn't you? You put her up to it, you little tramp." He began wildly swinging at Oliver. Then, before Oliver could react, Ludwig was on top of him, peering down, drool dripping from his mouth.

"I didn't say anything to her, sir. Honest!" Oliver protested.

Ludwig ignored the denial and began pounding on Oliver's face and chest. "I'll teach you to talk to the neighbors about me!" he screamed. Convinced his attack was not punishing enough, he clasped both hands together and, with all his strength, struck Oliver in the midsection. Oliver doubled in pain. Ludwig panicked when he saw his son gasping for breath. Certain he had hurt him, he jumped to his feet, rolled Oliver over, snatched the billfold from Oliver's rear pocket, removed the two dollars Oliver had been saving towards the purchase of a ball glove, and ran down the street towards the tavern.

Oliver lay on the floor several minutes before the cramps in his stomach eased and he could breathe again. After, what seemed to be minutes, he rose, hobbled into the bathroom, splashed water on his face, and looked at himself in the mirror. Already his left eye was beginning to swell and turn red. He was almost certain it would blacken. Once more he would have to worry about what his friends would say. It didn't seem fair. He wondered how he could hide it.

All weekend he tried to keep to himself. He delivered the Saturday afternoon papers while everyone was eating dinner and the Sunday morning papers before anyone was awake. No one saw him until Monday at school. By then the swelling had gone down and the eye was not quite as noticeable. Most of his classmates, aware of his recurring embarrassments, discreetly ignored the black eye. But Ann, not knowing of Oliver's abject home life, expressed concern when she saw him. Oliver assured her it was nothing, said he had bumped into an overhanging tree branch riding down the sidewalk on Saturday.

Ann believed him.

That evening, Oliver's thoughts were only partially on the headlines as he scanned the newspaper. Suddenly, one headline caught his attention. "*Germans Sink City of Benares*," it said.

He began to read, *Liverpool, England: It was reported here today that a German submarine had torpedoed the passenger ship* City of Benares *on Saturday. The ship left Liverpool on the 13th and was 600 miles out of England. There were 406 passengers on board including 98 English children. The exact toll is still unknown, but authorities believe that 83 children were among those who have perished. The children were English evacuees headed for the U.S. and Canada as part of the Children's Overseas Relocation Board (CORB) program created to provide safe refuge for children from bomb ravaged Britain. CORB officials are stunned. Unconfirmed reports indicate that one family lost all five of its children.*

Officials hope to find more survivors but caution not to expect many. Survival is difficult in the North Atlantic due to the cold water temperatures.

"Never before has the evacuation program suffered so terrible a tragedy," a CORB official was quoted as saying. "It is true there have been several instances of passenger ship sinkings, but never before has CORB lost a child."

Prime Minister Churchill has not commented publicly on the sinking but it is reported that he is inclined toward curtailing the program before there are any additional tragedies of this sort.

Sir Geoffrey Shakespeare, director of CORB, could not be reached for comment.

The article upset Oliver. It was the first time he had read a news story with so close a connection to someone he knew. He had never thought seriously about the danger Ann was under when she crossed the Atlantic. He had naively supposed it was a routine and relatively safe trip. He knew the Germans were sinking ships every day, but he had never before connected it to Ann.

He wondered if Ann had heard about the sinking and what her reaction would be. "I bet it will frighten her," he thought, "and her parents must be enormously happy knowing Ann made it safely to America."

He had not realized before how different the war must seem to the evacuees than it did to the children in Dexter Hills. The war had suddenly become more personal. He would discuss all this with Ann in the morning, including his recent dream he had about her.

Chapter 47

Friday, 27 September 1940

The *City of Benares* tragedy was still troubling Ann. Her parents had told her that crossing the North Atlantic was dangerous but they had never actually said she might drown. She should have realized the danger after being on the *Caerleon*, but even then, she hadn't. It was true, the lifeboat drills had scared her and she had been especially frightened after the two ships in her convoy sank. The sinking should have been enough to make her fully aware, but there had never been any official report of actual drownings, all she knew was that two dirty, old, gray ships had sunk. Even when she read about the *Volendam,* she hadn't completely recognized the real danger. After all, no children had drowned, everyone had made it safely back to England.

But on the *Benares* there were casualties. The deaths were real. Children had died. Evacuees–children just like Ann, Graham, and the others–were now dead. She could no longer deny that her trip had been dangerous.

She found some comfort in knowing she was not alone with her feelings. Although he said he wasn't, she knew Graham had been troubled by it too. He kept mentioning their crossing each time they had talked since then.

One good thing had come from the news, however. Many of her classmates now seemed to have a somewhat different attitude toward her. It was as if they suddenly realized she had been part of the war in Europe–or, at least, had been involved in some of its dangers.

Oliver, in particular, seemed to be more understanding–more sympathetic. His concern almost embarrassed her. He talked with her in homeroom, between classes, at noon, and even after school. Lately he had been asking her about things other than England–things of a more personal nature–such as her hobbies, her ambitions, and what she did after school.

Although Ann appreciated Oliver's increased attention, she worried whenever they talked. On several occasions Vicky had made it clear that Oliver was, as she said, "off limits to her." She intended to honor Vicky's wishes. She did not want to antagonize her. Her friendship was too important. It was almost a prerequisites to becoming popular at Dexter Hills Junior High, and Ann didn't want to interfere with anything that might lead to additional friends. She still felt quite lonely.

There was, however, one gnawing problem about establishing new friendships. She knew that someday she would be going home, that someday she would be leaving Dexter Hills. When that time came, if she had any close relationships, she would once again need to go through the pain and sadness of those terrible good-byes. She had already been through all that once. She was not going through it again. She simply would need to keep everyone at arms' length, just make their acquaintance, not develop any close friendships. Yes, that was it, she would keep everyone at arm's length. It was the only safe thing to do.

However, today she had other more pressing worries than the *Benares* and her friends. Mr. Teasley had asked her to explain the British sterling to the class during the current affairs session in homeroom.

At first, she thought it would be an easy assignment, but as she organized the material, and especially during her presentation, she found it quite difficult. Her plan had been to explain the system, then compare it to the American dollar. She would define the different money units, list the slang words commonly used for each coin, and lastly give several examples of addition and subtraction

She started by telling them the pound was much like the dollar, except worth much more. Some of the classmates immediately took exception to her comparison. Not understanding the concept of currency exchange, they thought she was bragging; they thought she was saying the pound was better than the dollar. Mr. Teasley had to interrupt and explain what exchange rates meant.

She told them twenty shillings equaled one pound, each of which was equivalent to twelve pence. She explained that the English often referred to the pound as a quid, the shilling as a bob, and the pence as a penny. Several argued it made no sense. They said it would take two hundred forty pennies to equal a pound. That seemed wrong to them, one hundred pennies equaled a dollar or equivalently, two hundred forty pennies equaled two and two-fifths dollars. But she had already told them the pound was worth more than four dollars. Mr. Teasley had to once again explain currency exchange rates.

She next listed the common English coins: the half-penny commonly called the ha'penny, the penny, the one-penny-ha'penny, the three penny known as the thrup'ney bit, the sixpence, the shilling or bob, the florin equivalent to two shillings, and the half crown equal to two and a half shillings. Many said it sounded far too complicated. "That's not the worst of it," she said, "prices are often quoted in guineas. There are no coins or notes equal to a guinea. It represents twenty-one shillings." There was a collective moan by the class when they heard this. She decided against mentioning that four farthings was once equivalent to a penny.

When Vicky kept complaining that Ann's explanations were unclear and requested further clarification, Ann decided not to talk about addition and subtraction. Although it seemed simple enough, she knew she would have difficulty explaining it, particularly since talking in front of all these foreigners made her frightfully nervous. She also was certain if she continued some of Vicky's friends would join in the attempt to discredit her explanation.

She shouldn't have worried, her presentation went well. In fact, it went too well, the compliments she received, especially those from Oliver, angered Vicky even more. Ann felt bad but didn't think there was anything she could do about it. But still, she had to admit, all the accolades were nice to receive, especially after all the negative comments she'd been receiving from everyone over the past three weeks.

On the bus ride home, Ann had a new concern. She knew she shouldn't have encouraged Oliver to visit the farm. At the time it seemed perfectly logical, but now she wasn't so certain. She and Oliver had been discussing some of the differences between English and American culture. When he suggested they needed more time to sort it out, she agreed and had invited him to continue the discussion tomorrow. Now that she had reflected on what she had done, she was no longer certain it was the wisest thing to do. She knew word would get back to Vicky, who most assuredly would think there was something more sinister in it than two friends meeting to share ideas. She also wondered how Aunt Ida would react to the invitation. What would she say when she heard Ann had a boy visitor?

She hoped Oliver would change his mind before then and cancel his visit.

This certainly wasn't the type of problem she had encountered in England. This coeducational school seemed to be producing all sorts of new difficulties for her. Boys and girls in the same class seemed to create situations not found when only girls were there. Of course, she was younger and less aware of boys last year. That might explain part of it.

The discussion with Oliver today about the cultural differences between England and the U.S. had also triggered renewed thoughts about her mum and dad. "Surely," Ann hoped, "there will be a letter waiting in the mailbox when I get back to the farm."

It had been exactly seven weeks since she left Pinnington. That should have been more than ample time for a letter to reach Dexter Hills. In that period she had traveled to the English coast, waited a day to board the ship, sailed across the Atlantic, traveled to McKinley Heights, waited over two weeks before finding a home, and spent three full weeks in school. She ran from the bus to the mailbox, but once again there was no letter. Her disappointment deepened. "How could you, Mum?" she asked as she closed the mailbox lid.

Ida sensed the frustration as Ann came into the house. "Why don't you and Ned have a look in the northeast corner of the hayloft?" she whispered, her demeanor suggesting it was some sort of secret. "I think it will be worth your time." Ann had very little interest in going to the barn. She was feeling terribly homesick, but went anyway, simply to please Ida.

As Ned and Ann entered the barn they heard several feeble whimpers coming from the hayloft. Ned, immediately knew what it was, and suggested Ann have a look. At first Ann could not find anything, but finally noticed movement behind a large clump of hay. "Oh, Ned, look! There are four puppies!" she cried, then corrected herself, "No! There are five!

"Oh the poor dears! Look how tiny they are. Will Queenie be angry if I hold one, Ned?"

"You'd better not. It's best if we don't disturb them until they're a little older."

Ann could hardly contain herself. "Look at that darling little one!" she exclaimed. "He's so much smaller than the others."

"He's what we call the runt, Ann. There often is one much smaller than the others in a litter."

Ann had never seen such young puppies before and watched, entranced, as they nursed. "Oh, Ned, Queenie's going to lay on them! You had better help the black and white one."

"No need. They'll be okay. That's the way a bitch treats her young puppies," he answered, trying to assure her everything would be all right.

Ann was reluctant to leave the pups when Ida called them for supper. She talked excitedly as she entered the kitchen. "Queenie has such lovely puppies, Aunt Ida. I've never seen any that were so beautiful," she noted. It was true, the only dog she had ever been around in the past was the one the family had before they moved to Pinnington, and it was already grown by the earliest time she could remember.

During supper, Ann talked continually about the pups. She described their pretty colors, their cute little tails, and their timid whimpers. She tried to imagine how they would look when they grew up, how big they would be, how quickly Queenie would wean them, what they ate once she did, and, most importantly, what was to become of them.

"We'll try to sell them. If that doesn't work, we'll give them away." Jack answered. He thought for a minute, looked at Ida for approval and said, "I tell you what, Ann; if you wish, you may pick one of them as a pet. I think it would do you a world of ..."

"Oh, Uncle Jack!" she interrupted. "You mean it? I can have a puppy? A puppy of my very own?"

"Yes, Ann," he laughed. "As I was trying to say, I think it would be good for you to have a pet of your own. You must understand, though; it will be your responsibility to take care of it, to feed it, train it, and do whatever else is necessary to make it a healthy, useful farm dog."

"I already know which one I'll pick!" she mused, not paying too much attention to what Jack was saying. She didn't care what she had to do, just so long as she had her very own dog.

"The runt?" Ned guessed.

"How did you know? Yes, I want that cute little one with the black face. May I go out and fetch him now?" she asked, quickly pushing her chair away from the table.

"No, not yet," Ida cautioned. "You must wait until Queenie weans him. Until then, you must be patient."

Ann was not certain she could. When she finished drying the dishes she ran back to the barn and sat for a long period watching the pups, particularly the runt. "What shall I name you?" she asked. "Let's see! Since your mother was Queenie, Prince sounds like a good name for you."

Ned laughed as he walked past and overheard her decision. "But what if he turns out to be she?" he asked.

Ann thought for a few minutes. "Then I guess I'll call her Lady," she answered.

After Ned had gone, she looked more carefully and decided it would be appropriate to name her Lady. At least she was pretty sure.

Chapter 48

Saturday, 28 September 1940

Ann opened her eyes with a start. It was Aunt Ida. "Good morning, Ann, time to get up! It's Saturday, no school today, just chores, home-work, and play."

Ann pulled the covers over her head, partially to shield the light from Ida's lantern, and partially to hide the tears on her cheeks. She had been dreaming of home. Mum had just told her there would be no let-ters; she had decided not to write. Ann knew it was a dream and there was no truth to it. Still, it produced a tiny feeling of uncertainty. It could be true. She hadn't received any letters so far. "By now, I would surely think I should have received at least one letter," she told herself.

"Come on, child," Ida insisted. "Get out of bed!"

Ann wiped her eyes and slipped one leg out from under the quilt. The cold air made her shiver. Ida had told her to expect much colder winters in Ohio than those in England. But it was only September. Was this a precursor of things to come? If so, ice and snow could not be far behind. The thought made her even more depressed.

But Ann had little time to feel sorry for herself. Ida and Jack had planned a busy morning of chores. By noontime, fatigue had begun to replace melancholy. Every muscle in her body ached; she had never worked so hard or been so hungry. "What have you done to that child, Jack?" Ida asked. "Have you ever seen anyone with such an appetite?"

"Yes, I have," Jack laughed, "her brother."

"You'd better go easy on her, Dad," Ned quipped. "If you work her any harder there won't be any food left."

Ann blushed.

"I had to work her much harder than usual this morning. That boyfriend of hers is coming this afternoon," Jack said, pretending to be upset. "Once he arrives, there won't be any more work from her. She'll be too gaga-eyed and giddy."

"Ann has a boyfriend? Already?" Ned asked, pretending to be surprised. "It didn't take her long, did it?"

"He's not a boyfriend. He's only a friend. We have homework to do." Everyone smiled. "We're comparing American and English cultures," she quickly added, blushing once again.

"Sure you are," Ned teased, giving her a sly look and grinning.

"Oh, I just remembered," Jack said, his face turning serious. "I want you to go with me to the co-op this afternoon, Ann. I need help filling the feedbags." He looked at Ida and continued, "Send her beau packing when he gets here. Tell him there'll be no hanky-panky today, she has to earn her keep."

"Stop it, you two. Leave the poor girl alone," Ida ordered. "If you keep teasing she'll never invite anyone again."

"Don't worry, Aunt Ida, I know what they're up to. I don't mind," Ann said, trying to conceal her discomfort. She knew they were teasing, but, all the same, it bothered her. She had been awfully silly yesterday; she shouldn't have invited Oliver. She certainly wouldn't invite him again. Especially if his visits caused this much embarrassment.

Oliver arrived shortly after lunch. Ann was resting on the porch swing, thinking about the absence of letters from home, hoping today's mail would finally contain what she was waiting for. She first spotted him riding up the lane on his bicycle. She couldn't help notice what a handsome boy he was. Momentarily she considered how it would feel if they were sweethearts but then quickly dismissed the thought. He was coming to talk about England, absolutely nothing else.

At first there was little talk. Neither knew what to say. Somehow, being together at school was different than being together on the farm— especially when they were alone. It made them shy and unsure of themselves. Finally, Ann broke the silence by asking him if he cared to see Queenie's new pups. By the time they arrived at the hayloft, they had forgotten their initial embarrassment and were talking and laughing uninhibitedly.

Ann was pleased when Oliver worried, as Ned had, that he might harm the puppies and especially when he was so careful not to hold any of them. Instead, he scratched Queenie behind the ears and told her what fine pups she had. When Ann introduced him to Lady he agreed with her, Lady was certainly the best of the litter. All this tenderness surprised Ann. It was a facet of his character she had not noticed before. He was a kind and caring person, not the rough-and-tumble boy his interest in athletics had suggested.

After watching the pups, they wandered around the farm and talked about England, Dexter Hills, and their classmates, teachers, and classes. Ann showed him her favorite hideaway and, much to her surprise, he showed her a special place too. He had found it during one of the work breaks while helping with the potatoes this year.

The time passed quickly and soon it was time to deliver the afternoon papers. "Can we do this again, Ann?" he asked, "I really enjoyed it today."

"I did too, Oliver, but I don't think we should. I really have too many chores to do."

She wasn't certain why she was refusing him, perhaps because of the teasing by Jack and Ned, perhaps because Vicky was his steady; or perhaps because she worried about the impropriety of an English girl roaming about the countryside with an American boy. It never occurred to her she might be avoiding another visit out of fear that it might lead to an attachment she could not easily leave someday–a day when it would be almost impossible to say good-bye. She had suffered through one of those already, and that was enough.

Her refusal disappointed Oliver. He was certain the visit had been special for them both. It was a shame not do it again, but he would follow her wishes–it was the gentlemanly thing to do.

He told her he understood and left.

As soon as he was gone, Ann eagerly ran down the lane to check the mailbox. Once again, to her increasing despair, the box contained no letter from home. It nearly broke her heart. She had been so certain she would receive a letter today.

Ida could see from Ann's disappointed look that there was nothing again. Ida, too, began to have doubts about Ann's parents. "When will that poor soul hear from them? Why would it take so long?" she wondered. "Here, Ann, help me pick the pinfeathers off this chicken," she said, trying to distract Ann from feeling so low.

They had worked only a few minutes when an auto came up the lane, followed shortly by a rap on the door. "Anyone home?" the postman asked, through the screen door. "Special delivery package for Miss Ann Montgomery."

Ann and Ida looked at each other, screamed with delight, and rushed to the door. The postman looked at Ann, winked at Ida, and asked, "Are you Miss Montgomery?"

"Yes, yes! I am!" exclaimed Ann. She pushed open the screen door, almost toppling the postman. He handed Ann a brown envelope. Her heart sank, it was from Bender Electric, not from her parents. She wondered why Bender Electric would be sending her mail, and quickly opened the seal. Inside were three envelopes from her mum and dad and a note from Stanley Roberts. In his note Stan explained he had received a special package mailed from the Pinnington plant late Friday afternoon. It contained letters for the evacuees from their parents. Knowing they would be eager to get them, he was forwarding them, by special delivery mail, to each addressee.

"Can you believe it? They're letters from my mum and dad!" Ann squealed. Without waiting for Ida's comment, she ran quickly to her room.

Ida, with great will power, forced herself not to follow. She wanted desperately to hear what they contained but thought Ann should read her letters in private. Perhaps Ann would share the contents afterwards. At least she hoped so.

Ann looked at the envelopes for a long time. She was somewhat hesitant to open them. It was difficult to dismiss the recent worry that her parents no longer cared about her. The letters might confirm these misgivings. Finally, with muted expectations, she began opening them. One contained two letters written by Diane and addressed to Graham and her. The other two envelopes contained letters addressed only to her. A stamp on the last one indicated a Government agent had censored it, several sections had been cut away.

The first letter pleased Ann. It carried a date of August 11, the Sunday after she left Pinnington. It was a short letter. It seemed to Ann her mum had found it awkward to say anything personal. It mostly talked about the weather and Diane's frustration of not knowing what address to use. She said she would not be able to post it until Bender Limited supplied an address. The sparse content and delay didn't matter; her mum had written–only two days after Graham and she left. She had not neglected to write; that was what was most important. Ann could not believe she had ever doubted her mum.

Ann smiled when Diane's second letter said that she hoped to have it waiting for Ann and Graham when they arrived in America. It had missed the mark by more than a month. Diane had dated the letter August 18 and had just learned the company was collecting all the letters for the evacuees and would bundle them together and forward them to America. The company hadn't posted the collection until near the end of August. That explained the long delay and the two letters in the same envelope.

Unlike the first letter, there was a sentence indicating how lonely the house seemed and another saying she missed Ann and Graham. Ann read it over again, several times, to make certain she could remember her mum's words precisely. Her words, "I miss you," made Ann feel very good.

She then picked up the third letter and read:

Wednesday, 21 August 1940.

Dear Ann,

What a glorious day it is! Your father just telephoned from the office to say you and Graham have safely landed in New York City and will be in McKinley Heights within a few days. I believe I can reveal to you now, both Dad and I were extremely apprehensive about your perilous journey across the North Atlantic. Now we can relax. You are in America and are safe!

In America! It is still difficult for me to believe you children are eating ice cream and watching the American cowboys lasso the villains.

By the time you read this letter, I imagine you and Graham will already be settled in with a wonderful American family and are having scads of fun. Actually, as Dad reminded me last night, if the post is slow you may be in school by the time you read this. If so, I hope you are happy with your studies, are making many friends, and are enjoying every minute of your great adventure. It is a wonderful opportunity to do many things you could not have done had you remained here in Britain. Please take full advantage of every opportunity you can while there. Try to compare the advantages (and disadvantages) of the two cultures. It should serve you well in future years. Above all, always be courteous and respectful. Leave the Americans with a good opinion of us Britons. (Listen to me, I am beginning to sound like a prime minister. Ha! Ha!)

Things continue to be hectic here. The long hours everyone is working and the persistent worry about an invasion have given everyone the jitters. Bombs are now falling on southeastern England at a terrible rate. Fortunately, Pinnington has escaped major attack (so far) and has suffered no damage. The biggest problem has been the numerous air raid alerts. They keep us inside the Anderson shelter almost every night now. It's a good thing Dad took the time to have our shelter built properly. Those poor people who did not are in trouble. I understand many shelters flood whenever it rains. Rain water simply drains away from ours. Your dad is a wonderful man. He anticipated the problem and took care of it beforehand. Bless his soul.

Well, dear, I must prepare dinner and will close with a promise to write again very soon. Take care of Graham and think often of your old mum and dad. I love you. If your dad were home I know he would send his love too.

Love and kisses,

Mum

P.S. Please share this letter with Graham. I have asked him to do the same with my letter to him.

Ann read the paragraph containing the expression of love several times then held the letter to her heart. "They do love us," she thought fondly.

"I hope they'll be all right," she added, thinking about the air raids.

She thought about yesterday's homeroom discussion. Mr. Teasley had spent time explaining the events in Europe, how Hitler had come to power, how the other European governments had attempted to appease him, and how, one-by-one, he had systematically conquered each country. Her classmates had looked at her sympathetically when he told how perilous the situation was in England. England expected a German invasion any day. He said everyone hoped the recent U.S. government assistance would be in time to help. If not, England would surely lose. "Even if Hitler is stopped," he said, "it would be at least a year before England could hope to have the situation firmly under control."

Until yesterday, Ann had never permitted herself to consider the possibility England could lose. Her mum hadn't said anything in the letter about that possibility either. Probably she didn't wish to worry Ann. Perhaps her mentioning the German bombings was a hint. She fought desperately to keep the thought of England losing and its effect on her parents from her mind. Unfortunately, she found it too difficult. Try as she would, it stayed with her.

She considered how long Mr. Teasley thought it could take, "Surely one year is wrong. I miss Mum and Dad too much. I can't stay here an entire year." If it is that long, it would mean she and Graham would not be going home until next autumn–or even next winter. That was simply unacceptable. For what seemed to her to be the hundredth time since she left home, a tear formed on her cheek.

Pinnington, Middlesex, England
Sunday, 25 August 1940

Dear Ann,

Here it is Sunday afternoon and, as I said I would, I am sitting here at the dining table writing to you again. (Am I not a good mum?) I hope this letter reaches you quickly and it finds you happy and well

It has now been over two weeks since you left! It is very frustrating not having heard from either of you. (I hope the two of you have been writing?? Remember, you promised!) Each day when I arrive home from work I find myself eagerly searching the post deliveries for a letter, which, of course, is nonsense–it is entirely too soon for a letter coming all the way from America.

Poor Dad is never home anymore. He is working much too much, and I so hope he soon finds a way to cut back a bit. Whenever I say anything, he scolds me and says he must do it for the war effort. "We must help all we can," has become one of his favorite expressions. Being forced to sleep in the bomb shelter each night has not helped the poor man either. He is beginning to look peaked from the lack of sleep. But not to worry, he is a strong and determined man and I know nothing will bring him down–especially not the Jerries.

The air raid alerts continue nightly. We heard the first actual bombers overhead last night. It was a worry, hearing those wretched bombs screaming down and not knowing when or where they would land. Suddenly, we could hear explosions in the distance. It was frightening. Fortunately, all went well. None exploded close to us. It is difficult to know if the ones we heard caused any damage–the newspapers no longer publish details. I suppose they don't want the Jerries to know what havoc they are causing.

As you can see, the war continues unabated, but please don't worry. We are managing to get along all right. Perhaps I should not have told you about the bombing, but I thought being honest would set your mind at ease. If I painted the picture too rosy you would suspect I was fibbing and would worry even more.

Yvonne finally received her defence assignment. She is now working six days a week at the Rolls plant. She cannot tell us what she is doing–for security reasons. She also continues to help at St. John's. I think, like her dad, she is trying to do too much. It is beginning to get the best of her. The poor girl comes home exhausted. The last few mornings (she works the night shift) she has come home and promptly gone to bed. Of course, like all of us, she only sleeps until the air raid sirens sound, then must trudge down to the shelter.

Because the raids are so regular now (one thing you can say for Jerry–he is methodical), Dad and I recently began spending the entire night in the shelter and have finally mastered sleeping in the bunk beds. It seems to tire us less than running back and forth. Poor Yvonne has not been able to do the same. The shelter is too warm during the day. There seems to be many more disruptions during the day too. The officials apparently are somewhat less quick to sound the alarm at night.

Oh yes! I must tell you! We had a letter from Henry on Thursday. He says he is feeling good and getting along well. He and his buddies are in high spirits and are looking forward to finishing this horrid war soon and returning to England. He could not say where they have stationed his unit but from what he wrote we think he is in ... Here a section of Diane's letter was missing. Ann discussed this later with Jack and Ida. They decided the censor had removed it. ... *Henry has asked about you. I know he would enjoy hearing from you children. I have enclosed his address. Please drop him a line.*

- - -

The sirens sounded about an hour ago and I had to drop my pen and rush to the shelter. Dad was at work, so Yvonne and I were in the shelter alone. I suppose I should have taken this with me and continued it there, but these raids are fearsome, and without Dad, I am too nervous to do anything, let alone write. Today we could see the German fighters coming and watched as our RAF boys battled them. I suppose we should have entered the shelter sooner, but the fight held us spellbound. It reminded us of a group of bees buzzing overhead. Occasionally a German fighter would explode and fall helplessly toward the ground. We felt like cheering but could not. The thought of the poor lads who were in those fighters made us sad. After all, they are the sons of a mum and dad somewhere, obeying orders just like Henry. How could we cheer? Unfortunately some of our chaps also came down spinning. While we watched we counted ... Here again there was a cutout. ... So you can see, we will beat those Nazi's yet.

I fear the raid has made me too nervous to add anything more so I will sign off with a promise to write again very soon. I hope you plan to do so too. Tell us something about the wonderful family who is taking care of Graham and you. We are eager to hear about your living quarters, your new friends–anything that concerns the two of you.

Love,

Mum

P.S. I have just read this letter again and fear I may have given you the wrong impression of life here in Britain. Please know, even with the terrible war, we are well and happy and find many things for which we can be grateful. We often smile when we recall some of the wonderful times we had before you left. We know you must already be providing your <u>new</u> family with many fond memories as well. Have a wonderful time in America!

There was another note enclosed:.

Hi Princess,

I just got in from work.

How are you doing? As Mum says, I hope you're finding your stay in America a wonderful, enjoyable experience. Everything here is fine. Don't believe your mum, I'm not working too hard. You know your old man! He never works hard. Actually, most of the time I'm at the "Boar & Whistle" having a few pints of bitters. I must keep my pipes lubricated, you know. Ha! Ha!

I imagine all the American lads are looking dreamy eyed at you and plying you with all sorts of bonbons and tokens to win your love and devotion. It must be difficult to have such a lovely thing close by. You should be careful, dear. Who can resist a lass as attractive as you?

Take care of yourself and always know we miss you. Let's hope you can return before too much longer.

Love,

Dad

Finally, after nearly an hour reading and re-reading the letters, she opened her door, went to the kitchen, and found the Schaefer family, waiting, somewhat impatiently, to learn what her family had said. Reluctant to leave go of the letters, even momentarily, Ann chose to read them aloud.

There were many exclamations and sighs as she read. Everyone could sense the melancholy, the feeling of parental loss, the loneliness, the horror of war. They wanted to help, to do something about it, but no one knew what. All they could think of was to hug Ann after she finished.

Later, Jack suggested Ann telephone Graham from the Ekenwilders'. At almost the same instant someone knocked at the door. It was Mr. Ekenwilder. He had just received a telephone call from Graham. He wanted Ann to call him.

They had a lengthy conversation. Graham had also received his letters. Thinking her children were still together and could easily share her letters, Diane had written different things to each child. Once they realized this, neither would hang up until they were certain they had digested everything from the other's letters. Even then, they had to promise to have the letters with them the next time they visited.

Afterwards, the Schaefers took Ann, Graham, Karen, Meg, and Ned to a movie in McKinley Heights. The outing was intended to be a celebration, but instead, it served more as an way to wind down after a day filled with so much excitement.

Ann took Diane's fourth letter to class with her on Monday and, at the encouragement of Mr. Teasley, read it to the class–leaving out the more personal parts. Her classmates found it difficult to believe that the Londoners needed to huddle in bomb shelters each night. The European war was too remote to believe it was actually happening.

Afterwards, Oliver reported on the Sunday news article describing the additional boatload of *City of Benares* survivors found still drifting in the North Atlantic. Friday's count of survivors included thirteen children. Eighty-five English children were almost assuredly dead. The class was somewhat indifferent to the news. It had so little to do with their own lives.

Ann felt much differently.

There would be no more English evacuees coming to America. The sinking of the *Volendam* and, especially, the *City of Benares* caused

CORB to officially suspend the program on Thursday, October 3. The final count of children sent to the U.S. under the official auspices of CORB numbered only thirteen hundred fifteen. The only other English children to enter the U.S. were those privately evacuated. Ann and Graham, who of course had no knowledge of these numbers, were part of a very select group.

Chapter 49

Sunday, 13 October 1940

It had been over two weeks since Ann had talked to Graham. Such a long time was really no one's fault; school functions, chores, and other activities always seemed to interfere with any plans she made to call him. She supposed he had the same problem.

By now, she had sent another letter to her parents and, more importantly, had received one more from her mum. It was dated September 1, almost one year since the start of the war between England and Germany. So much had happened since last September. The war news seemed to be growing worse each day and any hope for an early settlement was rapidly disappearing. And each day her concern for her family's welfare was increasing.

For over a month, the reports had been more and more worrisome. Apparently, Hitler had shifted his air assault from the English airfields and coastal cities to the city of London. Nightly bombing raids, frequently exacerbated with additional raids during the daytime, had been going on, with no letup, since September 7. This terrifying series of raids, now referred to as the Blitz, had been in the headlines almost daily for many weeks, each day describing, in gruesome detail, more horror than the previous day.

The Germans were dropping large quantities of incendiary bombs which started many uncontrollable fires that were made more horrible by their indiscriminate and random nature. Bombs were as likely to fall on civilian facilities as on strategic targets. No place was safe. It included schools, churches, residential flats, and individual homes. Thousands of people became homeless. Even clearly marked hospitals, where injured soldiers and civilians were being treated, were not spared. Londoners had to station guards on rooftops to put out any fires and prevent them from spreading. Broken water mains and downed light and power lines regularly interrupted road and rail routes into the city. Ruptured gas mains often caused additional fires and explosions and contributed to the bedlam. Hundreds of thousands of people crowded into shelters each night. Conditions in these shelters were terrible, often unsafe and unsanitary.

Surprisingly, the city continued to function. People went about their business as best they could. Morale remained high, even though no one knew how long these nightly bombing attacks would continue.

"Pinnington is only a suburb of London," Ann reasoned "It is possible it missed the bombing–but unlikely." Ann had no way of knowing. Diane had not mentioned the Blitz in her letter, but that meant little, everything Ann had received had been written before the Blitz started.

Graham should also have a letter by now. She hoped she would hear from him soon so she could know for certain and, of course, read it, or at least have him read it to her.

In spite of all the careful attention she had paid to the newspaper articles and newsreels recently, Ann could not fully comprehend, or completely believe, what the war in Pinnington was like. She only knew it must be horrible. She began to feel guilty. She should have been part of it, not an evacuee harbored safe and secure in America. She was not suffering the way her family must surely be. It affected her studies. Everyone was beginning to notice the change in her disposition. She was not laughing as much as she had when she first arrived.

She would have felt better had she known Graham, and most of the other evacuees, had similar reactions. The only thing she knew for certain was she needed to talk with Graham. "He will assure me that it was all right for us to come here," she kept trying to convince herself.

By the time Stan Roberts called Tom Derringer, Ann still had not talked to Graham. Little did she know that as a result of Tom's phone call she and Graham would be together before evening. Bender Electric had just received a cable from England. The Royal family was planning a message to all overseas evacuees via shortwave wireless. Princess Elizabeth would deliver the message on the *BBC Children's Hour*. It could be heard in America on a good shortwave receiver.

Stan told Tom that at first he had planned to invite the evacuees into the plant to hear the message. Unfortunately, it would be difficult for almost eighty children to listen simultaneously to one radio. He had been trying since then to locate alternate sites, sites with shortwave receivers, where some of the children could listen. He had heard Tom owned a good receiver and wondered if he would host a few of the children while they listened to the broadcast. Without hesitation Tom volunteered. They agreed he would invite Graham, Ann, and several of the other children to his house.

That night, while Tom patiently tuned the radio through the short-wave bands, the children had much to talk about, so much so that they nearly neglected to listen to the broadcast. Finally, Tom found the station and, the children, along with Ken, Louise, Victoria, and the other foster families, huddled near the radio speaker.

Her Royal Highness, Princess Elizabeth, began her message:

In wishing you all good evening, I know that I am speaking to friends and companions who have shared with my sister and myself many a happy "Children's Hour." Thousands of you in this country have had to leave home and be separated from your fathers and mothers. My sister Margaret Rose and I feel so much for you, as we know from experience what it means to be away from those we love most of all. To you living in new surroundings we send a message of true sympathy, and at the same time we would like to thank the kind people who have welcomed you to their homes in the country.

All of us children who are still at home think continually of our friends and relations who have gone overseas to find a wartime home and a kindly welcome in Canada, Australia, New Zealand, South Africa, and the United States of America.

My sister and I feel we know quite a lot about these countries. Our father and mother have so often talked to us of their visits to different parts of the world, so it is not difficult for us to picture the sort of life you are leading, and to think of all the sights you must be seeing and the adventures you must be having, but I am sure that you too are often thinking of the old country. I know you won't forget us. It is just that we are not forgetting you but want on behalf of all the children at home to send you our love and best wishes, to you and your kind hosts as well.

Before I finish, I can truthfully say to you all that we children at home are full of cheerfulness and courage. And we are trying to do all we can to help our gallant sailors, soldiers and airmen. And we are trying, too, to bear our own share of the danger and sadness of war. We know, every one of us, that in the end, all will be well, for God will care for us and give us victory and peace. And though peace comes, remember, it will be for us, the children of today, to make the world tomorrow a better and happier place.

My sister is by my side and we are both going to say good night to you. Come on Margaret ...

Margaret said simply, *Good night children.*

Elizabeth then ended with, *Good night and good luck to you all.*

The speech made everyone nostalgic. The children talked for a long time about London and its month of very heavy bombing, about their families still in England, about their wonderful new foster families, and about their good fortune of having come to America. Although it grew late, the parents did nothing to terminate the conversation. They sensed it beneficial to let the children talk about it thoroughly. It was an opportunity for each child to shed some of his guilt over his own safety and sadness for the agonies his family was being forced to bear at home.

The decision to talk on was a good one. When Ann went to bed at twelve-thirty, she felt much better. It was as if someone had removed a heavy weight from her shoulders.

Although she normally took Lady back to the barn before she went to bed, this night she didn't. Instead, Lady slept by her side, with only her nose sticking out of the covers. Both the girl and the dog slept well.

Chapter 50

Tuesday, 29 October 1940

Edith was glad she had come to America, happier than she could ever have imagined back in July and August. She had been living with her McKinley Heights foster family now for nearly two months. During that brief period she had grown quite fond of Clara and Brad Holtzman. They treated her with love and respect, something she never would have thought possible after having lived with her inconsiderate father all those years.

Perhaps it had to do with their relatively young ages. Clara was twenty-four and Brad was twenty-six. She supposed it could also have been their modern approach and attitude towards child rearing. They left many of the decisions to her judgment and dealt with her as if she were a grownup. Above all, they displayed a sincere interest in her dreams and ambitions. When she told them she someday hoped to become a chemist, they were excited and encouraged her to keep after her goal. If she worked hard, they assured her, eventually she would have the career she wanted.

As happy as they seemed to be, Edith suspected everything was not as rosy as they pretended. Their major problem seemed to be Brad's income. Apparently, it was barely enough to live on. Several times she had inadvertently overheard them discussing the mortgage payments and often noticed how Brad worried about their finances. He seemed to always be pointing out to Clara ways to save, but, as poor as he was, he would never admit it or complain openly to Edith. One had to admire both of them; they never brought up the cost of keeping her, or denied her anything she truly needed. They seemed genuinely concerned for her and always gave high priority to her welfare.

The first shopping trip was a good example of their generosity. Just before school started Clara had taken Edith shopping and, as Edith now realized, spent much more for her school outfits than the Holtzmans could afford.

Edith had never been in a store quite like *Bon Marché*. Its elegance impressed her. She imagined it comparable to *Harrods* in Knightsbridge, or even one of the fancy shops on Regent Street. She couldn't be sure which, she had never been in any of them. "Mum and Dad usually bought my clothes at the outdoor markets, places like Petticoat Lane and Camden Passage," she told Clara. "I could never try on any of the clothes to see if they fit properly, everything was sized by guess and luck. It certainly doesn't compare with *Bon Marché*, with its fancy dressing rooms and helpful clerks."

Clara and Edith had a grand time selecting Edith's wardrobe. They giggled each time Edith put on something particularly attractive. Clara, at first, wanted to buy everything but, once she looked at the price tags, settled for a few basic school ensembles. Even with the budgetary restriction Edith was ecstatic with all they had purchased. She had never had such nice clothes. Not even the clothes she wore to church were as pretty. There was little doubt in her mind, she would be the envy of all her classmates. "You should have seen the pretty dresses I tried on at *Bon Marché*!" she exclaimed excitedly to Brad that evening. "And they had a full length mirror so I could see how well I looked."

She had no idea why Brad had laughed at this, but she really didn't care. Brad could do almost anything and she wouldn't mind. She thought he was such a fine man, and handsome too. He was so different from her father, so kind and considerate. His knowledge of science particularly impressed her. Although Brad had wanted to be an engineer, he couldn't afford college. Instead he had taken a correspondence course and, studying entirely by himself, had become a radio repairman. After working for someone long enough to accumulate the necessary capital, he had opened his own repair shop. Clara told Edith, with a great deal of pride, that the shop had been an almost instant success. "The McKinley Heights residents consider him capable, honest, and, perhaps most importantly, his prices are reasonable," she boasted.

Brad was also an avid fisherman and had promised Edith he would take her fishing one day–once he caught up with his work. Clara laughed when she heard this. She told Edith not to expect it anytime soon. "Lately he hasn't had time for much of anything except business," she complained. "He never takes a day off, in fact, he hasn't taken a vacation since he opened the shop."

"Now that I have a family," he said, looking at Edith, "I'm going to change. Just you wait, you'll see. I'm going to arrange my schedule so I can spend more time at home, with my wife and my daughter. Don't you worry, Edith, I'll make a fisherman out of you yet."

"And a wife out of me?" Clara asked, looking at him wistfully and with a silly grin. "That will be wonderful. It would be nice to have a real husband at home once again."

It had been over a month now and they still had not gone fishing. But Edith was not particularly disappointed; she wasn't certain she would enjoy it anyway. She especially had her doubts about "putting those wiggly worms on the hook."

But fishing was far from everyone's thoughts today. There existed a definite possibility Brad might be called into military service. Today's newspaper would answer that, and they were anxiously awaiting its delivery. It would contain the order of induction for all Selective Service registrants. Brad would finally know if he had been chosen to serve as a soldier in the United States Army.

It had been a long, anxious wait. In early September, the government had a huge debate concerning the war in Europe and, in particular, the future involvement of the U.S. There were many who actively called for the U.S. to do whatever was necessary to keep out of the scrap. Senator Taft of Ohio was a leader of this isolationist movement. He insisted European problems were of no particular concern to America.

It upset Clara, an avid Roosevelt supporter, when, in September, Brad had shown her the newspaper article quoting the American First Committee. They claimed the Jewish-British-Capitalists-Roosevelt conspiracy aimed to plunge the country into war. She particularly did not agree with the Committee's objection to F.D.R.'s offer of further support to England and, especially with their personal attack on him. The article quoted congressman Curtis of Nebraska who stated that because the U.S. had no stake in the conflict, President Roosevelt's actions could be explained only as someone whose lust for power made him the rival of Stalin, Hitler, and Mussolini. Brad had to convince Clara most Americans were not as negative towards F.D.R., Britain, or the war in Europe as the article seemed to indicate. Although, no great fan of F.D.R., he did not believe Roosevelt was a warmonger.

Before she arrived at the Holtzmans', Edith had been almost completely unaware America had any interest in the war in Europe. Since then she had listened to many of Brad and Clara's dinnertime discussions and had closely followed the war related articles and editorials in the newspaper. By now she was somewhat knowledgeable and had her own opinions about all that was happening. In her mind, the warmongers were beginning to have too much of their own way. Only days after she had arrived the U.S. had mobilized the National Guard, with the first contingent of these so called citizen-soldiers ordered by F.D.R. to "report to colors" on September 16 for one year of regular army active duty. Then, on September 14, Congress approved the Burke-Wadsworth Peacetime Conscription Bill and sent it to the White House for the President's signature. The Bill called for the registration of all men between the ages of twenty-one and thirty-five. The first seventy-five thousand draftees were to report to camp in November. Also included in the Bill were provisions for the president to take over industrial plants, on a rental basis, when necessary to fill defense orders expediently. The president signed the Bill immediately, and registration had occurred on October 16. Brad was one of those required to register.

All this worried Edith. Indeed, the U.S. seemed to be definitely gearing up for war. Although she had escaped the war in Europe, she realized it now threatened to follow her to the U.S.

Escalation was even more apparent toward the end of September when Nipponese soldiers invaded Indochina, and Roosevelt responded by imposing a total embargo on the shipment of iron and steel to Japan. A day later Japan signed a treaty of alliance with the Rome-Berlin Axis. The Tripartite Pact, as they called it, explicitly linked events in Europe and the Far East and further reinforced the animosity between the Axis and the U.S.

Brad, when he first read about the Selective Service Act in the newspaper, thought it a good decision for the U.S. "Finally we're beginning to do something to beef up our defenses," he told Clara and Edith. Clara, less of an F.D.R. supporter now than she had been a few weeks before, did not agree. The distinct possibility Brad could be drafted concerned her. He was not an employee of a defense plant and his radio repair work was not considered critical to national defense. Neither would make him eligible for deferment. There was presently an exemption for married men, but there was talk that even that might soon change. The only real chance to keep him out of the army was to draw a high number in the draft lottery.

The process was somewhat complicated. It began with the distribution of identical sets of registration numbers to each local draft board.

They assigned these numbers to each man as he registered at his local polling place. Then on October 26, Secretary of War, Simpson, blind-folded, reached into a fishbowl and drew the first registration number. The number signified which registrants would be inducted first. The next number drawn identified the second group to be called, and so on, until all numbers had been ranked. The list was scheduled to appear in local newspapers today.

When the paper arrived, Brad, Clara, and Edith nervously scanned the list to find Brad's number.

"I found it!" Edith exclaimed. "It's here, near the middle."

"Oh, Brad, does that mean you'll be called?" Clara asked.

"I don't believe so," Brad answered, somewhat relieved. "The last number needed to satisfy seventy-five thousand men should be well ahead of my number. Of course, if they need additional men the number could get closer to the top. Let's hope there's no need for any more call-ups. Of course I'll not go even then, unless they decide to call married men."

"Oh, Brad, they can't take you! I depend on you too much," Clara sobbed. She grabbed Brad and Edith and held them tightly in her arms. It especially moved Edith to know Clara had included her in her embrace. It felt so comfortable, as if she were truly part of the Holtzman family. For a moment she almost forgot her mum and dad, Brad and Clara had nearly taken their places. As they continued to hug, she realized how fortuitous it had been to have found such a wonderful home. She, indeed, had been lucky. She snuggled even closer to Clara and wrapped her arms tighter around both of them. She hoped she could stay with them forever; the war in Europe would never reach America, and the U.S. Government would never induct Brad.

These wishes would not be fulfilled. In the coming early spring Congress would make plans to slash War Department appropriations, but by October they would have a change of heart and would vote over seventeen million dollars for defense. World conditions would slowly encroach on America's intention of remaining neutral, and with it, an even more critical need for a bigger army.

Chapter 51

Sunday, 3 November 1940

The Battle of Britain had been raging for over two and a half months, and Diane and Chad were tired. It seemed each day was worse than the one before. Had someone told them back in August they could live through such an ordeal they would not have believed them. Yet, somehow, they had managed. The only question now was how much longer they could endure the hardships.

The character of the battle had assumed many forms since its onset. In mid August, the first phase of the German air assault, a few raids occurred north of the Wash, most concentrated on targets in the South. Almost all these southern raids focused on the convoys in the Channel and on the Kent promontory and Channel coast. No bombs dropped near Pinnington.

In late August, the Germans changed their tactics and began attacking the air fields in southern England. Their attempt to destroy the British Air Force was unsuccessful, but they caused major damage to the sector stations south and southeast of London. Among the particularly hard hit areas were the airfields at Manston and Beggin Hill. The fighter commands located at the fields near Pinnington were also under heavy attack which brought the raids closer to the Montgomerys and forced them to use the Anderson shelter regularly. Even then, however, bombing was sporadic, occurring mostly in the daytime while they were at work. Yvonne was usually the one forced to huddle in the shelter for long periods.

Then, on September 7, Goring publicly took command of the air battle and shifted the German air campaign, emphasizing nightly bombing runs. London was the primary target. Although there were still frequent daylight air raids, the nighttime raids were heavy and caused major devastation. On the first day of Goring's new plan, three hundred fifty German bombers attacked London during the day followed by approximately two hundred fifty that night. It was on this September night that the Montgomerys experienced the horror of bombs dropping around their home for the first time and several windows in their house were broken. During the next fifty-seven days the Germans bombed London every night using an average of over two hundred bombers. Fortunately, Ann and Graham were not there. They were safe in America.

Chad could recall the September 7 raid particularly well. It seemed as if the entire city was on fire. There were more than one thousand fires, some raging out of control for hours and burning entire districts.

While fires blazed on the ground, an air battle raged overhead. Citizens watched with horror as the British Spitfires and Hurricanes battled the German Luftwaffe's ME-110 bombers during the day and the British Blendheims and Defiants battled the Heinkel-111 heavy bombers during the night. These air battles continued for some time until the defense forces moved their antiaircraft guns and searchlights from coastal emplacements into London. At first, the people cheered to see these weapons added to the defense of their city. Soon, however, their happiness turned to frustration. Although the guns were reassuring, the din created by these antiaircraft weapons added to the noise and chaos of the raids and proved unnerving to everyone. Nevertheless, even though they never grew accustomed to the noise, the Montgomerys stoically learned to tolerate these added defenses.

September 8 was an especially traumatic day for everyone. The church bells, which were to be used only as a warning of an invasion, began ringing. In response, Chad and his Home Guard companions rushed to their duty stations, expecting at any moment to meet German paratroopers or soldiers. To everyone's relief it was a false alarm. Chad felt particularly upset by his performance during the alert; he had been much more frightened than he had thought he would be and was ashamed of himself. He hoped no one had noticed and vowed he would react differently–that is braver–if it ever happened again.

Although the London raids concentrated on the dock areas and the airfields around London, there were sufficient raids over the Pinnington area to cause considerable damage to houses and to make citizens stay in their shelters for exorbitantly long periods. Serious damage to the Montgomery house occurred Sunday, September 15, during the Luftwaffe's greatest concentrated daylight attack on London. The concussion from a nearby bomb violently shook the house foundation, broke most of its windows, and caused major cracks in the walls. No injuries occurred; everyone had been in the shelter. Neither Chad nor Diane ever mentioned these damages in their letters–they did not want the children to worry.

Dave and Gladys were not as lucky. A delayed-action bomb destroyed their East End flat in late September. The bomb exploded only minutes after a UXB official had ordered them out of their flat. Gladys still had nightmares about the explosion. The thought of those poor men being blown up while attempting to deactivate the bomb was almost more than she could bear.

Because the Haskells could no longer live in their flat they stayed in makeshift quarters provided by the government and routinely used a nearby Underground station as a bomb shelter each night. It was during this time that Gladys and Dave wished they had not withdrawn the children from the evacuation program–especially when they learned the area where they had gone during their brief participation had remained untouched by the bombing. Gladys seldom spoke to her brother after the Blitz began. The special opportunity to evacuate the Montgomery children to America had made her jealous. She thought it unfair her children were in danger, while Ann and Graham were safe. Chad and Diane, learning this, tried to make amends with offers of some of their children's old clothing. Gladys stubbornly declined. Envy and pride had replaced sisterly love.

In October, the Germans again changed their tactics. They no longer concentrated on the dock areas, instead they began indiscriminate bombing of all of London. It was during this phase that Pinnington came under its fiercest attack. One of the heaviest attacks of all occurred on October 15. Along with the more conventional bombs, on this one day alone, the Germans dropped over seventy-thousand incendiary bombs. These incendiaries created new problems for the residents. To keep the fires under control the National Fire Service had created an organization of fire watchers. All three members of the Montgomery family were assigned to the local brigade. Their duty, to sit on the roofs of important buildings, watch for fires, and douse them wherever they could. The assignment frightened Diane. Each time bombs began to fall she would become fearful and nearly hysterical, wanting desperately to vacate the roof before any fires started. Fortunately, no bombs ever fell near her building, there was never a fire, and she had no need to use her bucket of sand.

By the fourth of November, no Londoner doubted the phony war had ended. Everyone was well aware England was engaged in a serious war. However, even with no end in sight to this awful London Blitz, morale remained surprisingly high.

Chapter 52

Monday, 4 November 1940

"Wake up, Chad! It's a quarter past seven. We overslept! We're late for work." Diane said, as she jumped hurriedly out of bed.

"Quarter past seven? What happened? Why is it so late?" Chad asked, sitting up and rubbing his eyes.

"I forgot to set the alarm last night. I must have been too sleepy, or thought I would do it after the raids," she speculated, "but they didn't wake me. "I don't understand it."

"Did we have a raid last night?"

"Maybe we didn't."

"That certainly is odd. Jerry has been coming over every night for ever so long. When was it he first started his nightly visits?

"Nearly two months ago," he said, answering his own question. "Could we have grown so accustomed that we slept through one without noticing?"

"I don't think so, Chad. Those horrible things always wake me. There must not have been any," she postulated. "Wouldn't it be wonderful if Hitler finally came to his senses and decided to stop this stupid war."

"There's little chance of that, dear. I know we've been shooting down huge numbers of his aircraft each time they fly over, but, from what the *Times* says, he still has many more to send. It's unlikely even his recent losses would dissuade him. I don't like to be a doomsayer, but there could be another reason. Maybe the invasion has started. It would explain the change in tactics. Or perhaps he changed his target again, has chosen some place other than London. He's done that sort of thing a number of times before.

"Whatever the reason, we should be thankful for the one night of uninterrupted sleep. Now if only my supervisor will forgive me for being late. He really should, you know. When he notices how much more alert and efficient I am after an entire night's rest, he won't be able to complain too much. In any case, we had better leave as soon as we can.

"If there were no raids last night a lot of people probably overslept. He'll need to forgive an awful large number of workers," Chad chuckled.

Chad, as he usually did whenever he left the house, looked forlornly at the cracked walls and broken windows covered with boards. He wondered if they should attempt repairs during the lull in the raids. Then quickly reminded himself, "One night without a raid doesn't mean things have changed. Besides, even if the lull continues, there is no one available, or enough building materials, to make the repairs." He decided they would need to make do with the simple temporary fixes he had already completed. It would probably be better to wait anyway. He had just learned that the Chancellor of the Exchequer was preparing an insurance scheme whereby the government would, as Churchill had instructed, "pay, in full and at once, all damage from the fire of the enemy." The funds were to be available shortly.

As he closed the door, he looked at the pictures of Ann and Graham on the mantel. He quickly looked away. He still could not bear to look at them. He missed them so much.

Diane was also thinking of Ann and Graham. She wondered what they were doing at that moment. With the time difference, they would most likely be asleep. She could imagine her little girl and boy snuggled under their eiderdowns. "What precious children," she thought, "if only they were here with us!" She looked at the bomb-destroyed vacant house next door and changed her mind. "No, it's better they're not. They don't need to put up with terrifying air raids, damaged buildings, severe shortages, and strict rationing. I'm glad they're in America–safe and secure."

She looked up at Ann's bedroom window, "Oh, no I'm not. Oh, Ann! I wish you were here," she sobbed. "I am to blame. I'm the one who sent you away." The decision still troubled her. She still had doubts that it had been the correct thing to do. "I probably will never be certain," she thought, "at least not until they safely return home– whenever that is." Some people were now estimating the children would be gone for at least a year. She was beginning to think it would be much longer. She hadn't mentioned this to anyone, not even Chad; she was afraid repeating it out loud might, somehow, validate her hypothesis.

As she did every morning, she hoped there would be another letter from Ann or Graham waiting in the postbox when she returned home after work. Those letters meant so much to her. The last one was from Ann. It had come on Saturday. It told about Graham's visit to the farm. At least Graham and Ann could visit each other often, that was something. It still upset her when she thought how the company had separated Ann and Graham. Although, from what Ann said, it sounded as if she liked farm life. That surprised Diane. She found it difficult to visualize her sweet, delicate little girl gathering eggs, milking cows, and working in the hayfield. She hoped they didn't ask Ann to do too many of those kinds of chores every day.

From Ida's letter, it sounded as if the Schaefers were treating Ann nicely; that was a relief. Diane liked what Ida had said; she sounded sweet and sincere and, more importantly, concerned for Ann's welfare. It certainly hadn't sounded as if they had asked Ann to do anything they wouldn't expect from their own children. She promised herself she would write to Ida after dinner, something she should have done long ago. It had been nearly two weeks since she received Ida's letter.

Graham's last letter suggested things were going well for him, too, but it was difficult to know for certain. He didn't write often, and when he did, his letters were usually brief. She had to smile when she thought how much he talked about Meg in his letters. He obviously likes his foster sister. "Too bad he's not as fond of Yvonne," she thought. Then, as if trying to assure herself, her thoughts returned to Meg, "The longer he knows her, the more squabbles they'll likely have. More than likely they will be at odds with each other before long. Isn't that the way it is with brothers and sisters?" Fred seemed like a good companion for Graham. She was glad he lived next door. It was almost the same as having a brother nearby.

Her mind shifted to Henry. Although she knew it was a fruitless wish, she wanted him home. She missed him and worried for his safety, more and more each day. He couldn't tell them where he was, but it was fairly obvious he was in a hot, dry region. Chad and she had long ago concluded he was somewhere in North Africa.

She hoped they were mistaken. North Africa was not the best place to be these past five months. In June, Mussolini declared war on England, and almost immediately intense fighting had broken out between British and Italian troops on the road between Tobruk and Bardia near the Egyptian-Libya border. Although the fight ended within a few days and British losses were light, Diane and Chad had many anxious moments waiting to receive a letter from him. The lull lasted until the Italian forces made a major push across the Egyptian frontier in mid September. Four days later the Italians were in Sidi Barrani. Since then, the action had settled down to a series of small skirmishes. British casualties continued to be light compared to the Italians', but Chad and Diane took little solace in the news. Their concern for Henry's safety grew with each new engagement reported.

"What're you two still doing here?" Yvonne asked, as she met them on the front walkway. She looked much more cheerful than she had for some time. "Shouldn't you be at work?"

"We forgot to set the alarm," Chad said, looking somewhat sheepish. "We planned to do it after the raid. Either we slept through it, or there wasn't a raid last night."

"Nary a one. Can you imagine? Everyone at the factory was talking about it this morning. They can't understand what made them suddenly stop," Yvonne reported enthusiastically.

"It is strange," Chad agreed.

"I hope it continues today. I'm badly in need of a day of uninterrupted sleep," Yvonne said, wistfully. "Wouldn't it be wonderful if those wretched raids were over?" Almost as an afterthought, she added, "By the way, I plan to skip St. John's this afternoon."

"Why?" inquired Diane.

"Because I'm bloody well tired of rolling bandages, Mum. I made plans to meet some friends at the *Boar & Whistle* instead."

"You know your work at St. John's is important, Yvonne. You can't simply stop. They need you." complained Diane. "If nothing else, think of your brother Henry. He can't decide when he has had enough. He can't simply stop soldiering whenever he feels like it. The Army wouldn't permit it. What, heaven forbid, if the bandage you didn't roll was the one he needed?"

"Don't do that, Mum. I don't need a bunch of bloody guilts piled on me. I'm tired. I need some rest and, especially, some relaxation. Don't tell me what I can and can't do. We've already been through all that. If I'm old enough to work, I should be old enough to make my own decisions."

"But, Yvonne ..."

"To bloody hell with the volunteer work," Yvonne snapped. "Forget it. I don't need it!"

"Don't talk to your mother that way," Chad ordered.

"To hell with you too! I would not have had to work, or roll those damn bandages, if you had sent me to America with Ann and Graham," she cried, then stormed up the steps to her bedroom.

"Oh, Chad! What has happened to Yvonne? Have we lost her, too?" Diane sobbed.

"It's just this terrible war, Diane. Everybody is on edge. Yvonne will be all right–once we return to normal times. Don't worry."

"I hope you're right, Chad. I hope you're right!"

As bus number 297 wound its way along Castlebar Road, Chad stared absentmindedly at the seatback in front of him. He was deep in thought. He was worried about Yvonne's increasing hostility and rebellion. It had to be more than just a result of the war. Part of it was due to not going to America, he was certain of that much. Another part was probably his refusal to let her continue her schooling. He was sorry about that, but what could he do? Diane and he could not afford an additional two or more years of school expenses. The family really needed Yvonne's income, just to stay solvent. Besides, what good would an education do her? She could never hope to go to university, her destiny was either ordinary factory work or some other menial work. The futility of working-class daughters pursuing additional education was one thing George and he agreed about.

He worried about Henry too. If the war did not end soon, the chances were huge that Henry would serve on one too many combat patrols and become one more entry on the growing list of casualties. Chad had seen it in the Great War. A chap only lasted so long, eventually almost everyone had bad luck.

He had to quit thinking about Henry. It depressed him too much.

He thought about Graham and little Ann. Tears came to his eyes.

He quickly switched his thoughts to Diane. It didn't help much. He was worried about her too. Her excessive concern for her children was beginning to show. She was not as healthy as she once was. She blamed it on the work at the factory and the many hours spent in the bomb shelter, but he knew it was really the despondency caused by her missing children. He wished he could do something to ease her mind, but there seemed to be nothing. It had been horrible the last several months. "The bloody war is causing too many problems," he sighed. He wished it either would end soon, or Hitler and Churchill would at least agree to end the air raids on each other's cities. One would think they could find some sort of compromise. Hadn't there been a lull last night? Maybe it was a good sign–or perhaps Hitler had a new plan in mind.

In a way, Chad got his wish that day. The "Battle of Britain" had once again entered a new phase. Unfortunately, the change would not help Diane and Chad. The German bombardment would last for six more months, this time, not only London, but the entire island was subjected to air attacks.

A letter was waiting in the post box when Diane returned from work. She quickly opened it and began reading.

No 9
RFD #1, Dexter Hills, Ohio, USA
Saturday, 28 September 1940

Dear Mum and Dad,

Your first five letters arrived today–four from you, Mum, and the note from Dad! They arrived at the Bender factory yesterday afternoon and were immediately sent special delivery to the farm. They arrived this afternoon! How wonderful to finally hear from you. You will never know how lonely it has been without a letter. Even though Aunt Ida, Uncle Jack, Karen, and Ned are all treating me wonderfully, I still miss you sooo ... much!!!

After I read your letter (over and over again), they called me to the telephone (at the Ekenwilders–our neighbors on the farm next to us). Graham had called. He had received letters too. He had only two, since Benders sent the two addressed to both of us to me. We shared your letters with each other and talked a long time about how lovely it was hearing from you. Afterwards, the Schaefers took me to the cinema in McKinley Heights–in celebration of receiving your letters. We saw "Rebecca" starring Lawrence Oliver. It was good to hear someone talking proper English again. Everyone here talks with that terrible American accent. (Can you imagine, they all say I'm the one who has the accent. How ridiculous!)

"How homesick she must be," Diane thought as she continued to read.

There was a newsreel at the cinema last night. It showed people who were in a unit called the Civil Defence Service. They said it included former members of the Fire Guard, Air Raid Precautions, and the Home Guard. The uniforms they wore were quite handsome. I'll bet Dad looks extremely spiffy in his new uniform.

"I hope they don't show the children pictures of all the death and destruction caused by the Blitz. We sent them to America to escape the war–not to see pictures of it in the newsreels," she thought somewhat bitterly.

School is going well. I plan to take your letters to school on Monday to share it with the class. That is, if the class shows interest and Mr. Teasley (my homeroom teacher) permits it.

"At least she seems to be doing well in school. It's odd though, she has not said anything about any school chums. I hope this is only an oversight. I imagine she has many good friends by now."

Living with two separate families is still working well. Graham seems to have found a good family and I certainly have. Aunt Ida has invited Graham to our farm again very soon. (We have not set a definite date yet.) One thing though, Graham keeps worrying you are angry because he let them assign us to different homes. Please don't be–it is perfectly all right. Perhaps you could say something to assure him in your next letter? Your approval certainly would ease the poor boy's mind.

"That brave little soldier! I know not living with Graham bothers her, even though she says it doesn't. Although the Schaefers must be grand people–and the letters from both Ann and Mrs. Schaefer say she is getting along splendidly–it still would have been better if the children had stayed together."

Her eyes began to cloud as she continued to read.

The puppy Uncle Jack gave me is growing rapidly. Ned corrected me when I first called the puppy Prince. I now call HER Lady–if you know what I mean. Ha, Ha. HER eyes opened not too long ago. Uncle Jack says she is about four weeks old now.

"That sweet little girl! She is beginning to learn about the birds and the bees," Diane sobbed. "Before long she will be a young woman–and I'll not be there to give her the much needed motherly advice. Why, oh why, did we send those children away?"

Well, dears, it is terribly late (I am writing this by kerosene light after the cinema) so I will say good-bye for now. I just wanted to drop you a note so you would know I received your letters. Take care.

Love,

Ann

P.S. Now that you sent his address, I will write to Henry. Soon!

Chad read Ann's letter when he arrived home. Afterwards, Diane and he held each other for several minutes and cried. They had just regained their composure when Yvonne came downstairs, ready to go to the *Boar & Whistle*. "Look, Yvonne, we received another letter from Ann today. She says she has received the first of our letters," Diane said eagerly.

Yvonne scanned the letter briefly, then threw it on the table. "I don't wish to read any more of this rubbish," she said, contemptuously. "The little snip doesn't want me to read it. I see she addressed the letter to just the two of you."

"Don't be silly. It's for you too. She just addressed it to us because she was responding to our letter. You don't think your sister would purposely snub you, do you?" Diane asked, almost pleading.

"Yes I do. She would have included my name had she intended it for me," Yvonne retorted.

"Stop it, Miss High and Mighty!" Chad scolded. "All of her other letters–all eight of them–all but this one, included your name. What do you expect from her? How often have you written?"

"I never wrote! What's more, I have no intention of writing to the little brat," she shouted and rushed out the door, slamming it behind her.

"What are we going to do, Chad?" Diane sobbed. "Isn't it bad enough we have one child in the Army, maybe–Heaven forbid–wounded, and two children in America, homesick and lonely? Do we need a sassy and unruly one here at home?"

"Calm down, Diane. It was only a family spat. She's simply tired and frustrated. She'll get over it."

"No, Chad, I don't think so. I think God is trying to punish us for sending our two youngest away."

There were no air raid alerts that night either–but neither Chad nor Diane were able to get much sleep.

Chapter 53

Wednesday, 6 November 1940

The Schaefers had discussed the presidential election many times since Ann first arrived at the farm. As the election grew close, the debates increased noticeably. The family ate few dinners without an argument over the qualifications of the candidates. Everyone thought their candidate was best. Karen wanted to see President Roosevelt, or F.D.R. as everyone called him, re-elected. Ida, Jack and Ned said two terms were enough and wanted Republican candidate, Willkie, and his running mate, McNary, to win.

The election was a prevalent topic at school as well. Mr. Teasley, towards the end of October, chose the election campaign as a homeroom topic and asked everyone to study the newspapers and prepare a list of issues in favor of whichever candidate they chose. After debating the issues, the class would cast ballots in a mock election.

Ann had no difficulty with the assignment; the Schaefer dinnertime debates had taught her well. She thought of herself almost as an expert and felt little need to study. She chose Willkie, mainly because he was Jack and Ida's choice.

The election was obviously a concern everywhere that fall. The discussions were as intense at school as they had been on the farm. Almost everyone at school had firm opinions about their choice, repeating, like Ann, mostly the arguments heard at home. Some did not believe F.D.R. should run for a third term since no president had ever done it before. Others thought Roosevelt deserved more time to make his New Deal programs work. Some complained his programs did little to end the Depression, were poorly conceived, were failure prone, caused too much strife and sloth, and should be canceled. They argued if he did not halt them soon America would lose its potential for greatness. Others argued that the American economy was beginning to improve, thanks to the New Deal, and further that any premature changes would negate all the gains already realized. Some countered with statements that the gains were only temporary and the programs terribly expensive.

The war in Europe also formed a major part of the debate. Some said the U.S. should not help England. It was too costly and already too late. Others complained Europe should have worried about Germany sooner and because of that deserved all that had happened. Still others said the war might go on for many months, with Germany eventually occupying England; it would be senseless to give them more assistance. Almost all agreed that the United States should not enter the war and focused mostly on which candidate proposed the best method to keep the U.S. out of it.

Few realized how much these discussions were bothering Ann, especially the negative statements concerning England. She had difficulty concentrating on the election each time she heard one of these comments. She feared for her parents' safety and wanted even more than ever to be with them as soon as possible. But what were the chances of that? Already going home next summer seemed slim. There was even a possibility Graham and she might not see their parents until the following Christmas. It was a horrible thought and made it difficult to keep her composure.

She resolved not to give up hope. She would pray a little harder for an end to the conflict and a quick return home. She decided to pick the candidate who would send her home the quickest, the one most likely to involve the U.S. in the war. As in the Great War before, she believed America's involvement would help England tremendously. Still the choice would be difficult to make. The more she heard the more confused she became. She definitely no longer felt like an expert. Both candidates claimed they would keep the nation out of the war, but neither announced plans that convinced her one way or the other. She had to admit it, she was still uncertain who had the better qualifications.

On the day of the mock election, a group of her classmates challenged her right to vote. They said it improper for an English citizen to vote in an American election. A heated debate followed. Many children made impassioned speeches, arguing against her right. Oliver pointed out that, as a *bona fide* Dexter Hills student, Ann should be permitted to vote. Vicky argued against it. Finally Mr. Teasley resolved the dispute. He decreed Ann could vote.

Ann voted for Roosevelt. It was a speech by Oliver, just before balloting started, that made up her mind. He had done his homework well and had presented a strong case for Roosevelt. Oliver also seemed to take the sincerest interest in Britain's success and expressed an interest in a quick end to the conflict. If he was voting for Roosevelt, she would too.

When they counted the votes, Wendell Willkie won by a narrow margin. The result disappointed Ann, not because she had lost, it really didn't matter much, but because Oliver had lost. For a reason she could not explain, she felt a growing bond with him.

After their vote, Mr. Teasley compared the electoral college system used to elect the president with the procedures used to determine the heads of state in other countries. Ann was thankful he did not ask her how England chose its prime minister. Somehow Mr. Teasley had known she couldn't answer. It was not the first time he had been so perceptive. She was beginning, in spite of her initial aversion to his stern manner, to think he was an outstanding, empathic teacher. She wished she had more closely followed the election of Prime Minister Churchill last May, perhaps she could have responded to Mr. Teasley's question.

Although the straw vote ended the formal homeroom discussions, the debate continued both at school and at home. At dinner one evening Jack complained F.D.R. was claiming too much credit for the economic upturn. "The economy," he said, "is simply beginning to respond to war orders, and, with or without F.D.R., the European war and its need for war materiel will soon create an employment boom in the U.S. It's high time there is someone in office willing to decrease the costly subsidies instituted by F.D.R.."

Karen argued everyone was living better today than they had at any time since the 20's. "Yes," said Ned. "Look how well off we are. Here we are with an old rickety coal furnace, no inside plumbing, and no electricity. Roosevelt has really made a difference."

"What has he done for us?" Jack asked, expanding on Ned's comment. "If we had a president in the White House with industrial experience it could make a big difference. We need someone who knows how to manage, a person who appreciates farming. Remember, Willkie has experience as president of Commonwealth and Southern Corporation. He also owns two farms."

"That's nonsense, Dad," responded Karen. "Willkie is an Indiana lawyer and a politician, just like all the others. They say he was a lifelong Democrat, voted for F.D.R. in '32. We should stick with someone we know, someone who doesn't change his mind, someone we can trust. Look at all the people F.D.R. has put to work on WPA, and all the improvements made by the CCC. Do we want another Republican in there? Remember what Hoover did to us in 1929."

"Roosevelt doesn't change his mind?" Jack asked, laughing and ignoring her comment about Hoover. "What's Roosevelt doing with

Henry Wallace as his new running mate? Why didn't he stick with Vice President Garner?"

"Because Garner and he have different philosophies," Karen defended.

"No. It's because he believes Wallace can deliver more votes than Garner. Old Franklin wants to win a third term so badly that he doesn't care who he tramps on to get there. His claim of not actively seeking a third term is a big charade. The draft Roosevelt hoopla at the Chicago convention was a well orchestrated sham," Ned argued. "You know as well as I that the PWA, the WPA, and all the other agencies he created are just the first steps towards his plan to socialize America. Handouts and welfare are not what made America. It was good old raw capitalism that did it, the concept of free enterprise. It was the opportunity for people to do whatever they were capable of doing–and wanted to do–that made us great. Constraint by government regulations and–no offense to you, Ann–limits imposed by a class-based society did not make us strong."

Ann did not understand all Ned had said. If "limits" meant being held back from advanced studies because one belonged to the working class, as Yvonne was–and as she, Edith and all the others in their class would someday be–then she guessed Ned had a point. She would ask him to explain it more fully someday.

"You see, Ann," Ida interrupted. "This is how we Americans go about electing our government officials. Everyone has his own opinion about the candidates, most of which are the result of false rumor and simple speculation. We argue amongst ourselves, sometimes say mean things we shouldn't, and, finally, vote our conscience. Somehow the process works. We end up with good, reasonable men in office."

"Except the last two elections," Ned corrected. Everyone but Karen laughed.

The Schaefers had not discussed the candidates' positions about involvement in the war. That surprised Ann. She wondered whether they thought it unimportant, or simply did not want to bring up things involving England–did not want to alarm her. She was sorry they hadn't discussed it because it seemed awfully important. She knew Willkie had charged the New Deal with leaving the nation vulnerable by "promoting internal disunity, squandering billions on unproductive projects, and shamefully neglecting defenses." She had read his Sunday quote claiming "all of us–Republicans, Democrats, and Independents–believe in giving aid to the heroic British people. We must make available to them the products of our industry." After Ann recalled that, she wondered if she should change her mind again and favor Willkie.

Still, she was uncertain whether he would really support England as well as Roosevelt would. After all, they were saying McNary was an isolationist. Willkie had chosen him as his running mate, what did that make Willkie? Besides, Roosevelt had said in Cleveland last Saturday, "Our policy is to give all possible material to nations that still resist aggression across the Atlantic and Pacific oceans." England was certainly one of those nations. That made her favor Roosevelt once more.

"Hadn't Willkie claimed he was the guarantor of peace? And hadn't he claimed Roosevelt was a warmonger?" she thought. Some were saying that even though F.D.R. was promising that America would not enter the war, based on his past neglected pledges, the U.S. would be at war by spring. That in itself made her think Roosevelt was a better choice. Everyone admitted if the U.S. entered the war, England would benefit. It seemed to her he was England's only hope.

She did not tell the Schaefers about her final choice. She did not think it proper for a guest to express her opinion about so important a matter. Besides, she was just a little English girl. What did she really know about American politics?

It was thus a pleasant feeling to awake and find Franklin Delano Roosevelt in office for a third term. The newspapers reported the popular vote was twenty-seven million for Roosevelt, twenty-two million for Willkie. The final electoral college vote was four-hundred forty-nine to eighty-two. She still did not understand why there was an electoral college.

Two days later President Roosevelt announced his "rule of thumb" whereby the U.S. would divide weapons coming off the production line, roughly fifty percent for U.S. forces and fifty percent for British and Canadian forces. Ann hoped this would make everyone in England, particularly her family, happy.

She was glad America had elected President Roosevelt again.

Chapter 54

Saturday, 9 November 1940

The northeastern Ohio autumn lingered much later than usual in 1940. By early November, the days remained unseasonably mild and pleasant, a few scattered pockets of frost, mostly in the lowlands, were the only hints that winter was on its way. Many of the leaves still clung stubbornly to the trees, the landscape still dotted with an unusual mixture of brilliant yellows and reds. Throughout October, even the rainfall had shown restraint. Only a few scattered showers were large enough to dampen the outside activities of the children. It was almost as if the weather was trying to prove it could be as temperate in Ohio as it usually was in London.

But by Friday evening, a cold front had moved in from the northwest, and with it came a sudden and significant drop in temperature. Snow flurries started early in the evening, increased in intensity throughout the night, and by midnight the temperature had dropped into the teens and several inches of snow blanketed the ground. Then, in early morning, as if to apologize for the sudden change, the storm passed on and the sky became cloudless. Only in the low areas did wispy puffs of mist rise from the freezing ponds and icy streams to dull the clear air. Elsewhere shiny bright stars sparkled downward in the still dark sky, their tiny dots of light reflecting upward to form sparkling crystals in the snow. With the snow, came a soft, almost eerie, still.

The signs of dawn had just begun to illuminate the room when the first wake up crow of the Schaefer rooster interrupted the silence. It did not wake Ann–she was already awake. She had been lying for some time, snuggled under the hand quilted feather comforter, thinking of England, and hoping Ida would not call her–not on such a cold morning. She could tell it was cold, frost covered most of the window panes and her breath was clearly visible each time she exhaled. While questioning her courage to throw off the covers, she heard Jack in the cellar stoking the furnace. If she remained in bed just a little longer the house would be warm and cozy; or at least she hoped so, it was so terribly cold in her room.

Ann had almost convinced herself that the cold would not be too bad, so long as she made every move count–planned everything carefully–wasted no time dressing, grabbed every article of warm clothing she had. Then she remembered the outhouse. How would she ever find the courage to run outside this morning? She hoped Ida would have some good advice on how to survive that icy adventure.

As she lay contemplating all this she felt the nudge of a wet nose under her arm. She laughed and affectionately rubbed Lady's tummy. Lady, in response, playfully nipped at her hand and gave a slight whimper. "Quiet, Lady," Ann cautioned, "We don't want Aunt Ida to know you're here."

For over two weeks now, long enough for it to become almost routine, Ann had ignored her conscience and had been sneaking the dog into her bedroom at night. She knew she shouldn't, Lady was only a puppy and probably should still be with her mother at night. Perhaps even more important, the visit was still not authorized, Ida had never given her official consent. But Lady had grown so rapidly, and Ann had been lonely at night; she couldn't resist. So far, to Ann's relief, nothing had been said, there were even times when she suspected Ida was aware of this secret nighttime sojourn. Whatever the reason, it was good it had continued. The growing bond between the girl and her dog had helped make her a little less homesick, and a little more content.

As they lay in bed playing, Ann could hear the muffled voices of Jack and Ida talking in the kitchen below. She tried to make out what they were saying but failed.

"Installing electric power would greatly improve things, especially on these cold winter mornings," Jack said wistfully.

"But can we afford it?" Ida asked.

"I think we can, if we're careful with our money, if it's a good year for maple syrup, and if the bank will give us a loan."

"That's an awful lot of ifs, Jack. Don't forget, now that winter is here, Ann will need more clothes. The poor thing can't continue to wear Karen's old school jumpers and blouses. They're too light for this winter weather. Besides, they were nearly ready for the rag bin when we gave them to her."

Ida was silent for a few minutes, thinking carefully about what she would say next. "She's such a nice girl and I love her very dearly, but maybe we shouldn't have invited her to stay with us. The way things look in England now it could be a long time before she goes home. Maybe we can't afford to keep her that long."

"You're not serious, are you, Ida? Of course we should have asked her to stay with us," Jack scolded. He then added, "I don't care how long she remains; we'll keep her as long as necessary. Darn it, Ida, I love that little girl–just as you do. She's such a sweetheart. Buy whatever she needs, we'll make do. It won't bankrupt us. We still should be able to install the electricity next spring. We'll simply be a little more careful. Perhaps we can buy a few less appliances to start with, or perhaps delay installing some of the light fixtures."

"I know you love her, Jack. Maybe we can delay the bedroom curtains too–or maybe I can sew them myself. There have been some lovely patterns on the feed sacks lately. The next time you go for feed I'll go with you to see if there's a pattern I could use."

"Don't overdo the scrimping and saving, Ida. With everyone going into defense work these days there are fewer farm workers available.

That portends higher farm prices next year, just about the time our crops and cattle are ready for market. We should get considerably more for them than we budgeted," Jack assured her.

"I've been thinking," he said, changing the subject. "With all the heavy bombing reported in London lately, there's a chance Ann's parents could be killed."

"Oh, Jack! Don't say such a horrible thing!"

"No, we need to consider that possibility. We must face reality, it could happen. The war is killing people every day." He thought for a moment, then continued, "I was thinking, maybe we should write to Ann's folks; discuss the possibility of their death, and ask their advice on what to do with Ann in such an event."

"I certainly won't write a letter like that, Jack," Ida shuddered.

"What I think we should do is offer to continue caring for Ann if they both should die. Or better yet, we could offer to adopt her. It might be a relief for them–to know she would be legally looked after. Naturally, we would leave it entirely up to them. We would simply make the offer and wait for their response."

"How would you phrase such a letter?" Ida asked contemptuously. "Would you say, 'if you die we want your child' or maybe 'we love your child so much we want to steal her, make her our own. The last thing we should do is make them think we have even the slightest inclination of taking their child from them. Besides, even if you find a polite way to ask them they still might be insulted. If anyone suggested adopting Karen or Ned I know I would be. Let's forget it."

She tried to change the topic. "Karen told me she saw my brother, Ted, at Klink's Tavern last evening. She said he was acting quite mean again. I don't know what we're going to do with that man. Every time he has a few drinks, he seems to do stupid things. I pity his poor wife."

"I'll think of some way to say it without insulting them," Jack continued, ignoring her attempt to talk about something else. "We don't want to give a false impression; we must assure them we're only thinking of Ann's welfare. I'll write to Mr. Montgomery, perhaps that would be the best way to do it."

"Well I'm not going to think about it any more. It's time to call the children," she said as she left the kitchen, a disgusted look on her face.

Ann could not recall ever seeing so much snow. The snowfalls in Pinnington seemed mere flurries compared to what she was looking at. Perhaps they had snowfalls as deep in the mountains of Scotland, or Wales, but she had never been to those places. She thought it marvelously beautiful. Most impressive were the trees bordering the meadow. The snow, because it was the first of the season, was wet, and as it fell, it had attached itself to the individual tree branches, creating a huge matrix of white silhouettes. Now, with each wind gust, large chunks of snow fell from the branches and created, what Ann romanticized as, an animated forest. She hoped everything would stay as it was until she completed her chores so she could run through the snowdrifts and explore the odd looking trees up close.

As she worked, she thought about her mum and dad's latest letters. Five more had arrived since the initial batch. In mid September, Bender Electric had provided Diane and Chad with Ann and Graham's new addresses. Diane immediately began addressing her letters directly to the farm which shortened the delivery time by a few days. They were arriving now on a more or less regular, once-a-week, schedule.

Ann also thought of her promise to post a letter to Henry. She had been frightfully derelict in fulfilling that promise. She would delay it no longer.

With this new sense of duty and her planned walk postponed, she sat down as soon as her chores were over and began writing:

> *% Jack Schaefer*
> *RFD #1, Dexter Hills, Ohio, USA*
> *Saturday, 9 November 1940*

Dear Henry,

Please forgive me for not having written sooner. I only received your address from Mum a little while ago. ...

In truth, this was a fib. It had been more than a month since she received it. She thought Henry would be happier if she did not reveal how tardy she had been.

... I hope this letter finds you well, rested, with food in your tummy, and stationed far behind the front line. Above all, let's hope this war ends soon so you, Graham, and I can meet back to Pinnington. I especially don't want you fighting anymore. Please tell your commanding officer I said that. Tell him I know how much you hated your fight in Europe this spring and believe you should be relieved of further duty—that battle in Dunkirk should be all the fighting any soldier must endure.

As I am certain Mum has already told you, Graham and I are now in America but not living in the same billet as we had planned. We are staying with separate families. The family I am with is very nice. Their names are Ida and Jack Schaefer, I call them Aunt Ida and Uncle Jack. They have two children. Karen is eighteen. She has red hair and is <u>very</u>

pretty–you would like her! Perhaps someday I can introduce you to her? Who knows what would come of that! Ha, ha! Ned is fifteen. He is a very handsome chap. No, he is not my boyfriend–and not my brother either. No one can replace you or Graham. As you can see, even here, I am again the baby of the family. We live on a farm and, even though I have many farm chores to do, it is a wonderful place to live. Can you believe it? Your "Little Annie" is milking cows!

The best thing here is the food. There certainly is no shortage of food in America. We have more to eat than anyone could ever want, nothing like the English shortages. I eat so much I'll probably look like a bloated pig when you see me again. Ha, ha!

I attend school in Dexter Hills. I'm in the seventh grade, which the Americans call the first year of junior high school. The children are nice and the subjects are interesting and moderately difficult. I am taking English, geography, general math, home economics, general science, art, and music (chorus). The last two, art and music meet on alternate days. It is a fairly tough schedule, but I enjoy all the studies and believe I am performing satisfactorily–in spite of a few difficulties caused by the transition to the new American curriculum. It is quite different from our school in England. I received my first progress assessment (it's called a report card in America) a few weeks back. It was not as good as I had hoped, but I plan to do better next time–now that I have caught up on all my deficiencies. There are some areas where we are ahead of the Americans too. I can coast whenever we come to one of those. Unfortunately they do not come up often.

In any case, do not worry whether I study enough. I will continue to do so–as you instructed. I promise! I well remember how you stressed the importance of an education and will not disappoint you. After all, you are my big brother, and I always try to listen to the advice of such a nice person.

Well, dear, it is almost time for supper so I should close this letter. I will write again–soon. Please drop me a line when you can. I would love to hear from you. But only do it if it doesn't take away from the more important things–like shooting Germans and ducking bullets.

Take good care of yourself! God bless you.

Love,
Ann

"After every major snowfall," Karen told Ann during supper, "the Dexter Hills merchants block off Station Street so we can go sledding. It's great sport. Would you care to join us this evening?"

"Could I, Aunt Ida?" Ann asked.

"Of course, child, but first I must find you something warm to wear."

As Karen, Ned, and Ann rode down the lane with the sled bouncing in the back of the truck, Ann had on so many clothes it was difficult to recognize her. She quickly began to remove some of the items. After she had taken off one of the coats, the earmuffs, and several scarves she gave a big sigh of relief, and told them she was thankful she hadn't died of heat prostration. Everyone laughed.

When their truck approached Station Street, Ann could hear the children shouting and saw the sleds racing down the hill. She thought of Graham and wondered if he was sledding too. She hoped he felt as excited about the new snow as she did.

Oliver was thinking too. His thoughts were about Ann, as they had been ever since he watched her school bus leave the school grounds on Friday. He couldn't help himself, he missed being around her. He loved to hear her charming accent, enjoyed seeing her with her striking good looks and liked talking with her because of her interesting ideas and thoughts. He found her charming, witty, and wonderfully intelligent. It was too bad she didn't feel the same about him. Recently, even talking to Ann had been difficult for him; for some reason his words always seemed to get twisted. On many of these occasions she certainly must have thought he was a simpleton. He somehow had to let her know he wasn't really that inept, let her know how interested he was in her.

He supposed it had started when she first arrived in Dexter Hills. It certainly had grown more serious recently, especially after Ann forbade his visits to the farm. He wanted to know her better. He needed to tell her how he felt, needed an excuse to meet with her, somewhere outside school, someplace where they could have a long, uninterrupted talk. It was true, she still sat beside him in homeroom, and they were together in geography class. Seeing her every day was better than not seeing her at all, but it was still too restrictive. A few words between classes, a few whispers during class were all well and good but not very satisfying. He had to be alone with her. He didn't know why. He had never felt quite like this before, not even with Vicky.

However, he had to be careful not to antagonize Vicky. She seemed always to be lurking nearby whenever he tried to talk with Ann. For reasons he could not understand, Vicky had developed an apparent dislike for her and acted odd any time she found the two of them together. But the petty jealousy of a steady girlfriend was not going to interfere with this rare opportunity to befriend an interesting foreigner. He saw no justification for Vicky resenting an innocent friendship, especially since Ann's stay in Dexter Hills would undoubtedly be for such a brief period. She would be returning to England before long and out of his life for good.

It, therefore, came as a pleasant surprise when he saw the Schaefer truck pull into the parking lot, with Ann inside. "Hi, Ned. Hi, Karen. Hi, Ann," he said, as they began unloading the sled. He had been careful to greet Ann last. It would not do to appear too eager.

"Hi, Oliver," Ned answered. "How's the snow?"

"It's great. It's about as slick as it ever gets. Gee, you only have one sled. If you want to, you may sled with me, Ann."

Ned smiled, realizing almost immediately this was no casual, spur of the moment invitation, but a clever ploy to pair up. "That sounds great, Oliver. Karen and I will use this one. Go ahead, Ann, ride with Oliver, if you wish."

"Come on, Ann," Oliver shouted, turning around and running toward the top of the hill. "I'll race you to the top," he said, hoping desperately that Ann would follow.

Ann tried to catch Oliver, but he had too great a lead. She arrived at the top several steps behind. As soon as she caught her breath, she pleaded, "I've never seen such a steep hill. Are you certain it's safe for sledding?"

"You needn't worry. There's nothing to it. I've gone down many times already. Never had a spill," he boasted. "Hardly anyone ever falls off their sled. Besides, if they do, they can't hurt themselves–the snow along the edges is deep enough to soften any spill. It's perfectly safe. Come on, sit behind me. Let's go. Let's see if we can beat Karen and Ned."

As they sped down the hill Ann could feel the wind in her face. She giggled with joy, and when they nearly beat Karen and Ned, she laughed and shouted, "Come on, Oliver, we can beat them next time."

They repeated the run many times and with each trip Ann became less afraid of the hill and more willing to take risks. On several occasions they went down in what Oliver called a "belly-flopper." He laid down, his stomach on the sled, Ann lay on top of him. It surprised Ann to see how fast the snow seemed to whiz by when her eyes were so close to the ground.

After awhile, Ann was ready to try it on her own. She mounted the sled and asked Oliver to give her a push. His push was much harder than she anticipated, and she immediately lost control. She was halfway down the hill before she regained control, but as she did she spied, out of the corner of her eye, a sled veering across her path. Both sled riders attempted to swerve but failed to do so and crashed into each other. The impact tossed them into the snow banks beside the sled run.

The first voice she heard as she pulled herself out of the snow bank was from the other rider. "You really should watch where you are going, Ann," laughed Vicky. "You could have hurt someone."

Ann was not certain how to respond. She didn't know whether Vicky was teasing or serious. She decided to simply laugh and apologize, "Sorry, Vicky. It was my first trip alone. I guess I have much to learn."

By then a crowd had gathered, a few were asking if anyone was hurt or needed help. When Oliver joined the crowd, he was laughing. "What happened?" he asked.

"You know, Ollie, you really are a rotten teacher. You nearly sent Ann and me to the hospital," Vicky giggled.

They picked up their sleds and trudged back up the hill, Vicky now an integral member of the group. Although the laughter continued and everyone appeared to be having a good time, Ann decided to stop sledding. She did not particularly enjoy, as she called it, "going gooseberry." Vicky was monopolizing Oliver. He no longer paid much attention to Ann, did not seem to notice she was no longer taking her turn down the hill. "How fickle you are, Oliver," she thought. "A few minutes ago, you wanted me with you every minute. Now you barely know I exist."

Ann gave a little sigh of relief when it came time to leave; she had had enough of the gushiness of Vicky and Oliver for one day. Just as Ann turned to go, an obviously drunken man stumbled up the hill, bumping into people and almost falling as he came. "There's the little tramp," he said, looking directly at Oliver, or as directly as he could in his near stupor. "Why aren't you home, boy? Who said you could go sledding tonight?"

"Go home, Dad," Oliver ordered, blushing with embarrassment. "I'll be home later."

"Don't tell me where to go, you smart-ass kid. No one gives me orders. Particularly not my pimple-faced boy. Now get your rear end home or I'll thrash you from here to hell and back."

Ann began to shiver. She was scared and felt sorry for Oliver. So this was his father, this was the person who had been treating Oliver so dreadfully. She could understand how embarrassed Oliver must be. She had to say something in his defense. "Please, sir. He didn't mean any disrespect. It's all right."

"All right? Is that what you said? I can barely understand anything you're saying. Who are you? One of those stupid English children, I'll bet. Get out of here! Go back to England where you belong," he screamed, trying to shake his fist in her face. He leaned too far forward and fell to his knees. Embarrassed, his face grew red with rage. He rose to his feet and lunged at Ann. "You crummy limey! I'll teach you to push me."

"I didn't push you, sir," Ann said, flinching, and trying desperately to evade her attacker.

Before his dad could strike at her again, Oliver interceded. He pushed him backwards into the snow. "Leave her alone, Dad. Don't you dare hurt her." As his dad fell, he grabbed Oliver and they tumbled into the snow together. A brief tussle followed. Ludwig rolled over on top of Oliver, sat up, and began rubbing snow in Oliver's face. Oliver swung his hands wildly, trying desperately to defend himself. Several times he hit his dad in the chest. "Oh no you don't," Ludwig cried, as he grabbed Oliver by the neck and began choking him.

"Stop! You'll hurt him!" cried Vicky. She jumped on Ludwig's back and began beating him with her hands.

"Get off me, you crummy vixen!" Ludwig cried. He caught Vicky's hand, pulled her around in front of him and began slapping her.

"Stop it!" Ann sobbed, "Don't hit her!" She lunged at Ludwig and began punching him with both fists. He released Vicky and raised his arm to ward off Ann's vicious attack. The distraction was all Vicky needed, and she joined her friend in battle. The arms of the two girls thrashed at Ludwig like a swarm of bees. He could do little more than raise his arms in a hopeless attempt to defend himself.

The fight ended when Oliver, Ned, and some of the older boys grabbed Ludwig and held his head on the snowy surface. "Go on home, old man! Cool off," one of them said. By then Ludwig had passed beyond sensible awareness, the effects of booze and the strain from all the exercise was in control of his senses. He offered no more resistance and began to sob and uttered random words that no longer formed meaningful sentences. "I'll take him," Oliver offered. "Come on, Dad, it's time to go." They left together, the father now silent and subdued. The son did not look back. His dad had been too much of an embarrassment.

Vicky looked at Ann. Ann looked at Vicky. They hugged and said nothing. Neither could explain why, but a special bonding had just occurred, a special friendship had emerged.

*   *   *

Ann was quiet on the way home. She was thinking about Oliver. She was worried about him. She hoped he would not have any more problems with his father. Both Ned and Karen understood her silence. Neither knew how to help. They rode all the way in silence.

Jack was sitting at the table looking rather solemn when they arrived. "I'm sorry, Ann. The evening newspaper says Neville Chamberlain died today." He looked at Ann and added, "He was a great prime minister. Even if he did believe in appeasement, he was a good man. England will miss him."

Ann knew little about Mr. Chamberlain but feared his passing portended many new heartaches for England. She went to bed troubled and worried. "Too many bad things happened this evening," she told Lady as they snuggled close together.

The entire class was laughing.

Mr. Teasley stood in the rear of the room. "Stand straight," he ordered. "Let us look at the two of you. Don't squirm, Ann! Turn around, Graham!"

"How odd they look!" observed Vicky.

"Have you ever seen anything like it?" Oliver snickered.

"How could they? Imagine dressing that way every day," Bonnie exclaimed.

"What's the matter with us, Graham?" Ann whispered.

"Ignore them, Ann. They're jealous. They're envious of our school uniforms," Graham answered.

"School uniforms? What do you mean? What school uniforms?" Ann asked.

"The ones we're wearing," Graham laughed, startled to learn Ann did not know what she had on.

Ann looked at Graham. His clothes were different from the other boys. They were the school clothes he wore in England. She looked at herself. She was wearing her English school clothes too. She laughed. They looked so different from her American contemporaries.

She had on a navy serge gymslip with three box pleats in the front and back, a matching blazer, navy knickers, a white blouse, a red school tie, brown stockings held up by garters, and brown laced shoes. Draped over her arm was a double-breasted navy nap coat. She wore a small navy colored cap on her head.

Graham's uniform consisted of a gray suit with short trousers and blazer, white shirt, red tie, three-quarter length hose, brown shoes, and a cap similar to Ann's.

Ann looked at her classmates. The girls wore brightly colored cotton dresses, white anklets, and brown and white saddle shoes. The boys wore blue denim trousers, light colored pullovers, and tennis shoes.

She looked so different from the others. She began to cry. "I'm so ashamed! I don't want to be different. I want to be one of you. May I?" she asked, looking pleadingly at her friends.

There was no answer. They turned to face the blackboard and began conjugating sentences. Even Oliver no longer looked at her.

"Let this be a lesson to you," Mr. Teasley scolded. "Never come to school dressed in those horrible clothes again."

"But Graham does not belong here," Ann reminded him. "He belongs in Oakton."

"No longer, child. The Germans bombed Oakton last evening. It no longer exists."

Ann woke with a start. "What an odd dream," she thought.

Chapter 55

Saturday, 23 November 1940

"You really shouldn't work so hard," Sarah said, as she placed a plate of bacon, eggs, and potatoes in front of Fred. "You can't expect to complete all your chores and still play basketball, it keeps you too busy. Your studies will suffer.

"Why don't you talk to Dr. Derringer about it? I know he's a task master, but he's not unreasonable. Ask him to cutback on your duties–at least until basketball season is over. Perhaps I gave you a false impression when you first arrived. He's not a Simon Legree; he's really a very considerate man. Although he's demanding he has always been fair.

"He's quite proud you're doing so well in school and already on the junior varsity team. You are aware of that, aren't you? Why, just the other day I overheard him boasting about you and your athletic ability. I'm certain he doesn't want work here at home interfering with school."

"I know, Sarah, but Dr. and Mrs. Derringer have done so much for me already, giving me a place to stay and everything. I feel I should do all I can to show my gratitude. Besides, shoveling the snow off the driveway was my idea. He didn't ask me to do it. I just wanted to surprise him."

"Then for heaven's sake, don't add it to your list. It's much too ambitious. Do you realize how long the driveway is? He paid someone to shovel it last year and probably intends to do the same this year."

"Oh, it's really not so bad; the snow isn't very deep. It shouldn't take too long and the exercise will be good for me. If I hurry, I might be able to finish before he leaves. Wouldn't he be surprised if it were done when he left for the office?

"Anyway, today is special," he added, "I won't always be this busy. We have a team meeting this morning, a game this afternoon, and the Bender banquet this evening."

He gulped down his last piece of jellied toast and hurried out the door. "I would think basketball would provide all the exercise you'd need," Sarah shouted after him. He didn't hear her.

"My goodness! Did you shovel the driveway, Fred?" Tom asked, as he opened the garage door. "You didn't have to do that. I would have hired it done. It was awfully nice of you though; I appreciate it. Thanks.

"But why so early? Don't you know growing boys need their sleep? You could have waited until later. Why not stay in bed a little longer on these snowy winter mornings?"

"We have a game this afternoon," Fred answered. "With the team meeting and everything else, it's the only time I had to finish it.

"Oh, that's right, there's a game. I nearly forgot. By the way, congratulations. I hear you made the team."

"It's only the junior varsity, sir."

"For someone who is only in eight grade and has never played basketball before, that still is mighty impressive. Sorry, I can't be there, I have office hours, but I'll be thinking about you. Good luck." He paused for a moment, then added, "Don't get too tired. Forget your other chores today. Save your energy; it's important you whip those Buccaneers."

"Thank you, sir, but everything's under control. I've nearly finished everything."

Fred was about to enter the tool shed when a snowball struck his back. He turned to see Graham walking up the driveway, his hands in his pockets. He look innocently at Fred, then laughed. "Gotcha," he said as he started to make another snowball.

Fred dropped his shovel and quickly responded with a snowball of his own. A battle followed, accompanied with shouting, laughter, and many more snowballs. In the excitement, few hit their target. The boys soon tired of the game and sank down in the snow, gasping for breath. "I've not seen many of the others since we left camp," Graham said. "It'll be great seeing everyone tonight."

"It sure will be," Fred agreed. "Besides Sandy at the fair, and Ann and the others during Princess Elizabeth's talk last month, you're the only other person from England I've seen."

"Do you ever get homesick anymore?" Graham asked.

"Do I! Sometimes it seems all I can think about is England and home. It embarrasses me. Seems a bloke should be able to get over those feelings after being away three months."

"I think we will, Fred. Eventually. I don't think I feel quite as bad now as I did a month ago. It's only those quiet moments, when there's lots of time to think. That's when I still feel the pain. To make matters worse, I recently started thinking about my brother, Henry. I don't know why. He just seems to keep popping into my mind lately, for no apparent reason."

"He's in the Army, isn't he?"

"Yes. My parents think he's in North Africa, probably seeing action against the Italians."

"Gee, combat must be rough–being shot at and having to shoot back. It's hard to imagine. I think I would be scared to death."

"I know what you mean," Graham agreed. "I'd be scared too. Even so, as soon as I can, I'm going to join the RAF and do my bit for England."

"By the time you're old enough to enlist, the war will be over."

"Maybe not! Mr. Nelson says it's beginning to look as if Britain is stronger than anyone thought. The war could continue for a long time, especially, now that British bombers are causing so much damage to the German cities. They'll do a lot more, too–once the Americans figure out the best way to help us."

"But you're only fifteen. The war would have to last three more years before you'd be eligible to enlist. It can't possibly last that long!"

"You're probably right. Actually, it's only around two and a half years. My birthday is in June. Believe me, if there's still a need by then, I'm joining." Just then he spotted Meg. "Look! Here comes Meg. Let's snowball her!"

At first, the fight was between Meg and the two boys. Then it turned into a disorganized melee with much shouting and giggling and everyone throwing snowballs at everyone else. A few more minutes and Fred was no longer a target; Meg and Graham started aiming all their snowballs at each other. Finally, Meg caught the back of Graham's coat, pulled him toward her, then pushed him, face down, into the snow. Laughing, she pounced on top and tried to put snow down his back. They wrestled until exhausted, stopped, lay on their backs, and laughed even harder. Fred, subconsciously noticing the bond that was developing between Graham and Meg, sat down beside them and smiled. He thought it nice to see a brother and sister having so much fun with each other. He wished he had a sister.

"Let's make some hot cocoa," Meg suggested.

The two boys, who never refused an offer of food or drink, willingly followed her into the kitchen. Ken and Louise were still sitting at the table, having just finished their breakfast. "Look at the three of you," Louise exclaimed. "You're covered with snow, from head to toe! What have you been doing?"

As the children drank their cocoa, Fred could see how proud Ken and Louise were of Meg and how fond they were of Graham. What he did not know was how worried Louise was. She feared the war might end soon and she would lose Graham. If only Germany would win and the children had to stay here. She knew it was a selfish thing to wish, certainly not something to make her proud, but what could she do, she wanted Graham to stay in Oakton—forever.

On the way to the Thanksgiving party, Fred had the most pleasant conversation he had ever had with Tom and Victoria. Tom was particularly friendly. He asked about the basketball game and showed a special interest in Fred's point totals and rebounds. Even Victoria seemed less reserved than she had always been. She asked him about his parents and volunteered to write a letter to them "so the two families might become better acquainted." Fred enthusiastically encouraged her, while secretly wondering if she really meant it. He was already aware of Victoria's tendency to make promises she had no intention of keeping.

Without exception, everyone gave a startled gasp when they first entered the banquet hall. Stan Roberts, with help from Miss Perkins, had worked long hours preparing for the party. They had decorated the hall in a Thanksgiving motif. Corn-in-the-shock and huge orange pumpkins stood at intervals along each wall. Orange and brown crepe paper ribbons radiated outward from the central light fixtures towards the edges of the wall. There were so many that they nearly blanketed the ceiling. Paper pumpkins hung from each light fixture. Real pumpkins, hollowed out with candles burning inside, rested on mats made of pine boughs and served as the centerpieces for each table. Favors at each place setting were turkey shaped figures fashioned from native pine cones with orange cardboard heads, tails, and feet.

Each attendee wore a name tag: large black pilgrim tags for the evacuees and orange pumpkins for each member of the foster families. As the crowd gathered, the noise in the hall grew louder. There were shouts of joy and emotional hugs as friend met friend, and cordial handshakes as the children introduced their foster families. Prevalent were remarks about how much the children had gained in weight, squeals of delight when they saw each other's new American clothes, and giggles when they heard each other's new, partially developed, American accents. It was quickly apparent that the children had begun to change; they had, to a small extent, already become Americanized.

When Captain Ben arrived, there was a noticeable cry from the throng and a rush to greet him. The children swarmed around him like bees, each eager to give their thanks, to wish him well, and to assure themselves he still was their friend and benefactor.

The excitement ran particularly high for Ann, Graham, Fred, and the few other children who lived outside McKinley Heights and had not had much opportunity to see many of their English friends. Ann was busy talking with the Nelsons when she saw Edith. It was the first time she had seen her since they had left camp. "Edith!" she screamed and ran to her, giving her a big hug.

"Oh, Ann," Edith sobbed. "I missed you so much."

After several minutes of excited talk, the two girls realized they had been ignoring their families and made the necessary introductions. Then quickly slipped away and continued to share stories about their families, their schools, and their homes. Edith talked very affectionately about Brad and Clara and told Ann how lucky she was to have the Holtzmans as foster parents. When Ann talked about the Schaefers, Edith was quick to say she thought Ned was awfully cute. Ann agreed.

Ann had just finished telling Edith about Lady, and was starting to describe life on the farm when Sandy interrupted her. "Hi, Ann. Hi, Edith. I'd like you to meet my parents, Mr. and Mrs. Maurer."

Ann was happy for Sandy, it looked as if she had found outstanding parents, too. The attention Lucy Maurer showered on Sandy was particularly impressive. Perhaps a wee bit too much, Ann thought, but kept it to herself; it really was none of her business. What Sandy told her next truly amazed her. The Maurers had promised her a riding horse in the spring–that was, of course, if she were still in America by spring. Ann could not believe it. A horse of her own. The only horses on the Schaefer farm were work horses. Jack had let her ride one of them one day while he was plowing, but that certainly was different from having one's very own riding horse. She momentarily felt a twinge of jealousy.

Before long, the entire shipboard "gang" were together. Ann, Edith, Sandy, Graham, and Fred had joined with Elizabeth, Steve and Stewart. They were busy sharing all the latest news when Stan asked everyone to find their places at the tables. All the children, evacuees and their foster siblings, sat at tables immediately in front of the speaker's dais. The foster parents sat at the surrounding tables.

Captain Ben began the festivities by reading a well-prepared blessing and followed it by saying, "Let the fun begin!" Everyone laughed and began talking to their neighbors, as the waiters served a fruit cocktail punch and special Thanksgiving Day hors d'oeuvres. The chef had prepared an excellent meal. Included was corn which, this time, no one found strange or called pig food.

Among the many conversations were several prevalent topics. The children worried about their families back home, about the state of the war in England, how soon it would end, and when they might return home. The parents bragged about each of their English tots and how lucky they had been to have been given the nicest of all the evacuees.

At the children's table, Graham talked knowledgeably about the state of the war and made Meg proud to be his foster sister. At one of the grown-up tables, Tom Derringer boasted about Fred's basketball exploits and his splendid help around the house. There were many at the other tables saying much the same sort of thing as Graham and Tom. Others, more modest like the Schaefers, said little; although, in their hearts they were certain their foster child far outshone all the others.

The after-dinner program was short. Captain Ben told the children how much everyone enjoyed them and thanked the foster parents for their continued generosity and support. He then surprised the children, announcing a special 78 rpm recording session in December. Each child was invited to record a message to be sent to their families in England. After the applause stopped, he told them to think about what their parents would appreciate hearing and prepare a little talk beforehand. The mention of their parents momentarily sobered the children, but soon they were once again laughing and having a good time. The formal program ended with the children singing *Roll out the Barrel*, several patriotic songs, and the U.S. and English anthems while facing the American flag and Union Jack.

Afterwards, the children played games and the talk of the grown-ups soon turned to the war. Many were worried about its slow progress and feared it could become a stalemate similar to what had happened during the Great War. Their greatest fear was that eventually America would find itself directly involved.

Although they did not share it with the children, they were concerned for the safety of the English parents and discussed Hitler's apparent change in tactic. Ever since the devastating Coventry Blitz in mid-November, he had been bombing a much broader selection of targets. Now all of England was under attack. Although the Pinnington area had escaped the major brunt of the Blitz, they feared it would not continue to be so fortunate.

It was difficult to believe that anyone survived the Blitz. According to one newspaper article, approximately five hundred German aircraft dropped an estimated six hundred tons of high explosives and thousands of incendiaries on the city center of Coventry during one night and the following morning. More than four-hundred people died and many thousand were injured.

Afterwards, Hitler promised other cities would be similarly "Coventrated". He kept his word; five days later, a four day attack began on the city of Birmingham. In that raid, there were two thousand people injured and eight hundred killed. According to one news source, they buried the dead in a mass grave. Amazingly, by the end of the Birmingham raid, Coventry industries and businesses were functioning once again.

While hoping America would remain at peace, nearly everyone agreed the U.S. should help Britain in some manner. The concern was how to do it without increasing the risk of war. Some were troubled by Secretary of Navy, Frank Knox's statement that "the English are not going to win this war without our help, I mean our military help." They feared it meant the U.S. involvement was almost a certainty. Others quoted William Allen White's statement, "The dictators are greedy for our wealth and have scorn for our liberty. Sooner or later we shall have to meet them with arms, how and when I do not know." They said there was little choice, the U.S. was eventually going to be involved. The discussion left everyone depressed. They were relieved when the conversation finally turned to other topics.

During the good-byes, Jack and Ida invited Edith for a visit. Ned thought it an excellent idea. "I hope it's soon," he said, enthusiastically, as he looked at Edith. Although Jack did not mention it to anyone,

Ned's look intrigued him, there was obviously more to the wish than polite hospitality. The look on Ned's face reminded him of how he felt when he first saw Ida. He bet a romance was in the making.

He would have to keep a close watch for it.

Chapter 56

Sunday, 29 December 1940

By the end of December the situation in Great Britain was serious. Dire shortages existed everywhere, and bomber attacks were continuing unrelentingly. The Germans had recently caused major damage to the ports of Bristol, Southampton, and Liverpool. Other cities had also weathered heavy raids; included were Plymouth, Birmingham, Sheffield, Manchester, Leeds, and Glasgow. Despite the increased German attention to areas elsewhere, London continued to be a prime target. There were few signs of relief. The delay of the island invasion, the support President Roosevelt was finally beginning to muster in America, and the scattered reports of victories by British troops in North Africa dominated what little satisfaction and hope there was.

One of these British victories occurred in western Egypt. It started in early December after many weeks of extensive training and maneuvers. In what they thought was another training hike, Henry, and his nearly twenty-five thousand fellow combatants, engaged in a forty mile forced march westward. After a day's rest and another westward march, they went into battle, this time at Sidi Barrani. The fighting was fierce, but successful. By Tuesday, the British had large numbers of Italian forces confined in a hastily established desert compound. It was part of Henry's task to help guard this compound.

Henry had never seen so many prisoners. There were nearly five acres of officers and twenty acres of lesser ranks. Rumors began spreading that the British had all but driven the Italians from Egypt and Britain was on the verge of winning the war in North Africa. "Now, perhaps," Henry speculated hopefully, "I can go home."

However, the rumors would prove false. The English were still facing a major force, and fighting would continue. During the first week in January, Henry's unit would assist the Australians with the capture of Bardia, and on January 22, after intensive fighting, they would take Tobruk. Only after these battles would Henry's hopes of going home reappear. By then, the British army would have advanced two hundred miles and along the way, captured one hundred thirteen thousand prisoners and seven hundred guns; and the Italian army would no longer be a threat in North Africa. But all this was still to come.

It was soon after the capture of Sidi Barrani that Ann's letter caught up with Henry. How thrilled he was when he read it and how pleased he was to learn she and Graham could continue their schooling in America. He had heard schools there were excellent. If so, the kiddies would receive what he had wished he could have had, a good education. Even more importantly, they were safe from the terrible horrors of war. He would tell them in a letter how happy he was for them–whenever there was a long enough lull in the fighting to freshen up and get at least one good night's sleep.

The news of the victory at Sidi Barrani came to the U.S. only a few days before President Roosevelt's press conference on December 17. In the conference, he explained his new proposal with an illustration. *"Suppose my neighbor's house catches fire,"* he said, *"and I have a length of garden hose four or five hundred feet away. If he can take my garden hose and connect it up with his hydrant, I may help him to put out the fire. Now what do I do? I don't say to him before that operation, 'Neighbor, my garden hose cost me fifteen dollars; you have to pay me fifteen dollars for it.' No! What is the transaction that goes on? I don't want fifteen dollars–I want my garden hose back after the fire is over."*

He further explained, *"There is absolutely no doubt in the mind of a very overwhelming number of Americans that the best immediate defense of the United States is the success of Great Britain defending itself and that therefore, quite aside from our historic and current interest in survival of Democracy in the world as a whole, it is equally important from a selfish point of view and of American defense that we should do everything possible to help the British Empire to defend itself."*

The following day he proposed the Lend-Lease Bill. It vested sweeping powers in the president *"to make or procure any defense article the president deems vital to the defense of the United States; to sell or transfer or exchange or lease or lend any such article to any such government; to repair or outfit any such defense article for any such government. The president would also have the full authority over arranging terms, if any, with such governments."*

The idea thrilled the British people while the Americans were more cautious. Great debates arose both in Congress and in American homes. Some were for the Bill, some against it. The same was true at the Schaefers. Ida, Karen and Ann were for it. Jack and Ned thought it would bankrupt the nation. The arguments persisted for many weeks. It would be March before Congress reached its final decision and approved it.

Meanwhile, the activities of the Bender divisions on both sides of the Atlantic were increasingly more concerned with war related projects. Among these was a highly classified contract, sponsored by both the U.S. Navy Department and the British Admiralty Office. Its purpose: to develop proximity fuses. It was a joint effort between the McKinley Heights and Pinnington plants. The plan, once the development phase ended, was to manufacture the fuses in both plants.

As part of this effort, E.J. Newton journeyed to McKinley Heights in mid December to ensure the necessary program coordination. He received top priority seating on military aircraft flying between the two countries and had scheduled his return to leave immediately after completing his work in the U.S. However, W.T. Bender had other ideas. He insisted E.J. wait until the children finished their recording sessions. Although E.J. protested, he was not as upset as he pretended. It gave him several additional days to visit with his children whom he had not seen since last July.

E.J.'s need to return to England as soon as possible meant the evacuee's scheduled recording session date had to be moved forward. Not unexpectedly, W.T. called on Stan Roberts to coordinate the change. It meant locating suitable equipment and finding a new date suitable for the sessions. Finding the equipment was not easy, a shift to a warlike production was already producing scarcities of U.S. electrical equipment. After a frantic search, Stan finally obtained an agreement with the McKinley Heights radio station; the children would do all recording there.

It was a heart-rending scene at the studio that evening. While most children had no difficulty thinking of things to tell their parents, others could think of nothing to say. Stan had to prompt these children, sometimes with a few words of encouragement, other times with quickly prepared scripts. Operating in this manner, they recorded all messages, and E. J. was soon on his way back to England.

The English parents heard the recordings for the first time a few days before Christmas. Their reaction came as no surprise. It had been nearly four and one-half months since their children had departed. Hearing their voices, with few exceptions, caused most to break down and cry. It was one of the most difficult days of E.J.'s life. He had never anticipated what a soul-wrenching experience the playback session would be.

*   *   *

It had been four days since Christmas and the Schaefer family had spent only a few minutes listening to their new battery powered radio. Tonight the president was addressing the nation over the radio. The newspapers described it as a "fireside chat." It was a first, something the Schaefers did not want to miss.

The entire family, including Ann, assembled in the living room and eagerly listened to the static, segments of music, and interrupted commentators as Jack twiddled the knobs and scanned the dial. He finally stopped at station WTAM out of Cleveland, Ohio. The president's speech had just started. *"This is not a fireside chat on war,"* he said. *"It is a talk on national security because the nub of the whole purpose of your president is to keep you now, and your children later, and your grandchildren much later, out of a last-ditch war for the preservation of American independence and all the things that American independence means to you and to me and to ours."*

He then cautioned, *"Never before since Jamestown and Plymouth Rock has our American civilization been in such danger as now. The Nazi masters of Germany have made it clear that they intend not only to dominate all life and thought in their own country but also to enslave the whole of Europe, and then to use the resources of Europe to dominate the rest of the world."* Ann thought about her mum and dad.

"The past two years have proven beyond doubt that no nation can appease the Nazis. No man can tame a tiger into a kitten by stroking it." Ann thought of Prime Minister Chamberlain and what he had tried to do.

"Thinking in terms of today and tomorrow, I make the direct statement to the American people that there is far less chance of the United States getting into war if we do all we can now to support the nations defending themselves against attack by the Axis than if we acquiesce in their defeat, submit tamely to an Axis victory, and wait our turn to be the object of attack in another war later on." With a shutter, Ida suddenly realized her son, or maybe even her husband, could someday serve in such a war.

"If we are completely honest with ourselves, we must admit that there is risk in any course we may take. But I deeply believe that the great majority of our people agree that the course that I advocate involves less risk now and the greatest hope for world peace in the future." Jack wondered if the president was being completely honest about the risk.

"Our national policy is not directed toward war. Its sole purpose is to keep war away from our country and our people." Everyone smiled when he said this. They felt more secure. He continued, *"We must be*

the great arsenal of democracy. For us, this is an emergency as serious
as war itself.*"

*"There will be no 'bottlenecks' in our determination to aid Great
Britain. No dictator, no combination of dictators, will weaken that determination by threats of how they will construe that determination."* It
pleased Ann when she heard him say he would aid Great Britain.

*"I believe that the Axis powers are not going to win this war. I base
that belief on the latest and best information."* They all wondered if this
was just political rhetoric or whether he really knew.

He ended his talk, *"As president of the United States I call for that
national effort. I call for it in the name of this nation which we love and
honor and which we are privileged and proud to serve. I call upon our
people with absolute confidence that our common cause will greatly
succeed."*

Not only were most Americans listening to this speech but so were
the Europeans. After it was over, the Londoners walked away with renewed hope. The speech had led them to believe America would soon
help. Perhaps then, the awful raids would end.

But the Germans quickly squelched these hopes. Whether by coincidence or design, they inflicted a horrible raid on London that night. At
the outset, very heavy high explosive parachute mines broke the water
mains cutting off the supply of water to all the fire hydrants. An incendiary raid followed. Nearly fifteen thousand fires resulted with no water
to douse them. Damage to railway stations and docks was serious and
eight Wren churches were destroyed or damaged. There was heavy
damage to Guidhall and only heroic efforts of dedicated firefighters
saved St. Paul's Cathedral.

Morale would have been much worse had the king and queen not
paid a special visit to the scene in the aftermath. The visit provided
much needed encouragement to the British people.

Chapter 57

Thursday, 2 January 1941

It was a terrible day in London. The German Luftwaffe launched
one of their, now rare, daylight bombing runs. Widespread destruction
and devastation followed, especially in the East End.

In Pinnington the alert sirens sounded, but no bombs fell and the
Bender employees remained at their workstations. They had become

accustomed to alerts and no longer fled to the shelters, not until they heard the actual sound of exploding bombs. Still, they were mindful of the danger and their productivity always went down, returning to normal only after the all clear signal.

The loss in productivity concerned Chad. Bender Limited had made him a supervisor in December after they received the proximity fuse contract. Since then he had been trying desperately to bring his un-trained crew up to the demanding skills needed to machine the complicated torpedo parts. Yesterday, for the first time, the crew had obtained the level he sought. Now, here they were, slipping behind again, all because of the air raid and the inability of his machinists to concentrate.

George had particularly upset Chad recently. He had begun taking advantage of their friendship to avoid the increasingly demanding workload. At first, Chad had privately urged George to work harder, but his prodding made little difference, and George's output continued to lag. Then this past week, when George's sloth caused a delay in the entire machining activity, Chad finally was forced to publicly reprimand him. What was most exasperating was George's false notion that the machinists considered him a hero. George was certain they approved of his clever ploys to shut down the operation. Although no one had ever told him so, he was pretty sure they appreciated the convenient work breaks he kept creating.

Now George had come up with a new excuse. He claimed the latest alert caused him greater anxiety than any of the previous ones. He said he feared for his life and asked if a bomb had to explode on the factory floor before management would permit its employees to seek shelter. He demanded if not everyone, at least he, be permitted to take shelter immediately. He used as his excuse his growing premonition that "a bomb had his name on it and was going to kill him."

"Damn it, George," Chad said in a harsh tone, "you know these parts are critical. If they aren't finished on time the entire contract will be in jeopardy. We have spotters on all the roofs. Should they hear or see aircraft approaching they'll sound the alarm; then we'll take shelter. The shelter's not far away. We'll have ample time to get there."

Chad's argument did no good. George continued to protest, and the argument grew more heated. Finally, much to Chad's chagrin, the factory superintendent had to intercede. He told George that if he did not remain at his workstation he would be fired. Reluctantly, George accepted the edict, but spent the remainder of the day assuring Chad they were no longer friends. "I'll even the score—the first chance I get—you wait and see," he snarled at Chad bitterly.

To compound his frustrations, it was Chad's turn for neighborhood fire watch; he would get very little sleep during the night. All this had put him in a particularly angry mood when he arrived home after work. The letter from Jack Schaefer was nearly the last straw. It proposed the Schaefers be appointed legal guardians for Ann should something happen to Chad and Diane. It was a generous offer, and, obviously, from the tenor of the letter, done only with the best of intentions, but it irritated Chad. The suggestion of taking Ann away was too reprehensible to consider any further.

However, try as he would, he could not forget the proposal. By the time Diane arrived home, Chad had worked himself into a highly agitated state. "They're not going to take my daughter from me, Diane. I don't care what Jack says. She's _my_ little girl, not the daughter of some stranger in America. Next, I suppose we'll receive a similar suggestion from the Nelsons concerning Graham."

"What if something really did happen to both of us, Chad? It could, you know! Just last week that delayed action bomb killed that nice couple standing outside the greengrocer's in the high street area. They both died instantly."

"It's not going to happen to us, Diane. We won't be that unlucky."

"How can you be so certain, Chad? It would be nice to die knowing our children, at least Ann and Graham, would be looked after. It's a gracious offer, and quite a compliment to Ann. Imagine the Schaefers taking in our little Ann, a stranger, and then only a few months later, volunteering to look out for her, possibly adopt her. Think about it, consider what a major burden it would be if they had to assume full responsibility for raising another child."

"You're undoubtedly right, Diane, but, all the same, I refuse to consider it any further. I'll write a letter thanking Jack for his kind offer but I'm going to tell him we don't wish to pursue it. I'll say we refuse to even think of such a terrible scenario, all we want is to see our children safely back with us in Pinnington," he said, still showing signs of irritation.

After a few moments of additional thought, he modified his stand slightly. "I'll do one thing though, I'll talk it over with E.J. tomorrow; see what the legal ramifications would be if we should die while the kids are in America."

"Thank you at least for that, Chad. As you know, in the past I've expressed few opinions and not made many demands concerning this horrid evacuation but, for once, I believe, wholeheartedly, that we should do all we can to assure their future welfare and happiness. I couldn't sleep at night if we didn't explore any opportunity to help them. I'll be eager to learn what Mr. Newton has to say. Now don't forget!"

"I won't, Diane. I promise."

"And don't say anything in your letter to upset the Schaefers. Their offer must represent a huge sacrifice on their part. I'd hate it if your refusal changed their attitude towards Ann. They've been taking such good care of her up until now."

When Chad talked to E. J. the next day, he was surprised to learn how interested E.J. was. "You know, Chad, I'm ashamed to admit it but it's something we overlooked. Truthfully, we have no plan in place for such a horrible circumstance. We've really only considered the children's safety, never the possibility of both parents dying. It's something we'll certainly look into, immediately. There are other disasters with serious consequences, too," he said, thinking out loud. "For instance, what if one of the children should get deathly ill? If they had to wait for the parents' consent before, say, an emergency operation, it might take too long. The child's life could be endangered. We better think of as many dreadful situations as we can and develop contingency plans for all of them."

Chad shuddered at the idea of Ann or Graham needing an operation. He had never considered the possibility of either of them getting sick and dying while in America. He had always thought of America simply as a safe haven from the air raids and invasion. He had, of course, considered the possibility of losing them as they crossed the Atlantic, but that was over. He hadn't given their safety any thought since then.

"Thanks, Chad. I assure you, we'll look into this and take the necessary actions. Soon! You have done a great service to the program," E.J. said as they shook hands.

"It really was the American, Jack Schaefer, who suggested it," Chad corrected.

As he walked back to the machine shop, he worried if he had said too much to E.J. He wondered if, out of this conversation, Jack would get his selfish wish, would someday, somehow, adopt Ann. He wished he hadn't gone to see E.J.

Chapter 58

Saturday, 11 January 1941

The president's speech to the joint session of Congress on January 6 quickly became the topic of many conversations. In it, he warned that any further appeasement would spell disaster for America and the rest of the world and urged the nation to reject those who wanted to placate the aggressors. He then introduced what he called the *Four Freedoms*: freedom of speech and expression, freedom for every person to worship God in his own way, freedom from want, and freedom from fear. He called for a reduction of world armament *"to such a point and in such a thorough fashion that no nation will be in a position to commit an act of physical aggression against any neighbor"* and to establish a world-wide economic understanding sufficient to secure *"for the inhabitants of every nation a healthy peacetime life."*

Ann first heard about the speech at school when Mr. Teasley told the class it had all the earmarks of a classic and would probably be remembered for many years to come. He said its basic message was important and assigned it as a homeroom study project.

That evening Ann carefully read the newspaper account of President Roosevelt's speech. Not only did it talk about his reference to the four freedoms but also outlined his appeal to Congress for increased appropriations to manufacture munitions and war supplies. She was particularly pleased to note the president would use this increased production not only to build the strength of the American Army but also to support those nations now in the act of war with the aggressors. Those nations, of course, included Britain. She hoped the support could hasten the day she would return home.

Because she had studied the article so thoroughly, she felt qualified to introduce the subject at the dinner table. She did so by describing what she had read and ended with a summary of her feelings about the speech and how she thought the president had recommended the best plan to bring the war to a quick resolution.

Ida was proud of Ann's authoritative command of the subject. She couldn't help notice how much Ann had matured in the past four months. She smiled when she thought about how proud Diane and Chad would be if they could have heard their little girl, but nearly wept when she thought how terrible it was that her parents could not watch, first hand, their little girl's maturation from child to young lady.

Karen agreed with Ann. She thought it was a good speech and said F.D.R.'s proposal was a good start towards peace in the world. Jack and Ned immediately disagreed. They said Roosevelt made these proposals, not as an act of good will, but as a ruse to promote his Lend Lease program. They called him a socialist and repeated what they had said many times before; his New Deal was slowly destroying America's will to work. The argument continued for some time, with Ned and Jack arguing for a capitalistic system and Karen arguing for expansion of social welfare and price support.

Ann was amazed. What she had thought was a truly benevolent speech and proposal, apparently could be construed as another political ploy, another idea that would elicit highly emotional debate. She could not understand why grownups were so opinionated and fixed in their beliefs. She wished they would concentrate on the important issues, finding ways to stop this horrible war and to be more sympathetic and supportive of the needs of her country. Would they ever stop arguing? She wished she hadn't mentioned the speech by Roosevelt at all.

Eventually, Ida stopped the debate. She declared everyone had said enough and insisted they talk of something else, hopefully something more pleasant.

Even when it was only good natured banter, Ann did not like it when the Schaefers argued. As she waited for Edith to arrive she was still thinking about this morning. The most impressive thing from her point of view was the way Ida had stopped the debate. Once she had heard enough, Ida simply told them to stop, and they did. They did so not because they feared Ida but because they loved her. Ann hoped, if she ever had a family, they would love and respect her as much.

Of course, having a family was pure conjecture. She actually had no intention of marrying and rearing a family. As young girls her age often did, she had, only last week, vowed there would be no time for such foolery. She believed she was destined to do great and worldly things. If it meant she must become an old maid—or maybe even a nun—so be it. She was prepared to make the sacrifice. Unless, of course, she found a special someone who could make it worthwhile being a wife and mother. In that case, if he were special enough, a prince charming, she might find it in her heart to deny the world her special gifts, give up her career, and live happily ever after.

Ned had not expected to see anyone in the front lawn when he came around the side of the barn. He had not heard the Holtzmans' auto come up the lane. When he saw Edith busily talking with Ann he quickly retreated from view. For some reason, he wasn't certain why, he considered it fortunate neither girl had noticed him. He would welcome Edith later in the day.

"Oh, Ann, this place is wonderful!" Edith said, her eyes wide with excitement. "I never imagined the farm would look this lovely. It's so neat and orderly."

"That's because Aunt Ida and Uncle Jack are super people. They believe in working hard and take pride in everything they do. You can't imagine how industrious everyone is around here," Ann bragged. "At first I thought they'd work me to death but now, after adjusting to it, I actually enjoy doing the farm work. At least most of it. There are a few chores I could do without, particularly on these cold mornings, but, overall, I won't complain."

"I've never spent any time on a farm, Ann," Edith confessed. "You must show me all around, and explain what everything is and does."

"I hadn't either! Fortunately, it didn't take long to learn. It's really quite wonderful. Especially on days when I have free time and can play with the animals, explore the fields, or simply find a remote spot to sit and think."

"Let's get started!" Edith urged, bubbling over with enthusiasm and excitement.

"Ho, girls," Ida called, "before you begin whatever it is you are thinking of doing, please come in for a glass of milk and some cookies?"

Ann would have preferred starting immediately but quickly saw that the cookies and milk offer appealed to Edith. "Come on, Edith," she said, "I'll race you to the door!"

After the quick snack, the girls rushed to the barn. One of the first things Ann showed Edith was Lady and the two, still unsold, pups remaining from Queenie's litter. Edith almost immediately became enamored with the playful dogs and was reluctant to leave them, but Ann insisted. They went inside the chicken coop next. Edith did not like the smell but laughed when Ann showed her how the brooders protected their eggs and how the hens ran when she tossed a handful of corn on the floor. Ann next demonstrated how to milk and how to squirt a stream of milk directly at the waiting cats. They were still giggling when Ned came in from the barnyard. "Oh, hello, girls. I didn't know you were in here," he said, blushing slightly.

"Hi, Ned," Ann replied. "You remember Edith, don't you?"

"Yes. Yes I do," Ned replied in as casual a manner as he could muster. "How are you, Edith?"

Edith thought Ned looked strange in his bib overalls, mackinaw coat, and knit stocking hat. She had only seen pictures in magazines of people dressed that way. She had always assumed the pictures were exaggerations of what real farmers wore and had never imagined they actually put on such silly outfits. "Still," she thought, "he is quite handsome."

"I was just going to show Edith the milk house. She's never seen a separator before," Ann explained.

"I'll go with you," Ned replied, nonchalantly. "She may have some questions I can answer."

While they were in the milk house Ned began to talk about the farm machinery and asked Edith if she had ever ridden on a tractor. When she said she hadn't he asked her if she would like to go for a ride.

Soon after, Ann found herself standing in the barn alone, watching Edith and Ned riding around the barnyard, laughing and shouting. At first she was upset. Edith was her guest, and Ned had rudely interfered. As she watched, she began to smile. She began to realize Ned had taken a liking to Edith and was doing these things to impress her. She decided to have some fun. "Did you enjoy that?" she coyly asked Edith as she climbed down from the tractor. "Next I'll show you my favorite thinking place–if you're ready. That way Ned can get back to work. I know he's terribly busy."

"That's all right," Ned quickly responded. "I don't have much to do until Dad gets back from the co-op. I'll tag along!"

"No way, Ned," Ann countered, pretending to sound upset. "I'm not going to show you where my hiding place is. If I did, it would no longer be a secret."

Ned wasn't certain how to reply. He didn't want to sound too eager and yet he didn't want to miss an opportunity to remain with Edith a little longer. Reluctantly he said, "All right, you two go on, I'll finish greasing the binder. I'll see the two of you at lunchtime.

"So long, for now, Edith," he said as he headed for the barn.

"Good-bye, Ned," Edith said, giving him a sweet smile, "see you at lunch."

"You know, Edith," Ann said afterwards, "I think Ned likes you. I've never seen him act quite like he just did."

Edith giggled, "Do you think so, Ann? He is rather cute, isn't he?"

Once they reached Ann's hideaway, the girls talked about home and school but, most of all, they talked about boys. Ann teased Edith about Ned. Edith admitted she was thrilled to think Ned might be attracted to her, to think that a boy so much older might show an interest. What was he? Three? Four years older than she? She asked Ann if she had found a boyfriend yet. Ann simply replied that she hadn't. She did admit that Oliver had hinted he liked her. He was a nice boy, but they were only good friends, certainly not sweethearts.

At lunch, much to the amusement of the girls, Ned found an excuse to sit next to Edith and spent much of the meal talking with her. As the meal was ending, Ned suggested it might be fun to play in the hayloft.

Ida cautioned them to be careful. "Be certain to look before you leap," she warned. "You can really hurt yourselves if you miss the soft hay."

"Oh, don't worry, Mom," Ned chided. "We'll be careful. Besides, the loft is still pretty full, there're aren't many bare spots."

After lunch and, upon the insistence of Ida, a brief rest, the children ran to the hayloft and before Edith realized what was happening Ned had climbed onto one of the beams and jumped into the hay below. "Come on, girls. I'll bet you can't do that!"

Not one to refuse a dare, Edith immediately climbed to the beam, looked down, and jumped, landing close to Ned. Ann, a much more timid girl, gingerly climbed up to the beam, looked down, lost her nerve, and was almost ready to retreat back down the ladder when Ned and Edith shouted, "Come on fraidy cat. You can do it!"

Solely from fear of being thought a prude, she ignored rational sense and leaped in what she was certain would be a fatal act. When her body hit the hay she fully expected a huge grisly pain. Instead, the landing was soft and gentle. She burst out laughing. "What a silly person I've been!" she exclaimed, "That was really exhilarating! Wasn't it?"

But Ned and Edith had lost interest in Ann. They sat there staring in each others eyes, slightly embarrassed, each waiting for the other to say something.

As far as Ann was concerned, she might as well have spent the remainder of the afternoon alone. Although she continued to tag along, Ned and Edith, for the most part, politely ignored her, focusing their attention on each other. It somewhat disappointed Ann that Ned had stolen her playmate away from her, but she forgave him, realizing something special had happened between the two that afternoon. They had fallen in love; that is if it is possible for a twelve year old girl and a sixteen year old boy to be in love.

During dinner, Jack complained he was tired and suggested Ned drive Edith home; a suggestion Ned and Edith readily accepted. Their newfound bliss was quickly dampened when Ida commented on how nice it would be for Ann to see where Edith lived and suggested Ann go with them. Neither dared to object. They accepted the unwelcomed passenger without comment.

On the way to Edith's, Ned and Edith argued about the benefits and dangers of socialism. Ned argued strongly in favor of capitalism while Edith favored the socialistic system. Ann chose to remain neutral and stay out of the discussion. She thought it prudent to give them opportunity to ignore her. By the time they reached Edith's house, Edith was almost convinced capitalism was not as bad as she had thought. After all, if Ned approved of it, it couldn't be so bad; he was such a nice, well-informed boy.

Chapter 59

Wednesday, 2 April 1941

Ann had been at Dexter Hills Junior High for almost seven months now, but still did not feel her classmates fully accepted her. Although they no longer teased her or did things specifically to annoy her, almost everyone still treated her as an outsider. Perhaps it was her English ac-cent–many thought it made her sound aloof; perhaps it was her inherent timidity and shyness–she had always had difficulty making new friends easily; or perhaps her classmates were intrinsically unfriendly to all strangers–after all, they came from a small, close-knit town. Whatever it was, Ann felt uncomfortable and sad at school. It was true, Vicky had treated her with more civility since the sled riding incident, but her only true friends were Oliver and Bonnie, and neither of them were after-school friends, although Oliver would have been if she had let him. To fill this void, she depended–perhaps more than she should have–on Ida and Jack for love and encouragement and on Karen and Ned for compan-ionship and rapport. Still, it was Lady that she turned to most often for comfort and solace, especially at those times when she felt lonely and friendless.

It was not the same for Graham, he had many friends at Oakton High and seemed pretty well adjusted. If he still harbored any remnants of homesickness it was not outwardly apparent. Ann was not as fortunate, she was still quite homesick and it occasionally showed. Although she had learned to hide it most days, the nights were often different. Once she and Lady were in bed, it was not unusual for her to lose self-control. On those melancholy nights, she would hold Lady close to her and cry, wanting desperately to return home to her real family, and wondering how much longer until the war would end.

But the war continued, and every day the signs of peace were less encouraging. With each new report, the day when she might expect to go home would seem to be a little more distant. In fact, there were days when it seemed questionable if England had any hope of victory at all. At those times she would wonder if she would ever get back home.

Although she was still writing to her mum and dad regularly, the in-terval between her letters was growing longer and their length shorter with each letter. Diane, however, continued to write weekly. Her letters were arriving now on a nearly predictable basis, most often in the Friday or Saturday mail, but they no longer satisfied Ann. She didn't just want letters; they never contained what she really wanted. She wanted to see her parents in person, wanted to feel their hugs and kisses, wanted to talk with them, tell them all about everything, hold them, or simply sit beside them, look at them, remember what they looked like. Even so, the letters from Yvonne and Henry were a welcomed surprise. She had not been expecting to hear from either of them, especially from Yvonne.

Yvonne's letter was very formal. She said how lucky Ann was to have escaped all the terrible bombing and scarcities in England. She told Ann how busy she had been, how much she hated her work, and how difficult it had been for her to give up the idea of going on to school. She said she would be happy when she turned eighteen and could join the Women's Land Army and made it clear her decision to enlist was not based on patriotism, instead she said it demonstrated how frustrated she had become with her life. She hoped, once she was in the WLA, they would serve chocolate candy and fresh fruit as part of the menu, something she had craved for such a long, long time. She then reproached Ann for having gone to America, a land of wonderful things to eat, beautiful clothes to wear, and no air raids. Finally, she teased Ann about living on a farm and how horrible it must be to milk cows and ted hay. By the time Ann had completed reading Yvonne's letter, she almost wished she had not opened it.

On the other hand, Henry's letter was sweet and filled with love and good will. He said he did not mind army life and found the other lads in his outfit to be super blokes. He encouraged Ann to make the most of the wonderful opportunities in America, to get a good education, to worship God regularly, and to remember him in her prayers. He said he hoped, and truly expected, the war to end soon. He signed the letter with love and kisses and included a wish for the Montgomerys to all be reunited soon. Ann held the letter to her heart for a long time afterwards, remembering past moments with Henry, and then sat down and wrote a long, upbeat letter to him. Yvonne received no reply.

In Ann's next letter to her parents, she mentioned the letters she had received and how happy Henry had sounded. She then shared some exciting news.

... We now have electricity here on the farm!! Isn't that wonderful? It would have been installed sooner had it not been for the difficulty of obtaining the right-of-way for the electric lines across the property of an old crotchety neighbor. But what a grand thing it is to have electric lights at night! (We have no blackouts here so we can turn them on without drawing the curtains.) The Schaefers have already bought some

of the modern appliances (toaster, iron, refrigerator, and radio) but must be careful with their budget. They hope to buy an electric stove before the end of the year. Now that we have electricity I have begun listening to the radio more regularly. My favorite programs (serials) are: "Little Orphan Annie" and "Jack Armstrong, the All-American Boy."

The evening news always updates the state of the war in Europe. It has all been so dismal lately! I do hope the situation improves for England soon. ...

Ann was correct about the war situation. Things were still looking bleak in Europe. On the first of March the Germans began to move into Bulgaria while the Bulgarian army massed its troops along the Greek frontier. The world trembled for it looked as if Greece was about to fall. The situation in North Africa was no better. Although the British Army had steadily advanced westward across North Africa during the first three months of the year and by the end of March was in El Aghaila, the situation had quickly changed. It was in El Aghaila that Rommel launched his counterattack on March 31. Using a tactic of relentless bomber and fighter attacks he soon had the British armored units seriously disorganized and suffering heavy losses. By the first week of April the British were in full retreat.

The most positive event was the signing of the Lend-Lease Bill by F.D.R. on March 11. It had passed Congress overwhelmingly after an intense debate. At least England would be getting additional munitions and war supplies.

... Everything is going well here. Now that I have caught up with the things I missed from the lower grades, school has become much easier. I expect to receive a good report next period. I'll let you know how I do.

Ann signed her letter with love and kisses and repeated how much she wished she were back in Pinnington. She did not tell them about the poor treatment she was receiving from her classmates.

Chapter 60

Friday, 4 April 1941

Meg looked up from her Latin book and smiled. Graham had just popped a large bubble from the gum she had offered him a few minutes before. "He certainly has come a long way since last September," she thought. It was remarkable how quickly he had assimilated into

American culture. He was not only chewing gum now, but he was using words such as "yeah" and "guys" and, with the influence of American clothes and an American haircut, he no longer looked as British as she had once thought. As a matter of fact, as she sat there looking at him, she could not help but think what a handsome boy he was.

She liked Graham; he was such a well mannered boy and smart as well. She could not count the number of times his explanations had helped her. What seemed particularly difficult for her was usually easy for him. He seemed to excel in everything they studied. Until recently, she thought she was good at conjugating Latin verbs, but even so, his ability far exceeded hers, particularly in the case of the irregular ones. They were presently translating *Ulysses* and there was little doubt his Latin vocabulary was much larger than hers; he always completed the assignment long before she did and often had to help her find an appropriate translation for a particularly difficult sentence. By her estimation, his help during the semester increased her overall grade by one, or perhaps two, marks.

But mostly she liked Graham's sense of humor. He was always saying funny things and telling wild stories, all of which were obviously fabricated although he swore they were true. He was a big tease, too, and usually kept the Nelsons laughing all through dinner. There was little doubt the entire Nelson family had fallen in love with him. He certainly had brought Louise back from those terrible days when she could think of nothing but the loss of Tommy. Meg felt he had done much the same for her. If she had wished for a nicer brother she would never have found one. Someday she would tell him how she felt, but, for now, that would wait.

"That's enough Latin for me tonight," Graham sighed as he threw the textbook on the table. "*Vini, veni, vinco. Amo, amas, amant.* By Jove, I wish Homer had been born in London. If he had he would have written the *Odyssey* in English, and it would have been much easier to read the works of that bugger."

"But do you think he would have written it had he been English?"

"Of course he would," Graham countered. "Had he been an Englishman, Ulysses would have been an even better explorer. There's no doubt in my mind. Look at our great Empire, almost all of it is the result of English explorers."

"But what if he had been born in England?" Meg chortled. "Then all those additional explorations would have made his story even longer than it already is. I'm glad he wasn't English."

"Perhaps," Graham replied as he wadded a piece of scrap paper into a small ball and tossed it across the desk at Meg. A minor skirmish followed with Meg throwing paper balls at him and both children ducking and running around the room laughing.

"Stop that fighting, you two," came the voice of Louise. "Won't you ever grow up?"

Meg and Graham quit, but sat there snickering and trying vainly to keep Louise from knowing how funny everything still was. The paper fight almost escalated once again when Graham surreptitiously tossed another ball at Meg. This time Meg did not return it. "Stop that!" she whispered, and exhaled another small burst of giggles.

Later, when the two children came into the living room where Ken and Louise were sitting, Louise reminded them Ann would be visiting tomorrow. She hoped they both had completed all their work so they could properly entertain her. "My sister doesn't need entertainment," Graham professed proudly. "She's content simply sitting by herself. I've seen her sit for hours at home, quietly playing with her doll."

"But it wouldn't be hospitable to just let her sit, Graham. We certainly want her to feel welcomed."

"Oh don't mind him, Mother," Meg laughed. "He's only teasing."

Ann arrived after lunch on Saturday. It was an unusually warm April day and the children spent much of the afternoon talking and playing outside. Ann and Graham, as they always did when they visited each other, had letters from home to share and many things to tell each other. Graham was particularly interested in the latest letter from Henry. He told Ann he worried because of the worsening situation in North Africa. He knew British losses were high but didn't mention it. He didn't want to worry Ann any more than she already was. What he feared most was the possibility Henry would be hurt, especially if he had been in El Aghaila. But on the other hand, he really could not imagine anything happening to Henry. Nothing that terrible ever happened to a Montgomery.

Later in the afternoon Ann borrowed Meg's bicycle and she and Graham, using the secondhand bike Ken and Louise had bought for him, went for a ride around Oakton. Even though the tree limbs were still bare and the grass had not turned green, Ann thought the town was pretty—with its neatly kept homes and their well-maintained gardens. Had it not been for the style of the houses, she could easily have imagined she was in a sleepy Cornish village. For a moment, she wished she had been sent to a foster home in Oakton too, but then she remembered Ida and Jack. She was glad she was on the farm; it was her home now—at least until it was time to return to Pinnington.

Graham planned their ride to end at Jeffersons' Malt Shop. He knew Ann was fond of strawberry ice cream sodas and wanted to treat her. He had planned it a week ago when she had called to tell him she was coming. They sat at the soda bar, sipped their sodas, and listened to the dance band records playing on the juke box. Graham liked Benny Goodman. Ann preferred Glenn Miller. Graham described what the Oakton kids did on Friday nights, how they would often meet at the malt shop and dance to the latest tunes. He said he and Meg had done it a number of times. The idea of so much convenience made Ann a little jealous. For a brief moment she again wanted to live in town, not on the farm. She wanted to dance and do all the other things town folks did.

After dinner, Louise suggested it might be fun to play Chinese checkers. "Oh, I don't know," Graham bragged, "it might be boring for me, since I'll probably whomp all of you every game."

"We'll see about that, young fellow," Ken replied, a frown on his face, pretending he was angry. "No one ever beats this old pro."

But neither of them were right. Meg won most of the games, while Ann and Louise split the remaining victories. "The game must have been fixed," Ken mused looking at Graham. "Can you imagine, the womenfolk won every game?"

"No I can't," Graham answered, trying vainly to hide his disappointment.

Louise, returning from the kitchen, interrupted the banter. She carried a tray with five plates of peach up-side-down cake, each covered with a heaping scoop of vanilla ice cream. They soon forgot who won and who lost as everyone began to eat.

On the way back from taking Ann home, and with Meg and Graham asleep in the back seat, Louise remarked, "Isn't Ann a sweet little thing, Ken?"

"She certainly is," Ken answered.

"It's too bad we couldn't have had both children live with us. She must get awfully lonely waiting to see Graham."

"Maybe not, Louise. She seems to like Jack and Ida very much. But I'm not surprised. Have you ever met such nice people? They're so friendly and down-to-earth. There's no doubt she has a good home."

"Did you see her with her little dog. Weren't the two of them together a wonderful sight to see? What did she call her dog? Oh yes, Lady."

"They'll miss Ann when it's time for the children to go back to England."

"Not any more than we'll miss Graham. I know this is selfish of me, Ken, but I do hope they aren't required to return home for a long, long time."

"You needn't worry about that. The way the war is going it could be another year, or more," Ken guessed.

Ken's guess was justified. The next day, in retaliation for the refusal of the Yugoslavian people to surrender to Germany, Hitler launched a heavy bombing attack on Belgrade. By April 8 nearly seventeen-thousand Yugoslavian citizens had been killed. On the thirteenth, the German Army entered Belgrade and seven days later Yugoslavia capitulated in spite of the valiant resistance of its citizens. Four days more and Greece surrendered. With that, the Germans were in control of Hungary, Yugoslavia, Romania, Bulgaria, Albania, and Greece in southwestern Europe. Only Turkey remained to be taken.

With the fall of Greece, the English found themselves once again evacuating their troops from a foreign soil. The losses were heavy. Twenty-six ships were sunk and, although over fifty-thousand men were successfully evacuated, over eleven-thousand troops were left behind.

On Sunday, the sixth of April, while Yugoslavia was falling to the Germans, spring had begun to peek through in northeastern Ohio. It was one of those balmy days when everyone wants to be outside enjoying the warm gentle winds and trying to forget the harsh winter with its ice and snow. In Oakton, Meg and Graham had decided to picnic in the park next to the pavilion in the town center. In Dexter Hills, Ann and Oliver agreed to study geography together in the shelter house at the local park. Neither couple worried much about the events in Europe on that particular day.

"Listen to that cardinal, Meg. Isn't that a lovely song?" Graham said as he lay on the blanket, the sun warming his body while his hat shielded his eyes.

"We must be bothering her. I'll bet she has a nest somewhere close by," Meg said as she placed the last dish back in the picnic basket. Afterwards, she lay down beside Graham and put her arm over her face to cover her eyes. As she did her hand brushed his and a strange feeling overcame her. She had never before felt anything quite like it. Suddenly, she looked at Graham and, for reasons unbeknownst to her, began to think how nice he was. Graham had felt their hands touch, too, and also momentarily felt a slight tingle. These strange feelings were brief and soon forgotten by both children. Before they knew it, they were back on their bicycles, riding home.

*   *   *

Oliver had arrived at the shelter early and was waiting when Ann rode up on Karen's bicycle. After only a few words of greeting, they opened their books and began studying. Within minutes Vicky rode by. "Hi, Ann. Hi, Oliver," she said, hiding any concern she might have had about finding them there. "What are you two doing on this wonderful afternoon? Not studying, I hope!"

They explained they needed to spend some extra time preparing for the geography test on Monday. Vicky did not believe them. She was almost certain studying was not the real reason they were together. "More than likely it's a lame excuse to meet," she said, then, no longer professing any interest in Oliver, left. She had given up any claim to him, now that she and Ann had become friends and, more importantly, once Oliver had told her how he felt about Ann. After she was gone, both found it difficult to concentrate on geography. Although neither child would say it, each was wondering if what Vicky had said was true.

On Monday, neither Ann nor Oliver did particularly well on the exam.

"Ahoy there, mates!" the captain said. "Look out below."

Ann ducked her head, as lifeboats tumbled all around. A scramble for remaining seats ensued. "Out of my way," Vicky cried, pushing Ann aside. "It's my seat. I saw it first."

"Objection. Objection," Mr. Teasley zestfully implored, pounding a yardstick across his desk. "The boat is full. You must walk."

"I beg your pardon," Fred complained. "Ann cannot walk, the sea is much too deep."

"Nonsense, m'lad. There is no sea," Teasley corrected.

"Then come along," Oliver begged, "I love you, my pet. Walk with me. You are a true friend."

"Yes, yes, I will," Ann cooed. "But first, we must find our seats."

"Hurry, the show is about to start. Quick, the cartoon is on."

"What funny birds! Are they drawn in zest?"

The feature followed shortly thereafter.

She felt his hand slip around her waist. "What are you doing?" she coyly asked.

"Simply trying to love you, my dear," he cooed.

"No. Please?" she begged, "I'm too young for that."

"One kiss right now? That's all, I need. Will you? Please?"

"No, not today. Perhaps next week."

"But days are weeks and weeks are years when one's in love."

Suddenly they were sitting on a porch swing, slowly swinging, his arm around her. At first she resisted, then snuggled close. "Oh, Oliver," she sighed. It's you."

"Of course it is. You can always count on me."

"Can you truly promise such a thing?"

"Certainly, for someone nice as you."

"Then here's the kiss I promised."

Ann awoke with a start. Lady's nose was next to her face. When she repeated her name, Lady licked her cheek. Ann smiled and fell back asleep.

Chapter 61

Saturday, 10 May 1941

Edith watched Brad as he rowed their boat into the small bay and tossed the anchor overboard. "What a nice man," she thought.

"There, that should do it," Brad said. "If I'm not mistaken this should be the perfect spot to catch our limit of bluegills." Looking at the early morning sky, he added, "They should start biting any minute now. Let's get our lines ready. Here's the can of night crawlers."

Edith looked at the can with horror. "He can't possibly expect me to touch those slimy disgusting things? Can he? Maybe he isn't as nice as I thought." But not wishing to be uncooperative, she reluctantly pulled out a crawler and gingerly held the wiggling thing between her fingers–wondering what to do next.

As she watched, Brad took the can from her, found a worm for himself, and began to pass the fish hook through it. A small amount of blood squirted from its body. She was horrified. Maybe she could bring herself to holding one of those slimy creatures in her bare hand but there was no way she would ever shove a hook through it.

From the expression on Edith's face Brad realized she had never baited a fish hook before and, chuckling, said, "Looks like you need some help. Here let me bait it for you." With relief, Edith placed the poor little worm back in the can and handed her line to Brad.

Next Brad showed her how to attach the bobber and pointed to what he said was the best place to toss her line. Almost immediately Edith felt a nibble, yanked violently, and expected to land the biggest fish anyone had ever caught. Instead the bobber and hook came flying out of the water and over the boat, just missing an overhanging tree branch. Brad laughed. "Wait until you're pretty certain the fish has taken the bait; not just nibbled on it," he instructed. "Then give it a little jerk. That will set the hook so the fish can't shake loose. Then worry about bringing him into the boat.

Slightly embarrassed, Edith tossed her line back in the lake and sat waiting for another chance to prove she could master the art of fishing. The next several nibbles were on Brad's line; then suddenly he had one securely on his line. She watched as he brought it up to the side of boat, netted it, and scooped it in. She felt guilty seeing how valiantly the fish battled while in the water and how hopelessly it flopped in the bottom of the boat. "The poor little thing," she said, as Brad placed it on the stringer. "He doesn't want to be caught. He wants to be safe and free, the same as we do." Brad only laughed. She began to have doubts about fishing. She wasn't going to like it if she had to hurt those poor creatures.

Finally, after nearly half an hour, she felt a nibble. This time she heeded Brad's instructions. She waited until she felt a stronger tug, yanked on her pole, felt a flutter, and saw the fish jump out of the water, vigorously shake its head, and try to pull free. Unsuccessful, and still on the end of her line, it splashed back into the water. She began pulling with all her might, trying to bring the fish to the side of the boat. It pulled so strongly she was certain she had hooked a whale. Suddenly it turned and rushed toward her leaving the line slack, then just as rapidly swam away from the boat, almost ripping the pole from her hands.

After what seemed like minutes to Edith, and after many repeated maneuvers to avoid capture, the fish began to tire and she finally managed to bring it close to the boat where, with a swift motion, Brad netted it.

What a rush of excitement she felt as she eagerly looked to see what she was certain would be a prize catch. Instead she saw a tiny fish nearly half the size of either of the two Brad had caught. "Sorry, Edith," Brad apologized. "It's not a keeper. We'll have to put it back."

Edith was certain there had been a mistake. It should have been much bigger. It felt so strong while she was landing it. What would a big one feel like, she wondered. She could barely wait until Brad had baited her hook again. She wanted her line back in the water so she could catch another one. She had changed her mind; she decided she liked fishing. "Come on, fish, let the next one be a keeper," she challenged.

By the time the sun was above the treetops, Edith had become an expert fisher. In her haste to get her line back into the water, she had grown impatient waiting for Brad to bait her hook and had gradually taken over the task. Looking over the side of the boat, she could see the fish she had caught on the stringer. She started having conflicting feelings. On one hand, she was eager to take her fish home and show them to Clara. On the other, she wanted to stay so she could catch more.

She was just about to decide there was no limit to the number of fish she could catch when they quit biting. Brad and she sat for a long time, neither with as much as a nibble. Finally, he suggested they leave their hooks in the water and eat the snack Clara had prepared. As they ate, they talked. He told her how he thought the government should be run. He said he thought America needed to be more socialistic. He believed it was the only way it would ever reach its true potential. He considered most of F.D.R.'s policies to be right on track while others weren't. "There is still an awfully long way to go before we reach Utopia. However," he said, "if we keep trying, I still think the U.S. will eventually get there."

Although what Brad was saying made good sense, she remembered what Ned had told her and tacitly wondered if Brad's conclusions were entirely correct.

As they finished their lunch, he teased her about Ned. "I think you're kind of sweet on him," he said. "I saw the way the two of you were looking at each other the other day. I'd wager he's your boyfriend."

Blushing, Edith denied she had any feelings for Ned, admitting only that she thought he was an nice boy. Brad did not pursue it further, although he was certain she was not being entirely truthful. He and Clara had talked about the relationship. He agreed with Clara when she said, "It's only a matter of time until those two become a couple."

By the time Brad and Edith pulled up anchor and headed back to shore, Edith had a nice catch of bluegill and one small bass. When they arrived home, she proudly showed the catch to Clara. "Oh, Clara!" she said, "What a lovely day this has been! I don't know when I've had so much fun. America is such a grand place to live. I hope we can keep it this way forever."

"So do I, Edith," Clara agreed. "Let's hope nothing happens to change things." She was thinking about Brad and the draft. She hoped the president would continue to keep America out of the war. "If only the war in Europe would stabilize," she thought.

But her wish was in vain. On May 20, the Germans launched a large-scale air attack on the island of Crete in the Mediterranean. The following afternoon German parachute drops began. Although the British put up strong resistance, the losses were large and on the twenty-sixth the decision was made to evacuate the island. By the twenty-ninth, the last troops were removed. The remaining five thousand British and Imperial troops left behind were told to capitulate.

The news of the loss of Crete was not the only thing troubling the American people. On May 27, the American freighter *Robin Moore* was boarded by the crew of a German U-boat and plane parts were discovered. The *Robin Moore* crew were ordered into lifeboats and the freighter torpedoed and sunk. Incensed by this attack, the U.S. Government froze all German and Italian assets in the U.S.

The situation in North Africa had also been deteriorating rapidly. By the twenty-seventh of May, General Rommel and his Fifteenth Panzer Division was in control of Halfaya and Tobruk was in jeopardy. A degree of hope followed on June 15 when the British launched operation "Battleaxe" against the Germans, but by the seventeenth, the attack had failed and the British had retreated. The eventual defeat of Britain by Germany seemed assured to most Americans who closely followed the war. Everyone wondered what America would do next.

Chapter 62

Friday, 27 June 1941

Harriet was tired as she rode the No. 207 bus home from Uxbridge. It had been a long day, and she still was not completely used to working in the munitions factory. She sat looking out the small opening in the window without paying attention to the passing view. It had been a particularly unpleasant day. She had not wanted to get those two lads in trouble, but they insisted on continuing, even after she warned them she would put them on report. When they wouldn't listen, she had no alternative but to tell her supervisor. It was the only thing she could do, she wanted the war to be over soon–she wanted Edith back home. Nothing else mattered. She missed her daughter. Besides she had no truck for anyone not trying to do their best, even if it had not been something that hurt the war effort.

"Weren't we told to report any suspicious activity? Wasn't it my patriotic duty?" she asked herself, trying to justify her actions. She hoped the two blokes understood that. The reaction to her report had been rapid and decisive. She couldn't believe how swiftly the authorities had come to her work area. In an instant, they took the two Communists away, almost before anyone at the factory had noticed.

"What an effect the war is having on everyone," she mused. "Everyone is so quick to judge nowadays. No one gets a second chance. Even I–no especially I–don't give second chances any longer. Perhaps I shouldn't have treated George the way I did, maybe I should have given him a second chance, been more forgiving. Maybe it's living with the ever present danger–this blasted war–that's making me so intolerant.

"No, it's not that. There hasn't been any air raids for over a month. I've felt reasonably safe and have been able to sleep at night. No, that's not it. It's George. I don't have to endure his abuses any longer. I've done it long enough. If he wants peace with me, he will have to apologize and drastically change his ways. Not me!"

She couldn't understand what had happened last week, what it was that caused her to fight back suddenly. He had hit her many times before, and she hadn't reacted that way. He had been doing it ever since they were married. She had never complained when he struck her before, or when he humiliated her and called her embarrassing names. She should have put her foot down when he told Edith she had to give up her schooling, when he said she couldn't be a chemist, and, most certainly, when he sent her away.

But those days were over. Since she started working, she had gained a modicum of self-esteem and now had gained a willingness to look out for herself. She simply wasn't going to take it any longer. She had rights too. He would not dominate her anymore. As far as she was concerned, she would never speak to him again.

She smiled when she thought about the day she decided she would go to work. It was the nearly unbearable loneliness after Edith left that finally triggered her decision, that and the nagging feeling she should contribute to the war effort. When she told George, he had screamed at her, said no wife of his would ever work in a factory. He was quite startled when she slapped him. It had never occurred to him that she would. It took several moments before he recovered.

They had a terrible fight afterwards. For the first time, she stood up to him and fought back. Of course, the beating was awful, but it was worth it. He would never strike her again. Never again would he dominate her. It was their final fight. As far as she was concerned, he was dead; he no longer existed. He had threatened to divorce her. He was surprised when she said she could hardly wait. She wished the old fool would have left, but he hadn't. He stayed on in spite of her wishes. He still could live in the house, it being so difficult to find housing these days, but she would pay absolutely no attention to him. She would cook his meals, when she had a mind to, but she would not talk to him, would not look at him, and most certainly would never sleep with him again. "And now, the old fool is talking about joining the Communist party. Let him do it," she thought, "I'll turn him in the first time he does anything illegal–just like I did those blokes today."

When she arrived home, she found one of those rare letters from Edith in the post box. She tore it open and read it before removing her jacket. The letter was not the same as previous ones. It sounded happier. It praised the Holtzmans for being such nice people and raved about the loving care she was receiving. "Isn't it ironic?" Harriet thought, "George's meanness has turned out to be to Edith's benefit. It wasn't at all what George had planned." In a way, in spite of how much she missed her, Harriet was pleased George had sent Edith to America. Her little girl had a much better life now. She immediately wrote a reply and posted it before dinner. It was upbeat. There was no mention of the rift between George and her. She only wrote about the good things, about the cessation of the bombing raids over Ealing; and all the fun she had at the pub with the gang every Friday evening after work. She didn't mention how much she missed Edith, or how she had cried while writing the letter. It would do no good to make her little girl worry.

When George came home, she did not mention the letter–nor did she mention any of the others she got from that day on. They were just some of the many secrets she would never share with him.

In Ohio, at nearly the same time, Ned Schaefer was begging his dad for permission to take the car to the drive-in. "It should be a good movie, Dad. Humphrey Bogart is in it. It's called the *Maltese Falcon*, a detective story. If you let me take the car, Ann can go with me. She hasn't been to a drive-in movie yet. It will be a new experience for her." He then added, as if an afterthought, "We'll ask Edith to go with us–so Ann doesn't feel strange." It was the only excuse he could think of; he truthfully had no idea why Ann should feel strange. He hoped his dad wouldn't ask him.

"I suppose so. Ask your mother if it's okay for Ann to go."

"Yes, sir!" Ned answered, trying to hide his excitement. He quickly excused himself and rushed into the kitchen. "Mom, Dad says I can take Ann to the drive-in movie, if it's okay with you?"

Ida looked at her son and wondered why he was so excited. She had never known him to be quite this eager to go to a movie, although, heaven only knew, he had always been eager to take the car whenever he could. "I don't know," she answered, "it would keep Ann out rather late. Does she want to go?"

"I haven't asked her yet. I didn't want to get her hopes up until I knew it was all right with you and Dad. But I'm certain she will. I'm asking Edith to go with us.

"As company for Ann," he quickly added.

Now Ida knew why the excitement. It was an excuse for Ned to take Edith to a movie. "What's playing? Do you think the girls would enjoy it?" she asked, wanting to tease him for a minute or two.

"Oh, I'm certain they would. It's the *Maltese Falcon*," he replied, emphasizing the title as if it should mean something special. "Bogart's in it," he added.

Ida chuckled to herself. Her son was growing up; he was becoming interested in girls. How quickly they grow, she thought. "I suppose it will be okay, but you had better ask Karen to go along. I'm sure she'd enjoy it too."

Ned's heart sank. If his sister went with them it would spoil everything. But then he remembered, Karen had said she had a date this evening. "That's a good idea, Mom. It would be great to have Karen with us–she's always so much fun."

He quickly talked to Ann and told her to invite Edith. Ann said she would and ran next door. It would be one of the few remaining times she would need to phone from next door. Last night Jack had announced he had ordered a telephone. Ann was still excited about that. For the first time in her entire life, there would be a telephone in her own home. She would be able to call Graham and Edith whenever she wished. She would never need to bother the Ekenwilders again.

It took a bit of coaxing before Clara granted permission. She argued that a thirteen year old should not be "dating"–even if accompanied by a girlfriend. Another reason, which she was reluctant to openly address, was the fear that her little girl was finding outside interests. Edith might be going back to England someday, and Clara had no desire to share the little remaining time with others. Had Brad not encouraged it, she probably would never have agreed.

That evening, after Ned and Ann left to pickup Edith, Jack turned to Ida and said, "I think our son is in love."

"Don't be silly, he's much too young to be in love."

"We'll see, Ida. We'll see."

They arrived at the drive-in nearly one-half hour before the movie was scheduled to start. After a few minutes of playing spotlight tag on the blank screen, Ned went to the concession stand for Cokes and popcorn. On his way back, he saw several of his classmates standing along side the car. "Look at that," one of them said, "Aren't those two limeys in Ned's car? He's turning into a real limey lover. Isn't he?"

"Yea," said another. "He's too snooty to date one of our American girls nowadays. He has to fetch them all the way from England–and two of them, no less!"

"Back off, fellows," Ned growled, as he passed the popcorn and Cokes through the side window of the car. "I'm sure you know this is my foster sister, Ann. The other is her close friend. They're not dates."

"Don't feed us that malarkey, Ned. We know you plan to neck with them after the show starts, especially that cute blondie there next to your ..." he paused. "Foster sister? Pretty nice. Isn't it, boys? Daddy fixed him up with a limey sister to play house with.

"They're over here sponging off us, eating our food, sleeping in our beds, taking up space in our schools. Isn't it just like old Winnie Churchill, taking advantage of President Roosevelt and our American hospitality. I say we send the whole lot of them back to England, back where they belong. Eh, boys? Let them take care of their own problems. Like my daddy says, no need to give them any more handouts."

Ned's face turned red with rage. He was preparing to strike the classmate closest to him when Oliver and several of his buddies walked up. "Hi, Ned. How's it going, old buddy? Hi, guys," he said, staring at Ned's classmates. "Looking forward to the movie tonight?"

They sensed they were outnumbered now. Oliver had too many friends with him. "Yea, it looks like a thriller all right," the leader replied. "It's getting dark. We'd better get back to our car so we can see the cartoon and newsreel."

"Thanks, Oliver," Ned said, after they had gone. "I'd like you to meet Edith, Ann's girlfriend from England."

"Hi, Edith, glad to meet you. Hi, Ann," he said, looking at her, and hoping she would invite him to watch the movie with her.

"Thank you, Oliver. Things were getting rather tense," Ann said. "See you on Monday."

After Oliver left, Ned apologized for the brash rudeness of his classmates. "They're just ignorant boys who live with bigoted parents. Don't draw any general conclusions about all Americans from boys like that. You'll find that most of us do our best to be gentlemen."

Edith laughed, "I know what a bigot is, Ned. I have a father who is a classic example. Your classmates are tame compared to him. Don't be embarrassed. We understand. Don't we, Ann?"

Ann agreed.

"The movie is about to start! Why don't you sit in the back, Ann? That'll give us more room to watch. Edith and I can sit here in front. We'll scoot down so our heads aren't in your way."

Ann saw nothing wrong with Ned's suggestion and crawled over the backrest. They all laughed at how awkward she looked as she flopped onto the back seat. Just then, the screen lit up with the faint image of *Donald Duck*. It would be several more minutes before the twilight turned into darkness and the screen could be seen easily.

After the cartoon there were clips of the latest events in Europe; the German declaration of war on Russia, dominated the newsreel. It showed pictures of the German Reichstag and explained how Ribbentrop had, on the twenty-second, delivered the formal declaration of war to the Russian ambassador in Berlin. The pictures that followed were said to have been taken during the early morning hours on the day the Germans launched their massive attack on Russia. The commentator said it explained the halt in bombing raids over England this past month. Apparently the Germans had been preparing for this attack during the lull. He also said it was too early to predict the outcome of this unexpected turn of events, although some were speculating that Hitler could not afford to fight on two fronts. With his decision to attack his former ally, there appeared to be less possibility of an invasion of Britain.

That prompted some excited talk. If it were true that there was no longer a threat of an invasion and the bombing lull continued, then their parents would be safe; perhaps the girls would be returning to England before long. They were still talking when the previews ended and the movie started. It was not *Maltese Falcon* as Ann had expected but the second feature, about a poor family living on a farm in Southern Illinois. "What a grand bargain," exclaimed Ann. "Two features for the price of one!" Everyone laughed.

Part way through the movie, Ned moved closer to Edith, and later still, put his arm around her. Ann could not understand it. Why didn't Edith complain? It looked terribly uncomfortable. Ann hoped Edith would soon take his arm away, their heads greatly interfered with her view. She had to slide over to one side in order to see the screen. Later still she noticed they had apparently completely lost interest in the movie. They seemed to be more interested in whispering and giggling. Between features she asked Edith if she liked the movie. The only response was a somewhat disgusted, "Yes, Ann."

Still later, in the middle of the main feature, Ann thought she heard them kissing, but she wasn't sure. She couldn't believe they would do that while the movie was running. It seemed to her Humphrey Bogart was too good an actor for them to miss even one minute of the film. "And besides, why would they kiss? They were still much too young for that sort of silly thing."

Ned walked Edith to the door after the movie. Ann thought it took an awfully long time before he returned and would have blown the car horn if it hadn't been so late. She didn't want to wake the Holtzmans and make them angry. When Ned came back, she thought he acted rather peculiar. He seemed to be staring into space–almost as if he were in a daze. She hoped he would soon snap out of it so he could drive her home safely.

As they drove through the country, she could see the mist lying in the low areas and could here the croaking of the frogs. That, coupled with the bright moonlight produced a nostalgic mood. "Funny," she thought, "here I am on my way home–and it's not to Pinnington, it's to a farm near Dexter Hills. In America! It's odd, I've been thinking more about Aunt Ida and Uncle Jack lately than I have about my own mother and father. Sitting here beside my foster brother I'm almost as happy as if he were my real brother." Tears gathered in her eyes. "Am I a traitor? Have I forsaken my birth parents for my foster parents? Graham for Ned? Might I, someday, not want to go home to England? Could that ever happen?" She certainly hoped not.

Just then, through the static of the car radio, the announcer interrupted the music to comment on the Japanese attack on Indochina and the effect it would have on Britain and the U.S. There followed a panel discussion of how the attitude of the Communists had changed in Britain. Only a few days ago they were sabotaging the British factories and denouncing the "capitalist and imperialist war" but, now that Germany had assaulted Russia, they wanted Britain to attack Germany from the west. They had started scrawling slogans of encouragement on factory walls; things such as 'A Second Front Now.' "Of course," the moderator explained, "England is in no condition to initiate an offensive campaign in Western Europe so long as it has its hands full in North Africa, and now in Indochina."

"See how the Communists do, Ann?" Ned said. "They adjust their ideals and actions to benefit their needs. They have no firm ideology." Ann wasn't certain what all this meant but she agreed with him anyway. She wanted to make him think she understood.

A few miles further along, he turned to Ann and said, "Edith is nice. Isn't she? She's someone very special." He then asked that Ann not mention what he and Edith had done at the drive-in. He said it would only upset his mom and dad. "Besides," he added, "it didn't do any harm. It's natural for a boy and girl to kiss at the drive-in.

"It's done all the time," he added.

It didn't seem natural to Ann, but she didn't want to cause him, or Edith for that matter, any trouble. She promised not to tell. Nevertheless, she worried about it—until she talked to Edith on the Schaefers' new telephone a few days later. She couldn't believe how excited Edith was about Ned.

Chapter 63

Friday, 29 August 1941

As if to show off its best face, the weather was warm and balmy in McKinley Heights and its surrounds throughout most of the summer of 1941. Thus the evacuees enjoyed a pleasant school vacation with ample opportunity to explore the hills and dales around their American homes. They hiked; swam; played softball, baseball, basketball, and soccer; jumped rope; played marbles; rode bicycles; chewed bubble gum; ate ice cream cones; drank Cokes, Pepsi's, and root beers; stuffed themselves at family barbecues and picnics; and, at every chance, went barefooted.

Mostly, it was an opportunity to become more and more assimilated into the northeastern Ohio's social and cultural structure. The children congregated with their American friends at the malt shops and soda fountains; they danced together at the town socials, went to movies, collected stamps and butterflies, read comic books, and sang at the park hootenannies. On rainy days, they visited their friends and played checkers, Parcheesi, Crokinoles, Monopoly, and table tennis.

But all was not fun and games. Some of the children grew more responsible with assigned chores at home while others, the more enterprising in the group, mowed lawns, peddled papers, baby sat, or did whatever other odd jobs they could find to augment their allowances.

American slang crept into the evacuees' vocabularies; their clothes and attitudes were Americanized, and their accents more closely mimicked that of their American friends. Their bodies grew stronger, taller, heavier, and tanner. Maturation set in for some of the children with the boys' voices growing deeper and the girls' bodies beginning to display more shapely figures. Had their parents in England met these children on the street, many would already have had difficulty recognizing them.

Even with all these enjoyable activities and pleasant changes, all but the youngest spent a good part of their time still thinking of their beloved English families and homes, and constantly wondering how soon they could return. It had now been over a year since they left home. In spite of their happy faces, they remained inwardly sad, sent many impassioned letters back home, and hugged their pillows tightly at night, trying to fall asleep without crying.

In England during the Summer of 1941, people were becoming accustomed to once again sleeping though the night without the bombing raids. All were thankful for this much needed reprieve. Without this relief, they now felt it would have been impossible to continue working at the demanding pace of the past two years. This, of course, was not true. War production had increased, and would have continued to increase, regardless of the wartime conditions around them; their strong determination and tireless will to win, no matter what the costs, would have pulled them through.

Although cheerful faces were everywhere, this was a clever subterfuge, a method of hiding the lessening, but still lingering, fear of a German invasion and the tribulations of the severe shortages of almost everything needed to subsist. They grew veggies in their victory gardens, planned their meals carefully, and dressed less fashionably. Their faces aged and their shoulders stooped from the hard toil, constant fear, and, as the number of military casualties steadily grew, the worry for loved ones in the military. Almost every family had at least one member serving in the British armed forces. Many had already lost a son or father.

Doubly troubled were the parents who had sent their children to overseas billets. They pined to have their children with them once more, but knew it impossible to bring them home safely until the war was over. Until such time as the children came back, the parents had to suffer huge pangs of guilt and nearly unbearable angst, vainly wishing they could revoke their decision to send them away. But they plodded on, not telling the children in their letters how they felt, how bad things were, or how much they missed them.

*   *   *

The governments of Britain and America worried as well. By the end of July the Japanese had completed their occupation of Indochina. In response, President Roosevelt, by executive order, froze all Japanese assets in America until such time as Japan withdrew all its troops and neutralized Indochina. Two days later the British did the same. On August ninth, Roosevelt and Churchill met on a cruiser in Placentia Bay in Newfoundland. On the twelfth, they announced the *Atlantic Charter* which called for freedom among all territories and people, full economic collaboration between all nations, destruction of the Nazi tyranny, peace, and disarmament.

It was also during the summer of 1941 that Bender Electric drew up a parent consent form which, in the case of death of an evacuee's parents or the sudden illness of one of the evacuees, designated W. T. Bender as the child's guardian. It authorized him to legally act in their best interest, alone, and without additional consent. Some of the parents quickly signed the form without concern, while others required several days to reflect on its implication. Chad and Diane were among those who required several days. Not only did the thought of such a disaster bother them, but it also reminded them that it was possible Ann and Graham could be lost to England forever. In the end, however, they decided it was the only choice they had and signed, while continuing to pray it would never apply to either of their children.

By the first of June, when classes were over for the summer, the strained relationship between Ann and her classmates had essentially disappeared. Ann had her wish; she had become "one of the gang." Some of this improvement was because they had grown used to having her around; some was because of Ann's success in her courses–she had ended the semester either first or second in every class and had received respect, and even awe, from almost everyone; some was because she had made a concerted effort to win their friendship; but mostly, it was simply because they had decided she was not much different from them, in spite of her English heritage.

Bonnie, in particular, had become an especially good friend. The two girls visited each other often and sometimes had sleepovers at each other's house. Bonnie lived in the middle of Dexter Hills which Ann thought neat since from Bonnie's house they had easy access to all the popular hangouts and could walk quickly to the stores. Bonnie envied Ann as well; Ann lived on a farm and had all the animals to play with, had woods to explore, fields to play in, and could wade barefooted in the creek.

Sometimes the girls met at the swimming hole just north of town, often bringing a picnic basket and eating lunch in a nearby shaded alcove. Occasionally other friends would bring baskets too and they would make a party out of it. Ann enjoyed that. She liked the feeling of camaraderie that resulted and was content to sit and talk, often to the dismay of Bonnie who was more interested in swimming. By the end of the July however, in spite of Bonnie's complaints and Ann's predilection to talking, they had spent sufficient time in the water for Ann to be nearly as good a swimmer as Bonnie.

Wednesday evenings, when Ann was staying over or when farm work didn't keep the Schaefer family at home, Ann would attend the free outdoor movie sponsored by the local Dexter Hills merchants. Ann especially enjoyed those nights. The children brought blankets, which they spread on the grass near the screen. The older folks brought portable chairs and sat further back. Although almost everyone enjoyed the cartoon and the *Buck Rogers* serial, many of the features were old class B pictures and often not very good. When the movie was bad it was not uncommon, much to the consternation of the older folks, for the children to lose interest in the film and begin talking or teasing each other.

It was at one of these movies in early August when Ann and Bonnie ran into Oliver and Vicky. They were sharing a blanket in a rather secluded section of the lawn. It was Bonnie who noticed them first. "Look, Ann," she said, "There's Oliver and Vicky."

Ann looked up just in time to see Vicky putting her arm around Oliver and placing her head on his shoulder. It was a surprise seeing them together again, apparently on a date. It bothered her, but she wasn't certain why. What difference did it make? It was their business, not hers. "Hi, Vicky. Hi, Oliver," she whispered. "It's not a very good movie tonight, is it?"

"Oh. Hi, Ann," they said. "Nice to see you here."

Just then the movie scene changed and the plot recaptured Ann's attention. For a few minutes she forgot about Oliver and Vicky. When she looked back, they had gone. She wondered where but said nothing to Bonnie. "After all, what do I care about where they went, or what they do?" she tried to convince herself.

Just before school opened, Kirk and Lucy gave Sandy a party for her twelfth birthday. Among the invitees, at Sandy's request, were her cabin mates from the *S.S. Caerleon*: Ann, Edith and Elizabeth; and her special shipboard friends: Graham, Fred, Steve, and Stewart. It was the first time the group had visited together since the Bender Thanksgiving party and a good opportunity to share experiences.

It didn't take long for everyone to notice how overindulgent the Maurers were with Sandy. No one could mention a popular toy, doll, or game that Lucy and Kirk had not already given her. There were no movies or places of interest in northeastern Ohio that Sandy had not already visited; no candy bars, ice cream flavors, or American dishes that Sandy had not tasted. The group feared all this special attention would spoil Sandy, but surprisingly she still seemed as sweet and friendly as she had always been. Apparently the excesses had not affected her, but the group still worried. They were certain such doting foster parents would ultimately lead to unpleasant consequences.

Thus, it came as no real surprise to anyone when, after the ice cream and cake had been served, and the candles blown out, Lucy announced they were giving Sandy the riding horse they had promised her as a special birthday present. They also had enrolled her in an equestrian school, hoping she would develop into a champion rider someday. After the party everyone was invited to accompany them to the riding academy to see the horse. All the children were thrilled at Sandy's good fortune; although some were a little jealous.

Ann felt especially sorry for Sandy. The Schaefers had no riding horses but they had work horses and Ann knew how much effort it took to take care of them. She wondered if Sandy would enjoy that part of ownership. She also couldn't imagine training for an hour or so each day. Sitting on a horse that long couldn't be much fun. But, if it made Sandy happy, that was all that really mattered. Her well-being and happiness were the most important things.

On the Friday before school started, Ann saw Oliver again. He had been picking potatoes all morning and was sitting on the farm wagon finishing his lunch when she came down the path. "Hi!" she said, stopping to talk to him. "Are you ready for school next week?"

"Yea." he responded. "It'll be good to be back in school, away from all this hard work. What subjects are you taking this fall?"

"English II, American history, arithmetic, art, music, physical science, typing, and maybe band, if they have an instrument I can borrow."

"I'll be taking English II, American history, arithmetic and physical science too. Could we maybe sit together in those classes?" he asked, looking at Ann with a hopeful countenance.

"It depends on where Bonnie wants to sit. We promised we would sit beside each other, but I wouldn't object to sitting near you too, if possible. It would be especially nice in American history. I'll probably need some help with that one. I still don't know much about America's past." She hesitated, then asked, "But wouldn't you rather sit with Vicky?"

"With the grades you've been receiving I can't imagine you needing any help," he said, ignoring the question. Then he added, "But I'd be happy to help whenever I can."

"I'd best get on now. Uncle Jack wants me to help sort and sack potatoes this afternoon. See you in school," she said as she walked away.

Oliver watched Ann until she turned the corner. There was something about her that still fascinated him. He couldn't quite decide what it was, but there was no doubt that she was special. He promised himself he would do everything he could to sit beside her.

Chapter 64

Monday, 6 October 1941

Oliver, whose loyalty to the American League was almost as great as his devotion to the Cleveland Indians, was elated; the New York Yankees had beaten the Brooklyn Dodgers four games to one in the World Series. There had been much excitement at the barbershop when the Series ended. Almost everyone had cheered after the final Dodger out. Only the barber, "Digger" Hartline–Oliver had never heard why they called him Digger–had cursed the outcome. He argued the National League should have won, "There's no doubt," he said, "it's the stronger conference."

The argument confirmed what Oliver had always suspected, Digger supported whichever team was the least popular with his customers. It was an excellent way to generate an argument, and arguments entertained the men waiting for haircuts. There was no other explanation for why Digger would suddenly abandon his beloved Yankees. All the same, Oliver had to admit, the ploy was successful, almost anytime he stopped by there was an argument underway and everyone seemed to have an opinion. Usually the debate was over which team was better, the Indians or the Yankees in the summertime and the local high school basketball teams in the winter. Even though Oliver knew it was a cleverly contrived plot, it still irritated him when Digger made disparaging remarks about one of the Cleveland players, especially when it was about his favorite pitcher, Bob Feller. He had to admit, DiMaggio was a good fielder and an excellent batter, but he tired of Digger always claiming DiMaggio was a much better hitter than Feller was a pitcher.

There was little doubt, though, the barbershop was the favorite hangout for most of the men whenever they had leisure time to kill. Everyone hated the Yankees, the most unpopular team in town, and seemed to enjoy the good natured banter Digger generated. Those that didn't could always join the game of Jass, usually underway in the backroom.

There had been a noticeable change in the conversation in recent months, however. Where before it centered almost exclusively on baseball and the other popular sports, or occasionally on the effects of the Depression, the talk recently was mostly about the war in Europe and the fear of America becoming involved. Among the regulars were several who had served in France during the Great War, and they wanted no part in another one.

Oliver could still recall the bitterness of some of the men when the Selective Service Act passed last year. They drafted two men from Dexter Hills shortly after Secretary Simpson pulled the numbers from the fish bowl. Both had looked forward to getting home in November, after their year of training, but had their hopes dashed when Congress passed the Selective Service Extension Act in August, it extended their service an extra six months. One of them still had hopes of getting home early; all men over twenty-eight were going to be released, and he'd be twenty-eight in January.

The men at the barbershop still talked about the misfortune of those two and worried about other groups being called. The limit of nine-hundred thousand inductees had been removed in August and some of their sons with low numbers expected to go in the next call-up. One man had teased Oliver, telling him he might be called too, "if," as he said, "Congress continues to pass more of those silly Acts." Oliver laughed at the suggestion; he didn't think they'd call thirteen year old boys. "Don't laugh, Sonny," the man cautioned. "The limit's twenty-one now but sooner or later it will be eighteen, or maybe sixteen–or even fourteen. You'll be old enough before you know it."

For several days in September, spirits rose when Roosevelt declared publicly that the Russian front would hold and Moscow would not be taken. Still many thought this was mere propaganda, simply designed to ease growing concerns about America's involvement. They predicted Germany would defeat Russia in a few weeks.

Another major topic of discussion at the Dexter Hills barbershop during 1941 was the large number of people stricken with tuberculosis.

By mid fall, it had become epidemic with the number of cases increasing at an alarming rate. No city or area had been spared. By August, there were two cases in Dexter Hills, which, because of its small population, represented a much larger percentage than in either Oakton or McKinley Heights.

Coincidentally, while Oliver was at the barbershop Monday afternoon listening to the latest concerns about the TB epidemic, Ann and Graham were on the telephone talking about Bobby Preston, one of their fellow evacuees. Only the day before, Bobby had been diagnosed as having TB and had been immediately rushed to the sanitarium. Everyone was speculating his stay would be quite lengthy, TB was not easily cured.

"I've heard that Captain Ben is upset about Bobby," Graham said, his voice reflecting his concern. "He's saying that, as long as he has anything to do with it, Bobby is the last of his English children who will fall deathly ill. He has vowed that all of them, including Bobby, will return to England after the war ends, happy and healthy, no matter what the cost. He is personally guaranteeing it."

"That seems to be an extremely difficult promise to keep," Ann argued, questioning the wisdom of such a bold statement. "It's very noble of him. I hope he's correct, but I don't see how anyone can guarantee no more illnesses or injuries. It's just too uncertain to guarantee."

"What he really is saying, Ann, is that he will do everything within his means to keep us healthy. It certainly makes me feel better to know he feels personally responsible for us. It must be reassuring for our parents as well–knowing their children will be looked after, regardless of the cost. Dad Nelson says Captain Ben cabled Bobby's parents last night with the prognosis and an explanation of the planned treatment. They must have been relieved to receive his personal cable."

"Captain Ben certainly is a peach. Not many people would go to the bother and expense he has to ensure his charges receive the best of care," Ann observed, then asked Graham what Bobby's symptoms were.

"They say just before he went to bed he had a bad coughing spell. He had been nursing what everyone thought was a bad cold for the past several weeks. When he started coughing up blood, his foster parents rushed him to the hospital. It took the doctors only a few minutes to determine, with almost certainty, that it was TB. That's why they immediately sent him to the sanitarium."

"No one had time to think about what was happening," Graham added. "Almost before anyone knew what was going on, he had been admitted."

"Golly, Graham," Ann worried. "I hope we don't come down with a terrible disease like that. It's bad enough worrying about the polio epidemic. Must we now worry about TB also?"

"They say TB is quite contagious, you get it by being around someone who has it. Fortunately, we haven't been around Bobby since the last Bender party. So we have no cause to worry."

"I hope not, Graham."

"How's school going?" he asked, changing the subject.

"Pretty good, so far! Eighth grade looks as if it will be quite pleasant, especially since I made it into band this year. I borrowed a clarinet from school and am practicing whenever I can. So far I mostly sit while all the other band members are playing. They play so fast I don't think I'll ever be able to keep up with them. Mr. Spencer says not to worry. He assures me that's the way everyone feels in the beginning, but I fear my ineptitude may be a special case."

"I wouldn't worry, Ann. He probably knows what he's talking about. I think it's great, but I must admit, it's difficult to imagine you playing in a band. By the time we go back to England you'll probably want to join the King's Guard Band," Graham teased. "Of course you'll need to cut your hair and pretend you're a man."

"I don't plan to make a career out of playing, Graham. I just want the experience of being in an American band. It's something unique, something I can always point to when we go back home."

After she hung up, Ann sat down immediately and wrote a letter to Chad and Diane, a task that was getting harder and harder to do each week. There always seemed to be more pressing chores, or interesting activities, to consume her time. What was worse, she no longer felt as obligated to write as she had a year ago. The indifference worried her. She didn't quite understand why writing to her parents had become so difficult. She still loved them and missed them dearly, but, in truth, the real reason she wrote was to keep her mum's letters coming. It embarrassed her. She had vowed, over and over again, to get back to a regular schedule, but it just didn't seem as important as it once did.

Anyway, this afternoon she was writing and that was at least a start towards getting back to a regular schedule. There was so much to tell them. She told them about her school courses and about her classmates. She told them who she was sitting with in her various classes, talked at great length about her friend Bonnie, and wrote nearly half a page describing the band program and how proud she was to be in it. Although she wasn't certain why, she even included a brief description of Oliver and how he had gone out for junior varsity football, how he was helping her with American history, and what a nice boy he was. Then, because she knew her dad would tease her, she told them Oliver had a girlfriend named Vicky. As an added precaution she included a special assurance that he definitely was not her boyfriend.

By the time she sealed the envelope, she was crying. Writing home seemed to do that to her, even now, after almost fourteen months. She quit crying soon after Lady nuzzled up to her. "You're here for me, aren't you, girl?" she sobbed, as she held Lady close and scratched her between the ears. "You wouldn't send me away. You'd not do that to a friend, would you?"

At nearly the same moment Ann was writing her letter, Oliver was thinking about her and how nice it was to sit beside her in American history. Being there and helping was one of the highlights of his day. Too bad Vicky had managed to sit in between them in English and the teachers had assigned seats alphabetically in arithmetic and physical science. He only had this one opportunity each day. He supposed it was better than nothing.

His thoughts then turned to how well things were going this fall. He was almost certain he'd be a starter on the junior varsity football team soon. He had just started to plan his exercise regimen when his Dad staggered in. "What're you doin' at home, boy?" he asked, his words slurred by the alcohol, "Why aren't you out peddlin' your papers, or doin' somethin' more productive than sittin' around the house?"

"Everything's done, Dad. Coach says we should get plenty of rest so we can do our best tomorrow night at the football game."

"Football game? Rest? What does that stupid Coach know?" Ludwig said, fumbling with the words and confused by the alcohol. "Doesn't he know I need you to work around the house. Does he expect a father to do everythin'?"

He continued to ramble on about the incompetence of the coach, Oliver, the government, and everything else he could think of and continued to get angrier with each new object he found to curse. Finally his anger overwhelmed him. He grabbed Oliver by the right arm and with a violent effort pulled him out of his chair and hurled him half way across the room. Oliver could hear the crack as he landed. The pain in his arm was so intense he nearly fainted. "You damn lazy bum!" his Dad shouted. "Get out of here and get to work. Show some respect for your old man! Earn some money–some cash. Aren't you ashamed of yourself, boy? Don't you know your dad has debts? Only this afternoon Klink told me if I didn't pay my tab, there'd be no more booze." He altered his voice, tried to make it sound sweet and loving. "And, son, you don't want to see your old man goin' thirsty, do you?" he sobbed.

With an effort, Oliver picked himself off the floor and, holding his arm as best he could, ran from the room without uttering a sound. He roamed the streets for what seemed like hours. The pain in his arm was excruciating, he knew he needed medical help but was reluctant to go to Dr. Carter's office. How would he explain what had happened? Finally, the pain became too unbearable to delay any longer. He staggered up to Dr. Carter's office door and rang the bell. "Doc, you've got to help me," he said when the door opened, "I've had a fall and think I broke my arm." Having said that, he could hold out no longer; he passed out in the doctor's arms.

The broken arm put and end to Oliver's participation in junior varsity football for the season. Had it not been for several of his friends who helped deliver his papers during the first weeks of his recovery, he would have lost his paper route as well. Normally with the spare time created by the absence of football practice Oliver would have tried to find some sort of work to do, but with a broken arm, work was difficult to find. Instead, he used the time for additional study, a habit that would serve him well the remainder of his life.

Things were better for Fred. He had made the varsity football team and by the third game had won a starting position as a wide receiver. Last week, he became a local hero scoring the winning touchdown catch in the waning moments of the Emerson High School game. The catch had been spectacular enough to be written about in the *Oakton Sunday Press*. Not only had the *Press* described the catch but also told about Fred's evacuation from England. It said he was staying with Dr. and Mrs. Thomas Derringer, much to Victoria's pleasure.

Victoria was so pleased that she invited Fred to join Tom and her for dinner on Sunday evening, the first time in several months he had eaten with them. She was immediately impressed with the way Fred was maturing and his excellent manners. Long before the dinner was over she had decided to invite Fred to dinner more often. In fact, she was beginning to really enjoy talking with him and began to think of him more as a son than as a foreign visitor.

After dinner, Graham was outside shooting baskets when he spotted Fred. "Hey, Fred! That was some game on Saturday," he yelled. "What a spectacular catch you made. I thought for sure we were going to lose that game. Then you came to the rescue. Way to go!"

"It wasn't as great as everyone is saying," Fred replied, somewhat embarrassed. "I just did what the coaches have been telling us to do during practice. If anyone should get the credit it's our quarterback, Smith. Smitty put that ball exactly where it had to be. Anyone could have caught his pass. It was perfect, right on the numbers."

"I think you're being too modest, Fred," Graham protested. "Boy, I wish I had your ability."

"Don't be silly, Graham. Your game's coming along. As far as I'm concerned, there's no question you'll make the varsity next year. You just need more experience before you get there. Besides, I'd gladly trade my athletic skills for your scholastic abilities." And then he added, "If we did trade, I would get the better of the bargain. I've heard how well you're doing in school. If I only had half the grades you have, I'd consider myself a super student."

The praise embarrassed Graham. To change the subject he asked, "Have you heard anything from your folks lately?"

"Yes, I received a letter from my mum and dad on Friday. Everything seems to be going better for them lately. It's been sometime since they've been bombed. Maybe with the Germans fighting the Russians now, things will begin to improve in England."

"That's what my parents are saying too. England certainly hasn't won the war but at least Jerry isn't bombing them anymore. Let's hope the moratorium lasts!"

The two boys discussed other news from home. Fred had learned that his father was now serving in the Civil Defence Service, the same as Graham's, although not in the same unit. They talked about their mothers and soon became rather sad. To change the mood, Graham mentioned Yvonne's work in the Rolls-Royce plant and bragged about Henry's service in North Africa. The boys agreed it was their duty, like Henry's and Yvonne's, to help their country. They vowed to return to England and join the RAF as soon as they were old enough.

Chapter 65

Saturday, 18 October 1941

Ned and Karen had invited Ann to go with them to the Dexter Hills Saturday afternoon football game. It would be Ann's first game. Last fall she had little interest in American sports and had chosen not to attend any of the games. This year was different. She wanted to attend now that she knew many of the cheerleaders and team players and would be in the marching band next year. That is, she would march provided she successfully completed eighth grade band–which was not all that certain–and, of course, if she hadn't gone back to England.

One of the first people they saw when they arrived was Oliver, his arm still in the cast, standing by the refreshment booth. "Hi, Oliver," Ann said when she saw him. "How's that arm coming? Does it still hurt?"

"Not so much anymore," Oliver replied, trying to act nonchalant about the injury. "I'm getting used to it already. The main difficulty is that I can't button my clothes and have a real problem writing with the left hand."

"It's too bad you broke it. It's such a shame, breaking it right after you made the team. Will you be able to play again?" she asked.

"That shouldn't be a problem," Oliver replied. "I talked it over with the doctor and he said I'd be as good as new long before next season. Of course I won't be able to play any more this year."

"I'm sorry to hear that. You must be terribly disappointed," Ann sympathized. "By the way, you never really did tell me how it happen. What did you do?"

Oliver ignored Ann's question. "I'm disappointed all right, but maybe it'll be a good thing. Now that I can't play football, or take on any more work until it heals, there's more time to study–and you know how badly I need to study."

"Don't be silly, Oliver, you're a good student. I know you'll do well in all your classes this year. If I can help you with any of your assign-ments–provide a hand to write with or something–just let me know."

Oliver's eyes lit up. "Thanks. I just might do that. I talked to my teacher about getting help with the term paper. She said I could get someone to pen it for me." He quickly added, "As long as I certify it's my own words and ideas."

Ann laughed. "Don't worry, I wouldn't cheat. I'll just write what-ever you tell me to write–without making any suggestions. Of course, we have always discussed the assignments before we started to write–I don't see anything wrong with continuing to do the same. Do you?"

When the game was about to begin she invited Oliver to sit with Ned, Karen and her. Mumbling something about Vicky needing to help the varsity cheerleaders, Oliver eagerly accepted Ann's invitation.

American football surprised Ann. Although she was no expert on English sports, it was immediately obvious this game was entirely different from what they called football in England. She thought American football was an odd game. The players seemed to simply line up, run for a few seconds, then pile on top of each other. It made almost no sense to her. "Why, pray tell, does the crowd scream each time the first fellow gets the ball? He always either quickly throws it or hands it to someone else. Is he afraid or something? Does he think all those boys running after him are going to hurt him?" Everyone laughed, especially Ned and Oliver.

With considerable patience Oliver tried to explain the game to Ann. Although there were still many rules and concepts not covered, Ann was pleased when the final whistle blew; Oliver had been a good teacher. He had given her a fair understanding of the underlying principles of this complicated game of football. How proud she would be when she went back to England with all this newfound knowledge. Of course it was knowledge that would, in all likelihood, serve no useful purpose, but at least it would make her unique among her peers. She would need to find some way to reward him.

Oliver was also pleased. His mission had been successfully completed. It had been an easier task than he had anticipated. As usual, Ann had been eager to learn and easy to teach. More importantly, he had been able to look carefully into her eyes as he explained the rules, those beautiful dark brown eyes, eyes filled with such excitement, so interested in whatever he said. He had never seen eyes quite like hers. They caused something strange to come over him. His body almost wilted. It was a grand feeling.

Without questioning it further, and in spite of his current relationship with Vicky, he asked Ann if they could meet tomorrow after church and go for a walk along the old canal towpath. Knowing Ann's fondness for animals, he hastened to add that through years of disuse much of the canal bed was now swampy. He told her there would be many interesting critters and creatures to study along the way.

She blushed when she noticed Ned and Karen grinning. "Had they heard what he had asked?" She finally regained her composure and asked about Vicky.

"Don't worry about her, we're just good friends," Oliver tried to assure her. "Besides," he was quick to add, "She'll be at her grandmother's tomorrow."

Ann told him she would love to but needed Ida and Jack's permission first. They parted with an understanding Oliver would wait for her at the old springhouse, north of town. If she wasn't there by half past one, he would assume she wasn't coming.

*   *   *

"Ann's got a date!" Ned teased on the way home from the game.

"What a handsome lad he is," Karen added. "Why, if I were a few years younger I'd be jealous. I'll bet he's a dandy date."

"It's a good thing he has a broken arm," Ned noted. "I'd hate to see them walking together on that deserted towpath if he had both arms free–she'd be kissed for sure," he said and laughed.

"I can think of worse things," Karen said, laughing with him. "I wouldn't mind a kiss from that lovely fellow."

Ann blushed again but said nothing. She wasn't certain how to respond to teasing of that sort. She knew one thing though, she had never kissed, or been kissed, by a boy–other than her brothers–and she had no intention of starting tomorrow. It would merely be a pleasant walk, looking at the frogs, turtles, and other swamp creatures.

Ann was relieved when Ned and Karen did not say anything when she asked permission that evening. Although Ida was somewhat reluctant to let her "little Annie" meet a boy on the towpath, she eventually consented after agreeing with Jack that Oliver was an awfully nice boy.

That night Ann retired early. She eagerly looked forward to the walk and wanted to be fresh. With Lady snuggled by her side, she caressed her gently as she dreamed of football games, turtles, frogs, England, and kissing boys.

Oliver had been waiting for nearly forty minutes when Ann arrived. She was only five minutes late. Oliver had worried she wouldn't come. Ann had worried he would be gone. Neither quite understood why. After all, it was no big deal, they were merely going for a walk. Nevertheless, they were both elated to see each other.

The afternoon sped quickly by. They walked and talked and thoroughly explored the bog. They watched the birds, threw stones at the frogs, and watched the fish and tadpoles swimming. Oliver showed Ann the remains of one of the old canal locks and explained how it had worked. She laughed at his sense of humor and was greatly impressed with his serious side, especially his thoughtful plans and ambitions. She had never met a boy who had a clearer picture of where he wanted to go or how he would get there. He talked about airplanes and engineering, the colleges best known for aircraft engineering, the need for him to do well in his high school mathematics and sciences courses, and how important it was to save a sizable bank account if he had any hope of going to one of the more prestigious institutes.

It surprised Ann to learn that college admission policies gave almost no consideration to one's social standing; they based everything on one's intelligence and chances of success. It was so different from the system in England. She told him about Yvonne's disappointment, how her dad had not wanted her to accept a scholarship because they were only a working-class family. Oliver couldn't understand what that had to do with going on to school, even after she tried to explain that higher education was reserved almost entirely for the gentry. He could understand how the ability to pay could be a consideration, but if Yvonne had a scholarship that shouldn't have been a problem.

As the day went on, Ann told Oliver about Henry and how proud she was of him, how he had fought at Dunkirk, and how he was now in North Africa. She talked about the shortages in England and how much better off everyone was in the U.S., even though there were beginning to be some shortages in the U.S. too. They discussed many of the different customs in the two countries, particularly how the English ate with the knife in their right hand and the fork in their left while the Americans switched the utensils after cutting their meat. They compared the meaning of words in the two countries. They were particularly amused at words such as draughts versus checkers, larder versus pantry, bonnet versus hood, braces versus suspenders, pudding versus dessert, wireless versus radio, and many more.

They made each other laugh when Ann said, "ta ta" instead of good-bye and Oliver replied, "So long." But their laughter quickly turned serious when they realized the awkwardness of the situation. Both felt an unexplained urge to do more than simply say good-bye. But neither knew exactly what it was.

That evening Ann felt strange. She could not quite decide what was wrong. She had no particular pain, nor any other specific symptoms. She simply did not feel right. It was only during her evening bath that she discovered her difficulty. She was bleeding! She did not understand what was wrong. Her first thought was of Bobby Preston and TB. She knew he had coughed up blood just before they had admitted him to the sanitarium, but this wasn't quite the same. She thought of polio, but had never heard anyone mention blood in connection with polio. It was embarrassing. She wished there was someone to ask. If she were back home in England, she could have asked her mum. She could ask Ida, but this seemed far too personal to share with her, even as nice and helpful as she was. Instead she washed thoroughly, put on a pair of panties, her nightgown, and went to bed.

It was a long night for Ann. She got little sleep. She worried about what was happening to her and felt certain it was some sort of horrible disease, something Captain Ben, with all his good intentions, could not prevent. "Would she be the one to spoil his guarantee? Would she be the one to die in America?" By morning there was little doubt it was something serious. She once again washed carefully but afterwards decided she could not go to school and climbed back into bed. When Ida came in to ask why she hadn't come down to breakfast Ann complained of stomach cramps and said she was too sick to get up. Ida took her temperature, and even though it was normal, agreed she could stay in bed. Ann had always been too conscientious to be pretending now.

After Karen and Ned left and Jack had gone to the barn, Ida returned to Ann's room, determined to either discover what was ailing Ann or take her to see Dr. Carter. "What's the matter, child?" Ida asked, a worried look on her face. "Tell Aunt Ida what is wrong."

Ann didn't quite know how to respond. She needed help but was too embarrassed to tell. "It's nothing, Aunt Ida. Just an upset stomach. I'm sure I'll be better in a day or two."

"Tell me exactly where it hurts," Ida pleaded, putting her hand on Ann's stomach. "Does it hurt here? You don't have appendicitis, do you?"

"I don't believe so," Ann replied. "There's no pain."

"But you just said you had stomach cramps," Ida scolded. "Don't lie to me. Tell me what's wrong."

"Oh, Aunt Ida!" Ann cried, "I think I have TB!"

"What makes you think that, child?"

"Because I'm bleeding, Aunt Ida," Ann confessed, her face turning red.

"You aren't coughing up blood are you?" Ida asked, a look of alarm on her face. Suddenly Ida realized what it was. "Oh, you poor child," she said, pulling Ann close to her. "Why didn't you tell me sooner? There's nothing wrong with you. It's just part of becoming a woman!"

"What do you mean, Aunt Ida?" Ann sobbed.

It took considerable time for Ida to explain. Much the same as it had with Karen. There were many questions and much consoling before Ann was convinced it was a normal event in a young girl's life. When Ida left, she felt sad, the talk she had just had was something that should have been between Ann and her real mother. "How unfair this evacuation scheme is. Diane should have been here to share such an important and intimate time with her daughter. I'll miss Ann so terribly when she goes home, but what a happy day it will be for Diane."

*   *   *

On the shortwave radio later that evening Ann came across a BBC broadcast of greetings from English parents to their children overseas. Six London families had been selected on this particular night. None were parents of Bender evacuees. Still, she listened intently to the entire show, hoping a mistake had been made, hoping one of the voices would be that of her mum or dad. She heard neither and was emotionally spent by the end of the program. Nevertheless, she planned to listen to all future programs–sooner or later, she was almost certain someday one of the messages would be a greeting from home. At least she hoped so.

When Ann returned to school on Tuesday, she found Oliver worrying about her. He was certain he had somehow been responsible for her absence. She did not explain. Instead, she asked about American history and what she had missed. Much to her relief, there had not been much new material and the bell rang before he could ask her again why she had stayed home.

The following weekend, Ida suggested Karen take Ann to a movie. It was a welcomed assignment for Karen, she needed the diversion after completing a trying week at Klink's. They chose the newly released movie, *Dumbo*. Before the movie started there was a short plea for patrons to buy *US Defense Savings Stamps*. Karen laughed when Ann suggested perhaps they should buy some. "You'll be back in England long before they mature," Karen cautioned.

"But it seems like a proper thing to do," Ann countered, then pestered no more.

The following Thursday night, the US destroyer, *Reuben James*, part of convoy SC-48, was torpedoed by a German submarine wolfpack 400 miles south of Ireland. It was the first sinking of a U.S. warship in action. Although no one in the U.S. was ready to panic, the sale of *U.S. Defense Savings Bonds* increased significantly the following week. Within the next few weeks, several merchant ships would also be torpedoed and sunk. The U.S. did little more than issue a formal protest.

With her first paycheck, Karen purchased an entire book of stamps for eighteen dollars and seventy-five cents, then immediately converted them into a twenty-five dollar *Defense Savings Bond*. She said she had done it to help Ann get home.

Ann was pleased.

The phantom rose from the searing sand. It was dressed in black.

It's eyes flashed brilliant green. Smoke belched from it's mouth. Slowly it crept closer. Lady did not see it until it was too late. It snatched her and threw her into a burning caldron.

Ann heard Lady yelp, but could not see where she had gone. "It is I who snatched your dog. Next it will be somebody you love," the ogre threatened.

Ann woke with a start, "Oh, Lady. You're here! It must have been a dream." She rolled over and was soon back asleep.

"The phantom reappeared. "It's not that easy. I always get them, no matter what they do. When I want something, I take it."

"Why do you want someone else?" Ann asked. "Don't take anyone, I want everybody here with me–for ever so long."

"I'm sorry, little lass. It's written down in blood, you see. It's some soldier's fortune to go with me."

Chapter 66

Friday, 7 November 1941

The cast of the Young Thespians Guild had been looking forward to this night with mixed feelings. In September, at the start of rehearsals, everyone was certain the play would be one of the best comedies ever presented at Oakton High. Then, as the opening night loomed closer, they began to fear the play would be a disaster. By opening night, they were certain it would be the worst play ever presented at Oakton High.

No one believed Miss Brown, the Guild advisor, when she told them final rehearsals often seemed to go poorly. "It is normal," she said, "to miss lines and cues during these last few tense practices. When you walk on stage Friday night the adrenaline will flow and everything will be okay." This increased their confidence level until she added, "That is, if you remain calm and don't panic."

But she had been right. When the cast took its final bows, the many cheers and thunderous applause confirmed it.

Afterwards, the actors broke into a wild and gleeful frenzy, laughing, cheering, repeatedly congratulating each other, and giving hearty hand-shakes. "There now, Graham, aren't you glad I talked you into joining the Guild? You were the hit of the show," Meg said, after running across the stage, grabbing him, and giving him a big hug. "You rascal, why did you wait until tonight to say your lines that way? Your timing was perfect. It was all those little pauses that captivated the audience. You seemed to know just how to make them laugh."

"You weren't so bad yourself," Graham said, returning her hug and compliment. "I thought you told me last night you couldn't remember any of your lines and probably would stand on the stage speechless, making a fool of yourself. You never missed a cue or muffed a line."

"But you're the one the people really liked."

"My lines were funnier. That's what did it," Graham argued, trying his best to be humble. "Did you hear what Suzy said? She said the audience would have laughed twice as hard if they had understood more of what I was saying. She told me I should start talking like an American and quit sounding so foreign. She thinks everyone is getting tired of listening to my accent."

"That's nonsense. The crowd wouldn't have laughed if they hadn't understood you. Suzy is jealous. She wanted to be the star tonight, she probably thought she'd get all of the attention. It must have made her angry when you got more applause than she did."

"Why do people keep reminding me I'm a foreigner? I appreciate everything you Americans are doing for me, but, darn it, I'm still an Englishman–and proud of it. I have no desire to become an American, or to change my way of talking; even if I could. I'll go home just as I came, and as soon as I can. I think that's the way most evacuees feel."

"Please don't be upset," Meg admonished. "One or two rotten eggs in a basket doesn't make the basket rotten. Most of us love you and are happy you're here. Unfortunately, we Americans have our prejudices. Ever notice how we treat the Orientals? The Irish? And especially the Negroes? We're far from perfect. But I'll bet there are groups that aren't treated very nice in England too. I don't suppose every Englishman is crazy about the Americans."

Just then Ken and Louise arrived backstage. "You were wonderful, children! What a great show!" Ken said, a huge grin on his face. "You made a dad proud."

"Oh, Graham, I thought you were so funny. You're quite the jester. I didn't know you had it in you," Louise bubbled.

"I was just doing what comes naturally," Graham replied, mimicking the recent hit song. Everyone laughed.

"Can we treat you kids to an ice cream soda to celebrate?" Ken asked.

"Gee, Dad, I'm sorry but the cast is meeting at the malt shop for a cast party in half an hour. We'd love to go with you, but we really should go with the gang."

"That's all right, Meg. We understand. You kids run along. We'll talk some more when you get home. Now change your clothes. You don't want to be late for your party."

After Ken and Louise left, Graham turned to Meg, "Your parents are such nice people. They're so understanding. I'm lucky to have the three of you."

"We're the lucky ones, Graham. We love you so much. You've been a good son ... and brother. You've made us so happy, been such a gentlemen, and had such an important part in bringing Mom back to health. She finally accepts Tommy's death. The only thing is, she's become so attached to you. I can't imagine how she'll ever let you go when the time comes for you to go home." She paused, then added, "I'll miss you too. Maybe you shouldn't go?"

Graham laughed.

When they arrived at the malt shop, it was already filled. The jukebox was playing and several members of the cast were dancing. "Come on, Meg, let's dance," Graham coaxed as soon as they had found a seat and ordered their Cokes.

They spent most of the evening dancing with others in the cast, laughing, and celebrating their success. As the party began to wind down Graham put a quarter in the jukebox and selected several sentimental tunes. "These are the songs I like," he told Meg, "the slow and romantic tunes. Will you dance to them with me?"

As each song played they talked less and less, held each other tighter and tighter, and looked at each other with dreamy eyes, oblivious to the others still on the dance floor. By the time the last song was playing they were the only couple still dancing. "Hey, kids, it's time to close the shop," the proprietor finally said, tapping Graham on the shoulder.

Graham and Meg looked around and blushed. "I had no idea it was so late," Graham said, smiling at Meg. "We're sorry if we kept you. Please forgive us?"

On the way home they held hands as they walked along the street. Neither had much to say. They both were deep in thought.

The following day Ken and Louise treated them to the movie, *Sergeant York*, and to banana splits afterwards. Louise didn't like the movie, she complained it glorified war. Graham thought it keen, especially when York captured, single-handedly, all the German soldiers.

"We're going to run up to Wooster to visit Aunt Catherine tomorrow, would you kids like to ride along?" Ken asked that evening.

"Gee, Dad, I'd love to but play practice has been interfering with homework. I'd better stay here and study tomorrow afternoon," Meg apologized.

Graham declined, too. He also was behind in his studies.

The afternoon began with Meg and Graham sitting at the dining room table absorbed in their schoolbooks. However, as the afternoon dragged on they started to tire and began teasing each other. Graham started it, tossing a small gum eraser at Meg. Meg quickly retaliated. She shot several rubber bands at Graham. When one of the bands hit Graham on the side of the face he jumped up and started chasing her. "Now you're going to get it!" he shouted.

Meg quickly sprang from her chair and ran out of the room, Graham in pursuit. He cornered her in the living room and grabbed her around the waist. Laughing, they fell on the sofa. Meg began to tickle him. He quickly released his grip trying to defend himself. In the ensuing struggle their two bodies touched. Suddenly they were no longer laughing. Almost without realizing what he was doing, Graham kissed Meg. For a brief moment Meg returned it passionately, then quickly jumped to her feet. "Graham!" she screamed, "we can't do that. We're brother and sister!"

"No we're not," Graham protested, his face turning cherry red. "We're not related. You're not my sister."

"But I'm your foster sister," Meg countered, emphasizing the word sister and began to sob. "We just can't!"

"I'm sorry, Meg. You know I wouldn't do anything to hurt you. Please forgive me? I won't do it again." Then he added, "It's just that ... Well ... I think I like you ... Very much."

"You mustn't think such thoughts. It's incestuous," she warned.

That evening when Ken and Louise returned they sensed something amiss. There was nothing specific, just an underlying tension not there when they had left earlier. "Anything wrong?" Louise asked. "You both look odd."

"No. Nothing I'm aware of," Meg answered.

"No. We've been studying all day," Graham agreed.

That was all that was said. Still, Ken and Louise wondered what had happened.

*　*　*

On Thursday, the American Neutrality Act was amended. For the first time, it permitted the arming of all American merchantmen and gave them free passage to the war zones. It was another in a long sequence of steps the United States was taking to help Britain in her time of need.

Chapter 67

Thursday, 27 November 1941

Henry crouched behind the revetment tired, scared, and angry. This latest German barrage had been going on for some time, and its unceasing intensity had finally affected him. Ever since the battle started a week ago last Tuesday, there had been few opportunities to rest and many occasions to be frightened, but today certainly qualified as one of the worst. The anger he now harbored for Jerry surpassed anything he had ever felt before. He had thought he hated the Germans during the battle of Dunkirk but that was nothing compared to now. There had been too many casualties here in Tobruk; too many of his mates had been butchered by Rommel's heavy armor. He would have gladly used a machine-gun on the whole bloody lot if he could, but machine guns were ineffective against tanks.

Just then a shell burst nearby and Henry flinched from the impact of the concussion; the sound of the explosion caused a sharp pain in his ears. It momentarily eclipsed the earache he had had since the rocket attack two days before. Relief came a few minutes later when the shelling ceased. Henry took a cigarette from his pocket, lit it, and took a long drag. His mind raced back to all that had happened in Tobruk since he first joined the garrison in February. That was the day they had attached him to the 9th Australian Division.

Everyone blamed General Wavell when Rommel launched his offensive in March. By then Wavell had sent most of his veteran troops to Greece, leaving only the 2nd Armoured to defend their positions in western Egypt. The Second was poorly trained and no match for Rommel's newly formed Afrika Korps. Rommel, or the Desert Fox as he was now called, took El Aghelia on the Tripolitanian border on March 31, had recaptured Benghazi by April 6, and was in Tobruk by the fourteenth. The fighting had been fierce. Had it not been for the heavy artillery emplacements and the anti-tank guns Tobruk would have fallen. Instead Rommel had been forced to withdraw and to redirect his attack toward the Egyptian frontier. By the time the battle was over, the

Tobruk garrison had bravely and successfully withstood two more assaults by Rommel's tanks and had captured two thousand prisoners, but Rommel finished in control of the land between the garrison and Egypt. As a result, much of Tobruk lay in ruin and Henry's garrison had been isolated from the remainder of the Allied armies. The only way in and out was by sea.

The irony was that the troops sent to Greece by Wavell had failed miserably. By the end of April an evacuation had to be mounted to get fifty-thousand Allied troops out of Greece, many of them the troops sent from North Africa. "Had they stayed here," thought Henry, "they just might have prevented the isolation of Tobruk. The transfer might have done some good, but who knew? Being a foot soldier and not understanding many of the decisions sent down from the upper echelons was frustrating."

General Wavell had attempted, in June, to free the "Rats of Tobruk" as Henry's unit now called themselves. Wavell attacked Rommel at Halfaya Pass in an operation code named Battleaxe but the plan failed, Rommel's Afrika Korps defeated him decisively.

By then, Tobruk had become an obsession with Rommel; he was determined to capture it. He sent the Luftwaffe on nightly bombing raids and continuously caused havoc with his artillery and tank probes. It was nearly impossible to sleep during those nights. Added to Henry's misery was his diet. His unit survived mostly on bully beef, tinned stew, and canned fruit supplemented with vitamin pills. Water was rationed, only six pints allocated to each man per day. Any supplies they got had to be brought in by ferry at night.

Other than a daring naval operation in August that brought in additional troops, there was no relief for Tobruk until the Allies reorganized into the Eighth Army under General Cunningham and, on November 18, started another offensive thrust against Rommel. The Tobruk garrison was called on to do its part in this operation. Its task was a simultaneous assault on the forces surrounding them. Major fighting had gone on ever since with Henry in the thick of it all. The successes of the fight vacillated between the two armies. By the nineteenth, the British Army was in Sidi Rezegh, and on the twenty-second the Germans had recaptured it. On the twenty-sixth, General Ritchie took over command of the Eighth and had, just this morning, retaken Sidi Rezegh.

Then last night, the New Zealanders joined hands with the Tobruk garrison. Rumor had it that Rommel, who now had lost most of his air force, was in retreat and heading for Bardia. Henry hoped this was the beginning of the end of this campaign. He so wanted to rest, clean up, and feel relatively safe again.

*　　*　　*

Today was going to be a special treat for Ann. Jack and Ida had invited Graham and the Nelsons for Thanksgiving dinner. Although the feast, in itself, promised to be a grand occasion, Ann had not seen Graham for some time and looked forward to their meeting almost more than she did to the dinner. She had several letters to share and it would be nice simply to talk for awhile. For some reason, she was feeling homesick lately and talking with her brother might ease the pain a little.

When the Nelsons arrived, Ann and Graham quickly excused themselves from the main conversation and went to Ann's room to exchange information about home. "Everyone seems to be working so hard," Graham lamented. "I hope they're all okay. At least the bombing has stopped. That's a blessing."

"Poor Yvonne," Ann volunteered. "I haven't received a letter since the one last spring–she must be quite upset. She was very disappointed that she couldn't go on for more schooling, and now, working at Rolls-Royce and helping at St. Johns apparently hasn't improved her attitude. Mum says Yvonne has changed her mind again. She no longer has any interest in the WLA and fears she might be drafted into the Home Guard. There are rumors around that all boys and girls sixteen and older will be asked to register for the Home Guard. They are already encouraging boys to join the Cadets when they turn sixteen. Yvonne's saying now she wants no part of any government service, not the WLA or the Home Guard, claims it's not her war, it's Churchill's and the other government blokes. Mum also said Yvonne probably will change her mind again tomorrow–she's been changing it so often lately."

"I don't understand why she's so opposed to serving her country," Graham complained, "I certainly plan to join, just as soon as I can. I'll be eighteen in less than two years and, believe me, I'll be back in England and signed up just as quickly as I can after that."

"Surely there won't be a need for you to join in '43, Graham," Ann worried. "I would hope the war is settled long before then so we can go back to Mum and Dad together. Besides, I already have one brother in the Army. I certainly don't want you to be the second."

"I hope the war is over soon, just as much as you do, Ann," Graham agreed, "but things haven't been going well lately. They're saying Hitler's fight with Russia is draining his resources and spreading him pretty thin, but even though the Russian front has reduced the fear of an invasion of England, Germany still is a major force to be reckoned with. It may take a long time to bring this war to an end. It's entirely possible the fighting may still be going on in early '43. If so, I'll see if I can't join at seventeen. I'd like to shoot a few Jerries before it's over."

"Don't talk that way, Graham!" Ann scolded. "Let's talk about going home together, just as soon as possible. And let's hope Henry is home from North Africa–or wherever he is–when we get there."

"Speaking of North Africa, have you been reading about it?" Graham asked. "The reports are that there's a big battle going on–between the Allied Eighth Army and Rommel's Afrika Korps. No one seems to know exactly what's happening. One day they say Rommel is winning, and the next day it's the Allies. It's quite confusing. They're fighting most of the battles with tanks. Never before have armies moved so quickly. Some say it's comparable to sea warfare with the tanks rapidly changing position on the desert sand, just like battleships at sea."

"Oh, Graham! What if Henry is part of that battle?" Ann worried. "What if he gets hurt?"

"No need to fret, Ann. Henry can take care of himself. I'll bet he's giving those Jerries a lesson or two. Besides, no one knows for certain where he is. It's only a guess that he's in North Africa. He could just as easily be somewhere else."

"I hope you're right, Graham."

They were interrupted by Ida calling dinner. "I see there's major military activity in North Africa, Graham," Jack said as they walked into the room.

"Yes, sir," Graham replied. "That's where we believe our brother Henry is stationed."

"I know, son. I hope everything is going well for him." There followed a brief discussion about the North Africa situation among the menfolk, with Ann interrupting occasionally to make certain they didn't forget Henry's role in the engagement.

Before they ate, Jack offered a prayer of thanksgiving. He finished with, "... and please, Lord, protect all our loved ones who cannot be with us today; especially bless Diane and Chad Montgomery of Pinnington, England, and their daughter Yvonne. And please, dear Lord, pay particular attention to Henry, Ann and Graham's brother, who is now serving with the British Army and who needs your help to bring him safely home. We ask this all, in your name. Amen."

"Amen," agreed Ann and Graham, along with all the others sitting at the table. Both children were pleased Jack had included Henry in his prayer. It relieved them knowing that God had been asked to watch over him.

At that same moment, without the others knowing, Meg's hand clasped Graham's under the table. She too was glad.

*   *   *

Rommel was not to be denied. In a bold move, and in spite of heavy losses, he reversed his direction and recaptured Sidi Rezegh. The New Zealand Brigade lost over three thousand more in that battle and the Tobruk garrison was once again isolated.

Henry had been dozing inside a lorry when Rommel's counterattack began. He awoke with a start as the first of the incoming artillery arrived. The concussion of the first explosion caused his helmet to nearly fly off. He grabbed it, placed it firmly on his head, and sat up erect. He knew he had to get back to the machine-gun emplacement as quickly as possible, but fearing for his life, waited for a break in the shelling. When the lull finally came he opened the lorry door and leaped to the ground. Immediately he was pushed violently backwards from what felt like a huge weight on his chest, then he slumped to the ground. He had heard no sound. "That's queer!" he thought, "I wonder what that was?"

His first instinct was to get up, but quickly realized he couldn't, at least not until he could feel his legs again. He felt strangely disconnected from his lower body. He lay there for several minutes before suddenly feeling a sharp pain in his abdomen. He reached down to hold his stomach. It felt wet. Pulling his hand back he saw it was covered with blood. "My God! I've bloody well been hit!" he cried.

As he lay there, tears streaming from his eyes, he heard someone shout, "Medic! Medic!" One of the last things he saw before he faded into unconsciousness was the setting sun. The reflection of the sun off the dust particles in the sky formed a brilliant orange background for the few white puffy clouds floating over the desert sand. Golden rays shot upward from around the clouds. The rays covered most of the western sky. It was one of those beautiful sunsets no one can ever quite forget.

"Heaven must look like that," he thought.

Chapter 68

Saturday, 29 November 1941

The second Bender Thanksgiving party was another gala affair. Stan Roberts and his committee, under orders from W.T. Bender, had done everything they could to make the children feel welcomed. They had decorated the camp dinning hall in a Thanksgiving motif featuring silhouettes of turkeys, the Pilgrims, American Indians, and displays of numerous cornucopia filled with foods of all kinds. Orange and black banners hung profusely between every chandelier and lamp fixture. Having been responsible for the previous banquets, they now considered the chef an expert on the foods the children liked and gave him complete freedom to select a menu he thought most pleasing. He selected apple cider for a beginning cocktail and followed it with a cranberry gelatin salad topped with mayonnaise, served on a lettuce bed. For the main meal he chose ham, meat loaf, roast turkey, a spicy stuffing, mashed and fried potatoes, gravy, dried corn, green beans, peas, and applesauce. The dessert was a choice of pumpkin or mincemeat pie, both served à la mode. Drinks included chocolate or white milk, tea, and coffee. Gingerbread cookies and more cider were available after dinner for those who wished to munch while they talked and renewed old friendships.

By this time, many of the foster families had become close friends and many conversations filled the hall, both before and after the dinner. Conversations focused on the children's schooling, the war in Europe and North Africa, America's expanding role in the war, speculation over the return date of the children and what conditions to expect once they returned home.

Most agreed that the evacuees were fortunate to be enrolled in U.S. schools. Letters from England indicated their schooling would have been disrupted had they remained there. Many English schools either had reduced school hours or were shut down altogether. An extreme shortage of teachers was also contributing to the curtailments. Classrooms, particularly in the larger cities, were in short supply since many school buildings were being used as civil defense depots, forcing churches or pubs to be used as alternative schoolhouses. Even school supplies were at a premium. The scarcity forced students to share pencils and eliminate margins in all their written work. There were reports geography was now being taught by following troop movements and tending to victory gardens had replaced games.

There also were long discussions concerning Lord Halifax, the British ambassador to America, who had recently been struck by eggs and tomatoes while on tour of Detroit's Arms Production Center. Although everyone agreed it was a poor method of protesting, there were some foster fathers and mothers who said it was high time America took a firm stand to stay out of the war. Having lived with the Schaefers, Ann had been unaware how negative some Americans could be towards England; she was horrified to hear all the anti-English sentiment. She particularly felt sorry for the children living with the parents who felt that way. If they thought that, she wondered why they had agreed to serve as hosts to the evacuees, but decided she shouldn't ask any of them.

The war talk centered on the recent military actions in North Africa and the vacillating balance of power in the Mediterranean. It was unclear which side was winning. The loss of Greece was a severe blow for the Allies but reports of the brave defense of Tobruk and yesterday's capture of German General von Ravenstein, commander of the 21st Panzer Division, were somewhat comforting. It was during this discussion that Graham said his brother was more than likely serving in North Africa and undoubtedly was one of the Tobruk defenders. Most of the men smiled when he said this, knowing how improbable it would be for Henry to be there. Ann, having overheard Graham's boast, could not help being proud. Her pride diminished however when the discussion turned to some of the other Allied losses. It was bad enough when they talked about the recent disastrous raid on Rommel's headquarters but the sinking of Britain's aircraft carrier *Ark Royal* by a German U-boat off the coast of Gibraltar particularly upset her. She wanted to believe the Royal Navy was invincible.

Throughout the evening, Captain Ben circulated among the evacuees and carried on long conversations with everyone. It was clear he had a sincere concern for their welfare. This was particularly evident when in his after-dinner speech he included a prayer for the return to good health of Bobby Preston who was still in the sanitarium. When he prayed for the safe return of all the evacuee family members presently serving their country, both Ann and Graham felt a great sense of pride, particularly when he talked specifically about Henry.

On the following Monday evening, Chad laid the newspaper and Atlas carefully out in front of him, trying to understand exactly what was happening in North Africa. He was unfamiliar with places such as Sidi Rezegh, Bardia, and Belhammed but had long ago decided if his son was serving there the least he could do was follow the events and try to assess the situation. With the huge amount of censorship imposed by the government, it was difficult to gain a clear picture of the activity, but at least he had a vague notion of what was happening. It was nearly impossible to track the day-to-day movements since the tank units advanced, and retreated so rapidly, but he tried as best he could. He knew Tobruk had been under siege for a long time and that Rommel was the commander of the German North African forces but was completely unaware General Ritchie had now assumed command of the British Eighth. He still thought General Wavell was in charge, never suspecting that General Cunningham had served as commander for a brief spell between Ritchie and Wavell.

The paper had just announced that Rommel had reversed his retreat reported yesterday and had succeeded in driving the New Zealanders off Sidi Rezegh ridge. The link into Tobruk had once again been severed. Chad thought about Tobruk and wondered if anything remained of the city. Probably not, it was inconceivable any city could withstand such an intense fight for such a long period.

For a brief moment, he wondered if Henry might be in Tobruk but dismissed it as a thought without basis and not worth further worry. "The boy will be home before we know it," he assured himself, "and when he is he will be able to fill in all the details. Then maybe I'll finally understand all that has happened in North Africa." He then laughed and thought how ridiculous his idea was. He knew full well how little Henry, as one of the troops, would know. Armies were like that, fought by soldiers who had no idea of what was going on strategically. He imagined Henry would know little more than what he read in the newspapers.

Chad had just put away the Atlas when he heard the knock at the door. Before he could answer it, Diane had gone to the door and opened it. Her scream sent shivers down his spine. He had never heard Diane cry that way before. He hurried to the door, but before he had to ask what had happened, he knew. Standing in the doorway was a British army officer, his bicycle propped against the gate outside.

"Chad! Oh, Chad!" Diane screamed. "It's Henry! He's been hurt!"

"I'm sorry, sir," the officer apologized. "I have the unpleasant duty to inform you that your son has been fatally wounded in the African theater."

"Fatally wounded?" Diane shrieked. "You mean he's dead? No! No, it can't be!"

Chad was numb. He could not think. He knew he should comfort Diane, but he couldn't move. "Not my son. Not Henry!" he sobbed.

As had now become an almost standard procedure for him, the officer caught Diane as she collapsed. "What dreadful duty," he thought. "I'd rather be out there getting shot at than suffering through this so many times each day." He thought about the three other names remaining in his bicycle saddle-bags. Three other families who would mourn; more mothers who would faint, three more fathers who would be angry—all thanks to messages he had to deliver—it wasn't fair. He still had to deliver those three before returning to his barracks. He wondered if he could do it.

Seeing Diane fall, Chad snapped out of his stupor and helped the officer carry Diane to the divan. "I'm sorry. I really am. She will be all right in a few minutes. I've seen this happen many times."

"You son of a bitch!" Chad thought. "You have no idea what it is to be told your son's been killed. Don't tell me how sorry you are!" He started massaging Diane's hands and face, trying to bring her back to consciousness. It didn't help. "Unless you have something more constructive to say–something more helpful–get out!" he screamed.

The officer had seen this reaction before but was never quite prepared for it. "I'll leave the papers here on the table, sir," he said. "It has the name and address of the military officer who will provide further assistance–when you're ready. Just ring the number at the top of the page."

"Get out!" Chad screamed. "Get out! Please leave."

Diane had just regained consciousness when Yvonne came home. "What's wrong with Mum?" she asked.

"Go next door and ask Mrs. Wilson if she could come over and help us. Tell her it's an emergency, your mother needs some medical attention."

"What happened to her?" Yvonne asked again.

"Just go, girl. Just go!" Chad shouted.

Yvonne imagined all sorts of things as she ran next door. She had just reached the Wilson front gate when she met Mrs. Wilson rushing toward her. "Oh, you poor child," Mrs. Wilson cried grabbing Yvonne's arms. "What happened? Was it Henry?"

"What do you mean, Mrs. Wilson?" Yvonne asked. "Mum's been hurt. Or is sick. That's all I know. I just arrived home and Dad told me to fetch you. How did you know?"

"I saw the army officer at your door, Yvonne. I'm afraid something dreadful has happened to your brother!"

Yvonne felt light headed and nearly fell, finally regaining her balance. "Oh, bloody hell!" was all she could say, tears forming in her eyes. She thought of the last time Henry was on leave, how Chad had asked her to visit with him on his last night home. She recalled she had gone to the pub instead. How was she to know it would be his last night home? The last time to be with him, to talk to him–ever? She cursed the wretched war and everything that was happening. Life was definitely unfair!

Chad was worried about Diane. It had been a day now; she had only said a few words. She simply continued to lay on the divan and stare at the ceiling. Several of the neighbors had visited, but she refused to acknowledge any of them. He was not certain what to do next. When he finally convinced himself that he could do little more to comfort her, his thoughts turned to Ann and Graham. He knew he must, somehow, get the word to them. But how? He dreaded telling them. He had no idea how to do it gently.

Finally, he called E.J. Newton and talked for a long time. E.J. told him Bender Electric would do whatever they could to help but thought Chad should handle it personally. He suggested Chad send a cablegram to Ken Nelson or Jack Schaefer and ask them to tell Graham and Ann in person. He thought it would be more effective than cabling the children, or calling them direct.

It was Wednesday morning when Chad finally mustered the courage to send the cable. Since he could not decide which child to tell first, he sent telegrams to both Ken and Jack. Included in the telegrams were instructions to do whatever they thought best for the children. Once the cables had been sent he felt somewhat relieved and returned his full attention to Diane who still lay in a near trance.

After numerous telephone calls back and forth, Ken and Jack decided to delay telling the children until Friday evening, it would give them the weekend for their first days of mourning. The Schaefers would invite Ann into Oakton for dinner and would tell them while they were together. It would give them a chance to console each other. Ken suggested Ann bring Lady. He'd say Louise wanted to see her–that they were thinking of getting a dog, or some excuse of that sort. They agreed not to tell Meg, Ned or Karen ahead of time, in case the children might not be able to keep it from Ann and Graham.

It was a long and sad time for the Schaefer and Nelson grownups thinking about Henry and waiting for the dreaded Friday evening meeting. They were almost glad when Friday finally came. After a somewhat subdued dinner, the children played briefly with Lady until Ken called everyone into the living room.

It came as a shock to both. Neither child had ever truly faced up to the possibility Henry might be killed. They were terribly shaken. Ann burst into tears and lay on the floor next to Lady and cried. Graham tried desperately to hold back his tears but couldn't, he held on to Meg who was also crying. Louise and Ida tried to comfort them, but nothing they did seemed to help. Finally, they gave up, left them alone, left them to sort it our for themselves.

On the way home, Ann thought about Henry, the good times they had together, the things he had done for her, his last letter, and how she wished she had written to him more often. Her intentions had always been good; it was all those silly, unimportant other things that always seemed to prevent her from sitting down to write. She began to sob again.

As she climbed into bed, she tried to remember how Henry looked, but, try as she might, she could not recall his face clearly. "What kind of sister am I?" she asked herself. "I don't even remember my brother's face." She held Lady tight and cried for nearly an hour. Finally, exhausted, she fell asleep. She dreamed of climbing onto the rafters above the hayloft in the barn. There was no hay below; she called for Henry to help her. He would not answer her call. She was just about to jump when she woke. She began crying again.

Ida heard the sobs from her bedroom. "Oh, Jack. This is so horrible," she cried. There was no premium on tears in either the Schaefer or Nelson households that night, everyone knew how to cry.

Tobruk was relieved once again on December 10. This time there was a brief opportunity to repair some of the damages done and to take care of details neglected during the siege. Henry's body could have been sent home, but because of the need to transport urgent war materiel, he was buried in Tobruk. A small white cross marked his grave.

III - Japan

Chapter 69

Sunday, 7 December 1941

Edith had difficulty concentrating on Reverend Hanson's sermon. She kept thinking of Ann and Graham, wishing she could have done something to help. Henry's death had been so tragic. She could not imagine how Ann and Graham were coping with the loss of a brother. "It must be awful," she thought.

She had telephoned Ann yesterday. It was only a brief call. The conversation had been awkward. Ann had been so sad and had cried almost the entire time. She told Ann how sorry she was, but her words had all seemed so inadequate. Edith wished she could have done something more, made a bigger difference, been more empathtic and helpful, but she didn't know how. She was ill-prepared to provide consolation. She had never lost a close relative. But then, neither had Ann or Graham. She wiped away her tears with the handkerchief Clara had discretely handed to her.

When Ned called yesterday to relay the sad news they both had cried. Afterwards, once they had stopped and were in better control of their emotions, Ned suggested they take in a movie. He thought it might help boost their spirits. She said no. She didn't think it proper to enjoy herself while Ann and Graham were still in mourning.

But that was not the only reason. Clara had asked her to limit her dates with Ned, especially when no one else was with them. She had made it quite clear, she thought they had been seeing too much of each other lately. It wasn't that she didn't like Ned, she just didn't think Edith was old enough to have a steady boyfriend. In the past, she had been more lenient about it but recently she worried they were becoming too serious and had become much less tolerant. It had started just after she received that last letter from Edith's mum. Since then, she had apparently felt a greater responsibility for Edith. She had insisted they take their time, let their friendship grow more slowly, remain good friends, not date so often–at least not until she was a little older.

Edith was not entirely pleased with this new set of rules but reluctantly accepted them. "It's reassuring to know she worries so much about me, and is concerned for my well being–not like that crazy ogre in England," she told herself as she reflected momentarily on her father. She quickly scolded herself, "I had better quit thinking about Dad; one shouldn't have such profane thoughts here in church."

Her attention reverted to Reverend Hanson. He was talking about the horrors of the European war and the sacrifices so many were now making. "Some," he said, "had given their life in order that peace could someday return to the world." He then said a prayer for Henry, "the British soldier who had been killed in North Africa," and asked the congregation to pray for his brother and sister, "two of the community's adopted evacuees from Britain." Edith looked at Clara; she was crying. It was too much, seeing Clara so sad made her start to sob again.

It was only after Brad put his arm around both of them and hugged them tightly that they were able to control their grief, and it was not until they were leaving the church that Edith finally felt confident enough to return Clara's handkerchief.

Sunday dinner was a quiet affair for the Holtzmans that day. Everyone ate silently, thinking about Ann and Graham and wondering what else they could do to help. It was around two o'clock when Brad turned on the radio, hoping to hear some pleasant music, something to soothe the prevailing sadness. As the filaments warmed he heard the announcer, "... early reports indicate damage has been extensive, although, as you might expect, the reports are still unreliable. All we know is that many of the ships have been severely damaged. Preliminary reports list destroyers, escorts, and, although not verified, at least one battleship–perhaps, two. Some of the ships are said to have already sunk or are sinking as I speak. Many personnel were killed or injured by explosion and aircraft strafing. I repeat, for those of you who may have tuned in late: although it is too early to tell precisely what has happened, it appears Japanese aircraft have attacked our naval force at Pearl Harbor in the Hawaiian Islands. This vicious sneak attack has caught everyone by surprise. It started sometime this morning and is still going on. It appears the United States has herself a war, whether she wants it or not. Japan has made the decision for her."

Brad was stunned. "Clara! Edith! Come here. Quickly! Listen to this," he shouted.

This news did not come as a complete surprise to the Holtzmans, there had been discussions in the newspapers recently about the imminence of war. They knew the country had been moving toward it for some time, but the reality of it still came as a terrible shock. Everyone sat in stunned silence, listening as the commentator droned on.

"What a dreadful thing!" Clara cried, ending her silence. "What will we do?"

"We are switching now to the White House," the announcer continued. "What can you tell us, Ed?" he asked, addressing the correspondent reporting from the scene.

"Nothing much, David," came the reply. "A large crowd has been gathering here in front of the White House gate, expecting some sort of report. However, there has been no additional word from anyone for quite some time. Several minutes ago a number of top-level government officials entered the White House, presumably to meet with President Roosevelt. Among those seen entering were Speaker of the House Sam Rayburn and Republican Leader Joe Martin. Earlier, Secretaries Stimpson and Hull were also seen hurrying in. As far as anyone knows, the meeting is apparently still going on. No one has left. There has been no official notification of exactly what they are discussing. There can be little doubt, however, that it certainly must concern today's unprovoked attacked on our naval base at Pearl Harbor."

The microphone switch backed to the Washington studio. "In case you have just tuned in, the U.S. naval station at Pearl Harbor–near Honolulu, the largest city in the Hawaii Islands–was savagely attack by Japanese aircraft around 7:30 a.m. local time. That would be 12:30 p.m. here in Washington. Damage to our forces has been heavy. Many ships, including battleships and cruisers, have apparently been sunk and many U.S. aircraft have been destroyed. Although our boys mounted a valiant effort to engage the enemy, the suddenness of this surprise attack apparently has caught our services off guard. Many airplanes remained on the ground, and quite a few gunner stations were left unmanned throughout the entire sortie. We will be bringing you more details as they become available. Please stay tuned. In the interim we will return you to your local station for regular programming now in process."

"Due to the gravity of the situation," the local station announced, "we will momentarily be switching to the Mayor's Office for important instructions and comments. Until then, we will continue with recorded music." he added. The first song played was *God Bless America*.

The Holtzmans kept the radio on the remainder of the afternoon. After each new bit of news they discussed the situation, speculating on the inevitability of a declaration of war and its effects on McKinley Heights, the United States, England, and, particularly, on Edith and the other evacuees. "I would think the children will stay in America," Brad guessed. "It certainly will be impossible to send them safely across the

Atlantic now. There is little doubt, once we declare war on Japan we'll also be pulled into the war with Germany. That will make the Atlantic even more treacherous than ever." He looked at Edith, laughed, and teasingly said, "I guess we're stuck with you until our war is over."

Edith should have been unhappy with the idea of an extended stay–most of the other evacuees were that day–instead, not too surprisingly, she was pleased. At least now she could put off living with her dad for a little longer. She smiled and answered, "I suppose so."

It was what Clara asked that sobered her. "Gosh, Brad, what effect is this going to have on your selective service status? Do you suppose they'll draft you now?"

"The last change in the Selective Service Act increased the manpower pool to well over a million men. That's a lot of men, I wouldn't think they would need many more than that," he responded, trying to sound reassuring. Then, thinking aloud, he added, "You know, Clara, if war is declared Uncle Sam will need all the help he can get. They'll be calling up more men from the pool any day now. Perhaps it's my duty to go now, not wait to be called? Maybe I should volunteer. Maybe I should enlist. Maybe they need people with skills like mine. After all, I know something about radios."

Edith was dumbfounded. She had never once given any thought to Brad volunteering. How horrible, just when she finally had a "father" she liked, one who treated her well, he was thinking of leaving. She was just about to protest when Clara screamed, "No, Brad. Not you! There are plenty of others who can serve. There's absolutely no reason for you to go. I didn't want them to take you away when they passed the Selective Service Act, and I certainly don't want you leaving voluntarily now. Besides, you won't be called, you have a child to support. They aren't taking fathers with dependents."

"I'm afraid that won't make a difference to the draft board. It's true, Edith is my responsibility, but she is not my child. She is merely a foster child and, in reality, not even officially that. We never legally took her in, she's here simply as a favor to Bender Electric. We cannot claim to be her legal parents. As far as the board is concerned we have no children."

"Well, just put any thought of enlistment right out of your mind," Clara stated emphatically.

They spent the remainder of the day listening to additional descriptions of what had happened at Pearl Harbor and listening to analyses of why the Japanese had launched such a vicious attack and what it meant to the future of the United States.

*   *   *

There was a flurry of telephone calls between Bender evacuees after the first announcement that afternoon, mostly comparing what each had heard and speculating about its effect on them. Some thought it terrible, some had cried. They were certain it meant a much longer stay than anyone had ever imagined only one week before at the Thanksgiving party.

A few were elated. These were the ones who, after sixteen months in America, had lost some of their passion for returning to England. Their memories of their homeland had dimmed, replaced by a growing fondness for their new country and their new friends and families. They, in much the same manner as Edith, had found a more enjoyable life. Now they had an honorable excuse to extend their stay–America was going to war.

Graham, Meg, and Fred spent much of the evening reviewing all that had happened in the past few days and worrying how it would affect their lives. Graham reaffirmed his resolve to return to England as soon as possible and join the British armed forces–especially now that he had Henry's death to avenge. Meg found it upsetting to think that Graham would be so cavalier about joining the service and hoped none of the other Oakton boys had similar foolish notions; she certainly had no desire to lose Graham or anyone else. As far as she was concerned, Henry's loss was enough wartime tragedy for her. Fred agreed. He assured her he had recently decided he would never be so foolish as to enlist, then turned pale, thinking what his father would say if he ever learned what an unpatriotic coward his son had become. There followed a somewhat emotional debate about their new responsibilities now that America was entering the war. The only point they completely agreed on was the serious impact Japan's attack would have on their future–but even so, no one fully realized what grave consequences were in store for them.

The excitement continued in school the next morning. Everyone was talking about what had happened and its significance to themselves, their families, the community, and the nation. Ann and Graham, in spite of the news of Henry, both had decided it would be better to go to school rather than stay home and mourn. Although the classroom discussions did not mend their grief, it occupied some of their thoughts and helped to distract them from their enormous sadness.

Meanwhile the president, speaking to Congress in the House chamber, said, *"Yesterday, December 7, 1941–a date which shall live in infamy–the United States of America was suddenly and deliberately at-tacked by naval and air forces of the Empire of Japan.*" He talked about the deliberate nature of the attack and then said, "*Yesterday the Japa-nese Government also launched an attack against Malaya.*

"*Last night Japanese forces attacked Hong Kong.*

"*Last night Japanese forces attacked Guam.*

"*Last night Japanese forces attacked the Philippine Islands.*

"*Last night Japanese forces attacked Wake Island.*"

He continued with a discussion about his responsibilities as commander in chief and the will of the people to gain ultimate victory and finished, saying, "*I ask that the Congress declare that since the unprovoked and dastardly attack by Japan on Sunday, December 7, 1941, a state of war has existed between the United States and the Japanese Empire.*"

With little debate, the war resolution passed in the House by a vote of three hundred eighty-eight to one and in the Senate, without debate, by eighty-two votes. By five-fifteen in the afternoon the president had signed the resolution and the United States was at war with Japan. Al-though most of the nation was solidly behind the president there were a few dissenters. Some isolationists urged America to resist. One senator even went so far as to suggest the attack was "*what Britain had planned*" to get the U.S. involved

At nearly the same time, Britain declared war on Japan in response to Japan's attack on Malaya. On December 9, China declared war against Japan, Germany, and Italy. On December 11, Hitler, encouraged by Japan's attack, declared war on the United States and ordered his navy to attack American ships wherever found. The U.S. immediately retaliated by declaring war on Germany and Italy.

By December 12, twenty-five countries formed the Allied partner-ship and eight countries made up the Axis alliance. It had now become the second world war.

Chapter 70

Sunday, 14 December 1941

It had been a hectic and patriotic week in America. Almost every thought and action had a connection to the newly declared war. Long lines of men eager to enlist formed at the Army, Navy and Marine re-cruiting stations; cities intensified their civil defense preparations with increased emphasis on blackout rules and further definitions of air warden responsibilities and authority; foreigners suspected of espionage and those who failed to register as foreign agents were arrested and quickly put on trial; war production efforts intensified; the president issued a call for an end to all labor disputes while the war continued; and, in spite of the urgent need for war materiel in America, the White House issued assurances that lend-lease shipments would continue.

A grim and solemn Congress quickly passed legislation to permit servicemen, including National Guardsmen, to serve outside the Western Hemisphere; extended the terms of all enlistees and selectees for the duration of the war plus six months; began debate on registration of all men ages 18 through 44 for training and service in the military and all others 17 through 64 for other defense duties; and began work on the passage of a ten billion dollar defense supplemental appropriations bill.

Although suffering a loss of nearly half of their air force in the Philippines, American armed forces managed to retaliate by sinking a Japanese battleship, a cruiser, and a destroyer and, in spite of heavy naval bombardment and air attack, held on to the islands of Wake and Midway. But the threat of further major territorial losses in the Pacific was serious. The Philippines were under heavy attack by Japanese aircraft, troops had landed northeast of Manila and at Legaspi in Southern Luzon; Malaya had been invaded, and its northern regions seized; Thailand was on the verge of capitulation; Hong Kong was under siege; and the island of Guam was reported lost. One of the few bright hopes for the American public was assurances from General Douglas MacArthur that his Philippine forces were fully in control of the invasion threat and that his air force was capable of dispersing all Japanese raiders headed for Manila.

But Jack at the moment was more concerned about Ann. It had been more than a week since learning of Henry's death. He realized a week was not a long time, but even so, he thought the deep mourning had gone on long enough. It was time she began showing signs of improvement. But nothing was changing, each night he could hear her crying, and each day she continued to mope around, showed no interest in anything, and hardly ever talked to anyone. Nearly all her free time was spent with Queenie, Lady, and the other pups. It wasn't the neglect of her chores he minded, he could take care of those things, it was how she had withdrawn from everything. He worried that it wasn't healthy and wanted desperately to do something to ease her pain.

The letter from Diane received last Friday, dated before Henry's death, had made Ann's mood sink even lower. Most of it was about Henry. Diane said she was looking forward to the day when all of her children would be home again. She talked about the good times they would have and assured Ann that all the sad memories of the war would fade once the family was back together. It was one of the few times since Ann had learned of Henry's death that she had gone to Ida for solace and reassurance. That had been a difficult moment for Ida. Poor Ida. Although she was pleased Ann had finally asked for help, it took all her willpower to maintain her composure. She had cried afterwards and again that night. She finally fell asleep after Jack held her tightly in his arms for a long, long time.

"Perhaps today will be better," Jack hoped. "Perhaps this is the day Ann will begin to improve." It was Sunday morning, everyone was scurrying about preparing for the trip to Cleveland. Ann and Graham, along with children from five other Bender evacuee families, had been invited to participate in a program, sponsored by the BBC in London. The program, known as *Children Calling Home,* was the one Ann had first heard on the shortwave radio back in October. Its purpose, to let evacuees from all parts of the world talk with their English parents, live, and on the air. Out of sheer luck, Ann and the others had been recently contacted and asked to participate this afternoon. They were to be at the Cleveland radio station by one o'clock.

Jack had originally agreed to transport the Montgomery children along with several other evacuees to Cleveland but, as time grew short, the entire Schaefer family asked to go along. It took several frantic, last minute, telephone calls to arrange for additional transportation, but finally everything was set. They left before eight for the three hour drive– no one wanted to be late.

It was the first time either Ann or Graham had been to Cleveland but neither child was interested in looking at the scenery on this particular morning. They were too busy thinking about the upcoming talk and how it would be to hear their mum and dad's voices again. They both were trying desperately to decide what they would say. There were so many things they wanted to tell them, but the time allocated was limited, so much so that it would be difficult to say much of anything.

But when they arrived they were terribly disappointed. The station manager had scrubbed their part. He told them it was due to technical difficulties at BBC. What he did not tell them was that Diane, at the last minute, had refused to participate. She said if she could not talk to all of her children–including Henry–she did not want to talk to any of them. Chad had tried to coax her into changing her mind, but she had stubbornly refused. He had pleaded with the program director to let him talk with Ann and Graham by himself, but the director insisted both parents be involved. "Without the mother," he said, "the program would not generate sufficient interest to hold the listening public's attention."

The disappointed Schaefer family did not stay to hear the other children talk, instead, they immediately left for home. There was little talk along the way, all were in deep thought. It seemed their troubles had been multiplying much too rapidly during the past several weeks.

After this latest adversity, Jack was even more concerned than ever that they should do something for Ann. When he discussed it with Ida she assured him it would be better if Ann worked it out in her own way and in her own time. She was almost certain they would begin to see improvement before long.

And just as she had predicted, a few days before Christmas Ann began to get better. Although she still had brief periods of depression, for the most part she started to regain her old vigor and vitality. Jack was amazed. It seemed time and the dogs had provided the therapeutic remedy needed. He was glad he had listened to Ida and not interfered.

It snowed on Christmas eve and by Christmas morning there was a white blanket covering everything. The Schaefer family rose early, quickly attended to their farm chores, and opened their presents. They spent the remainder of the day eating, playing games, talking to siblings and friends on the telephone, but mostly simply enjoying each other's company.

Among the calls was one from Graham. Ann and he excitedly described the gifts they had gotten. Their favorites were the airgraphs each had received on Saturday. The reassuring words from home were especially pleasing, but both chose not to mention that only Chad's signature appeared on their letters and that no mention was made of Diane, other than to say she sent her love. They suspected something was wrong but were afraid to discuss it, they would admit it to no one, not even to themselves.

Later in the afternoon, Ann received a call from Oliver who wished her a merry Christmas and, rather shyly, told her he missed seeing her during the school holidays. He assured her his arm was much better and said he hoped it would be strong enough for him to play baseball in the spring, then laughed and jokingly suggested he couldn't join the Army if he didn't recover. He said they wouldn't want a cripple. Ann good-naturedly scolded him for making fun of the handicapped and then turned serious. She didn't think he should worry about the service. She reminded him that he was only thirteen; the war would be over long before he reached the legal age. "Maybe I'll lie about my age," he teased, "and join next year when I'm fourteen."

"Come to think about it," he added, "they'd probably take me anyway. What do they care if I don't have a good arm? It's probably good enough already to hold a gun. Trying to shield myself with a bad arm would be just as ineffective as with a good one, the Germans could shoot me just as easily." He laughed, thinking he had said something clever.

Ann did not reply. There was only a frigid silence. Almost immediately he realized what he had done was most inappropriate. Ann had just lost her brother. Her brother had probably been shot by a German soldier. He was embarrassed and wished he hadn't mentioned guns, or Germans, or shooting. He quickly asked which classes she was planning to select next semester. A few minutes later they said good-bye.

Edith called next. She began by asking Ann about her gifts, but it soon became apparent that presents were not the main reason she had called. She was really more interested in talking to Ned. Realizing this, Ann called him to the telephone. She said there was someone who wanted to talk to him, someone very special. As she left the room, Ned begin to giggle. "He's just like a small schoolboy when he talks to Edith," she thought, smiling to herself.

Shortly after Ned hung up, he left in the family car. "Where's he going?" Karen asked.

"To Edith's. He wants to give her present to her while it's still Christmas," Ida answered.

"What's he giving?" Ann asked.

"One of Queenie's pups–the one with the black patch on his eye."

"Oh, that's super!" Ann exclaimed. "Edith will love that one. He's the cutest one left. I wish I had known Ned was going to Edith's. I would have gone along."

"I don't think Ned would have welcomed you this evening," Jack said, smiling.

Ann didn't understand why Jack had winked, but thought no more of it; she was too happy for Edith. A dog of her own, it was the perfect gift. She was certain Edith would like it. She was always saying how much she wished she could have a dog, a dog like Lady. Now she does. "Let me think," Ann chuckled, "Edith's dog is Lady's sister. Does that make Edith a relative of mine?"

That evening the Schaefer family sat in the living room and sang Christmas songs while Ida accompanied them on the piano. Ann particularly liked the song *O'Little Town of Bethlehem*. She had never heard it before. She thought maybe it wasn't sung in England. Some of the other songs made her sad, they made her think about Henry. Tears came to her eyes. Apparently she was still mourning Henry much more than she thought.

Partially because of the death of one of the brothers of "his children" and partially because of the low morale of the evacuees, Ben threw another evacuee party on New Year's Eve. Originally, he thought it best for the families and their children to interact at home and had decided against it, but the news had continued to be so troublesome that at the last minute he changed his mind. The lateness of the decision, caused Stan much additional work. However, he was used to W.T. changing schedules on short notice. He quickly rolled up his sleeves and, with much help from Miss Perkins, managed to finish on time. Everyone was impressed when they arrived on Wednesday evening, December 31. The trimmings were magnificent and once again the dinner excellent.

Much of the talk before the banquet was about the War Powers Act signed by the president on the nineteenth. It lowered the minimum age for military service from twenty-one to nineteen and gave the president the right to organize the executive branch however he wanted in order to prosecute the war. Many believed this went too far. They complained it gave the president dictatorial powers. Others were equally convinced it was necessary to insure an early end to the war.

Among those arguing against the Act was Ned. Edith could not understand his concern. She thought presidents, like monarchs, should have all the authority needed to do whatever was necessary for the overall good of the country. What did he mean when he complained about a president exceeding his Constitutional powers? She had lived in a monarchy all her life and saw nothing wrong with someone having absolute power. Ned tried to explain that the British government was a parliamentary form of government, not too unlike America's; and that English monarchs had very little say in running the government. She was not convinced. In fact, a rather heated argument followed. Fortunately, the call to be seated interrupted the argument. Had dinner been served a few minutes later, they might not have eaten together that evening.

After dinner, before the dancing started, Ben said a few words of sympathy for Bobby Preston, the boy in the sanitarium, then surprised everyone with the announcement that each child should prepare a brief, personal note to be sent by cablegram to their parents.

Because there was so little time to compose their thoughts, the messages were candid and diverse. Some children talked about ice cream, some about living conditions, some simply said they were well, while others sent their love. Ann said she hoped everyone would write soon.

Graham assured them everything was "fine in America and he was ready to help England beat Hitler, Mussolini, and Tojo." Edith included only her mum's name in the address and assured her school was going well. Fred told about his athletic accomplishments. Sandy talked about her horse.

The children left the party in a much better mood than when they arrived. The party had been the success Ben had hoped it would be.

By the end of December, the British Eighth Army had captured Benghazi and Rommel was once more in retreat. Unfortunately, this did not signal an end to the Nazis presence in North Africa. Badly needed Allied reinforcements were being diverted to the Far East; most of the British Navy in the Mediterranean had been destroyed; the Luftwaffe still had mastery over the sea routes, and General Auchinleck, with war weary troops and equipment badly in need of repair, chose not to press on into Tripoli.

In the Far East, the Japanese onslaught continued. Hong Kong had fallen, Australia was preparing for an anticipated Japanese invasion, and the Allies faced the expected loss of the Philippines and Singapore.

To discuss the situation, Prime Minister Churchill visited with President Roosevelt in the White House over Christmas. Both men were worried and foresaw a long and difficult Allied struggle ahead. Neither entertained any hope for a quick end to the war.

Chapter 71

Saturday, 17 January 1942

In the past month and a half, America had changed from a nation halfheartedly preparing itself for a possible war to a nation enthusiastically committed to winning a war. Enlistments in the armed forces had increased dramatically; military production was expanding at a rapid pace; salvage programs were collecting vitally needed resources such as scrap iron, rubber, and paper; and many new workers, including a large number of women, were either already employed in war plants or seriously considering joining the work force. Wherever people congregated, their talk focused mostly on the war.

Although Bender Electric had only one large defense contract weeks before, new contracts were now rapidly coming on-line. In only a few months, the company had changed from a manufacturer of commercial products to one almost entirely under Navy contract. Nearly every employee was on a six-day workweek, with some, including Ken Nelson, at the plant seven days. Among the new employees was Karen Schaefer. She had started the first of January, had been quickly trained to wind motors, and was already putting in many overtime hours too.

The changes had a profound influence on the evacuees as well. Not only had the war affected their everyday lives but it, surprisingly, had increased their self-respect. The embarrassment the children had always subconsciously harbored over having left England in its time of need had eased. Although no bombs had dropped in Ohio and there was no immediate threat to their personal safety, the shame of leaving their friends and family to suffer all the horrors of war no longer preyed quite as heavily on their minds. They now had their own war to contend with; they were once again sharing in at least some of the same hardships as those back in England. But still this was only a small compensation considering all the new concerns, fears, and depression everyone had been feeling since the attack at Pearl Harbor.

Henry's death had made it even more difficult for Ann and Graham. The dire consequences of war were felt much more vividly by them than by any of the other evacuees; they already knew what it was like to lose a brother. This loss, coupled with the increased absences of Karen and Ken, caused them many moments of despondency.

Graham, who closely followed the progress of the war in the newspapers, was in one of those depressed moods on this particular January afternoon. He had been crying. The news recently had seemed especially troubling. Although President Roosevelt had announced on January 6 that the U.S. would send land, sea and air forces to England, Graham could find little else to assure him that America's involvement would do anything to speed his return to his homeland. The Far East was nothing but one military disaster after another: Jasselton had fallen in Borneo; Allied divisions were retreating in Malaya; Bataan was reportedly under heavy attack; and Kuala Lumpur had fallen to the Japanese Army on the twelfth. The newspapers were even reporting many German U-boat sightings off the shores of eastern United States. Even the German retreat on the Russian front was of little consolation—everyone still expected Germany to eventually prevail.

Ken was still at work and Louise was at the local church helping to organize an Oakton paper drive when Graham sat down at the dining room table. He still had to complete his science assignment and hoped a few hours of intense study would somehow ease his doldrums, although he doubted it. Tears were still evident on his face when Meg came into the room. "What's wrong?" Meg asked, a look of concern on her face.

"Nothing, Meg. I'll be all right," he replied, looking down at his book and trying, unsuccessfully, to avoid looking at her.

"Have you been crying?" she asked.

Graham, realizing Meg had guessed his mood and knowing she would offer a sympathetic ear–much as his mother would–could contain his emotions no longer. He burst into convulsive sobs.

"Oh, Graham," Meg exclaimed, as she put her arms around him. "Tell me, what's wrong?" She begged.

"I'm sorry, Meg," he replied, still sobbing. "It's just this bloody war. It's killed my brother, my mother is apparently overcome with grief, my sister tells me she can't quit crying at night thinking of them, and now, America is at war. All those terrible things we could have experienced in England has caught up with us here. Men will go into the service, bombs will fall, and people will die. The entire world is going to change. Forever! We'll never get home to England. I'll never be part of a family again."

"Oh, you poor dear. Of course you will. Ann has the Schaefers and you have us, Graham. You are part of our family now," she said emphasizing "our family" as she drew him closer to her and gently kissed him on the forehead.

He tried to return her kiss, but she was standing above him, and as he turned toward her, his lips brushed against the folds of her dress between her breasts. She felt soft and warm. He detected a slight scent of perfume. He knew he should quickly move his head but didn't. She did not protest, instead held him tighter. She felt sorry for him and wanted to do something to comfort him–to mother him. After a few minutes she gently moved away, taking his hand in hers and, without a word, urged him to follow her into the living room. They collapsed on the sofa, arms around each other. For what seemed like an eternity they lay there embracing. Neither saying anything.

Finally, Meg released him and gently placed her lips on his and kissed him. He returned the kiss with an ardor he had never known before. Neither quite understood what was happening. "My baby," she sighed. "My baby!"

"I love you, Meg," he said. He was afraid he had said the wrong thing. He feared she would push him away.

"I know," she replied. "I love you too."

They lay there for a long time, enjoying the warmth of each other's body and repeatedly kissing–sometimes gently and sometimes with great passion and intensity. They continued to say nothing. Finally Meg broke the silence. "We can't tell Mom and Dad about this, Graham. It must remain our secret," she warned.

"I know, Meg, I know!" Graham sighed. "Oh, Meg, it doesn't really matter. We're not brother and sister." He paused then added, "I love you so."

"But, it isn't right," she protested. "We shouldn't be doing this. If Mom and Dad ever find out they'll never leave us alone by ourselves again. I couldn't stand that, I love you too much."

Slowly the couple untangled and regained a degree of composure.

Meg had just finished smoothing her dress and Graham had combed his hair when Louise walked in. "Hello, you two. Have you had a good afternoon?" she asked innocently, then turned to Graham. "Do you think you could spare a few hours next Saturday?" she asked. "The church is sponsoring a paper drive and we need help collecting the paper."

"Sure. That would be fun, Mom," he responded. "I'll ask Fred to join me. I'm sure he will be glad to help." Graham, smiled to himself; only an hour ago he was feeling terribly gloomy and now everything seemed so much brighter. He looked at Meg as if to say, "I love you." She looked at him and understood. "I love you too," her returned glance told him.

Louise was busy taking off her hat. She did not notice this exchange.

Chapter 72

Tuesday, 31 March 1942

Diane was terrified when she opened the postbox. It contained a letter from Louise and Ken Nelson. There could be no question about it, whatever was in it would be bad news. That seemed to be the only kind of news she received lately.

"Something had happened to Graham! That was it. Or maybe it was Ann! The Schaefers probably asked the Nelsons to tell us about it," she guessed as she stared at the envelope. She began to cry and rushed into the house, hoping the neighbors hadn't seen her. She knew she had been acting wretchedly these past four months, ever since they had heard about Henry. She truly wanted to be over her grief. But it wasn't easy. She had lost her son! Her first born! For God's sake, what was a mother to do? What did people expect?

The thought riled her, took her back to that horrible day, the day the officer had delivered the news. The more she dwelled on it, the more ashamed she felt. She should have written to Henry more often, should have told him more about how she felt: how much she loved him, how much she missed him, how proud she was of him. Now it was too late. She could never tell him any of those things, could never share anything with him–no matter how much she wished it. She thought of Ann and Graham. She had written to them regularly–until that dreadful day. Since then only a few notes, and all of those had been extremely short. They all had been so cold–contained so little emotion. None of them had said anything about how much she loved them. No doubt the kids could tell they were only written to fulfill a duty–not to tell them how much she cared, how much she missed them. "Was it too late?" she wondered. Would she once again rue her negligence? Had she once again been remiss in sharing her feelings? She knew she should write more often, write better, more loving letters, but whenever she had tried she could never think of the right way to say it; she always tore them up and threw them in the wastebasket.

Her thoughts returned to the unopened Nelson letter. But try as she would, she could not bring herself to open it. She left it on the bureau, in a prominent place where Chad would be quick to spot it when he arrived home. He'd be the first to read the horrible news. Maybe he would be more gentle in breaking it to her.

It was a mistake, no doubt about that. She returned to the letter all evening, even picked it up a few times, but always panicked and left it on the bureau unopened. She should have done it when she first saw it. Now it lay there, begging to be read. But she couldn't. "Where is Chad?" she asked herself. "Why hasn't he come home before this?" She knew it was a silly question. He had said he would be late tonight– something to do with a new jig he had to install. "How late will he be?" She had paid almost no attention to him this morning. Now she wished she had; then she would know when she could expect him.

Finally, exhausted from worry and despair, she climbed into bed and eventually fell asleep. It was half past two when she awoke with a start. "Where's Chad? Why didn't he come home last night? Has he been hurt?" She moved her arm. It touched something. It was Chad–he was lying there beside her. Then she saw the letter. It had been opened, lying near where she had left it. "Why didn't he call me?" Then it struck her–the news must have been so terrible he hadn't wanted to tell her. He probably wanted her to have a good night's sleep first–before he told her that dreadful thing–whatever it was. She supposed, now that it was open, she should read it but still couldn't quite bring herself to do it.

Instead, she tried to go back to sleep. She couldn't. She lay there thinking about her two evacuated children. "Those poor dears. What have I done to them? Most unmercifully sent them to that far away land. Alone! By now, undoubtedly devastated by having been deserted by their mum. Those poor children," she repeated.

The alarm sounded promptly at half past six. She watched while Chad slowly woke up. She waited until he was wide awake, then trying to sound casual, said, "I see you opened the Nelson letter."

"Why didn't you open it last night?" he asked.

"I thought it would be nice for you to do it this time," she lied. "Did they have anything important to say?"

"You really should have opened it, Diane. It contained two nice letters, one from Louise and one from Ken. Louise says Graham is growing like a weed and we would hardly recognize him now. She says he grows out of his trousers almost as fast as they fit him with new ones. Poor souls, he must be costing them a fortune. He's doing quite well in school too. In fact, Ken says he is on the Honor Roll now. I believe the Honor Roll is America's way of designating the top group of students at each level. He's into all types of school activities, too. Louise says our son is a real help around the house and has become quite a trooper in the war salvaging efforts now under way in the States.

"Ken also said they saw Ann last week. She's looking healthy and fit. He says if he were a young lad he would have an eye on Ann–says she has blossomed into a charming young lady. They both say we should be quite proud of our children.

"You really must read the letters, Diane. They're such fine people. We owe them a great deal for all the wonderful things they're doing for our son."

Diane burst into tears. Her children were all right–her worry had been for naught. "I'm so relieved!" she confessed. "I was certain the letter held bad news. I just couldn't open it last night."

"You must stop worrying about them so much," Chad scolded. "They're in America, Diane. They're safe and happy there. Everything we hear confirms it."

"But they should be here with us. We sent them away," she argued. "We should have kept them here. We're going to be punished for that misdeed–you'll see. Henry's death won't be the end of our punishment."

"You know full well, had they remained here, they could have been hurt during the Blitz. Who's to say the Blitz won't start again? Just be-cause the Germans have shifted their air raids away from London to other cities is no guarantee they won't return one of these nights. No,

Diane, I still believe we did the correct thing. Ann and Graham are safe and sound and that's what we wished for them in 1940."

"But America is at war now. The children could be bombed, and we wouldn't be there to protect them," she complained.

"That's nonsense. America is a long way from Germany and Japan. Except for regions along the coast within range of aircraft launched from carriers, there's little chance for air raids over many American cities. Interior regions have almost nothing to worry about. Ohio is hundreds of miles from the Atlantic, far away from danger. The children should be quite safe where they are.

"You can also rest assured, the Nelsons and Schaefers are fine substitute parents. They're good people, Diane. They're looking after our children with the utmost of concern. You know perfectly well that Ann and Graham have nothing but the highest praise for their foster parents."

"That's another thing, Chad," Diane continued to lament, "they're stealing our children. You can tell that from the children's letters. They no longer miss us—or have any feelings for us. All they talk about in their letters are their playmates, their school activities, and their foster parents. They no longer say anything about missing us or wanting to come home."

"That is as much your fault as it is theirs. You haven't sent any loving letters to them lately. I'm certain they sense a problem here in Pinnington and have avoided writing anything that might worry you."

He then brought up what had really been gnawing at him for months, "It was you who refused to talk with them on the BBC last December. How do you think they felt? Imagine, having a mum that wouldn't talk to you when she had the opportunity to do so. They must have felt awful. I have tried in my letters to explain it and make amends for it, but it's painfully obvious, Diane, you have broken their hearts."

Diane burst into tears, this time with convulsive sobs. The crying was not out of sadness for having been reprimanded but from the sudden shift in mood she felt. Chad's chastisement had apparently come at the correct moment. It provided just what was needed to snap her out of her melancholy; it made her see the terrible way she had been acting. She knew he was right. She realized she had acted horridly since Henry's death. She was ashamed. She had been letting Ann and Graham down; she had been letting Chad and Yvonne down too; in fact she had been letting everyone down. It was time she gain control of her emotions, time to act like the mum she was supposed to be. "You're right! I've been acting wretchedly. I know that now. Please forgive me?" she said as she threw her arms around Chad and kissed him.

Chad could hardly believe what had just happened; it was the first she had kissed him this year. He truthfully had not expected a reaction of this sort. He had always supposed a scolding would depress her even more, would only make matters worse. He had tried to hold his tongue this time too, but he had reached the end of his patience, he had done it without thinking, had said it out of sheer frustration and hopelessness.

But all that didn't matter now, it felt good holding his wife in his arms again. It had been such a long time. "I tell you what we're going to do," he said, looking into her eyes and smiling. "Tonight I'm going to come home from work early–I'll make up some excuse to get off. You do the same. We're going to go out to dinner tonight. We're going to celebrate your return."

"Oh that would be wonderful!" she sighed.

"Now don't expect anything very fancy. They tell me it's self-service at the *Lord and Fox* these days.

"But, at least it will be one night–perhaps–without wheatmeal bread," he joked.

"Let's forget about soap rationing for one night. Let's use all the soap we want when we bathe," Diane responded, catching the festive mood. "For once, I'm going to just lie in a tub full of water, surrounded with suds! Maybe even spilling over a little. Let Mr. Hitler have his old war–tonight we'll forget about it."

Unfortunately, the night did not go as well as planned. The temperature continually fell throughout the day and by evening it was well below normal. Because of the severe rationing of coal, the pub owner had not fired the fireplace and Diane and Chad sat shivering throughout most of the meal. Had it not been for the endless drafts of brown ale, they probably would not have stayed for the plum pudding. Afterwards, while Chad smoked his pipe, they talked. Chad had tried to keep the conversation gay and light-hearted but, try as he would, he could not keep from talking about the war. It was the first time since the loss of Henry that Diane had permitted such talk. He complained about the censorship now imposed on the newspapers and wondered what was happening around the world–what was really true. He said censorship was the sort of thing Hitler would do and wondered if Churchill had the same sort of dictatorial ambitions too. He talked about the American forces supposedly stationed in Northern Ireland and the regular bombing of German cities by the RAF. Recent reports indicated Emden, Hamburg, Kiel, Cologne and Mannheim had been hit and severely damaged. It made them both feel good to know that England was finally returning some of Jerry's own medicine, but still it made them wonder if what little they were told was true.

But then again, maybe it could be. After all, the newspapers were filled with descriptions of less happy events as well. There were reports of the damage the German submarine wolfpacks were inflicting on the U.S. convoys in the Atlantic and how Rommel was fighting back in North Africa, once again causing all sorts of problems to the Allied forces there. Although Chad did not tell Diane, he was thankful Henry no longer had to suffer through all those rotten North African battles. "At least he's at peace," he rationalized to himself.

They walked home in the moonlight, holding hands like two young lovers. Their conversation no longer focused on the war. Instead they talked about the future and the wonderful things they would do once peace had returned, the good times they would have, and the happiness they could expect. Tired and happy, they went quickly to bed after they arrived.

Later, Chad smoked a cigarette. The day would have been near perfect had his thoughts not now turned to Yvonne. He had no idea what to do about her. She had become almost totally incorrigible lately. They seldom saw her these days. She normally left for work before either he or Diane returned home in the evening and seldom was home before they left in the morning. Some days Yvonne stayed with friends and did not come home at all. They knew little about those friends but suspected they were a rowdy lot. He feared she was headed for serious trouble, but there seemed little he could do.

They were losing her, no doubt about it, if they hadn't already. He blamed it on the war, not on anything he had done. How could he make her understand that he and Diane loved her? How could he convince her they would have sent her to America if they could have, given her an advanced education if they had been of the right class? He only hoped she would come to her senses before it was too late.

He doused his cigarette and finally fell asleep.

Chapter 73

Saturday, 4 April 1942

Ann could not believe what she had been reading in the newspapers, hearing on the radio, and seeing at the theaters. She thought America was invincible, at least that was how she had interpreted her American history books. They all seemed to take pride in America's reputation for never having lost a war. But it didn't look good for America this time–at least not from what she could glean from the vague and often confusing reports. There were plenty of articles describing America's military power and the rapid build up of munitions and equipment, many stories of heroic efforts by American servicemen, and numerous examples of American industrial ingenuity and productivity, but almost every news item and map reporting on actual battles either described, or at least hinted at, humiliating losses and retreat.

There seemed little doubt the war in the Pacific was going Japan's way. They had chased MacArthur from the Philippines, and from all reports, the remaining troops left to defend it were on the verge of sur-render. Japan was in control of most of the Dutch East Indies; the Mala-yan coast had been evacuated; Java had surrendered; Hong Kong had been captured, and major Japanese inroads had been made into Burma. The Allied stronghold at Singapore had been forced to surrender in Feb-ruary, and there were fears the forces at Corregidor could not hold out much longer. Australia, although still not invaded, was coming under increasingly heavy bomb attacks.

In the Atlantic, things were not much better. Although America was not part of any of the armed conflicts in Europe, German U-boats con-tinued to cause havoc to U.S. shipping. The total tonnage lost was growing rapidly.

The only positive war news Ann had seen recently were reports of the German difficulties on the Russian frontier and Britain's successful bombing raids over German cities. But Ann had mixed feelings about those raids. She agreed with the news analysts who feared they would lead to further retaliation by Hitler. If this happened, one could expect renewed air raids over Pinnington. From her point of view it was fortu-nate that Germany was ignoring London and its suburbs and concentrat-ing on other British industrial cities. This meant her parents were safe. While it offered some consolation, it also made her feel guilty. She was putting the safety of her parents above the overall welfare of the British Isles. She feared it was a terribly selfish attitude and certainly grossly improper for someone loyal to the king.

Ann discussed her concerns with Jack as they motored towards McKinley Heights. He told her to expect setbacks while America was tooling up its military capability and assured her America would soon have the goods and production capabilities needed to successfully carry out the fight. Once the buildup was complete, he felt confident the Al-lies would quickly put the Japanese and German armies on the run. He also advised her not to feel guilty about putting the safety of her loved ones ahead of all else; he assured her it was a natural thing to do. Although he had not convinced her, she knew she had his support. On the other hand, she suspected he was as worried about the war as she was. That certainly did not ease her mind.

There was something else that was troubling her. She was beginning to think of the house in Pinnington as her parents' home, not hers. Somehow, much to her embarrassment, she was beginning to have a much greater attachment to the Schaefer house than to the one in Pinnington. She had to face it, the farm seemed much more like her home lately. Of course she would never admit this, not even to Jack.

Ann and Jack were on their way to visit Edith. Several serious shortages were impeding the war effort. Particularly critical was aluminum used in the manufacture of military aircraft. To help ease this shortage a plea had been issued for the donation of aluminum pots and pans. In response, the McKinley Heights Junior High eighth grade class had organized an aluminum scrap drive. Edith had volunteered to help with the collection. Partially to visit, but mostly in the hope that Ned would bring her, Edith had asked Ann to help.

Although the girls had much to tell each other, Edith was mostly interested in Ned. She wanted to know what he had been doing, asked about his health, repeatedly found excuses to turn every topic into one that involved him, and soon was telling Ann how she felt about him and some of the romantic things that had happened on their last date. "Did he really kiss you that way?" Ann asked incredulously. "It must have been awful!"

"No it wasn't. It felt really wonderful," Edith assured her, rolling her eyes towards the ceiling as she spoke. "It produced feelings I've never known before. Sort of a dreamy, numb sensation. Haven't you ever had a boy kiss you?"

"Never! I would never let anyone kiss me that way–it's too icky. I don't think I'll ever let a boy kiss me, not even if it's just a peck," Ann said in disgust.

"You will if you love him," Edith cooed.

"Do you really believe you love Ned?" Ann asked, half expecting a negative answer.

"Oh, yes! I'm in love, Ann. He's so nice–and so handsome!"

"Don't you think you should wait? Aren't you too young to be getting so serious?"

"You're never too young when the right man comes along."

Ann was both amused and disgusted. She was amused at how silly Edith was acting over a boy–even if it were Ned–and disgusted Edith had so little control of herself. She couldn't understand why Edith made all the fuss about how she felt around Ned. Ann decided to drop the subject. "How's that puppy of yours getting along?" she asked.

"You mean Spotty?" Edith responded, somewhat excitedly. "He's such a darling. He sleeps with me all the time now. You'll be surprised to see how smart he is. He does all sorts of tricks–and it didn't take any time until he was housebroken. Everyone else loves him too. Brad says he belongs in the circus, as many tricks as he can already perform. Clara says he is just like another child; she thinks he's sweet. I don't know what I would do without him, Ann. He's such a companion."

"I know what you mean. I'd miss Lady terribly if I ever had to part with her."

"Spotty is just one more reason why I'm determined not to go back to England when our evacuation is over," she added, with a snicker, "of course Ned is an even better reason."

After the scrap drive, Clara asked Ann to stay for dinner. It was a lovely meal. Ann was impressed with Clara's attention to every little detail. Everything she did was prim and proper. Even more impressive was the way Clara and Brad treated Edith. Ann had no doubt there was a deep and loving bond amongst the three of them. Everyone seemed so happy. She was pleased Edith had found such a good home. After all the terrible things her father had done in Ealing, it was time she had a better life. But Ann was not envious, she thought Jack and Ida were equally as loving, if not more so.

That evening when Ned came for Ann it amused her to watch how Edith and he acted. It was almost as if seeing each other turned them into different people, they seemed so giddy and happy. But the relationship between Ned and Clara was less than perfect. She couldn't understand why Clara treated him with such noticeable reserve. Couldn't she see how good Ned was to Edith? And how happy he made her?

It was rather late before Ned reluctantly consented to leave. They drove home in silence. Ned apparently did not wish to talk. He was thinking about something. Ann supposed, from the smile on his face, that it was Edith.

Chapter 74

Friday, 15 May 1942

Friday, 15 May 1942

Dear Graham,

I could hardly believe it when Dad came in waving your letter written 1 April. We were both extremely pleased to receive it–it has been such a long time since your last one. I immediately tore it open and–with Dad looking over my shoulder–we both read it together.

You naughty boy! You had both of us worried when you said you had quit school and had found employment in the local mill. You can imagine how relieved we were when you said it was only an April Fool's Day fib. Afterwards, we had a jolly laugh over it.

When you mentioned returning to England however, we quickly turned serious. It is a terribly important decision. Rest assured we would love to see you again, but are extremely concerned with all the dangers associated with returning right now–the trip across the ocean, the wartime hardships, the threat of more air raids, service to your country, etc. should not be ignored. It is not a decision one should make quickly, or take lightly. Your first consideration should be your own safety and welfare. However, as you requested, Dad will talk to the chaps at the factory today. But don't get up your hopes; he suspects it is nigh impossible to obtain passage. There is too much U-boat activity in the Atlantic these days. Nevertheless, he will ask and will write to you when he has something definite to report.

You cannot believe how excited your request has made me feel. It would be so nice to have you back here with us! It is difficult to imagine hearing your voice again or seeing you sitting at the dinner table here in Pinnington. It would be wonderful and I truly would look forward to it. Although, from what Mrs. Nelson tells us, I fear it would be difficult to recognize you. She says you have been growing like a weed and even your voice has changed since you arrived. But, not to worry! A mother always recognizes her son–no matter how much he has changed.

HOWEVER! Dad and I spent a long time last night discussing it and neither of us are certain you should be considering coming back at the moment. There are <u>many</u> negatives to offset the positives.

First of all, there is Ann. If you were to come back you would be leaving her alone in America. We know she is with an excellent family and that the Schaefers will continue to take good care of her, but we would still worry with you not there to look out for her interests.

Secondly—as we understand it—you will be in the eleventh grade this autumn and will not complete your American schooling until May of '44. Neither Dad nor I can conceive of the war lasting until then—but what if it does? We both agree you should obtain as much education as you possibly can while you have the chance. Things are changing rapidly here. Everything is in need of repair and reconstruction and it will take a major effort to return things to normal. Dad now believes, with all the rebuilding required, there will be many supervisory and skilled positions available after the war for those with a good education. It will be a wonderful opportunity for a working-class bloke to attain a higher standard of living than he could ever have dreamed of before. But one must be educated to obtain these positions and since once you return there will be little hope of any additional schooling you would be well advised to stay in school as long as you can. We realize now that we should have done things differently with Yvonne. We should have permitted her to continue on after she matriculated. Alas, it is too late for her now. Poor thing! But there is still time for you and Ann.

Thirdly, you are still a boy. My goodness, you aren't even 17 years old yet—at least not until next month! You shouldn't be so concerned about the war here in England. Even if you were home there is little you could do to help. And for goodness sakes, don't talk about joining the service, wait as long as possible. The Montgomerys have already given one son. No one expects us to give another!

I have missed you, Graham. You will never know how often I wished you and Ann were here with me. I love you and would do anything to have all of us together once more, but your safety is far more important! Stay in America! God must have had a reason for taking Henry from us. He surely will return you, Ann, and Yvonne to us—in due time.

There was a smudge on the letter here—the ink had smeared—as if something damp had dripped on it.

Sunday, 17 May 1942

Sorry for the delay. I had no time to write any more on Friday. Please forgive me?

I mentioned that conditions have deteriorated in England. You wouldn't believe how much. For example, it is no longer possible to purchase fine fabrics. There are only a few basic utility materials and patterns available. Except for those wearing ragged pre-war clothes, the church on Sunday is filled with ladies all dressed in frocks of similar design. It makes us all look alike–as if we are in uniform. Silk stockings are nearly a thing of the past, too. Some of the ladies have begun painting their legs with a brown stain to make it look as if they are wearing hose. My solution is simply to wear short stockings. (It makes me appear to be an old woman trying to look young again. But what else can I do? I am old–and wish I could look young again.) Even our intimate ladies' undergarments have been affected. There is no longer any attached lace or frills. Of course, you wouldn't know about such things. Would you? Ha! Ha!

Not that it makes much difference what styles or materials are available. No one can afford them anyway. In April our purchase tax was raised to 66 per cent! Yes, you read that correctly–we must now add two-thirds the cost to all the non-essential goods we buy. Thank goodness it does not include food. If it did, Dad and I would be destitute by now–although, to think about it–with rationing limiting the quantities so severely it might not cause too serious a dent in our budget anyway.

-   -   -

Here, inserted in the margins, was a penciled note from Chad. It complained that the price of beer had increased by two pence a pint and whiskey now cost one pound two and six. He added, *"Blimey, this war is getting out of hand. These excessive beer and whiskey prices represent a war atrocity too serious to go unanswered. They should hang Hitler for all the inconveniences he has caused!"*

-   -   -

The Government is being much harder on slackers lately. Last month they began prosecuting women who refuse to enter the National Service. Soon the only people left on the home front will be us old folks. All the youth will be either in one of the military or the national services. It is so dreary here with so many of the young people gone. Even Princess Elizabeth registered for war service after her sixteenth birthday last month. The newspapers all carried pictures of her. She looked rather spiffy in her Girl Guides uniform. I can't imagine the Ministry of Labour calling her for interview, but one never knows in these very different wartime conditions.

I'm glad you are not shirking your duty there. You sound very busy with all your volunteer activities: salvaging paper, metal, and other scrap materials. You pal, Fred, sounds like a super chap. It's nice that the two of you are neighbors and can do things together. It must help to have a little bit of the homeland so close at hand. It does sound as if

Fred is quite the ladies' man, however. Perhaps too much so? I trust you are minding your manners and not following in his footsteps–remember, you represent England and must always put on a good show, make Americans think of you as the gentleman I know you are.

I guess I am beginning to sound like the vicar with all these admonishments and had better close this letter–before I say something that turns you against your dear old mother. I know I have been rather derelict in writing this past half year but, you must admit, I have improved recently. I promise I shall do even better hereafter.

Love,

  Mum

P.S. (Monday evening, 18 May) Dad wants you to know he has submitted your request to the Bender executives but it will be some time before there is any resolution. If you are truly serious about coming, Mr. Roberts suggested you talk to Mr. Bender. It may help to expedite the request.

Now I will finally post this. Sorry for the delay.

Love again,

  Mum

Scribbled at bottom of the letter was the following in Diane's handwriting:

I strongly suggest you not share this letter with Ann. When I re-read it I found it contained many things that would probably only serve to upset her. It is better if she were unaware of any possibility of your return to England. That is, if you haven't already shared your wishes with her.

Chapter 75

Monday, 18 May 1942

Clara was already awake when the alarm clock sounded. She had been thinking about yesterday's picnic and how wonderful it had been. Everyone had such a good time. Edith had been even happier than usual, and Brad was in better spirits than he had been in almost as long as she could remember.

The decision to give up his radio repair business had been a good one. Because of the war, components were getting unbelievably difficult to obtain. Had he stayed in business any longer he would not have had the parts he needed to fix radios anyway. Instead, he now had a good job at Bender Electric. Taking the Defense Pre-employment and Refresher Program had certainly been a good decision. It had really improved their life. Finishing at the top of the class in the electrician's course had not hurt matters either. It was the reason Bender Electric hired him.

She was proud of Brad, after only three months they had promoted him to his present supervisory position, and with it had come a wonderful salary increase. A year ago they never could have imagined paychecks as large as his were now. His salary, coupled with her wages from United Assembly, made them feel almost wealthy. In a matter of only a few months, they had gone from barely being able to meet their expenses to a family with a rapidly growing savings account and regular monthly purchases of U.S. War Bonds.

She thought about all those days before joining Bender Electric, especially the ones after Edith came to live with them, when they worried if they were going to be able to meet all their expenses. It was during those difficult times when she had worried that they might have made a mistake taking in an evacuee, but now those worries were behind them. They could easily afford Edith. Only last Saturday, she had taken Edith downtown McKinley Heights on a grand shopping spree. They spent most of the day trying on clothes and came home with a bundle of new things. Brad had laughed when he saw their packages and teased them by asking if they had left anything for the other customers.

Edith certainly was a happy and contented girl; and so good-natured and helpful. She had been that way from the day she arrived. She had fit in quite comfortably with Brad and her. The three of them had shared many good times since then. It was wonderful how Edith had quickly accepted them as her father and mother–although recently, she had to confess, Edith had seemed more like a sister than a daughter. Even Edith's dog had become a treasured member of the Holtzman family. Admittedly, at first she was somewhat concerned when Ned brought Spot; she thought a dog in the house would be too much of a nuisance, but soon he had won her heart, along with everyone else's. She really liked that little dog now. At times she was almost jealous that it was Edith's pet and not hers.

The one thing that troubled her was the relationship between Edith and Ned. The way they had been acting toward each other recently caused her considerable concern. She could recall how she and Brad had been when they were that age. She remembered the urges they had and how easily it had been to lose control. She didn't want that to happen to Edith. She had tried to restrict Edith's dating but that hadn't always worked. There were too many opportunities for young people to be together these days. She felt more drastic measures were needed–before they became too involved–but could not decide what was the best approach to take. She considered being more restrictive about their seeing each other but she knew that would only lead to hard feelings and trouble. She also thought about sitting down with Edith and explaining certain facts every young woman should know. She probably owed that much to Edith's parents. But Brad had talked her out of it. He insisted there was no cause for alarm; they were both good, well-behaved children who would act sensibly and responsibly. In a way, she was glad he had. She really hadn't known how, or for that matter, what to tell Edith.

Brad's insistence of bringing up news of the war was the one thing that marred yesterday's good time. She didn't like to discuss the war. It was simply too depressing. Why did everyone insist on analyzing all the battles the Allies were losing? Although the Americans had had their first major success this past week in the Coral Sea and General Doolittle had bombed Tokyo in April, most of the news was about horrible losses and depressing withdrawals. The Allies were also still losing ships in the Pacific at an alarming rate. The carrier Lexington was the latest reported casualty–the Japanese had sunk it in the Coral Sea. The Coral Sea was somewhere northeast of Australia she thought, although she couldn't be certain. Brad would know where it was; he kept track of such things. Bataan had fallen in April; Corregidor had surrendered the first week in May, and much of Burma was now reportedly under Japanese control. Particularly troubling to Clara were the reports, which were appearing more and more frequently in the newspapers lately, of the terrible atrocities the Japanese were committing on Allied prisoners. She could not imagine anyone being so cruel, not even the Japs–as everyone was now derisively calling the Japanese. She shuddered when she thought of what their poor prisoners had to endure.

At least in Europe the reports were better, although not much. The English were still reporting successful air raids over Germany, but a resolution was far from being decided and the eventual outcome was still in doubt. And what about the poor people in all those occupied countries who had to put up with that awful Nazi tyranny? It was too horrible to think about.

Clara's thoughts shifted to Brad's status with the local selective service board. She hoped the next time they had a call-up they would take into consideration his new job. Working for Bender Electric certainly was more vital to the war effort than his radio repair business. As far as she was concerned, it was enough to keep him out of the service. "But what if it wasn't?"

Fortunately, it was time to call Brad. They both had to be at work before eight. She wouldn't have any more time to think about such dreadful possibilities. She called him and quickly put his selective service status out of her mind.

That evening Clara arrived home rather late. Being in a hurry to start preparing dinner, she ignored the newspaper on the front lawn and the mail in the mailbox and went directly inside. Edith was sitting on the divan playing with Spot. "Hi, Edith," Clara said. "How was your day?"

"Super!" answered Edith. "There's only one more week of classes, a few days of final exams, and then school will be over until autumn."

"My goodness. I hadn't realized time was so short. It's difficult to believe, in just a few more weeks, you will be ready for high school. It seems such a short time since you came here and began the seventh grade. Is it possible it's been nearly two years?"

"Isn't it great? A couple more weeks and I can say good-bye to McKinley Heights Junior High. I'll finally be able to look down my nose at all those younger, and much dumber, junior high kids," she joked. "I'll be eligible for varsity cheerleading and all the other great things high school kids get to do."

They were interrupted by Brad, who came in reading the news. "Well, it's definite. The paper reports gasoline rationing started today. They say many stations ran out of gas last weekend because everyone was trying to fill their tanks before the deadline. I can't imagine how we will get along on such a small weekly ration. They need to find a way somehow to consider those of us who live a long way from work. Otherwise we won't be able to make it into work every day. At least one thing's good though, the price of gasoline should stay stable. Thank goodness President Roosevelt froze the prices of all essential goods several weeks ago."

"They were discussing the possibility of forming car pools at work today. That should stretch the gasoline tanks a little," Clara observed. "By the way, did you get the mail?"

"Yes, I took it out of the mailbox, but the article on gasoline rationing upset me so much I haven't looked at it yet." Suddenly Brad's face turned ashen.

"What's wrong, dear?" Clara asked.

"There's a letter here from the Selective Service Board," he groaned as he tore open the envelope.

"Good heavens!" He began to read out loud, "Greetings. Your friends and neighbors are pleased to inform you that you have been chosen to serve your country as a member of the armed services. You are to report to the county courthouse at 0630 hours on Monday, June 1, 1942. At that time you will board busses and proceed to an assigned military base to undergo a medical examination. If you are found physically fit, you will be sworn into the Army of the United States of America for a minimum service period of one year or the duration of the war plus six months, whichever is longer.

"Please bring the necessary toiletries and other personal items and one change of undergarments. Only one small travel bag will be permitted.

"All good-byes must be said prior to the reporting time.

"Signed, G. D. Metzger, President, Local Selective Service Board No. 121."

"What are you reading, Brad?" Clara asked, a look of horror on her face.

"It's my induction notice, Clara. I've been drafted!"

"They can't be serious. It's some sort of mistake. You just started your war work in February. You're needed at Bender Electric."

"I'm afraid that doesn't count. Last month they took Ben Young. He was a highly skilled tool and die maker. The company tried to keep him out but were unsuccessful. My job is no where near as critical as his, so I can't expect an industrial deferment."

"But you're a married man!"

"So was Ben."

Clara sank onto a chair and began to cry.

Edith tried to comfort her, but Clara resisted all attempts. She rudely pushed Edith away and cried harder. "Brad," Edith said, "what can I do to help her?"

"Oh, Brad, what are we going to do?" Clara interrupted.

"Sorry, honey," he replied, "there's not much any of us can do. I guess I'm in the Army now!" He laughed, but everyone knew he was not amused.

Chapter 76

Saturday, 30 May 1942

The thirtieth of May was a beautiful day. There were only a few clouds in the sky, the temperature was a balmy seventy-two degrees. It was a day when everyone found an excuse to be outdoors. The more enterprising began neglected landscape projects or repaired damage to dwellings caused by the past harsh winter. The less ambitious planned picnics, pickup ballgames, special outings, or whatever they could think of for outdoor fun and relaxation.

Sandy, as was her regular Saturday morning routine, rose early and was due at the Richmond stables when they opened at eight o'clock. Her plan: to ride as much as possible. Her first riding contest was only two weeks away. If she hoped to make a presentable showing, she needed much more practice.

Normally Sandy walked to the stables on Saturdays. It was only two miles and Kirk thought the short walk was good for her. He said it would exercise muscles she didn't use while riding. Sandy, not particularly keen on any form of extra exercise, did not agree with his theory but reluctantly put up with it—she wanted nothing to interfere with riding her horse. On this particular morning, however, Lucy had a breakfast with some of the girls. Since she would pass near the stables, she offered Sandy a ride. Consequently, Sandy arrived a little earlier than usual and, for quite some time, had the stables to herself.

The visit to the stables was routine for her; she had been riding weekly ever since Kirk and Lucy had given her the horse. Wishing to ride as soon as possible and knowing the stables always required it before each ride, she immediately began to groom her horse. When she finished, James, the trainer, had still not arrived so Sandy, although she had never done it before, proceeded to saddle her horse. She was just completing the task and was tightening the cinch when James walked into the paddock. "You're already here," he observed. "You've been busy. I see you're all saddled and ready to ride. That's good. I like to see my students taking the initiative that way." He added, almost as an afterthought, "Make certain you have that cinch tightened securely. You wouldn't want it to slip while riding."

He had intended to check Sandy's work before she rode off, but, just as he was about to do so, several girls relatively new to the stable arrived and began excitedly asking him all sorts of questions. In the confusion, he forgot about Sandy.

Sandy had not entered the steeplechase event. James and the other trainers still considered her unqualified to jump obstacles in competition. Sandy had agreed with their assessment but, bored with simply parading her horse around the field, was eager to qualify someday for the more difficult event. Thus, not surprisingly, when she found herself all alone on the field, the first hurdle caught her eye. It looked innocuous enough, something she was certain would not be a difficult jump.

If she were ever going to be a jumper, there had to a first time. "Why not now?" she asked herself. "Before anyone else comes onto the field; before anyone is here to see me make a mistake." She rode up to the hurdle, inspected it to make certain she understood what she needed to do, rode a considerable distance up the track, turned, and with great enthusiasm and wild excitement, coaxed her horse into a fast gallop toward the hurdle. When she reached the point she judged right for jumping, she pulled back on the reins and encouraged the horse to leap. The horse, responding well, obeyed, and the two went flying through the air. Exhilarated by the leap, she gave a squeal of delight as the horse's feet landed beyond the hurdle. She had successfully completed her first jump.

However, as they hit the ground, the cinch, which was not secured as tightly as she had thought, slipped suddenly and the saddle shifted. It was just enough to cause her to slide backward off the saddle and onto the bareback of the horse. The horse, feeling the change in her position, broke into a gallop, jerking Sandy even further backwards. Sandy tried desperately to hold on to the reins but was jostled about too severely. She lost her grip, tried to grab hold of the horse's mane and failed. As she fell her left foot remained caught, momentarily, in the stirrup which catapulted her toward the ground. After she landed, she continued somersaulting head over heels until finally coming to rest several yards beyond the hurdle.

The last thing Sandy saw was green grass coming rapidly towards her, followed by everything turning black.

The telephone call reached Kirk just as he was about to begin cleaning the wash shed. He heard the telephone ringing and had almost decided to ignore it, but something in the way the telephone operator rang the bell sounded different. He decided it might be important. Later he would hardly be able to recall what had happened next. James had asked for a Mr. Maurer. After Kirk identified himself, James said simply, "I believe you should get over here right away, sir. Your daughter has been in an accident and we think it's serious. We have called the doctor, but he is on another emergency call. It may be sometime before he gets here."

"My God!" Kirk cried. "What happened?"

"We're not quite certain, sir," the trainer answered, somewhat defensively. "We found her lying in the field. Apparently she was thrown from her horse. We're doing everything we can for her, but I think you'd better come right now."

"I'll be there as quickly as I can. My wife has the car, so I'm not certain how I'll get there but I'll be there–even if I must run all the way!" Kirk, in a near trance, hung up the telephone, looked across the street and, spying his neighbor, asked to be taken to the stables.

When they arrived, he knew immediately where Sandy was by the crowd that had gathered in the field. He rushed to her. "How is she?" he asked.

"We don't know, Mr. Maurer. She hasn't regained consciousness. We made her as comfortable as possible, but we couldn't do much. We're afraid to move her before the doctor arrives."

Kirk looked at Sandy. She lay there, her eyes closed, looking so pale. Her chest moved irregularly. She was having difficulty breathing. Kirk feared she would die. "Oh please, God, don't take this innocent little girl. She has so much to live for. She can't die so far from home. Please, please! Let her get well so someday she might return to England." Kirk kneeled on the ground beside Sandy and held her limp hand.

It was nearly nine-thirty before the doctor arrived. He spent only a few minutes examining her. The prognosis looked bleak; he wasn't certain he could save her. He secured her face and body as best he could in a makeshift splint, hoping to keep her neck as rigid as possible, and instructed the volunteer firemen to load her carefully onto the stretcher and rush her to the hospital. He looked at Kirk, "I'm afraid it's quite serious. It's difficult to tell exactly what the damage is, but it may very well be a broken neck. We must get her to the hospital quickly, or she will die for certain."

"By all means! Go!" Kirk agreed, almost hysterically.

"But moving her risks further damage. We could cause permanent paralysis if a nerve in the spinal cord is severed, or, worse yet, we might kill her. There is no guarantee, but I don't know what else to do. We'll be as careful as we can, but you must understand the risk that is involved."

"I understand, doc. Just do your best. That's all we can ask of you."

They loaded Sandy on the back of a flatbed truck and were just leaving when Lucy arrived. "What's happened, Kirk?" she asked. "What's happened to Sandy? Will she be all right?"

"We don't know, Lucy. She had a bad spill. The doctor doesn't know how serious the injury is. She may have a broken neck."

"A broken neck! Will she die?"

"We hope not! He says we must wait and see."

Lucy broke into tears. "You'd better notify Mr. Bender," she said, between sobs. "He'll want to know. Maybe he'll know how we can get in contact with her parents in England. They really must be told about this. She's their daughter!"

Chapter 77

Sunday, 31 May 1942

News of Sandy's accident spread quickly among the evacuees. Stewart received a call from Elizabeth whose foster mother was a close friend of the Maurers. He called Fred, who relayed the information to Graham, and Graham called Ann. "They don't know what the outcome will be," Graham told her. "Sandy is still in a coma. She hasn't regained consciousness since the accident. No one knows for certain what happened–only that she fell from her horse. They believe she was trying to jump a hurdle when she took the spill."

"Have they sent word to Sandy's parents?" Ann asked. "I would think they should be told as quickly as possible."

"I believe Captain Ben sent them a cablegram. At least Stewart thought so."

"I'll tell Edith. She's here with me this weekend."

"For the weekend? Why is that?"

"Mr. Holtzman leaves tomorrow morning for basic training. We invited Edith to stay with us so the Holtzmans could spend some time alone."

"Mr. Holtzman is going into the service? That's too bad. I suppose Mrs. Holtzman is all broken up about her husband leaving?"

"She's devastated. Edith says she's been a different person since his induction notice arrived," Ann answered, her voice filled with sympathy. "Edith is feeling pretty low, too. She likes Mr. Holtzman very much. She tells me he was more of a father to her than her dad ever was. She wanted to be there this weekend, to say good-bye, but Mrs. Holtzman would not hear of it. She didn't want anyone, not even Edith, interfering with their last weekend together."

"That seems like a reasonable request."

"I suppose it is, but it's rather selfish. She should realize there are others who need to say good-bye, too."

"When will he be back?"

"Uncle Jack says it's usual for the boys to come home on leave after they complete their basic training. That would make it about eight or nine weeks, but that's only a guess."

"That doesn't seem like such a long wait."

"I guess it is when you've been married to someone for so long–and love him very much. The worst part, once his leave is over he'll probably go back for advanced training and then directly on to his final duty station. In many cases now, Uncle Jack tells me, that is somewhere overseas."

"Yea!" replied Graham, an Americanism slipping into his vocabulary. "It could be almost anywhere. I understand American troops have been stationed in Australia since March, and just this past week, a large contingent of GIs landed in Ireland."

"Uncle Jack thinks most American soldiers are being sent to the Pacific now. That's where America is most involved. Edith says Mrs. Holtzman is especially worried that is where they will send Mr. Holtzman. She prays not. The newspapers are full of reports of horrible atrocities over there and she doesn't want him in danger of that sort of treatment."

"Wouldn't it be something if he were sent to England? He could visit some of the evacuees' families. Maybe even our mum and dad."

"I hardly think that would ever happen, Graham. That would be too much of a coincidence."

"Anything can happen these days, Ann. Who would have believed, two years ago, we'd have been in America all this time?"

"You're right. We hadn't even thought of ever seeing the United States back then."

"How are you and Oliver getting along?" Graham asked, abruptly changing the subject.

"What makes you ask? I haven't seen him since school ended a week ago. How should I be getting along with him?" Ann asked, in a somewhat cross tone.

"I thought you were sweet on him?"

"I definitely am not," she replied. "I don't know why you thought that."

"I've heard reports that the two of you are sweethearts, and they came from pretty reliable sources," he teased.

"I assure you! It's not true. He's a nice boy and I like him very much but we definitely are not sweethearts!"

He laughed. "Okay. I was merely checking."

When the children hung up, Ann called to Edith, "Things are getting so difficult these days. Let's take a walk–to my secret hiding place. Spot and Lady need some exercise. Besides, I think we need some time alone—now that we have something else to worry about. Graham just told me Sandy's been hurt."

Chapter 78

Sunday, 31 May 1942

Despite what had happened to Sandy, the war raged on. The Russians and Germans fought a fierce battle in Kharkov, the outcome of which was still in question; the Japanese had overrun Kinhwa, the capital of China's Chekiang province, and Rommel had just initiated a new offense in the western desert of North Africa. The only good news was the successful nighttime bombing of Cologne by a large armada of RAF bombers.

But no one who knew Sandy was at the moment thinking about the war; they were too worried. To everyone's relief, x-rays had shown she did not have a broken neck or any signs of damage to her vertebrae. But surprisingly, she still remained unconscious. Particularly concerned was Ben who had been at the hospital ever since they called him from his golf game on Saturday morning. Although the doctors said there was nothing he could do and suggested he go home and rest, he refused to leave. He was still there Sunday morning when Tom Derringer and Fred arrived at the hospital. "Hello Mr. Bender," Tom said, looking quite anxious. "How's Sandy this morning? Has there been any change?"

"Hello, Dr. Derringer. Hello, Fred," Ben replied. "They won't tell me much. All I know is that apparently she has suffered a severe concussion. I've asked them what I could do, but no one will give me an answer."

"Perhaps I can help. I'll talk to them and try to get a better idea of her condition," Tom volunteered.

"I'd appreciate that," Ben replied. "I'm willing to do anything to help her. Remember, cost is not a consideration, they should do all they can."

Fred could not help noticing Ben's clothes. In the past, he had always dressed impeccably, was never in anything but carefully tailored and pressed dress suits. To see him in wrinkled golf clothes, no tie, and badly in need of a shave was surprising. Fred thought this new image better suited him than what he had seen before. He had always thought Ben's formal, almost stuffy, dress belied the friendly, down-to-earth way he had always treated the evacuees.

"Have you had anything to eat this morning, sir?" Fred asked.

"Yes, I had a cup of coffee and a sweet roll," he answered. "It's nice of you to ask. You're staying with the Derringers, aren't you? How do you like your home?"

"Yes, sir, I live with them," Fred answered. "I couldn't ask for anything nicer. They have treated me superbly. There is one thing though ... None of us planned on such a long stay in America. We would all appreciate it if you could find a way to get us home. Soon!" Fred chuckled after saying that.

"Yes, I know how difficult it must be for all of you. It's a shame this nasty war keeps extending your stay. It's hard to guess when it will end, but rest assured, we'll get you home just as soon as we possibly can."

"I'm sure you will, sir. All of us appreciate the wonderful hospitality everyone has shown us and are sorry for all the inconveniences we have caused."

"Nonsense. You children are no bother. We're most happy to have you here with us–for as long as necessary. To tell the truth, some of the families tell me they're not looking forward to the day when you leave. They say it will be difficult to let you go; you children have become so much a part of their families."

"We feel the same way," Fred agreed. "Even though I'm looking forward to seeing my mum and dad again, it's going to make me terribly unhappy to leave the Derringers. I'm not looking forward to saying good-bye."

"I've just talked to Sandy's doctors; they are still uncertain what to do," interrupted Tom, coming back from Sandy's room. "We talked about the possibility of transferring her to the Cleveland Clinic where they have better diagnostic and treatment facilities. We finally agreed taking her there would be a worthwhile thing to do. Everyone thinks the advantages offset the danger of transporting her. But there is a risk. The final decision must be yours."

"No, not mine alone. I know I have legal authorization, but the Maurers should have a say in this as well. Go ahead and begin making the necessary arrangements. In the meantime, I'll call Kirk and Lucy; they just left a few minutes ago but should be home by now."

W.T. made two telephone calls, one to the Maurers and one to Stan Roberts. The Maurers agreed to the transfer and asked to accompany Sandy in the ambulance. Stan was told it was time to send a cablegram to Sandy's parents in Uxbridge. He was asked to come to the hospital to help compose it.

The first cablegram arrived in Uxbridge early Monday morning.

MCKINLEY HEIGHTS OHIO 31 MAY 1942 0900 HRS

MR AND MRS HAROLD MEYERS
265 RATHBURNE ROAD
UXBRIDGE MIDDLESEX ENGLAND

REGRET TO INFORM YOU SANDY HAS BEEN IN AN ACCIDENT STOP SHE IS PRESENTLY RESTING COMFORTABLY BUT HAS APPARENTLY SUFFERED A SEVERE CONCUSSION AND IS COMATOSE STOP DOCTORS ADVISE US THERE IS EXCELLENT CHANCE SHE WILL RECOVER BUT ARE TAKING HER TO CLEVELAND FOR FURTHER DIAGNOSTICS STOP KIRK AND LUCY MAURER WILL ACCOMPANY HER STOP WE WILL KEEP YOU INFORMED AS SOON AS MORE TO REPORT STOP PLEASE DO NOT WORRY SHE WILL HAVE THE BEST TREATMENT POSSIBLE STOP MORE INFORMATION CONCERNING THE ACCIDENT WILL FOLLOW STOP

W T BENDER

Jessica nearly fainted when she read the cablegram. "Oh, Harold, what do you suppose happened to her? She's unconscious! Are they telling us everything?"

Harold was near panic but knew he must remain strong for Jessica's sake. "Now don't worry, Mr. Bender will see that everything possible is done for her. American hospitals are excellent. If there is any place she can receive good treatment, it is there. I am certain she'll recover," he assured her in a confident tone. He did not, however, believe a word of what he said.

"How can we find out more? she asked. "How can we contact them for more information?"

"I don't know, dear. It's nearly impossible to get a message through to America these days, but I'll ask at the factory to see what can be done," he promised.

That afternoon they received a second cable.

MCKINLEY HEIGHTS OHIO 31 MAY 1942 1600 HRS

MR AND MRS HAROLD MEYERS
265 RATHBURNE ROAD
UXBRIDGE MIDDLESEX ENGLAND

SANDY HAS BEEN SUCCESSFULLY TRANSPORTED TO CLEVELAND STOP UNDERGOING EXTENSIVE DIAGNOSTIC EXAMINATION STOP WILL REPORT AS SOON AS DIAGNOSIS AVAILABLE STOP

W T BENDER

The cablegram did little to allay their fears.

The Tuesday morning newspaper headline read, "Japanese Bombers Raid Sydney; Concern grows that Australia will be invaded." The newspaper went unread at the Meyers' house; shortly after it arrived they received the third cablegram.

MCKINLEY HEIGHTS OHIO 31 MAY 1942 2430 HRS

MR AND MRS HAROLD MEYERS
265 RATHBURNE ROAD
UXBRIDGE MIDDLESEX ENGLAND

DOCTORS HAVE COMPLETED THEIR EXAMINATION AND REPORT THAT NOTHING CAN BE FOUND OTHER THAN CONCUSSION STOP CAN ONLY WAIT UNTIL SHE REGAINS CONSCIOUSNESS FOR FURTHER TREATMENT STOP HER CONDITION WILL BE CONSTANTLY MONITORED AND ANY CHANGES WILL BE IMMEDIATELY ADMINISTERED TO STOP UNDERSTAND YOUR ANXIETY RE ACCIDENT STOP SANDY FELL FROM HORSE STOP ATTEMPTING TO ARRANGE TRANSATLANTIC TELEPHONE LINK SO YOU AND MAURERS CAN TALK STOP PLEASE STAND BY STOP

W T BENDER

The knowledge of the fall and promise of a telephone link only added to their angst.

The telephone connection proved difficult to arrange and several additional cablegrams–none with anything new to report–passed across the Atlantic before Stan finally established the telephone link. To do it, he first needed government approval. He justified the phone call as necessary to resolve several technical questions concerning the proximity fuse program. He had never done anything like that before, had never lied to the authorities. He rationalized to himself that it was only a slight bending of the truth. By arranging to begin the call with a conference between American and British engineers, he had legitimatized it; at least that is what he told himself. Midway through the conferences, the phones were handed to the families while the engineers waited to resume their discussions. He hoped the parents' conversation would go unnoticed.

"I'm so sorry, Jessica! It's my fault. We should never have given the horse to Sandy, but it made her so happy and her training was progressing so nicely. We fully expected her to win her first trophy in the upcoming contest. We don't know exactly how the accident happened. They found her lying on the ground, apparently thrown by the horse. She must have hit her head. Please forgive me? Please, please forgive me?" Lucy repeated. "I love her so much. I never wanted anything bad to happen to her."

Jessica was relieved to finally learn the details of the accident and pleased to hear how deeply everyone cared. She felt especially sorry for Kirk and Lucy. She did not blame them; it wasn't their fault. They had only been trying to please her. "Now don't you fret about it, Lucy. Harold and I know you love our daughter and only have her best interests at heart. Your past letters convinced us of that. Accidents do happen! We are extremely saddened by it but don't hold you responsible."

"But you should, Jessica," Lucy protested. "I should have been there–I should have been with her. I should have been a more protective guardian."

"Nonsense! It was no one's fault. God must have had a reason for it. Who knows, had Sandy remained in Uxbridge something even worse might have happened. We have had so many heavy air raids. They even hit one of our theaters. Many people were killed in that one. She might have been one of them if the two of you hadn't so graciously taken her into your home–and into your hearts," she said, meaning every word, but subconsciously still resenting what they had just done to her little girl.

"I can only promise we will do everything we possibly can to help Sandy get well. And we'll keep you informed whenever there is a change in her condition–even if it is only a little change. You can rest assured we will tell you everything," she told them, "everything good–or bad. I'll write often but, as you know, there is nearly a six week delay for letters to cross the Atlantic. Perhaps we can make use of the air-grams for quicker reports, and most certainly we will continue to send cablegrams while the crisis continues. Mr. Bender, bless his soul, has provided an open account at the telegraph office, so we can call in the messages via the telephone."

"I know you'll do your best and will keep us informed," Jessica assured her, then added, "We are so thankful for Mr. Bender. He has been so helpful and reassuring. Our hats are off to him. Please tell him that."

Afterwards Jessica turned to Harold. "Oh, Harold," she cried, "our little daughter is hurt! Will we lose her?"

"I firmly don't think so, darling," he lied. "There's no reason God should call her home."

Stan slept poorly for several nights afterwards, fearing someone had monitored the call. He knew they could fire him for the security infraction, or, at a minimum, the Navy project officer in charge of the program might reprimand him. Fortunately, the violation was not discovered, "or more likely," Stan thought, "the project officer chose to overlook it–he probably has children too."

Chapter 79

Tuesday, 9 June 1942

MCKINLEY HEIGHTS OHIO USA 9 JUNE 1942 1635 HRS

MR AND MRS HAROLD MEYERS
265 RATHBURNE ROAD
UXBRIDGE MIDDLESEX ENGLAND

SANDY CONTINUES IN COMA STOP DOCTORS SAY SHE STILL IS NOT RESPONDING TO STIMULI BUT ARE ENCOURAGED WITH HER VITAL SIGNS STOP WE PRAY FOR HER CONSTANTLY STOP

KIRK AND LUCY

* * *

UXBRIDGE MIDDLESEX ENGLAND 10 JUNE 1942 1012 HRS

MR AND MRS KIRK MEYERS
19 SHADY DALE LANE
MCKINLEY HEIGHTS OHIO USA

THANK YOU FOR UPDATE STOP KNOW YOU ARE DOING ALL
POSSIBLE AND APPRECIATE IT STOP WE PRAY TOO STOP

HAROLD

*   *   *

Edith was impatiently waiting for Ann to pick her up. They were to
go to Kirk and Lucy Maurer's house. Elizabeth was also to meet them
there. Kirk and Lucy had invited the girls to visit Sandy at the Cleveland
Clinic. The doctors thought it might, somehow, help Sandy if she heard
familiar English voices. They had little hope the experiment would succeed but had few other ideas–by now, anything was worth a try.

"You must help Clara all you can," Mrs. Martin, Clara's mother,
was instructing Edith. "She needs all our support now that Brad is in the
service. The poor dear was so dependent upon him and can't seem to
adjust to his not being here."

Edith was only partially listening to her. Clara's mother and father
had arrived last Friday. Ever since, she had heard repeatedly how terrible it was that Brad had been drafted, how unfair it was to Clara, and
how precious their daughter was. Edith wished they would stop. She
had their concerns memorized by now. Besides, she understood how
terrible Brad's absence was–long before they told her. Didn't they realize his absence discouraged and depressed her too? She loved Brad and
missed him, just as much as anyone. No one seemed to appreciate what
she was feeling. She was only the foster child, the evacuee. Hadn't it
occurred to them she loved him too? She did. Terribly. His departure
affected her almost as much as if she had lost her mother–not her father,
she didn't care what happened to that old goat.

Only Spot was there to comfort her. Ned had wanted to come see
her, but Clara wouldn't permit it. Edith hardly ever saw Ned now that
Brad was gone. Clara had been demanding nearly all of her attention
and became nearly hysterical every time Ned telephoned. Whenever he
asked to visit, Clara would scream at Edith and accuse her of not appre-
ciating all the sacrifices Brad was making. "After all, the wonderful
man is serving in the armed forces of his country," she would say. She
accused Edith of disregarding his patriotic contribution; told her because
she was English she could not possibly understand what the Americans
were enduring–all due to England's inability to settle its own dispute
with Hitler. Although the accusation hurt, Edith did not complain. She
had hoped, with the arrival of Mr. and Mrs. Martin, things would improve. But they hadn't. They only made matters worse. The Martins
always sided with their daughter and, in many cases, were even more
abusive than Clara.

Edith looked at the clock and wished Ann would hurry, not so much in an eagerness to get started for Cleveland, mostly to escape the Holtz-man household for a few hours and to see Ned–if he brought Ann. "Thank goodness Mrs. Martin has gone into the kitchen, at least now I won't need to listen to all her advice," she thought, as she peered out the window.

While she waited, she overheard a conversation between Clara and her father. He was advising her not to give up her work at United Assembly. "Be reasonable, Clara. You must have an income. With Brad gone, how would you live? The income of an army wife is so small it contributes next to nothing to your budget. You'll go broke if you quit," he argued, and then added, "You can't come live with your mother and me. We just don't have room for both of you."

"But, Daddy, I can't go back to that place anymore. Everyone treats me so rudely. No one ever sympathizes with me. No one knows how terrible I have it with Brad gone," she whined. "It's as if they don't care about me. They act as if they don't know my husband was drafted."

"Face it, Clara, you're not the only one with a husband in the service. I wouldn't be surprised if a lot of the girls at your plant have husbands in the service now. The sooner you accept the fact that you are not unique, the better off you'll be. Be thankful you have Edith here to keep you company."

Clara apparently did not realize Edith could hear the conversation. "She's not much company these days. She spends all her time talking on the telephone–to that horrid boy from the Dexter Hills farm. Mark my word, that affair is going to lead to something dreadful. The next thing you know she'll tell us she's pregnant. I'd be better off if I got rid of her before she disgraces me. Besides, it's too expensive to keep her any longer. The pittance from Bender Electric doesn't begin to cover what she costs me. I've just about decided to ask them to take her away."

Edith was shocked. She thought Clara loved her, like a mother loves her child. "How could she turn on me that way? Does it really have to do with finances, or is it because Brad is in the service?" she wondered.

"Don't do anything hasty," Mr. Martin begged. "Edith seems like a nice girl and you've gotten along so well with her all this time. And don't fret about the boyfriend, kids are much better behaved than you think. Remember, you and Brad dated in high school. You didn't get into any trouble, did you?"

"But we were different, Dad. We were more grown up than those two are."

Mr. Martin laughed. "I don't think so, Clara. You were no more grown up than they are. You're just looking at it from a different perspective now."

Just then Ann and Ned drove into the driveway and blew their horn. "I must go now," Edith shouted as she grabbed her hat and raced out the door, tears in her eyes.

"Give my love to Sandy," Clara shouted. "Tell that poor child we're all hoping she is up and about real soon."

Edith barely heard what Clara said. Her previous words were still reverberating in her ears. She didn't quite know what to do. "Hi, Ann. Hi, Ned," she said.

When they arrived at the Maurers' Edith remained in the car with Ned while Ann went to the front door. "Tell them I'll be there in a jiff," she said, "I want to talk to Ned for a few minutes."

The girl's visit to Sandy was disappointing. Sandy did not respond to their greetings and, much to their embarrassment, they found it much more difficult than they had expected to look at Sandy, lying there, just staring into space. It took them several minutes before they overcame their discomfort and were able to engage in the chatter and banter the doctors wanted. But, sadly, when they did, there was no response. Finally, to the disappointment of all, the doctors asked them to leave, telling them there was no use proceeding any further with the experiment. It had failed. Lucy was so disheartened she broke into tears and left the room crying. Ann tried to offer comfort but could do no more than put her hand on Lucy's shoulder and wait until the crying stopped.

On the way back to McKinley Heights, Ann could not help but think of her last trip to Cleveland. This was almost the same as then, the visit ended in nothing but disappointment, followed by a trip home in near silence, with everyone quiet and deep in thought.

Later that evening, after Ann was home, Ned asked if Edith had said anything about Mrs. Holtzman's conversation with her dad.

"Only a little. Isn't it terrible?" Ann replied. "Can you imagine wanting to get rid of Edith?"

They discussed Edith's problem until the late evening news on the radio. It mostly reported on the sea battle raging off an island in the Pacific called Midway. Japanese losses were said to be heavy with unconfirmed reports that Japan had lost four aircraft carriers. The U.S. had lost the carrier Yorktown and many servicemen. While all this was happening, Japan had also struck at U.S. bases in the Aleutian Islands off the coast of Alaska. "An apparent diversionary attempt," the newscaster speculated.

Ann had difficulty going to sleep that night. She was uncertain whether it was Sandy's coma, Edith's problems with Clara, or the war news that never seemed to get better. Fortunately, Lady was there to keep her company. By half-past midnight Ann finally fell asleep.

MCKINLEY HEIGHTS OHIO, USA, 11 JUNE 1942 2306 HRS

MR AND MRS HAROLD MEYERS
265 RATHBURNE ROAD
UXBRIDGE MIDDLESEX ENGLAND

SANDY VISITED BY THREE ENGLISH CHUMS TODAY STOP SHE DID NOT RESPOND STOP WE CONTINUE TO HOPE FOR CHANGE STOP

KIRK AND LUCY

Chapter 80

Tuesday, 16 June 1942

Cleveland, Ohio
16 June 1942

Dear Jessica and Harold,

Oh happy, happy day! Our little girl has come back to us! I realize you will already know she is better from the cablegram Harold is sending as I write, but I wanted you to know the details. Hence, this letter written from Sandy's hospital room on <u>the day she woke up</u>.

The sweet thing is sleeping peacefully now after a <u>very</u> exciting day. We received a telephone call about three forty-five this morning from Sandy's doctor. He told us there had been a remarkable change in her condition and believed we should come to Cleveland right away. Kirk asked him what had happened. He laughed and told him our little girl had opened her eyes and was talking to the nurses. Can you imagine— talking to the nurses! We both were so happy we grabbed each other and jumped with joy. It's good we had the shades pulled, if our neighbors had seen us they would have thought we'd gone mad.

Anyway–we quickly dressed and drove as rapidly as we could to Cleveland. When we arrived we found Sandy lying there, talking almost

as if nothing had happened. The nurses told us they heard a voice from Sandy's room about two this morning. When they investigate they found her calling out for her mum. They asked her if she knew where she was and what had happened. She promptly repeated her name, but couldn't recall much of that terrible morning, only that she had gone to the stables early. Then, almost immediately, she started complaining about how hungry she was. The poor girl must have been starved, she had been on an intravenous feeding ever since the accident. But she had to wait, the nurses couldn't feed her until the doctor completed his examination. As you might imagine, they had a difficult time keeping her happy. Finally, after a thorough examination, he authorized broth and fruit gels. When they came, she gulped them down, begged for more, and, since then, has been eating everything she's offered.

It was such a good feeling to see her eating again and especially to hear her talking.

All the nurses have fallen in love with that sweet child. They are so impressed with her good manners and have had many good laughs with her already, she's such a tease! The two of you reared her well.

The doctor tells us if she continues to improve, and barring setbacks, we should be able to take her back to McKinley Heights in two or three days. What a grand day that will be! They still want her to remain in the hospital for a little while down there, but everyone assures us we will have her home in about two weeks!

Now that the worst seems over, I must confess that Harold has worried about the number of trips we have made to Cleveland. They are causing us a serious gasoline (Sandy says you call it petrol) shortage. We have rationed gasoline now. (Twenty-five gals per month for those who work.) It doesn't take us very far when you consider Kirk drives to the Bender plant every day. We would have been in real trouble getting to the clinic except for our neighbors who pitched in and gave us some of their allotment. It was quite a complicated undertaking. Our service station attendant, bless his soul, devised a system whereby each time one of them bought gasoline he gave them a smaller amount than their ration stamps covered. He kept a record and gave us the difference. I suppose it's illegal. (If they censor my letter I'm afraid they'll know we're criminals. If so, I may be writing my next letter from jail! Ha, ha.) But at least we have been able to get to Cleveland during this crisis. Also, Mr. Bender gave Kirk paid time off for each trip. Can you imagine? His support certainly has been super since Sandy's illness. In fact, the entire community has been superb! God bless them all! We owe everyone a great big thank you.

Well, dears, it's getting late and Kirk has just come back from the cable office and wants to leave for McKinley Heights. He needs a little sleep before going to work tomorrow. Rest assured we will continue the cablegrams until Sandy has recovered fully.

Love, Lucy

The newspaper headlines that evening stressed more troublesome news. A Japanese submarine had shelled Newcastle and Sydney; Russia had suffered heavy losses at Sevastopol, and the U.S. had agreed to another lend-lease bill, the latter causing a serious national debate. The bill, which supplied arms to Russia, was similar to the one signed with Britain back in March of '41. Many questioned the wisdom of doing this. No one could forget what Russia had done to Poland and the other Baltic nations or that she had been part of the Axis group and an enemy not too long ago.

Lucy should have been upset by this news, but she slept sounder than she had for over two weeks. Her little girl was going to recover! But the euphoria did not last long. They brought Sandy back to the McKinley Heights hospital on Friday. Unexpectedly, the following Monday she slipped back into another coma.

MCKINLEY HEIGHTS OHIO USA 22 JUNE 1942 1846 HRS

MR AND MRS HAROLD MEYERS
265 RATHBURNE ROAD
UXBRIDGE MIDDLESEX ENGLAND

SANDY IS ONCE AGAIN COMATOSE STOP DOCTORS ARE PUZZLED STOP ARE RUNNING NEW TESTS STOP WILL NOTIFY YOU AS SOON AS THERE IS ANY CHANGE STOP

KIRK AND LUCY

Chapter 81

Sunday, 12 July 1942

As the Schaefer family motored to the Bender campgrounds, Ida thought about yesterday's McKinley Heights shopping. She had taken Ann into town to look for a new outfit for today's picnic. Ann had been growing so rapidly lately, the poor girl had outgrown almost everything.

She certainly was not going to send any child of hers to the Bender picnic with clothes that were too small. Thank goodness they found something. She frowned thinking how much poorer the summer selection had been. The war certainly was having a major effect on the lives of Americans. The requirement to use ration books for gasoline and sugar purchases was a good example–and more rationing was likely to be announced soon.

But the war had produced a few benefits as well. She smiled when she thought about the change in the Schaefer family budget. Although it was still tight, it no longer was the limiting factor in their daily life. Ever since Jack had taken the tool and die maker course offered evenings at Dexter Hills High and gone to work at the war plant, their income had improved considerably. Of course it meant more of the farm work fell on her shoulders, but with the help of Ned and Ann, and with Karen and Jack pitching in whenever they could, they were still keeping up with most of it. That is, if they didn't count the fields taken out of production. Leaving land idle seemed somewhat unpatriotic, especially with the government vigorously encouraging increased farm production. As concerned citizens, it embarrassed them to be shirking their farming responsibilities, but what else could they do? Jack had answered the government's call for volunteers. If working in the war plant wasn't more important then they shouldn't have accepted him. Besides, she and Jack had planted a huge victory garden this spring. It would make them nearly self-sufficient as far as food was concerned. In fact, the expected crop yield would probably mean they could sell some of it. That, in itself, would attest to their patriotism–they were still contributors to the nation's effort to lessen the shortage of food.

After they had selected a cute flowered blouse, a pair of pretty white shorts, white socks, and a pair of brown and white saddle oxfords, Ida encouraged Ann to try on one of the new bathing suits. She nearly laughed out loud when she thought about it now. Ann had been in the dressing room for quite some time when she had called to her, "What's the matter, Ann? Are you having difficulty?"

After a brief delay, a timid voice answered, "No ma'am."

"Then come out and let's look at you."

"Must I?" came the reluctant reply.

After further coaxing, Ann finally emerged. She was blushing and had her arms wrapped around her body. "I look awful," she complained.

"Stand up straight, Ann. Put your arms down. Let's see how you look."

It was at that moment that Ida realized her little girl was becoming a young woman. Last year's suit had no shape, this year it displayed a much more curvaceous body. There was no denying the difference.

"I can't wear this, Aunt Ida. Just look at me! I look horrible!"

"Nonsense. You look lovely. You've become quite a handsome young lady."

It took a lengthy discussion about the attributes of womanhood before she was finally able to convince Ann the swim suit fit properly. She had gone ahead and purchased it, even though Ann still thought she looked horrid in it. She would not let either Jack or Ned see it that evening when she tried everything on.

As Jack turned the auto into the camp driveway, Ida wondered whether Ann would keep her promise to wear it, even Karen's reassurance seemed to have done little to dispel Ann's apprehension about how she looked.

A noticeable pall hung over the attendees at the picnic. The major topic was Sandy. No one could believe she was still in a coma–it would be four weeks, next Tuesday, since that day she had slipped back into unconsciousness. There was criticism of the doctors for not having done more and for not having been more careful, and all sorts of speculation about what had caused the relapse. Some were saying it most likely meant she never would recover. Others, including Ann, Edith, and Elizabeth were still hopeful for a full recovery. But no one thought it would be soon.

There was even criticism of Ben. Some thought, out of respect for Sandy, he should not have had the picnic. Others argued Sandy's illness should not have had any bearing on whether to hold it or not. They believed life had to go on, despite the unfortunate distractions that always seemed to come up. Sad as it was, Sandy was just one more casualty of the war. The defenders of Ben pointed out that he was not at the picnic; he was at Sandy's bedside. In fact, he had been spending almost all his spare time at the hospital. He was almost never at home, preferring instead to be near by, just in case there was something he could do to help.

When not talking about Sandy, the conversation usually turned to the war. The Russian front seemed to be a disaster; the Germans were now claiming the capture of Sevastapol, and rumors were circulating of a major German offensive launched in the Balkans, once again using the Blitzkrieg as a major tactic in their offensive thrusts.

Elsewhere things were not going well either. Severe losses were being suffered by Allied naval forces in the Mediterranean; Malta had been heavily bombed by German war planes; the Middle East oil supply was feared in jeopardy; Rommel had recently made considerable gains in North Africa, and Germany was still causing major havoc in England with its bombing raids. To make matters worse, German U-boats were continuing to inflict heavy losses on Allied shipping in the Atlantic and, only this past week, the major portion of a convoy headed for Russia had been sunk in the Bering Sea.

And even closer to everyone's heart, McKinley Heights had its first reported casualty of the war, a victim of a German U-boat. A recent high school graduate, he had enlisted in the Merchant Marines last summer, and his parents had just received notice that he had been killed at sea. It was not known where the tragedy occurred, only that it was somewhere in the Atlantic. The parents had taken it hard. They had gone into seclusion and refused to talk to reporters about their son.

The newsreels were beginning to run clips featuring American boys who had enlisted in the British RAF. A boy from McKinley Heights was reportedly flying with the British on their raids over Germany, but there was no official confirmation of the story. Some attributed the success of the recent British bombing runs to American volunteers like him. Most, however, were skeptical. They argued the number of boys who had joined was too small to make any major difference.

On the political scene, Prime Minister Churchill had successfully beaten a vote of censure in the House of Commons; General Dwight Eisenhower had recently been named commander of the U.S. forces in Europe, and many residents of McKinley Heights were upset with the latest FBI arrests of purported members of the Nazi Party. They feared the next step would be the arrest, or internment, of first generation German Americans. If so, it would endanger many from McKinley Heights and the surrounding communities. The older evacuees, who could still recall details of English politics, were surprised by all this questioning of legal authority. It seemed Americans were quicker to mistrust their government officials and less enthusiastic about the operation of the government agencies than they recalled their English parents and friends had been. They wondered if it had anything to do with the difference between representative versus parliamentary forms of government but were not interested enough to pursue it further.

After the afternoon swim, Graham and Ann went for a stroll. Graham talked almost continuously about Meg, how wonderful she was and how much he loved her. It upset Ann. She thought Graham was wrong to think of Meg in any way other than as a sister. She thought it incestuous to think of her in the manner he had implied. She begged him to stop. He said he couldn't. He told her they had fallen in love and there was nothing either Meg or he could do about it. He argued there was nothing wrong with how they felt. "We are not biologically related," he said. "And besides," he added, "we're only kissing. It isn't as if we were going all the way."

Ann's face reddened. She had been on the farm long enough to know what Graham meant. Being a farmer or not, she did not feel comfortable talking about that sort of thing with a boy–even if it was her brother. She tried to change the subject, "You're English, Graham. We've been sent over here to represent England. To act as ambassadors, as Mr. Shakespeare told us before we left. As Englishmen we must stay faithful to England. Excessive fraternization will demean our nationalism. Falling in love with an American is wrong, Graham. It's just plain wrong!"

Graham was about to answer when Fred came running down the path. "Have you heard the news?" he asked, nearly out of breath. "Captain Ben has just arrived in camp. He says Sandy woke up this morning. She was awake long enough to recognize Mrs. Maurer. Although she fell back asleep, the doctors say she apparently is out of the coma. Her recovery, hopefully, has once again begun.

"You should see Captain Ben. He's beside himself. I've never seen him so happy or excited. Everyone in camp is celebrating. Come on back and join in the excitement."

MCKINLEY HEIGHTS OHIO USA 12 JULY 1942 1348 HRS

MR AND MRS HAROLD MEYERS
265 RATHBURNE ROAD
UXBRIDGE MIDDLESEX ENGLAND

YOUR LITTLE GIRL IS AWAKE STOP SHE WOKE UP AT 1203 TODAY RECOGNIZED LUCY MAURER AND WENT BACK TO SLEEP STOP DOCTORS ASSURE US SHE IS NOW ON ROAD BACK TO HEALTH STOP BUT WARN THAT WE MUST NOT EXPECT COMPLETE RECOVERY IMMEDIATELY STOP THEY SAY IT WILL BE A SLOW PROCESS BUT IT WILL HAPPEN EVENTUALLY STOP EVERYONE HERE OVERJOYED STOP

WALTER T BENDER

Although no one could see them since the blackout curtains were drawn, the lights in the Meyers house on Rathburne Road stayed on late into the night. Harold and Jessica could not sleep. They talked about their daughter. They recalled many fond memories of her and speculated on how long it would be until she returned to school, how long until she returned to England and how happy they would be when they met her at the train station.

But most important of all, they basked in the knowledge that their little girl was going to get well!

Chapter 82

Monday, 10 August 1942

Edith was wiping the top of the ice cream chest when Stewart entered the Star Diner. She had only one hour left before the end of her shift. Although she enjoyed working at the diner, especially when some of the gang from school came in, she was eager to go home this particular afternoon. Brad was arriving on leave. He had wired Clara last Friday, said he would complete basic training on Saturday and, beginning Sunday, would be on leave for ten days. He planned to leave camp by bus, catch the overnight train, and arrive in McKinley Heights sometime late today. She wanted to be there when he arrived.

Edith missed Brad. She had written letters to him regularly. Surprisingly, his only replies were a few brief, impersonal notes enclosed with his letters to Clara. It was very disappointing. She knew he was busy, with training and everything but, after all, she was now his foster daughter. It wouldn't have seemed quite as bad had she been able to read the letters he sent Clara but Clara refused to share them, said they were intended only for her eyes. There were only a few occasions when Clara related something Brad had written. Edith understood her desire for privacy but didn't think seeing parts of a letter–those parts that were not intimate–would cause any harm. However, she hadn't complained or said anything. She knew better than to argue with Clara these days.

Things had changed radically since Brad had gone into the Army. Clara had become extremely demanding. It was one of the major reasons Edith was now working at the diner. Clara had insisted Edith find summer employment, "To help support the two of us," she said. Her wage was only thirty-five cents an hour. With a weekly schedule of twenty hours, she earned seven dollars a week. Clara took six dollars of it to pay for part of the groceries. But it still was a pretty good arrangement, the remaining dollar was more spending money than Edith had ever had. She spent it mostly on magazines and movies.

Edith didn't mind working. As a matter of fact, she enjoyed it. It gave her an opportunity to visit with her school friends and eat all the food she wanted. Food was a great perquisite. Since she started two weeks ago, she had talked to almost everyone and had more Cokes, sodas, and candy bars than she had ever dreamed possible. The only cost to her was a noticeable increase in weight, which was beginning to worry her. "I hear Sandy is up and around now," Stewart said, as he sipped on a cherry-flavored Coca-Cola. "She spent yesterday afternoon sitting on the Maurers' front porch. Steve told me he stopped by and chatted with her for quite a while. He told me she's looking chipper and is eager to get out and about. She hopes the walks she is scheduled to begin within a few days will help speed her recovery."

"That's good to hear," Edith replied. "I imagine she is tired of all the weeks of confinement."

"Indeed she is. She hopes to be back in school soon after it starts in September. If she continues to make as much progress as she has lately, the doctor told her she should be able to do almost everything by mid September–except ride horses. She told Steve she didn't mind that restriction; she's not too keen on riding just yet."

"I would imagine not. It must be difficult getting back on a horse after the fall she took. She must feel awfully lucky though. She could have been killed–or at least paralyzed."

"Lucky? She certainly must," Stewart agreed.

As Edith walked up the sidewalk, she looked at the flag hanging in the window of her house. The blue star stood out on the white background with the red border. Edith was proud of that star. Flags like that were now beginning to appear in many McKinley Heights windows. They indicated someone from the house was serving in one of the military branches. In a few homes, several flags hung side by side, and in others, the flags sported multiple stars. Brad's star had been there for only a few days. She was glad Clara finally had bought it. She had worried it wouldn't be there when Brad came home. She had even once asked Clara if she could buy one herself, but like everything else these days, Clara did not want anyone doing anything for Brad but her.

Edith found Clara in a frenzy. She had started to clean the living room; the vacuum cleaner was in the middle of the floor. She had started to bake a cake; the mixing bowl was on the counter with the cake half mixed. Flour covered most of the counter and some was spilled on the floor. She had decided to take a bath and wash her hair; she was in her bathrobe, her hair wrapped in a towel. She was on the telephone talking to the ticket agent at the railway station trying to determine when

Brad's train would arrive. The agent could not give her a firm time, all the trains were running late. "What kind of a railway are you running?" she screamed into the phone and hung up. She did not seem to notice Edith.

"Hi, Clara." Edith said, trying to sound happy.

"Where have you been?" demanded Clara. "You should have been home hours ago."

"It's only four-fifteen," Edith answered. "I didn't get off work until four and I had to pick up your dress at the dry cleaners."

"Give it to me!" demanded Clara. "I need to get dressed. Brad will be here any minute now."

"What can I do to help?" Edith asked.

Clara ignored Edith and rushed into her bedroom. While Clara was dressing Edith finished vacuuming the living room, put away the sweeper, wiped the counter, and swept the kitchen floor. She was studying the recipe for the cake when Clara came back into the kitchen. "Is this the cake you were going to bake?" Edith asked, pointing to the recipe book.

Clara, realizing she had been in one of her foul moods, replied apologetically, "Yes, it's his favorite. I think I should keep my dress neat in case we hear from him. Would you mind helping? We can bake it together." Then she added, "Thanks for cleaning everything. You've been a big help. Forgive me for the horrible way I've been acting lately. I know I've been difficult to live with; I suppose it's because I miss him so much!" She began to cry.

Edith ignored the tears. Instead, she studied the recipe and, in a deliberate manner, began adding the remaining ingredients. Once Clara stopped crying, she helped. Soon the cake was in the oven. "I suppose it would be silly to go to the train station until we've heard from him," Clara mused. "The agent was uncertain how late the train would be. He said the war had completely disrupted all the schedules–too many people, too many high priority freight trains, and too few operators and engineers left to run the railway."

With nothing to do but wait, Clara decided to turn on the radio for the five o'clock news. It had just begun. The announcer was telling about the battle raging at Guadalcanal. He said U.S. Marines had landed on Friday. Everyone in Washington was excited. After so many months of Allied withdrawals and defeats, an offensive operation had finally been launched in the Pacific. "Maybe it will partially make up for the losses suffered in New Guinea in July and during the Japanese advance toward Port Moresby," the commentator speculated. "Everyone," he noted, "hopes the Guadalcanal campaign will signal the end of Japanese aggression and curtail the threat of an invasion of Australia."

"Unfortunately," he continued, "although Guadalcanal has all the earmarks of bringing about the turnaround everyone has been hoping for, extremely heavy naval losses in the Solomon's on Saturday have already placed that dream in jeopardy."

The commentator turned next to the European theater where the situation was still looking bleak. Russia was being forced back by the Germans and Rommel was winning additional fights in North Africa.

Clara turned off the radio. She did not want to think about the war anymore. Things were bad in both Europe and the Pacific. It didn't seem to matter where they sent Brad, he would be in real danger in either theater. Her only hope was that Brad might be assigned to a duty station in the U.S. She knew it was a lot to hope for; they had been sending most of the draftees overseas recently.

Edith was playing with Spot when the telephone rang. It was Brad. He had arrived at the McKinley Heights station. Clara grabbed her purse and was out the door almost before she had the receiver back on its hook. Edith wanted to go with her, but Clara said it would be too con-fusing–she wanted to greet Brad by herself. As she climbed into the car, she shouted to Edith, "Call Ida Schaefer. See if you can stay with Ann tonight. Ask them to pick you up. Don't wait for us, we might stop at a restaurant on the way home. If the Schaefers get here before we do don't worry, we'll know where you went."

Clara had never said anything about not going to the station before. The order stunned Edith. She had expected to go with her to the station. She had thought she would be there with her to greet Brad. She had even put on one of her prettier dresses. But now Clara was sending her away. It wasn't fair. But she had no choice, she had to follow Clara's wishes–or suffer Clara's terrible wrath. She made the telephone call. The Schaefers said they would be happy to have her stay overnight.

What Clara had not counted on was Ned coming alone to get Edith. Because of unfinished barn work, Ann did not come with him. It might have been Clara's strong opposition to Ned, or perhaps because of Edith's disappointment in not being home to greet Brad, whatever the reason, Edith climbed in beside Ned, hugged him tightly, kissed him passionately, and began to cry. "What's wrong?" Ned asked.

"I love you," she said simply. "Please hold me tight."

Ned was taken aback by her actions. The car was in the Holtzmans' driveway, in plain sight of the neighbors. He was aware of Clara's feel-ings about the two of them, he worried what she would do if someone saw them kissing. He politely, though reluctantly, withdrew from Edith, "I love you too, Edith, but we shouldn't be doing this here. The neighbors will see us. They'll tell Mrs. Holtzman."

"I don't care! What difference will it make? She hates me anyway."

"Do you mind if we talk about it later?" he asked, pulling free and starting the engine.

It was not until they reached the farm and were parked in the driveway that Edith finally answered him. They remained in the car for a long time. No one bothered them. Ann had heard their car come up the lane but had not mentioned it to either Jack or Ida. Instead, she suggested a game of Chinese checkers which occupied everyone until Ned and Edith finally came in.

So many people filled the train station, waiting to catch trains or waiting to meet someone, that Clara did not see Brad at first. When she did, she ran to him, her arms outstretched; he looked so handsome in his uniform. They kissed for several minutes while some of the onlookers smiled at the happy reunion, anticipating a similar greeting when the next train arrived. Others had tears in their eyes, recalling the sad good-bye they had just been through.

Clara and Brad did not go to the restaurant–that had only been a ruse thought up at the last moment by Clara. Instead they headed quickly towards home. On the way, Brad talked about the overcrowded trains, the difficulty in getting a ticket and finding a seat, and about the rigors of basic training. He complained about the "grub," as he called it, and called his first sergeant a name Clara would not repeat, even if she had been listening. She hadn't heard much of what he had said, being too busy looking at him and thinking how much she loved him.

When they entered the house, Spot greeted them enthusiastically. They barely noticed. Brad grabbed Clara and they embraced once again, but this time, with even greater passion than at the train station.

Much later Clara took the cake from the cake saver. "You must be hungry," she said.

"I hadn't noticed," he replied.

The following morning Clara and Brad drove to the Schaefer farm. When Edith saw the car turn in the driveway, she rushed out the door and was down the path and at the car door almost before anyone realized the car was coming. Brad's greeting disappointed Edith. He was much more reserved, much more formal than she had expected. Not at all as she had imagined. To make matters worse, his feeble, but cherished, greeting was rudely interrupted by the greetings and handshakes of the Schaefer family. When she left for her shift at the diner that afternoon, she still had not given him, what she considered to be, a proper welcome home.

She was still feeling her disappointment on the eighteenth when Brad left on the five o'clock train departing for Pittsburgh. By then, the Germans had arrived at the gates of Stalingrad; the First Marine Division was left stranded on the shores at Guadalcanal, and Churchill had formulated new war plans with Roosevelt in Washington and with Stalin in Moscow. As a result, the Army scheduled Brad to ship overseas immediately after completion of advanced infantry training. Everyone wondered if they would ever see him in McKinley Heights again.

Chapter 83

Thursday, 3 September 1942

Among the many letters that arrived in Ohio on Thursday were three addressed to evacuees. One was opened almost immediately, its content eagerly anticipated. The other two were less enthusiastically received and remained unopened for more than a day.

Victoria handed Fred his letter as he sat down at the dinner table. He could barely contain himself while Tom said the blessing and the food was being served. He had not received a letter from home for over a month and was eager to learn how his parents were and all that had been happening. When Victoria said he needn't wait–gave him permission to open it at the table–he was greatly relieved.

Graham was helping Ken paint the house when the postman delivered his letter. His hands had too much paint on them to read it immediately, and he was too tired after they finished. The letter remained on his bureau, nearly forgotten, until the following evening.

When Edith came home from the diner, she hadn't had time to open her letter. Clara was in another of her moods and had started nagging the minute Edith walked in the door. By the time Edith had cleaned the house, fixed supper, washed the dishes, and had finished arguing with Clara, she was too exhausted to read her letter. She placed it in the drawer of her nightstand next to her bed. It remained there, unread, until Friday night.

*   *   *

"Why don't you read it to us?" Victoria asked, smiling at Fred.

Fred was now a full member of the Derringer family. He ate all his meals in the dining room with Tom and Victoria; often sat with them in the parlor at night listening to the radio, playing chess, or simply talking; used Tom's den to study and write letters; and had his own bedroom on the second floor. They took him with them to concerts and plays, showed great interest in his schooling, attended many of his games last year and looked forward to season tickets this fall. He no longer had specific household chores, instead helped out only if it suited him. His life had certainly improved since he first arrived.

He had to admit, however, there were times when he missed the less formal life in the basement with Sarah. She had not insisted he wash as carefully and dress in spotlessly clean clothes before sitting down to a meal; it had been perfectly acceptable to quickly wash and come to the table with whatever he had on, soiled or not. She did not scold him if he was late getting home and said nothing when he stayed up late listening to the radio, reading, or building model airplanes.

But it was nice to be part of a family again, to share what he had done each day; to discuss his ideas, dreams, and ambitions, and to seek advice and counsel. Most importantly, it felt as if he had a real mum and dad again, even if they weren't as loving as his own parents had been. That was the only thing that bothered him, he often wished they would give him a hug–not be so formal. But he wasn't complaining, the interest Tom showed in his sports and the concern Victoria had for his schooling more than made up for the absence of overt affection.

"Mum says Dad is working ever so hard these days; apparently due to the tremendous increase in production at Bender Electric this past year," Fred observed after reading for a brief moment. Quoting directly from the letter, he continued, *"In spite of the production increase there have been no additions to the shipping and receiving department staff in over a year. There is such a shortage of workers in England now that it is difficult to hire anyone. To staff all the hard-to-fill positions, they have started requiring all young women to either enter the military service or work in some form of civilian activity. One common practice is to place them in the Women's Land Army, or WLA for short. These poor souls are sent off to work on farms, in the offices at the mines, or other similar places, and must do all sorts of menial tasks. An article in the paper last week indicated their beginning weekly wage is only eighteen shillings. I can't imagine being required to live such a long way from home and do work of that sort for so little pay. Of course they are provided food and lodging."*

"That's not much of a wage. A little less than four dollars a week," Tom guessed. "Then again, that seems reasonable when you consider our GIs earn twenty-one dollars a month as buck privates."

"We had quite a scare here in late July when Tobruk surrendered," Fred continued to read. *"The House of Commons became quite concerned about Prime Minister Churchill's performance and voted to censure him. Fortunately, it was overwhelmingly defeated. Churchill has been such an inspirational leader. It is Dad's and my feeling that England could not get along without him.*

"Can you imagine? Here we are in a war affecting almost the entire world and Mahatma Gandhi is making all that fuss in India. We can understand why India wants her independence, but it's a poor time to take up the cause–while a nation is under threat of attack. Then, I guess the same sort of thing is going on in Northern Ireland, too.

"We are beginning to hear reports about the Japanese and their horrible treatment of our boys held prisoner of war. It must be terrible for our boys. Such barbarianism. I can't imagine why any nation would act in such an inhumane manner.

"The world is a strange place these days. There's so much death, hate, and chaos everywhere. And compounding it: our dear child is far away–across the sea, in America. At least you have a lovely place to stay, we're thankful for that. Dr. and Mrs. Derringer sound like such fine people. You are certainly a lucky lad."

Tom blushed slightly as Fred read this last paragraph. Victoria smiled, certain Fred's mother was correct in her assessment of Tom and her. She wished the members of her club could hear this; but, try as she would, she could not think of any way to share it without being thought of as a braggart.

"We were pleased you enclosed the picture in your last letter (June 10). My, what a handsome young man you are. You must be driving all the young girls mad with your good looks. I know you would affect me that way if I were a young girl! Dad and I agree that we would not have recognized you had we met you on the street. It's been so long since we saw you. You've grown so much."

Fred blushed at his mum's statement. It embarrassed him to read aloud about what a handsome young man he was–even though it probably was true. He was also worried, for he too, would have difficulty recognizing his parents. The truth was, he could no longer remember how they looked. It had been such a long time since he had seen them.

Graham had just gotten into bed when he recalled Diane's letter. He turned on his bed lamp and opened it. It started with a reprimand.

You naughty boy. We have not received a letter from you for nearly a month! Is everything all right? We assume so since Ann said nothing in any of her letters to suggest otherwise. However, she doesn't write as often either. I guess the two of you have been away from home so long you have begun to forget your dear old mum and dad.

Please be careful! It's such a terrible tragedy, what happened to Sandy. As we understand it, she is now on the road to recovery, although the word at the factory is that she has a long way to go before she can return to school. The poor child! We hope by the time you receive this, she will be much, much better. Please tell her we send our love and best wishes for a speedy and permanent recovery.

You will be surprised to learn we have been entertaining some American boys in our home here in Pinnington. Yvonne met a Yank several weeks ago and brought him, along with one of his chums, home for dinner one evening. They are officers attached to the RAF who, I suppose it is permissible to say, are part of an advanced contingent of an American Air Force unit planning to fly out of Britain shortly. (Graham found this paragraph particularly interesting. In mid August, an article in the newspaper described a B-17 bomber group stationed in England. They were reportedly planning daylight bombing raids over Europe.)

Truthfully, we were not too keen on the visit when Yvonne first suggested it. We are still having difficulty controlling her and worry about the trouble she might get into next. Having Americans dating her was particularly worrisome. There is already growing resentment amongst many of the town folk towards the Americans. They act so cocky and sure of themselves. There's a humorous saying popular here now. It goes: "The Yanks are over paid, over sexed, and over here." Apparently, the government has decided to treat Americans differently than our own British boys. If it's true, it will only make feelings worse. The House of Commons just passed a bill declaring U.S. servicemen subject only to American law–not British law. It has caused grave concern.

Anyway, it turns out these guests are quite nice chaps. In fact, we have become rather fond of them and have invited them back several times since. Although we have repeatedly begged them not to, they always bring a gift–usually some sort of foodstuff not available in the shops but available in the American post exchange, or, as they say, PX. We had our first sweets in ages last week, thanks to our American boys.

The strange thing is now that Dad and I have gotten to know, and like, these chaps, Yvonne has lost interest in them. Lately, she always manages to be gone during their visits. Your sister has become a real rebel. We are not certain what will become of her. But enough about her!

Your school work really pleases us. Ann and you are both making us quite proud. My goodness, the two of you will be coming back with such good schooling you will probably be reluctant to speak to two old ignorant sods like us. We are happy for you and hope you keep at your studies. We both agree you should forget that nonsense about wanting to return before the war ends. We much prefer you to better yourselves while you have the opportunity. Once you come back to England there will be nothing but work for a long time to come. There has been so much damage and destruction. It will take the country years and years before it will be looking as beautiful and picturesque as it once did.

Diane ended her letter with a row of X's and O's and repeated over and over that she loved Graham. It made him cry. He promised himself he would write more often, even though it was increasingly more diffi-cult to find anything interesting to say. His parents were beginning to feel more and more like strangers. Ken and Louise seemed more like his true parents now. The thought was difficult to accept, but there was an awful lot of truth in it. He tried to think of more positive things about home, but he couldn't. He remained awake a long time before falling asleep. He dreamed of a prince who had been expelled from his castle.

"Well, Spot," Edith said as she rubbed him between his ears. "it's time we open Mum's letter and see what she has to tell us." Spot nuz-zled her, as if to offer his support.

Harriet told Edith how much she missed her and pleaded with her to write more often. She asked about her schooling and hoped she was choosing her subjects this autumn with the thought of pursuing advanced studies. "Good old Mum," she thought, "always concerned about my schooling, always thinking of my interest in becoming a chemist. This time however, there was a small, almost imperceptible, change in the way she talked about continued schooling As Edith continued to read she momentarily thought, "It is almost as if there's no longer any doubt I will be able to pursue my dream when I returned to England."

A large part of Harriet's letter described the impact scarcities were having on life in Britain, particularly the recent rationing of chocolates and sweets, and how thankful everyone was that the bombing raids had not resumed over Ealing.

She talked about her work and ended with a second plea that Edith write more often.

As Edith and Spot romped on the bed, she suddenly realized there had been no mention of her dad. Harriet never had much to say about him but this time there was absolutely nothing. Edith wondered if the omission had any significance, then dismissed it when Clara stuck her head in the door and demanded she play more quietly. Clara had been nauseated most of the day and was going to bed early. She told Edith if she was not up in the morning to call her supervisor and tell him she was sick and would not be in. Edith reminded Ida that she had already received a reprimand for taking too many days off, especially while Brad was home. Clara paid no attention to the scolding. "Don't argue. When I'm sick, I'm sick," she insisted. "I can't reschedule my illnesses, simply to please my boss."

"But you can quit complaining so much," Edith said, under her breath. "Everyone knows you are faking most of the time. They're going to sack you if you aren't careful. Then where will you be? As you've said yourself, Brad's pay is not sufficient to support you. How do you think you would live? You're such a baby." But she shared none of this with Clara. Instead, she answered in as sweet a voice as she could muster, "Get yourself a good night's rest. Maybe you'll feel better in the morning."

But Clara did not feel better. Edith could hear her retching long before it was time to get up.

Chapter 84

Saturday, 12 September 1942

"I hate you, you damn Americans," Yvonne cursed, as she took another large gulp of her pint of bitters.

She was sitting at a dirty table in a dimly lit, smoke filled room located in a dockside cabaret in London's East End. A bomb crater outside partially blocked the entrance and boards covered the broken glass panes in the two front windows. The proprietor had made only a token effort to clean the room; he preferred to do as little as possible, so long as the customers kept coming. Portions of the ceiling hung down and dust-covered rubble lay piled in one corner. An out-of-tune piano and a tinny sounding saxophone accompanied a middle-aged, throaty voiced singer. She wore excessive makeup and a soiled, gaudy costume and tried to imitate Vera Lynn's rendition of *We'll Meet Again*. No one paid any attention to the condition of the cabaret or her failed emulation; they had only two interests: drinking and women.

Tex looked at Yvonne, "You really think you can insult me,

sweetie?" he drawled in an accent that Yvonne found difficult to understand. "Honey, I don't care what you say, just as long as you promise to take care of my needs properly. You do know what I mean, don't you?" He paused a moment, then added, "No, you're too drunk to know if you can please me or not."

Yvonne pushed the remains of the cigarette she was smoking into a puddle of beer on the bare table. It sizzled as it went out. "Don't tell me what I know. I know I can please a stupid sailor like you." She looked at him in disgust, yanked the cigarette from his mouth and used it to light herself another. She threw his cigarette on the table and turned her head towards the singer. "I hate sailors. I hate Germans. I hate Russians. I hate my dad. I hate my mum. I hate the whole bloody world," she screamed, tears running down her cheeks.

Tex grabbed her by the throat and swung her head around until she faced him. "Pick up that fag, you dumb-assed broad. Pick it up before I blacken your two eyes." His grip on her throat made Yvonne gasp for air.

Yvonne realized he was serious. He had a look of rage that frightened her; she had never seen a man look quite like that before. She struggled to pick up the discarded cigarette. Just as the tip of her fingers touched the cigarette, she felt the force of his fist crushing her hand against the table. She was almost certain he had broken it. As she pulled her throbbing hand away, she saw his other fist coming directly at her face. There was a sudden flash of light and then blackness.

When she awoke she could feel dampness on her face. She tried to wipe it off. It was blood. The singer was singing a different song now, a peppy tune–something Yvonne thought she knew–but the words sounded distorted. She could not decide what the name of it was, she was too confused. She saw Tex still sitting in the chair next to her. He laughed as he playfully jabbed his finger into the side of one of his sailor buddies and said something that made everyone laugh. He paid no attention to her. As she lay there, the cobwebs of her mind slowly receding, she began to remember who she was, where she was, and how she got there.

She had come home from her night shift on Wednesday morning. Diane and Chad had already left for work. That was not always what she did, sometimes she went directly to the local pub, or to the house of one of her friends where she often stayed until time for her next shift. On this particular day; she felt tired and went straight home. She was about to get into bed when she heard the postman drop mail in the postbox. She had almost ignored it but changed her mind. She wished now she had.

One of the items was a letter from the Ministry of Labour. They had accepted her application to the Women's Land Army. She was to report no later than 1600 hours on Wednesday, the 16th of September. She was heartsick. She had sent in her application, mostly out of spite, after one of her frequent fights with her parents. She had never actually meant to go through with it; had only wanted to upset Chad and Diane. She had planned to secretly withdraw it the next day, on the basis of her work at Rolls, but, somehow, she had neglected to follow through. Now it was too late. They had accepted her, and there was no easy way to withdraw from one of these government programs once you were in them. On the other hand, she was tired of her boring assignment at the factory and did not like her boss. Maybe the change would actually turn out to be a welcomed alternative. It depended on where she was assigned–but who could tell what godforsaken place that would be.

She was too upset to sleep after reading the letter; she needed something to settle her nerves and decided to go to the *Boar and Whistle* for a pint. She grabbed her coat and bolted out of the door, not bothering to fasten it securely, the letter left lying on the floor.

That evening she had met the RAF flight lieutenant as she sat brooding in the *Fox and Hounds*. He had noticed her sitting alone, offered to buy her a drink, described his home town in Yorkshire, and related some of his wartime adventures, often embellishing them with witty remarks. He seemed to be a pleasant enough chap. She was delighted to accept his offer to take her to his flat. It was a wild and exciting night. On Thursday, they picnicked along the Thames. In her happiness, she had nearly forgot her WLA obligation. That night they bought scotch whiskey and returned to the flat. She could only recall the earlier part of the evening clearly, everything else remained hazy until Saturday morning. She had a vague recollection of a fight, but could not make much sense of the little she could remember. What she knew for certain was how awful she felt and how terrible she looked on Saturday morning. Her hair was matted, her dress was torn, her coat was missing, and she had unexplained bruises on her thighs and back.

It was shortly before noon when she met Tex. She was almost immediately attracted to him. He had a good sense of humor, offered to buy her some food and drinks, seemed genuinely concerned about her well-being, and offered to help her cure her hangover. They had gone to quite a few pubs and cabarets before ending up in this trashy hole. Now Tex had turned on her just like the–what was his name?–flight lieutenant. She realized she hadn't even bothered to ask the lieutenant what his name was.

*   *   *

As her mind came into sharper focus, she decided she had had enough and was ready to leave–to go home to her mum and dad. She started to get up. Tex grabbed her and pulled her down. "Where do you think you're going, bitch?" he snarled. "You're not going anywhere–till I tell you it's okay. Sit there until I say you can get up."

Tex meant it. He kept her sitting while he slowly drank himself almost into a stupor. "Come on, honey," he finally mumbled with a thick tongue. "We're going for a little walk and then I'm going for a little ride." He laughed at his use of what, to him, was a clever metaphor.

He took her to a nearby small, roach infested hotel where he spent the night satisfying his pleasures. Yvonne, in great agony, finally, and blessedly, passed out. When she awoke it was early morning, the room was empty. Tex was gone. She tried to wash her face but no water came from the rusty spigot. She tried to tidy her clothes and comb her hair but everything she tried made little difference. Finally, in disgust, she left the room, crept past the sleeping man at the registration desk, and left the hotel. She had no money, a bus ride home was out of the question. She went down to the river and tried to wash her face. It did not improve her appearance. She tried begging. No one gave her even a penny or would have anything to do with her. It was not that she blamed them, the way she looked, had she passed herself on the street, she would not have given anything either. As day turned into night she decided she could not walk home. London remained under a total blackout and, with the rubble still laying in many places, it was too risky, and much too far. She had to go somewhere. Finally, she remembered Dave and Gladys. They lived in the East End, not too far away.

It was nearly ten o'clock Monday morning when she finally dragged herself to the bomb scarred front door of the Haskell flat. "My God!" Gladys exclaimed when she pushed the door open and saw Yvonne. "Is that you, Yvonne?" she asked. "What has happened to you, child?"

Diane and Chad had found the door ajar when they returned on Wednesday evening. It took only a few minutes to piece together why Yvonne had departed in such haste. They worried when she did not return before going to work, but made no attempt to find her; not coming home was not unusual for Yvonne. By Friday morning, they had become truly concerned and had talked to the local constable. The constable had not been helpful. He had many other duties he ranked more urgent and of greater importance. It was not until Monday, when Chad telephoned the Rolls factory and made some additional inquires around the neighborhood, that he finally pieced together part of what had happened. She had gone from home to the local pub where she had a number of drinks while sitting in a corner, brooding over her misfortune. From the pub, she had apparently gone to the factory and had given her notice. The superintendent had tried to determine why she was leaving and had even encouraged her to take back her notice. Instead, she turned and stomped out of his office. Chad could trace her trail no farther; that was until Gladys called.

By the time Diane and Chad arrived, Gladys had, with the help of Fran and Ernie, managed to wash Yvonne, tend to her cuts and bruises, and make her lie down. "She's sleeping now, poor thing. I'm not certain what happened, but she must have gone through a terrible ordeal," Gladys told them. Diane and Chad had different reactions to their daughter's escapade. Diane rushed to Yvonne's bedside, sat on the edge of the bed, gently smoothed her hair, and wept while she watched Yvonne sleep. Chad refused to go into the bedroom and wouldn't talk to Yvonne when Diane and she finally came out. He continued to say nothing throughout the tube and bus trip back to Pinnington.

Although not fully recovered, Yvonne reported for WLA duty on Wednesday afternoon after a tearful good-bye with Diane. Chad, although greatly concerned about his daughter, continued his silent treatment, did not even wish her well the morning she was to report. Instead, he purposely left for work early, long before his usual time and long before Yvonne got up. Diane stayed home. She helped Yvonne pack and waited with her at the bus stop. They had much to say to each other and many apologies to make, so much so that they had not finished before the bus arrived. There was time only for one long passionate embrace and a quick declaration of their love for each other.

The WLA gave Yvonne a choice of assignments. She chose a farm in Cumbria at the standard eighteen shillings per week plus room and board. "It's ironic," she thought, as she boarded the bus for the journey north, "I teased Ann about farm work and here I am headed for the same sort of life. Anyway, I'll be far from the city, and most importantly, from my dad."

16 September 1942

Dear Ann,

My sweet little girl. How I love you. You were always such a good girl when you were here at home. I just know you continue to be obedient and thoughtful, always doing whatever Mr. and Mrs. Schaefer tell you to do, are nice to your little friends, mind your manners, and represent Britain as we told you to do and in a way to make us proud.

How pretty you must be in your new clothes. Mrs. Schaefer tells us you had a splendid time shopping for the Bender picnic. She says you have grown and are becoming quite the pretty young lady. I wish I could see you in your new bathing suit.

Oh, Ann! How I wish you were here with Dad and me. Never mind that things are scarce or that the fear of more air raids over Pinnington still remains. Just having all of us that remain together again would be so wonderful. We would talk and hug–for hours and hours.

Diane could write no more. She was soiling the paper with her tears. She laid down the pen. "There will be time tomorrow. I'll finish it then," she promised herself. She went to the kitchen and began cleaning the cupboard. Work always had a therapeutic effect on her, especially when she became homesick for her children. Now she had all four of them gone: Henry was dead; Ann and Graham were in America; and Yvonne was working somewhere up north, as a Land Army girl.

Diane re-read her letter, crumpled it, and threw it in the wastebasket. She would try again.

17 September 1942

Yvonne is now in the Women's Land Army program. She left yesterday. Dad and I do not know where they will station her. She has promised to write and tell us. Her plan is to ask for a farm assignment, somewhere away from city life, most likely up north somewhere. She says all she wants is some peace, quiet, and solitude for a change. The poor dear was working terribly hard at the factory and is in need of a good rest. I will send you her address once I know it.

I suppose you are laughing at my phrase, "in need of a good rest." "How can she rest on a farm?" you might ask. From what you tell us in your letters farm life can be plenty tiring–all those chores to do, hay to make, etc., etc. However, I wager it's still more restful than working in a factory, and makes for a much healthier and happier person–at least I hope so, for both of your sakes.

Well, it's getting late and I had best get on to other things before bedtime. Please write soon–even if it's only a postcard.

Love,   Mum

P.S. Excuse the smudges. I laid the letter on the washboard and it got a little damp.

* * *

Diane did not think her little smudge fib was too evil. She thought it was justified. She didn't want Ann to know it was made by tears or how terribly homesick she was for Graham and her.

Friday, 18 September 1942

Dear Graham,

Good news! I have just come home from Bender Electric with an answer to your question about returning to England. They say that boys (men) seventeen and over may apply for return to the United Kingdom as long as they have <u>both</u> their parents and their foster parents' consent. If, and when, approval is granted you will be transported back to England by the first available means. You can expect, however, considerable delay. To avoid missing these scarce accommodations, the returnee must be prepared to arrive at the embarkation point within a week–or in some cases less–once a notice is issued. The type of ship used will depend upon availability. It may be a merchant ship in convoy, a naval vessel, a ship of a neutral nation, or maybe even some other way. The cost of transportation is primarily the responsibility of the individual traveler, however, E.J. Newton has said Bender Electric will assume responsibility for all costs.

If you continue to be interested, you are to contact Mr. Stanley Roberts at our McKinley Heights facility. He will make all the arrangements. Of course you have our blessing and our approval to make the trip. The signed approval form is already on file at the factory.

I do, however, want you to understand the risks involved. Our government reports that losses in the Atlantic are presently as heavy as they have ever been so there is a real danger the ship you come back on could be torpedoed and sunk. They assure us all Allied ships used will sail in well protected convoys. If it is a ship flying a neutral flag, it is protected by international treaty, but German U-boats have often violated these protective treaties so a danger still exists.

I have not shared these dire U-boat statistics with your mother since I do not wish to worry her. Please do not pass the information on to either her or Ann. I have also not told her about the last condition on your return. Should you return, you <u>must</u> serve in the British military service as soon as you turn eighteen. This is another point that your mother is not aware of, she thinks there is a good chance that because of your bother you might be able to apply for service in some civilian capacity rather than go into the military. For now we will keep that a secret. Okay?

The decision on whether to return or not is entirely up to you. Mother and I will accept either and will remain proud of you, no matter what your choice is. Nevertheless, I believe, as a father, I owe you a few words of advice. On the down side is the danger you will encounter crossing the Atlantic and the perils you will face in the armed forces. You are, however, an Englishman and have a duty to your country–to serve her as best as you know how. It is you, and lads like you, who will determine the ultimate destiny of our little island. You should feel it both an honor and an obligation to have the opportunity to serve in the military. Although I rue the day we learned of your brother's death, I am still proud of what he did and, if I had it to do over today, I still would advise him to serve. It's what is expected of us all.

On the up side, Mum and I will see you once again. We have missed you, our son, and would love to have you here with us, if only until you leave for the service.

Well, son, it's time to end this letter. I fear I have left you with a terrible dilemma. I am sorry to have relegated such an important decision to you, but feel confident you will do what is best. I shall stand by you, whatever you choose.

Love,

Dad

Chapter 85

Friday, 16 October 1942

"Go Pirates, go!" Ann cheered, as the Dexter Hills football team charged onto the field. "Tromp those Cats!"

No stranger would have known she was English. Her accent was nearly gone. She had a hot dog in one hand and a Coke in the other. She wore a white blouse with long sleeves under a blue sleeveless pullover and a knee-length plaid skirt. White bobby socks and brown and white saddle shoes covered her feet. Her jacket was dark blue with cream colored arms and the letters "DH" embroidered on the back. A soft yellow hat, perched cockily on the back of her head, completed her ensemble. The others in her coterie, including her best friend Bonnie, wore similar outfits.

It was Dexter High's third home game, the most important of the season, against the arch rival Miller City Polecats, but only the first game for Ann this fall. With Jack and Karen working long hours and

Ned involved with after school senior class play rehearsals, most farm chores fell on Ann's shoulders. There was so much to do she normally couldn't finish in time to get to the games. She would have missed again but Bonnie's parents offered to give her a ride and Ida had felt sorry for her and volunteered to finish the remaining chores.

When the team ran on the field, she almost immediately spied Oliver. He was wearing number eighty-eight. He looked much bigger in his uniform and it was difficult to recognize his facial features under the huge helmet, but even so, she thought he was quite handsome. She was delighted that he had decided to play football this fall. He had been somewhat reluctant to try out for the team, even though his arm was now fully recovered. He said it would be better if he worked since he needed to start saving if there was any hope of going on to college. She had argued that he shouldn't be so serious, college was four years away, there was still plenty of time. She thought he was too good at sports. Having fun was more important right now. Her encouragement had been largely responsible for his trying out. "Now here he was, on the varsity and only a freshman," she boasted to herself. Subconsciously, however, she wasn't entirely certain she had given good advice; she knew college was terribly important.

She had not seen much of Oliver during the summer. She was busy on the farm and he was busy with his paper route, mowing lawns, and his other odd jobs. They had gone with the gang to several of the outdoor movies and she had seen him while he picked potatoes on the farm, but they had few opportunities to be alone together–except for the walks along the towpath, an activity they both treasured.

Since school had started, things had been a little better; they managed to sit next to each other in homeroom and English classes. It gave them an opportunity to see each other and talk, but there was hardly enough time to enhance their friendship. As a result, Oliver had been spending increasingly more time with Vicky. "It was just as well," Ann told Graham, "I'm not keen on having a steady this year. I'd rather spend my time concentrating on my studies. Besides," she rationalized, "one of these days I'll be going back to England. It would be awkward to leave a boyfriend here with no chance of ever seeing him again. It would make me feel awful."

Graham had disagreed, he told her he didn't think establishing close friendships with Americans was such a bad idea. If she did fall in love with Oliver someday, or some other American boy, it seemed perfectly all right to him. But he was prejudiced, she knew how he felt about Meg. At least she was being consistent, she didn't approve of his relationship and she didn't want to become involved with Oliver either.

She truly had wanted to study. She had received good grades in eighth grade but still worried she might not be able to do as well in high school. Studying was the best way to ensure success. English, general math, general science, Latin, American politics, chorus, and orchestra seemed a heavy load, at least it had at the beginning of the year–before she had adjusted to the high school routine.

Because she enjoyed orchestra music more than band music she had chosen orchestra this year. Now, as she sat on the bleachers cheering for the team, she wished she had elected band. If she had she would be down on the field, marching with them. More importantly, she also would not have to face the upcoming solo. Mr. Spencer had chosen her to play it at the November concert, and it was creating quite a worry. She didn't think she was good enough for a solo. She thought he really should have waited; he should have given her more time to develop her skills. Two years ago she would never have agreed to play, even if she had been good enough. She had been too much of an outsider back then. But those feelings had pretty much gone away. Lately, she felt she truly had been accepted by her classmates and friends.

There was, however, one remaining small difficulty. At times she wished she lived in town. Living on a farm kept her from participating in many of the after school activities. Not that it was a common problem, it didn't seem to bother the other farm children. Ned and Karen were farmers and they got along okay, but it did make her feel somewhat isolated. Anyway, those old classmate prejudices toward her English origin no longer prevented them from considering her "one of the girls." They liked her now; at least she was pretty certain they did.

She hoped things were going equally well for Sandy. "How lucky I am to be healthy," she thought. "It must be difficult for her. She didn't get back to school until the fifth of this month, much later than expected. The poor girl." Ann wondered how Sandy would make up all the missed work. As she understood it, Sandy had assistance from her classmates and had been able to work on many of the subjects at home while recuperating. "Still," Ann thought, "it must be horrible to miss out on all the school activities. In any event, Sandy's social life must certainly be better than Edith's. Poor Edith. Ever since Mrs. Holtzman realized she was pregnant, Edith hadn't had a very nice life. She insisted Edith spend all her free time at home, helping out around the house. I wonder if she'll even let Edith attend the Bender Thanksgiving party next month?"

Just then the coach substituted Oliver, his first opportunity to play against Miller City. It was the last few minutes of the first half and Dexter Hills was trailing seven to twelve. For several plays the Pirates failed to move the football. On third down, the quarterback was about to be tackled behind the line of scrimmage when he spied Oliver down field. In a desperate last minute effort, he tossed the football in Oliver's direction. Oliver had to stretch and even so it nearly slipped through his fingers. Somehow he managed to hold on, to keep his balance, and to begin running down field. Evading the defensive back, he lunged toward the goal line. "He's in!" Ann screamed. "He's scored a touchdown!" The crowd roared while Ann and Bonnie hugged each other and squealed with delight. The scoreboard changed to Pirates - 13, Cats - 12. The kicker missed the extra point. There was no more scoring for the remainder of the game. Oliver had scored the winning point.

After the game, everyone met at the malt shop. Oliver, the star of the moment, received many congratulations. Some of the senior team members, fearing he might become too arrogant from all the attention, began to tease. They reminded him of the passes he had dropped during practice. They said if he continued to show improvement the coach might consider substituting him again sometime, but he shouldn't count on it. They would no longer give him a free ride during practice. They promised to tackle him much harder from now on. They laughed and said that if he ever got better they might, someday, even consider including him in one of their weekend trips to the McKinley Heights burlesque show. They supposed he was old enough to see Rosie wiggle her ass and shake her tits. Oliver knew Ann was listening and blushed. It was not the sort of thing he thought she should hear; she was too nice a girl.

Soon afterwards, someone put a nickel in the jukebox and they started to dance. Oliver danced first with Vicky, then with Bonnie, and finally with Ann. While dancing with Ann, he asked her if she wanted to double-date. They would be going to a movie on Sunday afternoon with one of the senior boys who had a car. She was thrilled. It would be her first formal date. "I would love to go, but I must ask Aunt Ida first. May I call you tomorrow?"

"I had better call you," Oliver warned. "My dad might answer the phone. Depending on his mood he might say something nasty or, worse yet, not tell me you called. You never know what he'll do." It made Ann sad to think how terrible it must be for Oliver, living with such an inconsiderate parent.

As soon as she arrived home, she told Ida about the winning touchdown, the party at the malt shop, and her date with Oliver. "We're going to see *In Which We Serve*. I've especially wanted to see that one. Noel Coward wrote, directed, and is playing in it. Did you know he's from England?"

Ida frowned, "You're still so young, honey. There's plenty of time to date. I think it best if you tell Oliver you can't go."

"But, Aunt Ida," Ann protested. "Oliver is a nice boy. We see each other in class every day. What's the harm in going to a movie with him on a Sunday afternoon?"

"There's no telling where the boys might take you afterwards, Ann. I just don't think being alone with a boy, in an auto, is a proper thing for a fourteen year old girl. Besides we don't know who the other fellow is. He might be one of those reckless hooligans we see racing around."

Ann seldom argued or talked back to Ida. This time, however, she did. "That's unreasonable! It's not fair. I don't see what could possibly happen."

"That's just it. You're so naive. My gracious, child, you've so much to learn. Call me old fashioned, if you must, but I just can't see you going on a date in a car until you're older."

"But you let Ned go out with Edith, and Edith is no older than me."

"That's different. We know Ned. Besides, those weren't double-dates. You always went along as a chaperon." Ida realized her argument was weak, but it was the best she could offer at the moment. She wanted to be liberal with Ann and give her the same upbringing and privileges she had given her own children, but she couldn't. The trust Diane and Chad had given her compelled her to take extra precautions. She couldn't afford any mistakes with Ann.

"You just don't know what young boys are like, Ann. At that age they sometimes act in bad ways, do things they shouldn't–especially when they're alone with girls."

"I know all about that," Ann continued to protest. "I know what boys do. The girls talk about it all the time at school. I'd never let any-thing like that happen. Besides, Oliver is a nice boy. He would never treat me like that."

"How do you know?"

"I just know."

"I'm sorry. I can't let you go. That's final! If you want to meet them at the theater and have us pick you up afterwards that would be all right, but not a date with two boys and another girl–alone in an auto."

Ann gave Oliver the bad news when he called. She sulked the re-mainder of the weekend, especially when she heard later that Oliver had taken Vicky.

Ida also felt bad all weekend. She knew she was treating Ann dif-ferently than she had Karen, but she kept coming back to her responsi-bility as a foster parent. Perhaps, had she known that many of the other foster mothers with teenage girls were having similar misgivings, it would have eased her mind. She discussed it with Jack. He did not totally agree. "She's a good girl. You need to show her you trust her," he argued. "Give her some freedom so she can prove to you she can act responsibly."

His advice was not what she wanted to hear. Finally, she wrote a letter to Diane asking her opinion. She did not know it but she also was not the first foster mother who had written the same sort of letter.

Chapter 86

Tuesday, 17 November 1942

By mid November, U.S. naval losses in the Pacific had been substantial, especially in the Solomon Islands. In September, the aircraft carrier *U.S.S. Wasp* was torpedoed and sunk; in October, north of Santa Cruz Island, the carrier *Hornet* was bombed, torpedoed, and sunk and the carrier *Enterprise* severely damaged; and during one particularly bad night, November 13, the United States lost five destroyers and two cruisers. But losses to Japan were even greater, and the U.S. Army had been able to relieve the battered Marines on Guadalcanal. Although the battle still raged on at the Canal and the outcome was still very much in doubt, the war in the Pacific had taken an imperceptible turn in favor of the Allies.

In North Africa, major changes were also taking place. By the first of November, Montgomery had Rommel on the run. Tobruk was recaptured on November 12, and by the fifteenth, the victory at El Alamein was celebrated throughout Britain with the ringing of church bells, a practice which previously had been prohibited except to warn of an invasion.

On the eighth of November, Allied forces, in spite of resistance by the French, successfully landed on the west coast of North Africa. Four days later, the Allies were racing across Algeria although encountering increasingly greater German resistance. In England Churchill, speaking of the new Allied offensive in North Africa, uttered what was destined to become one of his classic remarks, *"This is not the end. It is not even the beginning of the end. But it is, perhaps, the end of the beginning."*

In Europe, British RAF and U.S. war planes were now routinely bombing German cities both night and day and Russia–although still under intense pressure from the brutal German assault on its western front–had been bombing Berlin and Danzig since August.

But all was not well. The Germans took Nalchik on the second of November; Malta was still under siege in mid November; German troops marched into unoccupied France on November eleventh, and German U-boats were still inflicting heavy damage on Allied convoys.

All these events, especially the positive ones, should have had an effect on the evacuees, but it went almost unnoticed. The children had become disillusioned with favorable war news, none of which had gotten any of them back to England. The war could have become an abstract and forgotten entity in their lives had it not been for the scrap metal and war bond drives, the friends and acquaintances who were being drafted into the service, the increasingly austere rationing of goods, and, of course, the letters from home. It was only a few who closely followed the progress of the war and worried about the outcome of each event. Graham was one of those who did.

After an inexplicably long time in transit, Chad's letter finally arrived on November 11. With it came the need for Graham to make his final decision. It was something he had to do himself since he had never told anyone about his plans. He wavered for several days; some times determined to return home, other times equally determined to stay in America–at least until he graduated from high school. Then, on the 17th of November he made a decision. The news describing the rapid advance of the Allies through North Africa made him think of Henry buried at Tobruk and raised the patriotism he felt towards England to a new high. He decided he would return home, and once there, he would enlist in the RAF as soon as he could, certainly before they drafted him. All that remained was to ask Mr. Roberts to make the arrangements and, of course, to obtain the Nelsons' approval.

He did not go to school the following morning. Instead, he made the long trip by bicycle to the Bender plant. He had no difficulty getting in to see Stan; Stan had already been alerted from the Pinnington office that he could expect Graham. They discussed at great length the many ramifications of returning to England and were soon joined by Captain Ben. At first, Ben encouraged Graham to wait; however, once Graham convinced him of his sincerity, he somewhat reluctantly consented. Since Graham already had his parents' approval the next step would be to obtain the Nelsons' permission. Once he had that, Stan would arrange transportation. It was to be done as soon as possible. Graham would be notified when a berth was found and was to be prepared to leave on a one day notice. The departure date could be as soon as a few weeks, or as late as several months.

As he pedaled back to Oakton, Graham decided not to include

Louise and Meg in his initial conversation with Ken, they would be too emotional and might scuttle the approval he needed. It was the next evening before he was able to talk with Ken privately. "You can't be serious, Graham!" Ken exclaimed, an incredulous look on his face. "You want to go back to England and join the RAF? You're much too young. You're only a boy. If nothing else, couldn't you wait until you complete high school? Or at least your junior year?"

"No, sir, I can't." Graham answered with a look of firm determination. "Many chaps are joining the service these days. I feel it's my duty, as an English citizen, to enlist just as they have. I want to go, sir. I'm seventeen now. I'll be eighteen next June. I'll enlist then, before I'm drafted. If I leave now, I'll have a few months with my parents before I'm off to the service."

It took Ken a long time to persuade himself he should send his "son" back to England and, most likely, into battle. It wasn't fair; he didn't want to lose Graham. Realistically though, he knew Graham was right. It made perfect sense. Now that he would be old enough, it was natural for him to want to join his fellow countrymen in serving his country. After all, Ken had done the same thing in 1917. But he hated to see this boy go. He had always known the time would come when Graham would leave; he just hadn't thought it would happen so soon, or so suddenly. He wasn't prepared for it. "Frankly, I don't know how Mother will respond," he said. "She still has periods when she mourns the loss of Tommy. If she loses you now–it just might be too much for her."

"I know. I feel truly bad about that, but isn't it what all the boys are doing these days? I know plenty of Oakton boys who have signed up. We've already lost several from the senior class and even some from my class are talking about volunteering. Most of their parents support their decision. If I were your son, wouldn't you feel obliged to let me enlist if I wanted to?"

"Honestly? No. I would insist you complete high school first. I wish you'd reconsider. At least put it off until you graduate."

"That would be a year and a half from now. That's too long. Besides, receiving an American high school diploma will have limited value in Britain. In all probability, if I hadn't come over here I would already have finished my schooling after turning sixteen. Looking at it that way makes graduation seem much less important."

"I firmly believe you're making a mistake, but you're entitled to do what you think best–for both you and your country. Since you already have your parents consent, I don't see how I can say no. I'll talk to Mother and try to convince her. I'll let you know what we decide. In the meantime, I don't think we should tell Meg. It'll just make her un-happy–she thinks so much of you."

"I agree, sir."

Surprisingly, although she was taken aback by Graham's request, Louise did not protest too much. She was determined not to counter-mand Diane's decision. "I know how that poor woman must feel," she empathized. "The poor dear is eager to have her son back–and well she should. But God only knows how I'll ever say good-bye to him. It's going to be awfully difficult, Ken."

"I know, Louise, I feel the same. I love that boy. I really don't know if I'll be able to let him go either."

What Ken and Louise did not know was that Diane had not been told Graham would be required to join the service as soon as he was eight-een. Knowledge of that might have changed the Montgomerys' deci-sion. Diane certainly would have had greater difficulty agreeing to his return had she known.

Now that he had the necessary approvals, Graham found himself even more troubled than before. He had to tell Ann and Meg soon. He decided to do it during the Thanksgiving party. Ann would be there. He would tell them whenever he could get each of them alone.

On the day of the party, Louise fell ill shortly after lunch, and Ken had gone to work. Graham and Meg had to go without them. A notice-able number of the other parents and siblings were missing as well. Many of the women now worked in the defense plants and were either at work or at home trying to catch up on their housework. Some of the men, like Brad, were in the service while others were working overtime.

Clara refused to attend without Brad. She told Edith to either stay home or find some other way to get there. This suited Edith just fine; it gave her an excuse to go with Ned. Ned had just bought an old Essex and they had planned to go to the party by themselves. But at the last minute, Jack was called into work so he had to take Ida and Ann with him.

Edith was quite disappointed when they arrived at her house and she saw they would not be alone. She vented her unhappiness by starting a silly argument with Ned. It involved the differences between the English system of government, with its House of Lords and House of Commons, and the U.S. system, with its Senate and House of Representatives. Edith claimed the gentry should have the major say in governing a na-tion. She thought members of the educated upper class were much better qualified than ordinary citizens to make critical decisions. Ned insisted it was important that all people, no matter what their social, economic, or educational status, should have an equal right to participate in, or at least be represented by, the nation's government. The intensity of the argument amused Ann and Ida. They thought both arguments sounded superficial. Certainly, neither had carefully thought through what they were saying. It almost seemed as if the two were disagreeing more for the sake of making a point than presenting thoughtful comparisons of the two systems. Ann and Ida were careful not to express their own views; they did not want to seem partial towards either side.

There were the usual enthusiastic greetings between the evacuees as each arrived, particularly with Sandy, who received many special hugs. Everyone asked about her recovery and sympathized with the difficulty she was having trying to catch up in her studies. Many offered their help. It did not take long, however, before they began to notice how much more protective of Sandy Kirk and Lucy had become. It made them wonder whether the Maurers weren't overdoing it. "Lucy's acting just like a mother hen," one of them noted. Ann felt sorry for Sandy. If Ida treated her the way Lucy was treating Sandy it would make her feel horribly smothered.

It was not long after they met that Graham took Ann aside and told her of his decision to return home. "I don't see why you should go back now," Ann said. "You're not the only evacuee who is seventeen. I'm almost certain Cindy is seventeen. Why shouldn't she go back, too?"

Without thinking Graham answered, "She isn't needed in the service."

"What do you mean?" Ann asked, alarm showing on her face.

Graham stammered a bit then finally admitted that he planned to enlist once he was home and turned 18–if he didn't he would be conscripted anyway. He said he wanted to be sure he got in the RAF.

Ann was distressed. "Not you, Graham! Isn't it bad enough that Henry had to serve? And had to be killed! Do you want to risk being killed, too? You know how hard it was on Mum when Henry died. She couldn't go through losing another son."

"Don't be silly, Ann. I'm not going to die. Enlisting in the RAF doesn't automatically mean I'll be killed."

"No, not automatically, but the risk is certainly there. Please don't go back. Stay here where it's safe."

"It's too late. I've signed the papers, and Mr. Roberts is already searching for a ship for my return."

Ann gave a shudder and began to cry. "When do you expect to leave?" she asked, a quiver in her voice.

"No one knows. It depends upon when they can find a way to get me home. It could be as soon as a month from now, or as far away as next summer. I'll just have to wait and see." Graham paused, then asked, "You'll be okay staying here by yourself, won't you? I know I promised to look out for you while we were here, but I really must go back—and help out wherever I can."

"Don't worry about me. I'll be okay. I'll miss you and will be looking forward to following you, just as soon as possible, but I'll be okay. What does Mum say about your returning?"

"She's excited and looking forward to it," Graham assured her, then added, "But Mum doesn't know I'm committed to going into the service soon after I get there. Dad only told her I was returning. Please don't tell her. Dad thinks we should keep it from her as long as we can, hopefully until I walk into their front door."

"I'll not tell," she promised, "but, woe be the day when she finds out she has another son in the service."

As secrets have a way of doing, it was not long before the party was abuzz with talk of Graham's return. When the word got to Ben, he decided to announce it during his after-dinner speech. "Ladies and gentlemen," he said. "We have among us tonight a true hero of the United Kingdom. A lad who came to McKinley Heights over two years ago. One who has been an exemplary English representative throughout that entire period. It is with great pleasure that I mention some of Mr. Graham Montgomery's fine accomplishments. He has been an outstanding student, a good citizen, and a valued friend. He has been on the Oakton High honor roll each semester since he arrived, has been an active participant in Oakton athletics; he and Fred Andrews—another of our evacuees—have just received a special commendation from the Oakton city council for their outstanding efforts in the scrap metal, newspaper, and tinfoil collection programs; and his foster parents, Ken and Louise Nelson, report he has always been a fine, industrious, obedient son, a son they love very much." Graham blushed as Ben paused to take a sip of water. Some of the people sitting near his table looked at him and smiled. Others wondered why he had been singled out.

Ben continued, "All of us, who have had the privilege of knowing Graham agree with the Nelsons. It is now my pleasure to announce an additional milestone in his still short life. Graham will be the first of our English guests to return to England. He will leave on the first available ship. Just as soon as we can book passage."

There was a collective gasp. No one had heard that Graham was planning to leave. Some patted him on the back. Others looked at Ann. A murmur arose in the hall as people exchanged surprised comments. "Graham will be eighteen next June," Ben continued, "and feels it important to exercise his responsibility, as a loyal English subject, to contribute to the defense of his country. Because of his intense devotion to duty and to satisfy the final requirement for his return, he plans to join a branch of the military service soon after he lands on English soil. Let me be the first to wish Graham God speed and good luck. May his decision be fruitful for the continued good fortune for him, his family, and his country. Please join me in this wish." There was a thunderous applause and a large crowd gathered around Graham, offering him their own personal congratulations.

Meg was dumbfounded. Graham had said nothing to her about this. "How could he do this to me?" she thought, dejectedly. Why hadn't he confided in her? Hadn't he told her he loved her? He must not have meant it. Didn't he know how terrible she would feel? Why didn't he ask her what she thought before making such an important decision? She sat in her chair, her face ashen. She responded mechanically to the people who congratulated her on her foster brother's decision. What they said barely registered with her.

Meg said little during the remainder of the party. Afterwards, preferring to think about what had happened, she climbed into the car and rested her head on the seat back. She said nothing as Graham backed out of the parking space. "Where are you going?" Meg asked when she noticed he had turned the corner in a direction opposite to the road home.

"We must talk, Meg. We can't talk at home. Fred told me of a place down by Mill Creek that's quiet and remote. Lots of the kids have parked there. I'm going there—unless you object."

Meg knew about parking places; some of the more ornery girls talked about them. She was aware of what often went on at those places. Several of the boys she had dated had tried to talk her into parking. She had always refused, telling them she was not permitted to do that, which, of course, was the truth. Louise had often warned her not to park with boys. It only led to naughty things she had cautioned. This time, however, Meg did not object, she wanted to talk, as much as Graham did.

The place was deserted. It was late and if any others had been there, they had already left; or they had found a warmer place to "neck" on such a chilly night. Because the temperature had fallen throughout the day, it was too cold to remain in the car without the heater. Graham eased the car into an alcove, well out of sight of the main highway, and turned off the ignition but left the heater fan running. In only a few minutes, the windows were steamed and the two had complete privacy.

"Meg, you must understand. I'm English, and have a duty to my country. I know it's difficult for you to comprehend, but all my life I have felt a deep sense of patriotism. It's something I can't explain. I wrote to my parents a long time ago and asked permission to return. A few weeks ago I received their answer, along with instructions on how to proceed. Frankly, Meg, it wasn't an easy decision to make. On one hand, I wanted to return home, on the other, I have a wonderful home here. More importantly, I have you here; and I love you and don't want to leave you–ever. Then, when I heard about the Allies landing in North Africa and their rapid advance through Algeria, I thought about Henry and how his body was lying in a grave in Tobruk, put there by the Germans. I made up my mind right then. I have to go back to England and join one of the services, hopefully the RAF, and strike back at those rotten Nazis. I just have to, Meg. I'm not at all certain why I feel so strongly about this, but I must do it!"

Meg looked at Graham. She could see in his eyes a look she had never seen in the eyes of anyone before. It was a look, she supposed, connected with determination and patriotism. She could not argue against patriotism. "You poor boy," she said. "It's not fair, is it? You've had such a rotten deal, sent away from your parents–from your home–not knowing when, if ever, you could return, losing a brother in this terrible war, and now, feeling compelled to return and fight for your country. It must be horrible how all this must prey on your mind. I guess I understand, Graham. I'm sorry. Please forgive me?"

"Of course I forgive you, Meg. But it's you who should forgive me. It's a terrible thing I've done to you. You must have felt awful, hearing it from Captain Ben instead of from me. I honestly had planned to tell you tonight, Ben just beat me to it. I apologize. I love you so much!" He put his arm out and pulled her close to him.

As the night wore on, a second layer of frost collected on the windows. They had sealed their love with a passion more intense–or so they thought–than any other lovers had ever experienced.

It was late when they came home. "Where have you been?" Louise called from the upstairs bedroom.

"We stopped off at Elizabeth's after the party and talked. Sorry it's so late. We don't know where the time went."

Fortunately, Louise never questioned Elizabeth, or her parents, about Meg's answer.

Chapter 87

Friday, 25 December 1942

Christmas had always been a happy occasion for the Nelsons. It began with the entire family attending the United Congregational church midnight vespers on Christmas Eve. On Christmas they opened their gifts, ate an early brunch, invited a few friends for an afternoon get-together, and finished the day gathered around the fireplace drinking eggnog cocktails and quietly reflecting on their happiness and good fortune. The Christmas of 1942 was different, a pall hung over the celebration. Graham would soon be gone, likely never to return.

To the puzzlement of Ken and Louise, Graham's impending departure seemed to be particularly difficult for Meg. They had expected her to be sad, after all she was losing the equivalent of a brother, but they had not anticipated how extreme her reaction would be. Instead of her normal good nature and optimism, she appeared to have lost much of her sparkle. She hardly ever laughed, usually harbored a sour attitude, and found fault with almost everything. Graham was the only one who seemed capable of bringing her out of the doldrums. When he was around, she was witty and bright; when he wasn't she was morose and discontented.

Ken tried vainly to keep the holiday upbeat. He teased Graham about his recent induction into the secret school fraternity. "I can't understand why they label it secret," he teased. "Everyone knows it exists. We can even tell who the members are simply by reading the list of organizations under each senior's picture in the yearbook."

Graham simply smiled.

"Come on, son, tell us about it. What do they do during the initiation? What goes on in your meetings?" Ken coaxed. Graham, faithful to the solemn oath of secrecy he had taken, steadfastly remained silent and revealed nothing. Both Ken and Louise laughed, pleased to see how loyal and resolved he could be. Meg left the room. She refused to be present if they were going to tease him. She did not like to see him treated so flippantly–not when he would soon be gone. But that wasn't the worst thing they did. What bothered her even more was how they seemed so unconcerned about his leaving.

Of course Louise's laughter was a deception, inwardly she was nearly as heartbroken as Meg. Once again she was losing a son. She considered it terribly unjust. "But nothing these days is just," she reminded herself as she discretely wiped away a tear.

The number of gifts exchanged this year was smaller. Although no one had wittingly restricted their gift giving, the shortages caused by the war and the realization Graham could not take much with him had contributed to the restraint. One of the gifts was a gold locket Graham had given Meg. It had Graham's picture in one side and a snippet of a love sonnet by Elizabeth Barrett Browning written in miniature in the other. Ken had laughed when he tried to read it. "Small print is not meant for old fogies like me. It takes a better pair of eyes than I'll ever have again. Why don't you read it to us, Meg?" he suggested.

Somewhat embarrassed, Meg read it softly, hoping no one would hear and trying desperately to hold back her tears. When she finished, she looked at it lovingly, held it to her breast, and said, "Thank you, Graham, it means a great deal to me. I shall always treasure it and keep it close to my heart. I'll think of you whenever I look at it."

Ken wondered why she was being so sentimental. Little did he realize it represented much more than a simple sonnet, it was Graham's private way of professing his love to her.

Meg's words about holding it close to her heart brought tears to Graham's eyes. "That's odd," Louise thought. "Why should those two act like that? It's only a piece of jewelry. If I know Meg, within a few months it will lay in one of her jewel boxes, forgotten and unused." She looked at the locket, turned to Graham and said, "It looks lovely, dear. What a nice present. I'm sure it will always remind Meg of you." A tear ran down her cheek too.

Meg gave Graham a small vest-pocket Bible. "It's something you can carry with you; something to carry while in the service. Think of me whenever you read it," she said.

More tears formed in Louise's eyes. She thought of Graham in the RAF. "My precious little boy, in an air force uniform, fighting the Germans, or Italians, or ..." She stopped. She would not, could not, think any more about Graham and war. It was too horrible.

Because it was Graham's last Christmas in Oakton, Louise suggested a small, informal afternoon tea for a few of his closest friends. She asked Fred, Edith, and Ann, and, at Meg's suggestion, Betty Lou, Ned, and Oliver. The list was meant to provide everyone with a partner including, of course, Graham paired with her. She did not explain her reasoning to Louise, especially not the part about Graham.

Edith, to the chagrin of Louise, who did not like pets in her house, brought Spot. "I'm sorry, Mrs. Nelson," she said when she arrived. "Mrs. Holtzman was feeling poorly again today and insisted I get him out of the house. There was nothing else I could do with him. But don't you worry, he shouldn't cause any trouble. Honest. He's housebroken and well behaved."

"That's quite all right, dear, don't fret about it. We like pets. I'm sure he will be just fine," Louise lied politely. She turned in time to see Spot poking his nose in the Christmas presents and worried about all the other mischief he could get into. Fearing she might somehow reveal how she really felt about dogs in her house, she quickly changed the subject, "What do you hear from Mr. Holtzman?"

"He completed his advanced training in early November and almost immediately shipped out. Mrs. Holtzman has received only two V-mail letters from him since then. He couldn't say where he was or what he was doing. All we know is that he has a Pacific APO address."

"Oh, the poor boy!" Louise exclaimed. "The Pacific theater means dealing with those barbaric Japanese. I do hope he's never captured. The newspapers are filled with such terrible stories about the way the Japanese treat their prisoners. If only half of what they say is true, it must be horrible."

Louise saw the look of horror on Edith's face and realized she should not have brought up any of those horrible rumors about Japanese atrocities. In an effort to correct her mistake, she added, "But chances are, Mr. Holtzman will never see any combat. There must be many assignments they could give him far removed from the battlefield. More than likely he'll be stationed in a place where he's safe. His skills are much too valuable to send him into combat and have him shot." She realized she was making things worse with every sentence and quickly asked about Clara.

"She's been frightfully sick. The doctor says it's a bad pregnancy and her work at the plant is only aggravating her condition. There is a good possibility she'll have to quit in order to rest," Edith answered, with a concerned look. "It's too bad Mr. Holtzman had to go into the service. If he were home there'd be no question about it, she'd be home right now, taking care of herself and the baby. With Mr. Holtzman gone, the budget is pretty tight. She has to keep working just to make ends meet. Having to feed me is a real drain on her finances too."

"Nonsense! You must be a great help and good company for her. I'm certain Clara doesn't mind the additional expense, with all the help you've been."

"Sometimes I wonder. She's very cross with me most of the time now. She's always complaining that I'm such a bother!" Edith blurted out before she realized what she was doing. Her face reddened.

"I wouldn't worry about the things she says. She isn't feeling well. Heaven only knows, I said some pretty vile things when I was pregnant with Meg and Tommy. I assure you Mr. Nelson had a difficult time with me too. Bad attitudes often go with difficult pregnancies."

Edith did not often find a sympathetic ear these days, she considered talking about her problem further, then decided against it. She looked at Spot, "Perhaps I should take Spot for a walk, Mrs. Nelson." She turned to Ned and asked, "Will you go with me?"

"Have you heard that Captain Ben's son has enlisted in the Navy?" Ned asked as they strolled through the park.

"Why would he do that?" Edith wondered. "It's so unfair to Captain Ben. Why would his son want to join now? Captain Ben must have enough influence to keep him out of the Army."

"It's his son's duty to volunteer," Ned scolded. "It's something most of us want to do."

"What do you mean, 'most of us want to do'?" Edith asked, a quizzical look on her face.

"The fellows in my class have been talking. Most of us believe–like Graham–we have a sacred duty to perform, a duty to fight for our country. Some will be joining right away, others plan to wait until they graduate."

"And what are you going to do?" Edith asked, defiantly.

"I'm going to wait until after graduation. I plan to enlist in June."

"Oh, no! Please don't!" she begged. "Don't volunteer. Let others go into the service. Stay here. At home, with me. You could, you know. Remember, you work on the farm. You should qualify for a farm deferment, especially since you are an only son."

"But I want to go. If Mr. Holtzman and Graham can serve, I should be willing to do my duty as well."

"To the devil with your duty," she said bitterly. "I want you here. You're the best friend I have. I need you. You say you love me. You wouldn't enlist if you truly meant it."

"You can't be serious! You mean to tell me that I should put my personal concerns ahead of those of my country?" he asked, loosely quoting what he had heard William Bendix say last weekend in a movie.

When the two returned, Ann could tell they had been quarreling. Edith was noticeably quiet and Ned spent most of his time talking and joking with the boys, an unusual thing for him whenever Edith was nearby. She felt she should do something but had no idea what. She'd ask Ned what had happened on the way home. Maybe then she could figure something out.

It was different with Ann and Oliver. They were nearly inseparable the entire afternoon. They teased each other, laughed at the same things, and, when the group played games, chose each other as partners. It was one of those rare opportunities to spend a significant amount of time together, and so much more pleasurable than those few brief moments they had during school. As the day progressed, Oliver decided to ask Ann for a date. "Surely Mrs. Schaefer can't object forever," he reasoned. "After all, we're freshmen now. Almost all our classmates are allowed to date this year." He'd wait until the right time, then ask her.

Later in the afternoon, after Ken and Louise had left to visit with some of the neighbors, Fred suggested they play Spin-the-Bottle. After a short debate, accompanied by much laughing and giggling, Meg found a bottle in the kitchen. Because he had suggested the game, Fred was chosen to spin first. The bottle stopped, pointing at Graham. "Oh, no you don't, old man," Graham said, laughing. "You're not going to kiss me. Spin it again. Quickly!"

Everyone laughed as Fred tried again. This time it pointed at Meg. All the girls moaned and the boys cheered. "Poor Meg!" they teased. "She gets Fred's first kiss!"

"Ugh!" complained Meg, but good naturedly faced Fred, put out her chin, and closed her eyes. Fred approached Meg gingerly, gave her a very formal kiss on the cheek and, along with Meg, blushed.

"Now spin it again. See who gets the next turn," someone said.

The bottle this time pointed at Edith. She pretended to be indignant, grabbed the bottle and spun it vigorously. When the bottle stopped it pointed towards Ned. "Oooo!" they all squealed at once. "Ned and Edith! How appropriate! Come on, you two, it's time to make up." Edith, blushing slightly, leaned over to Ned and kissed him on the lips. Ned returned her kiss, more passionately than the group had expected. Everyone cheered.

Although Ann laughed along with the rest, each time the bottle spun by her she was terrified. She certainly did not want it to stop pointed at her. While these thoughts were going through her mind, Oliver kept hoping it would point at him; he wanted a chance to spin. Finally, just as he had almost given up hope, his turn came. He looked at Ann, gauged the appropriate amount of force needed to fulfill his goal, and carefully gave it a whirl. His estimate was perfect, the bottle stopped, pointing directly at Ann. Edith smiled. She knew Ann was petrified. "Come on, Ann. Don't be backward. Let Oliver kiss you. That's the rule," she teased.

Oliver rose to his knees and put a hand on each of Ann's shoulders and drew her to him. Their lips touched. Ann felt a tingle. It was different than she had anticipated. It didn't feel anything like the kisses from Graham, or Ida, or any of the other members in the family. Perhaps it was different because all those had been on the cheek, not on the lips.

Oliver, too, felt a tingle. Ann's kiss was even better than what he had always imagined it would be.

They blushed and reluctantly returned to their places in the circle after Fred shouted, "Come on you two, let the rest of us play." They both now hoped they'd get another turn.

"Let's change the rules," Fred suggested. "Let's make it more like post office. When the bottle points at someone, that person must go into the closet with the spinner; and remain there until they deliver the mail– if you know what I mean?"

There was little enthusiasm for Fred's suggestion. Some were offended and others outright disgusted. "That's a stupid idea," Betty Lou complained.

"You didn't find it so stupid the other night when I delivered the mail at Mill Creek," Fred said, looking directly at her and laughing.

Betty Lou's face turned crimson. She knew, as well as Fred, that they had never been to Mill Creek. She couldn't understand why he would accuse her of such a dreadful thing. She thought he liked her. Hadn't he told her so on many occasions? Now here he was, insinuating they had been lovers. "It's time for me to leave," she said. "Meg will you and Graham take me home? Please?"

Betty Lou had come to the party with her parents. They had planned to pick her up afterwards. Meg knew they would wonder what had happened if she brought Betty Lou home early, but she also sympathized with Betty, knew how embarrassed she was. "Sure, we'll take you. The party's over, folks. It's time for everyone to leave." No one objected. Fred had spoiled the party and everybody, including Fred, knew it.

Oliver was especially disappointed; he had not found the nerve to ask for that date and now it was too late.

On the car radio the Andrews Sisters were singing *Don't Sit Under the Apple Tree* as Meg drove home from Betty Lou's. She looked at Graham sitting there quietly beside her. He was such a handsome fellow. She wondered how she would ever let him go when the time finally came. "Only time would tell," was the only assurance she had left.

Her thoughts were interrupted by a special radio announcement. Admiral Francois Darlan had been assassinated in Algiers. It had happened on Christmas Eve. "He was, at the time of his death," the announcer said, "the high commissioner for French North Africa and the former commander who ordered the cease-fire of all the Vichy-French troops in North Africa. The authorities believe his assassin is a student– an extreme right-winger. The assassination could have been motivated by Darlan's aborted attempt to turn the French fleet, harbored in Toulon, over to Allied forces last month. Although his orders could not be carried out and the Allies had to sink the fleet, the Admiral was held accountable by the Vichy-French of South France. It is expected that General Henri Giraud will be named his successor. General Giraud is the French general who escaped from a German prison camp earlier this year."

Meg wondered if somehow all this would mean the end to the war. "Perhaps it will be over before Graham has to go into battle," she told herself. It seemed all she had left was a little hope.

Chapter 88

Tuesday, 5 January 1943

Diane was embarrassed. She did not want Mrs. Wilson to know why Yvonne had called. She chose her words carefully, trying not to say anything that might reveal what her daughter was telling her, but it was difficult. There were so many questions she wanted to ask, so much advice she wanted to offer. "What can I do?" was the only thing she could think to ask.

"I've already told you, Mother. Weren't you listening? I'm pregnant and awfully sick. The doctor hopes I can leave the hospital in several days, but says I must remain in bed until the baby comes. But I can't do it here, the family I've been working for refuses to take care of me. They say they need someone who can work, not someone needing a nurse. They asked that I be replaced. The WLA has already assigned someone else. Now they have placed me on leave–until the baby comes."

"Where are you going to stay, Yvonne?"

"That's just it, I want to come home–if you'll have me. I need your help, Mum."

"Of course we will," Diane quickly answered.

"But I'm too sick to travel alone. Would you come up here and bring me back? The doctor says, if I'm extremely careful, I should be able to withstand a train ride as far as Pinnington."

"I'll need a day, or two, to get off work."

"Just get here as soon as you can, Mum. I really need you."

"I will, dear. I will," Diane promised.

"Is there something wrong, Diane?" Mrs. Wilson asked after Diane hung up.

"I'm afraid so. She has taken ill, wants me to go up to Cumbria and accompany her home."

"I hope it's nothing serious," Mrs. Wilson worried.

"Oh, she'll be all right. She's just exhausted and needs a little rest. Apparently the farm assignment was a little too much for her," Diane lied. "Once she's back in Pinnington–under her mother's care–I'm certain she'll recover just fine."

Chad was angry when Diane told him what was wrong. "What the bloody hell has that girl done now?" he ranted, unsympathetically. "Gotten pregnant, has she? We should leave her up there. Let her solve her own problems. She didn't want anything to do with us while she was conceiving the little bastard. Why should we help her now?"

"Stop it, Chad! We must take care of her–she's our child. We're her parents. She's pregnant, and needs our help. She wouldn't say exactly what the trouble is. She said she didn't want to talk about it on the telephone, but it's something serious. I just know it is!"

Chad refused to change his mind and continued to argue against helping his daughter. But Diane remained adamant, and in spite of his protests, started making plans to leave for Cumbria. Although he still had no sympathy for Yvonne, he didn't want to make Diane's life any more difficult than it already was and agreed to pick up her train tickets. It was good he did. People, desperately trying to reach their destinations, crowded the station. At first he pleaded with the ticket agent, explaining he needed to bring a sick, expectant mother home to Pinnington. It did no good. There were simply too many expectant mothers in England these days. "Those damn Yanks!" the agent said, disgustedly. It took several telephone calls, a telegram from Yvonne's Cumbrian doctor, and one from the WLA affirming Yvonne's leave before the priority level was high enough to purchase the tickets.

It was late Friday before Diane and Yvonne arrived back in

Pinnington. Yvonne looked thin and frail, much sicker than Diane had anticipated. Even Chad was shocked when he saw her. In spite of his resolve to remain indifferent, he held her tightly for several minutes and worried that she looked sick enough to die.

Early the following morning Diane and Yvonne visited the doctor. Afterwards, the doctor took Diane aside and told her Yvonne was much sicker than he had first expected. Although he thought she would live, he did not anticipate the pregnancy reaching full-term, she would probably abort soon. Then he surprised Diane. "At least I hope so," he said, "if she doesn't, the baby, most likely, will be born with major defects and disabilities. You know your daughter has VD, don't you?"

Diane was taken aback. "Are you certain, doctor?" she asked.

"There is no question about it, Mrs. Montgomery. It's one of the worst cases I have ever seen, and believe me I have seen all sorts recently. The disease is running rampant these days. I'm afraid the war is having a terrible effect on our young people. They seemed to have lost all their mores. It's a real pity."

"Do you honestly believe she will get better?" Diane asked.

"I hope so. But it will take time to get this disease in check. Fortunately there are some recently discovered drugs I can administer. But even if we do manage to cure her, I doubt she will ever be able to conceive again."

Six days later Yvonne lost the baby. It was only then that Diane told Chad what the real cause of the problem had been. There followed another terrible argument between Chad and his daughter. Yvonne blamed her rebellion and improprieties on her disappointment over not going with Ann and Graham to America. Chad called that nonsense, pointing out the many other English children who had also been denied that opportunity. They hadn't gotten into trouble. "No, there is absolutely no excuse for your behavior," Chad insisted. "Look at Graham, he made the trip to America you're so envious of, and now he wants to come home. It can't be so wonderful if he's coming back when he could stay longer." He knew he was stretching the truth but wanted to make his point. He asked her why she hadn't grown up, hadn't settled down, and hadn't given more support to ending the war–to make the country peaceful again–the way almost everyone in Great Britain was doing.

"Why aren't you willing to make a contribution like Graham plans to make?" he continued. "Graham is willing to make sacrifices for his country. Why else would he be planning to join the RAF as soon as he gets here."

"There you go again, telling me how great Graham is. Next thing, you'll be saying is what a great trooper Ann is. You've always done that. You've always said how much better they are compared to me. I'm tired of it."

By the end of the argument, Chad had promised never to speak to her again and said, if anyone ever asked him, he would deny she had ever been his daughter.

"Then you're no longer my father," she screamed.

When Diane came home and saw the results of these bitter words it shattered her last hope of ever seeing her remaining family together again. She wondered what had happened to this once caring and loving family. If she hadn't sent Ann and Graham to America would they have had this terrible rift? Perhaps that was it. Perhaps she was being punished for that foolish decision. Was she in the final throes of losing another child, the only child still here in England with her? She decided to give up. She no longer had the strength and fortitude necessary to try to set things right. She would simply accept a future devoid of any relationship between her husband and daughter.

She thought about Graham and wondered if he would get home this year as planned. Probably not. She thought about Ann. She questioned whether she would ever see her again. She supposed not. Everything seemed so hopeless now.

From that moment on, she devoted even more of her energies to nursing Yvonne back to health.

Yvonne left home again on March 12. She was assigned to another farm in Cumbria. She still hated farm work but was pleased to be away from her father and her home. She no longer wanted any part of a household with as much enmity as she felt in the Montgomery home.

Chapter 89

Saturday, 13 March 1943

Brad was a tired, seasoned veteran by mid March. He had joined the 32nd Division in New Guinea the first week of January, just after they took Buna. Within days, he found himself fighting through the pestilential swamps of Sanananda and by the tenth of February was at the mouth of the Kumusi river. On the ninth of March, he had suffered through the air attack at Wau and was now crouched in a foxhole partially filled with water, awaiting orders to attack once again.

He reached in his pocket, pulled out his mildewed billfold, and looked lovingly at Clara's photo and sighed. Although wrinkled and torn, he could still make out her pretty face, her lovely brunette hair, and, most of all, her wonderful smile. She reminded him–always had–of a Greek goddess. He had lost almost everything during the Jap counterattack yesterday. Thank God he still had the picture. At times, particularly after a major battle with the Nips, he found it difficult to remember exactly how she looked, how beautiful she was. It was always reassuring to see her smiling face again. But being able to conjure up Clara's image was not what really mattered; she loved him, that was the most important thing.

He was momentarily distracted by a leech that had fastened itself to the back of his hand. He hated leeches, almost as much as snakes. It was the snakes that bothered him the most. "Funny," he thought, "snakes were the one thing I really couldn't stand back home, and here I am, in a hellhole crawling with them." The only thing that kept him from screaming each time he encountered one, and that occurred much too often, was the fear his buddies would make fun of him, call him a coward. "Perhaps I am!" he said to himself. "I shouldn't be here. I'm too scared. They should have kept me in McKinley Heights, working as a civilian. I'd have served them much better there." He had already forgotten how effective he had been during the recent fighting, the patrols he had led, the Japs he had killed, the buddies he had saved–it was almost as if he had blotted it from his mind.

Malaria was the other major concern for Brad. He wanted to stay healthy so he could return to Clara as a whole man, not some decrepit, quinine dependent, broken man. He had seen how Malaria affected some of the men of his company and wanted no part of that disease. The trouble was, if he remained in this godforsaken country long enough, under these conditions, he would be stricken too. It made him shiver.

Then he remembered Clara's letter. It was the only one he had received since they had come ashore. No one had been getting much mail; some in fact had yet to receive any letters, so he was thankful for at least the one. He felt awful when he lost it, along with all his other personal things yesterday, but it didn't really matter, he had memorized most of it, having read it so many times. It was so full of love.

The only thing though, it would have been nice to learn more about what had been happening at home. He was worried about her health, how the pregnancy was going, and if she were keeping up with the bills. He was so ashamed of how poorly he was providing for her these days. He was constantly trying to think of ways to ease her financial problems, but there weren't many alternatives available to a GI in a foxhole in New

Guinea. He had written to her several weeks ago and suggested she cancel her support for Edith. She probably hadn't received that letter yet. In it he had said it was unreasonable for Bender Electric to hold them to their agreement. After all, when it was signed no one expected he would be called into the Army. That should be a sufficient excuse. He suggested she contact Stan Roberts. If only he could get word to her quicker. "Perhaps," he thought, "if I concentrate hard enough she'll receive my idea by telepathy."

Just then the sergeant hollered, "Move 'em out!" There was no more time to think about Clara. As he rose to his feet and let some of the water run off his poncho, he hoped the war would end soon so he could go home. He was not the only one thinking those thoughts. There were men, both Allied and Axis, all over the world involved in similar fights and almost everyone entertained the same thought.

There was at least a little hope now that their war might someday be over. In the South Pacific, the six month battle of Guadalcanal had ended in February with an Allied victory. The Battle of Bismark Sea, the first week of March, had inflicted heavy damage on the Japanese forces. In the North Pacific, U.S. troops had braved the bitter cold to begin the retake of Kiska Island in the Aleutians. In the Far East, the Burma Road had finally been completed permitting the transport of critically needed supplies over the Himalayas to the Army of Chang Kaishek. In North Africa, there had been rapid Allied advances into Tunisia, only to be delayed when Rommel counterattacked at the Kasserine Pass. In Russia, the Germans were defeated at Stalingrad and the railroad lines between Moscow and besieged Lenningrad were reopened. In Europe, English and American bombers were systematically raiding German cities night and day.

However, even with all this Allied progress, there was still much to do before anyone could foresee when the war would end, or even if, an Allied victory was assured. Guadalcanal had only been one of many battles still to be fought before superiority could be claimed in the South Pacific; there were other Aluetian islands still to be recaptured; China was too weak to oust Japan from her country; Germany still occupied western Russia with the final result far from determined; Allied air losses over Germany were prohibitively high; and even though the Allies had Rommel mainly on the run, other obstacles remained and the fate of North Africa still was not certain.

Because of Allied government propaganda published in the newspapers, newsreels, and movies, there was, however, less uncertainty among the civilian population as to the final outcome. They began to think in terms of when–not if–the Allies would win. The evacuees, and their American classmates, who were too involved in their daily activities and problems to realize how perilous the war situation was, worried even less. But the evacuees, long ago, had ceased to count the number of days until their return to England–which perhaps was good, for it permitted them to live nearly ordinary lives, at least as ordinary as any of their American counterparts living under the wartime restrictions.

No. 31
Dexter Hills, Ohio
13 March 1943

Dear Mum and Dad,

What a time I've had today! My best friend Bonnie visited the farm and after playing with Lady for a while we rode our bicycles into Dexter Hills and helped the local church women prepare "Bundles for Britain" packages. I hope someday you receive one of these. It's too bad that we can't designate who gets them. If we could, be assured your name would go on <u>all</u> my boxes. Sending so many to my family might sound selfish, but they are such lovely packages with all kinds of goodies inside and I know you would gobble the sweets as soon as they arrived.

With the scarcity of sugar, sweets have become limited over here, too–but, I suspect, the shortage is nowhere near as severe as yours. There are still sweets (we call them candy bars) in the shops (stores to us) so I still get my share. I'm afraid you would find it difficult to recognize me now. I've grown so much (around the middle, <u>not</u> up). The scales registers 101 pounds (7 stone 3)! Oh well, not to mind. Aunt Ida says I am a healthy young girl. Uncle jack says all the young boys must think I'm a good catch–but not to worry, Dad, there are no boys in my life. Well, at least not any who would make a difference.

Yes, Bonnie is my best friend. She is such a nice person. I really love her. People see us together so much of the time now that they are beginning to say we remind them of sisters, or perhaps twins. Lately, if she isn't visiting the farm, I am at her house. That is, of course, when we are not in school together. (We are in almost all the same classes this semester.) I love going to her house. It's in town so we can visit the apothecary (drug store). They have such a lovely soda fountain there. It's where most of the "gang" meet. Of course that's why I am getting so chubby (I won't call it fat)–all those Cokes and ice cream sodas. They have a jukebox and we play it often, and dance to the latest tunes. I'm just crazy about Frankie Sinatra. He makes all of us swoon. Actually I simply like his tone, but to be one of the girls I always join in with all that craziness and pretend to swoon. Some of his latest hits are

"Night and Day" and *"Fools Rush In."* Have you heard either of them in England?

Bonnie and I also go to the movies together whenever we have the chance. Last weekend, while her mother shopped in McKinley Heights, we saw *"Gone with the Wind."* Boy! Was it long. We thought it would never end. But it was worth it! That Clark Gable is something else. Too bad he's in the Army now, else I would be after him. Ha! Ha! No, actually my *"dream boat"* is Robert Hutton.

Graham still hasn't heard when he is scheduled to leave. I guess they haven't found a safe way back to England yet. Now don't you worry about me. I'll be okay here by myself. Actually, I won't feel very lonely after he leaves. I have so many good friends now. There's Bonnie and a chap called Oliver (we often study together), Karen, Ned, and, of course, Aunt Ida and Uncle Jack. There are many others but those are the most important ones. Since Edith (Dad, you might remember her. She's the daughter of Mr. Dickson.) and Ned are sweet on each other, I also see her quite frequently. Ned often brings her to the farm, and sometimes I go with them to the movies.

And naturally I see Graham's family every time I visit him. They are such nice people. Graham is fortunate to have been assigned to live with them. His sister Meg is a super person. We get along splendidly. I also see Graham's next door neighbor, Fred (an evacuee), since they are quite good chums.

Fred has done quite well here in America. He quickly adapted to their athletic games and has become quite a sports celebrity in Oakton. He has been a star in the high school football, basketball, and baseball programs. Almost everyone in Oakton knows Fred, or at least has heard of him. The truly amazing thing is Fred is not only a sports star but is also doing very well with his academics. He has been on the Honor Roll almost every semester. (Of course Graham and I have also done that, but neither of us have excelled in sports the way Fred has.)

My goodness look at the clock! Lady just stuck her snout under my arm to remind me that it is bedtime and I have a busy day scheduled for tomorrow. After church, Ned, Edith, Bonnie and I are going to the movie *"Wake Island."* They say it's another war movie which isn't exactly what I relish seeing nowadays, but it has been quite popular–and besides that is about the only subject on the movie screen this year.

Give my love to everyone.

Love,

Ann

* * *

McKinley Heights, Ohio
13 March 1943

Dear Mother,

Thank you for your letter. I enjoyed reading it very much. It was a nice letter. I was pleased to learn that you and Father are feeling fine and getting on with everything. Things are fine here. Most of the pain is gone from my legs now. The doctor says I will be good as new in a few more months. He says I should be able to ride a horse again late this spring although Mom and Dad are not so certain they want me to ride anymore–after the accident. I have assured them that I learned my lesson well and will be <u>much</u> more careful hereafter. I hope, when the time comes, they will have a change of heart and will give their permission.

Mom has just finished redecorating my bedroom. It's very pretty– much nicer than my room in Uxbridge. She made pale pink curtains to match the bedspread, which goes nicely with the pretty light blue wallpaper. The ceiling wallpaper is white with a small lightly colored golden star pattern. I feel like a princess every time I walk into the room. She also bought a writing desk. I am using it to write this letter.

I'm glad I came to America. It's a super place to live. There are so many nice things to buy, so many nice things to do, and so many lovely places to visit. I could live here forever! Daddy says he will take me camping this next summer and promises we will go swimming often. I can hardly wait!

It's time to leave for our usual Saturday night shopping trip. Mom has promised me a new dress and a pair of shoes!

I hope everything goes well with you.

Love,

Sandy

When Jessica read Sandy's letter she shuddered. Not only were Sandy's letters shorter now but she was repeatedly mentioning all the nice "things" Kirk and Lucy were giving her. She even was saying now that she could stay in McKinley Heights forever. Apparently she no longer missed Uxbridge. It seemed to Jessica that Kirk and Lucy were spoiling Sandy. She also noticed Sandy was calling Lucy "Mom"–not "Mum," but "Mom!"–and Kirk was Daddy!

"Am I losing Sandy? Am I losing my sweet little girl?" she asked herself. She decided she would ask Harold when he came home, see if he agreed. If he did then they surely had to do something to rectify it.

Chapter 90

Saturday, 3 April 1943

Edith could not believe how rapidly her life was changing. It had been little more than two months since President Roosevelt had ordered the longer workweek for all employees in critical war plants. The order increased Clara's work schedule to six long days each week. At first it had pleased her, with the time and a half overtime rate for all the additional hours and the fifteen percent cost-of-living increase that had recently gone into effect, Clara, for the first time since Brad left, had begun to think she might be able to cover her expenses.

But the physical strain of all the extra hours eventually became too great, especially with it being so close to her final months of pregnancy. She came home one evening and announced she had turned in her resignation. She had her fill of working and had decided to move in with her parents. "I'm sorry, Edith," she said, "I simply can't do it any longer. Heaven knows, the last thing I want is to live with my folks again, but I have no choice. I just don't feel well enough to keep on working." She then added, as if it was an afterthought, "Of course it would be unfair to ask them to take care of you, too. So I guess it means you'll need to find another place to stay. My last day at work is two weeks from now. I'll be moving home that same weekend. That means you should plan to settle into a new home no later than Saturday, the third of April."

Edith was dumbfounded. She knew her relationship with Clara had deteriorated over the months since Brad had left. For some time she had felt fairly certain Clara would ask her to leave someday. She just hadn't expected it to be so soon. She thought Clara would wait until after the baby was born. She had thought Clara would want her to help take care of it.

Things had moved rapidly after that. Stan Roberts, once again with the help of Dorothy Studer, began an immediate search for a family willing to take in Edith. It took a few days until they finally located the Adams family, and several days more before a suitable time could be arranged for Edith to meet them. Dorothy and Stan wanted to make certain they were compatible with each other.

Jim and Hazel lived in a small two bedroom bungalow south of McKinley Heights, a considerable distance from Clara and Brad's house. They had an eight year old daughter named Becky and appeared to be a nice family. The interview went reasonably well. Jim was a rather stern man who apparently worked hard as an engineer at Bender Electric where he spent most of his daytime hours. He had a deferment from the draft lottery because of Becky. Hazel seemed exceptionally well mannered and polite. She told Edith she did not work outside the home, preferring instead to be home with Becky and do a little volunteer work at church and the local Red Cross. Becky was rather rude which didn't surprise Edith; after all many young, precocious girls acted that way.

Edith's overall assessment of the Adams' was mediocre. She found nothing specifically wrong but had an uneasy feeling. Under the circumstances however, she decided she had better agree to the move. There could be much worse accommodations–she recalled Ann's description of John and Flossie Mannheim. She would never be as close to Jim as she had been to Brad and Hazel was a bit too prissy, but she could live with that. The biggest disadvantages were school and Becky. Because the Adams' house was in a different district she would need to transfer to a new high school. That meant she would not see her friends as often. Perhaps even more troublesome, she and Becky would be sharing Becky's bedroom. The thought of living with Becky did not bode well. However, neither of these were insurmountable problems, and she made no mention of either during the final interview with Mrs. Studer.

Jim and Hazel found Edith to be intelligent and polite and decided she suited their needs well. The only problem was Spot. After much discussion it was agreed, reluctantly, that Edith could bring Spot, with one stipulation, he was not to be brought into the house. Jim promised to construct a nice doghouse for him.

A few days later Edith and Spot moved in with Jim, Hazel, and Becky and Clara went to live with her parents.

Almost from the start, there were quarrels and disagreements between Edith and the new family, nothing major, just a collection of annoying differences and misunderstandings. Jim and Hazel did not approve of Edith's casual attitude toward church and God. They continually nagged, telling her she should be more devout. It was a request difficult to honor, given Edith's agnostic upbringing at home–her dad had practically forced her to deny God's existence. Her only real church experience had been with Clara and Brad, and even then, she had not been a regular churchgoer.

Jim and Hazel asked her to think of them as her parents and to treat them with the love and respect demanded by the Ten Commandments, but failed to show any love and respect in return. Silly as it was, what troubled Edith even more was their refusal to tell her how they wanted to be addressed. In a recalcitrant and spiteful reaction, Edith decided not to call them anything. She made a point of avoiding any situation which required the use of a name whenever addressing either of them. It was a ploy successfully carried out during her entire stay–never once did she call them mother or father, or even mister or misses.

Becky added to the underlying tension. The first evening, as they were undressing for bed, she turned to Edith and said, "I hope you enjoyed your first day here. Tomorrow, as I am sure you've been told, you will be expected to help me. You know: sweep, dust, and tidy up my room regularly; help me get ready for school; wash and press my school clothes; help me with my homework; and whatever else I ask–or demand of you."

"Who do you think I am? Your servant?" Edith asked, indignantly.

"Of course. That's why you're here. You don't think my mother and father invited you simply as a goodwill gesture? As I'm certain they told you, it's almost impossible to hire any good maids these days. They only took you in as a means of getting some cheap help," she answered curtly.

"Furthermore, you should watch that mutt of yours," she went on, "if he so much as barks at night and wakes me, or jumps on me and soils my clothes, or snarls at me, I'll ask Daddy to take him to the vet and have him put to sleep."

Edith shuddered. If this was indicative of what they expected of her, she could foresee real problems ahead. Of course most of what Becky was saying was simply the mutterings of a small eight year old trying to sound grown up. The trouble was, Becky must have heard these things from Jim and Hazel. She didn't have enough imagination to think of all those things by herself. Edith held Spot close to her that evening before she fastened the chain to his collar and returned to the house.

Although it took great effort on everyone's part, within a short time things became more peaceful with only an occasional minor dispute. It was not until Ned asked Edith to go to a Saturday evening movie that the fragile truce began to disintegrate.

Ann had called Edith Friday evening, as she often did. When they finished she handed the phone to Ned. While they were talking, Becky came in, unnoticed, just as Edith said, "I'll have to ask, but it should be okay. I haven't been to a movie since I came here. My schoolwork is done and the chores they gave me to do shouldn't take too long tomorrow. Seven-thirty sounds fine. I'll call you back if for some reason I can't go."

As she hung up, she saw Becky run into the kitchen. "Mother, Mother!" Becky cried, "Edith has a date tomorrow night. At seven-thirty!"

"I don't think so," Hazel said with an indignant look at Edith as she entered the room. "What is this all about, Edith?"

"That bloody Becky," Edith thought. It was not exactly the way she had planned to ask permission but, thanks to Becky, she supposed it would have to do. "Ned Schaefer, Ann's foster brother, asked me to go with him to see *A Guy Named Joe*. It's supposed to be a good movie. He's picking me up at seven-thirty."

"Oh no he's not! You're only fourteen, entirely too young to be going on a date," Hazel snapped. "Clara Holtzman warned me we might have trouble with you and that boy. Well it's not going to happen, not while you're staying in my house."

"But I've dated him before. What's the objection? He is a very nice boy. He's Ann's foster brother."

"Don't repeat yourself. I know he's one of the Schaefer children. That doesn't mean a thing. It's improper for a fourteen year old to be dating, no matter how nice the boy happens to be. You have many years ahead of you for that sort of nonsense. As for now, you should be concentrating on your homework, and your Christian spirituality."

Becky snickered. She was delighted to see Edith being scolded. "It serves her right," she thought. "It's good for her—it will pay her back for taking up so much of my bedroom."

"But I've finished my schoolwork and I've been attending church and Sunday school regularly. Just like you asked," Edith protested. "What more do you want me to do?"

"Start thinking like a Christian, not just going through the motions. Going to church and Sunday school is not enough, young lady. You must truly believe in His teachings. A little more respect for your elders wouldn't hurt either. Besides, I don't need to justify my decisions. When I say you can't go, it means you can't go," Hazel retorted, almost shouting. "It's as simple as that. Now I'll hear no more about it!"

"You ... You, bitch," Edith screamed. It released much of the pent-up emotion that had been accumulating since she had moved in. She immediately wished she hadn't used that word. She hadn't intended to use a naughty word and was truly sorry.

Hazel's face turned white. "No one will speak to me that way. Go to your room. Mr. Adams will have more to say about this when he gets home."

Becky's snickers grew louder as she watched Edith reluctantly head for the bedroom. "Oh, Brad," Edith thought, as she shut the door behind her. "Why did you go into the Army? It was such a good life before you left. We were all so happy. This bloody war is messing up everything. Everything!" She would have shouted that last thought if it would have done any good.

When Edith visited Ann the next weekend they had a long talk about Jim and Hazel Adams. They agreed Edith was not as well off as she had been with the Holtzmans, but there was little to be done about it. It was not the sort of problem that would warrant a change in homes. They knew, if Edith complained, Mrs. Studer would talk to Hazel and would eventually conclude it was Edith who was at fault. Mrs. Studer would simply tell Edith to change her ways. By the time the girls had finished talking about her, Edith had resolved to be even more defiant towards Hazel than before. Becoming more and more obstinate was something she was doing more and more of lately. After all, it had been an almost daily practice since arriving at the Adams house. She wondered how much longer she would have to continue before Hazel became more reasonable. She mentioned none of this to Ann however.

In spite of Hazel's specific instruction not to have anything to do with "that boy," as she now routinely called Ned, Edith spent the rest of the afternoon sitting with him on the front porch. When they went to Ida for advice she told them she shouldn't interfere but, confidentially, she understood how they felt and suggested they might invite some of Edith's friends to join them at the movies. It would make it appear less like a date and more like a casual gathering of schoolmates. She thought Ann should organize it. Since everyone would need a ride, she could ask Ned to pick up everybody. After the movie Edith could just as easily be the last one he took home. It was admittedly a devious thing to do, but she saw no harm in it–as long as Mrs. Adams never discovered it was her idea.

They thought it a grand suggestion and agreed to try it.

Ned and Ann drove Edith home after dinner. When Hazel saw Ned she immediately flew into a rage. "I thought I told you not to have anything to do with him," she screamed.

"But I had to get home. What else could I do? Ann isn't old enough to drive and Mr. and Mrs. Schaefer were busy. Mr. Schaefer asked Ned to bring me home. What else could I do? I couldn't be rude," Edith argued. "Ned and Ann had to come into town anyway, so it was the logical thing to do. I could hardly say no."

"I don't care if it was logical or not. What I'm concerned about is your being alone with that boy. You could have called us. We would have come for you," she snapped.

"That's rather silly, isn't it, Hazel?" Jim said, putting down his newspaper. "After all, they were together for just a few minutes. It would have made no sense for me to drive all the way out to the farm when he was coming into town anyway. Especially this weekend. I used the last of my gasoline ration stamps today. Until we get the next set, we can't afford any extra trips. We need to keep the car in the garage as much as possible until then. Besides, Ann was with them. They certainly weren't alone, they had a chaperone."

"Ann doesn't make a very good chaperone, if you ask me," Hazel countered angrily, ignoring his worry about the gasoline. "She's Edith's girlfriend and lives with that boy and his family. You know how friends look out for each other. That kind of tomfoolery will come to no good. Mark my word."

Edith sensed she might have found an ally in Jim. "Ann and several of the other kids are going to the movies tomorrow afternoon," she interjected. "She invited me to go with them. Would it be okay?" She paused to let them consider the question, then added, "Mr. Schaefer has given the gang permission to use his car. Karen, Ann's sister, will be working so Ned will have to drive again."

Hazel's face turned red. "Didn't I just say I didn't want you and that boy in a car together?"

"Be reasonable, Hazel," Jim pleaded. "If a group of kids are going to the movies, there can't be any harm in Edith tagging along. Let her go."

"I bet they'll stop for a hamburger afterwards," Becky chimed in. "And I bet Edith sits real close to Ned the whole time, especially in the dark theater."

"Do you hear that, Jim? Even Becky is not as naive as you are."

"It won't hurt a thing, Hazel. I say she can go. That's the way it will be–like it or not." He turned to Edith, "Get on the phone. Tell Ann we said it was okay."

Hazel glared at Jim, turned, went into their bedroom, and slammed the door.

That night Edith could hear Jim and Hazel arguing. "How dare you undermine my authority today?" Hazel complained.

"You're way out of line, Hazel. She's a young girl and needs a chance to develop socially, as well as physically." Edith smiled. She was asleep long before they settled their argument.

Seven weeks later Clara had her baby. It was an eight pound, four ounce girl with a cute little nose and round face. It reminded Clara of Brad.

That same day, Brad was on jungle patrol near Lae, on the east coast of New Guinea, probing the Japanese airport defenses. Tired and hungry, his patrol had finished their reconnoiter and were returning to the home base when the sniper bullet rang out. Desperately seeking protection, he threw himself onto the damp wet ground behind a fallen tree. "Get the yellow bastard," the sergeant yelled, "Can you see him?" Brad looked in the direction where he had heard the shot and momentarily spied a glint high in the tree.

"I see him," he whispered, as he took careful aim with his M-1 carbine.

He watched with mixed emotion as the sniper fell from the tree. On the one hand, he was glad that there was one less Jap to shoot at him; on the other, he was horrified. He had once again been a brutal killer and, as a result, there was now one less human being in the world.

What he did not know was that his daughter was born at the same instant the man had died. Had he known, perhaps he would have considered it an acceptable exchange–one life for another.

Chapter 91

Saturday, 15 May 1943

Unbeknownst to anyone in McKinley Heights, a fierce battle between convoy *ONS-5* and German U-boat wolfpack *Fink* took place in the North Atlantic on May 4. By the time it was over, thirteen merchant ships had been sunk and a large number of brave, young men from Allied homes on both sides of the sea lay dead on its bottom. Later in the month, a Japanese submarine sank the Australian hospital ship *Centaur* off the coast of Brisbane and two hundred sixty-eight mothers soon wept for their sons and daughters. While all this was going on, Allied air forces were increasing their raids on the German Ruhr Valley and elsewhere in Germany. Afterwards, even more sweethearts and mothers began mourning the loss of the brave lovers and sons who did not return.

In North Africa, a phase of the war had ended on Thursday the thirteenth with the capitulation of Italian General Meese, and the day before of German General von Armim. Allied forces had control of more than two hundred fifty thousand Axis prisoners of war. No longer would these solemn, defeated men kill or maim Allied soldiers.

On Friday evening, Ann heard the news of North Africa and thought about Henry. Had he survived until now, with fighting finally over, he might have lived to see the end of this terrible war. She cried briefly; then tended to her barnyard chores as she always did on Friday evenings.

Ann had been looking forward to this day for some time. She hurried through her work. It was a very special day, the Saturday of the annual Dexter Hills freshman class picnic. Bonnie would be stopping in a few minutes. Her father was dropping them off on his way to work. She and Bonnie were in charge of entertainment and were going to the park early to arrange the decorations and to take care of all the other little remaining details. The committee had collected food stamps from everyone, and the local grocer and butcher had bent the rules and accepted the loose ration stamps, so there would be plenty of food. The school had loaned them athletic equipment, so there would be plenty of games. One of the parents had loaned them a wind-up Victrola and a collection of Woody Herman and Glen Miller records, so there would be plenty of dancing. Most of her close classmates would be there, so there would be plenty of camaraderie. All in all, it promised to be a splendid picnic.

Ann and Bonnie had just finished tacking red and white checkered paper tablecloths on the picnic tables when the classmates began arriving. One of the first was Oliver. He immediately approached Ann. "Hi," he said. "The place really looks nice. The two of you have certainly done a nice job. I'll bet it'll be the best class picnic ever."

Ann knew he was somewhat prejudiced but appreciated hearing the compliment anyway. "Thanks," she answered, "but it's mostly Bonnie's doing. She's the one who asked the local merchants to donate the trimmings."

"Come on now, Ann," Bonnie modestly disagreed, "you know everything I collected had been chosen by you beforehand. Ann was the artist behind everything you see here."

"But Bonnie was the one who thought to borrow the athletic equipment," Ann added. "Had she not arranged it there wouldn't be any softball this afternoon."

"Were going to play softball? That's super. I'll always be grateful to you," Oliver said, smiling at Bonnie. He turned to Ann and with a serious look on his face said, "I made the community baseball team yesterday, but it's going to be difficult to continue once the school vacation starts. The games are scheduled throughout the summer and sometimes they interfere with my work at Elmer's garage. Elmer follows sports pretty closely. I think he'll give me time off, but I'm not certain. Even if he does, I'm still going to feel guilty playing when I should be working."

"On the community team this summer? That's great I'm proud of you. Only fifteen and already almost a professional," Ann said, smiling. "But don't fret so much about play interfering with work. Good heavens, it seems as if all you do is work. Try to relax and enjoy yourself a little more. As Uncle Jack keeps telling me, you're only young once, so enjoy it."

"But my old man will be terribly upset if he hears I'm playing baseball this summer."

"Then don't tell him."

"This is a small town. He'll hear about it soon enough."

"Worry about it then. Tell him you'll do what you like. It's time you stood up to him."

She realized that advising him to challenge his dad was not the best advice to be giving. Ludwig could be awfully mean, but, darn it, she thought it time Oliver free himself from his dad's abuse. The thought brought back the terrible incident in '41 when he broke Oliver's arm. No one wanted to go through that again. For a moment she wondered if she should tell him she hadn't really meant it, that he shouldn't disobey his father. But she didn't. She really did want him to be rid of that man's mistreatment, once and for all.

In the afternoon, after the softball game, and after everyone had a second round of hamburgers, baked beans, potato salad, watermelon, soda pop, and ice cream drumsticks, some of the classmates settled down to the less strenuous games of checkers, chess, and dominoes. A few played pinochle. Others, those with a special fondness for each other, paired together and sat around talking or went for lazy strolls through the woods or along the towpath.

"Look at the frog!" Oliver whispered.

"Where?" Ann said, trying to see where he was pointing.

"Over there, under the log hanging over the water."

"I can't see him."

"Yes you can! Here let me show you," Oliver said holding Ann around the waist and turning her body slightly to face the log. As she turned, her face brushed his. Though both instinctively tried to pull away, neither could quite do it. As their cheeks touched they forgot the frog and began to think only of each other. Oliver could smell the lingering hint of perfume coming from behind Ann's ear, put there by Karen who, teasingly, had told her it would help get the attention of the boys. Ann sensed the strength of Oliver's arms, which were gripping her more firmly now.

Without quite realizing what he was doing, Oliver put his hand on Ann's face and gently turned it toward him. Their lips touched lightly. Almost involuntarily they turned toward each other, embraced, and kissed. The kiss was a new experience for both of them. They had kissed once before, at the Christmas party. That kiss had triggered certain feelings, but this time the feelings were much stronger, much more difficult to ignore. Never before had either felt this much passion. Although the embrace was brief, no longer than a few seconds, neither would ever forgot it.

Afterwards, Ann blushed. "We shouldn't have done that."

"Why not?" Oliver asked. "I like you. I always have, from the moment I first saw you in seventh grade."

"I like you too, but we're too young to do that sort of thing. If we do have any feelings for each other, they're only the result of what Aunt Ida calls puppy love. They're not serious feelings."

"But didn't you tell me Edith and Ned are in love? Isn't Edith the same age we are?"

"Yes, but that's different," Ann answered, but did not go on to explain the difference. "We'll just pretend it never happened, Oliver. We'll just go on like before–good friends–nothing more."

"That will be difficult. I like ..." he hesitated, stuttered, and finally continued, "No. I love you, Ann. I've known it for a long time."

When they returned to the picnic area the chaperones were lighting the bonfire and the children were beginning to gather around in preparation for the songs and dancing. Bonnie and Vicky were sitting together and talking. They waved to Ann and Oliver, "Come on over. We've saved seats for you."

As they sat down, Bonnie looked at Vicky and Vicky looked at Bonnie. They both smiled. "What have you two been up to?" Bonnie asked.

"From the look on your faces, I'd say you've been necking," Vicky teased.

Ann blushed and Oliver tried to look nonchalant. "No," he protested. "We were inspecting the canal lock. We saw it was getting late, so we ran back and probably look a little flushed. We didn't want to miss the singing. Did we, Ann?"

"No," Ann answered in a subdued voice, trying desperately to hide the truth.

"Come on, Ollie, you can tell me," Vicky teased. "Heavens, I should know how you look after you've been kissed. Haven't I seen you that way often enough? Why, just last month we kissed after the movie. Remember?"

"What are you talking about, Vicky?" Oliver protested, frowning angrily.

"You know! On the porch–after we saw Jimmy Cagney in *Yankee Doodle Dandy*."

He was furious. Vicky had deliberately embarrassed him. He knew she was right. He remembered the kiss, but that was different. They were just horsing around, having a good time. He didn't love Vicky. He loved Ann. The last thing he wanted was for Ann to learn that he had kissed Vicky. He had just professed his love to her, had finally told her. Now Vicky had ruined it, just after he had overcome his bashfulness and found the courage to finally do something about it.

He could imagine what Ann was thinking. Vicky had made him look like a real cad. "Don't listen to her, Ann. She's just confusing me with someone else. I took her to the movie, but I didn't kiss her, I swear I didn't," he lied.

Ann didn't believe him. She knew Oliver and Vicky were still seeing each other, had even heard they were serious. But it was okay; it really didn't matter. She liked Oliver, but she certainly was not in love with him. She was not his girlfriend. As far as she was concerned, he could kiss whomever he wished. She was not going to get deeply involved with him; not when she would be returning to England, hopefully before much longer. "Forget it, Oliver. I don't care whether you kissed her or not. It's none of my business." She then turned to Vicky and added, "For your information, we did not kiss this afternoon. It's only something Bonnie and you imagined. Besides, I don't own him. He can go with anyone–kiss anyone–he chooses. He means nothing to me."

The songfest and dance were the major successes of the freshman picnic. There was much hearty singing and dancing. For a few, however, there was only limited enthusiasm. Ann, Bonnie, Vicky and Oliver did not dance or sing a note.

*   *   *

On the way home, Ann thought about what had happened. She thought about the strange and wonderful feeling she had when Oliver kissed her. She wondered if Oliver had experienced the same thing. She recalled the embarrassment she felt when Bonnie and Vicky accused them. She thought about the jealousy she felt when she learned Oliver had kissed Vicky. She wondered if Vicky had felt the same about them. "Well, never mind," she scolded herself, "it makes no difference. I shan't do that again. As far as I'm concerned," she assured herself once again, "Oliver is a friend–a good friend–no more and no less."

Ann had difficulty sleeping that night. She supposed it was the excitement of the picnic. Yes! That was it. She was just let down because her work on the entertainment committee was over.

Chapter 92

Saturday, 22 May 1943

During the third week of May, Allied bombers carried out air raids over airfields in Italy, Sicily, and Sardinia destroying many Axis aircraft. These highly successful raids would be followed in a few months by an Allied landing in Sicily–the first step toward the invasion of Italy and France and, eventually, to the take back of Europe from the Nazi oppressors. As remote as this had seemed in May of '43, the life of a Dexter Hills family was destined to be greatly changed by these recent events.

On the twenty-second of May, Ned escorted Edith to his senior prom. It had been no easy task obtaining permission from Hazel. At first, she had been strongly opposed. She had given in only after Ida intervened, arguing it was a special, once in a lifetime occasion, and perhaps more importantly to Hazel, a well chaperoned event.

Surprisingly, once Hazel had consented, she devoted all her energy into helping prepare Edith for the affair. "No one from the Adams' house will be seen at a senior prom unless she looks as lovely as a princess and is judged one of the best dressed in attendance," she boasted. She helped select the gown, sewed all the alterations by hand, surprised Edith with a complete set of matching accessories, and fussed over every detail until she was convinced everything was perfect.

Ned was quite taken with how ravishingly beautiful Edith looked when he picked her up that evening. The yellow corsage he brought matched perfectly, pinned on her light blue gown it magnified her young girlish radiance and showed off her soft, slightly tanned complexion. He could never have hoped for a more perfect partner and spent the entire evening certain he was the envy of everyone. He danced nearly every dance with Edith, and refused to share her each time an admirer asked her to dance–which, not surprisingly, was quite often.

Afterwards they went for a short ride, stopped at a lonely spot along the way, exchanged a few kisses, and returned to the Adams' house by one-thirty in the morning. Hazel met Edith at the door, saying only that she hoped the evening had been pleasant.

"Maybe she's finally beginning to accept Ned," Edith speculated, as she climbed into bed. "Perhaps she'll let me see him more often now?"

Her expectations were quickly dispelled however. On the following Thursday when Ned called to invite her to the farm for an informal celebration of his graduation, Hazel refused to let her go, even when reminded that Ida and Jack would be there to act as chaperones. When Edith protested rather vehemently, Hazel matter-of-factly told her the prom had been sufficient partying for the time being. Then, in an obvious effort to appease her, she invited Edith to join the family for some cookies and ice cream. Edith, greatly upset, went to her room instead and almost immediately went to bed.

During the night, as she lay sulking, it occurred to her, however briefly, that Hazel, with her many unreasonable rules, was treating her much like her father had done. "But what was it he did that had been so terrible?" She suddenly realized she could barely remember those days so long ago. Even worse, she no longer could clearly picture either of her parents in her mind. "How awful!" she thought. "I can't recall how my own mum and dad look. How absurd. How could I forget that?"

It had been some time since she had heard from her mother. She wondered what had been going on at the Dickson residence since then. Had she known, she would have been quite surprised. Final papers for her parents' divorce had been signed on Friday. George and Harriet Dickens would no longer be husband and wife, effective the end of August.

Had Edith known, she would not have been too disappointed. She would have celebrated along with Harriet. The only thing though: Edith was no longer certain why she hated her father; it had all happened such a long time ago.

Chapter 93

Thursday, 27 May 1943

Graham could not believe he was still in Oakton. It had been seven months since he had applied to return, and still no date had been set. He had pestered everyone at Bender Electric every couple of weeks, but they had always told him the same thing, no transportation was available. He couldn't understand it. He knew there was a steady flow of war materiel across the Atlantic; the newspapers kept talking about it. He couldn't see how one additional passenger could make so much difference.

What Graham did not realize was how serious the U-boat menace still was–and would continue to be until almost the end of the war. Even after the B-24 Liberator aircraft had been deployed in early May to cover the remaining unprotected regions of the Atlantic, the fear of U-boat attacks was still there–and was justified with each new sinking. The officials did not want to chance losing a returning evacuee. They had learned their lesson with the sinking of the *City of Benares.* They thought the publicity might do too much damage to civilian morale. It was better to keep him in the U.S. rather than take any risk; especially since Graham was not a high priority passenger.

Frustrated as Graham was, there had been several advantages to the delay. Most importantly, he and Meg had become unofficially engaged on April 10–actually it was past midnight so it was April 11. Graham smiled every time he thought about that night. It was the best night of his entire life, and the best decision he had ever made. Although he was only seventeen, he already knew Meg was the person with whom he wanted to spend the rest of his life, and fortunately she felt the same about him.

It had happened after they left the dance at Potawami Lake. The Lawrence Welk Orchestra had been there that evening and a friend of Meg's had taught him how to polka. They had danced until they were both nearly exhausted. Afterwards, they had parked in their usual place near the old lime quarry, professed their love for each other, and afterwards had fallen asleep. It was nearly three o'clock when Graham woke. "Meg, Meg!" he exclaimed, "Look at the time!"

They had hurried home, hoping Ken and Louise would be asleep and would not know how late they had come home. Unfortunately, Louise heard them pull into the driveway. "Look what time it is," she scolded as they came through the kitchen door. "What have the two of you been doing so late at night?" She went to the stairs and shouted for Ken to come down.

For some time Ken and Louise had suspected something was going on between the children, something that undoubtedly went beyond socially acceptable limits. Until then it had only been a suspicion, and they had been reluctant to confront the children. But after coming in so late, they could no longer ignore it. The romance had undoubtedly gone too far, had become much too serious. Graham, realizing they were cross, and in an innocent attempt to defuse their anger, looked at Louise and said, "It's okay, Mother. You needn't worry. I'm going to marry Meg. As soon as I return from England after the war."

Meg was almost as surprised as Ken and Louise. Graham and she had discussed getting married someday, but it had only been talk, no promises had ever been made. He had never specifically asked her to marry him, and she certainly had never accepted any proposal of marriage. She, of course, would have, had he asked her, so she went along with what he had said. "We were going to tell you. We just had never found an easy time or way to do it."

"But you're so young. You're only children," Louise complained, although not nearly as displeased as she pretended. "You have an entire lifetime ahead of you. Don't rush into something as serious as marriage before you are absolutely certain."

What Graham had just said, surprised and upset Ken, so much so, all he could do was utter one huge, "Harrumph!"

"I love Meg," Graham told them. "If we were going to fall in love it had to be now. I'll be leaving for England any day and there's no telling how long this war might last. It could be years before I come back and we can marry. We may be too young now, but we won't be when all this is over."

"I love Graham, too," Meg interjected.

"Oh, children, you know we want only what is best for you, but think carefully before you take such an important step. So much can happen."

After a lengthy discussion they agreed to keep the engagement unofficial, not to announce it publicly, and, although neither Louise nor Ken entirely believed them, Meg and Graham promised to control their passions and delay consummating their love until after Graham returned when the war was over.

* * *

Graham smiled when he thought about the agreement. Everyone had kept their promise with regard to secrecy but he and Meg had not been as honest about containing their passions. He thought Ken and Louise suspected, but fortunately, they had never said anything, probably preferring to overlook it rather than make a fuss. One thing was for certain though, they seemed to have grown even closer now that he would one day be their son-in-law.

He had just walked in the door when the telephone rang. It was Stan Roberts. Stan had received word that transportation was available for his trip back to England. He would be returning on an RAF transport plane leaving Willow Run Airport, near Detroit, Michigan, next Sunday. He should be prepared to leave McKinley Heights in two days; that would be early Saturday morning.

Graham's first reaction was one of joy. The timing couldn't be more perfect, he had been able to complete his junior year at Oakton high, the classes had just ended; he could attend his fiancée's high school graduation, which was tomorrow evening; and he wouldn't be eighteen until next month, so he still could enlist before being drafted. What's more, not only was he finally on his way but he would be flying on an RAF plane. It would give him an opportunity to discuss, firsthand, with members of the RAF, what service in the Air Force was really like and exactly what he had to do to enlist.

His elation quickly turned to sadness when he thought of how little time there would be to say good-bye to everyone—especially to Meg with the graduation ceremony partially interfering with their last night together.

He spent the remainder of the day on the telephone making certain everything was ready to leave and calling everyone. When he talked to Ann, she had cried and said she wished she could go with him. Then Fred stopped by and stayed well into the evening. By the time he left, Graham and Meg had to settle for a few sad and emotional minutes alone together on the back porch swing.

Friday was even more hectic. Fred visited once again, Ann spent most of the day at the Nelsons' with Graham, and Edith and Ned stopped in for a lengthy chat. In the afternoon, Louise called a hastily prepared party with some of Graham's close friends, including many of the evacuees. Almost before Graham realized, it was time to leave for Meg's graduation ceremony.

Finally, after graduation, and at the encouragement of Ken, Graham and Meg were able to get away for a brief drive in the Nelsons' automobile. It was the only real chance they had had since the telephone call to be alone and to say good-bye. It proved to be much sadder and more emotional than either had anticipated. Meg was in tears almost from the moment they drove out of the driveway. On several occasions, Graham almost decided not to leave and had foolishly suggested they elope. At two o'clock, with heavy hearts, they returned home.

Almost before Graham could collect his wits on Saturday morning he found himself at the bus depot preparing to board. A large contingent of friends was there to see him off.

"Give those Jerries a good rap for me, old man," Fred said as he slapped Graham on the back.

"Give Mum and Dad a big hug for me," Ann reminded him as she hugged him for what must have been the tenth time in the final five minutes."

"We love you, son. Please come back as soon as you can. We'll be waiting for you," said Louise. "I'll be proud to have you as a son-in-law," she whispered.

"Had Tommy lived, I would have wanted him to be just like you," Ken told him. "In case you need something before you get on that plane, this is for you," he added, slipping Graham a five dollar bill.

"I love you!" Meg cried as she embraced Graham just before he boarded the bus. "I really love you, hurry back!"

"I love you too, Meg. I'll always love you!" He then added, "Even with an ocean between us!

"Good-bye, all," he said. And then he was gone.

Chapter 94

Sunday, 30 May 1943

Meg could not believe it had only been one day since Graham said good-bye. His absence was much more painful than she had ever thought possible, not only for her but for everyone else.

It had been particularly difficult for Louise. By the time they arrived back home on Saturday she was already noticeably depressed. By evening she had grown worse, enough so that Ken finally called Dr. Harris. After a thorough examination, the doctor gave her a sedative and told Ken he was not too concerned at the moment. Her symptoms were not uncommon, many mothers were reacting much the same when their sons left for the service. He assured Ken the prognosis was good; most recovered, or at least adjusted, after a brief period of mourning. His main worry was that her spirits not sink as low as they had after Tommy's death. Ken was to monitor her carefully and call him if she did not improve within two or three days. Above all, he should be patient; her return to normal would simply take time.

Ken could think of little else than that horrible period nearly three years ago. He certainly didn't want a repeat of that episode and did everything he could to restore her good spirits. Unfortunately, in doing so he began to neglect Meg–not recognizing she, too, needed consoling. As a result, Meg found herself pining for Graham and feeling very much alone.

Ann, too, had found the departure of Graham more difficult than she had anticipated. It seemed as if every thought somehow involved Graham. When she had a problem, her first impulse was to call him. When something nice happened, her first instinct was to share it with him. When she was uncertain how to handle a situation, she would first think of asking him. When she missed Diane and Chad and felt homesick, it was Graham she wished were there to help her through it and make her laugh again. But now, Graham was gone. For the first time she was in America on her own. Or was she? She had so many friends now, friends she could ask almost anything of, or say almost anything to, friends who were always there when she needed help. There was Bonnie, her best friend, and Edith, and Oliver; and, of course, Karen and Ned and Meg. Most important of all, there was Ida and Jack. How sweet they were. In a true sense they had replaced her mum and dad.

The following Sunday afternoon Ken called and invited Ann to visit for a few hours. Unfortunately, Louise had not made as much progress as everyone had hoped. He thought Ann's presence might help. She might serve as Graham's surrogate. "It could very well be the therapy Louise needs," he speculated. After talking it over with Jack and Ida, she agreed. The visit went surprisingly well. Louise even managed to laugh at several of Ann's little jokes.

Ken drove Ann home that evening. As she was about to get out of the car, he urged her to visit more often. "You will always be welcomed at our house, Ann. I would ask you to come live with us, but that would be unfair to Ida and Jack. Instead, I'll consider you our unofficial foster child. If there is anything–and I mean anything–we can ever do for you, or if there is anything we can help you with, please ask." He then hugged her and kissed her affectionately on the forehead. It was the same sort of kiss she had seen him give Graham.

"What lovely people," she thought. "They certainly love Graham as much as Aunt Ida and Uncle Jack love me. How could both Graham and I have been so lucky? How could we both have found such wonderful parents?" When she thought of John and Flossie Mannheim, she shuddered.

By the end of August, everyone had adjusted to Graham's departure. Louise, although not completely recovered, was once again attending to most of her household chores and, more importantly, was, on occasion, smiling, especially when Ann was around. Ken was busily working on budgets and contracts twelve hours a day, and six days a week. Meg was working as a file clerk at the local county office. It was temporary, until college started in September. The summer job, along with her regular nightly letter to Graham, kept her busy and occupied. By now Ann had become a regular weekend visitor at the Nelsons. Meg and she had become good friends, good enough for Meg to share some of her more intimate feelings toward Graham, and even a few of the more intimate details of their courtship. Ann liked Meg immensely and looked forward to having her as a sister-in-law.

Meg was about to leave the office one afternoon when Albert Robbins approached her. Albert had been a classmate of Meg's and was temporarily working at the county office too, until he left for school as part of the newly formed U.S. Navy technical training program. Upon graduation, he expected to receive a commission as an naval officer. Albert was a fine looking lad with excellent wit and a strong work ethic. "Hi, Meg," he said as he caught up with her. "It's a scorcher today. Isn't it? They say tomorrow will be even hotter." He paused, then added as if it were an afterthought, "By the way, I have tickets to the band concert this evening. There are many Sousa marches on the program. It should be a good concert. Would you care to join me?"

There had been a time when Meg would have given almost anything for a date with Albert Robbins. She couldn't count the times she had looked at him in study hall and fantasized how it would be to go out with him. But without hesitation she replied, "I'm sorry, Albert. Not this evening. I have oodles of things I must do before I leave for college."

"Well what about this weekend? Maybe we could go to a movie?"

"No. Sorry! There just won't be any time," she lied.

"I don't understand. Why won't you date me? I'm only asking for one teeny little innocent date. It's not a big deal–just an evening for the two of us to share a little fun before we both leave for college. What's wrong with two friends going somewhere together? Are you engaged or something?"

Fortunately, Albert did not notice the slight flush on Meg's face. "Don't be silly!" she said, and quickly looked away.

Monday, 6 September 1943

Dearest Graham,

How I dread the nights without you in my arms, my dearest lover. As I have told you so often lately, I miss you so much. (Too much!) I am impatiently waiting until you return to me. Until I can feel your body once again close to mine, can give you a thousand kisses, can love you a thousand ways! Oh, my darling, how much I want to be with you, and to love you, for evermore–for all eternity!

Am I counting the days? How can I count them when no one knows how many there will be? This dreadful war! I hate it! It has separated us. It keeps us apart. And yet... How can I hate it? It brought us to-gether. Had it never been, you would not have come to Oakton. Had you never come, we would never have met, would never have known each other. Without it we would never have been brother and sister; never have been best friends; never have been lovers; would never be man and wife. Oh, Graham. I love you so much! Come back, sweet prince. Hurry! I can't bear the loneliness much longer.

Perhaps tomorrow will be better. Perhaps once I leave for school, become involved in my studies, be away from all the reminders of you. Perhaps then I can overcome this evil curse. This unbearable separa-tion. Perhaps! I doubt it, my love.

Well, dear, think of me tomorrow, as I know you will, when I leave for my new adventure–college. Too bad you couldn't have stayed here, joined me next year, after your graduation. My parents would have paid your college expenses. They are already talking about your return to America. How they plan to send you to school. How you will become the great statesman you always talked so longingly about becoming. Let's hope the war ends in a few months. Perhaps by the time you read this letter?! Imagine how it will be to hear them say, "The war is over!" I know it's only a daydream. They are betting now it could last for years. But maybe, just maybe, a miracle will occur. After all, there have been miracles before–we found each other, didn't we, my sweet? Can there ever be anything more miraculous than that?

I shall close now, and then I shall go to bed; and as I lay there, I shall think of you, I shall hug my pillow, and when I finally fall asleep I will dream of you!

Love and kisses,

Meg

P.S. Your letter of July 24 arrived today. My heart goes out to you. Basic training must be horrid! Hang in there, and when that old nasty sergeant tries to give you too difficult a time just think of me, my dear. Remember how much I love you.

The following day, Meg left for college. Before her graduation, she would receive one of her wishes–the war would be over.

Chapter 95

Thursday, 3 June 1943

Graham's heart pounded as the plane bounced down the runway, slowly gaining speed, and finally lifting off the ground. He looked at the other passengers also strapped into the small pull-down seats hanging from the sides of the fuselage. He wondered if everyone had been as convinced as he had been, a few minutes before, that the plane was going too slow, would never lift off, was certain to crash in the cornfield at the northeast end of the runway. "Perhaps not," he thought, "after all they're probably all seasoned travelers and know how slowly these B-24 bombers take off." It had frightened him, there was no doubt about it. He had nearly given up his dream of joining the RAF. "But never mind," he assured himself, accompanied by a large sigh of relief, "we're airborne. Finally, I'm on my way home."

The past few days had been hectic. There were times when he doubted he should have come. He had arrived early Saturday evening, tired, hungry and expecting to simply board a plane and fly home. Instead there had been total confusion. No one seemed to know anything about his trip or could find any papers which authorized it. The American lieutenant on duty had not cooperated. He told him to wait until Sunday, or possibly Monday, when the CO was due back from Washington. He was the only one, according to the lieutenant, who could, "straighten out the mess." When Graham asked what he should do until then the lieutenant simply shrugged his shoulders and said it wasn't his problem.

Had it not been for the corporal sitting at the reception desk Graham would have been in trouble. "It's just another government snafu," the corporal whispered. "Don't mind the lieutenant. He's just a natural mean son-of-a-bitch."

Graham blushed. Swearing was not something he did himself, or was used too hearing. The Nelsons never swore, nor had his mum and dad. It would, however, not be the last time he heard swearing in his lifetime, especially once he joined the service.

"Do you have a place to stay?" the corporal asked.

"No, sir," Graham replied. As far as he knew, he had thought he would be on a flight to England that evening. There had been no in-structions, or provisions, in case of a delay. It had never occurred to him to ask about it before he left. Now he was in trouble. He had no money, other than the five dollars from Ken, to pay for either accommodations or food.

The corporal picked up the phone, talked to someone who apparently had a sense of humor since the corporal seemed to spend more time laughing and joking than talking seriously. Finally he hung up, smiled at Graham, and assured him everything had been arranged. "Just hang around a few minutes," he said. "When I get off duty we'll go to the mess hall and get you something to eat. Afterwards you can bunk in with me in the barracks. And don't worry, pal, we'll get you on a plane for merry old England. It shouldn't be too long a wait."

Graham didn't mind waiting. He was actually quite thrilled. He was going to eat in a mess hall—and sleep in an army barracks. "Boy would Fred be jealous if he knew," Graham mused. "I'm actually going to be living here for a day or so. I'll find out what military life is really like. What a jolly good experience this will be," he thought, then realized he had used "jolly" in a sentence. He hadn't used it in a long time. "I guess I really am headed back to England," he chuckled, and added, "and its customs."

The experience was different from what Graham had imagined. It was not anything like what he had seen in the movies. There were no parades, no men carrying weapons, no tanks, no artillery. In stead there was much more sitting around and waiting, much more confusion, and, except for the uniforms, the yellow buildings and an occasional salute, very little noticeable military decorum. It, surprisingly, seemed more like a civilian base than a military post.

Once they had eaten and had found a bunk for Graham, the corporal asked if he would like to go to the PX for a little R and R. Graham had no idea what a PX was, or what R and R meant. He answered simply, "Sure."

"Give my buddy here a brew," the corporal said to the barkeep.

"Hey, Pete. Who's the civilian?" one of the soldiers sitting at a nearby table asked.

"A new buddy of mine. Everyone, meet Graham Montgomery. He's on his way back to England. He's an Englishman. Says he's on his way to join the RAF."

"Here you go, Graham," he continued, shoving a bottle at him. "Here's to your health."

Graham had never tasted beer before. Fred had offered him one once, but he had refused; he hadn't wanted to upset Ken and Louise; they didn't condone drinking. This time he could not think of a respectable excuse, and not wishing to appear inexperienced in front of all these soldiers, he acknowledged the toast and took a small swallow. He nearly choked. He definitely did not like it, it was bitter and had a rather stale, almost musty, taste; not at all as he had imagined.

"Come on, fellow," one of his new companions laughed, "drink up. I'll buy the next round."

Graham felt he had to join in, or else they would think him a prude. He took another swig, this time a mouthful, trying to get it over with as quickly as possible. Almost immediately he began to feel lightheaded. He made himself swallow another gulp, laughed and joined in, as best he could, with all the frivolity and tomfoolery. Finally, just as he had nearly emptied the second bottle another soldier slapped him on the back and said, laughing, "Here you go, old man, have another."

Graham did not remember anything after the third bottle. The next morning he woke, lying on the bunk, still in his clothes, and with a terrible headache.

By Wednesday, Graham had become one of the regulars. He could drink six or seven bottles before feeling dizzy, ten before passing out. His only regret was that he had little money to buy many rounds himself–his five dollars had gone so quickly–but none of the soldiers, or GIs as he was now calling them, seemed to mind. They said their money would be of little use where they were going. "We might as well live it up and have a good time. No need to save it for a rainy day," they said. Graham thought he understood what they meant, something to do with them not returning, but he wasn't certain.

Suddenly, the airplane dropped violently. They had crossed the shoreline of Lake Erie and had hit one of the downdrafts. Graham tried desperately not to be sick. He should never have gone to the PX last evening, should have spent at least one night sobering up before boarding the plane. He vowed he would never again drink beer; by the time the plane landed in Greenland, he wasn't certain he would ever eat anything again.

When the plane landed in southwestern Kent, he was convinced he did not want to eat or drink for the rest of his life, in fact he didn't even want to live anymore. He vowed he would never fly again and had firmly resolved not to enlist in the RAF, it was obviously not the best branch for him. Stiff and tired, he lowered himself down from the plane hatch and, after a few minutes wobbling around to regain his ground legs, his airsickness began to subside. He began to feel normal once more. It was about then that the thought finally hit him, he was back in England. He was home!

It was a warm balmy day. A gentle southwesterly breeze caressed his face as it blew in across East Sussex from the south coast. Even with the fumes of the airplane petrol still lingering on the tarmac, Graham could tell he was in England, he could smell the English sea air. It reminded him of a time, years before, when he had smelled similar smells, felt similar breezes; seen the same dark green fields, a time when he had traveled with his dad to Eastbourne.

It was good to be back home. Other than the aerodrome, which undoubtedly had not been there when he was a boy, nothing seemed to have changed.

However, during the train ride into London he began to realize how mistaken he was. In spite of all the newspaper articles he had read and newsreel clips he had seen, Graham was ill prepared for what he saw. Antiaircraft installations were everywhere. In a few cases, he even saw the remains of crashed aircraft lying broken about the countryside. Fields, which he imagined once were grasslands filled with grazing sheep, were now busy army supply depots, filled with military vehicles skittering here and there. Many buildings in the cities and towns stood in ruin, evidence of the severity of the German air raids. Large empty areas, where, he supposed, houses and shops once had stood, could be seen everywhere. In some places, the rubble still remained. He could not believe the terrible destruction he saw. He began to feel guilty. He had missed all the horror that must have accompanied the raids; he had been so unaware, so naive about all this. Had it really happened during these past three years? He had read about it, but he hadn't known, hadn't understood. He nearly cried.

As the train neared the outskirts of London, he began to see evidence of even greater destruction. Before it entered the first of the tunnels which eventually led to the Hungerford Bridge, he was amazed. By the time it arrived at Charing Cross Station, he was distraught. He had never seen such devastation. Block after block of the city lay in ruins. He could barely recognize it. Landmarks he remembered as a boy had disappeared. The city, once neat and orderly, was in disarray. In some places, traffic inched past large craters nearly blocking the streets; in other places, streets were cordoned off without explanation, apparently too damaged to use. He started to cry. The bombing raids must have been awful. He wondered why his mum and dad had not described this in their letters. Then realized they had not told him, bless their souls, in order to protect him from the real horrors of the war.

Graham carried his baggage to the Embankment underground station and boarded the District Line tube for Ealing Broadway where, if things had not changed, he hoped to catch the No. 297 bus to Pinnington.

It was nearly dark when he walked up the pavement to his house. No light showed from the windows. He supposed the blackout curtains were still drawn and hoped that his mum and dad were at home. "Hello, Mum," Graham said when Diane answered the door, a big smile on his face.

"Graham?" questioned Diane, not recognizing her son at first. "Graham, is it you?" Then the doubt disappeared and she knew. "Chad!" she screamed. "It's Graham! He's home!"

Diane could not get over how much her son had grown. Her first reaction: how could he have changed from a little boy into a grown man overnight? But it hadn't been overnight; it had been nearly three years–three terribly long years–since she watched Ann and him disappear around the bend that dreadful morning in August. So long ago. Three years! She should have expected this much change in him. Ever since she had known he was coming back, she had tried to imagine how he would look–how he had changed. However, try as she would, she could never picture him any different than he had been way back then–a fifteen year old boy. In spite of his disheveled appearance, caused by the growth of a fairly heavy two day beard and badly wrinkled clothes, he looked so nice, so healthy. She had to admit, the Nelsons had done an excellent job of rearing him. He was a handsome, fine, healthy young man. It suddenly occurred to her that Graham, her son, had a mustache. She couldn't believe it.

"Son!" cried Chad as he wrapped his arms around him. "It's so good to see you! Welcome home." He wept unashamedly and Graham, seeing his dad cry, cried too. "I'm sorry, Graham. Not very manly of me, is it?" he apologized.

"Don't be silly, Dad, no need to apologize. It's good to see you, too."

They stayed up late the first night, bringing each other up-to-date and reminiscing about past times. It was nearly two in the morning before they turned out the lights. At three o'clock there was an air raid alert that woke Graham. He lay there wondering what he should do and why his parents didn't go to the shelter. It was not until after the all clear sounded an hour later that he finally fell back asleep. Neither Chad nor Diane had heard the air raid sirens.

There was more talk on Sunday, and eventually Chad told Graham about Yvonne's escapades and difficulties. Graham sensed a coolness in his dad's attitude. Something he had never seen before. Only after talking alone with Diane did he realize the seriousness of the rift between his dad and sister. By mid afternoon, there was little more for them to say, everyone had run out of things they had in common, an embarrassing silence descended on the household. By evening, Graham and Diane had their first argument. It was not a serious disagreement, but it made Graham compare, unintentionally, the Nelsons with his mum and dad. With a huge feeling of guilt, and for a brief moment, he thought he preferred the Nelsons over his own parents. It was a feeling that deeply distressed him. He quickly put it out of his mind.

Late that night he wrote a letter to Meg telling her about his trip, how glad he was to see his mum and dad, and about Yvonne–but most of the letter was about his love for her. When finished, he placed it on his dresser. In the morning, he awoke to find Diane reading it. "My, my, Graham," she said as she continued to read, "it sounds to me as if you are pretty serious about this girl. Shame on you. You're not old enough to be that serious about anyone."

"What are you doing, Mum? Reading my letter!" he asked, trying to snatch it from her hand. "You have no right to read my letter. It's personal."

"Come now, Graham. You're my son. Sons should have no secrets from their mothers."

Graham was just about to respond, describe to her how the Nelsons always respected his privacy, when he saw Diane's face grow pallid. "What's this about joining the RAF?" she asked. "What are you talking about? You're not going into the service right away? Are you?"

"I have to, Mum. It was one of the stipulations I had to agree to in order to return. I must sign up within the next month, or be conscripted."

"Why didn't someone tell me?" she moaned. "I would never–never– ever–have consented to your return home if I had known. I've lost Henry. Yvonne won't come home. Dad refuses to speak to her. Ann is in America. You've finally come home and now you're already leaving? I'll not have it! I'll not consent to you joining the military. Never!"

"I'm afraid it's out of your hands, Mum. I must. It's my obligation as an Englishman, as a man, and as a human being."

"You're no man. You're only a boy!" she argued.

Several days later Graham could barely stand to be in the house, his parents were getting on his nerves, all because of their excessive concern for his comfort. They were treating him like a little boy. He didn't like it. As an excuse to get away, he proposed visiting Yvonne before he enlisted. He felt certain he could do something to settle the feud between his dad and her. He had always been a good arbitrator of disputes in school, so why not here, he reasoned.

The visit proved to be a mistake. He expected Yvonne would be pleased to see him, but almost from the moment he walked in, she let it be known she still resented his evacuation to America. She complained that it had been extremely unfair that Ann and he had agreed to go when they knew she couldn't. When it became obvious he could contribute nothing towards peace in the family, he returned to Pinnington.

Chapter 96

Tuesday, 6 July 1943

Ned was nervous. He had visited the recruiting office before, but this time was different; he was signing his enlistment papers today. When he came out of the office, he would be a soldier in the United States Army. He wondered why he was so worried. It hadn't been a difficult decision. He could have waited until he was drafted, which he expected shortly, or he could enlist, those were the only options he had. From what the recruiting officer had said, there would be certain advantages to volunteering; mainly, he would have his choice of service branch and skill category. But the choices really didn't matter that much to him, mostly he simply wanted to get on with it. He wanted the uncertainty to end.

He didn't particularly care for sailing, that eliminated the Navy. As far as he was concerned, the Marines had been in too many fierce battles already. He had no desire to be a rough and tumble war hero; he would be just as happy fulfilling his duty in an honorable, and safe, manner. That eliminated the Marines. The Army was the only branch left, so he chose it. As far as gaining new skills, he really had no great ambition to learn a new trade. He planned to return to the farm afterwards, no matter what he learned. Since the Army didn't provide training opportunities in agriculture, he chose communications, not because it particularly interested him but because it might provide a convenient means of keeping in touch with Edith. He knew these were silly reasons, but they were the best he could come up with.

"Congratulations, son," the sergeant said at the end of the signing-in ceremony. "You are now in the United States Army. Report back here on Thursday, July 15, at 0630 hours." Ned looked puzzled. "That's six thirty in the morning, soldier," the sergeant added, grinning and thinking he had just recruited another bumpkin. "Don't be late. We don't take kindly to goldbrickers in this man's army. And come prepared to work, 'cause we're gon'na work your ass off, private. Now run along home, and say good-bye to your sweetheart. Better make it a special good-bye. It's the last you'll see of her for a long, long time."

Ned left the recruiting office wondering if he should have signed those enlistment papers. The attitude of the sergeant seemed to change quite drastically once his signature was on the paper. It was strange. He had seemed so friendly beforehand, had been so mean and bossy afterwards. "It was probably just my imagination," he tried to assure himself.

At dinner that evening, he announced what he had done and surprised no one. There had been many discussions about it beforehand, and everyone had expected it. They had all known he would be going in, one way or the other. It was the finality of it that got to them. Ida cried a little at first; Jack became exceptionally quiet; and Karen teased him, saying he could delay it no longer, he finally had to learn to tell the difference between his left foot and his right one. Ann reacted with the most emotion of all. "You can't leave the farm! We need you," she protested. "Aren't you a farmer? Go back and tell them you changed your mind. Maybe they'll give you back the papers you signed."

Ned laughed, "I don't think so. The sergeant made it pretty clear this morning. I'm in the Army, for the duration plus six, and have little say about anything I do until the day they let me out."

Ann fell silent. There was something troubling her, something she would never admit to anyone. She had not been nearly as upset when she first heard Graham was leaving. Ned's announcement seemed much worse. It didn't seem right. Graham was going into the service too. Graham was her brother; she should have been more concerned about her own brother than about some other boy, even if he was considered her brother in some sense. She didn't understand it. Was she being unfaithful to Graham? Maybe she was being disobedient to her mum and dad, maybe it was her way of getting back at them? Was she placing her foster family ahead of her birth family? "And what about England?" she asked herself, "Didn't I make a promise to Mr. Shakespeare the night we left? Am I forsaking my country?"

"Have you told Edith?" Ida asked him.

"Not yet, we haven't been able to meet for quite some time. Mrs. Adams still refuses to let us talk. Edith knew I was enlisting, though. We have talked about it many times."

"You had better let the poor dear know anyway."

"It's reached a point where we can't even talk on the telephone. Mrs. Adams absolutely forbids it."

"Then get on the phone, Ann. Call Edith. Invite her out to the farm. Today! She must be told right away."

The following weekend the family rented a lodge on nearby Lake Potawatomi. They asked Edith to join them, once more using Ann and Edith's friendship as an excuse to override Hazel's objections concerning Ned. It was a grand, but sad, weekend for everyone, filled with fishing, eating, campfires, and, most importantly, plenty of reminiscing, hugging, camaraderie, and simply spending time with Ned. A tear shed from time to time was not unusual.

On Saturday night, after the family had gone to bed, Edith and Ned went on a moonlight canoe ride. It was a warm night, not a cloud in the sky. The moon was in its first-quarter, and the stars seemed brighter than either had ever seen before. It was an perfect night for two people so much in love. They did not paddle far before they found a secluded cove with a grassy shore suitable for the blanket they had brought along. While sitting there, holding hands, and silently gazing at the sky, a shooting star raced overhead. "Did you see it?" Ned asked.

"Yes. Quick, make a wish—before the magic is gone," Edith whispered.

"I wish for us to be husband and wife someday soon," Ned said dreamily, "with the war over and the two of us together, living happily ever after."

"What a lovely thought. I wish for that, too. And may it be soon, and may we never again be parted," she added, kissing him tenderly on the cheek. "Oh, Ned. I don't think I'll be able to bear the loneliness after you're gone. What if we never see each other again? What if they send me back to England before you come home?"

"Then I'll come to England and find you," Ned assured her. "No matter where you go. No matter how long it takes. I'll be there to hold you, and love you. And then, I'll marry you and we'll be husband and wife. Forever."

"Do you promise?"

"Yes, my darling, I promise."

Their bodies ached for each other. They could no longer tolerate any space between them. They wrapped their arms around each other and kissed. "I love you!" they said in unison, each tightening the hold on the other. Ned's hand slipped to her thigh. She did not protest.

"Love me," she pleaded.

"I do," he responded.

Each could feel the contour of the other as he laid her gently on the blanket. Their breathing grew more rapid and their hearts pounded. "You are mine," he said, "And I am yours."

"Yes! Oh yes!" she answered.

"Let's wait, Edith. Let's wait until we are married."

"Will you love me if we do?"

"Yes. Oh yes. I'll love you. I'll love you even more!"

"Promise?"

"Yes."

"Will you wait for me?" he asked.

"I'll wait for you forever, Ned. I love you."

The air had turned chilly and a fog began gathering and hovered several feet above the lake as they made their way back to the lodge. Edith listened to the sound of the oar as Ned paddled. It was a sound–a moment–she wanted to remember forever. A loon cried in the distance. It sent chills down her spine. "My Ned," she thought as she looked at him, tears in her eyes, "my precious Ned. That sound will always remind me of you."

The following week was traumatic for everyone. Almost before they had time to think, Ned had gone. Although Ida and Jack pretended not to worry about sending their son to war, they quietly prayed for his safe return. Ann, embarrassed that Ned's departure had upset her more than Graham's, found her final hours with Ned awkward–on one hand she told herself she should treat him as she would any good friend, on the other, she wanted to love him as she would a brother. Edith pleaded to see Ned once more before he left but Hazel would not permit it, even on the last day when Edith begged to go to the train station for a final good-bye, Hazel said no.

Afterwards, Edith retaliated by looking for especially mean things to do and say whenever she could. She brought Becky to tears almost daily, found all sorts of nasty things to do to Hazel, mishandled all instructions, and when scolded would only laugh. Finally, thoroughly exasperated by her increasing contrariety, Hazel and Jim appealed to Stan Roberts. They asked to terminate their agreement, they claimed they could take it no longer, that they had lost control of "that despicable girl." Stan, concerned about the mounting number of recent complaints between evacuees and their foster families, denied their request–he told them to try harder, then wondered how much longer the Bender evacuee program could hold together. It had been three years–that was a long time for people to do things primarily out of their good graces.

Chapter 97

Tuesday, 6 July 1943

Graham signed the enlistment papers for the RAF soon after returning from his visit with Yvonne. While waiting for his notice to report, he began following the news of the war more closely, looking particularly for news of Air Force activity. He was proud to think he was now part of such an august organization, especially when he learned that the Allies had begun heavy bombing raids over Sicily, had increased their air attacks on the Italian mainland, and had expanded their air runs in the Ruhr valley. He daydreamed of his future role in these activities, trying to decide if he would be more effective as a pilot, bombardier, gunner, or mechanic. As the days passed, he became increasingly more excited and eager to receive the letter of acceptance. On the last day of June, it finally arrived. He quickly tore it open and was terribly disappointed. He had not passed the physical examination; his enlistment had been turned down.

The letter suggested he try another branch of the service. After several days of frustration, and with somewhat subdued enthusiasm, he enlisted in the British Army. It was the sixth of July, by coincidence the same day Ned had enlisted in the U.S. Army. After basic training he was assigned to the British 6th Airborne Division.

When he told Diane he had enlisted she was heartsick. She had hoped the RAF rejection meant he would not have any further service obligation. The Army had taken Henry from her. Now it might take Graham too. She could not see why they had to have her only remaining son, especially since the war appeared to be decisively shifting in the Allies' favor. "After all," she reasoned, "if our island is secure enough to replace all its signposts and road signs, it surely isn't in need of such a young boy." But she did not complain, instead she successfully hid her feelings until Graham left, then immediately went to bed and did not get up again for nearly two weeks.

In November, Graham was assigned duty in southern England and regularly began going home on weekend passes. Diane was relieved, especially after he told her he had a clerical assignment in his company which would keep him safely in England for a long time to come. He was sorry for the fib, but what could he do? It was what she needed to hear. At least his enlistment didn't trouble her as much this way.

Actually, Graham was simply obeying orders when he lied to his mother. All activities at his camp had been classified secret. No one was permitted to tell what they were doing. Had Diane known what his real duties were, she would have been quite upset. His division was undergoing highly specialized training in glider landings and beachhead assaults. Apparently they were preparing for some sort of major attack or invasion, although his superiors would never say precisely where or when it would start.

Meg also was pleased. In November she received the following cablegram:

6 NOVEMBER 1943

DARLING,

HAVE BEEN ASSIGNED DUTY NEAR HOME STOP ABLE TO SEE PARENTS OFTEN STOP LOVE YOU STOP

GRAHAM

"Graham has not been sent into combat. Instead, he will be staying in England where he should be safe!" she excitedly told her college classmates that afternoon. She cried after climbing into bed that night. She didn't understand why, perhaps the news was too good to believe.

At Meg's insistence, the Nelsons hung a silk service flag in their window a few days later. It was the same as the one the Schaefers had hanging in their window honoring Ned. Some Oakton residents objected to Graham's flag. They said the flags were reserved for the sons of American families; not English boys who happened to have lived for a brief time in Oakton. But Ken and Louise ignored all the derogatory comments and unfriendly innuendoes and continued to proudly display the flag. As far as they were concerned, Graham was–always would be– part of their family.

Chapter 98

Friday, 12 November 1943

"Who can tell us what happened in Sicily?" Mr. Cairns asked, looking somewhat pessimistically at his world history students. He was almost certain no one had been reading the newspaper. He knew they seldom took his assignments seriously. It was very discouraging. Their subpar scores on last Monday's quiz should have sent them a message. Didn't they realize they needed to study? "That's the trouble with kids today," he thought, "they're not as studious as they used to be. Why, in my time ..."

He was interrupted by Ann waving her hand, "I believe, sir, Sicily was invaded by the Allies on July 10 and by mid August it was under their control."

"That's right. Very good, Ann," he said, smiling. He turned his attention to the others, "Aren't you ashamed of yourselves. Don't any of you keep up with what's happening? Aren't you interested in the progress of our fighting men? Is Ann the only one with enough gumption to read the newspaper?"

Ann laughed to herself. It wasn't exactly gumption. She knew about Sicily because of her special interest in the Mediterranean area– ever since her folks thought Henry had been sent to North Africa. After Henry died, for reasons she couldn't explain, she had followed it even more closely. Other than that, there was little else in the newspaper that interested her. She wasn't reading as regularly as Mr. Cairns thought she was. She certainly was not the conscientious student he supposed. She wondered what he would say if he knew she was more interested in *Little Orphan Annie, Popeye,* and *Gasoline Alley.*

"Now, who can tell me the present status of Corsica?"

"It was liberated by the Free French in early October," Oliver answered confidently.

Several of his classmates smiled. A few snickers came from the back of the room. "He certainly showed old man Cairns we're not stupid," was a universal thought that spread quickly around the room.

But they weren't surprised, Oliver knew quite a bit about the war. He had been following it closely for several years. Perhaps it had something to do with Ann Montgomery and her being from England. They always seemed to be together in school, were always talking, which caused much speculation.

It was rumored they weren't just friends, although no one had any hard evidence to confirm it. They knew Oliver didn't drive so they couldn't be sparking at Spoon Hollow, and as far as anyone knew, Oliver never visited her on the farm. But still, most insisted they had been, and continued to be, lovers. The rumors had started last spring at the freshman picnic when they had gone on that walk along the towpath. Several classmates had seen the two together at the movies several times since. Admittedly, they couldn't have "made out" at the movies since one of the Schaefers had always been with them. But still, it was sufficient to fuel everyone's suspicion and cause the rumors to continue. The truth didn't seem to matter. Only a few would concede that the couple had never been on a real date, had never parked, and had never had any other opportunities to be lovers. However, no one could deny that Ann and Oliver liked each other.

"Now what about Italy?" Mr. Cairns continued. Only Oliver's hand went up. "Someone besides Oliver," he pleaded. Finally in exasperation, he said with a sigh, "Allied troops landed on the mainland of Italy on September third. On that same day, the Italians surrendered. What happened next?"

"The Germans moved in, to defend Italy themselves. They took Rome from the Italians shortly afterwards."

"Correct, Oliver," Mr. Cairns affirmed, somewhat displeased that Oliver was answering all his questions. "Unfortunately, fighting in Italy is far from over. The Allies made major landings along the west coast of Italy in early September, but it took until the first of October before they finally capture Naples. Now they're somewhere north of Naples, dug in along a line across Italy just south of Cassino. But it may well be a long and difficult task to advance any farther, especially now that Mussolini has set up his new fascist state in northern Italy."

"But my Dad says we're going to win the war. He told me last evening—while we were eating supper. The Allies have been really giving it to Germany. He says he doesn't see how the German people can withstand the intense bombing the Allies are dishing out," Timmy Jones added, a smug look on his face for having contributed something.

"That probably won't make much difference," Ann observed. "Look at the terrible damage German bombing raids have inflicted on England. It hasn't caused the British to give up. In fact, my dad says it simply made everyone angrier, more determined than ever to whip old Adolph."

"But Germany has difficulties in Russia too," Chuck Anderson added, much to the delight of Mr. Cairns; he finally had them discussing the situation. "The Russians have just recaptured Kiev—according to last night's paper. That should be worrying Hitler," Chuck continued.

Had he finally stimulated the class to participate? "What about the war in the Pacific?" Mr. Cairns asked, trying to keep the conversation going.

"Well, we're starting to make some headway in the Solomon Islands," Oliver volunteered. "Japan has evacuated New Georgia."

"That's true, but it's only a beginning. There's still a long way to go before peace can be restored in the Pacific," Mr. Cairns warned. Then, he thought he would inject a little personal interest, "We'll more than likely have Ann with us for a long time to come–perhaps even until this class graduates in '46."

This made Oliver happy. It meant he and Ann could graduate together. Also Ann would be in Dexter Hills long enough for him to ask her for a date, a real date–next April when he turned sixteen and finally had a driver's license. Then maybe some of the rumors floating around the school would be true. He looked at Ann and immediately was ashamed. He realized it had been a selfish thought; she undoubtedly wanted the war to quickly end, for her parents' sake.

Ann was stunned and saddened. Although she had long ago realized it would be some time before she would be going home, no one had ever suggested 1946. Three more years! She nearly cried, but caught herself. "Well, at least I'll be able to graduate," she thought, as she forced a small half-hearted smile.

Fortunately, there was little time to think about the additional years. She had orchestra practice next. It was the first of several full-blown rehearsals for the Saturday evening concert. More importantly, Saturday was when she was playing her clarinet solo. She was particularly nervous because Captain Ben would be there. She didn't want to make any mistakes, especially since he was bringing a visiting English dignitary, a Miss Hunnybun, from the Committee for the Care of European Children with him. As she walked into the rehearsal hall, she wished she had been a bit more conscientious about practicing. Maybe then she would have had a reasonable chance of getting through the solo without a mistake.

After another week of nervous concern, demanding rehearsals, and a considerable increase in the number of hours spent practicing, it was the night of the concert. Her solo was listed fourth on the program. Then, after a few extremely stressful minutes playing, minutes that seemed as if they would never end, she finished the solo.

She should not have worried, the audience gave her a nice warm ovation. Later, to her surprise, Captain Ben and Miss Hunnybun came backstage and congratulated her. Before leaving Ben asked if she would be willing to repeat her solo at the Thanksgiving party. She wasn't keen on playing in front of her fellow evacuees, but it was difficult to turn Captain Ben down, especially in front of Miss Hunnybun. After assurances that her performance was worth repeating, she agreed.

Afterwards, Jack and Ida held a small party at the farm ostensibly to celebrate Ann's solo. Invitees included Ida's younger brother, Ted, his wife, and several of the Schaefer neighbors and friends. None of Ann's schoolmates or friends were invited. It was good they weren't, for as the evening progressed several of the men visited the beer keg a little too often and became intoxicated and boisterous. When they started telling naughty stories and making vulgar jokes Ann decided she no longer belonged there. She excused herself, saying she was tired and was going to bed. Ted followed her into the hall. "Where are you going, honey?" he asked, slurring most of his words. "Why are you leaving Uncle Teddy so soon? Don't give up so easily, honey. I've been watching you carefully. Now don't try to deny it, I know what you were up to. You've been giving me the eye all evening. Haven't you? You think old Ted's kind'a sexy. I know you do. I can tell. And that's the gosh darn awful truth."

Ann was terrified. "I'm going to my room. I have schoolwork to finish," she lied. "You had better go back to the parlor. They'll be missing you."

"Parlor. That's what I like about you, Ann. Not 'living room,' not 'sitting room,' but 'parlor.' You use the cutest words," he smiled as he put both hands on the wall, one on each side of her waist. He had her trapped. "I like the way you talk and how pretty you look–you really are someone special. Do all English women look as pretty as you?"

He leaned closer. "You are a woman, aren't you?" he asked.

"Leave me alone, Ted. Please!" she pleaded.

"Come on now, my little cutie. Give Uncle Ted a kiss," he said grabbing Ann around the waist and pulling her close to him.

"Leave me alone," she sobbed as she felt his body pressing against hers. His breath smelled like a garbage can. It nearly made her sick.

"One little kiss! That's all I want," he demanded, putting his mouth on hers.

Ann could feel the spittle from his mouth running down her chin. "Maybe one more," he said as he stopped for breath then kissed her again, this time with more urgency. Ann tried to wiggle free, but her effort only served to excite him more. He pressed closer. His hand grabbed her skirt. He started to lift it.

"Don't!" Ann cried. "Stop it!" No one had ever treated her this way before. She had heard about things like this. She knew what was happening; the girls had talked about it at school. Using both hands and all her strength, she pushed desperately on his chest. He was too strong. She could not shove him away. Thoughts raced through her mind. She wondered what she should do. Should she scream? Cry? Fight harder?

By now her skirt was above her waist and his hand was on her panties. With a quick jerk he pulled them down. "Let's have a look," he said, as he released his hold on her and stepped back for a better view.

It was the chance Ann needed. With as much force as she could garner she smashed her knee into his groin. It happened so suddenly that he had no time to protect himself. He reeled backwards in agony; reflexively placing both hands at the focus of his pain. The distraction was sufficient for Ann to escape his grasp completely. She raced up the stairs and into her bedroom. There was no lock on the door. She quickly propped a chair underneath the doorknob hoping to keep him out; but certain it would be ineffective if he chose to force his way in. Fortunately, he decided he had taken too many liberties in the Schaefer household already. He abandoned pursuit and returned to the party, ignoring the throbbing pain and trying to appear as if nothing had happened.

Ann stood trembling at the door listening for his footsteps. She was certain he would followed her. It took nearly ten minutes before she convinced herself he was gone and the danger was over. It was only then that she yielded to her emotions and began to cry and shake violently.

Later, she carefully washed her entire body using the washbasin in her room; then, after finishing, she completely washed again. It did little to ease the shame. She felt dirty. She cried each time she thought about what had happened. She had heard about things like this but had never dreamed it would happen to her. She naively thought he had stolen her virginity. How could he do such a thing? She had planned on returning to England a virgin. Humiliated, saddened, and disappointed she continued to cry until finally she fell asleep.

"You look terrible," Karen told Ann when she came into the room to call her the next morning. "Don't you feel well?"

"There's nothing terribly wrong. I must have eaten too many sweets at the party," Ann answered, trying to straighten her hair with her hands. "I'll be okay, just as soon as I have my bath."

"Well, hurry. We overslept and still have the barn chores to do before going to church."

"I guess you're right, Karen. I guess I don't feel as well as I thought," she lied. "I think I'll skip church today. As soon as I finish my chores I'm going back to bed."

Karen was concerned. Ann was seldom sick, and almost never went back to bed once she finished her chores. When Ida found out she also asked Ann what was wrong. Ann's only answer was a simple noncommittal, "I'm just a little under the weather." Although she knew Ann was hiding something Ida decided it best not to pursue it further, at least not until Ann was ready to admit that was bothering her.

While the Schaefers were at church, Ann took two tub baths and still felt dirty. She didn't know what to do. She was ashamed to tell anyone what had happened, but desperately needed to share her secret with someone. "If only I hadn't come to America," she thought, "I'd have Mum to advise me. She'd know what to do."

When she got home from church, Ida repeatedly asked what was wrong. Each time Ann would insist she was better and Ida shouldn't worry. But she remained noticeably despondent, enough so that her classmates became concerned when they saw her on Monday. Both Bonnie and Oliver tried particularly hard to cheer her, but they couldn't. Oliver finally concluded her aloofness was caused by something he had said, it was almost as if she wanted to terminate their friendship.

The following Wednesday, Ann told Ida she thought it time she looked for a new foster home.

"For heavens sake, child," Ida replied, highly alarmed. "Whatever has come over you? Have we done something wrong? Are you upset with something we did or said?"

"No, ma'am," was Ann's simple answer. "I just think I've imposed on you long enough. It's time I burden some other family."

"First of all, Ann, you're no burden. None whatsoever. We enjoy having you here with us.

"Secondly, we all love you very much. In fact, we'd be happy if you stayed with us forever." She quickly modified her statement, "But don't accuse us of being selfish, of wanting you to remain here if it's not what's best for you.

"Thirdly, you are a great help here on the farm. With Jack and Karen working as much as they do and Ned in the service, I don't know how I'd get along without you. Now, what in heaven's name is wrong? Please tell me. Please?"

"There's nothing wrong. Honest!" Ann assured her. "I just think I need a change. It would be best for all of us. Please don't ask me to stay. I really want to go. Would you call Mrs. Studer? See if she can find a new home for me."

"Oh, Ann, if that is what you really want, of course I'll call—but please—please—reconsider."

Ann steadfastly refused to change her mind and the following morning Jack asked Dorothy Studer to start a search for a new home. While they waited for Dorothy to find a place, Ida cried every night in the privacy of their bedroom. "Oh Jack," she would say, "what have we done to make Ann so eager to leave?"

Jack did not have an answer. He had been so certain she had been happy on the farm. He cried too.

Chapter 99

Saturday, 27 November 1943

Attendance at the fourth Bender Electric Thanksgiving party differed considerably from the previous ones. Most significant, from Ann's point of view, was the absence of Graham and Ned, but there were many other changes. With Graham gone, the Nelsons had not been invited; Ned, along with many of the other foster brothers, a few sisters, and several of the fathers, were in the service and could not attend, and several original families had been replaced by new ones. Also new among the attendees were several members of the Bender board of directors and their families who, with E.J. Newton, were in town to discuss the need for increased production and cooperation between the American and English units.

The scarcities caused by rationing and the war were evident. The banquet food was a little more basic than in the past and clothes a little more subdued. Many of the women wore styles from the year before and, in some cases, worn the previous year—something no respectable woman would have ever considered in past years. For those women fortunate enough to have new dresses, shoulders were more padded than before and hemlines were above the knees. Even men's new trousers had changed, they no longer sported cuffs. Almost no one wore new shoes.

Although nearly everyone treated it with guarded caution and was reluctant to mention it, the length of their foster children's stay and, in some cases the request for a change in billet, was one of their main worries. Because they all thought their problem was unique, it usually came as a surprise when they discovered others with similar concerns.

Therefore, when Ida finally found the courage to allude to her difficulty with Ann she found many sympathetic ears. "I know what you mean," one mother said, "Doreen isn't happy anymore either."

"I guess we forget the girls are in their teens now," another remarked, "and you know how troublesome that time is for a young girl. How old is Ann?"

"Fifteen," Ida answered. "I suppose that could be the problem, but I doubt it. I just can't figure what is wrong."

"Doreen is fourteen," was the other's reply.

"Well that explains it!" someone else volunteered. "Heavens, you should have known my daughter when she was fifteen. She was unhappy with everything I did. She made my life nearly unbearable–and remember, she was at home, with her real parents. She wasn't in another country–away from home. Imagine how that must be. The poor dears." She looked at Ida and reassured her, "Don't worry, it's just a passing phase. She'll out grow it."

Ida thought better. It didn't make sense. Ann was not like that. True, Ann had her bad days and things had not always gone smoothly between them, but she was basically a happy girl. "No, it's not that," she said out loud. "There is something else that's troubling her."

Some of the women smiled, they were certain Ida was mistaken. Others thought about their own wards and wondered how this horrible war would play out and how long it would be until the children went home. For many, when they thought about the day their children would leave, felt panic in their hearts. They loved these children–too much to let them go. Somehow they needed to find an excuse to keep them. They could never say good-bye. They knew it was selfish to feel that way, but, still, they wanted to hold on to these children forever.

Ida decided to talk with Ann again after the party. She would try even harder than she had to persuade Ann not to leave. She wasn't going to give up. She would ask Jack to withdraw the request for a change in Ann's billet, he could do it the first thing Monday morning. She would talk to Mr. Roberts and Mrs. Studer too. Maybe the three of them could figure out what was wrong. Her thoughts were interrupted by the call to dinner.

After dinner Captain Ben tapped on his drinking glass and made his usual speech about how grateful everyone was to have these wonderful young visitors still here with them in McKinley Heights and how he hoped the war would end soon so everyone could return safely to their loved ones in Britain. He then surprised everyone by announcing "a small program put on by these wonderful children from England—especially for the members of the board of directors who honor us with their attendance here tonight"

After several dance performances and a poetry reading, it was Ann's turn. Although there was no orchestra to accompany her this time, her clarinet solo, once again, went well.

Afterwards, everyone congratulated the performers and praised them for their hard work and outstanding skills. Among those who congratulated Ann was Charles Jefferson. "Congratulations, Miss Montgomery," he said, shaking Ann's hand. "That was a superb performance. I enjoyed it immensely. Perhaps I will have the good fortune of hearing you play again some time?"

Ann could not believe he was talking to her. It was unthinkable. She was actually being congratulated by Charles Jefferson–Charles Throkmorton Jefferson, the son of a Bender director. Earlier in the evening the girls had noticed him. They had called him a 'real dreamboat'. They all agreed that he was someone they would do almost anything to meet. He was not only handsome but quite wealthy too. His father, a New York banker, was worth a fortune. Even the American girls, who were much less conscious of class distinctions than the evacuees, admitted Mr. Charles Throkmorton Jefferson was in a class far above any boy they had ever thought of, even in their wildest dreams. "I'd just die if he ever talked to me," someone had said. "Oh, yes! Wouldn't that be wonderful?" the others agreed, pretending to swoon.

"I'd be most honored to play for you again, sir," Ann replied, curtseying slightly, as she vaguely recalled that commoners were required to do when they met royalty.

"Please, Miss Montgomery, don't call me sir. My name is Charles and I hope to see you again," he said. "Real soon."

"Thank you, Charles. I hope so too."

Afterwards, the girls gathered around Ann and squealed, "Ooh, Ann! You actually touched his hand. How dreamy! How exciting!"

For the first time since that horrible Saturday, Ann felt alive again. She giggled and blushed and joined in the excitement. She was happy, not so much from meeting Charles, but because she had become the focus of all the attention–she felt important. They envied her, that was why–not because she was the butt of every joke, which she would be, if they ever found out what Ted had done to her. Remembering that horrible episode made her, once again, feel dirty and unclean.

"Oh, Edith," she complained, having gone off with her friend to a quiet corner of the hall. "I don't know what to do. It was so horrible! I don't know where to turn."

"What happened, Ann?" Edith asked, frowning and looking worried.

"I can't bother you with my troubles. You have troubles of you own. Good heavens, your foster parents sound horrible. How do you stand them?"

"They are terrible. Believe me. It's certainly different coming to these parties with that family. I really miss Brad and Clara. But what about you? I can't imagine you wanting to leave Mr. and Mrs. Schaefer. They're such sweet people. What did they do to you?"

"You don't understand, there's nothing wrong with Aunt Ida and Uncle Jack," Ann quickly corrected her. "They're as nice as ever. It's just that ... well ... it's just that I'm ashamed to continue living with them."

"Ashamed? Why on earth would you be ashamed?"

Ann hesitated for a few moments and then, with tears in her eyes, she blurted out, "I was raped, Edith! That's why! I was raped!"

"Oh, Ann, that's terrible! By whom?"

"By Aunt Ida's brother. It happened after the concert two weeks ago. Oh, Edith, it was horrible!"

"Have you told anyone?"

"I can't! I can't tell the Schaefers. They'd be so ashamed of me."

"Of you? You were raped, Ann. It wasn't your fault. It was Ida's brother's. For heavens sake! Tell them. If you won't, I will!"

"No, Edith! Please don't!"

Edith rose to her feet and started to move toward the table where Ida was talking with Kirk and Lucy Maurer. "Stop! Please stop. I didn't confide in you for you to tattle. If you're my friend you won't tell," Ann pleaded, grabbing Edith by the arm and pulling her back.

"All right, Ann, I won't say anything. Not tonight. But I'll keep quiet only for a little while. If you don't tell someone soon, I will. That bastard must not get away with what he did."

Edith and Ann were still discussing Ann's problem when Fred walked up, "Hi, everybody. Nice to see you again. Now that Graham's gone, I seldom see you. It's too bad. Have you heard anything from Graham?"

"I received a cablegram from him early this month," Ann volunteered. He's stationed in England, not far from home. Evidently he won't be directly involved in the fighting. He sees Mum and Dad pretty often now. He said he made it through training pretty well, but we wouldn't recognize him. His weight is nearly a stone more than when he left here, but he says it's not fat, claims it's all muscle."

"Yes, the Nelsons received a cablegram too. I believe Meg has received a number of letters since he left but she refuses to show any of them to me. I suppose they're too personal. They were very close just before he left. Do you know anything about that, Ann.?"

Ann chose to ignore Fred's question. She wasn't going to divulge what Meg had told her in confidence. "The only other correspondence I've received was a brief note written in September, while he was in training. Graham was never much of a letter writer."

"I imagine Edith already has received more letters from Ned than all the letters Graham has written in his lifetime," Fred interjected, trying to tease Edith.

Edith blushed, but did not admit she already had a whole shoebox full in her closet.

"I'll bet they are filled with his undying love," he added.

"You know," Fred said turning toward Ann. "Meg has Graham and Edith has Ned. Perhaps it's time you and I got together. Don't you think?" He put his arm around her and drew her close to him.

Fred's action brought back memories of Ted. The blood left Ann's face and she turned deathly white. "Quit it, Fred! Leave her alone!" Edith screamed at him.

"What did I do? I was only trying to be friendly. It's not as if I committed a terrible crime."

"Just stop it! Get out of here this instant!" she said, pushing him violently away.

"What's going on, children?" Ida said looking over at them.

"Nothing, ma'am," Edith lied. "We're just teasing each other."

Fred blushed and walked away and called to Steve, as if nothing had happened.

"As I was saying," Lucy continued, "we love Sandy so much. She loves us, too. I can't imagine why you people are having so much trouble with your children. Perhaps you're not trying hard enough?"

Ida could not believe what she had heard. She and Jack loved Ann as much as anyone. How dare Lucy accuse her of not trying? She loved Ann and would do anything to make her happy.

Chapter 100

Sunday, 5 December 1943

"Stop that, Bossy," Ann scolded. "It hurts when you hit me with your tail! I have enough troubles without you making it worse. I'll finish in a few minutes. It's your fault, you know? You're not giving much milk anymore. Just cooperate and I'll be done before you know it."

The steady "spurt, spurt" sound of the milk hitting the pail soon returned Ann to her angst. The incident with Ted still weighed heavily on her mind. She had no idea what she should do. The talk with Edith had not helped; she remained ashamed, embarrassed, and devastated by what had happened. She needed to talk to someone, knew she should confide in Ida but couldn't quite bring herself to do it; it was just too embarrassing. A sudden swish of Bossy's tail brought Ann back to reality. "Sorry, girl. You're right; there's no use continuing, you've given all you can. Haven't you, girl?"

After her chores were over Ann returned to her room. If she hurried there would be just enough time to write to her mum and dad before church.

Dear Mum and Dad,

Sorry for taking so long to write. There have been so many things happening here lately that I haven't had time. Nothing to worry about. Just many little things that keep your little girl from her duty of writing regularly to her mum and dad. Please forgive her? She is truly ashamed and promises to do better hereafter.

Graham sent a cable in November. Glad to learn he is remaining in England after his training. I imagine it makes both of you awfully happy. It must be nice having your son with you on weekends, even if one of your <u>other</u> children is still missing. Graham says he has gained some weight. I hope he doesn't look too fat. Ha! Ha! He must be busy with all his important military responsibilities but ask (no tell) him to please write soon. I wish he were here, it was always so nice to have a big brother to talk with when a problem arose–not that I have a problem. I just really miss him! But I understand why he returned. He felt a need to do his part for the Empire! Believe me I would do the same if I were a boy–and old enough.

By the time you receive this letter I may no longer be living with the Schaefers. I have decided, if I am going to make the most of this adventure in America, I need to see it from as many points of view as possible. Living with the same family for such a long time has limited my perspective. Don't you think? Anyway, I told Uncle Jack I wanted to be placed with another family for the remainder of my stay. He talked to Mr. Roberts at Bender Electric last month. They are looking for a new family as I write.

Now don't conclude there is anything wrong between Aunt Ida or Uncle Jack and me. They have been super people. As I said, it was simply time for a change.

I must admit though, at times, such as when milking cows on a cold wintry day, I can empathize with Yvonne's dislike of farms. But then there are all those other times: the long tramps through the woods on a snowy day with all its peaceful solitude; the warm cuddly farm kittens purring in your lap; the smell of apple butter cooking in the open vat; the cozy winter evenings sitting by the fireplace playing checkers; etc. I don't understand why she doesn't appreciate the farm more. Imagine how it would have been had she been assigned to work in the coal mines like some of the English men must do.

There was a note written in the margins here emphasizing the farm had nothing to do with her request to change billets.

I have written to Yvonne again but haven't received an answer. I guess I'll give up. She apparently has no interest in corresponding with me. What did I do to make her so angry? Doesn't she know I love her?

I gave a clarinet solo at school last month. Miss Hunnybun from the U.S. Committee for the Care of European Children was at the perform-ance. She came backstage afterward and congratulated me. She said she would be in touch with you when she returned to the U.K. Perhaps she has–by the time you read this letter. I wish letters traveled back and forth more rapidly. These horribly long delays are so dreadful. I wish there were some way to do away with them. But I guess I will be back home long before there's any change in the postal service–at least I hope I'll be back there by then!

Can you imagine? In four more days, we will celebrate (That's the wrong word. Should it be rue?) the second anniversary of the attack on Pearl Harbor. How terrible that was and how much has happened since. There are so many Dexter Hills boys now in the service. There seem to be service flags in almost every window nowadays. The Nelsons have one hanging in their window for Graham and, of course, the Schaefers have one for Ned.

Speaking of Ned, he completed his advanced training in November and has already received his orders to ship overseas. We don't know where (he isn't permitted to tell us directly because of the strict military secrecy), but we surmise from his letters he will be going east. Perhaps to England! He said he hoped he could visit you the next time he got home. (We think that was his coded way of telling us the country where he was headed.) Let us know if you hear from him. Wouldn't it be a strange and wonderful coincidence if he and Graham were to meet in Pinnington?

Aunt Ida has just said if I don't hurry I'll be late for church. I still need to change out of my farm clothes, wash, and get into my Sunday togs (else no one could sit in the pew beside me–Ha, ha) so I must hurriedly say good-bye. Lady says good-bye too–she is sitting here by my side. What a wonderful friend she is!

Love,

Ann

After lunch, according to plan, Jack challenged Karen to Chinese checkers in the parlor and Ida asked Ann to help her mend some things upstairs. The Schaefers had decided it was time to take a more forceful approach. Ida was determined to pry a confession from Ann, find out, once and for all, what was troubling her. She began by saying, "I thought you should know, Jack has asked Mr. Roberts to hold up your transfer."

"Why would you do that, Aunt Ida?"

"Because we need to know what has been troubling you. Otherwise the same thing might happen again."

"It won't. You can count on that!" Ann tried to assure her.

"How do we know for certain, Ann?"

"Because. Just because."

"No! That's not good enough. We're not going to leave this room until you tell me what I did that made you so determined to move."

"It was nothing you did. Honest."

"Then was it Uncle Jack?"

"No!"

"Karen?"

"No."

"For heavens sakes, child, tell me. Tell me what it was!"

"I can't, Aunt Ida. I can't!"

"Why not?"

"It's too embarrassing. It's too terrible."

Ida put her hands around Ann and drew her near. "You know I love you, Ann. I want to help you, but I can't if you won't confide in me." She paused, then asked, "Have I ever been unreasonable with you? Haven't I always listened to your problems? Didn't we always work them out together?"

Ida began to cry.

"Oh, Aunt Ida, please don't cry. Yes! You have always been good to me. I know you want to help but ... Well ... No, I can't tell anyone– not even you. It's too horrible."

"Please! Please, let me help you?" Ida pleaded, her sobs becoming more and more convulsive. "Tell me!" she said, as she firmly, but lovingly, shook Ann.

Ann began to cry too. They sat on the bed a long time, embraced, neither saying anything, both sobbing. Finally Ann broke the silence, "I was raped, Aunt Ida! I was raped!"

"Good God! When? By whom?"

"At the party, the Saturday evening after the band concert."

"In Dexter Hills? In the field?"

"No. Here in the house."

"In the house! How could that be? Where was I?"

"You were in the parlor. It was in the hall, outside the parlor. I had just said goodnight and was on my way to my room."

"Who?" Ida asked incredulously.

Ann hesitated. She looked at the floor, "It was ... Oh, I can't tell you, Aunt Ida."

"Tell me!" Ida demanded, her voice rose, reflecting her anger.

"Yo ... You ... Your brother Ted!" she finally blurted.

"Ted!" Ida shouted. "How could he? He wasn't out of the room all evening. Was he? Tell me exactly what happened."

Ann described the experience and when finished said, "Oh, Aunt Ida, I didn't want to lose my virginity. I wanted to remain a nice girl. Go back to England pure. Marry a nice man someday, and be his–only his."

"Oh, you poor child. Why didn't you tell me sooner? You're still a virgin. He didn't violate you. What he did was wrong and he must be punished for it–severely punished, but he did not take away your purity. You're still our sweet, gentle, little, innocent Ann."

They hugged and held each other tightly. "Oh, Mummy!" Ann said. "I love you, Mummy."

Ida could not believe what she had just heard. Ann had called her Mummy! Ann thought of her now as her mother, not her aunt. The child was now hers, not Diane's. She knew she should feel guilty–feel compassion for Diane–but she couldn't. She was too overjoyed, perhaps too selfish, but still overjoyed. Ann had become her daughter. Ann was hers. "There's no need for you to move. Everything will be all right," she whispered.

"But what about Ted?"

"Don't you worry your pretty little head about Ted. When I tell Jack about this I assure you he'll take care of your problem with Ted. Ted should never bother you again. There is no room in our family for someone of his ilk."

Tears continued to roll down Ann's cheeks as they held onto each other. Only after Lady put her nose in Ann's hand did Ann finally begin to smile. She would not be leaving the farm.

It was what she had wanted all the time; she just hadn't known how to stay.

Chapter 101

Wednesday, 2 February 1944

Graham was exhausted. He had just returned from another glider run; this time with full kit. It was only his third run and, like the others, the flight had made him quite queasy. He wondered if he would ever get used to those bumpy rides and, especially, to the rough landings. Afterwards, they had gone on a forced march for nearly ten miles before engaging mock enemy units dug in behind hedgerows. It had been a tough fight and had lasted for several hours. Fortunately, lorries were there to transport his unit back to the barracks; he wouldn't have made it on foot otherwise–at least he didn't think so. He was thankful the simulated assault was finally over; it had seemed so real and frightening. He wondered what actual combat would be like. "What if the blue army had been really aiming at me, instead of pretending? What if they had seriously been trying to kill me?" As it was, he had gotten quite sick with fear. His stomach was only now beginning to return to normal. He hoped no one had noticed how scared he had been.

*   *   *

2 February 1944

Dear Ann,

Please forgive the long delay in writing to you. As you might expect, it has been what I might best describe as "hell" since joining the Army. We have been in almost constant training and I have never worked so hard in my life. They will not permit me to tell you what type of training I am involved in but, suffice it to say, it is making a man out of me—perhaps a tired old man. It's strenuous, strenuous, strenuous! You wouldn't recognize me. I have muscles where I never knew muscles existed. Perhaps, with all the rough airborne talk, and the near absence of art and culture here in camp, I am growing more muscle between my ears too. Ha! Ha!

The only thing saving me culturally is the excellent music festivals at the local cathedral. Not too long ago I was lucky enough to obtain free tickets to see Pablo Casals playing "Elgar's Cello Concerto." Attending the festivals is one of the few perquisites we receive because we are English servicemen. If I were an American, I probably wouldn't have had such an opportunity. America seems to have so little culture. How many times did we see performance of that caliber in Oakton? On the other hand, maybe that's unfair. Had they evacuated us to New York City or one of the other major American cities, things might have been different, we might have been able to attend concerts of that sort. Oh well, America is past history for me.

I was home on a seventy-two hour leave the weekend before last and Mum and Dad showed me your letter of December 5. They are quite concerned about your decision to leave the farm. I hope you have reconsidered by now. None of us can think of any good reason for you to leave Ida and Jack. They are such nice people and have been so good to you. I truthfully don't believe you can find a better foster family—mom and Dad Nelson excepted, of course.

Yes, as you supposed, being home makes me quite happy. I highly recommend it! I love England and hope no one ever asks me to leave again. You will understand why when you get home.

As you noted in your letter to Mum, I am able to get home on occasion, although not as often as I would like. Mum still is an excellent cook, even though the poor dear has difficulty finding all the ingredients she needs for most of her old standbys. The food rationing is atrocious here, as is everything else. (Even toothbrushes are hard to find.) It's much worse than anything we had in America. Mum tried to have a turkey for Christmas but it was impossible to find one. We settled for roast lamb with pudding—which, if you recall, suits me just fine. It has always *been one of my favorites. We had a grand time at Christmas. After din-ner, Dad took Mum and me to see John Mills in "This Happy Breed." We were just coming out of the theater when the sirens sounded. There were no bombs dropped but what a fright it gave everyone. I can't imagine how our folks put up with all those months of air raids. How fortunate we were to have been evacuated. I realize I said–a paragraph earlier–that I recommend coming home. Indeed I do–but only after the war has ended!*

When you do, expect to find many changes–not only physical but social. The Labour Party is assuring us things will be different once they're back in power. Mr. Bevin, minister of labour, is talking about budgeting jobs and holding the government more responsible for the social welfare of the people. There is even talk about radical changes in education. Perhaps working-class people like us will be able to take better advantage of higher education someday, much as they do in America. One thing's certain: it won't be the same Britain it was when we left in 1940.

I would have loved to hear your clarinet solo. I'll bet everyone was pleased with your performance. I know afterwards I would have been strutting around the auditorium saying "She's my sister!. What a grand girl she is; almost as good as Casals."

By the bye, what's this I hear about a certain "Charles" at the Thanksgiving party? Fred tells me the two of you made quite a hit with each other. Way to go, sis–or should I call you Lady Ann? Find a rich American if you can. I highly recommend it. Ha! Ha! But, what about Oliver? I'll bet it didn't set too well with him; if my memory of what went on between the two of you is correct. Ha, ha, again!

I hope your guess that Ned is somewhere here in England is correct. If so, maybe we can somehow get together before long. When you write to him, remind him to look up Mum and Dad. Through them, perhaps we can arrange to meet. It would be nice to see someone from Ohio. As wonderful as it is to be home, I still have mixed feelings about leaving. I often wish I were back there among my friends and especially (Blush! Blush!) with Meg. We write to each other often, but it's no substitute for being with her. Perhaps, after the war, I'll be able to invite her over here? Who knows?

Well, Ann, the sergeant has just said lights will be out in ten min-utes, so I had better finish this quickly. Besides, this letter is much too long for your brother to be writing. If he's not careful he'll lose his reputation for only producing short notes.

It may be a long time before I have another free moment like this, but I'll do my best to write as soon as I can. In any case, please write to me–letters are always welcome.

Love,

Graham

As Graham climbed into his bunk and the lights went out he thought of Meg. He hadn't been completely honest with Ann. His plans for Meg were much more definite than he had hinted. He knew what he wanted; he wanted her to come to England, to live with him. She couldn't help but fall in love with England, once she saw its beautiful countryside and lovely towns. They would be married and live in one of those quaint Cotswold cottages, surrounded by all their children and a flower filled garden–filled with the same lovely flowers he remembered growing in his mum's garden. "Oh, dear, dear, Meg. It isn't fair," he sighed to himself, "you on one side of the ocean; with me on the other. No! It's completely unfair to have an ocean between us. Come to me, my love. Please make it soon!"

But he knew it would not be soon. There was still a war to settle, and that would take many months. It was true, things were looking better: the Russians were pushing the Germans back now; just a few days before, the Red Army had reportedly begun to gain an upper hand in Leningrad; the Allies, with the recent landing at Anzio, appeared ready to break the stalemate on the Italian front; and Allied forces were making slow, but steady, headway in the Pacific, evidenced by the recent assault at Saidor in New Guinea and the attack on the Marshall Islands.

But there was much left to be done. Graham suspected his unit was being trained to take a major role in some part of this. No one knew exactly what it would be but everyone in camp believed something big was not too far off. Stockpiles of equipment and supplies had recently been growing, and no one could deny the expanded intensity and realism in their training maneuvers. The exercise he had just completed was undoubtedly designed to simulate some sort of future military campaign. The increased number of bombers he heard taking off from the nearby airfield each day also suggested something was in the wind. It was obvious the bombing of Nazi occupied Europe had been stepped up appreciably. Apparently, the commanders were ignoring the growing public concern over the effectiveness of these raids. Whatever it was they were planning, Graham hoped it would bring a quick end to the war.

He was just leaving on a weekend furlough when the two letters arrived. One was from Fred, the other from Meg. Graham opened Fred's letter first so he could prolong the joy of having a new unopened letter from Meg in his pocket waiting to be read. As with all of Fred's letters, it started with a detailed description of his sports prowess, this time as a member of the basketball team. There was no denying that Fred was an outstanding athlete, he just wished Fred wouldn't brag so much about it. There was also an equally lengthy description of the problems Fred had with a recent girlfriend. It seemed she was pregnant and blamed it on him. He swore to Graham it was untrue. He said it couldn't be his, he had never "done it" with her. He suspected she had accused him because she thought the Derringers would help her financially. She probably thought they would want to keep everything quiet. It had been resolved after one of his teammates finally admitted to an involvement with her. Fred had used nearly a page to tell how Tom and Victoria had supported him throughout the ordeal, how they continued to encourage him in sports and studies, and how proud they were to have him as their son. Graham had to smile. He could recall Fred's initial relationship with the Derringers, how they had treated him like hired help. He marveled at the change nearly three and one half years had made.

Meg's letter described her college life, how much she enjoyed it, and how happy she was to be there. Although her school life interested him, happily, most of the letter was about how she missed him and wished they were together again. She encouraged him to be careful and told him to hurry back to her as soon as the war was over. She said she would gladly leave school, if necessary; if it would help get them back together sooner. As he read, his desire to hold her in his arms increased tenfold. Before leaving for Pinnington, he placed her letter in his shirt pocket, as close to his heart as possible. It was the only way he had to keep her close to him.

On the trip to Pinnington, the rail line passed many military depots. Although there was some attempt to hide everything, the large stockpiles of tanks, weapons, and other military equipment were still obvious. Graham wondered how and where the Army could use so much equipment. He was almost certain that somehow it was connected to the recent training exercises.

He did not mention the stockpiles when he arrived home. He thought it in the best interests of everyone if he said nothing.

The visit was one of the best since he had returned to England. Chad was in a happy mood all weekend and seemed to enjoy himself more than at any other time. Diane was extremely happy too and spent a great deal of time talking with him. They speculated about his future and Ann's return from America. He told Diane how he planned to bring Meg to Britain and to marry her. Diane was ecstatic. She had feared he would return to America after the war. Now she was fairly assured he wouldn't. "Oh happy day, you are going to live in England. With any luck, you'll settle near Pinnington. Now if Ann does the same, I'll finally have you two back where you belong; and this horrible evacuation will only be a bad memory," she said excitedly.

By the time Graham returned to the camp, all civilian travel was banned in an area extending ten miles inland from the sea. It stretched from Cornwall to the Wash. Graham was permitted into the area only because he had a pass which proved he was stationed there. He had a feeling it might be his last leave for some time.

Chapter 102

Saturday, 18 March 1944

The melancholy whistle woke Ned from his nap. He looked out the window from his third-class compartment, surprised to see daylight. It seemed as if only a few moments ago it had been dark outside. Apparently he had dozed off. He looked at his watch. It was seven o'clock. He had slept nearly three hours!

Thank goodness he had been able to sleep. He was fortunate to have been one of the first to board the train. It had become crowded soon afterwards and many were left standing. Some were still standing–the poor souls. Only a few, the lucky ones like himself, had found a seat or were able to curl up on the floor. He supposed he should have looked for some little old lady, or some other deserving person, and offered his seat, but he hadn't; his tired body had outvoted his good manners.

Truthfully, he shouldn't have been on the train. The maneuvers had left him too exhausted. It would have been better had he found a hotel room and rested instead of traveling all the way to London. The trouble was, there was a good possibility passes might be discontinued any day now; there were all sorts of rumors that something big was about to happen. If it did, he might never be able to visit Ann and Edith's parents. While he still could, he had decided to go, no matter how tired he was.

He couldn't believe he had only been in Armbaugh for three months. The duty had been tough which had made it seem much longer. He had been assigned to the Second Signal Company of the Second Infantry Division, a unit which had arrived in North Ireland last October, over two months ahead of him. Because he was one of the latecomers, most of his time had been spent learning additional combat techniques and mastering the signal equipment unique to his company. All that, combined with what seemed like an incessant number of field exercises, kept him overly busy. Even so, because he was determined to be fully prepared for combat, he had used most of his little remaining free time studying everything he could find on combat and communications. It left little time for writing letters to Edith, the one thing he had been determined to do no matter how busy he was. But he wouldn't even be able to do that if his schedule got any worse.

He had received two letters this week. His regular weekly letter from Edith and a letter from Ann. Edith's letter, besides expressing her love and affection for him, told of her worsening relationship with Hazel and Jim and her increasingly desperate need to find a new place to stay. The severity of the problem concerned him. He felt he had to do something, especially when Edith had sounded so depressed in her letters. The last letter was so bad that he had immediately requested one of the rare London passes that sometimes were available. Surprisingly, the first sergeant had issued it, even though he still considered Ned a newcomer. Apparently, although he would never admit it, the sergeant was a sentimentalist and had signed it after learning Ned wanted to visit his foster sister's English family. Ned hadn't told him he also would be visiting his girlfriend's parents. He thought that might make his request sound too suspicious. It must have been a good tactic, he got the pass.

The train arrived in Paddington Station around noon, nearly three hours behind schedule. It took another two hours until Ned was able to find his way to Pinnington. He was surprised when he saw Ann's house. There was clear evidence of major damage. The few repairs already attempted had obviously been made rapidly and were rather crude, although probably as good as could be expected. He wondered why Ann had never told him her home was so severely damaged. When he remarked to Chad about it, Chad admitted they had kept it from Ann. He said they had not wanted to worry her and hoped Ned would not tell her either.

The afternoon went by quickly. Ned told many anecdotes about Ann, amusing things that had happened to her on the farm. Diane showed him pictures in an old photo album. They were all of the family before 1940. "Oh dear," Diane suddenly remarked, "these are the last pictures of Ann and Graham. I have no record of the them since then. It will be four years in September. Almost four years of my little girl's life lost to me!" Ned thought he detected tears in her eyes.

Diane continued, "Never in our wildest dreams did we ever imagine she would be gone this long. I sometimes wonder if she will recognize us when she returns–and if we will recognize her. Lord knows, Graham has certainly changed. It has taken us such a long time to know each other again. Even though he has been home–well at least back in Britain–since last June, there are times he still seems almost like a stranger.

Certainly our relationship is not as it once was. Sometimes I think he misses America and wishes he were there instead of here.

"Even though he rightfully belongs here," she added.

Ned tried to brighten things a little. "Ann certainly has become a fine looking young lady, Mrs. Montgomery. You will be quite proud of her when she comes home. Be assured, she looks forward to coming. She is going to be extremely happy when that day comes."

"It shouldn't be too much longer, Mother," Chad assured Diane, looking at Ned, as if for confirmation. "Although there is still a tough road ahead, the end is nearly in sight–at least I hope so. Thanks to help from you Yanks, we're beginning to get the best of old Schickelgruber.

"Let's hope it's over before you and Graham see any action," he added, looking hopefully at Ned.

From all the training his outfit had been receiving, Ned was nearly certain Chad's wish would not come true. If Graham's unit was participating in the same sort of exercises as his was, they both were almost certain to see action. No one had ever told him why they were training, but whatever the reason, the massive buildup and intensity of the maneuvers made it clear something major was going to happen, and pretty soon. It would probably be bloody too, whatever it was. But the activities of his unit were confidential and he couldn't comment about them; he simply answered, "I hope so too."

He had planned to find lodging in a local hotel after leaving the Montgomerys, then visit Edith's folks the next morning but Diane would not hear of it. "Nonsense," she said, "you can stay here with us. Heaven knows we have enough room with all our children gone." She pondered a minute, then continued, "Perhaps Graham will make it home this evening. Maybe you should sleep in Ann's bed. Wouldn't it be nice if you and Graham could see each other?"

"It certainly would. I'd love to see him," Ned answered enthusiastically.

But Graham did not come home and after an excellent breakfast that must have used many of the Montgomery's precious ration coupons, Ned said good-bye to Diane and Chad and began his hike to Ealing. As he disappeared around the corner Diane burst into tears, "He's such a nice young boy," she sobbed. "Imagine! He's been living with our little girl for almost four years. He saw her every morning at breakfast. He went to school with her. He assisted her with her maths, listened to her play the clarinet, was there for her when she needed support, watched her grow up. ... Oh, Chad, we've missed everything!"

It was late Sunday night before Diane was able to get back to her normal routine.

"Hello, I'm Ned Schaefer. You must be Mrs. Dickson. I talked to you on the telephone on Friday. I know your daughter," Ned said when Harriet opened the door.

"Of course. Hello, Ned. I've been waiting for you. My, my! What a handsome lad you are!" she said, stepping back to have a better look. "No wonder Edith says such nice things about you. Please come in."

Ned immediately liked Harriet. Looking at her brought back memories of Edith. Although he saw little physical resemblance between them, there was no mistaking Harriet was Edith's mother. They had many of the same mannerisms; so many it nearly made him cry. Harriet liked Ned, too. His presence opened a flood of memories for her. She, too, had difficulty holding back her tears. In spite of their loneliness for Edith and their desire not to be reminded of her, she continued to be the main topic of their conversation. There were, however, topics they avoided. She did not mention George, and he did not say anything about Edith's problems with Jim and Hazel. The Edith she talked about was a child while the girl he described was the mature sweet young lady he adored. It was only after considerable good natured teasing from Harriet, that he finally admitted he loved Edith and hoped to marry her as soon as the war was over. He described his plans for the two of them living on a farm and raising a large family.

"Such a lovely plan," Harriet said. "I hope you do. It's easy to see you're a nice boy and love her very much. But, please? If you do marry someday, promise me you'll give her much love and respect and will always treat her nicely."

Ned could not understand why Harriet had emphasized this. "Of course I will, ma'am. I couldn't imagine treating her any other way."

"I'm sorry. Forgive me? I'm sure you will. You see I am particularly sensitive to the way a gent treats his mate. I haven't told Edith anything about this yet, but please, permit me to tell you. You see, George, that's Edith's father, and I were divorced last August. Edith must have told you how mean he was. I simply couldn't take it any longer. I finally sent him packing."

Ned did not quite know how to respond. "I'm sorry. Please accept my sympathy," he finally said after a few awkward moments.

"Sympathy isn't the right word. I'd say congratulations would be more appropriate," Harriet quipped, a smile on her face. "But please don't tell Edith. She has enough worries in America all by herself. I've been keeping it from her and don't plan to tell her until she comes home."

Ned was astounded. Yesterday Ann's parents had asked him not to tell about the bomb damage to their house. Now this. That made two secrets he had to keep. He wondered if all the parents of the evacuees were keeping things from their children. If so, he foresaw some terribly sad times ahead, especially when the children went home and had to face all these surprises. "I really believe you should tell her, Mrs. Dickson. You'd be surprised to see how grown up she is. I'm almost certain she would rather hear it now, instead of when she gets home."

"Perhaps you're right. I'll think on it." she promised, although fully certain she wouldn't change her mind. "But perhaps it won't matter anyway, maybe she won't ever come home? She's always threatened that she wouldn't. Maybe you'll marry her and keep her there yourself."

"Don't worry about that. She'll be back. I'm certain she is looking forward to it. Besides, I haven't formally asked her to marry me yet. When I do, she might not accept. And even if she does, I promise you, she'll come home first, just as soon as she can, to see you."

"It would be all right if she doesn't, just as long as she's happy. From her letters I think it's only her recent unhappiness with the family she is living with that has prompted all the talk about coming home. She certainly doesn't have anything nice to say about Mr. and Mrs. Adams. Of course, you no longer being there hasn't helped matters either. She misses you terribly.

"She seems to be happy with her schooling though. She is always writing wonderful things about all that she is learning and the wonderful opportunities to continue in college once she graduates. I really do believe she'd be better off making America her home. There would be a much greater opportunity to follow the career she wants. But I guess that isn't too important anymore since you plan to make her a farmer's wife."

"There will be plenty of time to discuss giving up a career to live on a farm," Ned assured her, laughing at her assumption that it was a forgone conclusion that Edith and he would marry. "I'm afraid this conversation has gone too far afield. There are no definite wedding plans yet."

"I only want what is best for my daughter. If the two of you should decide to marry you have my blessing. In fact I'd encourage it," she added. "Times are going to be tough here in Britain after the war–and for many years afterwards. There will be scarcities and deprivations for a long time. America should be a much better place to live."

Ned left that evening, impressed with Harriet's unselfishness and deep concern for her daughter. He liked Harriet and could see why Edith had such good qualities, obviously she inherited them from her mother. The only thing though, he was sorry Mrs. Dickson had pushed marriage so much. Not that there was any doubt about asking Edith to marry him, it was just that ... Well ... What if he didn't get home? What if something happened to him? What if he were killed? What if he were seriously wounded? He certainly didn't want Edith, or her mother, to be disappointed, or tied down with a cripple. It was better he kept his future plans with Edith somewhat uncertain.

Ned had no other opportunity to visit either Harriet or the Montgomerys again. He arrived back in Ireland just in time to participate with his unit in a training exercise much more intense than anything he had so far experienced. Then, in the middle of April, his division moved across the Irish sea to a camp near Tenby in south Wales. There they participated in additional realistic training exercises, including amphibious landings on the English coast at Slapton Sands. It was there that Ned received his first taste of deadly fire. A communications mix-up caused his unit to go ashore before the naval bombardment had stopped. There were many casualties that evening. Fortunately he escaped without injury, the only price, a deep concern about his courage. He had never been that scared before. He quickly concluded he was a coward, and was almost certain he would be of no use to his unit if it ever saw real action.

My Dearest Edith, he wrote a few nights later.

My thoughts are about you more than ever now. You are in my dreams whenever I sleep and on my mind whenever I'm awake. I love you, my sweet. If only I could count the days until you are in my arms again! But alas, in these troubled times that is quite impossible. It may be weeks, it may be months, or–heaven forbid–it may be years, but rest assured, if I survive, I will come back to you as soon as I possibly can. I promise! One day you will look up and see me knocking at your door and then, only a moment later, you'll once more be in my arms. How I love you, my precious kitten, my confidante, my lover!

But do I merit your love? Am I deserving of your affection? I think not. I am too spineless, too weak, too timid for someone as good as you. I can never be your knight, your defender, your champion ... I fear I am destined to fail in my quest to serve you, my darling. Forgive me? Please, please, forgive me?

Signed with all my love,

Ned.

*   *   *

When the letter arrived in McKinley Heights, Edith noticed the wrinkled spots where his tears had fallen. She lay awake late that night worrying. It was different from all his other letters. There was something in it besides the thoughts of a homesick, or lovesick, boy. It contained a hint of fatalism and self-deprecation. She wondered why. What did it mean?. She could not get it out of her mind. "Be careful, my dear," she sobbed into her pillow late that night. "Please come home–safely!"

Although it was not the day she normally wrote to Ned, she rose early the following morning and quickly jotted a note. Before leaving for school, she hid the letter in her blouse. If Hazel saw it she would go into another of her rages. She would once again repeat her demand that Edith stop wasting her time, stop writing to that stupid farm boy. Edith had heard enough of her diatribes. She was in no mood for another.

Chapter 103

Thursday, 13 April 1944

Oliver was nervous and excited as they sat in the Schaefer driveway. Nervous because he was about to ask Ann for a date, excited because it would be his first date in his own automobile.

It all began nearly two weeks ago, on his sixteenth birthday. Unexpectedly his dad had asked him if he was ready to take his driver's exam. If so, he would take him to the license bureau, as a birthday present. Oliver was delighted. He had been studying for sometime but had never known when he would be able to take the test or whose car he would use. Certainly he had never expected it would be his dad's.

He had played hooky that day; he wasn't very proud about that part. They left early in the morning and by noon he had his license. He had to smile when he thought of what the examiner had said. "I'm amazed," he said with a wink, "how fast you learn. You received your learner's permit only a few minutes ago and already you're a skillful driver. It's almost as if you had driven before." Oliver, of course, had plenty of practice. His dad had taught him to drive over a year ago, said it would be useful in case of a family emergency. Oliver couldn't count the number of times he had been called to the tavern late at night because his dad was too drunk to drive home himself.

"Drop me off at the tavern," his dad said on the way back from the bureau. "Then go to the Seed & Feed and pick up my order. Drop it off at John Summers'. Tell him I'll be by later today to begin planting his garden. Then come back to the tavern and park the car–you can walk home. I'll drive it home later." Suddenly it was obvious why his dad had been so eager to help; with a license he could use him as an errand boy.

By the time he got home, Oliver had decided to buy a car. It would take all the money he had been saving for school, but with a car he would have much greater independence. Then, perhaps, he could even find a part-time job outside Dexter Hills. With his own means of getting around there'd be no need to ask his dad for the family car, no need to suffer through all that embarrassment and humiliation, and more importantly, he could go on dates whenever he pleased. But it would not be easy finding one. Since they quit manufacturing autos in early '42, cars had become quite scarce. With no new ones available, no one was selling their old ones. It would take some real doing to find something, particularly something he could afford.

Three days later he bought an old 1929 Model-A Ford roadster. He found it at the junkyard. It was in terrible shape. The body was badly rusted, the fenders were missing, the tires were bald, the seat upholstery was badly torn, the electrical wires were bare in some places, one headlight was missing and the other badly damaged, and the engine crankshaft was frozen. But he was confident, with new valves, rings, main bearings, carburetor, fenders, tires, wiring, paint, and a lot of effort, he could restore it to running condition. By Thursday, after spending every available hour overhauling the engine, he had a working jalopy. Undaunted by its appearance, which still looked as if it belonged in the junkyard, he drove it to school and immediately won the admiration of his classmates, none of whom had their own car yet.

This somewhat surprising popularity made him feel good. Mostly though, it was Ann who he wanted to impress. He wanted her to be aware of his newfound freedom and maturity, and more importantly, he wanted her to be his first passenger. He decided to ask her to take a ride with him after school. He had worried all morning, afraid she would say no. If she turned him down, he had already made up his mind, he would coax and coax until she finally gave in, no matter how long it took. By fourth period he could delay it no longer, nervous or not, he had to ask. Blushing slightly and focusing his eyes on the ground rather than looking directly at her, he said, "I'd like you to be the first to ride in my new–well not new, just new to me–car. Would you go with me for a ride after school?"

"Yes, I saw your car in the parking lot this morning. I'd love to go, Oliver. That would be quite an honor. But we will have to go directly home, otherwise Aunt Ida will worry."

Oliver had been in heaven all the way to the farm. Things were looking up. Now here he was, in his car with Ann beside him, wondering, "Will she go on a date with me?" He had delayed long enough, he would swallow hard and ask.

"Would you care to go to the movies this evening?"

"I'd love too, Oliver. The only thing is, Aunt Ida doesn't want me to go out alone. She says I'm still too young. Could we invite Bonnie and John to go with us?"

"We can't. You can plainly see, it only seats two people; three if we squeeze together. Once I fix the rumble seat they could go, but I haven't been able to find the parts I need so far."

"Then I'm certain she'll not let me go."

"*So Proudly We Hail,* with Claudette Colbert, Paulette Goddard, and Veronica Lake is playing. It's at the Palace theater. I hear it's really a good movie. Isn't there some way we could convince her?"

Oliver asked her again at school the next morning. Ann was once again about to say no when Bonnie interrupted. "What are you two doing? Plotting some secret affair?" she asked and laughed.

"As a matter of fact, we are," Oliver said, trying to sound mysterious. "We're trying to figure a way to go to the movies without Ann's aunt knowing."

"No we're not, Oliver," Ann scolded, embarrassed at the notion they might be plotting against Ida.

"That's not a problem," Bonnie laughed. "You can stay at my house tonight, Ann. Oliver can pick you up there. My folks are going to a dance; they won't be home until quite late. They've already suggested I ask you to stay over–that's why I'm here. The movie doesn't last too long, you could easily get home ahead of them. They'd never know."

After a lengthy debate, they decided to do it.

Although the movie ranked among the best she had seen recently and Oliver generously kept returning to the refreshment stand for popcorn, candy, and Cokes, Ann did not enjoy herself. She couldn't stop worrying. She knew from the beginning that she was being dishonest. And her guilt worsened considerably when they arrived at the theater and found an exceptionally long line waiting to get in. The line was not unusual, everyone was going to the movies these days; there was almost always a wait–sometimes even through an entire feature–but she had hoped this evening would be the exception. The longer they stood the more likely someone would see them and tell Ida or Jack. What if they didn't make the next feature? It could be quite late before they got back to Bonnie's. It was entirely possible Bonnie's parents would be home ahead of them.

She was therefore greatly relieved when they made it back in time. Their secret was safe. Nevertheless, she vowed she would never do such a foolish thing again. She would never go on another date without permission. When they said good-night Oliver tried to kiss her, but she was upset and refused. She felt too ashamed of herself.

This indiscretion would prove to have a negative impact on their friendship. It would be some time before they would regain their self-respect, and an even longer time before they would rekindle the special feelings they had always shared towards each other.

Chapter 104

Saturday, 6 May 1944

Reveille sounded at three-thirty. By four-thirty Graham's platoon had eaten, dressed in full kit, and boarded their Airspeed Horsa gliders where they were anxiously awaiting the snap of the towline as it was pulled taunt by the Albemarle tow plane.

He sensed something different about the exercise this time. It was becoming obvious whatever it was they were preparing for was getting close at hand. Maybe it would be the invasion of France everyone had been talking about. Perhaps this was the final rehearsal. There must have been thousands of troops involved, even some from other countries. Never before had he seen so many men assembled, or so much activity. There was also a noticeable difference in the officers. He could not recall having ever received such a thorough briefing, or having seen them so nervous and serious about the importance of meeting schedules and objectives as they had been this morning.

The takeoff was particularly rough. Heavy usage during the past several months had severely damaged the runway. Its roughness, the ensuing choppy ride, and, perhaps most of all, the thought that the exercise foreshadowed an upcoming real operation, made him wish he had skipped breakfast.

The plan was for the company to land, quickly assemble, then secure an enemy held bridge approximately one mile south of the landing site. Under no circumstances were they to break radio silence. Units landing on a nearby beachhead were to eventually relieve them.

When the glider finally landed in the South Downs field, they quickly disembarked and took cover behind a hedgerow along the southern edge of the field next to the river. There they waited for the remainder of the company. After nearly a quarter hour, the platoon leader decided the other units were lost and dispatched a search patrol to look for them. It took Graham's squad nearly an hour to locate the others and another half hour before the company was assembled and ready to attack. By then, units advancing from the beach had captured the bridge themselves. Graham's company had failed to carry out its mission.

The field exercise lasted another four days, almost always in total chaos and confusion. So much so that when it ended Graham's company had failed to see any of the opposing forces. It was almost as if his company had been forgotten by his battalion commanders. If it was as bad as he thought, and if indeed it was the last exercise before the invasion, how could the real assault end in anything other than one huge cock-up? The absurdity of it all worried Graham. "If this is indicative of the planning that's gone into the invasion—heaven help us when we finally do go ashore," he told one of his mates. "With the exercise going as badly as this one, the real operation can lead to nothing but certain failure."

He almost wished he hadn't joined the British airborne, had not come back to England, had instead remained in Oakton. But there was little he could do about it now. At least his mum and dad wouldn't worry; he was pretty certain he had convinced them he was in a non-combatant company.

Unbeknownst to Graham, shortly after his glider landed in the fields of South Downs, Ned was wading ashore on the English seacoast just east of Weymouth. With the heavy surf pounding on his back, it took all his strength to keep from being bowled over and, with live ammunition whizzing overhead, all his willpower to keep moving forward. When he finally reached the shore, he fell to the ground exhausted, disillusioned, and disgusted. He knew instinctively the beach was not the place to be, especially if someone was shooting at him. Looking back he could see the LST he had just left, it had already turned and was heading back towards the transport. He wished he were on it. If this were the real thing, not an exercise, he was almost certain he would have swum out to it and climbed back on board. There was no point in participating in such a futile operation. How could he and his buddies be anything but sitting ducks here on the beach? He would gladly accept the label "coward" if, in trade, they'd let him go back to the safe confines of the ship.

"Get up, soldier. No time to rest," he heard an angry voice behind him shout. "You'd be mowed down by machine-gun fire in a minute if you stopped here, exposed as you are. Keep going–no matter what–it's your only chance. Maybe you don't care, but your buddies do, they're depending on you to stay alive–as you depend on them. Everyone needs all the support they can get."

He had no wish to jeopardize the safety of his pals and certainly no intention of doing something to lessen his own chances of survival. Besides, there was no turning back now, no ship to provide refuge. He rose to his feet and ran across the open beach to the cliff that lay ahead. As he had been trained to do, he shot a grappling hook up over the cliff edge, pulled on it until it was anchored securely, and began climbing. Bullets whined dangerously close to his head. "Damn," he thought, "I'm still scared to death; and this isn't even the real thing. What if they were really aiming to kill me? I certainly must be the coward I always thought I was."

During the next four days, Ned spent his time laying communications lines, trying to repair malfunctioning equipment, and serving as a messenger between company and division command posts, all under highly realistic simulated battlefield conditions. When it was over he and his buddies climbed into one of the waiting deuce-and-a-halfs and was so tired that he fell asleep sitting upright almost before they had started the engines. At the beginning of his dream he was sitting with Edith on the bank along the towpath. She looked beautiful. He could smell the perfume she always used. He took her in his arms and told her how much he loved her, how he would never let her go. She gave him a warm kiss and rested her head tenderly on his shoulder. When he awoke, the truck was pulling into camp, and the soldier next to him was asleep, leaning against him. Ned wished he had stayed asleep; he much preferred being in Dexter Hills with Edith than in England with some bearded, mangy GI sleeping on his shoulder.

"There is no doubt about it, Diane. Something major is about to happen. E.J. tried to leave for America yesterday. When he arrived at the gates of the aerodrome, they wouldn't let him in. They gave no explanation, even when he showed them his authorization papers which plainly stated the trip was to be given top priority. Apparently they have shut down all foreign travel. The rumor is that there are mile upon mile of weapons, armor, and other types of military equipment sitting in the fields, all along the southern coast of England. It looks as if the promised major assault on Hitler's army will happen soon."

"Do you think Graham will be part of it? Do you suppose that's why we haven't heard from him for such a long time?" Diane asked, with a worried look. "I don't know what I'll do if Graham is sent into combat. We can't lose another boy. Not our last son!"

"Nonsense! Don't you remember? When he was here the last time he assured us he didn't expect to be involved in any combat missions. He's involved in depot security, or something of that sort. It's performed far behind the frontlines," Chad tried to assure her, although he didn't believe a word of what Graham had told them. "Even if they do decide to change his assignment, he'll still need a good deal of retraining first."

"We haven't heard from Ned either–he said he would try to visit us again before he shipped out," she continued, looking for additional assurances.

"I wouldn't worry. He's probably been too busy having fun on his days off. More than likely he goes sightseeing whenever he gets a chance. Visiting us is probably not one of his highest priorities. I imagine he only did it before as a favor to Ann. After all, we're not his family. He's undoubtedly more interested in exploring the U.K. while he has the opportunity." He paused, then added, "Now don't fret. Before you know it this war will be over and everyone will be home, including Ann. They'll all be here except, of course, Yvonne. It's highly unlikely she will ever come home again. She's much too spiteful."

Diane's face quickly saddened. Chad wished he hadn't mentioned Yvonne. He tried to change to a more encouraging subject. "This war will surely end soon. Every day there is more talk about peace. Did you see today's newspaper article about some of the reconstruction expected to start shortly? I understand the government is beginning to formulate plans to provide many building subsidies and revamp our welfare system. No doubt, when peace comes we'll have full employment. Once that happens we can expect almost everyone's life to be better than it was before the war. They're even beginning to experiment with pre-fab housing to replace homes severely damaged during the Blitz. There's little doubt in my mind that grand times are definitely ahead for everybody. We only need to put up with all the inconveniences of war for a little while longer."

Diane understood what Chad was saying. She had been reading the newspapers too, but she didn't agree. She didn't believe the war would end as soon as he thought, there was bound to be much hardship and suffering before it was over. She didn't agree with him about Graham either. In spite of all his assurances, her motherly intuition told her he was about to be in grave danger. And certainly it was difficult to believe Yvonne would never come home. Somehow she had to change Chad and Yvonne's attitude towards each other and coax her home. It was only right that the entire family should once again be friends.

1 June 1944

Dearest, Darling Meg,

I sit here in a tired body, but with a warm heart. We have been terribly busy these past few weeks. When not attending lectures and demonstrations, we have been busy cleaning equipment and unloading and loading supplies. Surely one of these days they'll start issuing seventy-two hour passes again. When they do, the first thing I plan is to visit Mum and Dad. A three-day pass doesn't seem too unreasonable. Does it?

As tiring (and boring) as this military life is, I'm still happy as a lark. Thank you, thank you, thank you, for being so faithful in your letter writing. Your weekly letters are just the tonic needed to keep up my spirits. It is so interesting to learn all about your university life and, most especially, to be assured you still miss me. I read those sentences over and over.

I must confess I had little sympathy for you in your last letter–telling me how few civilian boys there are in your classes and how little free time the servicemen (the ones enrolled in those training programs) have to socialize. I guess I'm selfish, sweetheart, but I do not relish the thought of you dancing in the arms of someone else. Please dance only with me? Let me be the only one who holds you in his arms; the only one who walks with you in the park; the only one who kisses you in the dark, caresses you, loves you, ...

Stop that, Graham! You mustn't think thoughts like that! It does you no good! Keep those thought in abeyance until you see your beloved again. And then let yourself go. Release all those suppressed feelings and urges, for your loved one!

And love her! Love her fiercely, passionately, tenderly! Forever and ever!!

Yes, forever and ever, Meg. I want you to be my wife. To live in a quaint little cottage deep in a forest, or in a city, or wherever, just as long as we're together. Anyplace where we can live our lives, rear our children, know peace and tranquillity. Alone. No more thought of war, death, destruction, hate, recrimination, or any of those other dreadful things the wicked world is spewing forth these days. It can be in Oakton or in Pinnington or even Timbuktu–it matters not–just as long as I'm with you.

Well, dearest Meg, lights are going out and I must hurry. They tell us we will be busy the next several days and should post all letters by tomorrow. No one knows why. But who am I to question the wisdom of my superiors? I, just the same as my chums, am nothing more than a poor, uninformed Tommy.

I love you, I love you, I love you! Wait for me, my love. Wait for me until I return to your arms!

Love, kisses, and all else ...

Graham

Meg received his letter on the fourth of August.

Ned's steel helmet rested on the ground beside him; the burning taper fastened to its top with wax. He lay on a straw filled tick reading Edith's letter in the flickering candlelight. The weather was raw and damp with a heavy wind blowing outside the tent. He could hear the deuce-and-a-halfs still busy transporting remnants of the battalion out of camp. He had completed the final preparation of the communications equipment yesterday, in readiness for the anticipated boarding of the transport ships in the Bristol Channel. No one seemed to be certain when the final orders to board would come. Rumor had it that bad weather had delayed the division's plans and the entire operation had been scrubbed for at least a month. It was only one of many rumors circulating around the camp. The plain fact was that no one knew when, or if, the orders would be issued. One thing was certain though, no one had been permitted out of the marshaling area for the past several weeks; they couldn't even make telephone calls. The rumors also claimed that the restrictions would stay in place until they were underway, no matter how long it took.

He had received Edith's letter just after the noon mess but had no opportunity to read it until now.

Dear Ned,

I received another letter from you today! Hallelujah! What a wonderful thing, a letter from my soldier sweetheart! I must admit, whenever I receive one of your lovely letters I nearly swoon with joy. They mean so much to me: firstly, knowing you are well and happy–at least as happy as one might expect a soldier to be in these terrible times; secondly, reading those wonderful words of love. Thank God you love me. It would be horrible if it were one-sided and I were the only one in love.

Oh Yes, I still love you! You naughty boy. You should never accuse me of seeing other boys. Don't you ever say those nasty things again, not even in jest. (Besides there are no young men left here in McKinley Heights; except for the wispy 4-F's and the silly boys too young to go. How could any of them interest me? Ha! Ha.) Kidding aside, I was quite aghast when your last letter said you "expected a Dear John letter from me any day." You will <u>NEVER</u> receive such a terrible thing from me. Erase it from your mind. Please! I assure you, there is no other– can never be–who is such a perfect lover. I shall never meet another like you, my dear; even if I searched for a million years. I am yours, you are mine–forever!

I love you. I love you. I love you. I love you. I love you. I love you. I love you.

There I said it over and over again. That should convince you. I shall always love you, my sweet. You are my true love. My bell ringer. My knight in shining (U.S.) armor. My strength. My future. My boy, my man, my confidant and friend. My passion and my hope. My day, my night, my heart, my soul."

You would laugh to know I am not the only one who swoons when your letter arrives. Hazel does also–but, as you know, for a different reason. She still tries everything she can, barring downright theft, to prevent me from getting your letters. Fortunately, Jim has laid down the law. He told her she cannot keep them from me. I still do not understand why she is so against the two of us. What harm can we do to her? She is truly a weird person, the sooner I move, the better I'll like it.

Thank goodness I have Spot to give me comfort and to remind me of you. No, not because I think he looks like you (Ha! Ha!), but because you gave him to me. Thank you, dear. It was a lovely Christmas present. Without him I am certain I would not survive this, pardon the expression, "hellish" place.

But enough about my problems. I'll work them out.

I hope everything has been going well in England. I was glad to learn you were able to visit with the Montgomerys in March and, especially, my mum. About the same time your letter arrived telling about the visit, Ann received a letter from Mrs. Montgomery. We have compared notes and it sounds as if it was a pleasant visit. (You must have been telling the truth–we could find no discrepancies in the two letters. Ha! Ha!—I'm getting to be quite the comedian, am I not?)

It sounds as if it was a good visit with Mum, too. You must have made quite an impression on her. (I don't see why you wouldn't.) She's been talking about you ever since. I'll bet you simply applied your precious charm and won her over, much as you did me. (Come to think of it, you'd better keep that charm under wraps 'til we meet again. I wouldn't want you to charm some young English girl. I want you all to myself, mister.)

I have nothing new to report about Brad. As I told you earlier, Clara had reason to believe he is in New Guinea. She no longer writes to me, so she might have heard something different since then. The latest in the newspaper indicates U.S. forces have landed on Wakde Island and that fighting has been very heavy. I hope he is not in it! I pray he will come through all this unscathed. He is such a nice man, and as you know, I thought of him as if he were my father.

Speaking of fathers, I note neither you nor Mum mention my dad. Was he at work the day you visited? Actually, Mum hasn't talked about him for a long time. I suppose she simply prefers to ignore his existence. He has always treated her so beastly. It would be nice, though, if she told me something occasionally. Can you tell me anything?

Well, honey, it's getting late and I have rambled enough for one night. The newsreel ran a piece on all the GIs in England. They said they were being gathered there for an eventual assault on Hitler's western front. If you are ever called upon to participate in that, please be careful. I want you back with me safe and sound. I shall hold you to your promise that you <u>will</u> return. I have your word!

Good night, my love. I will dream of you tonight–and every night until I am once again in your arms.

Love you,

   Edith

Even though his bed was hard and lumpy, Ned slept soundly afterwards. He dreamed of walking up a pathway toward Edith. They were still embracing when he woke.

It was then he noticed, B company, next door, was moving out.

Chapter 105

Sunday, 4 June 1944

Green and white crepe paper ribbons were draped from the ceiling light fixture to each corner of the living room. A large green paper ball hung below the light. Tiny specks of light glistened off many little silver flakes glued on its surface. Large colored letter cutouts spelled happy birthday on the wall behind the piano. On the other side of the archway was the dining room table, covered with a white linen tablecloth and holding a large crystal bowl carefully placed at the precise center of the table and filled with pink colored fruit punch. Neatly assembled on either side of the bowl were crystal punch cups and pale green linen napkins. At one end of the table was a plate full of dainty triangular cut sandwiches of various meats and cheeses and an empty plate awaiting the huge stack of hamburger sandwiches Jack was planning to broil once the party started. Ida still hadn't quite gotten used to last month's end to rationing on most cuts of meat; it was the most meat they had served in a very long time. At the other end of the table was a two-layered white cake with pink icing and sixteen white candles. Filling most of the remaining table space was a generous assortment of fresh vegetables, relishes and condiments. Stacks of china plates of various sizes were neatly sitting on a card table set up in one corner of the room. A large stack of light blue frosted ice cream dishes waited patiently for someone to fill them with neapolitan ice cream still in the smoking dry ice container.

Ida stood in the center of the living room and inspected her work. She was satisfied. It showed promise of being the best party she had ever given, even better than Karen's twelfth birthday. There was no doubt it would be a very special day–just as she had planned. She had been thinking about it for a long; ever since that terrible incident with Ted. She hoped it would finally put to rest, conclusively, any doubts still lingering in Ann's mind about that horrible day.

But she didn't want to think about bad things–not today, not on Ann's birthday.

"How proud Diane and Chad would be if they could see their daughter today," she thought. "Ann is such a handsome young girl now; and so much more mature, so different from those days back in '40." She wondered if Ann's parents would recognize her. Her hair, straight when she first arrived, was now curly, the result of the permanent Ida's friend had given her last spring. Ann's reaction to the new hairstyle had been similar to Karen's when she was about to turn sixteen, they both started keeping it meticulously neat and prim. It seemed they were always brushing, curling, or washing it after that. Ann was much taller now, as well. Her face had filled out and her figure, which was almost too slender when she arrived, had filled out nicely and was beginning to hint at the plumpness so common in teenage high school girls. Although Ann complained about her weight almost every day, both Jack and Ida agreed, she looked so much healthier now than she had when she first arrived.

Not only had Ann blossomed into a beautiful young woman, but she seemed almost completely Americanized. Perhaps it was because most people were used to Ann's accent, or maybe Ann had indeed lost it. Whatever it was, no one ever commented, or seemed surprised, when they heard her talk.

Ann's taste in clothes had also changed. She was now attracted to the styles worn by her American contemporaries. In the beginning, Ann's fashion tastes were quite conservative, but eventually she was influenced by the latest American fads, as were all the other young girls her age. Plaid skirts and pedal pushers with bobby socks and saddle shoes were the latest craze. Clothing styles were one aspect Ida would have preferred left unchanged. She liked the original English outfits Ann had brought with her.

Ida loved Ann. There was no denying it. As she always did when she thought about the dreadful day when they would have to say goodbye, she wondered how she could ever get through it. But the more she worried about it, the more thought she had given to coming up with a plan, some way of preventing Ann from ever going home. She had scolded herself whenever such selfish ideas popped into her mind, but still she kept thinking about them. She knew Ann had not been receiving many letters lately. Perhaps Diane and Chad were losing interest in their daughter. If so, there was a chance, slim as it was, that they wouldn't mind if she simply kept her. But the dearth of letters lately was worrying Ann–for Ann's sake it was wrong to be wishing they would stop altogether. "Then, again, perhaps Ann wants to stay. We certainly have never discussed it. It could be true." She quickly put it out of her mind. Talking Ann into staying was too silly an idea to contemplate.

Besides, there was no time for that now. The party would start in a little less than half an hour. The guests would be arriving soon. It had been difficult to keep the party a secret from Ann. She had to make all the arrangements while Ann was in the field or with one of her friends. Last evening Karen had taken her to the movies. It gave her time to bake and prepare some of the food and decorations. This morning she had pretended to have a headache and didn't go to church. Jack took Ann with him and on the way home he planned to run an errand. That gave Ida a little more time to put up the decorations, put the final touches on the food, and greet the guests as they arrived.

Most of the guests were Ann's classmates from Dexter Hills. The only evacuee invited was Edith, but at the last minute she sent word she couldn't attend. The cancellation bothered Ida, she wondered if it had anything to do with Ned. Had Edith grown tired of Ned? It was the only explanation she could think of since Edith and Ann were such good friends. She hoped Edith wasn't going to act foolishly and send Ned one of those "Dear John" letters. "She had better not!" she thought, barely able to control the rage it caused. "She had better treat my son properly. If he was good enough for her while he was at home, he certainly should be good enough while he's in the service."

Her thoughts were interrupted when the first guest arrived.

"Surprise!" yelled everyone in unison as Ann walked into the room.

"Ooo!" squealed Ann. It had been a real surprise. She had no hint of the party beforehand. "Thank you! Thank you! All of you," she said as she hugged Ida.

There followed many congratulations and much gift opening, often followed by Ann shrieking with delight. Oliver gave Ann a silver bracelet with an amethyst inset. "Thank you, Ollie," she said fondly throwing him a kiss. He blushed and everyone laughed.

They played the wind-up Victrola; sang along with recordings by Vaughn Monroe, Frank Sinatra, Nat King Cole, and the Andrew Sisters; danced; ate; and gossiped about the classmates who were not there. There was laughter, good natured teasing, and a few moments of seriousness as they remembered relatives and friends in the service. As the party began to wind down, some of the guests paired with their special partners and sought places where they could sit and talk and be alone.

As everyone departed, they thanked Ida and Jack for the wonderful party and repeated their wish to Ann for a happy birthday and an early return to England. The last to leave was Oliver. Ann walked him to his car. "Thanks again for the lovely bracelet," she said smiling.

"I'm glad you like it."

"How's your job at the garage?" she asked. "I'm thinking of asking Aunt Ida and Uncle Jack if I can work at the soda fountain this summer. I've already talked to Mr. Winters and he said he'll hire me if it's okay with the Schaefers."

"That's swell, Ann! I hope they say yes. It would give us a chance to see each other now and then. I could drop in sometimes and we could talk," he said, his eyes sparkling. In his enthusiasm, he had completely forgotten her question about his job. "I miss talking to you already–and we've only been out of school a little over two weeks. I can imagine how dreary it will be if I don't see you all summer."

"Well don't count on it, yet. With all the work here on the farm I don't see how they can let me do it. It would be nice though, spending some time in town during the summer. Sometimes, I feel so isolated here on the farm."

"No need to feel isolated. You just say the word and I'll come out," he volunteered. "Look at my car now. I finished rebuilding it this last weekend. See how much nicer it is, all painted and everything. You shouldn't be ashamed to ride in it anymore. I could come almost any time," he reiterated, "and could take you anywhere you'd like to go. All you need do is ask.

"That is if my dad doesn't interfere. He still gets terribly mean, at times."

"That's too bad. He really has treated you badly over the years. I'd hate to have a father who acted that way."

"It's not so bad anymore. With my new job, I'm not around home much. I go to work at the garage before he wakes up and he leaves for the tavern long before I get home in the afternoon." He abruptly changed the subject, "Could I take you to a movie some night this coming week?"

"I don't think so. You know how Aunt Ida feels about dating. You remember the last time, don't you?"

"You're sixteen now. You should be old enough to date. I'd be happy to ask her? I think she likes me enough to give us her blessing," he boasted.

"No, don't ask her for me. I'll ask her when I'm ready."

"Be reasonable then. Ask her today. You know how badly I want to go out with you," he begged, fervently.

"Don't rush it, we have plenty of time," she scolded. "I like you, Oliver, but I'm not ready for serious dating. Don't ask me why. I can't explain it. Maybe it has something to do with expecting to return home before long. Maybe I don't want to get to know someone so well that I can't easily say good-bye when that time comes. Heaven knows I've had to say it too many times already: my mum and dad, my two brothers, Ned, my sister, and, soon, some of you kids and the Schaefers. Frankly I don't know how I'll ever say good-bye to Aunt Ida and Uncle Jack. As for you, I'd like us to remain simply good friends–it would be much easier that way.

"Then again, maybe it's because of that terrible date we had last April? I really don't know." She kissed him gently on the cheek, as a mother would her young child.

The kiss, although meant to be purely platonic, stirred great passion in Oliver. "That was a mistake. I admit it," he said. "I should never have talked you into sneaking off like that, but I've learned my lesson. Hereafter, things will be different. Any dates we have will be strictly above board."

"I appreciate your promise, and your offer, but I'm sorry, I just don't want to go out right now," she said. "Let's leave it at that."

Oliver knew he was losing the debate. He quit talking and instead held Ann by her shoulders and pulled her near to him and kissed her. It was a long and passionate kiss. Surprisingly, Ann did not resist. "I think you had better go," she said finally.

"Good-bye, Ann," he said as he released her and climbed into his car.

"Good-bye, Oliver" she said, then turned and walked into the house without looking back.

That evening, before going to bed, Ann sat at her dresser, looking in the mirror and brushing her hair. She was deep in thought. It had been such a lovely day. She really enjoyed the party and thought her gifts were super. She looked at the bracelet and thought about Oliver. He was a nice boy, the type of boy she had always dreamed about, but why was he so persistent? She wondered why boys acted that way. Dating wasn't that important to her. In due course she could probably get serious, but not now. She thought about kissing him on the cheek and wondered if that had made him grab her and kiss her so passionately. She hoped not. She had meant it only as a friendly gesture.

What disturbed her more was the way she felt during the kiss, that last one. She had to admit, it felt pretty special. She was afraid she might be falling in love–or perhaps was already in love. "Don't be daft, you silly twit. It's not love. You're too young. You were just caught off guard."

She thought about Edith and Ned's relationship, then about Meg and Graham's. She wondered if they felt the same when they kissed. She supposed not; probably it was much more spectacular; there probably were bells and whistles and fireworks–as the movies always led one to believe.

Her thoughts shifted to Ned and Graham. She wondered where they were right now. She hoped they were safe and secure. She didn't want anything to happen to either of her brothers, they both meant so much to her. It had been too long–entirely too long–since she had written to either. Tomorrow evening she would write a nice newsy letter to both of them.

"Come on, Lady, let's go to sleep. I'm tired!" she said as she turned off the light.

Ned was crouched in a corner of a cabin on the promenade deck. They had been at sea since just after the noon mess. The wind was blowing, and rain was coming down in sheets. The sea was rough–not unlike the last exercise. There was one big difference this time, however, this time it was not an exercise. The CO had made it clear when they boarded, this time they would be landing on a French beach, code named Omaha, near Colleville-sur-mer. There would be German soldiers shooting at them. The future peace of the world depended upon the success of their mission. All the division command posts were expected to be communicating with their battalion HQs within three hours of landing. That was one of his responsibilities. There was no margin for failure. If they failed, the division failed, and, with it, the entire operation. Ned felt sick. Perhaps it was the rough sea, more than likely it was the near hysteria he felt rumbling around through his entire body. That same fear he had during the last exercise; that stupid cowardice of his had come back. He hoped, whatever the conditions when they landed, his buddies would not notice how scared he was.

Graham, dressed in full kit, was once again sitting in the hangar waiting for the orders to board the glider. His CO had told them–just like Ned's CO had–that they were not playing war games; this time it was real. His platoon was to capture the bridge within minutes of landing. Their mission was vital to the operation. Many lives depended upon their success. The wind tore open a piece of tarpaulin, whipped around inside the hangar, and across Graham's face. In spite of the nighttime dampness and cold air, sweat rolled down his forehead. He placed his hand on his vest pocket. He felt the bible Meg had given him. For a brief moment it provided comfort. "I love you, Meg. I love you!"

"Let's load 'em up," the voice of the platoon sergeant screamed.

Approximately 850 miles away the U.S. Fifth Army cautiously, but determinedly, entered the city of Rome. By noon the celebration had begun. Rome had been liberated. Farther north, the Germans were being pursued by the British Eighth Army. Dramatic progress was being made on the Italian front.

Neither Ned nor Graham were aware of the good news from Italy that evening.

Chapter 106

Monday, 5 June 1944

The platoon was once again in a glider, awaiting the tug from the tow plane. "What a cock-up this is turning out to be," he thought. He hoped they would take off this time. "It better not be another aborted mission like last night. Maybe the brass will be able to make up their bloody minds tonight? So we can get this damn mission over with."

There was a sudden jerk. The glider started down the runway. "This is it. We're on our way. Heaven help us now. Nice to have known you, old man," the soldier sitting next to Graham whispered. Graham's disgust for the incompetence of his commanders turned instantly into fear. What horrors were waiting for him at the landing site. He tried to think of Meg ... Or Ann ... Or his mum ... Or his dad ... Or anybody ... Anyone to keep his mind off the upcoming battle. He couldn't. His thoughts kept returning to the Germans waiting at the bridge. They'd be shooting at him shortly. They'd be trying to kill him! "Ironic," he mused, "when I was a lad I was always pretending I was a soldier. I thought it was a great sport. Why in bloody blazes did I think that? Didn't I know I could be killed? I must have been out of my mind."

It was a few minutes past midnight when the glider began its final descent. Upon impact it skidded along the field and stopped just short of its target. Although he had braced himself for the landing, the force of the impact was much greater than he had expected. It hurled him first into the soldier across from him, then toward the front of the glider, and finally into a twisted pile of men lying in the center of the aisle. There followed a brief moment of complete silence, then great confusion as he collected his senses, inspected for broken bones, and, after convincing himself he was not hurt, climbed out of the warped remains of the glider. Some of the men followed him, shaking and fearful of what they would find waiting for them. Others remained behind, writhing with the pain of broken limbs and bleeding wounds. A few lay dead, no longer shivering or afraid.

For a few moments, the survivors sought refuge in a small ravine, where they crouched as low as they could and hurriedly assessed the situation. Sporadic gun fire could be heard some distance away. None of the other gliders could be seen, apparently they had missed their assigned landing sites. There was no time to wait for a link-up. "Come on, laddies, that's the bridge over there," the platoon leader shouted. "Captain Randolf couldn't have landed any closer. We can't wait for the others. Let's take it ourselves."

Graham unfastened the safety on his rifle and followed the platoon leader to the embankment on the near side of the canal. Bullets from the machine-gun emplacement began to whistle overhead. The platoon returned the fire. "This is no good! They'll blow it before we reach the other side," the platoon leader worried. "We need to get across it before they set off the charges. We can't wait."

"I'll go!" Graham shouted.

He jumped up and began zigzagging across the bridge floor. Bullets dug up the dirt all around him and ricocheted off the steel girders. He miraculously made his way to the base of the hill, immediately below the machine-gun bunker. Aided by a tremendous surge of adrenaline, he charged the bunker and tossed in a hand grenade. The explosion made his ears ache; the resultant death and carnage made his heart ache. Complete quiet followed. Graham couldn't help noticing the moon. It looked lovelier than he could ever remember. Or, maybe, it only seemed lovelier, because he was still alive, and could still see it.

"You did it, son. You did it! The bridge is ours. That apparently was the only gun emplacement they had guarding it. The Jerries must have been caught completely off guard. We've done our duty, thanks to you," the platoon leader said smiling.

"Christ!" Graham exclaimed, "I've wet my pants!" No one laughed.

"Now all we need do is dig in and wait for relief from our mates coming ashore at Sword," the leader continued. In the distance, the platoon could hear the first rounds of the battleship guns beginning to strike the beach. It was 0530 hours.

In spite of the fierce fighting in most of the areas around him, Graham saw no more action that day. His platoon, according to orders, remained in place, fully prepared to defend against any counterattacks and impatiently waiting to be relieved. Although confusion and chaos plagued almost every offensive unit in the sector, steady progress was made. By nightfall, the British Army was well established on Sword Beach and Graham's platoon had been relieved.

This relatively uneventful day for Graham's platoon was not indicative of what horrors lay ahead.

*   *   *

News of the Normandy invasion began filtering into Dexter Hills on Monday evening. It's effect on the residence depended upon their circumstance. Those who had loved ones stationed in England or Ireland worried for their safety. Those who did not, were elated the Allies had finally opened another front against the Nazis. To everyone, it signified a new impetus for the Allied forces and a new worry for Hitler and his troops.

The newspaper reporters, heavily restricted by the censors, filed sketchy accounts of the heroics and tactics employed by the troops landing on the Normandy beaches on June 6. In America, the news was dominated by the exploits of the Americans, the heroics of the other participating armies were reported with much less emphasis. Perhaps because of this biased reporting, perhaps because she believed Graham was still safely in England, or perhaps because of the change in her attitude, which had slowly been taking place, Ann only worried tangentially about Graham. Her immediate thoughts were for the safety of Ned. She hated to think he was in the middle of all this, but could not convince herself he wasn't. After all, he had been in Britain for many months, training, and waiting for something. Clearly this was what that something was. At dinner that evening she knew she had a right to worry when everyone agreed that Ned was undoubtedly involved. She nearly cried when Jack said he was extremely concerned for Ned's safety.

Edith heard the commentator recap the day's news on the radio just as she was going up to bed. "Oh, Ned," she exclaimed, "You're in trouble! Aren't you?"

She cried for nearly half an hour before she finally fell asleep. Hazel offered no comfort; she didn't even bother to go to her room or ask what was wrong. Instead she looked at Jim and complained, "That poor girl just won't give up. She's in her room crying, I suppose it has to do with the landing in Normandy. She probably thinks her 'lover' is one of the boys on that beach. She's still taking that puppy love of hers much too seriously."

"He probably is," Jim said looking up from his newspaper. "That's a nasty battle raging over there. Don't be so harsh on her, if he really is in it, there's a good possibility he could be killed."

"Maybe it would be a blessing," she suggested. "Maybe then Edith could forget all this silly nonsense. Maybe then she would quit throwing those horrid tantrums of hers. It's time she grew up."

Jim couldn't believe what he had just heard. "Hazel! How could you ever say such a thing?"

*　　*　　*

Most of the concern in the Nelson household was for Graham. When Meg heard the news at school, she immediately telephoned her mother and they talked for a long time about Graham and the landing. Each tried to convince the other Graham was not in the fight. Neither was successful. Meg said she couldn't ... shouldn't ... wouldn't continue her studies–she was too worried. Louise encouraged her not to give up. She argued it would be unfair to Graham if his girlfriend didn't remain brave and focused.

In Pinnington, Diane was once again distraught. "He's there! I'm sure of it; he's there!" she wailed.

Chad tried to assure her. "Now we don't know anything definite–give him time to contact us. I'm almost certain they would have clamped tight security restrictions on all the camps because of this. All telephone calls are probably banned. That's undoubtedly why we haven't heard from either Graham or Ned. Keeping everyone bottled up is the only way they possibly could have pulled this thing off without alerting the Germans to what was planned. Graham is probably sitting at his desk right now, worrying because he can't call and tell us he's okay."

"I'll not lose Graham!" she sobbed. "That's too unfair. They can't take him away from me!"

Chad held her in his arms. He could think of nothing to reassure her. He knew it was unfair, but war is filled with things that are unfair. He thought about all the people who had suffered so much more than Diane and he, but it didn't help, he knew Diane was right. It was terribly hard to accept the fact that another of their sons was fighting in a major battle. Losing Graham would be too much to ask of them, especially since they had already lost Henry and Yvonne. With Ann in America, for God only knew how much longer, it was almost too much to bear. He hoped Diane wasn't about to sink into another of her fits of depression. He didn't believe he could go through another one–especially if it was anything like the time they were told that Henry had been killed.

Ned had been on the cramped transport ship for nearly three days. It had seemed an eternity. The sea had been rough and he had been sick the entire time–as had almost everyone else. Then yesterday, before dawn, the shelling began. It had started with a long, incessant barrage from the battleship guns and was followed with wave after wave of aircraft dropping bombs. He had never seen so many aircraft and ships, or even known that many existed. The gun assault continued throughout the day, often answered by heavy return fire from the enemy shore batteries. Ned would shake uncontrollably whenever a shell exploded close by and was nearly overwhelmed with fear when near misses caused giant plumes of water to splash across the deck.

Scuttlebutt spread rampantly among the troops. Some said many waves of landing craft had successfully made it to shore, others said the landing craft had been repelled, that survivors had returned to their ships amid chaos and carnage. The one most persistent rumor, which seemed to be common in every report, was that the battle had been frightfully brutal and troop losses extremely high. It was all very troubling since no one could prove, or disprove, anything.

That night he watched the flashes as shells from the ships and bombs from the airplanes exploded beyond the horizon. Then, near midnight, German aircraft staged a raid on the transports in his area. The roar of bombs and antiaircraft guns was deafening as again and again the German bombers struck. He watched in fear as several barrage balloons close by burst into giant balls of fire, and cowered near a gunwale while flak fell like hail just aft of where he stood. Afterwards, the welcomed silence seemed almost eerie. He had never thought it could be so quiet.

Almost before he could find comfort in the lull, orders came to board the Big Rhino landing craft hovering alongside the ship. It was not going to be easy. The swells of the sea made it difficult to climb down the netting and nearly impossible to board the waiting craft. The heavy pack strapped to his back, the two bandoleers filled with ammunition and grenades, his canteen, bayonet, flashlight, and other equipment hanging from his belt, and the M-1 rifle dangling from his shoulder, were almost too much to carry, let alone to struggle down a fishnet ladder. If he fell, he most assuredly would drown from the extra weight. Finally, after several near slips, he managed to plant his feet firmly on the floor of the Big Rhino. Many were less fortunate and fell into the sea and sank; their war finished before they had a chance to set foot on French soil. With the shoreline still some distance away, Ned felt the landing craft come to a halt and heard the dreaded command, "Disembark!" The water was shoulder-deep. With his rifle held high above his head, spitting out huge mouthfuls of saltwater after each crest of a wave, he waded ashore, still groggy from the rolling transport.

Once on solid ground, he struggled through the macabre array of broken, twisted beach obstacles, smashed German gun fortifications, scattered life preservers and gas masks, piles of crushed and damaged equipment, huge disabled tanks and broken vehicles partially buried in the sand, and bodies. Dead bodies! It was those that caused near panic.

He momentarily stopped to retch, then continued across the beach. The rain of enemy fire constantly falling all around him made him want to run. The only problem, there was no place to run, no place to hide.

After what seemed like hours of crouching behind the hummocks beyond the shoreline and clinging to the cliffs, his unit, under heavy attack from enemy snipers, made its way through the mine fields and up the steep bluffs to the division assembly area. Upon arrival Ned, under almost continuous danger from enemy fire, began to lay communication lines between the command post and division field units.

The following day, in spite of the absence of supplies, his division was ordered to relieve the First Division north of the town of Treviers, then to attack south. The ensuing fight was ferocious and, hampered by the absence of machine-guns and other heavy weapons, the progress was slow. Finally, after painstaking and treacherous house-by-house fighting, the town was liberated. He nearly cried when the fighting stopped and he saw the dazed faces of the civilians. Unlike the North Africa liberation newsreel pictures he had seen in '43, no one was cheering here. They simply stood, as if stunned, and looked forlornly at their once beautiful town–now nothing but a shell-blasted ruin. It nearly broke his heart to look at these sad, sad people, but he couldn't dwell on their misfortune; he was too exhausted.

He slept that night on an overstuffed mattress stolen from a broken bed found among the remnants of an old hotel. During the night he dreamed Edith was with him. The fields were peaceful and green, the sun was shining and they were both laughing. He felt happy and secure.

Chapter 107

Monday, 12 June 1944

Ann was busy cleaning the electric mixer and did not see Oliver enter the drug store. She had not noticed the door open, partially because she was excited since it was her first day working for Mr. Winters, partially because she was thinking of all the money she would make, and partially because she was intent on getting the mixer sparkling clean. He startled her when he spoke. "Hi, Ann! I see Ida gave you permission to work here at the soda fountain."

"Oh! Hi, Ollie. I didn't see you come in. Yes, I'm a soda jerk now," she laughed, "at least for four hours on Monday through Thursday. That's all I can manage; I'm needed on the farm too much to be away any more than that. But sixteen hours a week will give me a little pin money."

"Let's see how good you are. I'd like a cherry Coke, miss." he teased. "Please?"

"All right, sir, coming right up!" she replied, sounding much more confident than she felt. "Let's see: first the glass, some ice, the Coke syrup, a little cherry flavoring, and then the soda water." She placed the glass on the counter and, with a grin, pushed it toward Oliver.

"That's pretty good. Now let's see how well you do with a chocolate ice cream soda," he laughed.

She looked at the glasses on the shelf, studied them for a moment, and finally selected one of the taller ones. "We'll start with one of these. Then we'll add ice cream." One of the scoops missed the glass and fell on the top of the ice cream chest. "Oops!" she laughed. "Silly old dopey me. A little more time and I'll get the hang of it." She quickly tossed the spilled ice cream in the sink, wiped the chest top, and continued concocting the soda. "Now we'll add the chocolate; then the carbonated water." They both listened to the fizz of the water as it filled the glass. "Now a little whipped cream, some nuts, the cherry on top, the biscuit, and finally, the spoon!"

"Great! You're going to be a wonderful jerk," he joked, laughing heartily. "You seem to have the knack for it. Except ... Where's the straw?"

"Oops! Here," she said, quickly handing him a straw. "I'm glad you didn't order a banana split or a malted milk. Mr. Winters hasn't told me how to make either of those, yet," she teased. She already knew how; she was simply trying to trick him into another challenge; and another sale for Mr. Winters.

"You had better learn quickly because I'm coming back later to order one of those."

"You'd better not. You'll be as fat as a pig if you keep gorging yourself," she quipped.

"Well then, I'll come in and just talk. It's going to be nice having you here all summer long."

"Don't come too often. We don't want to make Mr. Winters angry. He's paying me twenty-five cents an hour, and expects a good day's work," she hesitated, then added, with a smile, "well, at least half a day."

"I tell you what. If you agree to go to the dance with me next Saturday night, I'll not bother you here in the store–at least, not too often–say, only once, or twice, a day."

"Do you remember what I said the other day about dating?" she asked resolutely.

"But Artie Shaw will be here this weekend. You know how much fun it is to dance to his music. Please say yes?"

Ann remembered her birthday party and how she felt after he had kissed her. Her resolve began to weaken. "They serve liquor at the dance hall, don't they? We're only sixteen, can we get in?"

"That's not a problem. They're not checking ages much these days. Several of the gang went to see Woody Herman last month. They had no problem."

"We shouldn't be going to a place that sells liquor. We're minors."

"That's okay. We'll only order soda pop. Nobody minds kids coming to the dances anymore. They need all the dancers they can get—with all the boys away in the service."

"Isn't it expensive?"

"Don't worry about that. I'm doing quite well at the garage this summer, I'm making thirty-five cents an hour. I can afford it," he boasted. "You just ask permission to go. I'll take care of everything else."

"Well, okay! I'll ask Aunt Ida this afternoon. I'll tell you tomorrow—if you come in."

"Don't worry, I'll be here. Mr. Winters has a regular customer the entire summer—so long as you keep making these great chocolate sodas." He made the straw gurgle as he sipped the last of the contents from the bottom of the glass.

Ann asked Ida as soon as she got home. Although Ida was concerned about Ann and Oliver being too young, Artie Shaw had always been one of her favorites. If he was going to be there in person, she couldn't deprive Ann of an opportunity like that.

Ann told Oliver on Tuesday. He was delighted.

Chad was deep in thought as he walked up the pavement toward the house. The jig he had been designing had not worked as he had expected. Something needed to be changed, but it wasn't clear exactly what that something was. Suddenly, he heard a strange noise overhead. It sounded like a badly timed lorry engine with the muffler removed. He looked up and saw it. It appeared to be an airplane coming from the east. As it drew nearer, he could see its stubby wings and what looked like a funnel, or tube, mounted above its narrow fuselage. A yellow flame jetted from the rear of the tube. "What the bloody hell is that?" he asked out loud, even though no one was there to answer.

Just then the buzzing stopped, and an eerie silence replaced the curious sound. Suddenly, this strange looking contraption began plummeting toward the ground. There followed a tremendous flash of light, a loud explosion. It was nearby, close enough to feel the concussive force as it went off. Black smoke began rising over the rooftops immediately to the west of where he was standing. Chad wondered what it was. A few minutes later he could hear the wail of sirens as emergency crews rushed to the scene. Then the air raid alert sounded. It was the first air raid sirens he had heard in quite some time.

"What was that?" Diane asked as she came running to the door. "It sounded like a bomb. Why did they sound the warning after it hit? Didn't they know the planes were coming?"

"I don't know what it was. I saw it just before it exploded. It wasn't a plane. It looked rather queer, and made sort of a clattering sound. Whatever it was, we'd better get inside before something else happens."

No more explosions sounded and soon the all clear was given. Two more explosions occurred the next day.

By Saturday, the newspapers in both England and America carried sketchy reports of a new pilotless bomb falling sporadically in various parts of London. Reportedly these flying bombs were being launched by Hitler's forces from somewhere in western Europe. They carried high-explosive payloads and were causing major damage to the city. At first, it was thought they were aimed randomly but experts later agreed they were, in actuality, often falling miles from their intended targets—probably due to the inaccuracy of their onboard guidance system. It was greatly feared these new bombs could be the beginning of another London Blitz, possibly a blitz destined not only to cause major havoc and destruction, but, since their pattern was so random, one that could also seriously degrade citizen morale.

It did not take long before these bombs were called buzz bombs, because of the sound they made, and doodlebugs, because of their erratic flight patterns. There was talk about these doodlebugs at the dance on Saturday night. It greatly troubled Ann; she feared for her parents safety. Apparently her folks were going to be subjected to another horrible round of bombing attacks.

Oliver tried to ease her mind by telling her the Normandy invasion would soon put an end to the doodlebugs. "Once the Allies fight their way through western Europe," he said, trying to assure her, "Germany will no longer be close enough to threaten England." But it did no good.

Instead it only reminded her of Ned and Graham and all the dangers they were facing. She became even more upset. He tried to change the subject. He asked her what she thought about F.D.R. running for a fourth term. She answered simply that American politics no longer concerned her; all she wanted was to go home, back to England with its Labour and Tory parties. Then in a mood he had never seen before, she complained about the method used by America to elect its president. She said it made much more sense to select a leader from one of the members of the majority party, as they did in the House of Commons, than it did to use the complicated American electoral college system. Oliver wanted to argue with her but decided it would be better not to pursue it any further. "Let's dance," he said.

The couple said little after that. They danced several more times then left the ballroom. On the way home they stopped at a drive-in restaurant for a root beer, hot dog, and potato chips, and continued to talk very little. Ann seemed cold and aloof in spite of Oliver's attempts to cheer her. By the time he walked her to the door, he wondered why he had spent so much effort chasing after her. It didn't appear she had much interest in him, probably never would. He didn't stay long. He kissed her politely on the cheek, turned, and walked quickly back to his roadster. His ride home was particularly sad, lonely, and disappointing.

Ann was disappointed too, not in Oliver but in herself. She knew she had treated him badly. It had been happening whenever she was alone with him lately. For some reason, even though she looked forward to being with him and often dreamed of the good things they would do together, when they did get together she could never quite bring herself to act toward him–or even to find the words to express herself–the way she had planned. It was extremely frustrating; especially since she didn't understand why.

Her dreams turned into a nightmare that night. She dreamed a large black bear was pursuing her parents as she watched helplessly from the empty Dexter Hills football stadium. Her mum tripped and fell but her father kept running. The bear ferociously lunged at her mother, clawing and biting. Ann woke; covered in perspiration.

"But that sounds inconsistent, Gladys. Why would you evacuate Fran and Nancy? You know how much you and Dave hated the evacuation back in '39."

"It's different now, Chad. Last time the air raid sirens sounded before bombs started falling. We had time to take cover. This time the bombs just come out of the blue. They can explode any time, and anywhere. There's no chance to run to the shelter. There has already been an unbelievable number of civilians killed, not to mention the property damage."

"But the BBC is saying it hasn't had much effect. They say Londoners are taking it in their stride and have remained calm and unconcerned."

She disagreed, "That's nonsense. Those beastly, vicious bugs are causing all kinds of havoc in our end of town. The one that landed on the Guards Chapel at Wellington Barracks was a real disaster. Rumor has it over one hundred were killed, civilians as well as servicemen. Many more were injured. Dave and I believe it makes sense to send the children away again. We would send Ernie, too, but he is in the Army Cadet Corps now. We're only sending Fran and Nancy."

"Well do what you must, Gladys, but believe me, Diane and I would never send our children away again. We learned our lesson. You can't imagine how it has troubled us since that fateful day back in August of '40. Imagine! It's been nearly four years since we've seen Ann; and who knows how long until we finally have her home again. Our little girl is nearly a grownup now and she still isn't back. By the time she gets here, we probably will have missed all those wonderful teenage years of hers. Graham was here for a little while, but now he's gone again, probably fighting on the beaches of Normandy. I tell you, Gladys, I really think you should keep your children with you."

"I hear what you are saying, big brother, but we must do what we think best. We're going to send them, just as soon as possible."

"No, Gladys, you haven't heard me!" Chad almost shouted. "You don't understand what a terrible thing it is to give your children away. You're going to feel awful guilt. It was different for you the last time. You went with them. Believe me, before long you'll begin to hate yourself for what you've done. We decided to do it out of what we thought was love for our children, but now we realize it wasn't love that sent them away, it was some sort of selfish fear."

"But at least they're still alive. They could have been killed had they remained in England."

"True! But they could die while they're away too."

"I don't know, Diane. I tried to tell her how we feel but I couldn't make her understand."

"You tried, Chad. No one will ever fully appreciate how terrible we've felt these past lonely years: the guilt; the loneliness; that helpless feeling when we heard they were sick and not being able to nurse them or comfort them or make them happy; and the disappointment of not being with them to share their happiness when they do something to make us proud.

"I can still recall that terrible, terrible morning. When was it? Four years ago on August ninth. Seeing Ann looking back at me out of that rear window is something I can never forget. Oh Chad! Oh Cha ..." she said, bursting into tears.

Chapter 108

Wednesday, 28 June 1944

News of the war had a decidedly upbeat tone in the final weeks of June. In the Mariana Islands, U.S. troops on the Japanese held island of Saipan had made steady progress towards its complete capture and the U.S. Navy had won a major naval victory in the Philippine sea. Elsewhere the intensity and number of bomb runs by the U.S. Air Force on Japanese bases was continuing to increase; Allied troops in India had reopened vital road links between Imphal and Kohima; the Red Army was on the verge of taking the Byelorussian capital of Minsk from the Germans, and in Normandy, the Allies had consolidated their lines and liberated the city of Cherbourg.

But not all of the news was good. The damage to London caused by the German buzz bombs, or V1 bombs as they were officially known, was increasing daily; a British offensive in a bid to capture the town of Caen had failed, and the Japanese forces had defeated the Chinese Tenth Army in the battle for the Hengyang airfield in China.

In the United States, excitement for the upcoming presidential election was beginning to grow with the Republican nomination on June 28 of Governor Thomas E. Dewey of New York for president and Governor John W. Bricker of Ohio as his vice-presidential running mate. Roosevelt had to wait until July 20 before he was officially nominated as the Democratic candidate.

Ann was in her room writing a letter to Graham when the telephone rang. "Ho, Ann," Ida called. "It's a Mr. Charles Jefferson on the telephone. He asked to speak with you."

Ann was startled, if she remembered correctly, Charles Jefferson was Charles Throkmorton Jefferson, that dreamy boy who she had talked to at the Bender Christmas party last year. "Hello," she said hesitantly.

"Is this Miss Ann Montgomery?" the voice at the other end asked in a rather dignified manner.

"Yes, it is she," Ann answered politely.

"This is Charles, Charles Throkmorton Jefferson. I hope you remember me? We met at the Bender party last year. I talked to you after you played that lovely clarinet solo."

Ann certainly did remember. "Yes, I recall. What can I do for you?" she asked, wanting desperately to hide the excitement she was certain he could hear in her voice.

"I hope I'm not being overly presumptuous, or bad mannered for being so tardy in asking you, but I wish to invite you to be my guest at the Bender picnic on the fourth of July. I would truly be honored if you would say yes."

Ann's heart missed a few beats. She couldn't wait to tell Edith. She had just been asked for a date by none other than Charles Jefferson! "Well, that's very nice of you, Charles. I certainly appreciate the invite, but I'll need to check with my aunt before I can give you a definite answer."

"Of course, that's perfectly understandable," he assured her. "It's the only proper thing to do. I'll call you again tomorrow night for your answer; that is, if you don't mind my calling again? I would have you leave an answer with my valet, but I am calling from New York. It would be an expensive long distance telephone call for you."

"From New York. Now that's impressive. I'm being asked for a date by telephone, all the way from New York City," she thought.

"That is very thoughtful, Charles. Tomorrow evening will be fine. I'll ask my aunt tonight and will wait for your call tomorrow evening. Thank you ever so much for thinking of me."

After she hung up, she screamed so loudly that both Jack and Ida came running. "Gracious, child, what's wrong?" Ida asked.

"I've been invited to the Bender picnic by Charles Throkmorton Jefferson!" she said, almost swooning. "You remember him, don't you, Aunt Ida? He's the son of Mr. Jefferson, the New York banker, one of the Bender directors."

"Good heavens!" Ida said excitedly. "Why on earth would he invite you?"

"Because our Annie is a pretty young girl. Isn't that a good enough reason?" Jack offered, looking at Ann and smiling. "So your are going to hobnob with the high-and-mighty? Imagine, Mother! Our daughter is going to the picnic with the son of one of the board of directors."

"Did you tell him you would go?" Ida asked, a worried look on her face.

"No ma'am. I told him I had to get your permission first. He's going to call again tomorrow night for an answer."

"That's good, then you can still tell him no."

"No?" Why no?" Ann quickly questioned.

"Because it would not be proper for a tool and die maker's daughter to attend the company picnic with the son of a director. Even if that didn't matter, you have nothing good enough to wear."

Ann knew Ida had assessed it correctly. Charles belonged to the upper class, part of America's aristocracy. She was a commoner. Commoners were not expected to associate with aristocrats. She wondered if she had forgotten all her manners since leaving England. Why hadn't she turned him down immediately? It would have saved him the expense of calling back tomorrow night and the embarrassment of being kept waiting by a commoner.

"Look here," Jack interrupted, "neither of those are good excuses. No one is too good to take my daughter to a picnic. And if she needs new clothes, take her shopping, buy her what she needs. But I really don't think she needs any new things, she looks nice no matter what she wears."

The argument continued for several minutes. Ann was embarrassed. She hadn't intended to cause this much trouble. Finally, after Karen came home and added her support, Ida agreed to let Ann go. Ann hugged Lady closely that night. "I'm going to the Fourth of July picnic with a proper young man!" she said dreamily.

Ann watched as the long, black Packard with the shiny chrome grill pulled into the farm lane at precisely ten o'clock. "He certainly is prompt," she told Lady. "And quite handsome too" she added as Charles walked up the pathway. She quickly backed away from her bedroom window, lest he see her.

Ida had never been prouder. She thought Ann looked especially nice when she came into the parlor a few minutes later. Apparently Charles thought so too. "My, you look lovely," he said, with a somewhat bashful smile. Ann was wearing a new red flowered white jumper. Her blouse was a solid pale blue with short sleeves and an extra frill around the collar. A white cardigan was draped neatly over her arm. White bobby socks and brown and white saddle shoes completed her ensemble.

At the waiting limousine, the chauffeur hurriedly jumped out and opened the rear door for them. "Robert, this is Miss Montgomery," Charles said as they began to get in. "Good morning, Miss," Robert said, bowing slightly to her. "It's a fine morning for a picnic."

"Our little girl seems to fit right in with those rich folks," Ida laughingly told Jack, as she watched the Packard drive away. "So much so, even the clothes she was wearing complemented the gray mohair rear seat of that limousine?" she added with another chuckle.

Twenty minutes later, everyone gasped as the Packard drove into the picnic parking area. Charles Throkmorton Jefferson was attending the picnic, and he had Ann Montgomery with him! No one could believe it. Ann had a date with Charles Jefferson.

Throughout the afternoon, Ann was surprised by how much more friendly everyone seemed to be. There was almost always someone–often people she hardly knew–trying to strike up a conversation, especially when Charles was with her. She enjoyed the extra attention because, as she told Edith, it made her feel more important than she had ever felt before.

Fred was one of the few who disappointed her. He had little to say to either Charles or her, except when he invited Charles to join him in several of the pickup games played that afternoon. Much to Fred's annoyance, Charles refused the offer each time he was asked, always saying he preferred talking with Miss Montgomery over playing any games.

And so it was that Ann spent most of the afternoon with Charles; the only exception, the few minutes she spent with Edith discussing Edith's problem with Hazel. "If I were you I'd insist on a new home. No one should be treated the way you have been," Ann said indignantly, then promised to ask Jack if he had any idea how she could rectify the situation.

They also shared their letters from Ned and talked about him, often in tears. They worried for his safety and, anxious to know he was all right, hoped at least one of them would soon receive another letter. Before rejoining the other picnickers Ann, suggested Ned should start routing all his letters in care of her. It would prevent Hazel from opening–or worse yet–destroying them. Edith only promised to think about it; she was reluctant to introduce any further delay in an already lengthy process.

That evening, Charles walked Ann to the door and politely asked permission to call again for another date. Ann blushed and told him she would look forward to hearing from him–anytime. He thanked her, shook her hand, awkwardly backed off the porch, said good-bye, turned, and left. Ann stood on the porch and watched the Packard disappear down the road. She was disappointed. He had not tried to kiss her, not even one measly little time. It left her with nothing to brag to the girls about.

Inside, Ann found Ida, Jack and Karen waiting eagerly to hear about the picnic, or, more truthfully, about the date. Ann answered their questions politely, volunteered nothing extra, and later, when the conversation turned to other things, did not pay attention. She preferred to think about Charles instead.

"There's quite a difference between a Packard limousine and a Model A roadster," she told Lady as she undressed. "But I must admit, Oliver is as nice as Charles–perhaps even a little nicer, but so much poorer."

After brushing her teeth she added, "There's no question about it, Lady, if Charles were ever to marry me, there'd be no limit to what a grand life I could have. You wouldn't believe how rich and sophisticated he is."

She dreamed of Princesses Elizabeth and Margaret that night. She was at one of the Royal balls. Charles, her escort, had just finished dancing with them. He was dressed in a black tuxedo and wore a bright red cummerbund. Apparently, he had been a hero in the war; many medals covered his chest. Suddenly trumpeters blew their horns, the palace doors opened, and King George and Queen Elizabeth made a regal entrance. Ann watched as they approached one of the king's guardsmen. He was dressed in a scarlet jacket and wore a black bearskin busby. "Lance-Corporal Graham Montgomery," the king proclaimed, "I dub thee Sir Graham, knight of my court."

"Hurrah!" they all shouted.

Chapter 109

Thursday, 3 August 1944

Graham sank down beside the road, tired, hungry, and covered in mud. His life in Normandy had not been easy. The morning after his platoon took the canal bridge the German Twenty-first Panzer Division launched a counterattack which cut his unit off from the main British Army. It had taken several days of intense, sometimes hand-to-hand, fighting to rejoin the main forces and nearly two months before they saw the bridge again.

Casualties mounted during repeated heavy fighting north of Caen throughout those two months. It was almost a new company now, so many new troops had replaced those killed and wounded. Then on July 18, the British Army launched a major assault on Caen. During the morning hours, Graham's unit advanced nearly to the bridge, only to be forced back to their original position by mid afternoon. On July 31, another major assault was more successful. By the time it ended, they were well beyond the bridge, a number of miles southwest of Caen at the Vire-Tinchebray Road.

While Graham was fighting his way south through Normandy, Ned's division had also been involved in several major pushes south from Omaha. After a tough offensive push through the Cerisy forest, the division, in a temporary defensive stand, set up its headquarters command post south of the village of Cerisy-la-Forêt where Ned spent several days, and miles of wire, connecting the command switchboard to the fighting units. When not laying wire, Ned found himself either skirmishing with the enemy while on patrol or cowering from the strafing from German aircraft. What he dreaded most was night patrol, especially when someone triggered a tripwire. Standing there frozen in position, while the flares floated overhead, required almost more patience and courage than he could muster. He knew keeping perfectly still was the best way to avoid detection, but it made him feel so vulnerable. Standing there, under near daylight conditions–so exposed–always made him want to run to the nearest cover. He kept thinking of the German who surely must have him in his gun sight, about to pull the trigger. It always left him shaking afterwards, sometimes for hours.

In mid July, Ned's unit was thrust into another major offensive push, this time an assault on hill 192. The battle lasted two days. Many troops were lost, including one of Ned's best buddies.

Toward the end of July, one day after the fall of German defenses at St. Lo, Ned's division, supported by artillery and tanks, attacked across the St. Lo-Bayeux highway. As the attack began the battalion command post came under heavy fire from German light artillery and mortars. It was not long before many critical communications links had been destroyed. Under heavy fire, with little cover, and unmindful of the small piece of shrapnel that struck his thigh, Ned soon had communications restored. Although not serious enough to relieve him from duty, the wound earned him the Purple Heart medal and, more importantly, his behavior under fire gave him the confidence he had so badly needed. He no longer considered himself a coward.

By August 3, his division had crossed the Souleuvre River and, by late afternoon, secured the small town of Etouvy and, with it, an important crossroads on the St. Lo-Vire Highway six kilometers above Vire.

Once again the division moved its command post, this time to an orchard four kilometers north of the river. On its right flank were all the American forces in Normandy and, on its left, units of the British Second Army.

That evening Ned crossed into the British sector while laying lines between the American and British units. Once in the British sector, he thought of Graham and wondered if he might also be in Normandy, and if so, what the odds were of the two of them meeting. With this in mind, he entered the command post and asked the duty officer if there were any way to determine whether Graham was in Normandy. The lieutenant laughed and dismissed him with a simple, "I'm afraid not, Yank."

By shear coincidence, a lance-corporal sitting at the desk overheard them and interrupted, "I believe I know him, sir. I met him while I was on rotation to the rear for R and R. I think he's in the Sixth Airborne. I don't know which unit but, I might be able to find out by calling their CP."

He made the call and, within a few minutes, Ned was on his way to meet with Graham. It indeed had been an astounding and highly improbable coincidence, a story that Ned was certain he would share with his grandchildren someday.

They hugged each other, slapped each other on the back, and spent a good deal of time simply stepping back and looking at each other. After several emotional remarks about how good it was to be together again, the conversation turned to their families, and especially to Edith, Meg and Ann. Ned proudly showed the snapshot of Edith he carried with him and Graham shared parts of a letter he had received from Meg and another from Ann. As they talked they nearly finished a jug of fiery calvados Graham had discovered earlier that day in a nearby barn. Although he had thinned it with lemon powder from his field rations, it was still extremely potent and both men became increasingly more nostalgic with each additional swig. They cried as they told each other how much they loved Edith and Meg, and how much they missed the tenderness and caresses of their lovers.

When it became time for Ned to leave, it was difficult to say goodbye. They knew they were in different armies and afterwards would go back home to different countries. The chances of seeing each other again were very slim–that is, if they got home at all. They both were keenly aware of the huge number of casualties their units had suffered. There was a good possibility one of them might die before they left France. After all, they had to make it through the next battle, and the next, and the one after that, and who knew how many more, before they could go home.

"One more for the road," Graham urged, as he handed the jug to Ned one last time.

The following morning Graham's unit advanced under heavy artillery shelling against well-organized German opposition. Near the close of the day they began to dig-in, defending a Bailey bridge that earlier had been hastily thrown across the river. As they dug their foxholes, reconnaissance reported a column of German armor approaching on the left flank. To stop them, Graham's platoon, supported with an anti-tank squad, was ordered to intercept. They had not advanced far when they encountered intense machine-gun and rifle fire coming from behind a hedgerow. After the loss of three men and several fruitless attempts to destroy the gun with mortar fire, Graham decided he'd had enough. He crawled along a row of hedges, inched his way to the near side of the bunker protecting the gun, armed a grenade, and tossed it through the opening. After the explosion, he jumped up and began firing his automatic into the gun position at point-blank range. He killed three Germans before he was hit in the chest.

Afterwards, when they came to collect the dead, they found his body lying on the road in front of the hedgerow. His hand was clutching the bible Meg had given him. The bullet that had pierced his heart had also pierced the bible. A half written letter was found in his pocket. It began: *My dearest darling Meg,*

Please wait for me ...

On August 16, the Second Division went out of contact with the enemy. Fresh troops relieved it the next day while it fell back for a well deserved rest. Later, the division was transported to the Breton peninsula where it was attached to the Eighth Corps in preparation for the assault on Brest. They assembled around Lesnevens, to the northeast of Brest, and planned to attack downward toward the city. Although still limping from the effects of the wound suffered in July, Ned was one of the able-bodied troops assigned this new task. The attack began the following Monday.

It was on that same Monday that the Montgomerys were once again visited by a British Army officer on a bicycle. He came at dinnertime, just after Chad had arrived home from work. Chad answered the door. The officer simply said that the British government regretted to inform him that Graham had been killed in Normandy on the fourth of August. He said that Corporal Graham Montgomery had served his country well and would, by order of the king, be presented the Victoria Cross, post-humously, for bravery on the field of battle.

"Who was at the door?" Diane asked when Chad came back into the kitchen. But she needed no answer. From the look on Chad's face she knew. "No! My God, no!" she sobbed, "Not another one."

By ten o'clock, Diane was running a high fever and Chad decided it was time to call the doctor. When the doctor finally arrived and had examined Diane, he said, "I'm afraid the poor woman has had a breakdown. There's not much we can do now except give her a sedative and plenty of rest. But don't expect much improvement soon. Only time can heal a broken heart and many times even that is not enough. I've seen it so often, news arrives of the death of a soldier son, husband, or lover, and then we lose the survivor, sometimes temporarily, often forever. It's one of the terrible tragedies of war."

"How long before I can expect some change?" Chad asked.

"There's no telling. It could be days, months, or even years before she fully recovers," he answered.

Chad stayed home from work the following morning and made arrangements for a live-in maid to take care of Diane. He then, reluctantly, went to the factory and placed a transatlantic telephone call to Jack Schaefer who cried when Chad told him what had happened.

It was Jack's unpleasant task to relay the message to Ann and everyone else in America who had known Graham. Ann was the first to be told. She took the information calmly, refusing to show any emotion, which worried Jack since he knew it unnatural to accept the death of this second brother without displaying even a hint of remorse. Ida was the next to learn. She quickly began to bake a pie, mostly to work off some of her sadness, but also to have a gift ready for Ken and Louise when they were told. She had advised Jack to tell them in person, not to do it over the telephone. Upon hearing the news, Louise immediately removed Graham's service flag hanging in the window. "It's no longer appropriate to display this," she said. "The serviceman no longer exists," she added coldly.

They told Meg the next Saturday when she came home from school for a weekend visit. She sat in stunned silence. She could not believe it had happened–it couldn't have–not to Graham, her love. They hadn't planned it that way. They were supposed to marry, to live happily ever after. She began to sob, "No, Graham! Not you!" She lay on her bed and would not stop crying. Ken and Louise tried to comfort her. She refused their help. By morning she was quiet, she had convinced herself he was dead. She refused to talk to anyone, she simply turned away. "If Graham was dead, she should be, too!" she kept thinking.

The following week the Nelsons placed a new service flag in the window. This one had a white background surrounded by a red border, the same as the other. The star on the new one was gold. When Ann saw the flag she insisted the Schaefers do the same. She wanted everyone to know that her brother had been killed in the service.

A dark pall hung over the Schaefer and Nelson households throughout the remainder of 1944.

Chapter 110

Sunday, 17 September 1944

There was a definite chill in the air. It was one of those early autumn days when summer had lost its grip and winter was beginning to add its still impotent frosty breath to the scene. The wind gusted and pushed rain against the window pains as Chad looked at Diane asleep on the bed. He had lost two sons, a daughter, and, unless a miracle occurred, he would soon lose his wife. He affectionately, and with what had become habit by now, placed her hand in his and slowly began to caress her fingers. She opened her eyes. "Hello, Chad," she said, trying desperately to fight her depression. A barely perceptible smile appeared momentarily on her pale, thin face, then was gone.

"Anything I can get for you?" he asked.

"Just sit here beside me. Having you close by is what I need most. ... It must be Sunday? You're home, and it's still daylight. ... I miss you when you're at work. Won't they ever let you return to a normal work-week?"

He shook his head. "No. No normal hours yet. There is still much to do. We can barely keep up, and new orders are coming in faster than ever."

A frown crossed Diane's forehead. He hastened to add, "But someday soon. It's beginning to look more and more as if the Allies are on the verge of winning–and when they do, this nasty war will be over, and we'll live a normal life again."

"Normal? Life can never be normal again," she thought. "How can there ever be life without my two sons?" She said nothing. Chad continue to talk. None of it interested her, but it was still nice to hear his voice.

"So much is going on, it's difficult to stay current," he went on, struggling to validate his prediction of an Allied victory. "The Allies have made excellent headway since Normandy. Brussels was liberated a little over a week ago; Paris has been in Allied hands since the twenty-fourth of last month; and London is seeing fewer buzz bombs, apparently Allied advances have overrun most of the launch sites. The invasion in south France has also helped. They now control a large chunk of territory down there.

"It looks as if we finally have them on the run. The Americans have reached the German border north of Trier and the Russians are making great inroads in the Balkans. Even in the Pacific, things are improving. The Americans have finally retaken Guam. So you see, Diane, it's getting better every week."

She squeezed his hand and smiled, but said nothing.

"One thing I know for certain, the government agrees with me about the war coming to an end. The disbandment of the Home Guard is a good example. They certainly wouldn't be closing it down if there was the slightest possibility it would be needed again. Thank God I'm rid of that responsibility. It makes my workload much easier. I finally can be home with you every night. Isn't that wonderful?"

Diane smiled again.

"What this also means is that in only a matter of months our Annie will be coming home."

Diane's face lit up. "Oh, Chad," she said, "do you really believe she will? It would be so wonderful if it were true. If we could bring her back, at least our baby would be home."

"You can count on it, dear. You can count on it."

The promise of Ann's return had a significant effect on Diane's recovery. Recognizable improvements started almost immediately. The doctor was surprised and pleased with the almost miraculous improvements each day. He predicted, for the first time, that in a few short months she would be fully recovered.

On the following Thursday Diane wrote to Ann.

21 September 1944

Dear Ann,

Just a quick note to tell you not to worry. I am much better and will be going back to work shortly. The doctor is not certain what was ailing me. He said yesterday it must have been a heavy bout of influenza. I guess your mum is not as strong as she used to be–getting to be an old woman (Ha! Ha!) and susceptible to all kinds of illnesses.

Her report on the diagnosis was, of course, a lie. She refused to believe that Ann knew the real reason she had been sick.

With all the successes the Allies are having, they are beginning to relax restrictions here. For about a week now the blackouts have been replaced with dim-outs. It seems odd to see street lamps back on and motor cars traveling with their lamps fully lit. There is even talk about bringing all of you back home soon. Wouldn't that be a grand and glorious thing? I can just see my little girl coming up the pavement. I can hardly wait. I hope you feel the same. You haven't forgotten your dear old mum, have you?

The government has been thinking about your future, too. They recently passed an education act and it received Royal approval early last month. The minister of education said it would have far reaching effects. He says secondary education will be free and offered according to aptitude. It looks as if you will be able to continue your schooling once you are back home. Won't that be wonderful? Our little girl can resume her schooling and receive a fine English education–apparently not hindered, as you once were, by class, social, and financial circumstances–a much better situation than before. Wouldn't you say? Heaven knows, it would have been nice if we could have afforded the education Yvonne wanted–and deserved.

I will write again soon–a much longer letter once I have my faculties honed back to tip-top shape. Until then,

Love,

Mum

Two weeks later Diane went back to work on a part-time basis. She carefully avoided, as did all her friends, any mention of Graham or Henry.

The lobby was packed with customers waiting for the next show. The queue extended outside and halfway down the block. "I'm sorry, Oliver," Ann apologized, "I should have been ready when you arrived. I don't know what is wrong with me, I can't seem to get anything done quickly."

"Have you been feeling okay?"

"I suppose so. There doesn't seem to be anything wrong, physically. I just don't have the pep–or maybe it's the enthusiasm I once had. I'm sure it's nothing serious. Perhaps I'm just a little depressed."

"I can certainly understand why; losing a brother must be awfully difficult."

"That's part of it, but I believe I've pretty much come to terms with Graham's death. It's my mum that concerns me more."

"Has she had a hard time with it?"

"That's just the trouble. I don't know. She hasn't written since Graham was killed. The only news from home has been a few brief notes from Dad. He assures me she is okay, but I don't believe him."

"She is probably still in bereavement. I'm certain she'll get through it soon. It just takes time. Our next door neighbor's son contracted pneumonia and died last May. She is just now beginning to recover from her grief. Your mother will get better. You'll see. You shouldn't worry."

"You're probably right. Anyway, I'm sorry I made us so late."

"Don't worry about it. It's such a popular movie, we would have had to wait no matter when we got here. The boys say Ingrid Bergman looks really great with her short hair. I can't wait to see her."

"And Gary Cooper gives a great performance, at least that's what Bonnie tells me," Ann said, laughing and, at the same time, stepping forward as the line began to move.

Ann frowned and thought of Brad when the newsreel opened with pictures of MacArthur's forces invading Morotai in the Dutch East Indies and U.S. Marines landing on Peleliu Island. The GIs at Morotai were using flame-throwers against Japanese pillboxes. She carefully scanned their faces, wondering if she would see Brad. "That's silly," she told herself. "Out of all the places in the South Pacific, why would he be at Morotai?" She dismissed the idea.

The scene shifted to the European front. Pictures of the ruin and devastation left in Florence after the German retreat in Italy were shown first. Next, two senators were interviewed. They praised Russia for launching its drive through the Balkans but criticized it for its reluctance to assist the Poles in their fight against Germany. The senators said the Russians failed to provide the necessary air-drops required to adequately support the Polish fighters. The segment closed with scenes showing American units advancing through northern France. The fighting appeared to be intense. Ann looked for Ned and grimaced when she saw a GI fall, apparently struck by a bullet.

The scene changed to the meeting of President Roosevelt and Prime Minister Churchill in Quebec where plans were being formulated for increased military operations against Japan.

Next the commentator described a new weapon used by the Germans for the first time on September 8. Although it was still unclear exactly what it was, it appeared to be a new type of flying bomb. The first had fallen on Chiswick in west London, the second shortly afterwards in an open field in Epping. "Authorities believe," the commentator reported, "these new bombs are much more deadly than the buzz bombs that have been raining such terrible havoc on Britain over the past several months. There are two significant performance improvements. First of all, based on damage assessments, they apparently carry much greater explosive power. Secondly, recent Allied advances in western Europe were thought to have eliminated all the buzz bomb launch sites. If these bombs have been launched from sites behind the front lines, it means they have much longer range and will be difficult to eliminate."

"Perhaps even more alarming," the commentator continued, "is that witnesses are reporting that no sound preceded either explosion. If this is true, it will be nearly impossible to detect when they are coming with no opportunity to intercept them. If countermeasures are not found quickly, it looks as if London is in for still more horror and devastation before this war is brought to a close." He went on to say that this new threat had come at a most inopportune time. "Children, who recently fled the city to escape the buzz bomb attack are just now beginning to return home from the countryside. Must they turn around now, and go back?" he asked.

Ann began to fidget. She thought of her parents and wondered how safe they would be with these terrible new things falling all around. Was she going to lose her parents too? Would she soon be the only one left in the Montgomery family? She began to shiver. Oliver put his arm around her and tried to comfort her. She continued to shake.

An elderly woman sitting behind whispered to her friend, "Look at that, Mildred. Isn't it disgusting? Why can't he keep his hands off her?"

"The little slut," the other said loud enough to be heard by Oliver. "Just out for a good time. Doesn't she have a mother to teach her how to conduct herself? Mothers like hers don't deserve to have children."

It was all Oliver could do to ignore the remarks. He hoped Ann hadn't heard them.

Another U.S. senator was interviewed. He was confident the war would be over by Christmas. Ann quit shaking.

The news analyst said he thought the senator was being overly optimistic. He said prospects had been dampened by recent military setbacks. "General Montgomery's gamble," he went on, "could fail. The airborne offensive launched far behind the German lines at Arnheim in the Netherlands is meeting stiffer German resistance than had been expected. The final outcome is still very much in doubt." File pictures accompanied his comments. They showed pictures of British airborne troops landing in an open field and subsequently involved in a fierce small-arms fight. Several of the men were photographed as they were shot and fell to the ground.

Had it not been for the cartoon, Ann would have left the theater.

Much to Oliver's relief, the credits for the feature film, *For Whom the Bells Toll*, finally flashed across the screen. Now Ann could settle down, watch the story and forget all her problems. As the action began, he knew he hadn't chosen the movie wisely. When Cooper killed his companion to save him from the horrible torture by the Spanish Nationalists, Ann flinched. When Cooper entered the ruined city, she began to shake. When Cooper entered the tavern and bombs began exploding outside, she had to stop watching. She put her head in her hands and began to sob. She wondered if her mum and dad had had to suffer through that sort of horrible thing.

"Come on, Ann," Oliver offered. "Let's go home."

As they rose to leave, the woman behind them said, "Now what, Mildred? Don't they have sufficient manners to stay in their seats once the feature starts? Must they jump up and disturb everyone? I've a good mind to follow them and complain to the manager."

They ignored the woman.

Afterwards they sat on the sofa in Ann's front parlor. Ann sat with her back leaning on Oliver's chest. He held her gently in his arms. He could smell her hair. It smelled good. He could smell her perfume. It smelled good. He began to feel very passionate. "I'm so sorry," he said. "I wasn't thinking. I shouldn't have taken you to that movie."

"Not to worry, it wasn't your fault. Everyone recommended it. They said Gary Cooper is marvelous in it. How were you to know?" she assured him. "I've been a silly old biddy lately. I guess losing Graham affected me more than I realized." She then added, "Thanks for being so kind and helpful. You'll never know how much your kindness and support has meant to me these past few months. You should have dumped me back in June when I treated you so horribly. It's nice you have been so patient and forgiving, I really appreciate it."

"I wish I could have done more," he said softly.

For a few minutes they talked about Louise. At first she had seemed okay, but as time went on she had become increasingly more despondent. Graham's death had been extremely hard on her. It had brought back so many memories of Tommy's last days. Meg was soon forced to withdraw from school in order to take care of her. "Poor Meg," Ann said, "first she lost her lover, and now she's going to miss out on a college education too. She wanted so badly to get that degree. I guess she's just one of the many unfortunate, heartbroken victims of this war."

They fell silent, said nothing, simply watched the fireflies skittering back and forth outside the parlor window. And then a cloud began to cover the moon, and as the darkness increased so did their passion. But neither moved, they were satisfied simply to be with each other, absorbing the warmth and love each felt for the other.

Finally Oliver said, "It's time to go. Will you walk me to the door?"

At the door, they turned toward each other and embraced. It was a long, tender embrace and ended with a loving kiss. "I wish I could stay longer but I'd better say good-bye," Oliver sighed.

"Perhaps you will some other night."

"I love you. You know that, don't you?"

"Yes, I know, Oliver. Now good-bye."

Oliver whistled as he walked to his car. "I wonder what that is all about," Jack mused from his bedroom window. Ida smiled.

The next day being Sunday, Ann, as she had routinely been doing since Graham's death, visited the Nelsons.

Chapter 111

Monday, 25 September 1944

"Here, Spot. Here, Spot. Where are you, boy?" Edith shouted repeatedly.

She was worried. Spot was not on the front porch. It was strange, he always met her there after school. She asked Hazel if she had seen him.

"No, not today," Hazel replied, contemptuously. "But that doesn't mean a thing. I don't spend my day keeping track of that mongrel."

"I don't understand it. I've looked everywhere. He just doesn't seem to be anywhere," Edith complained, more worried than ever. "It's so unlike him not to greet me when I get home."

"Well, you'll have to look for him yourself. I'm much too busy to look for that mangy animal. Besides, if it were up to me, I'd just as soon he'd stay lost," Hazel said, turning back to her baking.

When Jim came home from work, he and Edith expanded the search to some of the nearby vacant lots. It was nearly seven-thirty before they found him. He was lying in a tall clump of grass, a few yards beyond their property line. The contorted position of his head made it obvious his neck had been broken. The right side of his face was covered with blood. Edith could hardly recognize him. "There's no doubt about it," Jim said, "someone repeatedly struck this dog with a heavy object. The poor thing. Whoever it was, must have been awfully angry."

They buried Spot on a shady knoll just beyond the victory garden. Hazel was not at the funeral. She said she was too busy to attend a funeral for a beast. "And besides," she said, "it's a silly thing to do."

Shortly afterwards, Edith and Hazel became embroiled in another of their frequent heated arguments. It started when Becky called Spot a stupid dog and said she had always believed it to be the craziest animal she had ever known. Edith had cried when she said the world would be a much prettier place now that Spot was buried. When Hazel began to chide Edith for crying, Edith retorted, "I have every right to be sad. I've just lost a wonderful pet."

"If you ask me, it's good riddance! That cur should have been put to sleep a long time ago. He has done nothing but make trouble. I've wanted to see him dead ever since you brought him here."

"How can you say such an evil thing?" Edith asked angrily. "You're nothing but a wicked witch. I hate you!"

"Don't you call me a witch, you ungrateful waif," Hazel shot back.

The look of hate she saw in Edith's eyes made Hazel lose control. Without thinking she sneered and began screaming, "If you must know, I killed that worthless mutt of yours. Someone had to do it. I should have done it long ago. He got into the house and soiled my kitchen floor today. How dare he? I had just waxed it when that mangy thing wet all over it. You should have trained him better, then maybe you'd still have a pet."

Edith was stunned. She knew Hazel detested Spot, but never imagined she hated him enough to kill him. Without another word, she turned, dashed out the door and, slamming it behind her, ran down the street. Out of breath, she finally stopped near the town square. She needed help. What should she do? It was getting chilly and she had no coat. She couldn't return to the house. She would telephone Ann. But how? She had no change. She would have to beg.

It took nearly fifteen minutes before she convinced a passerby to give her a nickel to make the call. Even then, she had to reverse the charges, Dexter Hills was a long distance call.

"Ann," she cried, when Ann answered, "Spot's dead. Hazel killed him."

"Killed him! Are you certain?" Ann asked, nearly in tears.

"Yes, I'm certain. She told me she did. I've run away, Ann and I'm never going back. Never!"

"But you can't run away," Ann argued.

"Yes I can! I've just done it."

Ann had Edith wait while she talked to Jack and Ida. When she returned she said, "Stay right where are you. Uncle Jack and I will be in to pick you up–just as soon as we can get there."

After many hurried calls between Jim Adams and Dorothy Studer, and then between Dorothy, Stan Roberts, and, finally, W.T. Bender, it was decided Edith should remain at the Schaefers for the night. On Tuesday morning, a Bender employee picked up Edith's things from Hazel and temporarily reserved a room for Edith in a McKinley Heights hotel so she would not miss any school. Edith hated the hotel; she felt so alone.

On Thursday night, during the Schaefers' visit to the Nelsons', Ken asked if Ann could come live with them. "She'd be the perfect replacement for Graham. Louise badly needs someone like her," Ken argued.

Ida was immediately upset, she thought Ken was selfish to ask, but did not openly object; she left the decision entirely up to Ann. Ann did not hesitate, she answered with a quick and emphatic, "No." She told them she had no intention of leaving the Schaefers. She would remain on the farm until she returned to England. "Don't you understand? They're as much my mum and dad as my real parents are now. I love them too much. It would make more sense," she volunteered, "if Edith would come live with you."

"Of course. Why didn't we think of that?" Ken said, realizing what an excellent idea it was. "Not only will it give Louise some new interests but it also would let Meg return to school. I'll talk with Stan Roberts in the morning."

By Saturday morning, Louise had a new daughter, Meg a new sister, and Edith a new and loving home.

The war did not go as expected during the following weeks. After many days of fighting with inadequate supplies and equipment, trapped British and Polish troops surrendered to the Germans at Arnheim; the

Germans defeated the Poles in Warsaw while the Russians stood by and watched; German Panzer divisions inflicted heavy casualties in a fierce battle with the Russians on the Hungarian plain near Debreen; stiff resistance was put up by the German 1st Parachute Division on the Romagna plain in Italy, and London once again was under heavy air attack, this time by the German V2 rockets.

The return to England of the evacuees needed to be delayed a little while longer.

Chapter 112

Tuesday, 21 November 1944

It was one of those early winter days when the cold north wind blows traces of snow across the frozen ground. Warmed by the wood stove, Ann was sitting at the kitchen table finishing her homework, a comparison between the English system of choosing a prime minister and the American system of electing a president by popular vote. It had been a fascinating assignment, one she had enjoyed. She was convinced she finally understood the entire American election process–much more than she had four years ago–thanks to the election two weeks ago and the recent newspaper article describing the electoral college procedure.

She liked American Government, there were so many things in this class that her friends back in England wouldn't have the slightest idea about. It would make her feel special once she was home. And she would need all the advantages she could muster when she got to Pinnington. It would all be so strange, being home, not knowing anybody, not being used to the English customs–especially since she could recall almost nothing about how it had been, it had been such a long time. Although she was looking forward to going, there was something frightening about it, so much so that she really didn't mind if those responsible took their time setting up the trip.

Her school chums here in Dexter Hills also had learned something most students in other communities hadn't. If not for her, they would never have studied the parliamentary process in this class. The teacher had assigned it because, as he had said, "It would be interesting to find out how Ann's government chooses its leaders." Some of her classmates were not too happy about the added work, but that was okay, even if they didn't appreciate the additional knowledge, it gave her a sense of importance and that pleased her.

The race for president, in itself, had been interesting. She thought it especially fortunate she was able to witness the election of the first president ever to have served a fourth term, an event that had stirred much controversy among the electorate during the campaign. Although they knew it would be a close race, most had expected Dewey and Bricker would win. No one was supposed to want a fourth term president, not even if it was F.D.R. Surprisingly, Roosevelt had won anyway.

Ann was pleased with her other classes as well. She was pleasantly challenged by the chemistry and first year algebra courses and found the American literature class of special interest since they were reading the works of many fine American authors, some of whom she had never heard of before. Orchestra still held the fascination it always had, and she already was showing Ida some good new recipes from her home economics class.

She had just closed the textbook and was scratching Lady's head when the telephone rang. It was Edith. It had been nearly a week since they had talked and Ann was pleased to find her in such good spirits. Edith could not say enough about Mom and Pop Nelson, they had proved to be superb foster parents. Meg had been wonderful too, she was treating Edith as if she were a long lost sister. Although no one would ever forget him, the healing process had definitely started at the Nelsons; they were beginning to accept Graham's death at last. Mom Nelson had started doing housework again and was smiling more and more each day–Edith had even heard her laugh on several occasions. Pop Nelson had finally been able to talk about his foster son without crying. Yesterday, at the dinner table, he had recalled an amusing anecdote about Graham and everyone had laughed–something unheard of only a few weeks before. Even Meg seemed more resigned to Graham not coming back; she now planned, thanks in part to Edith, to go back to school in January. Edith almost wished she hadn't encouraged her. She had just found this wonderful sister and already she was leaving. She was tired of having to make so many familial adaptations. She didn't think it fair. She wanted some stability in her life, the kind Ann had.

Edith had received two letters from Ned on Monday. He appeared to be all right. From several things he mentioned, he had probably passed through Paris, although it was difficult to be certain, they were still censoring all his letters. Edith was unwilling to share the rest of the contents. "Everything else," she told Ann, "is much too personal."

She did, however, describe a dream she had the night before. In it, Ned had been watching a group of girls. They were dressed in extremely skimpy clothes, dancing the cancan in a French cabaret. She said she woke feeling quite angry with him for watching those naughty girls.

Ann laughed and said, "Let's hope watching is all he does." Then added, "You don't need to worry about Ned. I'm certain he will remain true to you. He's such a sweet, innocent farm boy. He was so very much in love with you when he left, and I'm sure he still is."

"Just the same," Edith said, "you know what they say about France."

She then shifted the subject to Ann and Oliver. She asked Ann how her love life was coming along. "Not too well. I don't know what to do. As you know, I've been dating Oliver again. We're not steadies, or anything like that, but we have been seeing each other quite a lot lately."

"So what's the problem? Oliver seems like an awfully nice boy."

"Oh, he is! That's not what bothers me. It's just that I'm worried he's getting too serious–he keeps telling me he loves me. I don't know how many times he's asked me to go steady. He even tried to give me a friendship ring the other night. He said it would advertise to everyone that I was his girlfriend."

"There doesn't seem to be anything wrong with that? Aren't most of your classmates going steady?"

"Yes, it seems to be endemic in our class," she answered, laughing. "But I'm not ready for a steady just yet. I'd prefer to wait a little longer. I'm only a junior–only sixteen. I won't be seventeen until next June. I like him, but I don't love him." She hesitated, as if carefully considering whether she should say what she was about to say, then added, "I like the freedom to date other boys too. For instance, Charles Jefferson is bringing me to the party at Benders on Saturday."

"Ah ha! Now we are getting to the root of your problem. There's someone else!"

"Frankly, I don't know. I like Oliver very much; he's quite special to me. But there are things about Charles that are pretty special too. On the other hand, it's not too realistic to think of Charles as a boyfriend. He is much too rich. I was almost ashamed when he came to the farm; and took me to the picnic in that chauffeured limousine of his. I feel much more comfortable in Oliver's roadster."

"You mustn't think that way. Here in America no one pays much attention to class, certainly not like we did in England. If Graham were here I'm sure he would tell you to seize the opportunity while it's there."

Edith regretted her words almost immediately. She shouldn't have talked about receiving advice from Graham. It had slipped out accidentally. She was terribly sorry. She hoped, somehow, Ann wouldn't notice. But she did. Edith could hear Ann's voice start to quiver.

They had just started to talk about more pleasant things when Edith said excitedly, "Meg just came in. She's crying! I'd better see what happened. I'll talk to you later."

Edith looked at Meg. Seeing how upset she was, she beckoned to her with open arms. Meg immediately accepted the invitation, "Oh, Edith! He was horrible!"

"Who was?" Edith asked, holding her tightly and trying to comfort her.

"Fred!"

"Fred? Fred Andrews? What did he do?"

"I saw him in his front yard this evening and went over to chat. We talked about the Oakton football team and, as he always does, he bragged about all the great plays he made. Then we started talking about Graham. After a few minutes he told me I should forget Graham. He said Graham was dead and, tragic as it was, would never come back. I should accept it and get on with my life."

Meg continued, "Oh, Edith, I cried when he said that. I told him how much I loved Graham and didn't think I could ever find anyone as wonderful."

After a few more sobs she went on. "Then he told me what I said was rubbish. There was always someone else. There were many men who could make me happy."

She cried harder and continued, "He said I was just frustrated because I didn't have anyone to sleep with, all I needed was a good ...," she paused, "... man to take care of me. Then he grabbed me and kissed me! He kissed me, Edith. It was horrible!"

"My God! What's wrong with him?" Edith exclaimed.

"He tried to push up against me, but I broke loose and ran home."

"Let's tell your mother and father."

"No, don't!. Don't tell anyone. It's too embarrassing. Let's just keep it between us."

"That's a mistake. Someone should be told," Edith protested.

The girls sat for a long time hugging each other. "That bloody jackass!" Edith finally said, interrupting the awkward silence. "Who does he think he is? Doesn't he recall anything we were told before we left home? Doesn't he remember any of the instructions? Didn't they say we should make our country proud? His actions are a disgrace to England, not to mention what it's done to you."

*   *   *

The annual Bender Thanksgiving Party had changed even more than it had the previous year. The children had an aura of independence not seen before. Most of the boys had voices which either had already changed or were in the process of doing so. Many were shaving. The majority of the girls wore high heels, bras, and makeup. Some of the boys had even begun to smoke. Few of the foster parents were there. They were absent, not because of a disinterest in their children but because they realized the children were becoming adults. Few saw any need to go out of their way to bring them when they could drive themselves, and those children who couldn't had made it clear they preferred to come with those who could.

Another change was the optimism among all the attendees. There was little doubt the war in Europe was rapidly coming to a close. Certainly no one questioned who the victors would be. The only question was when the end would come. Many discussions focused on the more upbeat letters now arriving from Britain. Their parents told of the extra rations available this Christmas, the reopening of the theaters, and the general easing of restrictions.

But everyone knew the war was not over. Heartaches and tragedies still lay ahead. Particularly disheartening was the recent affirmation by Prime Minister Churchill that what the news had been reporting for some time was indeed true, the Germans were now firing long range V2 rockets at England. Most discouraging was the damage caused by the inaccuracy of these weapons. Like the doodlebugs before them, they were dropping randomly throughout London and its suburbs. No place was safe. The knowledge that their parents were once again being threatened caused grave concern and embarrassment among the children. While they remained safe and were enjoying many luxuries, their parents were still being subjected to the deadly dangers of war.

As usual, the shipboard group congregated at the party. Edith was the first to arrive; she had Meg with her. Sandy, seeing the girls, left her parents to join them. Steve and Stewart, who had walked to the park from their homes, came next, followed shortly afterwards by Elizabeth. Fred was last to arrive. He came in a newly painted '38 Ford sports roadster, extravagantly decorated with a turning knob on the steering wheel, a spotlight, fog lights, mud flaps, a radio antenna with a raccoon tail attached to its tip, and other highly ornamental but unneeded accessories. Tom and Victoria had given him the car on his seventeenth birthday. Edith saw him enter the room and quickly approached him before he had an opportunity to join the group. "Hi, Edith," he said, smiling in his usual good natured manner. "Where've you been? I haven't seen you all week. We see each other so seldom it's difficult to tell we're neighbors."

"Look here," she said, ignoring his attempt to be friendly, "I don't want you associating with the group this evening."

"Why not?" he asked, looking somewhat puzzled.

"How could you?" she asked. "How could you treat Meg the way you did?"

"What are you talking about?"

"You know perfectly well what I mean. Last Tuesday. What kind of pig are you? Don't you have any sense of decency? Meg has been upset ever since."

"Oh that. I thought it was something serious. All I did was give her a little kiss. Can't a fellow give a girl a kiss when he feels like it?"

"No, Fred, he can't. For heavens sake! Don't you have any respect for her? And what about Graham? He was your friend. She was his girlfriend. It was only a short time ago that we found out he had been killed, and already you've made a pass at his girl."

Fred continued to protest, assuring Edith his intentions had always been honorable. He admitted he was attracted to Meg–had always been. He was certain she felt the same about him. He had never said anything before, because of her commitment to Graham. He had merely assumed, now that Graham was gone, they had, for the first time, a chance to get together.

Edith grew angrier and angrier as he talked. He soon became aware of how she felt and what she wanted. He was not to socialize with the group that evening, in fact, as far as she was concerned, it was all right if he never talked to them again. When he turned away, he tried to act as if nothing had happened, as if Edith had not berated him. He casually joined a group discussing the McKinley Heights area football teams. Before long he had nearly forgotten the incident. He was too entranced by the comments about his skill as Oakton's quarterback and his heroic prowess throughout the season. When asked how he had done it, he attributed it to Tom and Victoria who provided the opportunity to play and to his dad and mom who passed on the genes that gave him such superior athletic abilities. The mention of his parents in England brought on a discussion of the V2 rocket threat in London. Because he had little interest in things of that sort, he soon wandered away and joined another group who were talking about football.

"Say hello to Charles," Ann said to the group when she and Charles approached them.

As Charles shook hands with everyone, he failed to notice Elizabeth and Sandy raising their eyebrows and their feigned swoons. Even Steve and Stewart were impressed. All this did not go unnoticed by Ann. She liked him even better than she had when she first saw him at the farm earlier that night. By the end of the party, she was convinced that no one could match Charles for charm, wit, social grace, and good looks, let alone wealth.

On the way back to the farm, Charles asked the chauffeur to stop the limousine in the lane leading up to her house. "Ann, there is something I must tell you," he said, holding her hand and looking quite serious. "I'll be leaving for the Army in another week. I have accepted a commission. That is to say they will give me one after I graduate from OCS in three months."

"You volunteered for the Army?" she asked, somewhat surprised. Jack had once told her that someone with Charles' social status and wealth would never have to serve in the armed forces.

"Well, in a way. You see I was about to be drafted and my father pulled a few strings. He arranged for me to sign-up for Officers Candidate School instead." He laughed and added, "It's better than going in without a guarantee of rising any higher than a buck private." He fidgeted for a moment, then continued, "I know this is awfully presumptuous of me but you must understand, going into the Army and all, I simply don't have time to follow the proper protocol."

"That is," he stumbled on, "I know we have only dated once before, but it was sufficient for me to realize you are the one with whom I sincerely would enjoy spending the rest of my life. What I'm trying to say is ..." he paused again, "... will you marry me? Will you consent to be my wife?"

Ann was dumbfounded. The thought of limousines, nice clothes, celebrity balls, and big homes immediately flitted through her mind. But the proposal seemed terribly premature. They barely knew each other. They had only been on one date before tonight, had never kissed. She liked him—in fact she thought he was pretty special—but certainly she was in no hurry to get married, or even engaged. She though of all those people who meant so much to her: Oliver, Edith, Ned, Meg, Ida, Jack, her mum and dad. What would they think? She wasn't prepared to disappoint them, especially not Oliver, by getting married.

"You're a nice boy, Charles, I like you very much, but I just can't. Not now. I'm not ready for marriage. My life is too unsettled. Not only am I too young but I'll be returning to England soon. There's no telling what I will find when I go home—or where my life will lead once I get there. No, Charles, it's not the right thing to do at this time. I'm sorry."

He tried to appeal to her sympathy. He said he didn't know what fate had in store for him either. They might send him to Europe or, more likely now, the South Pacific and–he emphasized this–he could be killed. Ann told him she was aware of that but would not–could not–change her mind. "Let's just be friends, Charles," she said. "I'll write to you while you're gone. Then, after the war, when things are back to normal, see if you still feel the same as you do now. If you do, then we can explore it further. My guess is, by then you'll have met someone else, someone more suited to you, someone who really deserves to be your fiancée. You'll be glad then that I said no tonight."

"No, please believe me. You are the girl with whom I want to spend my life. Please change your mind. Please say yes?"

"I'm sorry," she said kissing him gently on the forehead. "I can promise you nothing for now, other than a special friendship."

"You haven't heard the last of this," he said, taking her into his arms and kissing her tenderly. "I shall keep asking you, over and over, until you finally agree to it. I don't care if it takes a month, a year, or a life-time. I want you as my bride."

"Don't make promises you can't keep," she cautioned. "Perhaps you should take me home now."

Charles rolled down the privacy window separating them from the chauffeur and instructed him to continue on up the lane.

Although the air was cold and a gusty wind made their bodies shiver, they stood a long time at the door. Neither one quite willing to say good-bye.

Finally Ida called from her bedroom window, "Ann, it's one o'clock. It's time to come in. Say good-night."

With one final kiss they parted.

Chapter 113

Saturday, 25 November 1944

Ann had difficulty falling asleep. She kept thinking about Charles' proposal. She did not want to become engaged, they didn't know each other well enough to be married. She was certain of that much. But suppose she had been willing, what would have been the consequences?

First there was Oliver. He had never asked her to marry him. Of course not, they were much too young to think about marriage. She did have to admit though, on a number of occasions she had written the name Ann Schumacher in her notebook. Of course, that was merely to see how it would look, nothing more. Come to think about it, marriage wasn't completely out of the question. Tim and Kaye had married last summer–and they had just completed their junior year. No, that was a special case, they were going to have a baby; the whole town had talked about that affair. She certainly wasn't going to follow in their footsteps. On the other hand, she thought Oliver and she were well matched. They seemed to enjoy the same things and had some grand times together, walking along the towpath, going to the movies, studying, even just sitting on the porch talking quietly. No doubt about it, Oliver was the type of person she would feel comfortable with, someone she could spend her life with. She liked Oliver, that was a given. Should she ever decide to marry, he would be an excellent candidate.

But then there was Charles. He was handsome, had exceptional manners, was a pleasant sort of person, and, perhaps most important– although she shouldn't be considering such things–he was wealthy. She had no difficulty imagining how she could adjust to his style of living. Servants, clothes, travel, and all the other things that come with wealth would suit her just fine. On the other hand, she wondered if she would be accepted in his social circle. She was a working-class girl. She would need to learn so many things, things like proper manners and protocol, to have any chance with his friends. That could be a problem. No, it wouldn't. She could do it. She could learn those things. It wouldn't be so difficult. What could there be to learning a few silly rules and manners? Besides, maybe she owed it to her parents? How happy it would make her mum and dad if she were rich and could give them all sorts of nice presents. She began to think that maybe she had acted too hastily. She hoped Charles would keep his promise and ask her again. Perhaps her answer would be different the next time.

Maybe they wouldn't need to get married right away. Marriage seemed awfully radical. Maybe they could just become engaged; he had said he would keep asking her over and over again. That sounded as if he might wait for her, be satisfied with an engagement. She had used the excuse she was too young, but it really wasn't a good one. Several of her classmates were engaged. Even Meg and Graham and Edith and Ned had done it, although neither of those engagements had been announced publicly. But wasn't that because they were too poor? Didn't the boys want to wait until they had decent jobs? That, of course, was not a problem in Charles' case.

Come to think of it, becoming engaged seemed to be a good thing to do these days; now that so many boys were going into the service. It made the boys feel so much better knowing they had a sweetheart waiting for them at home. Still, many of the couples had rushed into engagements, without giving it serious thought beforehand. But in a great many cases, those engagements hadn't lasted. There was so much talk in the papers lately about the "Dear John" letters the girls were sending to their soldier and sailor sweethearts. Ann promised herself she would never be so irresponsible. She would never send her lover a letter breaking off their engagement. That would be entirely too cruel.

She supposed it was possible to fall out of love if your man was gone for too many months—it seemed to happen to so many girls. Wouldn't it be terrible if you no longer loved someone but could not break it off, just because he was in the service and you had made a promise? That is probably a sufficient justification to avoid an early engagement. Besides Aunt Ida and Uncle Jack would never agree to anything like that without consulting my mum and dad first. Getting their consent—even assuming that they approved, which they probably wouldn't—would take months of writing letters back and forth before anything could be finalized. Charles would already have left for the Army long before that.

It was a difficult question, no doubt about it. Thank goodness she had given Charles a definite no. But come to think about it, she hadn't shut the door entirely. She only said it wasn't the right thing to do at *this* time. There was always a *later* time. But anyway, there was nothing to worry about, she wasn't expecting to see him again before he left. She couldn't change her mind, even if she wanted to. For now, she would be content to write to him occasionally, as she promised, and see what happened after the war. She knew, even then, it would be difficult to decide. She really didn't love him—at least she didn't think she did.

Her thoughts about the end of the war led to thoughts about the return home and the reunion with her mum and dad. It should be a happy time, that is if they still loved her—and she loved them. Why would she question whether she loved them? Of course she loved them. She did have to admit though, it was going to be difficult saying good-bye to Ida and Jack. She wondered if she could do it; they seemed so much more like her real parents now. Then there were all the others: Oliver, Bonnie, Mr. and Mrs. Nelson, and Meg. Maybe she shouldn't leave, maybe she should try to find a way to remain in America?

With thoughts of engagements, reunions, and good-byes swimming in her head, she finally fell into an uneasy sleep. She dreamed of the *S. S. Caerleon* in New York harbor. People on shore were waving, and her friends on board were waving back. Everyone was laughing. Everyone except her, she was crying. She did not want to leave America.

Edith dreamed of Ned that night. She saw him lying in a war ravaged forest. The ground around him was barren, all that remained of the woods were jagged-edged tree trunks. Broken equipment and bodies lay everywhere. Wisps of smoke still lingered over the battleground. There was no sound, just an eerie silence. As she came closer she heard him. He was crying. His forearm and hand were missing. Blood was oozing from what remained of his elbow.

She screamed his name and knelt by his side. "My darling," she whispered as she cradled him in her arms. "Please don't die! Please come back."

Edith sat upright in bed. "My God! Ned's been hurt!" she screamed.

A few minutes later she was in the arms of Louise, "You poor child. It was only a dream, dear. It was only a dream."

At nearly the same instant a soldier was lying on a battlefield in the Palau Islands. Blood was oozing from a terrible wound. A medic was applying a tourniquet and powdering it with sulfa. "Hang in there, soldier. Don't give up. You'll be going home now. Home to your family."

The names Clara and Debby flashed through his mind just before he lost consciousness. He did not wake again until they had evacuated him to the medical ship.

"My arm!" he screamed. "My God! Where's my arm?"

On October 4, the Second Division was camped in the Ardennes forest near St. Vith not far from the Belgium-German border. Its mission, to hold the border and two small salients established earlier inside German territory. It was not an easy assignment. The thinly held front was 30 kilometers long and suffered under constant threat of hostile attack and infiltration. Dense conifer forests, steep hills, sharp gullies, and rough terrain dominated the area. Division headquarters was established in one of the shell damaged St. Vith hotels. The troops lived in surrounding foxholes and hated it. The camouflage covering the holes was troublesome and inconvenient, and for days at a time, heavy October rains kept the foxholes partially filled with water. Then in mid November it began to snow and, in spite of an issue of winter clothing, it became nearly impossible to stay warm. By November 25, only a few of the men had managed to escape the cold, most suffered frost bitten feet.

Ned's squad was one of the lucky ones. They had sometime ago commandeered a deserted farmhouse, and had lived in relative luxury. They used it to store their communications equipment and, much to Ned's good fortune, as a place to sleep. Even with the missing windows and shell torn roof it was much better than those abominable foxholes; at least it was dry. He was beginning to think the Almighty was looking out for him. He even believed, at times now, he would someday be able to return to Dexter Hills; someday he would see Edith again.

On this particular night, however, he wasn't feeling so fortunate; he was tired and nearly frozen. After having spent the day laying new wire along the front, he was one of the unlucky ones who had drawn guard duty in one of the forward posts.

"What was that? Are those artillery shells they're firing?" Ned asked, his teeth chattering from the cold and damp.

"Didn't you see it?" his buddy whispered. "It was one of those new German V2 flying bombs. It must have veered off course. I saw it start up, then fall back. It must have hit somewhere on the other side of hill 342. What you heard was it exploding."

"Those damn things aren't very reliable, are they?" Ned noted. "That must be the fifth one that's gone out of control since we first started seeing them fly over. You'd think, after nearly four weeks, they'd have figured out how to keep them from falling before they reach their target."

"Scuttlebutt says those that do are giving the Brits one hell of a time. They say things in London are nearly as bad as they were during the Blitz."

"It must be terrible. They fly so high you can't hear them and go so fast there's no warning before they hit," Ned said, shaking his head. He looked up just in time to see another heading west. "There's another. Man, oh man, look at that thing go."

He hoped it wasn't headed toward the Montgomery or Dickson homes.

Walt was feeling good. He and Alice had just received a letter from Fred. Fred had, as usual, included many details about his latest football game and how well he had done. Walt was proud of Fred and wished he could be there to watch one of his son's games. He knew little about American football, only that it differed quite a bit from English football. He was eager to hear Fred explain the rules once he came back. That was why he was so happy; with all the reported Allied victories, he was almost certain he wouldn't have to wait too much longer before Fred would be home.

"Although the U-boat menace in the Atlantic is far from over and we still have those confounded V2 bombs to contend with, the war can't go on much longer." he thought. "With the steady progress the Russians are continuing to make in the Balkans and with the major offense they launched this past week in Latvia, Hitler must be starting to feel the squeeze–especially with the nearly constant Allied bombing pressure on all the German cities these days. Even the Italian front is sounding more hopeful–in spite of the stalemate in the Po valley."

He looked at the sky, as if to assure himself no V2 bombs were headed his way. He knew it did no good to look, no one could see them– and even if they could, there'd be no place to hide; looking was something he did by habit.

He smiled as he entered Woolworth's. "I'll just stop in here first and find a little trinket for Alice before I pick up the Bender package," he said, feeling somewhat guilty for taking a few minutes off. Walt was in New Cross, on a special errand for the factory. He normally would have stuck strictly to business, but this assignment had interfered with the Saturday morning outing he had planned with Alice. The poor thing, she had been looking forward to it all week. The gift was intended as partial compensation for her disappointment.

Suddenly, he felt the concussion followed by the deafening sound. The building began to collapse. Walt felt the falling rubble land on top of him. He had only a second to think. He knew he was in trouble. "I love you, Alice," he said, just before the beam struck his head.

The next morning the newspaper headline read, *"Rocket bomb kills 160 in south London."* Walt never saw it.

Chapter 114

Saturday, 16 December 1944

Ned sat on the floor in a corner of the supply room, his head cradled in his arms, his arms folded across his knees. He thought about the letter from Edith in his breast pocket. It had been there ever since it arrived yesterday, he hadn't had time to read it, in fact he had not even opened it. There had been several times when he could have found a spare moment or two to scan it, but he hadn't. He felt bad about that. The truth was, he preferred reading it at his leisure; when he could savor its contents, not when he had to rush. Now here he was, finally, with some free time, but he still couldn't read it. He was simply too exhausted.

It had been a hectic past week. Just five days before, the Second Division had been pulled off the line and was reassigned as part of the long awaited Allied offensive. Ned, as a communications specialist, had been transferred to the Second Battalion of the 9th Infantry Regiment. His new unit's objective was to secure Dam Number 5 on the flooded Roer River. It had to be done quickly, before the Germans opened the floodgates and flooded the down river area. If his unit failed the Allied armor would be seriously delayed in its advance towards the Rhine.

On the day Edith's letter arrived, the division had been especially busy. After passing through the 99th Division, it encountered German forces and a fierce battle ensued. By the end of the fight, which had continued through most of the night, a command post had been established in the town of Krinkelt.

Then, at 0700 hours this morning–was it Saturday, Ned no longer knew for certain–his battalion had pushed on. After several anxious, but successful, encounters with enemy pillboxes, it had established a defensive circle east of Krinkelt. Within minutes things became chaotic when intense German heavy caliber artillery fire cut off communications between the battalion and the command post. Ned was ordered to retrace, and repair if possible, the disabled communication line. When he found his path into Krinkelt cut off by the Germans, he turned and started back towards his unit. But, by now, it was also blocked. After several narrow escapes, he made his way to the neighboring town of Bullingen where he joined with other members of his signal unit and was attached to the Second Battalion of the 23rd Infantry Regiment. The regiment was preparing another attack for early in the morning.

What he did not know, and what the commanders of the 23rd were slow to realize, was that on his way into Bullingen he had crossed over what was, at the time, a still thinly established German line. Thin as it was, it would prove to be the precursor to a new major German counter-offensive, which later would be nicknamed the Battle of the Bulge. Involved in the counterattack were two panzer divisions under Von Rundstedth. His mission, to break through to the English Channel and, as he advanced, to capture the large Allied supply depots assembled at points along the way.

When Ned awoke from his exhaustive sleep, it was morning. By then the 1st and 2nd Battalions were completely cut off from the remainder of the Second Division. He did not get an opportunity to read his letter that morning either. He, along with all other available men were deployed on the outskirts of Bullingen to battle the German armor. They fought the tanks with their rifles, machine-guns, and the few rocket launchers they had until finally they had to retreat back into town. The Germans followed, shelling the town unmercifully with their eighty-eight-millimeter guns. After a valiant effort to destroy what supplies remained, Ned's group returned to the building where their gear had been stored and from the top floor directed small arms fire into the oncoming enemy troops and tanks. Suddenly an enemy eighty-eight-millimeter shell struck the building, followed by another that passed through the hole created by the first one. "Let's get out of here," a sergeant screamed.

They had just taken refuge in the basement when German troops entered the building and began their search for prisoners. For some unexplained reason, they failed to notice the cellar entrance and left, believing the Americans had somehow managed to escape. Later, under cover of darkness, Ned and several of his companions, made their way back to the command post in Wirtzfeld, obtaining their bearing from the westward path of the V2 bombs flying overhead.

Shortly after arriving, Ned volunteered to lay a telephone line to an observation post being set up to direct fire on tanks and infantry approaching Wirtzfeld. Ned had just returned and was being congratulated by the division commander when the explosion occurred. "Son, I'm recommending you for the Distinguished Service Cross," was the last thing Ned heard.

The following morning as the wind blew through the rubble of what had been the command post a partially torn paper fluttered through one of the broken windows. At the lower right corner of the page was written, *All my love, Edith.*

It was the day before Christmas and the Schaefer family spirits were high. Ann and Ida were listening intently to Edith. She was reading the less personal parts of her letter from Ned.

Things have been going well here. Although we must spend some of our time on duty at the front most of it is much more mundane. The division has established an R and R area some miles behind the enemy lines and I have been fortunate to get back here quite often. Not only do they offer plenty of snacks and have lots of entertainment, mostly movies and music, but–more importantly–there is an opportunity to take <u>warm</u> showers and eat <u>hot</u> meals. You'd appreciate my need for a shower better if you could smell me after several days in the field. Even old porky smells better than I do then! Ha! Ha!

A few of the fellows have been given stateside furloughs this past month. It's a select group and each time they announce who will be the lucky ones we all stand around hoping. But, darn, so far my name hasn't been called. But I feel my luck is about to change. Before you know it I will be knocking at your door. Gosh, it will be grand to see Ohio again. And of course, to see Mom and Dad, Karen and Ann, and most of all, my darling, to see you. You know, Darling, that ...

Edith paused, read to herself for a few seconds, then apologized for skipping some of the–as she said–more personal parts." Then continued.

Everyone is talking about the end of the war now. Der Führer can't keep going much longer. We are just too strong and better supplied now. Scuttlebutt around here says the war could be over almost any day–it only depends on how stubborn Hitler is. Let's hope he wises up soon. When he does I'll be home just as quickly as I can and once again I'll hold you in my arms.

Edith blushed at having mistakenly read the last line, then continued.

Of course, by the time I get home they will probably have sent you back to England. But if you are gone, don't worry. I'll follow you to England, as quickly as I possibly can.

Edith had become so interested in what Ned was saying, she forgot to stop reading out loud.

And then, my dear, we will wed–and you will be my bride. And I will love you. Oh how I will love you! And we will settle down in one of those new ranch type homes they are beginning to talk about. Just you and me–and, of course, all our children.

Well, darling, it's time I wrap this up and get back to my war. Until later,

> *Oodles and oodles of love,*
> *No! ALL my love,*
> *Ned*

"My, my, Edith," Ida said, trying to tease a little, "it sounds as if you will soon be my daughter-in-law. I had better start thinking about a dress to wear to the wedding."

Edith did not know how to answer and began to blush again. Ann looked at Ida and laughed.

Later in the afternoon Ann and Edith trimmed the Christmas tree. "Gee, Edith," Ann said, "I've never heard you whistle before."

"That's because I'm happy! Everything finally seems to be working out quite wonderfully; Ned loves me, I'm living with a super family I love so very much, the war is winding down, Ned will be home shortly, and someday I will be living in America, permanently–with no obligation to return to England hanging over my head. I'll be the wife of a former serviceman, not an evacuee sponsored by Bender Electric."

"What's this whistling all about? Let's turn on the radio–see if we can find some better music to listen to," Jack joked as he entered the room.

Bing Crosby was singing "White Christmas" when the doorbell rang. Neither Ann nor Edith paid much attention to it, they were both more interested in hanging the final holly leaves on the branch tips.

"Mr. Jack Schaefer?" the messenger asked. "Sign here please."

Ann saw Jack close the door. His face was pale, a terrible look on it. In his trembling hand was an unopened telegram. Without saying anything he ripped off the top of the envelope. The telegram began,

We regret to inform you that your son, Ned Arthur Schaefer, was killed in action on December seventeenth.

Jack sank to his knees and began crying like a baby. Edith and Ann looked at each other and started crying too.

Chapter 115

Tuesday, 17 April 1945

By mid April, the war was rapidly coming to an end in Europe. The Allies, with air superiority now firmly established, were systematically punishing the Germans with highly destructive bombing raids. Among the cities that had suffered the brunt of these attacks were Dresden and Cologne, both of which had been almost totally ruined. In the East, Poland was under Russian control, Budapest had been captured, and the Russians had crossed the German frontier and were threatening Berlin. In the West, after an initial crossing at Remagen in early March, the Allies crossed the Rhine River in full force on March 24 and, with little resistance, advanced steadily toward central Germany. In the South, after four days of intense aerial attacks and heavy artillery barrages, the long awaited offensive push had started with the Allies crossing the Senio river in northern Italy. Within days the city of Bologna would be in Allied hands, within two weeks the Germans would agree to an unconditional surrender at Caserta and the war in Italy would be over. By April 27, the Americans and Russians would link forces on the River Elbe and a total Allied victory would be all but guaranteed.

In the Pacific, although a major war was still raging, the situation was steadily improving. MacArthur had, as promised, returned to the Philippines and had retaken Manila and Corregidor and American B-29 bombers were delivering devastating attacks on Japan. Especially hard hit were the cities of Ota and Tokyo. By March 26, after over a month of fighting and after exceedingly large losses, the Americans finally were in complete control of the island of Iwo Jima. Okinawa, an island only three hundred forty miles from the mainland of Japan and an ideal launch site for the planned Japanese invasion, was attacked on April 4. A fierce fight followed, with heavy casualties. The battle would finally be won on June 21.

But even with all the victories, there were still many hardships for English civilians. On March 17, after a temporary lull in V2 rocket attacks, the Germans launched a new series of assaults on England and Belgium. By the end of March, soon after a bomb had destroyed a block of flats in West Hampstead, the rocket offensive stopped. The air war was finally over for Chad and Diane.

The impending peace was also producing many positive effects on the people of England. Motorcar headlamps were unmasked, blackout curtains were removed, newspapers were permitted to report current news from the front and weather forecasts were once again printed. But surprisingly, controls on food and clothing became even more restrictive than they had ever been–even during the bleakest days of the war. The liberation of the continental European nations, and their subsequent need for large supplements of food and clothing, had decreased the available supplies once headed for England. It would take several more years before supply would meet demand in Britain.

Many changes were also beginning to be made in the governing forces in England. Although pressures were forever increasing to make a change in leadership, all efforts effectively stopped after the Labour party decided no changes would be appropriate until complete victory in Europe was won. It was by this action that Churchill retained his control until the end.

Other major changes were also happening: the antiquated educational system was under attack; there was a large movement to nationalize many industries, including transportation; and a particularly high priority effort had been mounted towards critically needed postwar reconstruction. Many families, including Diane and Chad Montgomery, were looking forward to the home repair assistance expected through this reconstruction program.

All these events led, finally, to a call for the evacuees to come home.

Ann and the other Bender children were told on Tuesday, April 17. The notices came only two days after America had buried President Roosevelt. He had died the previous Thursday and the nation was still in mourning over its loss and wondering what effect his successor, Harry Truman, would have on the remaining days of the war. Few of the evacuees were concerned about the presidency however; they had other things on their minds now. They were going home.

Ann's reaction to the notice, surprising even to herself, was mixed. She had always imagined when the news finally came she would be overwhelmed with joy. Instead, she found herself somewhat ambivalent. On one hand, she was relieved to be finally going home; on the other, she could not bear to leave Ida and Jack.

Poor Ida and Jack. It had been a terribly difficult year for them. Two gold stars now hung in their window, one for Ned and one for Graham. The one for Graham was of course out of deference to Ann, but the one for Ned meant so much more to them. She couldn't remember a day when she hadn't caught them looking at that star with a sad look in their eyes. Now, she was leaving, most likely never to see either of them again. In some ways it was almost the same as dying. Everyone felt almost as bad. She loved those people, and they loved her. How could they possibly separate now?

She, too, had been especially saddened by the loss of Ned. The thought of never seeing him again, never hearing his laughter after one of his awful jokes, and never seeing his muscular body working in the fields, filled her with a huge sense of loneliness, much more, she was ashamed to admit, than she had ever felt for Graham. She couldn't explain it. She had spent many hours trying to understand why she should have greater remorse for the death of Ned, a foster brother, than for Graham, her real brother. The guilt at times was nearly unbearable.

She thought of the grand times she had with the Schaefers, all those times working in the fields. How terribly tired she had been. But how invigorating it had been to work alongside all of them, with their wonderful sense of humor and healthy outlook on life. She recalled the long girl-to-girl talks she had with Karen, how Karen had helped her understand some of the strange feelings she had as she approached womanhood. She thought of the times she and Ned had spent in her secret hiding place, watching the clouds overhead and feeling the wind on their faces. How he had talked so enthusiastically about his ambitions and plans. How he hoped to marry Edith, and the family he planned on having. She thought of baking bread with Ida, of all the things Ida had taught her in the kitchen. How Ida taught her to sew, crochet and knit; how to keep the house neat and clean; and especially, how she was always there for her, as a mother and as a friend. She thought of Jack. How serious he was when he played checkers, cards, or any other parlor game. How he would laugh when he won and pretend he was upset when he lost. How hard he worked, but how he always had time to help with her schoolwork–or to fix a broken locket or trinket. How concerned he was for her well-being; and how he also was always there when she needed support or help.

Now here she was, about to return to England, to her mum and dad, and instead of being happy, all she could think of was how much she would miss Ida and Jack, Karen, the farm, and all the friends she had made during the past nearly five years. It wasn't fair.

"Oh, Lady," she said, as she sat in front of her dresser mirror looking at the tears streaming down her face. "How can I leave them? How can I leave you?" She began to cry harder.

Ann thought of Oliver. She recalled their last date. It was just last Saturday night. They had gone to the movies, a regular Saturday night routine for them these past several months. They had seen *Since You Went Away*. She had told Oliver she thought Robert Walker was groovy and laughed when she recalled how upset he had become. He said he didn't think Walker was so special and couldn't understand what the girls saw in that silly, curly-headed boy. She recalled how emotional he had been during some of the sadder scenes in the movie. She was quite impressed. She had only discovered recently how much of a romantic he was. It was something he had hidden well until their friendship had grown so close. He certainly was romantic during those wonderful times when they had parked in the alcove–just off the back road to Mason City. She recalled how passionate they had both been last Saturday night. It was getting difficult to keep their emotions in check. She was almost certain they would be taking the next step soon, but she wasn't quite ready for it–yet.

There was no question, she liked him. In fact, she was almost ready to admit she loved him. "It's rather ironic," she thought. "Just when I'm about to return to England we get involved; just in time to make it so terribly difficult to say good-bye. After all those years trying to avoid that very thing." She wondered if she would ever see him again, wondered how she would react to his not being there to talk to. "After all," she thought, "I've known him since the day I started at Dexter Hills Junior High. He was such a nice boy; he always treated me so nice, not like so many of the others who always seemed to be looking for ways to tease and embarrass me."

* * *

There was so much to do before leaving. Friday was only three days away. First on her list was to tell Oliver. She wouldn't be able to see him in school–they were on spring break. She wanted desperately to see him once more. She tried calling him at the garage but he wasn't there. Then, even though she knew she shouldn't, she called his house. His father answered.

"Mr. Schumacher?" she began.

"Yeth," came the answer.

She could tell he had been drinking from his slurred answer. "Is Oliver there?"

"Who'z callin?"

"It's Ann Montgomery, sir. Something important has come up. May I talk to Oliver. Please?"

"Oliver!" he shouted. There was a long pause. Finally he answered, "Guess not."

"May I leave a message then? Please tell him to call me as soon as he can."

"Have the hots for him, have you?" he gurgled.

"I must leave for England on Friday and would like to say good-bye. That's all, sir," she said, a hint of disgust creeping into her voice.

"Now ain't that just dandy?" came the reply. "We're finally getting rid of you limeys," he laughed.

"Just tell him. Please!" she begged.

"Oh? Right, honey. Or should I say right toe!" he laughed, mocking how he supposed the English would say it. "I'll tell him."

Ann quickly hung up. She had never talked to Ludwig on the telephone before. He was horrible. She now better understood why Oliver did not get along with him.

The next two days were hectic.

First, there was the meeting with Mr. Hartline. He was extremely cooperative. He gave her a certified list of all classes taken, including those she had presently elected and those she still needed to graduate. He made special note of how few required courses remained especially since she had always selected the maximum course load during each of her six high school semesters. He attached a detailed description of the college preparatory option she had pursued and said her scholarship had been exemplary and suggested she probably would have been the class valedictorian, or close to it, had she continued to earn the high marks.

He said that, in his opinion, she had all the intellectual attributes necessary to compete successfully at any American college or university and strongly recommended she be permitted to go on to more advanced studies. Before she left, he complimented her on having elected typing and shorthand. "Those two courses," he said, "will serve you well, no matter if you choose to go on to school–which I wholeheartedly encourage–or to go to work as a secretary."

Next, although Ann politely argued that it wasn't necessary, Ida insisted they go shopping. She said she refused to send Ann home dressed in shabby clothes. At the store she kept suggesting additional things to buy, which embarrassed Ann. She knew the Schaefers could ill afford such extravagance, especially after all that had happened in the past four terrible months. Besides Ned's death in December, Karen had contracted pneumonia in February. And only a month later, an electrical spark set the barn on fire. But, as she always had, Ida's wishes prevailed; they shopped until Ann thought she was about to collapse. By then, Ann had a completely new, and very lovely, wardrobe and Ida was able to proudly boast that now Ann looked like a proper young lady traveler. She thought Ann's parents would be very pleased when they saw her. Ann agreed wholeheartedly.

On the way home, Ida dropped Ann off at Bonnie's. It was a tearful time for the two girls. They found it difficult to imagine not being together anymore–not being able to share all those little things they had always found so important. As a token going away present, Bonnie bought Ann a banana split at the drug store. Ann, hoping Oliver would come in, dallied for as long as she could. But he never did; Mr. Winters was the only one she was able to say good-bye to that evening.

On Thursday, there seemed to be no time to do anything properly. Many of her friends stopped in to say a brief good-bye, and almost all their visits turned into lengthy stays. Ann and Ida had barely finished packing before it was time to visit the Nelsons.

By then, Ann still had not heard from Oliver. For all she knew, Oliver might not even be aware she was leaving. She knew how irresponsible his dad was, perhaps he hadn't given Oliver her message. She considered trying to reach Oliver again. On the other hand, maybe Oliver knew she was leaving. His silence could just as easily indicate he had already written her off as one of his friends. Maybe he figured if she was leaving he had no further need for her friendship. But that was a silly thought; hadn't he always been interested in her? Still ...

She probably would have tried harder if there had been more time. Or maybe she purposely hadn't tried. The honest truth was, she dreaded saying good-bye to Oliver, she might not even be able to do it, when she finally saw him. She decided not to try any more. She would simply leave without a good-bye. It was a decision she would regret for quite sometime.

It was a tearful evening at the Nelsons. Everyone was sorry to see Ann leave. Edith was especially sad because she was not leaving with Ann. The Nelsons, upon learning Edith was going home, had called Harriet and, with her approval, had successfully petitioned to keep Edith in Oakton until the end of the school year. By then she would be only a year away from a diploma. The long term plan was for her to return to England–as all evacuees were required to do, stay a short time, and then come back to America. She would complete her senior year, then earn a degree in pharmacology at some American college. Ken and Louise had offered to provide a home and financial support throughout her school years. It was an wonderful offer. Ann was happy for Edith.

On Friday morning, Ida called Ann early so she could be at the train station in ample time. Before she left, Ann, forgetting her earlier resolve, called the garage and asked for Oliver. They told her he had not been in to work all week. Reluctantly, she dialed Oliver's home. There was no answer.

The scenario that follow was surprisingly similar to the good-byes in 1940, but this time a foster family instead of a birth family was filled with sadness and anxiety. Ida kissed Ann, hugged her, and wished her happiness, but did not go to the train station. She, like Diane five years before, did not believe she could control her emotions. Karen did not go either; she had to work. She gave Ann a tremendous hug, wished her well, and quickly left. Ann did not see Karen's tears as Karen drove down the lane. Only Jack was left to escort Ann to the train station.

One of the last things Ann did before getting in the car was to say good-bye to Lady. "You be a good girl," she said as she put her arms around Lady's neck. "Aunt Ida and Uncle Jack will be taking care of you from now on. They love you, girl."

Ann looked at Ida as if she were seeking confirmation. "Now don't you fret, child," Ida said. "We'll take good care of her. She'll be here waiting when you come back."

"Oh, Aunt Ida," Ann sighed. "Do you really think I'll ever return? It's such a long distance."

"Yes, I'm certain of it. You'll come back, if not to stay, at least to visit."

With that, Ann hugged Ida for what must have been the tenth time and climbed into the auto. Jack quickly put it in gear and hurried down the lane; he didn't want to change his mind; he didn't want to disobey the officials and hide her somewhere on the farm.

Ann could not look back. She recalled how sad she felt five years ago watching her other mum disappear in the rear window. Had she looked back she would have seen Ida, her apron held to her eyes, weeping uncontrollably. Lady sat watching the car until it disappeared around the bend. For many weeks afterwards, Lady would often be found sitting on the front porch, apparently waiting for Ann to return.

On the way to the station they passed through Dexter Hills. They passed the school house; Ann thought about her school days and the friendship she and Oliver had. They crossed over the canal bridge; Ann thought about the walks Oliver and she had taken. They passed the drug store; Ann thought about that first cherry Coke she had made for Oliver. They passed the garage; she wondered if Oliver had finally come to work. They passed the hill where they had gone sled riding; she recalled her first time down the hill with Oliver. They passed the alcove just off the back road to Mason City; she thought of Oliver. She wished she could go there with him once more.

Back at the farm, Ida hung a small Union Jack in the window beside the two gold stars. "There," she sighed, looking at Lady with a look of pride on her face. "That will be our commemoration to our little girl."

All Lady could do was wag her tail.

Chapter 116

Friday, 20 April 1945

Ann was puzzled. She had expected to see the station bustling with evacuees and their families. It was true, the McKinley Heights railway station was bustling all right, people were everywhere, but few were fellow evacuees. "What's going on? Where are all the others?" she asked Steve who was standing with his family in front of the station.

"I guess there aren't many of us going today," Steve answered.

"I thought we were all going?"

"No, a few left yesterday; some are leaving today, and more will be leaving next week. There may even be a few after that. As I understand it, they couldn't find passages for all of us on one ship so they're sending us home separately, and at different times."

"Have you seen anyone else from our group?"

"The only ones I've seen so far are you and Fred. He's over there surrounded by all those people. I think almost everyone you see in the station is here to see him off. I know the band is from Oakton and I believe a number of his football and softball teammates are here. Some of the others are apparently fans."

"That's not surprising. Fred doesn't do anything in a small way, does he?" Ann said laughing. "He's become quite the local celebrity. I wonder how difficult it will be for him when he gets home and no one recognizes him."

"Yes, that will be a problem," Steve chuckled. "Do you know of anyone else who's going with us?"

"The only person I know anything about is Edith. She won't be going today, she's staying until school is out. She plans to leave sometime around the first of June. They decided to let her finish the school year before she leaves."

"That's interesting," Steve mused. "I didn't think anyone could stay behind. I thought the American government insisted everyone had to go home–something to do with their immigration laws. Several kids I know didn't want to leave–but they were told they had to go anyway. Amy Harden was one of them. Her foster parents have been trying frantically to find some way to keep her in the U.S. permanently. But why should they? Why do they think they can change the rules?"

"I agree, why would Amy's parents think they were special. We always knew, right from the start, we had to return–just as soon as the war was over. Edith's case is a little different. It's only a delay of six weeks–and for a very specific reason, to complete her schooling, not to stay in the U.S. forever"

"I suppose parting with Amy after five years seemed just too difficult. Her foster parents must have gotten desperate."

By now, several others had arrived and were greeting each other excitedly. Sandy and Stewart were the first to join Ann and Steve, followed soon afterwards by Fred and his family who had managed to tear themselves away from all of Fred's well-wishers. As they talked, Fred mentioned his mum and how eager he was to see her again. Victoria momentarily flinched hearing this, then quickly recovering her composure, she smiled and said brightly, "Yes, isn't it grand. You children will all be back with your parents before you know it. I can't begin to imagine how happy your parents must be–having you back after all this time."

Fred was about to agree with her when Captain Ben climbed onto one of the station benches and asked for everyone's attention. "I just want to say," he shouted, "how much we have enjoyed having you children here with us these past five years. Thank you for sharing your lives with us. Never in our wildest imagination could we have ever thought you would be as outstanding and responsible ladies and gentlemen as you have proven to be. All of you have been the exemplary citizens that I am certain your parents had hoped you would be. They should be very proud. We certainly are. It has been an honor for us to have had such a fine group of young people visit us. You have touched our hearts very dearly and we love you very much. We hope you leave here knowing that you will always be in our thoughts, always in our dreams, and, above all, always in our hearts. Please come back to visit us often. You will always be welcomed."

"We regret you had to be away from your families for such a long time," he continued. "But, on the other hand, we are pleased to have had the time to get to know you better. To us it seems such a short time. In our selfish hearts, we wish we could have kept you with us even longer.

"Now I know you are eager to say your individual good-byes so I will not keep you. God speed, and God bless you!"

"Excuse me, sir," Stewart said, as he climbed onto the bench beside Ben. "May I say something?" Ben looked surprised.

"On behalf of all the evacuees, I want to say how much we appreciate what you, and all the wonderful people of McKinley Heights, Oakton, Dexter Hills, and all the other communities, have done for us," Stewart shouted. "In a time of great need, you took us into your homes and made us feel we were part of your family. You fed us when we were hungry, clothed us when we needed warmth, nursed us when we were ill, consoled us when we were sad, shared our joy when we were happy, and, most importantly, loved us when we needed love. It was an unselfish and wonderful thing you did. We wish there were some way to repay you for your kindness. We have talked amongst ourselves, trying to think of what would be most appropriate, and have concluded no material gift could ever be grand enough to express our appreciation and gratitude. Instead we depart, with sadness for having to leave you but with happiness in our hearts for having known you, and simply bestow on you the greatest honor and gift we can give, one that comes most naturally and sincerely from our hearts. We give you a simple promise that we will think of you always as our very own special mums and dads, sisters and brothers, and friends. Thank you all."

As Stewart ended his speech, the Oakton band began playing *Rule Britannia*, followed by *America*–which the evacuees knew was meant to be *God Save the King*, and finally *The Star Spangled Banner*. Never had a crowd stood at attention as reverently as this one did.

Afterwards, Ann and the others spotted Sandy and her parents and called to them. Sandy had been crying. She did not want to go back to England and Lucy was not helping matters. "Don't let her go, Kirk," she pleaded.

"You know perfectly well there's nothing we can do, Lucy. I tried."

"There must be something! I understand the Dickson girl is not going. They say the Nelsons made a special plea and it was granted."

"It was only an extension until the end of next month, and only because she had agreed to serve as an escort for Bobby Preston. She was lucky, Bobby couldn't get his release from the sanitarium until late May. That was the only reason they permitted her to stay."

"Mummy! Daddy!" cried Sandy. "I don't want to go! Please do something. Can't we do something? What if I miss the train?"

"Stop it, Sandy! I've told you before, you have no choice," scolded Kirk, then tried to soften his reproach. "You're going home, Sandy. Think of it, in a few days you will be with your mother and father. You should be thrilled."

"I don't want them as my mother and father anymore. They didn't even care enough to keep me with them back when I was a little girl. Instead, they sent me away–they got rid of me," Sandy sobbed. "You're my mom and dad now–not them! They are strangers as far as I'm concerned."

Ann tried to bring up something else, "Gosh, Oakton must think highly of Fred, Sandy. Look at all the people here to see him off–that's quite a group. Isn't it? And a band to boot!" But the ruse did not work. Sandy and Lucy continued to fuss. Finally, Ann turned away and ignored them.

When the conductor shouted all aboard, Stan Roberts had to help Kirk separate Sandy from Lucy. As they forced her onto the train, there was a sudden and surprising change in her demeanor. Instead of continuing to reach out for Lucy, she looked at her with disgust and shouted, "I hate you! What have you ever done for me? You never gave me anything. You never permitted me to grow up, you always kept me practically in chains. You wouldn't even let me go out with a boy. I never went on any dates, not even once. I'm fifteen years old. My mum wouldn't have been so spiteful. She loves me, she'll let me do whatever I want. You'll see. She's a nice lady, not an evil person like you. You, you ... old hag!"

No one could believe what they were hearing. After all Lucy had done for her. Lucy collapsed in Kirk's arms. "See! She hates me! We shouldn't have let her go. We should have kept her here–with us. If we had, she wouldn't have said such spiteful things."

"I don't understand it," Steve told Fred. "I don't see why everyone is so emotional. What's all the fuss about? Why is everyone so sad about leaving? What was so great about America? The folks here have treated me admirably, but so will my parents. I'll be as happy there as I have been here. I could care less whether I go home or not. I have neither good nor bad feelings about leaving."

"Not me," replied Fred, "I'm eager to get home. With my dad gone, Mum needs me. I need to get home to help her as quickly as I can."

"I would have thought you'd be one of those eager to remain in America," Steve conjectured. "You've been terribly fortunate, with all your sports fame, that nice home, and those lovely people. You must have had a super time."

"That's true. Oakton has treated me as if I were some sort of a celebrity; it made me feel real special, and Dr. and Mrs. Derringer have been very good to me too. They made my stay a splendid one," he admitted. Then, not being able to resist an opportunity to brag, he added, "I'm even going home with quite a bit of pocket money. Dr. Derringer bought my thirty-eight Ford. He paid good money for it. That, plus all the money I saved from my allowance, gives me quite a bundle to take home.

"Anyway, Mum writes that she's desperate to have me home," he added, turning more serious, "She says she needs me and looks forward to our reunion. She is such a sweet woman. I don't know when I have been so eager to see someone–and to take care of her now that Dad's gone."

Just as Ann was climbing on board, Edith came running, "Ann. Ann! I was afraid I wouldn't catch you. I wanted to say good-bye again, to wish you a happy crossing, and to tell you how much I'll miss you."

"Oh, Edith, I'll miss you too. Let's vow, here and now, to continue our friendship once we're both back home. You have my address, call me just as soon as you arrive. Promise?"

"I promise. Oh, by the way, the Nelsons said you should be sure to tell your mum and dad they expect them to visit Oakton just as soon as possible. They said you all are welcomed to visit anytime and stay as long as you can."

"That's very sweet. The Schaefers said almost the same thing. Isn't it grand that we found such wonderful parents here?"

"Well at least some of them," Edith laughed. "I wouldn't say it has all been peaches and cream for us. Remember the Mannheims?"

"Don't remind me. All I could think of while I was there was going home. Thank goodness I moved. What if I would have had to stay with them for the entire five years!" She frowned, then added, "You had some good ones and some bad ones too. Didn't you? If you promise not to remind me of the Mannheims I promise not to remind you of the Adams," she said and laughed.

"You're right, I won't miss Hazel. She was something else. But I still miss Clara and Brad."

"I guess the world is full of all sorts of characters."

"You mean like my dad?" Edith quipped, then changed the subject. "Did you ever get a chance to tell Oliver you were leaving?"

"No, sadly, I never did. I left word several places, asked him to call me, but he didn't. Perhaps he is through with me, now that I'm leaving Dexter Hills."

"I hardly think that," Edith tried to assure her. "Everything you told me makes me think he's a boy in love. I wouldn't jump to any quick conclusion. Wait until you've heard from him before you decide."

Just then the train began to move. There were hurried good-byes, many hugs, and a wealth of tears as the last of the children climbed into the coach. Ann squeezed Jack's hand just before she boarded. "Thanks!" was all she managed to say. Tears welled in her eyes. She turned to Edith, "Oh, I nearly forgot. Here is something Ned sent me some time ago. He told me to pass it on to you at the appropriate time."

It had been enclosed in one of Ann's letters, but had arrived after she knew Ned had died. "I was taking it back to England and planned to give it to you later. I wasn't sure when to give it to you," she told Edith, "but I think you should have it now."

As the train pulled out, a boy came running around the corner of the station. It was Oliver. He had only a quick glimpse of the passengers looking out the coach windows. He saw Ann for a brief moment. It was a picture that would haunt him for the remainder of his life. "Drat!" he said, "I missed her. Why didn't she tell me she was leaving? Didn't she care enough to say good-bye?"

Ann sat by the window watching the hills of eastern Ohio gradually turn into the mountains of western Pennsylvania. She thought of the trip back in 1940. It was such a long time ago. So many things had happened, so many changes. Her thoughts sped eastward to Pinnington.

She imagined everyone, her mum and dad, Yvonne, Graham and Henry, sitting at the garden table laughing. She tried desperately to blot thoughts of her two dead brothers from her mind. She finally replaced them with images of her old playmates. She could see them playing in the garden–they hadn't changed, and they were much too young to be her playmates now. She saw her house. It was freshly painted, just as it had been when she left. The Anderson shelter was gone. Beautiful flowers blossomed in the garden just like before. The shiny red, double-decker buses were running up and down Bilton Road. Pinnington had never looked lovelier. It would be good to be home.

Edith opened the envelope Ann had handed her. In it was a hand written poem. She started to read. It began:

> *Oh beautiful lady–*
>> *With hair to match the golden sun,*
>> *And eyes as blue as summer's sky;*
>> *In waning night, once day is done,*
>> *Sweet thoughts of you, I shan't deny!*
> *Oh wonderful lady–*
>> *Sit by my side, make life be fun,*
>> *Please wed me soon, else I must die;*
>> *For what is life, unless I've w ...*

She could read no further. Perhaps later?

Chapter 117

Sunday, 22 April 1945

Although eager to be on their way to England, the children were pleased to learn their boat would not sail until Tuesday. Unlike their visit in 1940, it gave them time to explore New York City and, because they were older, to do their sightseeing unescorted. On Saturday, they had shopped at Macy's and Gimbel's, visited Times Square, walked through the theater district to Rockefeller Center, then strolled up 5th Avenue to Grand Central Park and down 8th Avenue to their hotel. To-day they planned to visit the Empire State Building, Chinatown, the Bowery, and the Statue of Liberty.

Ann had thoroughly enjoyed herself Saturday and was looking forward to visiting the other places when the telephone rang. She could not believe who was calling. It was Charles Jefferson.

"I just heard you were in New York," he said. "I'm stationed at Ft. Dix, over here in New Jersey, not too far away. I thought perhaps we could get together while you were in the area. Could we have dinner this evening?"

Ann's first thought was to say no, but as they continued chatting, she remembered how badly she had felt after he had left the last time and decided to accept his invitation. They agreed he would come to the hotel in early evening. He said he knew of a lovely Portuguese restaurant in the iron bound section of Newark. They would go there first, then, depending upon the hour–and if she agreed–they would take a ride along the Hudson. "The view of New York from the Palisades," he said, "is spectacular."

Ann paid little attention to the sights that afternoon; she was too concerned with what she would wear and what she would say when she met Charles. By the time they returned to the hotel it was late and she had to hurry. She quickly bathed, change her clothes, and wondered if he would be on time, be late, or not bother to come at all. Promptly at six the telephone rang, it was Charles. He said it would be improper for him to come to her room; she should come down to the lobby.

It was a night of many new experiences for Ann. When first she saw Charles, she was nearly speechless. She had forgotten he would be in uniform and couldn't get over how attractive he looked. He was the most stunningly handsome officer she had ever seen. After a moment to regain her composure, she shyly said hello and kissed him politely on the cheek. As he took her by the arm and escorted her from the hotel she nearly burst with pride. She had seen many servicemen on the streets of New York but none could compare to Charles; she was certain that, with her lieutenant on her arm, she was the envy of every woman who looked at them.

Charles apologized as they waited for his automobile. "Service has become exceptionally bad lately," he complained, "I hope it will get back to normal once the war ends." The car arrived in what she considered a reasonable time. Still Charles scolded the valet for being so slow then handed him a dollar bill. "That's a big enough tip for such an incompetent dullard," he told Ann as he helped her into his sparkling clean, yellow, 1942 DeSoto custom coupe convertible. A dollar seemed pretty generous to her–she wondered how much the attendant would have received had he been prompt.

It was an unseasonably warm evening and the air felt grand as they drove down 9th Avenue toward the Lincoln Tunnel. It was her first ride in a convertible. With the top down, the view of the skyscrapers was marvelous. She felt as if everyone was looking at them and wondered if they thought she was a movie star. As they motored through the tunnel, she told him she thought the car looked spiffy. "It's one of my favorites," he replied. "Dad bought it for me just before Chrysler changed over from manufacturing autos to building tanks. I had some difficulty getting permission to keep it on post but after dad intervened my CO finally gave his consent."

Ann was just about to ask him how it felt to receive so many special privileges when he said, with a little chuckle, "It really pays to have a dad like mine." She agreed that it must, but didn't tell him how she usually felt about people who received special favors just because they were rich.

After a dinner of veal parmigiana and several glasses of sangria, they drove along Henry Hudson Drive. Ann looked at the skyline of New York and sighed. She had never seen so many lights. It was beautiful. He parked at an outlook in Ft. Lee Park, near the George Washington Bridge. "Have you given any more thought to my proposal?" he asked, as he reached in his pocket and pulled out an engagement ring.

Ann was startled by the size and beauty of the diamond. She had never seen one quite so pretty, or as big and expensive looking. She could barely resist the urge to try it on. "The answer is still no, Charles. As I told you last November, I'm too young to be engaged. Besides," she added, "I'm on my way back to England. We leave on Tuesday and there is no telling what I'll find when I get there. England has been badly scarred by this horrible war. As a British citizen, I feel it my duty to help restore it to its old, glorious self. I mean to do my share, whatever they ask me to do."

"I don't know how long I'll be at Ft. Dix," he said, ignoring her argument. "They could ship me out almost any minute. Why, just the other day, one of guys–a good friend who went through OCS with me– was shipped to the Pacific. He probably will be fighting Japs on Okinawa, or some other godforsaken island, within weeks. I sure hope he doesn't get killed."

He paused, hoping the threat of death would appeal to her sympathy. "I expect my orders almost any day. Please marry me? We can't afford to wait."

"You make me feel so guilty," she complained. "I like you, I really do, and I appreciate your offer, but, as I said before, I want to see what the future has in store before I make any decisions about marriage. I'm sorry."

Charles tried again. He looked sad and dejected and suggested that he might die soon just like his buddy. "... just casualties of this rotten war," he continued, looking quite somber. He asked her how she would feel if one day she learned he had died and she hadn't given him this one chance for happiness? But Ann remained resolute and he eventually gave up.

"Then consider this: I'm on a three day pass and will be free all day tomorrow. Would you let me take you to see my parents on Long Island? It will be purely platonic. You'll miss some of the sights of New York, but I know my father would be happy to see you again, and I would love to have my mother meet you." He assured her she would be back in the hotel in plenty of time to do whatever she needed to do before the ship sailed on Tuesday.

At first Ann said she wouldn't, but during the drive back to the hotel she changed her mind. "Wear casual clothes and bring your bathing suit," he told her. "We'll try to get in a few sets of tennis and a swim while we're there. We'll dine with my parents in the evening–nothing formal, perhaps a nice dress."

They had a splendid time the following day. Charles taught her the fundamentals of tennis and they swam in the Jeffersons' indoor pool. Afterwards, they lazed on the poolside chaise lounges until it was time to dress for dinner. They dined on roast duck and Ann found Mr. and Mrs. Jefferson gracious hosts. She was particularly impressed with their elegance, good manners and style. Surprisingly, Charles did not escort her back to the hotel. He apologized saying he had several financial matters to attend to before going back to Ft. Dix and told her the chauffeur would take her.

They said good-bye in the parlor. "I will miss you, Ann," he sighed as he put his arms around her waist and kissed her.

"I will miss you too, Charles," she replied, returning his kiss.

A few more words of endearment and tender kisses and Ann tore herself away. "I really must go," she said, "Now!"

She quickly ran down the steps and climbed into the limousine, afraid she might change her mind. "Here is a little gift," Charles said through the car window as the engine started. "Open it on your way back to the city."

She had it open before the limousine was to the end of the driveway. It was a beautiful gold watch and two pair of hard to find silk stockings. On the back of the watch was engraved, *"To Ann, with love Charles.*

Always." Attached to the stockings was a note which read, *"These were difficult to get, but not nearly as difficult as you have been. Please change your mind?"*

By the time she arrived at the hotel, she was nearly in tears. There was a boy in Dexter Hills who she loved and who could, almost without question, provide a happy home and family; there was a young army lieutenant from Long Island who could provide wealth and contentment; there was a family on a farm in Ohio who loved her with all their hearts and offered her a wonderful loving home; and here she was leaving for England tomorrow, uncertain what was in store for her there. Why was she leaving all of this behind?. Perhaps she would find love and happiness waiting for her in Pinnington. Then again, maybe not.

"Where have you been, Ann? I have been worried sick. Do you realize how late it is? What, in heaven's name, have you been doing?"

"It's really none of your business," Ann scolded the escort. "I told you this morning I would be visiting with one of the Bender board of directors today. It would have been rude if I had left before they wanted me to. Wouldn't it?"

"Look at your dress! Why is it so wrinkled? What sort of hanky-panky have you been up to?"

"I'll hanky-panky you," Ann shouted down the hall as she opened her door, slamming it behind her. "I can't stand that woman. She treats me like a child!" she complained.

Sandy agreed. In her opinion, now that they were returning to England, they should be treated as grown-ups, not as runny-nosed little babies. "After all, we've grown up while we've been here," Sandy tried to assure herself. "They should at least consider that."

The first thing Sandy was going to do when she arrived in England was find herself a boyfriend. She wanted to experience, firsthand, all those dreamy feelings her girlfriends were always telling her about. No more of this "you're too young to date nonsense," she complained. "From now on, I'll date whomever–and whenever–I please.

"What did you do on your date?" she asked, a look of excited anticipation on her face. "Did you kiss him? Did he kiss you? Is that all you did? What does it feel like to be kissed?"

In the morning the children took a cab to the pier and immediately boarded their ship. The cab ride was much different from the New York bus rides back in 1940. No one treated them with candy or bubble gum or called them little darlings, no one hugged them or said hello. In fact, no one seemed to even notice them. This was not too surprising, there was nothing particularly unique in their appearance or in their journey; they looked like ordinary, normal, young American children starting out on an ocean voyage.

Among those not making this journey across the ocean at this time were two very unhappy men. Each was certain he had lost the love of his life. On board was an unhappy girl. She also feared she had lost the love of her life–the only difference in her case, she wasn't certain which one it was she loved the most.

Chapter 118

Tuesday, 8 May 1945

It had been a very confusing period, fueled, perhaps, by wishful thinking. For nearly two weeks there had been persistent reports the war in Europe was over. Some thought it ended on April 26 when the U.S. 69th Infantry Division linked with the Russian 58th Guards Division on the River Elbe. Again, on April 30, there were celebrations after the fall of Berlin and the reported deaths of Hitler and Mussolini. The report of the signing of a surrender of the German forces in all of northwest Germany, the Netherlands and Denmark on May 4 added further fuel to the speculation. But fighting still raged on in Czechoslovakia until May 5 and it would be May 9 before Prague was liberated. However, with the signing of the German unconditional surrender by General Jodl at Rheims on May 7, and with the cease-fire agreement effective May 8 at 2301 hours, the world could no longer contain its joy and exultation. The public celebration could finally officially begin in earnest and Tuesday, May 8, was formally declared Victory in Europe Day, or VE-Day as it was to eventually become known. Happy, shouting, thankful people poured onto the streets of cities in many parts of the world.

Edith could not believe the excitement it generated in Oakton and McKinley Heights. Schools were dismissed, people left their jobs, and the crowds went wild. The church bells rang and the sirens wailed as people danced in the streets, sang songs, sounded their horns, laughed, shouted, and in general had a wonderful time.

During the afternoon, there was a public meeting in the town center. The national anthem was played; the mayor gave a lengthy and boring speech, and a roll call of the names of all the county veterans either killed, reported missing, or held in prisoner of war camps was read. When Ned Schaefer's name was called, Edith burst into tears.

Graham's name was not among those called. Although Edith understood it was because he had never been an official resident of Oakton, she was annoyed just the same. He had served valiantly too, not only for England, but for all the Allies. Hadn't he lived and gone to school in Oakton just like many of the others? Didn't three years living in America count for something? The only difference, he was an English citizen, not an American. It seemed so unfair. She was glad Louise and Ken had not come to the celebration; she knew how upset they would have been had they known.

At the same time, a similar celebration was going on in Dexter Hills near the city hall. Among those in the crowd were Oliver and Vicky. "Oh, isn't it grand, Ollie?" Vicky exclaimed, as she hugged him and tried to kiss him.

"It sure is," he answered, smiling, but carefully tilting his head to avoid the kiss. "Too bad Ann isn't here for the celebration. It's rather sad. She spent five years with us, patiently waiting for the war to end, and now that it has, she's not here to celebrate."

"There you go again," complained Vicky. "Why can't you let it rest. She's gone. She won't be coming back. She's not your girlfriend any longer." Oliver gave no sign he had heard her. "Let's face it," Vicky continued, "she never really was your girlfriend. You dated her, but she never committed to you. I never heard her say she loved you. No one ever thought of you two as committed sweethearts."

She hesitated for a moment as if trying to decide if it was wise to continue, "Besides, she wasn't worthy of you. You are much too good for her. Admit it. She really wasn't very nice. Frankly, I never really cared for her. She was too stuck on herself, too cold, too indifferent. I was only nice to her because I felt sorry for her–and because that's what you wanted me to do."

"How could you?" Oliver shot back, his face turning red with anger. "How could you say that? She was a sweet, warm, intelligent girl. Anyone who knew her would agree."

"She was a Brit, Oliver. Just a crummy Brit!"

"Don't say that, Vicky!" Oliver came close to screaming, his voice shaking with rage. "Don't you ever say that again."

"Just ask anyone. They'll agree with me. She, along with all the other Bender evacuees, were a group of selfish, ungrateful, snobbish, ..." she paused, trying to think of some more derogatory adjectives, "... orphans whose only loyalties were to their precious England. They made fools of us, used us, finagled their way into our homes, just so they could escape the war—a war their country foolishly let happen. America was simply a convenient safe haven for them. Look how quickly they left."

Oliver walked away. It was the last he would ever talk to Vicky, except on school related matters, but even then, he was cold and aloof.

Sixteen days later, after Edith finished the semester with high honors, Mr. James, the principal, was almost certain she would qualify for a scholarship if she continued to do as well in her senior year. It was what she had always wanted, she could go on to school and become a chemist. All she had to do was accept the Nelsons' invitation to come back.

The irony was that she no longer was as eager to stay. The change of heart had come after her mum and she had talked on the telephone last month. Hearing her mum's voice made her realized how much she missed her. It certainly had come as a surprise. All through the years she never had any desire to go home. Now, if not for the Nelson family, there was no denying it, she passionately wanted to go home. The trouble was, she had fallen in love with the Nelsons, especially Louise. It was difficult to imagine not ever seeing them again.

But she also loved her mum, and loving your mum was the most important thing, so here it was, May 25, and she was leaving for New York City tomorrow with Ken, Louise and Meg. They were going a few days early so they could do some sightseeing. Bobby Preston, escorted by Miss Perkins, would arrive in New York on May 30. Edith would meet Bobby and a group of CORB evacuees who had been living in Canada at the pier just before they sailed for home.

When she answered the door, it was Oliver. He looked as if he had been hurrying. "I'm glad I caught you! I didn't think I'd make it," he gasped, trying to catch his breadth. "I wanted to congratulate you. I think it's really nice you could stay long enough to complete the school year. I wish Ann could have stayed too."

"Do you miss her?" Edith asked sympathetically.

He sighed, "Yes, I really do." It probably didn't sound sincere enough but it was the only way he knew to say it.

"Do you love her?"

"With all my heart," he answered, then, blushing slightly, tried to talk about something else. "I understand you're leaving in the morning? I wonder if you would take this gift to her? I bought it last month and wanted to give it to her before she left. But I didn't learn she was leaving until the last minute. I just missed her at the station. The train was pulling out when I got there. I didn't even get to tell her good-bye. I've been feeling awfully sad about it ever since."

"I'd be happy to take it to her," she said sympathetically. Looking at the package, she added, "My, it's small. May I ask what's in it?"

Oliver blushed. "It's a friendship ring. I thought it would be something to keep her from forgetting me. I hope she doesn't think it's silly."

"I don't think she will. Confidentially, I always hoped the two of you would have come to some kind of an understanding. You made such a handsome couple. You deserve each other. You're both so nice.

"Isn't it ironic, Oliver? We thought once Hitler was defeated all our troubles would be over. But now, he's gone and Germany has been defeated, yet the misery still continues. So much sadness and loneliness still remains. I'm afraid the effects of this wretched war may go on for a long, long time. I know I will never forget Ned; he will always be in my heart.

"But maybe things will work out better for you and Ann, maybe someday she'll return to America and the two of you can get together. If I can return to America, there's no reason she couldn't. But right now, I suppose all we can do is wait and see how everything works out."

Oliver smiled. Edith thought it was because she had given him a glimmer of hope. In truth, he thought it rather absurd. There was no way Ann would choose a boy from provincial, small town Dexter Hills, Ohio when she had all those sophisticated fellows in London to choose from. He was certain he would never see her again.

Edith and the Nelsons arrived in New York on Sunday evening and spent Monday and Tuesday sightseeing. High on their agenda was a visit to the Chrysler and Empire State buildings and the Statue of Liberty, places Edith still remembered seeing on the skyline from the sun deck of the *Caerleon* in 1940.

They had just returned to the hotel late Tuesday afternoon when the telephone rang. It was Clara Holtzman. Clara had heard Edith was on her way home; she wondered if they could get together before she left. Brad had been injured in the Carolines and was being treated in a local veterans' hospital. She had rented a flat in the Queens while he recuperated. She told Edith that Brad sent his love and assured her he was on the road to recovery, although he still needed some time to heal completely. They agreed to meet for dinner at a small restaurant in Greenwich Village.

Clara brought Debby with her. Debby was now two years old, precocious, and full of all sorts of energy. She was into all sorts of things while they ate. One of the first things Clara told Edith was that Debby's full name was Deborah Edith Holtzman. She had been named after Edith which pleased Edith immensely. Clara then apologized for her bad behavior during their final months together. She was ashamed of the way she had acted. She knew she had no right to act the way she had. It was all because she had been so upset and worried about Brad at the time.

"Anyway, now I have him back. That's the most important thing."

"How is he?" Edith asked. "How badly was he hurt?"

"Oh, not too bad. It could have been worse," she answered, a grave look on her face.

"Will he have any disabilities?"

After further hesitation and several feeble attempts to avoid answering, Clara burst into tears. "He lost his arm! Imagine, he has no arm!" she sobbed.

"Oh, Clara!" everyone sighed in unison. "How terrible!"

"But even without an arm, I'm terribly thankful. At least he's back home with me. Thank God for that. Even with the war over in Europe, there is still such terrible fighting going on in the Pacific. Brad thinks the fighting on Okinawa might go on for a long time yet. He says he feels guilty about it. He wishes he could be there to help. Can you imagine? He only has one arm and he talks about returning to the Pacific–to help his buddies." She began crying again.

Once Clara regained her composure, she said they planned to give him an artificial arm which, the doctors had assured them, would minimize his disability. "We're both confident we can get back to a near normal life once he's out of the hospital," Clara assured Edith.

Surprisingly–or perhaps because of Clara's continual, mostly self-centered chatter–there was no mention of either Ned or Graham. But that was all right, neither Edith nor the Nelsons particularly wanted to talk about what had happened to the boys–not as long as they could avoid it.

Clara and Debby left soon afterwards and Edith spent the remainder of the evening getting ready for her early morning departure.

They were met at the pier by the two Bender evacuees, Donna and June, who had gone on to Canada in 1940; the CORB evacuees; and Miss Perkins and Bobby Preston. Bobby looked pale and underweight. It had been nearly four years since he had gone into the sanitarium. He had little to say and was listless. Donna was the complete opposite, she was bubbly and terribly excited about leaving. Asked how she felt about going home, she answered, "Although I will always have fond memories of Canada and will certainly miss my foster family dearly, I am terribly excited about seeing my mum and dad again. My only desire now is to return to England and resume my life as an Englishwoman. I shan't return." June said just the opposite, she planned to go back to Canada as soon as possible. Most of the others agreed with Donna, only a few expressed sentiments similar to June's. Edith was one of the few with doubts about whether she wanted to return or not.

When the boarding signal came, there were many hugs and kisses.

Meg and Edith hugged like the sisters they had become.

Louise told Edith she loved her and wished her happiness. She said that although it seemed impossible now, she and Meg would eventually be able to recover from the loss of Ned and Graham. "I didn't think I would ever get over losing Tommy but, thanks to Graham, and now you, Edith, I did. I realize now there are others who can fill the void left by those dearly departed." She hastened to add, "But not the memories. One always keeps the memories."

Ken, hugged Edith, and said simply, "Come back. Come back and get that education you always wanted."

"I'll think about it," Edith said.

The last they saw of her she was smiling and waving vigorously as she walked up the gangplank.

With the departure of Edith and the others, an era had ended. As promised Bender Electric had returned all of the children, and for the first time in almost five years, there were no English evacuees in Canada or the United States. But that was only a temporary condition. Eventually, some would return to stay permanently, some would return for brief visits, and some would never set foot on the continent again. But regardless of what they did, the memory of these special children would remain forever in the hearts of their American families.

Chapter 119

Monday, 4 June 1945

A dark pall still hung over parts of eastern Ohio on June 4. In many homes, no one seemed completely satisfied anymore. It had nothing to do with the war in the Pacific.

At the Bender Electric headquarters there was a spark missing from Ben's eyes; he no longer possessed the bubbly spirit he had only a few months before. He reminded some of a father who had lost his only child. A strange silence enveloped many of the workers as well. Although they continued to laugh and joke, they seemed reluctant to leave when their shift was over. It was almost as if they dreaded going home to an empty house. All over town, lights burned well into the night; the lights of men and women who until recently had a child under their care.

The McKinley Heights Class of '45 valedictorian still had not quite gotten over her surprise. She could not believe she had won; everyone had expected Stewart Jamison to win–but he was disqualified when he left shortly before the end of the semester.

At a movie one evening, when the young boy and girl in the feature became sweethearts, Lucy worried that perhaps she had been too strict with Sandy; she wished she had it to do over. "The next time," she told Kirk, "I'll let her date. What can be wrong with that? Isn't it something all young people want to do? Wasn't it something you and I did?" The next day when Kirk passed the boarding farm where Sandy's horse had been stabled, he looked at the young riders, and wondered why he hadn't spend more time there. Why he hadn't watched her ride more often. What bothered him the most, he could barely remember what she looked like, and it had only been a little over a month since he had last seen her.

In Oakton, the high school softball team was in the middle of a losing streak; the first in nearly four years. There was a sadness in the eyes of the cheerleaders, as well as in the faces of many of the junior and senior high school girls; it was as if they had lost a dear friend.

Tom Derringer still went to the games and hoped they would win, but for some reason, he no longer cheered, instead he sat quietly and simply watched. Victoria preferred to stay home. She spent much time looking at the empty place setting on the table and wondered why she missed Fred so much. She didn't quite understand what it was that made her like him. His presence had long ago ceased to be an asset in her social circles and he, to say the least, had never quite mastered the proper rules of dining room etiquette, but she missed him just the same.

Ken and Louise were still feeling the resentment and petty jealousy of the other foster parents over their success at keeping Edith until the end of May. Almost everyone thought they should have been forced to give up their child in mid April, just like they had to do. The Nelsons ignored their snubs, thankful they were able to keep Edith for that one precious additional month, and continued to hope she would be back with them before long.

In Dexter Hills, the summer concert sounded slightly shallow; the lead clarinet did not sound as mellow as the lead had the year before. The electric mixer at the soda fountain was not as clean as it had been the previous summer. Mr. Winters, on numerous occasions, had to scold the new soda girl. He had hoped she would be more thorough and wondered if she would ever learn how to make chocolate ice cream sodas. There seemed to be fewer people ordering sodas and Cokes this spring; the most noticeable missing person was Oliver Schumacher. He hadn't been in for over a month.

Missing from many of the area homes was the laughter the folks had become used to, and gone was any evidence of the English accents they had grown so fond of hearing. Among the households experiencing the most change was that of Ida and Jack Schaefer. For the first time, in almost too many years to remember, Ida fed the chickens–there was no sweet little girl there to do it for her. Similarly, Jack was milking the cows–there was no pretty little milkmaid to do it for him either. Often, when he thought no one could hear him, Jack would whisper, "You miss her too, don't you, Bossy?" Fortunately, he had his red bandanna with him; it came in handy at times when he thought of Ann. Karen, who had never been particularly fond of dogs, found herself playing with Lady more than she had with any other animal. She even invited Lady to sleep on her bed at night, but Lady preferred to sleep on the floor in the room across the hall, the one where Ann had lived.

There was no doubt the Bender evacuees had made an impact when they came to Ohio, and perhaps even more so when they left. Things would never be the same. For most now there would always be an ocean between these children and their foster families.

IV - England

Chapter 120

Friday, 4 May 1945

"Oh, Chad, her room looks so shabby. I just know she won't like it. Isn't there something we can do to make it more homey?" Diane asked as she set the wash pail down and scanned Ann's room.

"Now don't you worry," Chad said, trying to assure her. "She'll like it just fine. Give your little girl some credit. She'll understand."

"How could she? We never told her how bad the bomb damage was, or that most of her things were destroyed. She probably expects the house to look as good as it did when she left," Diane worried. "Maybe we should have done more than make temporary fixes. It might have looked better. Then she wouldn't be so disappointed."

"You know I'm doing everything I can," Chad said defensively. "I'm trying to fix things as best I know how, but materials are so difficult to find. Even a coat of paint would help. The house wouldn't look as bad as it does if I'd been able to find paint. I even tried the black market. There simply isn't any to be found." A look of frustration came over him. "You know as well as I do," he continued, "with things as scarce as they have been and with everything still rationed, repairs are almost impossible."

"I know. I'm not blaming you. It's this wretched war."

"It's almost over, dear," Chad reckoned, a sparkle returning to his eyes. "It can't be more than a few days now before the war in Europe is over. Hitler and his mistress are dead, Berlin is in Russian hands, and the news last evening said the entire German army is on the verge of surrender. At least Ann will not be coming home to a land filled with fear and strife. She'll never have to sit in the shelter, horrified and cringing at the sound of bombs screaming down, or hear the buzz of the V1's, or the sudden explosion of a V2. Thank God, except for that one night in Liverpool, she never heard a bomb explode, never suffered through the terrible long nights of the Blitz, never knew the feelings of desperation, the pangs of hunger, the bitter cold nights without heat. Through it all, she was living on a pleasant farm, eating well, sleeping well, and surrounded by a loving and caring family.

"We did the right thing," Chad continued. "We sent them away, saved them from the terrible horrors of war. We at least made their lives more bearable."

"We didn't save Graham," Diane noted with a quivering voice.

"That wasn't because we sent him to America, Diane. It was because he came home—he came home too early," Chad argued defensively.

"I know we can rationalize it that way, but in my heart I still believe we should have kept them here—weathered it together—as a family. But we didn't, and what was the consequence? A daughter far away in a strange land, growing up without us, learning strange new customs, living with strangers, and, as you said, loving them. What if she loves Ida and Jack more than she loves us? What then, Chad? Will she turn around and hurry back to them? Will we lose her too?"

"You're talking nonsense. She's our daughter. She loves us. Certainly she'll always appreciate what the Schaefers did for her and love them for it, but we're her parents. We're the ones she really loves."

"I'm not all that certain. It's been such a long time. She was just a little girl when she left. Twelve years old! That was nearly five years ago. Five years! She was just a child. She's sixteen—seventeen next month. Why, she probably doesn't even remember how we look. Had it not been for our letters, she most likely would have forgotten us entirely by now. You know how different her letters have been this past year. There have been times when I wasn't certain I even knew who had written them."

"You're wrong, Diane. You wait and see. It will all work out when she arrives at Waterloo Station on Sunday."

The excitement of Ann's return, the evenings spent preparing for the reunion, and the long hours she was still spending at the factory were taking a heavy toll on Diane. She was near exhaustion, and things she normally would have taken lightly, weighed heavily on her mind, especially with her tendency to look at the dark side of everything. "What will we feed her?" she asked. "Food is so scarce, more so than ever before—even during the worst part of the war. What will she wear? There is so little to select from in the shops. Even if we found something suitable, we have so few ration coupons we probably couldn't buy it anyway. She will hate her life here, I just know she will. She's used to eating all kinds of goodies and wearing all sorts of fancy clothes. America is so much better off than we are."

You're just tired, Diane. Things will look rosier in the morning, after a good night's sleep."

"She probably hates us for sending her away and will leave us. I just know she will. Look at Yvonne. She left, didn't she? She never understood our reasons for doing what we did. Why would Ann be any different? She'll be the same, I just know it!"

"No she won't. Ann is not like Yvonne. She never was, and never will be. She'll understand. Haven't her letters always agreed with what we did? Hasn't she always been concerned about us? She loves us, Diane, I know she does."

"I hope so, Chad. I hope so. I'll do anything to make her love us. Anything!"

"You won't need to do anything. I assure you," Chad replied, trying hard to convince Diane that everything would work out.

"I promise you one thing. I'll never treat Ann the way we treated Yvonne. I'll agree to anything she wants, I'll give her anything, do everything I can for her. I want to be here for her from now on. Always, no matter what. I desperately want her to love us."

Chad worried about Diane. He had never seen her so insecure, so afraid Ann would not love her. He decided it best to say no more. Ann would prove him right—she would come home with more love for them than she had when she left.

The trouble was, he subconsciously wasn't very confident about all this. In truth, he hoped she hadn't been gone too long.

Alice was busy dusting the parlor furniture. She was whistling while she worked. It was the first time she had whistled in—what must have been—nearly five years. She hesitated as she dusted Fred's picture sitting on the piano. "My, look how you have grown. Aren't you the handsome lad," she cooed, "so pretty, so strong, so athletic."

She was looking at the picture Tom and Vicky Derringer had sent a few months earlier. Fred was wearing his football uniform, standing with his legs apart as if he were a soldier standing at parade rest. He held his helmet against his right hip and had an ornery grin on his face. A lock of curly hair hung down, partially covering his forehead. When she looked carefully, she could see a few whisker stubbles on his chin. Either he had neglected to shave or was making a rather poor attempt at growing a beard. Whichever it was, it would be some time yet before it would be dense enough to be manly. She marveled at how his body and face had changed. It reminded her of Walt, back when they were first married. "How much I loved that man," she remembered sadly. "But at least I still have you, Fred," she said, after crying for several minutes. She took the picture off the mantle and held it close to her bosom. "You're the man of the house now; you handsome young thing."

She opened the door to shake the duster and spied Mrs. Weatherby. "Betty," she yelled. "Fred's coming home. Can you imagine? My son is coming back! He'll finally be home on Sunday!"

"How nice," Betty replied rather coolly. She tried to be sympathetic but found it difficult to understand why Alice was so excited. She had never quite understood why Fred's absence had bothered Alice. It seemed to her there was nothing so terribly special about having one's son away on a visit, especially if it was for his safety. Wasn't it perfectly normal to want your child to be safe? Wasn't being in America better than being in Britain, threatened by the ravages of war? She never could quite understand why mothers were always talking about their children. Certainly if she had children she would never bore her friends with incessant talk about them. "I imagine you're quite happy," she said, trying to look interested. After hesitating briefly in order to think of something appropriate to say, she added, "I imagine he's eager to get home. Losing a father must have been a terrible blow."

"That's been a worry. I've tried to prepare him for the disappointment of not having a dad here to greet him, but I can't be certain he fully comprehends how much it will impact his life–at least none of his letters have indicated it does. My only hope is that I can shower him with all the love he'll need to compensate for the loss."

"Well, the best of luck to you, Alice!" Betty said as she hurried back into her kitchen, not wishing to hear any more about it.

"It looks nice," Harold observed, trying not to reveal his thoughts about what seemed to him to be Jessica's overly zealous remodeling. "Where did you find everything?"

"A friend of Gertrude gave me the name of a friend who has a friend in the home repair business. After quite a bit of negotiating, I finally managed to arrange for the materials."

"By arrange, I assume you mean pay?" Harold said, a frown on his face.

"It wasn't much. It's the least we can do for our daughter."

"Now don't you go spoiling her, Jessica," he scolded. "We want our daughter's love, but that doesn't mean we should buy it."

"Of course not!" she replied, a look of surprise on her face.

* * *

Ida's letter began:

Dear Ann,

I am sitting here at the kitchen table determined to write this letter–although it will be a challenge. Lady is sitting here beside me and is continually pushing her muzzle under my writing arm. It makes it difficult to write. But the poor thing seems to need so much attention lately. She misses you terribly. We all do.

She re-read the paragraph, tore it up, and threw it in the wastebasket. It sounded too melancholy. She knew she had to be more cheerful. She did not want to upset Ann. She had to make Ann believe she didn't miss her. It was going to be tough keeping that out of the letter. It was difficult to make someone believe you still loved them while telling them how happy you were they were gone. She felt so lonely. She felt just as bad as she had when Ned left for the army. "Let's face it," she groaned, "I've lost a daughter. Yes that's it! I lost another child! It's so unfair. Jack and I were only trying to be helpful when we volunteered to have Ann come live with us five years ago. Has it been five years? We simply wanted to do our part. Help those poor kids. If I had known then how attached I would become, I would never–no absolutely never–have agreed to take Ann."

"Oh, Annie," she sobbed. "Please come back. Come back–if only long enough to complete your schooling. Certainly, if your mom and dad don't have the funds, we can scrape the resources together, from someplace, and bring you back." As she wiped away the tears, Lady pushed her head once again onto her lap. "I know, girl, you miss her too. We'll have to comfort each other until we see her again. Won't we?" She cried even harder, then started another letter.

Dear Diane,

How could you? How could you take our little girl away from us? You gave her up in 1940? You deserted her–at a time when she was so young and so much in need of your undivided comfort and support? We were the ones willing to do those things for her. We were the ones who made the sacrifices, the ones who scrimped and saved so she could go to school dressed properly, who did without our ration of sugar so she could have more, who saw to it that she went to school every day, admonished her when she failed to do her homework, praised her when she earned good grades, saw to it she brushed her teeth, ...

"Shame on you," Ida scolded herself. "What made you write such a nasty note?" She tore it into small shreds and put it in the old cook stove, lit a match, and quickly burned it. She watched carefully to make certain no telltale evidence remained. "Thank goodness no one was here to read it." At least no one would ever know.

She started again:

Dear Ann,

What a fine day it is. You wouldn't believe what lovely weather we are having. The trees are just about in full leaf and the temperature is a balmy 65 degrees. The sky is a deep blue, big white puffy clouds are scattered here and there. Everything has been going well here on the farm. Karen has been helping with some of your chores and Jack and I have been doing the rest.

I imagine you are looking forward to seeing your parents soon. (How stupid of me! By the time you receive this, you will already be re-united with your family.) How happy all of you must be!

She finished the letter with a few more innocuous paragraphs, quickly put it in an envelope, and sealed it. She was determined not to risk saying anything that would make either she or Ann feel sad. She really did want Ann to be happy–even though she was so far away.

Chapter 121

Sunday, 6 May 1945

Ann was the first to see the southern coast. It was barely discernible through the morning fog. "Look over there," she exclaimed, pointing excitedly off the port side of the ship. "That must be England!"

As they watched impatiently the dark gray outline became more and more distinct. Finally, after what seemed a terribly long time, they began to make out the shapes of buildings scattered along the top of the bluffs. By the time the sun had risen above the horizon and the mist began to rise, they could clearly see the details of the skyline and were able to make out the little images of people scurrying about. "We must be almost there," Fred said. "The mess steward said we should be in sight of the harbor before nine o'clock."

"Do you think we should go to our cabins and get ready?" Sandy asked. "I don't want to be late. The sooner we're off this ship and I'm with my mum and dad again, the happier I'll be."

"There should be plenty of time," Steve guessed. "Once the ship enters the harbor we still must dock. I don't know what the rest of you are going to do, but I intend to stay here a little while longer and watch the view. It isn't every day one has the opportunity to view England from the sea. Besides, we haven't begun to see anything that resembles a harbor. We probably still have a long way to go"

They all thought he made sense and agreed to remained topside.

They had little else to say as they watched the changing scenery. They were just beginning to grasp the fact that they were, after so many years, actually looking at their own country again. It stirred many thoughts.

Steve thought of the past five years, how he had always felt different, had never really fit in, always been known as "that English boy, the one with the accent." At least now he would be among his own kind, treated not as an outsider but as one of them.

Sandy wondered about her mother. Would she be as sweet as she always sounded in her letters, or would she be mean and domineering? She wanted her to be a real pal, someone with whom she could talk and share experiences and ideas, someone who would be tolerant and kind. She wondered if her mother was pretty. Some of the other evacuees had received pictures, but her parents had never sent any. The only photograph Sandy had was the one she brought with her back when she was evacuated. It was now faded and ragged, so old and worn that it was difficult to recognize the facial features of her mum and dad. Their picture had become almost as obscure as her memory of them.

Ann thought about her mum and dad and what they had done. She wondered how different her life would have been had they never sent her away. She thought about Graham. Had he not come to the U.S. perhaps—yes perhaps—he might have been somewhere else on the day he was killed; he might still be alive. And certainly, if Graham and she had stayed home Yvonne would not have been so jealous and angry. Maybe, just maybe, she would not have deserted the family.

She wished they had never sent her. That was until she thought about Ida and Jack. Had she not gone to America she never would have known them, never would have loved them. She thought of Oliver and Charles, Ned and Edith, Karen, Bonnie, and Lady. It was good she had gone. "At least I think it's good. No, it's too complex," she told herself, "too paradoxical. I wish I had stayed home but am glad I went; happy I am on my way to meet my English family, but sad I had to leave my American family behind." She wasn't certain she could ever be completely happy again.

The blast of the ship's horn interrupted her thoughts. "Look!" exclaimed Stewart. "There's the pier."

"Where are the people?" Fred asked. "I thought there would at least be a welcoming committee to greet us. Do you suppose we arrived at the wrong time? Or the wrong place?"

Everyone had a different theory about the missing friends and family. It was not until they saw the train pull in that they realized their journey was not over. They still had a train ride ahead of them before they reached London. Presumably, their parents would be waiting for them there. They felt ashamed for having questioned why their parents hadn't been there to greet them. The truth was, they had not been forsaken, the meeting had only been delayed a little.

They tried to hide their embarrassment with witty remarks and laughter. Had anyone been watching, they might have mistaken them as a group of young people on a joy-filled afternoon picnic or some other equally pleasurable outing, not young adults who had not seen their families for five years. From their clothes and manner of speaking they also might have supposed they were American.

But soon, as the train passed through Southampton their demeanor turned more somber for they had never anticipated the devastation they saw everywhere. Although no one was familiar with how the city once was, it was apparent that it had suffered severe damage. Most of the rubble had been removed and, apparently, so had many of the buildings. There were large areas where, judging from the positions of the surrounding structures, buildings had either been destroyed or so badly mutilated they had to be torn down. In other areas, they saw buildings with large sections covered with ugly and presumably temporary patches. Even the areas that had escaped damage radiated an aura of deprivation and neglect. The few autos on the roadways were dusty and old, often with broken headlamps and windscreens.

"Blimey!" Steve exclaimed, uttering a word he hadn't used in years. "What's wrong with this town? I never thought Southampton was so poor."

"Maybe it isn't," Ann speculated. "Maybe it's the result of the bombing raids we've heard about."

Sandy disagreed, "I doubt if that is the cause. Bombs couldn't possibly do all that."

"They might," Stewart argued. "Haven't you seen any of the newsreels of people after a raid fighting fires and searching through the rubble? The pictures were mostly the results of Allied bombing over Germany, but the Germans must have done the same sort of thing to England. Maybe they haven't shown us what actually happened here. Maybe they didn't want the American public to know how bad it was."

Ann refused to believe this. She had followed the newsreels rather closely Mostly, as Stewart claimed, they were pictures of damage to German cities. Only a few showed pictures of the damage in England, certainly nothing to suggest anything as severe as this seemed to be.

The children discussed it at some length and finally decided Southampton, because it was a seaport and an important strategic target, had been especially hard hit. Surely their hometowns would not be as bad off. Their hopes seemed to be confirmed when they left the city and entered the countryside where evidence of bomb damage no longer could be seen.

As the train chugged through the Hampshire countryside Ann was pleasantly impressed with the forests and grasslands. The foliage seemed so much greener here and so many flowers were already in full bloom. It would be several more weeks before it would be as lovely in Ohio. It made her proud. She had always thought her country was prettier than America and this seemed to confirm it. The hills, however, were a disappointment. She had remembered the English countryside filled with tall and rolling hills. They were certainly rolling, but, surprisingly, they did not seem as tall. Had it been an illusion? Could it have been because she was comparing them to the hills of eastern Ohio and western Pennsylvania, or had she not remembered correctly? Had five years of propitious thinking of her beloved England made her memory wrong? In fact, very little of what she had seen since landing agreed with what she remembered. It was disturbing.

As the train passed through Winchester, Bassingstroke, Woking, and the other towns along the way, there was further evidence of bomb damage. They soon realized that Southampton had not been hit any harder than the other cities. Apparently every English city had suffered damage. And the closer they got to London the greater the damage appeared to be. They began to worry about their own homes. Could they have been damaged too? They tried to assure each other that nothing serious had happened. Wouldn't their parents have told them if it had? But fear soon crept back into their minds after someone suggested that their parents might not have been telling them everything. Perhaps they had tried to shield them from what had really happened? "Didn't we do that? Did we tell our folks how homesick we were? Hadn't we put mostly positive things in our letters?" Steve asked.

Fred thought of his dad: he had died as a result of a bomb. He thought of his mum: what a horrible life she must have had, suffering through those terrible years, then, just as the war was winding down, losing her husband. How awful it must have been. He thought of

Graham: he had volunteered for the army, and now he was dead–had died almost a year ago. He was only eighteen, much too young to be dead. He compared all these things to himself. While his parents were being bombed–and, in the case of his dad, killed–he felt safe and secure. While Graham was fighting in Europe, he was safe in America. When Graham was killed, he was playing summer ball, almost oblivious to the dangers in Europe. He could have–should have–volunteered to come home and gone into the service. Instead, he had stayed so he could finish his high school education, and, in truth, because he was afraid of the dangers he might face if he went home. He was ashamed of himself. How could he face his mum and all her old friends? And what about his friends? He wished he had stayed in America a little longer.

While Fred was chastising himself, Stewart was also thinking about Ohio. They had given him his high school diploma even though he hadn't completed the final month of classes. The principal had assured him there was no problem, his grades were good enough to carry him through the last month. Had he stayed he would have finished at the top of his class, but since he hadn't, Janice Kinzle was named valedictorian. Good for her, he was certain she deserved it more than he did.

Stewart had no problem with giving the award to Janice. She was a good student, and besides, he didn't believe he deserved it anyway. He knew how little he had studied and how much more he could have learned had he been better motivated. He blamed his indolence on the evacuation. Living with foster parents, instead of his birth parents, made him feel like an impostor. He liked his foster parents well enough. They certainly had treated him okay. He just didn't feel whole as a foster child. He was glad he was going home, to the place where he truly belonged. At least he hoped they still considered him part of the family. "It won't be long now. I'll soon find out," he assured himself.

The last part of the train trip was underground. They could not see the streets of London and could not assess how badly it had been damaged until they arrived at Waterloo station. It was much worse than they had expected. The condition of the station was the first thing noticed. Windows were broken and many sections, where walls once stood, were entirely gone. The second thing was the dreary clothes worn by the people. The colors were mostly gray or black. Many of the suits and dresses were soiled and wrinkled. Men's suits looked as if they had been ready for replacement many months ago. Women's dresses were plain and threadbare. Not a pair of silk stockings could be seen anywhere.

The evacuees, in contrast, were wearing neatly pressed and recently purchased clothing, most of it made with brightly colored material. Many of the girls wore suits or skirts with coordinated jackets. Those that did not, wore neat cotton dresses. Some carried formal overcoats and many wore perky little hats. Almost all the girls had on nylon stockings and neat pumps. The few who didn't wore saddle shoes with bobby socks. Recent hair permanents were evident on a few of the girls.

The boys had on either dress suits or sport coats with matching trousers. Nearly half wore dress shirts and ties while the rest were less formally dressed with sport shirts with the collars worn outside the lapels of their coats. A few of the boys sported fedora hats.

Fellow travelers gave uneasy glances at the group. A few of the children could be heard whispering, "spiv," as they tugged at their mother's arm.

There were no bands playing, no reception committees; just the friends and families of some of the returning evacuees. Sadly, several of the children had no one to greet them. It was not that these parents had lost interest in greeting their returning children, it was simply that pressing obligations prevented a reunion at the station.

Ann was one of the last to get off the train. She had purposely held back. She hadn't seen her parents when she looked for them through the coach window and, seeing so few people waiting, was certain no one had bothered to come to welcome her. She had no sooner set foot on the platform, however, when she heard, "Ann. Ann! Over here!"

She recognized him almost immediately, it was her father. "Daddy," she cried and rushed to him with open arms.

"Look at you, child," Chad said, stepping back after they had hugged for several moments. "Just look at you! My, how you have grown! Where is my little girl? She's changed into a fine young lady! A very pretty young lady, I might add," Chad was overcome with emotion. Ann reminded him of the way Diane looked when he first met her, back in '22. He couldn't believe the resemblance. Ann was Diane. There was no question about it. Diane would still look that lovely–even now– had it not been for those awful past six years of strain, worry and war. He hugged Ann again, only this time even more firmly.

"Couldn't Mum come to the station?" Ann asked, looking around disappointedly.

Chad laughed, "She's right here. Right here beside me. Don't you recognize her?"

Ann was taken aback, she had noticed the woman standing next to her father when he had called to her, but the woman didn't look like her mother. Ann had assumed she was merely a bystander, and paid no more attention to her. It had been difficult enough trying to convince herself it really was her father. She examined the woman more carefully. Of course, she recognized her now, it was her mum all right, no doubt about it. Except she looked so much older; and so tired. "Mum!" she cried. "Oh, Mum!"

"Ann!" was the most Diane could utter. The emotion had nearly overcome her.

Ann and Diane hugged each other tightly, broke their embrace to kiss, and then hugged each other again. It was several minutes before Chad finally spoke up. "That's enough now, girls. There will be ample time when we get home. Where's your luggage, Ann? I'll fetch it for you. How should I identify it?"

After he was gone, Ann studied Diane carefully. Her mum did not look well. She wondered what was wrong but did not ask.

While Ann was greeting her parents the others were doing the same, although not always with such happy results.

Steve recognized his dad immediately. "Hello, Father," were his first words, formal even after such a long time.

"How are you, son?" came his father's stiff reply. They shook hands. There was no other display of affection. "It's nice to see you again. You're looking well," he continued. "Mum sends her love. She couldn't come today. She had a meeting at church this morning and then had to hurry home. She is having a group of women in for tea this afternoon. You know how Mother is; she worries so about her teas."

"Yes, I recall, Father," Steve answered.

"Is this it?" he thought. "Is this my reception? Couldn't Mum even make time to greet me at the station? Her only son. Even after five years?" He was disappointed, almost angry, and wished he hadn't come back, wished he had stayed with his foster family. But, then again, they weren't very loving either. He wondered what was to become of him. He wondered if he'd ever be part of a nice, loving family, one that wasn't too reserved to display affection.

Harold and Jessica had come to the station with great expectations. They had planned a wild welcome. They were going to shout greetings and wave small hand-held Union Jacks as Sandy got off the train. They brought a large banner and hung it between lamp posts on the station platform. That was, until moments before the train arrived, when the station guard made them remove it. They were still attempting to hang it in the station lobby when the train pulled in and unfortunately did not see Sandy get off.

Sandy, seeing Ann greet her folks, and not seeing her own parents on the platform, immediately concluded they had not bothered to come. All she could think about was how unfair they had been to her. First, these so called "real" parents had sent her away when she hadn't wanted to go. Then, after so many years of separation, they had insisted she return home against her strong objections. Didn't they know she had truly wanted to remain with her American family? And now she was discovering that they were too rude to even come and greet her. "It's unfair," she thought, "especially when I've been so eager to see them. "Why should I be treated like this? Why haven't I been lucky like Ann? Why weren't my parents as loving and considerate?"

Had it not been for the *WELCOME HOME, SANDY* printed on the banner they might have missed each other altogether. Sandy saw it as she entered the main lobby. She nearly decided to ignore it after they had been so rude. And besides, those two people looking so intently at all the children as they passed by couldn't possibly be her parents. She couldn't recall them looking like that. They were so old and not nearly as handsome as she had remembered. But the excitement of seeing her name on a banner at Waterloo Station was too luring. After a few moments of hesitation, she finally garnered sufficient nerve to approach these unfamiliar looking persons, these plain people who apparently were her parents.

They did not recognize Sandy as she approached. She had weighed five stone, eight and was only four feet, nine when she left. She was now eight stone, two and had grown to a height of five feet, three. Sandy was no longer a little girl; she had changed in both face and body. When she continued to approach they wondered why.

Unfortunately, Sandy's initial reaction when she thought they were not there had put her in a sour mood. The meeting was not as happy as everyone had hoped.

"Look at you! How much you've grown," Harold and Jessica said, almost in unison, once Sandy had identified herself. "What a pretty young lady you've become," Jessica sighed. "We're so glad to have you home," Harold added.

They tried to hug her. "Hello, Mother. Hello, Father. Nice to see you again. Will you help me with my bags?" Sandy asked, then turned and walked towards the exit."

*   *   *

Fred and Alice saw each other at nearly the same instant. "Mother!" Fred gasped as he ran to her. "Forgive me?"

"What for?" Alice asked, covering him with kisses. "Why must I forgive you?"

"I should have been here. I should have come back when I turned seventeen. I should have been here to take care of you after Dad died." He burst into tears.

"Nonsense. You're here now. That's all that matters." She looked at Fred. He reminded her of Walt. "I love you," she added.

Fred looked at her. She was much younger than he had imagined. He hadn't remembered such a pretty face either. "I love you too," he said tenderly and held her close to him. His emotions were becoming confused. He grieved for his dead father; he grieved for the lost years away from England, and he grieved for all the years he had missed with his mother. But he no longer felt bad, he felt good. This wasn't the mother he remembered. This was someone else. He could really fall in love with this woman. The love he felt seemed much more than the love a son should feel towards his mother. He was going to thoroughly enjoy being home.

Stewart, too, had mixed feelings after greeting his parents. He was happy to be home and once again with his family, but he felt uncomfortable, he felt almost as if he were an outsider. There were too many little exchanges between his sisters and parents that had no meaning to him, too many innuendoes he could not understand, too many times he felt inferior. In spite of all their hugs, kisses, and warm greetings he felt out of place. He wished now he were back in McKinley Heights, back where he was considered part of the group; back where he was someone special, where he would have been first in his class. But it was too late for that now. Somehow he would have to adjust. But it was going to be difficult.

Ann looked at Diane's hair. It was snow white. It had been auburn when she left. The lines, now prominent on her face, attested to the great pain and suffering she must have gone through during all those years Ann had been away. She had grown old without Ann being there. "I'm sorry, Mum," she said, looking deeply, and lovingly, into Diane's eyes.

"What for, child?"

"For not being here to help."

"But you didn't choose to go. We sent you. We are the ones who should apologize."

*   *   *

The excitement soon abated and the reunited families quickly left the station. The last to leave was Harriet Dickson. No one had noticed her. She had been careful to remain in the shadows, concealed behind the newsstand in the rear of the lobby. It wasn't entirely clear, even to her, why she had visited that day. There was nothing for her there; she wasn't greeting anyone. Edith wouldn't be home for at least six more weeks. She supposed it was to see how these reunions went; perhaps just to gain a little self-assurance for the homecoming in June. She was afraid it would not go well between Edith and her. Edith was not a happy child when they sent her to America, and there was no telling how she would be now.

Unfortunately, watching the reunions did not help.

Chapter 122

Tuesday, 8 May 1945

The evacuees and their parents went through many highs and lows during the young people's first week at home. One of the highest of highs occurred two days after the children arrived. Everyone had been waiting for the war to end for weeks, each day more promising than the last. Finally, on Monday, after the Germans signed the unconditional surrender in Rheims, the pent-up emotions could be contained no longer and the celebrating began in earnest. By the following morning it had become a wild, joyous event; by three in the afternoon, after Churchill made the end of the European war official in a speech from No. 10 Downing Street, it reached a feverish pitch. There was no containing the crowds anymore. Joy and jubilation had taken over. VE-Day became one of the most festive celebrations anyone could remember.

Anticipating the fun and excitement, Chad and Diane stayed home from work on Tuesday and, as soon as the wireless confirmed the celebration was in full swing, the three of them, Ann, Diane and Chad, grabbed their hats, coats, and the little British flags they had used on Ann's arrival and rushed for the Underground. The trains were jam-packed. By the time they reached Green Park Station, their clothes were wrinkled and damp from perspiration. They looked as if they had just come from a hothouse, but no one seemed to mind. Their spirits still bursting with excitement, they followed the rush of the crowd, stopping at Buckingham Palace where they waited impatiently for the Royal family to appear on the balcony. People were shouting, blowing whistles, waving flags, and climbing every tree, lamppost, and structure that offered a better view. Ann, used to the openness and solitude of the farm, felt crushed by the enormity of the crowd and overwhelmed by its enthusiasm. She wished she were back at her secluded hideaway, far away from the throngs of people, but quickly forgot her discomfort when the king and queen appeared and waved to the crowd; and later still, when Mr. Churchill joined the Royal family on the balcony.

The Montgomerys, still caught up in the crowd's exuberance, stayed in central London much longer than they had planned. After seeing the king and queen, they made their way through St. James Park to the Horse Guards Parade Grounds where they listened to speeches by gentlemen they did not know, proceeded to Trafalgar Square where they watched the crowd climb over the still covered column honoring Lord Nelson, and then shoved their way to the London Pavilion at Picadilly Circus where they watched drunken servicemen from Britain, America, Canada and other Allied nations dance deliriously around Eros. They barely made the last train back to Ealing Common and were exhausted by the time the bus dropped them off in Pinnington. By then, neither Ann nor Diane had the energy to continue the petty arguments that had been occurring at increasingly shorter intervals almost from the moment Ann had arrived at Waterloo.

For the first time since she left New York, Ann was able to fall asleep as soon as she climbed into bed.

In Ohio that night, some five hours later, Ida and Jack in celebration of VE-Day had a quiet glass of wine before retiring for the night. Like Ann, they preferred solitude over the crowds of people they imagined were celebrating in McKinley Heights. "How do you suppose Ann spent the day?" Ida asked, as she climbed into bed.

"She probably went to Buckingham Palace and saw the king and queen," Jack quipped.

They both laughed at such a preposterous suggestion. "I hope she had a good time, whatever she did," Ida said. She paused and then added, "She's probably having the time of her life now that she is back home."

"Probably," was all Jack was able to say as he quickly snapped off the light. He was determined to conceal his true feelings–he had been doing it quite often lately. Never in his life had he shed so many tears as he had since Ann left.

The next day Ann and Diane resumed their bickering. It was really no one's fault, both wanted their relationship to succeed and neither tried to upset the other. It was just that neither really understood the other anymore, they had been apart too many years. Whatever one said, or did, the other thought was either silly or just plain wrong. They soon began questioning each other's sincerity, and once that happened, their failing relationship disintegrated even further. Both began to realize their dream of continuing where they had left off five years before was just a dream, and an unrealistic dream at that. Their future together was never going to be as sweet, or pure, as they had expected. Reestablishing the happy life they once had known was not going to be easy, if possible at all.

That's not to say there weren't times when the two shared a common bond. Whenever they talked about Graham, the mother-daughter bond of before would temporarily rekindle itself. For a few moments they would console each other and empathize with each other's grief. When Diane talked about the prewar years, Ann would listen intently and ask many questions: Where they had lived. What Ann had been like as a little child. What toys she had played with. Who her friends were.

When Ann talked about Oliver or Charles, Diane would become keenly interested, but even then, it usually ended in an argument. Each time Ann tried to explain her ambivalent feelings for the two boys, Diane could not understand why Ann harbored any doubts. There was an obvious answer: the boys were American, not English, Ann should have nothing to do with either. She should look for a nice English boy instead, someone who would not ask her to live in America. Although she never said it outright, any thought of Ann settling in America was something she could never tolerate.

But no matter what they discussed, Ann would usually end up accusing Diane of some sort of misunderstanding. This usually made Diane feel as if she had failed. She began to worry that she had lost her maternal instincts during the five-years of separation—or then again, maybe she never had any. She only had to look at the strained relationship between Yvonne and her to realize what a poor mother she was.

Matters grew even worse when Ann became discouraged after talking with the local headmaster. He had listened politely to her description of her American schooling, studied her transcripts with great interest, and asked many serious questions. "I'm sorry," he said afterwards. "It looks as if you have done quite well in your studies but unfortunately you will be seventeen next month. You are no longer eligible to continue in grammar school."

"But I don't understand, sir," Ann argued. "Some of my friends who are my age are still in school."

"That's true," he sympathized, "but they successfully matriculated. You didn't take the examination so you aren't qualified to continue."

"But didn't I do the equivalent of that in America?"

"Was there a specific examination that qualified you to go into—let's see—what do you call it? Oh, yes, high school?"

"No, other than the final examinations for each course we took at the end of eighth grade and again at the end of each year in high school."

"Sorry! That won't qualify."

"Well what about college? Could I enroll in some sort of makeup program? I was in a college preparatory curriculum, within a year of graduating from that program—and look here, Mr. Hartline wrote a letter saying I had nearly completed all the required credits to qualify for graduation. Can I somehow make up the few discrepancies and then enroll in a college or university?"

"No. That's out of the question. The only road into a university is with a higher school certificate from one of our grammar schools—or from one of the public schools." He then added, which made Ann furious, "Of course, you could never have gone through our public school system, your father does not have the proper credentials and income to qualify you for one of those highly respected institutions."

Perhaps, Ann should have pursued it further, but she was too frustrated to do so. She would only learn later that some of the others had been able to obtain special dispensations and continue their education. Instead, she talked it over with Chad and Diane and, although she was disappointed, they agreed she should go to work. Chad thought, with her typing and shorthand classes, she could probably find work at Bender Electric since many of the secretaries would be quitting, just as soon as their menfolk returned from the war.

Ann was beginning to realize that she had not returned to the wonderful dreamland she had expected. It was, in fact, much worse than the life she had left behind. There were many differences: shortages were much more severe; harsher rationing still existed, and, in general, living conditions were much more austere. Even more worrisome, she didn't love Diane and Chad the way she did Ida and Jack, nor did she now expect she ever would. It was a troubling conclusion, five years believing otherwise was difficult to overcome.

As the rifts intensified, she decided she needed to get away from the family long enough to sort out her plans for the future. As an excuse, she announced she would try to locate Yvonne. She knew Yvonne had not been friendly during Graham's visit, but, knowing him, he probably had not tried hard enough. As Yvonne's sister, she had a better chance of getting through to her. Besides, Yvonne might be able to give her some pointers on how to survive–independently–in Britain in these rapidly changing times. Even if she didn't hit it off with her sister, at least she would have tried.

Finding Yvonne would not be easy. The only hint of her whereabouts was Chad's recollection that some of the Land Girls had gone on strike in March. Chad thought it had something to do with the girls demanding a war gratuity from the government. It wasn't much to go on, but it was a clue. The next morning Ann started her search, determined to find a solution both to a family problem that had been festering for a long time and to her own growing discontent with life in England.

Sandy was also having problems adjusting. She found her parents much different from what she vaguely recalled and certainly not what she had expected. "Why do they treat me as if I'm still a child?" she wondered. "Don't they know I've grown up since leaving Uxbridge so long ago?"

"I wish they'd treat me the way the Maurers did," she would start to think, only to change her mind, convinced the Maurers had never really given her anything significant or done anything nice for her. She apparently had already forgotten all the nice things they had done: the vacations, the riding lessons, the new clothes, the toys, the new bicycle, and the myriad of other gifts they had constantly showered on her. It was only the unpleasant things she apparently wanted to remember now.

As for her present circumstance, she was particularly upset with her room. She knew they had gone to great trouble and expense to prepare it for her, but she couldn't believe how foolish they had been. How could they have done what they did? Her mother had pasted silhouettes of clowns and baby elephants on the walls and had arranged a huge menagerie of stuffed animals on her bureau and night stand. It was a nice gesture–redecorating and everything–but she was fifteen years old now, a little old for a circus motif in her room. What she really wanted was simple enough, she wanted their permission to date. It was time–past time. "I would have done it months ago, had Mom not been so stubborn," she assured herself.

Then she corrected herself, "I don't mean Mom, I meant Mrs. Maurer. I must get used to calling my new mother, Mom–or I should say Mum?" The idea of a new mum still seemed strange. It was Lucy who had nursed her after she had fallen; Lucy who had taken care of her when she contracted the measles; Lucy who insisted she bundle properly when she went out to play in the wintertime; Lucy who fed her when she had been hungry and hugged her when she had been blue. Her new mum had never done any of those things–at least not as far as she could remember. It did not seem right. Lucy was her mom, not this strange woman who she knew so little about and who knew so little about her.

On the other hand, the new mum was trying to please her, there was little doubt about that. She was always telling Sandy how much she loved her. Sandy decided she would need to try harder, find a way to accept her new mum and dad. But it was going to be difficult, especially since they were so stodgy and oppressive, much the same as the Maurers had been. They simply did not understand any of her needs. "Although Mrs. Maurers certainly tried harder than this mum seems to want to do," she told herself.

This mental conflict had a noticeable effect on Sandy. She began spending increasingly more time in her room as the days passed. It was becoming difficult for her to concentrate. She always seemed to be tired and sleepy.

Sandy's attitude troubled Harold and Jessica. They thought she was becoming too reclusive and sleeping entirely too much. On the other hand, and much to their embarrassment, they were thankful she did. Whenever she was awake, she was overbearing, demanding, and disagreeable; when she was in her room they at least had some peace and quiet. It seemed almost as if she were trying to punish them, perhaps for having sent her away in 1940, perhaps for not doing more for her now. Jessica tried to compensate. She did everything she could to make Sandy happy–remarkably, not much different from what Lucy had done. There were times when she would worry that she was being too generous, feared if she didn't curtail her generosity she would eventually spoil Sandy. But it was not easy to say no. Sandy was her child, her only child, the child she loved so very much, the child she had sent away. She worried that if she did not do everything just right now she might lose Sandy again, and, even worse, she realized nothing she had tried had worked. She cried night after night and prayed to improve as a mother.

Things were different in the Andrews household. Fred was in love with his mother. It had started the instant he saw her standing on the station platform. She had looked so sweet and loving, and it had continued after they arrived home. It wasn't as if he had planned it. He had merely wanted to provide her with all the compassion and sympathy he had to offer. He knew she was still mourning his father's death and that his support was sorely needed. But somehow everything had quickly gotten out of control. Suddenly his compassion and sympathy had changed. He had fallen in love, and it was not exactly a filial form of love either.

It had all been innocent enough. Shortly after entering the house he had cried. The mourning for his dad that he had so bravely suppressed for so many months finally came out. He needed his mother's comfort and she had taken him into her arms and held him close, her motherly love erupting after so many years in suspension. Fred felt that love. It was a love he had not known since leaving home. Victoria had never offered it to him–had never held him in her arms. Nor had he ever felt it with Betty Lou, or any of his other girlfriends. It felt good. He stopped crying. The feeling of his mother's warm breast so tenderly close to him made him sigh. "It's good to be home, Mother. I love you," he said. The manner in which he said it had been a surprise to both of them.

Alice, too, had strange feelings. Fred had reminded her of Walt the minute she spotted him at the station. He was a younger, much stronger Walt, but Walt just the same. From then on it was difficult for her to think of him as her little boy. She did not try to recall his childhood; she did not think about his long absence, instead, she welcomed this young and highly desirable man back into her life. Whenever they hugged, she had the feeling she was in the arms of a man again. It was a good feeling.

Alice and Fred were inseparable from that moment on. They could not do enough for each other. Fred would rise early, just to serve her tea and toast in bed. He would read the *Times* to her and soon was spending all his free time taking her to see their old friends, walking with her in the park, or whatever she wanted to do. Alice was ecstatic. She had not been so happy since that last time Walt held her in his arms–the morning of that terrible day when the bomb took him away. When her friends commented on how wonderful she looked, she told them it was because she had her boy back, but, secretly, she knew it was because she had a man in the house–her very own man. She loved Fred. She would never let him leave her again. Fred felt the same. He would never leave his mum either.

Chapter 123

Tuesday, 19 June 1945

Although the war in Europe had ended, the war in the Pacific seemed far from over. The U.S. had been battling for the island of Okinawa since April and progress had been painfully slow. Casualties were nearing twenty thousand and increasing daily. The Marines had taken its capital, Naha, on May 27 but the island was still not secure. In early June, Japan attacked the U.S. naval force off Okinawa in a series of *kamikaze* raids. The damage was heavy and a large number of ships and sailors were lost. In Japan, the thousands of tons of incendiaries dropped by the rapidly expanding American B-29 bomber raids were inflicting heavy damage, but there still was no sign of a Japanese surrender and U.S. morale remained low.

In England, life had begun to change. Although there was still great concern and worry over the war in the Pacific, focus was shifting towards the rebuilding of the country. German prisoners of war were put to work and signs of improvement were already beginning to show. But still there were many reminders that Britain had been through a terrible war: rationing was increasingly more severe; there were fears of huge layoffs in the workforce; and people were impatient for change and improvement. Urged on by the general dissatisfaction of the English population, Winston Churchill, on May 23, submitted his request to resign and end the wartime government. The king responded by dissolving Parliament and called for a general election on July 5. In the interim, the king asked Churchill to form a temporary coalition government. Clement Atlee, the leader of the Labour party, reluctantly agreed but a vicious political fight erupted almost immediately between the Labour and Tory parties. By the time it was over the Labour party was in control, Clement Atlee was the new prime minister, and Ernest Bevin the foreign secretary.

It was in this atmosphere that Edith, Bobby Preston, and the other CORB evacuees met their families and friends at Euston station on June 19 after twenty days en route. This time E.J. Newton was the only Bender representative to meet the children. He gave a brief speech in which he reminded everyone that W.T. Bender had kept his promise to safely return all Bender children to England. He added as an afterthought, "Although it took you several weeks longer to get here than the others." There were a few who laughed at his pitiful attempt at humor but most did not. They were eager for him to finish so they could continue greeting each other.

Bobby had a particularly warm welcome. His parents and many of his relatives were there. All were overjoyed to see him and to assure themselves he had indeed successfully concluded his long battle with tuberculosis. On the other hand, no one was there to greet Edith. Apparently her mum and dad had not thought enough of her to come to the station. She began to cry.

* * *

"Edith," Ann shouted as she made her way through the crowd.

"Ann!" Edith answered, pleased to see someone she knew. The two girls hugged as Edith asked, "What are you doing here?"

"Your mum couldn't come. She had to work. It was a last minute thing. Some special order that couldn't wait. She called me this morning and asked me to take her place. She said to tell you she is truly sorry. She really wanted to be here."

"What about Dad? Couldn't he come–or was he too busy too? Is he still the same inconsiderate man he always was?"

Ann ignored the question. "I'm glad you're finally here, I've needed a friend. You wouldn't believe how things have changed. I'm afraid they're not as wonderful as we imagined. The war has taken a terrible toll on everything. Everything is so ..." She hesitated, "I don't know ... So different? Yes, I suppose that's the proper word to describe it."

"It can't be that bad, can it?" Edith asked, trying to assure herself it was good to be home. "Wasn't it wonderful to see all your old chums?"

"Not as much as I thought. They all seem to resent me. I suppose it's because I went to America. Some have even accused me of running away. They claim I should have stayed here–weathered the storm–like they did."

"But we didn't ask to go. We weren't given a choice. We were told to go."

"That doesn't seem to make any difference."

Just then two small boys walked past the girls. "Listen to those two, Huey," one of them said. "A couple of Yanks, I'd wager."

"I'd say so," the other agreed. "They certainly sound like it. Listen to their funny accents. And look at their clothes! Have you ever seen anything so horrible?"

"See, Edith. Everyone thinks we're different. I started to work at Bender Electric last week and even there–at the factory that sponsored us no less–I found resentment. Some say it's unfair we went to America. They have even gone so far as to accuse me of being an American spy; sent here by Mr. Bender to make certain the UK factory isn't doing something contrary to company policy. Can you imagine?"

"You're working? What about school?" Edith asked, not believing what she had just heard.

"I can't go to school. They won't accept me. They say I don't qualify. I'm too old and didn't matriculate."

"But what about our American schooling?"

"Forget it. They won't recognize what we did over there. They say the American program is far inferior to ours."

"You don't paint a very pretty picture, Ann. Maybe I should turn right around and go back to Oakton."

"I'm sorry, Edith. I didn't plan to be so negative. It's just that you're the first one I've seen who I can talk to about this."

"But what about your family? Didn't you talk it over with them? Weren't they understanding?"

"Oh, they tried to understand, but it just hasn't worked. I don't know why. Perhaps I was away too long and our ideas differ too much. Or maybe I've grown too independent. Whatever it is, things just aren't going well. I even tried getting away—to think it through. I looked up Yvonne a couple of weeks ago and paid her a visit."

"You saw Yvonne? How lovely!"

Ann told Edith how she had to struggle just to find Yvonne, and once she did, how little they had in common. It was similar to what Graham had found during his visit. Even the day they met, Yvonne had little to say. She was too absorbed in her own activities and the politics of her radical friends. She called Ann a quasi-American and almost immediately became fractious. "She called America a hotbed of capitalists, told me if I were smart I'd recognize that the Communists will save the world. I left as soon as I could.

"But never mind all that. I've been looking out for myself lately, attempting to minimize my dependence on my family as much as possible. I'm already pretty self-sufficient. It seems to be a better way to live. But tell me, what's the news from Ohio?" Ann asked, her eyes brightening.

"Ida misses you. She and Jack told me they hope you'll find a way to get back to the farm. Lady still goes to the door looking for you every time a bus or car goes by. Ida says she can only coax her away for short periods. She's beginning to think Lady will never forget you.

"The Nelsons still insist that I go back and complete my last year of high school. Meg sends her love. She is back at the university now; and still misses Graham terribly—all the Nelsons do. And I really miss Ned."

Edith stopped talking. Tears welled in her eyes. "Oh, Ann. I miss him so much. I can't seem to get him out of my mind."

"I know, Edith, he was a wonderful boy," Ann said, holding her while she sobbed.

A few minutes later Edith wiped her eyes, and with a half-hearted, almost embarrassed laugh said, "I nearly forgot. I have a little present for you." She pulled out a neatly wrapped package. The one with Oliver's ring inside.

"For me?"

"Oliver gave it to me. He was extremely disappointed that he couldn't say good-bye when you left. He didn't know you were leaving until it was too late. He tried to see you at the station but the train was pulling out when he got there. He told me to tell you he was sorry and that he misses you very much."

Ann eagerly opened the package. "Isn't it lovely," she said, putting the ring on her finger. "What a sweet boy. I really do love him. I must write to him."

As they rode on the Central Line to Ealing, the two girls continued to talk about Ohio, their friends, and the changes in England. Ann told about meeting with Charles in New York, their visit to his Long Island home, and his second marriage proposal. Edith was somewhat amused when Ann complained. "That certainly is a problem," she laughed. "Two lovers. How will you ever decide?"

Ann was not as amused. She was quite serious.

Edith's reunion with her mother was tearful. She had not realized how much she missed her until she saw her sitting on the sofa. They hugged and kissed and sat for most of the day bringing each other up-to-date and recalling old times. Edith was shocked to learn Harriet had divorced her dad. "Why didn't you tell me, Mother?" Edith asked, finding it hard to believe she had finally found the courage to leave him.

"I didn't want to burden you. You were so far away. It just didn't seem right to tell you that you no longer had a daddy."

"But it would have been okay. He was a nasty old man. I'm glad you did it. It will make a big difference to me. I feel much more comfortable being back here now that I know he's gone."

Late that evening the telephone rang. It was George. He had heard Edith was home. "Could I stop by and see her?" he asked meekly.

"I don't believe you should," Harriet answered in an unfriendly tone. He did not argue, he simply thanked her and hung up.

Several days later a man stood in the shadows and watched Edith board the No. 207 for Shepherd's Bush. "I'm sorry, Edith," he said, although no one was there to hear him. "I wish things had been different. I wish I could have been different."

He turned and slowly walked away.

Chapter 124

Thursday, 22 November 1945

Many things had happened in the past six months. Demobilization of English servicemen had been underway since June; Prime Minister Clement Atlee and his Labour Socialist party had been in office since July; the war in the Pacific had been over since August; English brides of American servicemen had already started emigrating to the United States; and the world had begun to repair the damages caused by World War II.

The war had ended abruptly on August 14, just five days after the Americans dropped the second atomic bomb on Japan. VJ-Day, the celebration of the end of the war in the Pacific–and with it, World War II–was celebrated in London, New York, and all the other cities of the Allied world the following day. Although many people celebrated with too much dancing and drinking and paid dearly for it the next morning, all agreed the exuberance was well worth the discomfort. Among those who had an uncomfortable morning were Oliver and Fred, both of whom had, for the first time in their life, consumed much more alcohol than they could handle. In the case of Oliver, it was too much beer; in the case of Fred, too much ale. No one seemed to mind, however. The war was over, peace had come, and the future augured well.

But the ensuing times did not turn out as happy as everyone had hoped. Shortages continued; workers lost their jobs; those that didn't were unhappy; strikes became frequent; and lines of division were drawn between the western nations of Europe allied with America and the eastern European Bloc countries under the control of Russia. Particularly troublesome was the threat of nuclear technology. The atomic bombs dropped on Hiroshima and Nagasaki had caused horrendous and instantaneous devastation to the two cities. These bombs with their huge destructive force shook the surety, not only of the Japanese, but of the entire world. There was growing fear that a new war between the East and West might erupt at any moment, but this time using atomic weapons. If it did, some said, the world most assuredly would destroy itself.

It was under this atmosphere that a group of Bender evacuees arranged to gather at the *Fox and Hounds* for a pint–or two, to talk of old times, and to share recent news about themselves and their friends. Some had nothing but happy things to report, while others were less content and reported mostly unpleasant experiences. Among those who came were Fred, Stewart, Sandy, Elizabeth, Edith and Ann.

When Fred was asked what he had been doing and what girls he had dated he blushed. "My mother and I have moved to a cottage in the Cotswolds. I have a job there in a blacksmith's shop. Mum is no longer working." He then added, as if trying to exonerate himself, "I'm dating a girl named Elaine."

"Have you been playing any ruggers or cricket since you came home, Fred?" Stewart asked.

"I haven't had time. I plan to go to university this autumn and must work to save some money. I heard from Tom Derringer, my American dad, the other week. He tells me Oakton beat McKinley Heights last month, 9 to 7. You chaps never did have a good football team," he teased.

"How can you go to university?" Edith asked. "I tried and they told me I wasn't eligible. Ann was turned down too."

"Because I was credited with graduating from high school," Fred answered.

"That can't be it," Stewart volunteered. "They turned me down too. Even though I got credit for graduating just like you."

"You must not have had good enough grades," Fred suggested.

"No, I had excellent grades. I was told I would have been first in my class had I stayed the last month," Stewart assured him.

"It's really a mess," Ann interjected. "They passed the Education Act in '44, but they still haven't sorted out how to handle special cases like ours."

"They told me they might—and they emphasized might—have an opening next year," Stewart said.

"Then there's still a chance you could get in?" Edith asked. She paused for a moment, then said, "Maybe there's a reason why they turned Ann and me down? Maybe it has to do with discrimination against women?"

"Probably not," Ann said, a doubtful look on her face. "The Education Act was supposed to give women equal opportunity. But who knows what's going on."

"They let me go to grammar school," Elizabeth said. "Of course I'm not sixteen yet. That might have made a difference."

"Well, I've decided to give up trying. I've even been giving some thought to returning to the United States–to finish my high school work and then maybe go on to college," Ann admitted.

"That's great," Edith exclaimed. "I envy you. It would be nice to return and see everyone again, but I've decided to stay here. My mum needs me. And besides, I like it here. I'll never go back–except maybe for an occasional visit."

"I'll bet it has something to do with the Socialists being back in power," Stewart teased.

"No! I just like England. I think it's a great place to live. I'm glad I'm back," she assured him, then added, "However, I must admit, I was happy when the Labour party won. I definitely believe that socialism is the best chance for out future."

"You're a Socialist?" Ann asked, a look of surprise on her face. "I thought you were a Capitalist. Didn't Ned convince you?"

"Yes, he did, but the world has changed since then," she said simply. "But who really cares? We're all going to be blown to bits by an atomic bomb one of these days anyway."

"I certainly hope not," Sandy responded. "I've just begun to enjoy life."

"How's that?" Ann asked.

"I've finally begun dating boys, and I think it's grand. I've been making up for all the time I've missed and am truly enjoying all the new pleasures I've been experiencing."

Ann was surprised. She couldn't believe what Sandy was implying. "Are you seeing any one in particular?" she asked, trying to ignore Sandy's confession.

"Yes. His name is Ralph. He's an American GI, stationed here in England. He's here until next year. He plans to start a ranch after he's discharged. He wants to breed and train western horses. He's asked me to go back with him."

"You'd marry and go back?" Edith asked incredulously.

"I don't see why not. My life is no good here. Mum doesn't understand me. She makes me do all sort of things Lucy didn't. Anything would be better than living at home. I'd rather be a war bride than living with a tyrant for a mother."

"But she is permitting you to date, isn't she?"

"Not really. I haven't told her. Ralph says what she doesn't know won't hurt her."

"That's not a good idea," Ann scolded.

"Is that the Yank attached to the air base at Northolt?" the barmaid asked, slightly embarrassed for breaking in on the conversation.

"It very well might be. I know he's stationed at Northolt."

"You'd better chuck him, miss. I've heard only bad reports about him. They say he has a mean streak, particularly with women."

"Then it isn't him. My GI isn't a bad man. He's never been mean to me." She hesitated, then added, "Except when he drinks too much. He has knocked me about a bit then, but has always apologized afterwards. He's always been a perfect gentlemen about it."

Everyone looked startled, but no one was willing to pursue it further. They figured it was Sandy's business.

Later that evening, as Ann and Edith rode the Underground back home, Edith talked about Ned and Ann talked about Oliver and Charles. "Is that why you're going back, Ann? Are you going back to be with one of them?"

"Of course not," Ann answered indignantly. "If I go, it will be solely to complete my schooling."

"I don't believe you!" Edith said.

"Besides, which one would I choose, given a choice?"

"As I've said before, you do have a problem," Edith laughed.

When Ann arrived at home there were two letters waiting for her. One from Oliver and one from Charles. She read one of them and then the other, and then she read both of them again.

After going to sleep she dreamed. Both men were in those dreams, even though only one letter had been affectionately placed under her pillow.

Chapter 125

Thursday, 15 August 1946

From The McKinley Heights Free Press:

Miss Ann Montgomery from Pinnington, Middlesex, England, a suburb of London, arrived today in McKinley Heights. She will be making her new home with Mr. and Mrs. Jack Schaefer of RFD No. 2, Dexter Hills, Ohio. Miss Montgomery was one of the children brought here in 1940 by the Bender Electric Corporation as part of a program to evacuate children of employees working in its plant in Pinnington, England. She returned to England in 1945 after living with the Schaefers for almost 5 years. All of the 84 children originally evacuated by the Bender Corporation had returned by the end of the European conflict in 1945.

Miss Montgomery plans to continue her schooling and hopes to eventually obtain a degree in English history at Ohio State University.

Her brother, Graham, also an evacuee, returned in 1943 in order to enlist in the British Army. He took part in the Normandy invasion and was killed near the Vire River in France in August of 1944. Lance Corporal Montgomery was awarded the Victoria Cross.

Oliver saw the notice in the paper that evening after he returned from his day at the steel mill. "You've come back, Ann. Thank God, you've come back!" was his initial thought.

Charles saw the notice several days later, having been sent a clipping of the news item by a Bender employee. "You've come back," he said. "I knew you would!"

Chapter 126

Wednesday, 23 July 1947

Diane lay on the bed writhing in pain. She had been in ill health for nearly a year now. Chad was at her bedside holding her hand.

"Is God punishing me, Chad? Should I have kept my children with me?" she asked.

"No, dear. You're not being punished. You just caught a bad virus, that's all. The doctor said your pain will ease shortly," Chad assured her, gently rubbing her pale hand.

She gave a sigh and grimaced, "It hurts so much!"

"Can I get something for you, dear? Some more pain capsules, perhaps?"

Diane did not answer. The hand Chad held went limp.

"Oh, God! No!" Chad sobbed. "Don't take her. Please don't take her. It's me you should have taken instead? I'm the one who decided. But I thought it was best for my children, honestly I did. I didn't know any better."

Chad walked out of the room and sat on the parlor settee. He put his head in his hands and cried uncontrollably. It had been exactly seven years, to the day, that he had made that dreadful decision to send the children. Now they were all gone: his two sons, his two daughters, and his wife.

"Isn't that enough? Please don't punish me anymore," he begged.

Ann did not attend Diane's funeral. Crossing the Atlantic would have taken too long. She couldn't have been there in time.

"There always seems to be an ocean between," she complained to her husband.

Further Reading

I hope this novel has piqued your interest in the evacuation of the English children during World War II. If you would like to read more, the following bibliography may help. It was the source of my research and preparation for this novel. The brief comments associated with each reference will hopefully help focus on your particular interests. Please note that unless the word *Hoover* is included in the title or comments, the reference is *not* specifically about the Hoover Company evacuation.

Bibliography

Bailey, A., America: Lost & Found, Faber & Faber, 1981. The account of one evacuee's experience living in Dayton, Ohio. This person lived with well-to-do people and had a good experience. He eventually settled in the U.S.

Basner, Ruth Harpold, Open Homes, Open Hearts, The Evacuee Story, North Canton Heritage Society. Descriptions, photographs, and newspaper clippings of the Hoover Company evacuation scheme.

Beck, Kathryn, The British are Coming, Hoover Historical Center, 1990. (A presentation caught on video tape.) Describes the experiences of a foster family who billeted one of the Hoover evacuees.

Body, Alfred H., Children in Flight, Univ. of London Press, 1939. This was written immediately after the initial London evacuation and paints a very positive assessment of the project.

Breed, Bryan, I Know a Rotten Place: An Evacuee's Story, Arlington Press, 1975. This novel was based on an evacuee's personal experiences. It is entertaining and enlightening.

Burns, James MacGregor, Roosevelt: The Soldier of Freedom, Harcourt, Brace Jovanovich, 1970. A political history of the United States between 1940 and 1945 with an emphasis on President Roosevelt's part in it.

Busher, Hugh, Education Since 1800, Macmillan, 1986. A history of education in England from the 1800's until the present time.

Cary, Joyce, <u>Charley is My Darling</u>, Michael Joseph, 1962. A fictional story focusing on evacuees from London living in the reception areas. It is a story about the children of that era but contains no particular details about the evacuation process.

Chamberlain, E.R., <u>Life in Wartime Britain</u>, Batsford, 1972. The content agrees with the title. It contains quite a few pictures. It is a good reference of the WW II era. One brief chapter on evacuees—nothing beyond what was found in the other references.

Churchill, Winston S. and Editors of Life, <u>The Second World War</u>, Vols. I and II, Time Inc., 1959. The history of World War II from the English point of view.

Clout, Hugh (ed.), <u>The Times London History Atlas</u>, Harper Collins, 1991. Shows a few details of the effects of bombing raids on London during World War II.

Cohen, Stan, <u>V For Victory, America's Home Front During World War II</u>, Pictorial Histories, 1991. A chronicle of the visual history of America during World War II.

Compton, Richmal, <u>William the Film Star</u> (Formerly *William and the Evacuees*), Newness, 1956. This is a fictional story about William aimed at the young reader. It references the evacuees during WW II but is not an account of the evacuees experiences.

David, Kati, <u>A Child's War</u>, Four Walls Eight Windows, 1989. World War II through the eyes of children.

Fethney, Michael, <u>The Absurd and the Brave: CORB–the true account of a British Boy's WW 2 evacuation</u>, The Book Guild Ltd., 1990. This is about the CORB evacuation to Canada, S. Africa, and Australia. It gives an excellent summary of the difficulties encountered by the planners, children, and reception area personnel.

Fyson, Nance Lui, <u>Growing Up in the Second World War</u>, Batsford, 1981. Description of the conditions facing children in WW II in England. Good details.

Gershon, Charles, <u>We Came as Children</u>, Victor Gollancz, 1966. A collective autobiography of evacuated Jewish children.

Glover, Michael, <u>Invasion Scare 1940</u>, Leo Cooper, 1990. A look at England during the first year of World War II when it was feared Germany would invade the UK.

Harrison, Tom, <u>Living Through the Blitz</u>, Collins/Penquin Books, 1976. Based largely on unpublished material in the Mass-Observation Archive at the University of Sussex.

Heide, Robert and Gilman, John, Home Front America, Chronicle Books, 1995. A descriptions of American life during World War II. Gives many details of what things were like: rationing, movies, dance bands, etc.

Hays, Sharon (ed.), Hoover Remembers World War II, Hoover Historical Center. A pamphlet accompanying an exhibit by the same name. Contains a brief reference to the Hoover evacuation.

Isaacs, Susan (ed.), The Cambridge Evacuation Survey, Methune, 1941. A detailed study of the Cambridge evacuation from Tottenham and Islington. Chapter 4, "What the Children Say" gives many examples of the children's likes and dislikes. There are other chapters with examples of people's thoughts.

Jackson, Carlton, Who Will Take Our Children, The Story of the Evacuation of Britain 1939-45, Methuen, 1993. A very complete description of the entire evacuation process including the evacuees who came to America. This book was written by a college professor and hence is a more scholarly approach to the subject. It contains an excellent reference list.

Johnson, B.S., The Evacuees, Gollancz, 1986. A collection of 31 anecdotes written by participants in the evacuation process–mostly evacuees but also several accounts by the teachers who accompanied the evacuees.

Jones, Madeline, Life in Britain in World War II, Batsford, 1983. A children's book describing WW II. A somewhat confusing format (each topic in a separate paragraph) which made it difficult to study.

Klingaman, William K., 1941 Our Lives in a World on the Edge, Harper & Row, 1989. A thorough political history of America during 1941.

Lewis, Peter, A People's War, Methuen, 1986. Based on a BBC television series by the same name. Was extremely interesting. Discussed the entire war from the civilian point of view. Has a section devoted to the evacuation process.

Leuchtenburg, William E., Franklin D. Roosevelt and the New Deal, Harper & Row, 1963. An account of the Roosevelt administration from 1932 to 1940.

Lifton, Betty Jean, Journey of the Adopted Self, Harper Collins, 1994. The effect of adoption and fostering on children and parents. A scientific study.

Liverpool, Univ. of, Dept. of Social Science, <u>Our Wartime Guests–Opportunity or Menace</u>, Univ. Press of Liverpool, 1939. Statistics based on 412 interviews with persons involved in the evacuation process at the reception areas including workers, volunteers, and hosts.

————, <u>Preliminary Report on the Problems of Evacuation</u>, Univ. Press of Liverpool, 1939. Statistics based on a series of 356 interviews with persons evacuated, their families, and those who assisted them.

Longmate, Norman, <u>How We Lived Then</u>, Hutchinson/Arrow, 1971/1973. Detailed study of WW II. One chapter on evacuation.

Lorimer, Jean, <u>Pilgrim Children</u>, Muller, 1983. This was written in 1942 and is obviously an attempt to justify the CORB evacuation of the children to the U.S., Canada, Australia, and S. Africa. It includes letters between children, parents, and foster parents during their stay in the different countries.

Lumley, Joanna, <u>Forces Sweethearts</u>, Bloomsbury, 1993. A companion to a display at the British War Museum. An excellent book capable of generating many tears when one reads about wartime romances.

Maclean, Meta, <u>The Singing Ship</u>, Angus and Robertson, 1941. This describes the shipboard experience of the 480 children evacuated to Australia on the Polish ship Batory. An excellent description of the feelings, fears, and joys of the children, escorts, and crew during the 20,000 mile journey.

MacKenzie, S.P., <u>The Home Guard</u>, Oxford, 1996. A detailed history of the English Home Guard.

Massey, Victoria, <u>One Child's War</u>, London: British Broadcasting Corporation, 1978. Life during World War II.

Mathewson, Dorothy Warren, <u>Sweet Memories</u>, 1999. Not completed at press time, but it promises to be interesting. Ms. Mathewson was a Hoover evacuee who now lives in N. Canton, Ohio. She tells of her evacuation memories. Pictures are included.

Mercer, Derrik, <u>Chronicle of the Second Word War</u>, Longman, 1990. Major reference source used in *An Ocean Between* to identify the events and dates of World War II.

Miburn, Clara Emily, <u>Mrs. Milburn's Diaries</u>, London: Harrap, 1979. An Englishwoman's day-to-day reflections, 1939-45. Many references to what people were thinking during World War II.

Monham, Kathleen, <u>Growing Up in World War II</u>, Wayland, 1979. A children's book describing WW II. Many pictures. No mention of the evacuation.

Moss, Miriam, <u>How They Lived–A Schoolchild in World War II</u>, Wayland, 1988. A children's book. Pictures and prose. Devoted to WW II–not the evacuation.

New York Times, <u>Page One, The Front Page History of World War II As Presented in The New York Times</u>, Galahad Books, 1996. A collection of actual front pages from the New York Times.

Painter-Downes, Mollie, <u>Letter from England</u>, Little, Brown, and Co., 1940. A description of conditions in London from September '30 to September '40. A diary written in the form of letters.

Parsons, Martin, and Starns, Penny, <u>Evacuation–The True Story</u>, DSM Publishing, 1999. Based on a BBC radio series by the same name. It is a nostalgic look at some of the difficulties encountered during the evacuation of children in England.

Perry, C., <u>Boy in the Blitz</u>, Leo Cooper, 1972. This is an excellent diary of the bombing of London from the point of view of an 18 year old. It gives a good description of what went on during the Blitz.

Reynoldson, Fiona, <u>The Home Front: Evacuation</u>, Wayland, 1990. Although a book written for children, I found it interesting. It contains a large number of references.

————, <u>War at Home</u>, Heinemann Education, 1980. A book for children. Contains pictures and simplistic descriptions. Good overall view of the war. One short section on the evacuation.

Second Army Div., <u>Combat History of the Second Infantry Division in World War II</u>, Army & Navy Publishing Co., 1946. This was used for Graham & Ned's war scenes.

Statler, Jocelyn, <u>Special Relations</u>, Imperial War Museum, 1990. Poignant letters written between parents and children evacuated to America from England during World War II.

Strachey, Mrs. St. Loe, <u>Borrowed Children</u>, Murray, 1940. An account of some of the evacuee problems (e.g., lice and enuresis) and their remedies. Note: this was written in 1940 and agrees with material found in other references.

Titmuss, Richard M., <u>Problems of Social Policy</u>, MNSO and Longmans, 1950. A very detailed study of the social problems in England during World War II.

Tutle, William M. Jr., <u>Daddy's Gone to War</u>, Oxford, 1993. The lives of children whose fathers were sent to World War II and what effects it had on them. A scientific study. Tutle is a professor.

Wagner, Lady, <u>Children of the Empire</u>, Werdenfeld & Nicolson, 1992. This tells about the evacuation of children from Britain from 1600 to 1937. It does not discuss WW II evacuations.

Wells, Herbert George, <u>"Single Works", Shape of Things to Come</u>, Hutchinson & Co., 1935. Also, Gregg Press, 1975. (Reprint of the edition published by the Cresset Press, London.) A film story was based on this work.

Westfall, Robert, <u>Children of the Blitz</u>, Penguin, 1985. A brief recollection of events that happened during the war in England written by children who experienced them. Covers the entire period from August 1939 to the end of the war.

Wicks, Ben, <u>The Day They Took the Children</u>, Bloomsbury, 1989. This is a sequel to *No Time To Wave Goodbye*. It is a compilation of various evacuees' notes and experiences.

————, <u>No Time To Say Goodbye</u>, Bloomsbury, 1988. This book was written partially from experience and partially from comments assembled from other evacuees. Contains extracts from many personal letters and documents written by evacuees.

————, <u>Waiting For the All Clear</u>, Bloomsbury, 1990. True stories from survivors of the Blitz.